Books by Kent Halstead

Servant Leadership for Congregations

Novel Guide

Heat Stress

A Guide to Military Civic Action

Across America: 848 County Rankings

Wages, Amenities and Cost of Living

Tax Wealth in the Fifty States

Statewide Planning in Higher Education

Inflation Measures for Schools and Colleges

State Profiles: Financing Public Higher Education

Tuition Fact Book

Higher Education Report Card

Higher Education Revenues & Expenditures:
A Study of Institutional Costs

Rich Colleges, Poor Colleges

Three R's: Race Retention Rates by State

NOVEL GUIDE

Information and instruction on the selection of fictional prose 575 titles and favorite passages

Kent Halstead

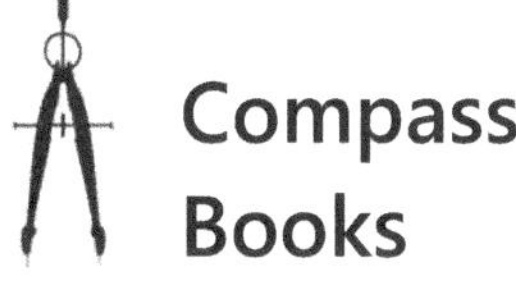

First Edition

Novel Guide

Printed in the United States of America
First Edition

Suggestions for improving this publication and contacting the author should be addressed to:

Research Associates of Washington
1200 North Nash Street, #1112
Arlington, Virginia 22209

Ordering
This book may be purchased at www.amazon.com or through your local bookstore.

Cataloging Data
Dewey number 809.3
ISBN 978-1-883298-09-8

Published in the United States by Compass Books, a division of Research Associates of Washington, Arlington, Virginia

Contents

Preface

If you like fiction, especially for the discerning reader, there arrives a point when one invariably becomes more judgmental, partly because of the sheer number of choices available; more often because of growing awareness of the rewards of critical selection. Why not read the best? While few will argue this premise, the difficulty is in the process. With such an outpouring of titles, let alone the multitude of classics, how does one begin? In fact, is knowledgeable selection actually possible?

The present volume should help, but there is no accounting for individual tastes. Personal discernment is naturally recognized and encouraged. Here, however, for readers seeking guidance, we turn to the selections of experts, commonly relied upon in matters of judgment. A majority of titles reported have appeared on at least two of seven "all-time best" lists compiled by literature specialists. A second large inclusion is award-winning titles from 1946 through 2009. To this central collection, the present author has added a number of supplemental titles believed equally noteworthy. The resulting 575 title total will obviously not include everyone's favorites, nor necessarily satisfy literary professionals. But the listing should invariably keep even voracious readers busy for some time.

Title selection, of course, involves more than perceived quality. The nature of the subject matter is often equally if not more important. We assist in such preferences by identifying each work by one of 15 subject descriptors. There is also the matter of book length, extended works sometimes simply too tedious an undertaking. We consequently report page length, and also publication date for those interested in literary period or recency. Readability may also be a factor. We combine readability with our initial more important concern, literary quality, appraised together by a simple 1-2-3 rating scheme. Hopefully, this personal judgment by the present author will reflect that of many contemporary readers, recognizing again that selection ultimately is a matter of individual preference.

If this study design strikes you as somewhat involved, we firmly believe that the results warrant the complexities involved, delivering close to an optimal reading list. Judge for yourself.

In closing, may I note that getting to know these fine authors and their works, even in this introductory manner, is more than sufficient reward for undertaking this study.

Kent Halstead

Book cover for *The Bed-Time Book* by Helen Hay Whitney, 1907
In charcoal, watercolor on board, 18 x 15" by Jessie Wilcox Smith

Introduction

"Great literature is simply language charged with meaning to the utmost possible degree." — Ezra Pound (1885-1972), American poet and critic

"Read any good books lately?" A typical casual question, seldom eliciting any response warranting more than a nod in passing. After all, an extraordinary 200,000 new titles are published in the United States each year including 25,000 fiction entries. And, in stark contrast, most readers have neither the same reading preferences nor much time to read. So any response of real value regarding "good books" necessarily requires deliberate study. This is the intention here, to provide an informed listing of the all-time best in fiction. Somewhat surprisingly, the task turns out to be fairly straight forward, recognizing, of course, that lists are often controversial and none can be error-free or complete. Recent fiction can be immediately narrowed to the 200 to 300 titles annually reviewed, and then further refined to the dozen or so yearly award-winners. Over extended periods coverage can be based on "top 100" lists. To this core the present author has added personal selections believed essential to any master list. Together a total of 575 titles are reported, a sizable number, but workable with further aids for selection. When combined with 15 subject identifiers as reported here, readers can develop a practical reading list of quality works matching their personal interests.

Titles are reported in three tables:

#1. All-Time Best, Award-Winners, & Supplement Titles, page 399. Reports 575 titles listed alphabetically by author together with year of publication, page length, type (subject identification), and evaluation grade. The number of citations are reported for the "All-Time Best" titles, awards received for the "Award Winners."

#2. Title & Author listed by Novel Type and Grade, page 413. Lists the 575 titles by their story type classification and evaluation grade.

#3. Bestsellers (*Publishers Weekly*), 1917-2009, 93 Titles, page 423.

Favorite Passages The favorite passages section, listed alphabetically by author (pages 94-398), cites content of particular quality and meaning, likely informative in title selection, and, as important, simply interesting to peruse. In many instances entries include photographs, selected art work, and commentary.

Together the three tables and favorite passages provide an encompassing reporting system to assist librarians in advising readers regarding selection, as well as of immediate value and interest to readers themsleves.

How should readers proceed? A number of options are available. One can simply choose a title from reading the "Favorite Passages." Or one can choose from the titles for a given author using Table 1.

Again using Table 1, readers valuing expert opinion can choose among the "All-Time Best" receiving the highest citation count (column 1). On this basis these 10 titles would be the first to read: *Invisible Man* (1947), *The Great Gatsby* (1925), *Catch 22* (1955), *Lolita* (1955), *1984* (1949), and *Catcher in the Rye* (1945), each receiving 11 citations; then *Ulysses* (1922) scoring 10; and lastly *The Sound and the Fury* (1929), *To Kill a Mockingbird* (1960), and *Grapes of Wrath* (1939), each with nine citations. One can then continue in descending order of citation count, choosing to read as one is so inclined, comfortable in the knowledge that all are likely winners.

On a par with the above citation winners are 57 titles from the British guide to fiction, *Novels and Novelists*, each receiving a maximum five stars in all four rating categories: Readability, Characterization, Plot, and Literary Merit. These titles are identified by a solid black vertical bar in Table 1.

One can also choose from among the more recently published "Award-Winners" of Table 1 (column 2), where the leaders with six awards are: *Billy Bathgate* (1989), *The Corrections* (2001), *A Flag for Sunrise* (1981), and *Dinner at the Homesick Restaurant* (1982); and these titles with five awards: *Humboldt's Gift* (1975), *Stories of John Cheever* (1978), *Underworld* (1997), *The March* (2005), *Ironweed* (1983), *Gilead* (2004), and *Rabbit is Rich* (1981).

A (>) mark in Table 1 identifies 54 "Supplement" titles selected by the present author as highly suitable for inclusion in this list. Most readers are likely to find real gems among these commonly overlooked titles.

Readers primarily interested in subject matter will find such a listing for 15 "type" classifications in Table 2. Also reported is the present author's assessment of literary quality.

A few choices among the "Bestsellers" list in Table 3 are invariably rewarding. Knowledgeable readers will want to be familiar with at least John Grisham, Stephen King, Tom Clancy, Jean Auel, James Michener, and James Clavell, among the most popular and, in some instances, prolific writers today.

There you have it, a number of means to create a starting list of high quality selections with minimal effort. And the process can continue by transferring from one list to another, and by gradually lowering the number of awards involved, or even paying more-or-less attention to the present author's ratings. Happy reading!

Aids to Literary Selection

This present study adds to the resources currently assisting readers in literary selection. All are useful and in concert provide a full complement of supporting services. Of course, leading any means of selection is cultivation of one's own personal search and judgment. To this we add four supplemental aids: Sunday newspaper book supplements, literary websites, text guides, and book clubs. Together the five constitute a full spectrum of aids to literary selection.

With regard to **personal judgment and appraisal**, consider the advice of Michael Dirda of *The Washington Post.*

"Bestseller lists work like blinders on a horse: They prevent people from seeing all the wonderful, odd, quirky and worthwhile books that might actually appeal to them far more than the list's largely commercial and standardized products. Think for yourself! Instead of picking up one of the top 10 titles, look around the bookshop. Ask your local booksellers what they've enjoyed lately. Read reviews. Talk to your friends. Above all, just wander along the shelves, take down a novel or a collection of poems or a work of history by an author you've never heard of and just read a few pages–you may discover a book that will change your life."

The most immediate and frequently used guidance are the **Sunday book supplements** of major newspapers. Readily available and invariably professional, these guides are typically among the best in the business.

Numerous fiction **websites** range in assistance from capsule summaries and brief assessment to, remarkably, total reprints. A most helpful site is *fictionawardwinners.com* with a complete listing of award winners and commentary, providing a readily accessible and recommended complement to the present study. Other useful sites are listed in the bibliography.

Text guides provide the most rigorous and, seemingly in conflict, entertaining demonstrations of the art of literary criticism. The bibliography lists ten such references in addition to this present study. Readers may readily be excused if they find on occasion as much enlightenment and enjoyment from these sources as they do from the very volumes they address.

The last source, personal and fun, is **book clubs**. To say that a club is in your immediate area is an understatement. The problem is likely more one of choosing than finding. Selecting a club typically depends on the convenience of meeting locations and times, compatibility with members, expected member participation, variety of selections, and nature of treatment. Three references in the bibliography will get you started.

Young Girl Reading, 1776, by Jean-Honore Fragonar
National Gallery of Art

The Elements of Fiction

"The final test for a novel will be our affection for it, as it is the test of our friends, and of anything else which we cannot define."

— E. M. Forster (1879-1970) British novelist and essayist

We intend to bring to your attention novels of *quality*. This assertion typically evokes the response, "What do you mean by quality?" With regard to fiction, a not so easily answered question, generally sidestepped with vague reference to being "found in the eyes of the beholder." Our response is straightforward–list the major elements of fiction, then describe their respective quality features. This chapter attends to this analysis. Then in the following chapter we explain how the titles in the present instance were selected, primarily by national critics, judgments hopefully based on the quality elements cited.

Over time the basic design components of the novel genre have evolved into a fairly detailed set of factors that may be summarily listed as follows:

1. Subject matter
2. Major elements–plot, characters, and setting
3. Writing style (pace, focus and continuity, complexity, etc.)
4. Mechanics (difficulty level, book length, and date of publication
5. Author
6. Popularity

1. Subject matter Clearly the world of fiction is too diverse to classify in any but the broadest descriptive categories. The 15 divisions listed below have largely been developed through trial testing.

Adventure	Culture	Horror
Character	History	Fantasy
Relations	Location	Military
Family	Frontier	Occupation
Youth	Crime/Mystery	Stories

Content distinctions are an independent means of classification without an inherent quality element. Subject popularity among readers, however, is well recognized and discussed in the next chapter along with some further details on the division categories themselves.

2. Major components refers to the presentation of plot, characterization, and setting that constitute the central core of any novel, and in perfection arouses and maintains reader interest, occasionally at a fever pitch. Excellence in these basics is developed through description, enriched by realism, intensity, intrigue, suspense, and innovation. In order of importance, plot precedes characterization, distantly followed by setting. Balance among the three is common, yet plot by itself carries many novels, characters occasionally, setting alone never.

In this present study, excellence in plot, characterization, and setting is reasonably understood through the expertise and creditability of the selecting individuals and organizations on which the title entries are dependent.

—Plot in literature refers to the degree to which the narration weaves a substantive, arresting, perhaps occasionally riveting, story. It is the essence of the novel genre. Plots are developed through the *events* that occur in a story. Main events are the significant experiences of characters or important situations in their lives. Plots invariably involve *conflicts* which lead to attempted resolution. The lesson or lessons involved constitute the story's *theme*.

Story enhancement is achieved by such ingredients as drama, intrigue, conflict, danger, anticipation, and suspense. Drawn-out, plodding drivel in contrast is the bane of good prose no matter how artfully phrased.

—Characterization is the portrayal of absorbing, memorable personages that arouse and hold attention. The "main" character is often the voice expressing the story. Three or four major characters and a few supporting individuals can generally be kept in mind; a cast of dozens is more often than not confusing.

Characters are developed through description of their appearance, their dialogue and responses to others, personal actions and reactions, and, in written context, their mental thoughts and processes. Good novelists can put the reader inside the mind of a character, an intimacy at once difficult if not impossible for other media.

Naturally, fictional characters can exhibit all human traits, attitudes, and feelings, whatever the author elects. Traits which combine to form temperament are most lasting, attitudes less so, and feelings occasioned by immediate events, may even be fleeting. Over time all aspects of emotional makeup may change for better or worse.

A writer succeeds if readers truly know and often care for the characters portrayed.

—Setting is the context and environment in which a story takes place—the prevailing conditions of geography, time, and culture. Both characters and action are invariably affected by the involved surroundings. Yet so well understood and seamlessly integrated are such factors that they seldom received much individual attention. Thus setting, however distinctive or important to the narration, seldom generates more than passing acknowledgment. There are vivid exceptions, the far north of Jack London, the Africa of Hemmingway, the Orient of Maugham and McKenna, the India of Rushdie, the grinding poverty of Steinbeck's *Grapes of Wrath*, and the South Pacific of Michener. How essential and enriching these settings!

3. Writing style is the author's manner of imaginative and distinctive expression and phrasing. At its best, good writing reflects insight and sensitivity, and at its rarest, constitutes an element of beauty. Great stylists portray subjects and events so intimately and real as to engage the reader's attention and psyche like a trap, occasionally so rigorous and durable as to last a lifetime. Such expression captures the mind and heart; on occasion, causing one to pause and reflect.

Composition of this quality level is understandably rare, yet remarkably varied. Consider these brief illustrations: Jack London's description of a lifetime friendship ending "...parting in the maw of a shark"; the startling incalculable conclusion of *All Quiet on the Western Front*; the exuberant joy of the black nursemaid reunited with her young ward, "Why God bless him, why chile, chile, ah believe you do remembuh!" by James Agee; and the bittersweet "Sleep tight, ya morons!" yelled by Holden Caufield in his final departure from school in J. D. Salinger's *The Catcher in the Rye*.

Use of figurative language to create sensory impressions is a matter of style. So also is choice in who's relating the tale, for the narrator's point of view may be highly significant.

How a novel ends is also a matter of style. Here we could do with a lot less depressing, tragic, and disappointing conclusions. Most readers would likely prefer the last page as good as the first, leaving a satisfied if not pleasant memory.

Finally, in addition to the cardinal components above, there are technical elements of style including focus and continuity, pace, clarity, phrasing or syntax, and diction (choice of words). This is writing that would pass your English teacher's examination. Most important are focus and pace, sticking to the story-line and moving right along. Few elements of a focused and well-paced novel can be removed without seriously jeopardizing the story. Continuity controls story coherence by minimizing distractions and divergence.

Quality in writing style is expected to be ensured in this collection of fiction, as is quality of plot, characters, and setting, as judged by the awarding agencies and selecting panels. The name and number of citations or awards received, evidence of these evaluations, are reported for each title in the listing tables.

4. Mechanics is the design or structural element of novels, dealing with reading difficulty, length of text, and date of publication.

Difficulty level refers to the complexity and extent of structure, plot, and character treatment that may tend to confuse and distract the reader. Some novels are simply hard to wade through, the 783 page *Ulysses* with a cast of dozens being a prime example, extolled by all, read by few. Difficulty level is not distinctively rated here, rather assumed as a determinant within the overall selection process of the cited reviewing agencies.

Length A good book is hard to put down regardless of length. Around 300 pages is commonly cited as "reasonable." Short reads, a rarity, are often wished to be longer. At the other extreme, long books may generate fatigue, even boredom. They can reflect lazy or less often, presumptuous writers. Authors may disclaim need for editing. Efficient wordsmithing is, after all, difficult and time-consuming. So readers will likely continue to suffer more from excess verbiage than too severe pruning.

Number of pages is reported for all listed volumes. Page count may vary by edition due to differences in type and page size.

Date of Publication This is a dubious concern in novel selection, primarily a factor within book clubs and among voracious readers able to operate at the cutting edge of current fiction. The slower pace of the vast majority of readers, however, permits a leisurely approach to selection, sifting through choices old and new. All volumes listed here include the year of publication.

5. Author Authorship justifies purchase by many readers. Who, for example, would not pick up a newly discovered writing by London, Hemmingway, or Fitzgerald, or a new title, if they were alive today? Yet excellence is difficult to sustain. Only 106 (less than one-in-three) of the 379 listed authors are cited for more than one title. Remarkably, a few have more than beaten the odds. Philip Roth has 11 listed titles, John Updike 10, William Faulkner 7, and Saul Bellows 6 titles.

6. Popularity While occasionally duped by aggressive sales hype and prone to crowd mentality, e.g., the two-year bestseller *Jonathan Livingston Seagull*, reader tastes more commonly reflect fairly deliberate selection based on published criticism and personal investigation. In response to the importance of popularity, bestsellers reported by *Publishers Weekly* are listed back to 1917 in Table 3.

Pen and ink chapter heading, *The Fables of Aesop*, 1909
Edward Julius Detmold

Listings

The list is the origin of culture. It's part of the history of art and literature." — Umberto Eco, Italian literary critic and novelist

The intent of this volume is seemingly simple, to bring novels of *quality* to the attention of readers. Yet the meaning of "quality" in this context, and the manner of its appraisal immediately arise. In the previous chapter we undertook to define literary excellence, abstracted from a number of interpretations. Now we attend to the *means* whereby such distinction may be assessed. And we find that in a field as subjective as fiction, the only recourse available and thus employed is dependence on professional judgment. This we have done with confidence, and begin this chapter by first explaining then evaluating the procedures employed in using four separate independent sources to identify 575 qualifying titles. In Table 1 the titles are listed by author, page 399; in Table 2 listed by subject type, page 413.

The chapter continues with the nation's "bestsellers" reported in Table 3, page 423.

A final component presents the 15 subject descriptors singularly assigned to each listed title to assist readers in identifying the subject novel's central theme or content.

Selection Procedures

If a book can't be set down, it's undoubtedly a good one, at least for the involved reader. Stories that elicit an emotional response, a pause to reflect, contemplate, even savor, are fiction at its best. Personal reactions are, of course, not always shared. Even among literary critics, opinions vary. Consequently, in assembling this collection intended for knowledgeable discerning readers, exceptional measures have been necessary.

All-Time Best Sources In determining the "All-Time Best" entries of Table 1 (cited in the first column) we have necessarily relied on the opinion of foremost literary experts. The professionals involved, both individuals and organizations, have clearly taken the task seriously, devoting considerable attention and study to the process. However, for added insurance we have required listing by at last *two* of our 12 sources before a title is cited as an "All-Time Best." Yet despite the apparent care exercised by each source, concurrence at even this minimal level turns out to be, surprisingly, remarkably rare. Of approximately 1,223 titles initially listed, our 12 expert sources agreed on only 220 selections, roughly 18 percent of the total. On the positive side, such rarity suggests that the few titles so uniquely distinguished are likely to be, in fact, exceptional.

Note: Entries in Table 1 are listed alphabetically by author, and include publication date, page count, and the present author's subject classification and overall quality grade.

Each of the "All-Time Best" sources conducted thoughtful, deliberate investigations. The results are possibly the best guides to quality literature available. Yet, the selection criteria employed are generally not announced and, as previously stated, the lists themselves only marginally agree. Much of this inconsistency is due, understandably, to the substantial number of excellent novels in existence, far more than can be contained on any typical single list. Limited selections consequently are bound to differ with so many alternative qualifying choices available.

The following 12 sources were used in compiling the "All-Time Best" selections. Each of the 12 appear to be of high quality based on the credentials of the individual or organization involved, and the apparent thorough and deliberate care exercised in list preparation.

– Anthony Burgess, *Ninety-Nine Novels: The Best in English Since 1939*, 1984.

– British Broadcasting Company, "Big Read" project listing the 100 most popular books nominated by a poll of viewers, 2003.

– College Board, *101 Great Books Recommended for College-Bound Readers* (not dated).

– Daniel S. Burt, *The Novel 100: A Ranking of the Greatest Novels of All Time*, 2004.

– Radcliffe Publishing Course, *100 Best Novels List* for The Modern Library, 1998.

– Norwegian Book Club, *The 100 Best Books in the History of Literature*. Titles cited most often from 10 nominations from each of 100 prominent authors, 2002.

– Random House's Modern Library, *100 Best Novels of the Century: The Board's List*, 2000.

– Random House's Modern Library, *100 Best Novels of the Century. The Reader's List*, 2000.

– Robert McCrum, *100 Greatest Books from The Observer*, 2003.

– TIME Magazine, *All-Time 100 Novels*. Selections since 1923 by TIME critics Lev Grossman and Richard Lacayo, 2005.

– Waterstone, *Top 100 Books of the Century*. Includes non-fiction. Based on the Waterstone's bookstore chain poll of over 25,000 people in the United Kingdom, Republic of Ireland and Europe, 1997.

– One Combination of Eight Short Lists (123 Titles)

Amazon Listmania! *The Ten Best Novels of Our Time*, 2004.

American Library Association, *Contemporary Classics 1944-1980* (includes 41 novels).

Clifton Fadiman, "Ten Best Books of Fiction," *The Book of Lists*, 1977.

Somerset Maugham, "Ten Greatest Novels Ever Written," *Great Novelists and Their Novels*, 1948.

New York Public Library, *50 Years of Books to Remember,* 2004, (includes 10 novels).

Readers of the Observer, "Ten Best Novels of All Time," *Observer*, October, 2003.

University of Virginia Library, *Cumulative Ten Best-Sellers by 1965*, 1965.

Jonathan Yardley, "The 22 Books of the Century," *The Washington Post,* February 1, 1982.

Titles from *Novels and Novelists* A second contributor to fiction of highest quality is the British reference *Novels and Novelists*, a work of exceptional coverage and excellence. This study is "must reading" for students of fiction. Of the 3,284 titles cited (1,348 authors), only 57, a modest 1.7 percent, receive a five-star rating in all four of the guide's appraisal factors–readability, characterization, plot, and literary merit. So limited to a perfect five-star score virtually assures quality. The 57, minus 20 already listed from the "All-Time Best" sources, result in a net 37 title addition to Table 1. All 57 *Novels and Novelists* titles are identified by a solid vertical black bar.

This modest initial use of *Novels and Novelists* most assuredly suggests more extended employment of this excellent source in future editions of the *Novel Guide*.

Award Winners The third component of Table 1, "Award-Winners," consists, as the name implies, of winners or finalists for two or more of seven major awards for fiction in English primarily by American authors (one or more of the three existing awards given prior to 1968). The fact that no more than ten titles have ever achieved this status in a given year (1981) strongly suggests the likelihood of excellence. Overall, during the 1946-2009 64-year period, 300 titles have been so distinguished; 264 net additions.

The seven awards from which selections have been made are: Pulitzer Prize, National Book Critics Circle Award, National Book Award, Man Booker Prize, Pen/Faulkner Award, *New York Times* Best Fiction Books, and *TIME* Magazine Best Fiction Books.

Note that the prestigious Nobel Prize in Literature is awarded to *individuals* for their collective work, not for specific titles. And the Man Booker Prize, awarded to citizens of the Commonwealth of Nations, Ireland, or Zimbabwe, is an exception to the other awards all exclusively for American authors.

The awards are:

– Pulitzer Prize (P) first awarded 1918, American author, preferably dealing with American life.

– National Book Critics Circle Award (C) first awarded 1975, published in English.
– National Book Award (N) first awarded 1950, American author.
– Pen/Faulkner Award (F) first awarded 1981, living American citizen.
– Man Booker Prize (B) first awarded 1969, citizen of the Commonwealth of Nations, Ireland, or Zimbabwe.
– *New York Times* Best Books (Y) first fiction identified as "Year's Best" 1968. No winner distinction.
– TIME Magazine Best Books (T) first fiction identified as "Year's Best" 1956. First winner distinction 1992.

The requirement of winner or finalists for *two* awards narrows the original listing from a total of roughly 25 titles per year to a typical and manageable six to eight volume count.

These awards constitute the current principal means of recognizing outstanding fiction in the novel genre. The assessment task is understandably time consuming at best, laborious at worst. Considering the hundreds of candidate titles involved, the fact that any given title is a winner or finalist for more than one award is exceptional. One explanation is the strength of popular acclaim and critical reviews which makes completely independent appraisal difficult if not impossible.

Supplement As a modest start to adding quality titles toward any theoretically ultimate list, the present author introduces 54 candidates, a fourth component of Table 1, each such entry identified by a (>) mark. These titles hopefully add entries possibly overlooked, under-valued, or seemingly warranting inclusion by their popularity alone.

Some of the older titles in the "Supplement" are slightly lower-ranked entries cited in *Novels and Novelists (N&N)*, adding to the 57 five-star novels from that source specifically so cited. It is understandable that a source of 3,284 titles such as *N&N* will undoubtedly include significantly more quality entries than the few top-ranked currently chosen. This source will consequently be further mined for additional entries in subsequent editions of this publication. Other inclusions in the "Supplement" are personal favorites, one surprisingly from the author's childhood, but clearly believed a classic. Finally, the "Supplement" contains titles simply because they are too popular to omit. It would be hard to explain, for example, the exclusion from any modern day list of fiction of such popular adventure/mystery authors as Ian Fleming, Mickey Spillane, Agatha Christie, and Ken Follett. The acceptance of their inclusion is left to the reader.

Readers may submit their own nominees by contacting the author.

Secondary Appraisal

This assessment, by the present author, is an evaluation of the listed titles in terms of modern day literary quality as might be judged by discriminate contemporary readers. Consistent with the subjective nature of criticism, the rating scheme is limited to a simple three-division scale: 1–outstanding, 2–superior, 3–notable. Mid-level interpretations are reported in the involved lower category. The grading results are reported in the last column of each of the listing tables. Needless to say, rigorous interpretation of the grading is discouraged.

Assessment has required that all the listed novels be carefully read, serving also in identifying an outstanding passage. The appraisals are hopefully impartial, judged according to the *qualitative* aspects of plot, characterization, setting, and writing style (see pages 5-7). However, any personal interpretation is subject to the reviewer's predisposition. While intending to be even-handed, we admit a propensity for fast action, interesting characters, and moderate length, hopefully none to excess. Readers are accordingly cautioned.

The author's appraisal has been deliberately rigorous, attempting to further distinguish among entries already refined. The resulting 24% – 41% – 35% rating distribution is evidence of this discernment, hopefully accurately and impartially administered.

The relationship between title sources and the present author's appraised literary quality is reported in the table below. The first three sources exhibit a remarkably consistent quality distribution. Naturally, the author's "Supplement," specifically intended to add otherwise excluded quality works, has the highest share of #1 ratings. Again, this is a simple exercise warranting no serious interpretation.

Title Source and Quality Ratings

Title Source	Quality Rating							Total	
	1-outstanding		2-superior		3-notable				
All-Time Best	**43**	20%	**99**	44%	**78**	36%	=	**220**	100%
Novels & Novelists (distinctive titles only)	**9**	20%	**13**	44%	**15**	36%	=	**37**	100%
Award Winners	**58**	22%	**99**	38%	**107**	40%	=	**264**	100%
Supplement	**29**	54%	**24**	44%	**1**	2%	=	**54**	100%
TOTAL	**139**	24%	**235**	41%	**201**	35%	=	**575**	100%

Bestsellers

Ninety-three "Bestseller" fiction titles reported by *Publishers Weekly* from 1917 through 2009 are reported in Table 3, page 423. Entries, listed chronologically by year of best seller status, report author, title, page length and subject type. The *Weekly's* hardcover "Bestseller" list is based on shipped and billed figures supplied by publishers for new books issued in the subject calendar year, and a few books issued in the previous year continuing their tenure on the best seller list for the subject year.

Best selling fiction reflects public tastes and, to a degree, the success of promotional efforts. Judicious selection within the listing will invariably result in some "good, solid, commercial fictions" as John Grisham describes his writing. And some satisfaction can be gained in keeping at the cutting edge of new literature. The negative side is that extravagant sales pitches, and a too easily stampeded public, can propel some fairly mediocre work to bestselling prominence. Cautious readers may well wait until the reviews are out.

Incidental to our yearly list of bestsellers is mention of the all-time champions. Alice P. Hackett and James Henry Burke report this phenomenon in their *Eighty Years of Best Sellers* (1977). The remarkably diverse top ten are: *The Godfather* (12.1 million), *The Exorcist* (11.7), *To Kill a Mockingbird* (11.1), *Peyton Place* (10.7), *Love Story* (9.9), *Valley of the Dolls* (9.5), *Jaws* (9.5), *Jonathan Livingstone Seagull* (9.1), *Gone with the Wind* (8.6), and *God's Little Acre* (8.3). Interpretation of this mishmash is left to the reader.

Finally, we might add "bestsellers" defined in terms of collective sales for a given author. John Sutherland's 1981 *Bestsellers* list is now out-of-date. As a guess, today's all-time bestselling authors might be topped by these ten: Agatha Christie, J. K. Rowling, Harold Robbins, Alistair MacLean, Frederick Forsyth, Mickey Spillane, James Michener, John Grisham, Barbara Cartland, and Mario Puzo. Hopefully, the interest of many will prompt publishers to provide an accurate update.

Assessment

Lists suffer the usual errors of complicity accompanying any compilation—too many entries, omissions, incorrect entries, and simple obsolescence. The title listings reported here are no exception. Excellence omitted is likely most disturbing. The 575 title total would seem adequate for many individual readers, but certainly makes no claim on comprehensive coverage.

Exclusions The underlying problems with lists of any sort are commonly the inherent biases of compilers and the invariably restricted coverage. In this instance, literary critics too often let their personal tastes interfere in making selections and are themselves typically under-read. Thus the remarkable dissimilarity among lists and the occasional surprising agreement. Fresh independent judgment and comprehensive study should always be hallmarks of literary compilations. Any so-called "master" list must necessarily be a team effort by representative critics subject to reader review and updating.

Consider this commentary regarding listing adequacy: Herbert Kupferberg asks "could a whole generation have been wrong about the quality of *Look Homeward Angel*" (1957) by Thomas Wolfe. He also would encourage "An injection of some humorous fiction" such as Anita Loos' *Gentlemen Prefer Blondes* (1953) or Ring Lardner's baseball classic *You Know Me Al* (1914). His other suggestions include Charles Jackson's *The Lost Weekend* (1945), Arthur Conan Doyle's *The Hound of the Baskervilles* (1939), and Norman Douglas' "exquisitely written" *South Wind* (1917).

Reviewing 25 years of fiction, *Book World* editor Michael Dirda cites a generous 109 authors that "to my mind, have been the truest mirrors to American society in our time, or have attempted innovative forms of story-telling, or revealed new subject matter, or generated schools of imitators, or done all of these." He also includes a few offerings that "simply ...won my heart." Among titles that "could and should become classics," he cites three, John Cheever's *Collected Stories* (1990), William Gaddis's *JR* (1975), and E. Annie Proulx's *Accordion Crimes* (1996). All three are excluded from our collection. Generous, perhaps to a fault, more than half the authors Dirda cites do not make our list.

The *Novel Guide* can also be faulted for inadequate regional coverage; for example, including only 15 titles from "The Top 25 Great Southern Books" (ageefilms.org). And every other type of "special coverage" is likely also underrepresented.

Perhaps most incriminating is the seeming inability of any two sources to agree on title selections. Consider the inconsistency between the top titles receiving five-stars in all four ratings as reported in *Novels and Novelists* and the "All-Time" best entries from primarily American sources. The five-star selections were made by an eminent panel of 19 British critics, literary editors, professors, and writers convened in 1980. Recognizing some variance in criteria employed and possible British bias, one would still think that such an eclectic and scholarly panel would choose wisely and broadly, which they did. Yet in listing 1,348 authors and 3,284 works of fiction, only 20 of their 57 five-star selections were also cited by our other experts in their top 100 compilations. In this instance, agreement is reached regarding the highest level of fiction only 35 percent of the time. Evidently this is as high a degree of consensus possible, concurrence dropping rapidly as expected as lower levels of fiction are introduced.

What about all-time bestsellers such as Barbara Taylor Bradford's *A Woman of Substance* (1979) 20 million, Mario Puzo's *The Godfather* (1969) 12 million, and John Grisham's *Pelican Brief* (1992) 11 million? Such popularity implies certain literary merit that cries for acknowledgement, but not on our list!

The upstart of all this is that there is a fine body of fictional literature outside this current combination of "best" lists. As a consequence, the task of assembling a true master list of exceptional fiction remains an open, daunting, and likely unaccepted challenge.

And More Deficiencies From another perspective, long-standing lists, by their very duration, become dated. Yet, who has the courage to exorcise legends, however antiquated?

Consider some details of the "All-Time Best" list which reflect its flawed stature. First, age. Well over half (59%) of the 220 total were written before 1946, over 60 years ago. Most inclusions, however, are "classics," possibly dated in one manner or another, but permanently quality works. Others are less defendable, likely "survivors," initially retained perhaps as a matter of historical record, then continued as an expected member. Such remnants are often rife with dated language, customs, and environment. Alone, such content is not overly distracting. However, when combined with an archaic plot, the sum may exceed most readers' tolerance level.

Second, and more serious, some early choices appear to this observer altogether unacceptable in the first place, an extreme example being *Naked Lunch* (1962). Such aberrations are possibly explained by the prominence of the author, yet obviously not in the *Lunch* case. In other instances, publicity and hype may have played a significant selling role. Their retention on any list is inexcusable.

Thus, despite its length and pedigree, no informed reader will likely find the core "All-Time Best" entries either complete or without questionable inclusions. The more recent "Award Winners" also have their faults, but seemingly less serious. The present author's many low personal ratings (35% overall) should provide some warning to readers regarding likely marginal inclusions in all the title listings.

Subject Classification

The *novel* genre is commonly and simply described as fictional prose narratives of considerable length. Included here are also collected short stories treated as a composite whole. Excluded are such specialties as children stories, crime/detective/mystery where the reader's main interest is in identifying the culprit, fantasy, humor, pulp fiction, romance, screen plays, serials, science fiction, sports, and Westerns. These and other excepted categories typically have their own reviewing body, award winners, listings, and websites. Their large fan base and often superb quality speak well for the diversity they represent.

Content descriptions of novels are available from numerous websites; see Bibliography "Plot Synopsis." As an immediate and necessarily minimal guide to content, this study employs 15 encompassing descriptive terms according to each entry's central theme or underlying conditions as follows:

Adventure (exciting, hazardous, or perilous experiences; drama, survival)

Character (memoir or biography of principally one person's life or portion thereof)

Crime/Mystery (crime, misbehavior, violence, mystery, detective, suspense, criminal law, drugs, slavery, imprisonment)

Culture (a way of life of a particular period, community, nationality, or race; society, a special manner of living)

Family (married life, parent-child relationships, patriarchy, kinship, heritage)

Fantasy (supernatural, ghost, futuristic, science fiction, surreal, speculative, creatures, myths, fairy tales, folklore, fables)

Frontier (explorers, pioneers, settlers, cowboy, homestead, gold rush, farm, animals)

History (underlying progression of events over time, sagas, epics, odysseys)

Horror (dark, frightening, ominous situations; danger, degradation, depravity, apocalyptic)

Location (strong geographical/national orientation, includes air and oceans, travel)

Military (combat and war related conditions and issues, soldiers, mercenaries, spy, espionage, terrorism)

Occupation (underlying theme of a certain type of work, e.g., law, politics, government, philosophy, religion, medicine, science, engineering, enterprise, farming, institutions)

Relations (interpersonal involvement and associations between and/or among individuals other than family, romance)

Stories (short stories)

Youth (young adults, adolescents, children)

Readers interested in a possible relationship between subject matter and literary quality may examine the table below. The author's secondary appraisal is explained on page 13. Discounting possible rater bias, novels dealing with military, youth, history, occupation, and crime/mystery together with the accompanying writing style appear to result in fiction of highest overall quality. Relationships, characters, locations, and fantasy are subject matter apparently most difficult to ably present. No serious interpretation is justified here, however, other than possibly prompting further study.

Subject Descriptions and Quality Ratings

Subject description	Quality Rating 1-outstanding		2-superior		3-notable			Total	
Adventure	**5**	25%	**12**	60%	**3**	15%	=	**20**	3%
Character	**11**	11%	**41**	40%	**51**	50%	=	**103**	18%
Crime/Mys	**15**	35%	**22**	51%	**6**	14%	=	**43**	7%
Culture	**13**	28%	**19**	40%	**15**	32%	=	**47**	8%
Family	**13**	21%	**23**	37%	**26**	42%	=	**62**	11%
Fantasy	**5**	17%	**11**	37%	**14**	47%	=	**30**	5%
Frontier	**5**	45%	**3**	27%	**3**	27%	=	**11**	2%
History	**10**	36%	**10**	36%	**8**	29%	=	**28**	5%
Horror	**5**	29%	**8**	47%	**4**	24%	=	**17**	3%
Location	**2**	17%	**4**	33%	**6**	50%	=	**12**	2%
Miltary	**12**	50%	**7**	29%	**5**	21%	=	**24**	4%
Occupation	**7**	35%	**11**	55%	**2**	10%	=	**20**	3%
Relations	**7**	9%	**33**	44%	**35**	47%	=	**75**	13%
Stories	**19**	33%	**21**	37%	**17**	30%	=	**57**	10%
Youth	**10**	38%	**10**	38%	**6**	23%	=	**26**	5%
TOTAL	**139**	24%	**235**	41%	**201**	35%		**575**	100%

Repeat titles are counted only once.

"Steerpike and Barquentine" by Mervyn Peake
Author's illustration for *Titus Groan*

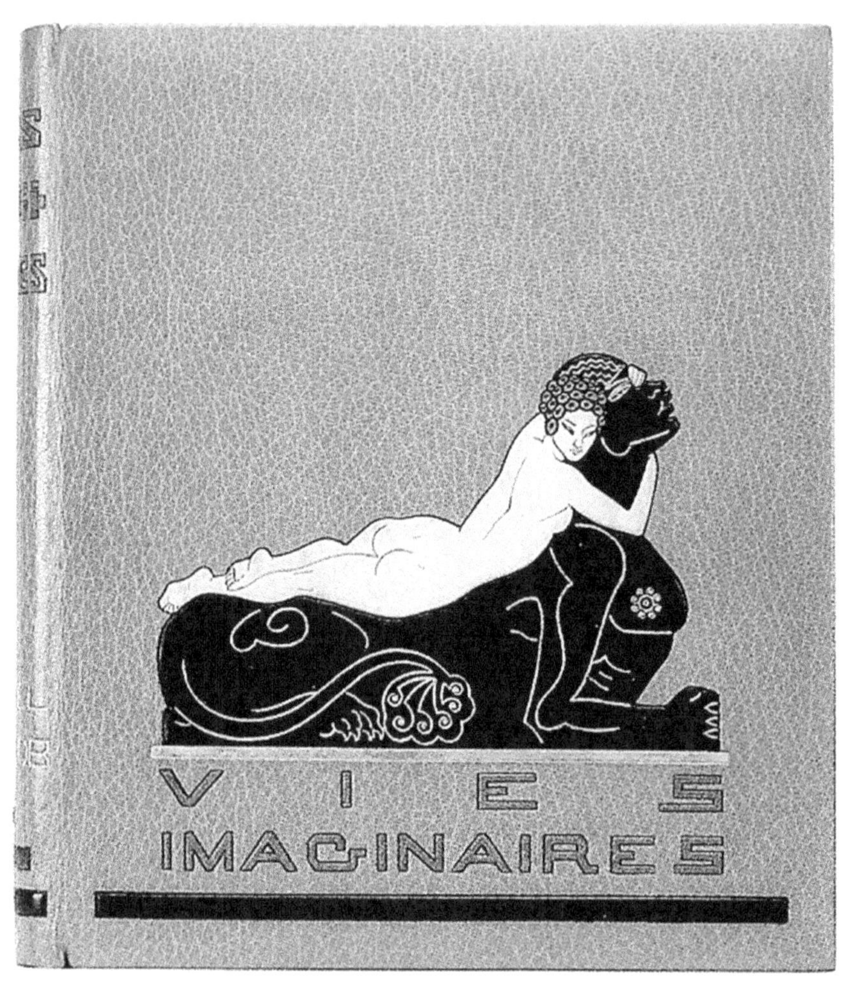

Art Deco book cover by Rene Aussourd, 1929
Inlays of leather with gold-tooling.
Art Nouveau and Art Deco Bookbinding
Alastair Duncan & Georges De Bartha

Commentary

Here is a compilation of supplementary material to expand and enhance your enjoyment of the novel genre. Perhaps as well as any scholarly treatise, these diverse observations and opinions, largely by pundits and critics, reflect our continual delight and concern with this noble art. Most fun and insightful are some of the wittiest and wisest commentary, judgments, and apropos quotations on the world of fiction by seemingly the cleverest observers. On the visual side, one need only view the sample illustrations to appreciate their value, now unfortunately a lost practice. Writers themselves might benefit, although not in every instance, from "The Writing Craft" section which quotes, among others, E. M. Forster's questionably helpful "How do I know what I think until I see what I say?" From "Tributes, Epitaphs, and Inscriptions" we cite Lou Reed's delightful "These are the tales of Edgar Allen Poe. Not exactly the boy next door." All-in-all it is remarkable how much meaning and pleasure can be obtained from such brief rhetoric.

I have taken license to considerably quote Jonathan Yardley and other *Washington Post* editors, due to their ready availability in my Sunday paper over the past 40 years, but more justifiably, by the recognized excellence of one of the all-time great reviewers and his associates. Also deserving special recognition is Steve King and his always welcome daily *Today in Literature* e-mailed to subscribers for our education and entertainment. Content examples are illustrated on page 25. We are indebted to Steve's research for a good number of the quotes used here.

The 22 components of "Commentary" are:

Readers and Reading
Collecting
Book Clubs
Writers' Lives
Pen Names
Awards and Lists
Literary Feuds
Deaths Too Early
Tributes, Epitaphs, and Inscriptions
The Novel Genre (State of the Art)
The Writing Craft
Titles
First and Last Lines
Artwork
Cartoons
Reviews and Criticism
Literary Extremes
The Publishing Industry
Rejections
Libraries
Films versus Books
Novel/Location/Film

Readers and Reading

• Roughly around the age of four, psychologists say, the human child develops a "theory of mind." The child suddenly grasps that other people have feelings, thoughts, just like the child's own. From this great mental leap comes a secondary, almost accidental talent: We can get inside the heads of people whom we never actually meet except in stories. This is why fiction works. Who says Huck Finn, Pooh, or Harry Potter aren't real? They seem real enough.

— Joel Achenbach, "The vestigial tale,"
The Washington Post. October 29, 2009

• Reading is to the mind what exercise is to the body.

— Joseph Addison (1672-1719) English politician and writer

• I read a book twice as fast as anybody else. First, I read the beginning, and then I read the ending, and then I start in the middle and read toward whatever end I like best.

— Gracie Allen (1902-1964) American comedienne

• Some books are to be tasted, others to be swallowed, and some few are to be chewed and digested.

— Francis Bacon (1561-1626) English philosopher

• Literature has many mansions and excellence is found in many forms—some of them unassuming and even fugitive . . . The true reader allows himself a balanced diet and moves easily through the categories from philosophy to humor . . .

— Jacques Barzun (1907-) American historian of ideas and culture

• Reading is one of the great pleasures that solitude can afford you.

— Harold Bloom (1930-) *O Magazine*, April, 2003

• A reader is not like a critic, who reads for professional judgment. The reader seeks pleasure, enlightenment, self-identification, seduction.

— Malcolm Bradbury (1932-2000) British author and academic

• It happened on a dark night, somewhere in the middle of Book IV. For three years, I had dutifully read the "Harry Potter" series to my daughter, my voice growing raspy with the effort, page after page. But lately, whole paragraphs of "Harry Potter and the Goblet of Fire" had started to slip by without my hearing a word. I'd snap back to attention and realize the action had moved from Harry's room to Hagrid's house, and I had no idea what was happening.

And that's when my daughter broke the spell: "Do we have to keep reading this?"

O, the shame of it: A 10-year-old girl and a book critic who had had enough of "Harry Potter." We were both a little sad, but also a little relieved.

— Ron Charles, "Harry Potter and the Death of Reading,"
The Washington Post, July 15, 2007

• I like being around books. It makes me feel civilized. The only way to do all the things you'd like to do is to read.

— Tom Clancy (1947-) American author

• There is no frigate like a book
  To take us lands away.
Nor any coursers like a page
  Of prancing poetry.
This traverse may the poorest take
  Without oppress of toll;
How frugal is the chariot
  That bears a human soul!

— Emily Dickinson (1830-1886) American lyric poet

• As with a love affair, the battered heart needs time to recover from a good work of fiction.

This is why rereading is so important. Once we know the plot and its surprises, we can appreciate a book's artistry without the usual confusion and sap flow of emotion, content to follow the action with tenderness and interest, all passion spent.

The beauty of words, the sound and fall of sentences, a writer's distinctive voice rising from the page—these, in the end, provide the greatest and most lasting pleasures of a reading life.

— Michael Dirda, *Book by Book*

• … the Semi-Colons, a gathering of men and women who met every Monday evening for parlor readings by the members, discussion, dancing, and refreshments.

— E. L. Doctorow (1931-) *Creationists: Selected Essays 1993-2006*

• Books are the quietest and most constant of friends; they are the most accessible and wisest of counselors, and the most patient of teachers.

— Charles W. Eliot (1834-1926) Harvard President, *The Happy Life*

• If we encounter a man of rare intellect, we should ask him what books he reads.

— Ralph Waldo Emerson (1803-1882) American essayist and poet

• The decline in reading among every segment of the adult population reflects a general collapse in advanced literacy. To lose this human capacity —and all the diverse benefits it fosters—impoverishes both cultural and civic life.

— Dana Gioia, Chairman, National Endowment for the Arts,
2002 NEA survey of American reading habits

The cold statistics confirm something that most readers know but have mostly been reluctant to declare as fact—books change lives for the better.

— National Endowment for the Arts, November, 2007

• I read part of it all the way through.

— Samuel Goldwyn (1882-1974) Hollywood motion picture producer

• The greatest gift is a passion for reading. It is cheap, it consoles, it distracts, it excites, it gives you the knowledge of the world and experience of a wide kind. It is a moral illumination.

— Elizabeth Hardwick (1916-) American writer

• I cannot understand the rage manifested by the greater part of the world for reading new books . . . If I have not read a book before, it is, to all intents and purposes, new to me, whether it was printed yesterday or three hundred years ago.

— William Hazlitt (1778-1830) British writer

• The time to read is any time: no apparatus, no appointment of time and place, is necessary. It is the only art which can be practiced at any hour of the day or night, whenever the time and inclination comes, that is your time for reading; in joy or sorrow, health or illness.

— Holbrook Jackson (1874-1948) British journalist

• I am a part of all that I have read.

— John Kieran (1892-1967) American writer

• . . . people like buying books more than they like reading them. And, of course, in the famous formulation (credited to Gloria Steinem, among others), writers don't like writing. They like having written.

— Michael Kinsley, *The Washington Post*

• To have read the latest literary wonders may enable one to prattle at tea-parties; but, had one only waited a year, they might all have blown away, like last year's leaves.

— F. L. Lucas (1894-1967) British literary critic

• The pleasure of reading is doubled when one lives with another who shares the same books.

— Katherine Mansfield (1888-1923) New Zealander modernist writer, *Letters*

• Knowing your likely appreciation, we bring to your attention the extraordinary literary newsletter *Today in Literature*, available each morning by e-mail from author Steve King. Begun in 2001 as a Canadian weekly radio series, the *TinL* website now receives over 25,000 visitors a day! Subscribers live throughout the world, including two, remarkably, residing on Bouvet Island in the Antarctic.

The newsletter has been described as "like fresh bread and fresh coffee for the soul..." Taking only a few minutes to read, each issue contains articles, stories, quotations, anniversaries, photos, and artwork about what happened in literature on that date sometime in the past. On the adjacent page are a few example entries. An archive contains 500 + articles and 500 + newsletters.

Today in
LITERATURE
Great Books, Good Stories, Every Day

Anita Loos died on this day in 1981. In *A Girl Like I*, her 1966 autobiography, Loos tells us that the 1,200 copies in the first edition of *Gentlemen Prefer Blondes* (1926) was sold out by noon, that the second edition numbered 65,000 copies, that there were forty-five more editions by 1966, and that the whole world was reading the novel in translation, though some had to rationalize the fun:

> When the book reached Russia, I was told by our then Ambassador, William Bullitt, that the Soviet authorities embraced it as evidence of the exploitation of helpless female blondes by predatory magnates of the capitalistic system. As such, the book had a wide sale, but Russia never sent me any royalties, which seems rather like the exploitation of a helpless brunette author by a predatory Soviet regime.

F. Scott Fitzgerald's *This Side of Paradise* was accepted for publication on this day in 1919. Fitzgerald was five days away from his twenty-fourth birthday, and the publication of his first book – by far the most financially successful one in his lifetime – would springboard him to fame, as he predicted:

> I know I'll wake some morning and find that the debutantes have made me famous over night. I really believe that no one else could have written so searchingly the story of the youth of our generation.

Advertised at Fitzgerald's request as "a novel about flappers for philosophers," Scribner's first edition (left) of 3000 copies sold out in three days. In his review, Robert Benchley said that he was "inclined to hail as a genius" a young author who "can think up something new and say it in a new way." Benchley's ominous conclusion: "Mr. Fitzgerald deserves a crown of something expensive."

> "If you saw Atlas, the giant who holds the world on his shoulders, if you saw that he stood, blood running down his chest, his knees buckling, his arms trembling but still trying to hold the world aloft with the last of his strength, and the greater the effort the heavier the world bore down upon his shoulders—what would you tell him to do?"
> "I...don't know. What...could he do? What would you tell him?"
> "To shrug."

— From **Ayn Rand**'s *Atlas Shrugged* (1957), which she says she began writing on this day in 1946; right, the Atlas in Rockefeller Center, New York City

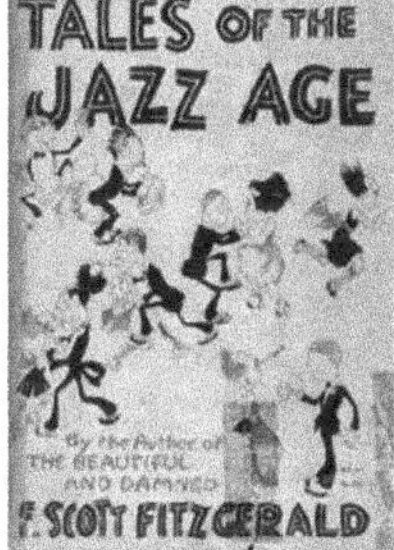

F. Scott Fitzgerald's *Tales of the Jazz Age* was published on this day in 1922. In his introductory comments on "The Curious Tale of Benjamin Button," one of the stories in the collection, Fitzgerald includes "this startling [and misspelled] letter from an anonymous admirer in Cincinnati":

> Sir—
> I have r Button in *Colliers* and I wish to say that as a short story writer you would make a good luna ead the story Benjamin tic. I have seen many peices of cheese in my life but of all the pieces of cheese I have ever seen you are the biggest peice. I hate to waste a peice of stationary on you but I will.

Left, John Held Jr.'s first edition cover

• In literature as in love, we are astonished at what is chosen by others.

— Andre Maurois (1885-1967) French author and man of letters

• Reading is the sole means by which we slip, involuntarily, often helplessly, into another's skin, another's voice, another's soul.

— Joyce Carol Oates (1938-) American author

• The proper METHOD for studying poetry and good letters is the method of contemporary biologists, that is careful first-hand examination of the matter, and continual COMPARISON of one 'slide' or specimen with another.

— Ezra Pound (1885-1972) American expatriate poet, critic, and major figure in the Modernist movement, *A B C of Reading*

• Life being very short, and the quiet hours of it few, we ought to waste none of them in reading valueless books.

— John Ruskin (1819-1900) British art and social critic

• If ever there were a teaching conundrum, today's high-school English teachers are smack in the middle of it. It's our job to take digital natives—teens saturated with images in video games and on YouTube—and get them to strike up a relationship with pictureless chains of black print and focus on the decidedly internal rewards of classical literature. More and more, this mission feels like blind idealism. . . .

. . . Until we do a better job of introducing contemporary culture into our reading lists, matching books to readers and getting our students to buy in to the whole process, literature teachers will continue to fuel the reading crisis.

— Nancy Schnog, "To Get Teens Reading, We Need to Turn the Page," August 24, 2008, *The Washington Post*

• We shouldn't teach great books; we should teach a love of reading.

— B. F. Skinner (1904-1990) American psychologist

• Books are good enough in their own way but they are a mighty bloodless substitute for life.

— Robert Lewis Stevenson (1850-1894) Scottish novelist and poet

• Read the best books first, or you may not have a chance to read them all.

— Henry David Thoreau (1817-1862) American author and naturalist

• As for the literary pundits, the high priests of the Temple of Letters, it is interesting and helpful occasionally, for an acolyte to swing them a good hard one with an incense-burner, and cut and run, for a change, to something outside the rubrics.

— H. W. Tomlinson (1873-1958) British writer and journalist

• Never force yourself to read a book that you do not enjoy. There are so many good books in the world that it is foolish to waste time on one that does not give you pleasure.

— Atwood H. Townsend, Professor of English, New York University

• The reading of detective stories is simply a kind of vice that, for silliness and minor harmfulness, ranks somewhere between smoking and crossword puzzles.

— Edmund Wilson (1895-1972) American writer

• Persons attempting to find a motive in this narrative will be prosecuted; persons attempting to find a moral in it will be banished; persons attempting to find a plot in it will be shot.

— Mark Twain (1835-1910) American author, *Huckleberry Finn*

• It can be argued that the kinds of works being published by literary presses in the United States today are very much a reflection of the interests and concerns of this typical [middle-aged white female living in a Western or Midwestern city] reader.

— Nicholas Zill and Marianne Winglee, "Literature Reading in the United States: Data From National Surveys and Their Policy Implications," 1989

Art Nouveau book cover by Emile Carayon, 1906
Inlays of leather with gold-tooling, and incised and tinted panel. *Art Nouveau and Art Deco Bookbinding*
Alastair Duncan & Georges De Bartha

Collecting

- My Pop is always buying books:
  So that Mom says his study looks
  Just like an old bookstore. The bookshelves are so full and tall
  They hide the paper on the wall,
    And there are books just everywhere,
    On table, window-seat, and chair,
  And books right on the floor.
  And every little while he buys
  More books, and brings them home and tries
  To find a place where they will fit,
  And has an awful time of it.

  Once, when I asked him why he got
  So many books, he said, "Why not?"
  I've puzzled over that a lot.

  — Ralph Bergengren (1871-1947) in *Jane, Joseph and John*

- When I get a little money I buy books; and if any is left, I buy food and clothes.

  — Desiderius Erasmus (1466-1536) Known as Erasmus of Rotterdam, humanist and theologian

- Never lend books—nobody ever returns them; the only books I have in my library are those which people have lent me.

  — Anatole France (1844-1924) French author

- There are 10,000 books in my library, and it will keep growing until I die. This has exasperated my daughters, amused my friends, and baffled my accountant. If I had not picked up this habit in the library long ago, I would have more money in the bank today; I would not be richer.

  — Pete Hamill (1935-) novelist, essayist and journalist

- Mr. [Irvin] Cobb took me into his library and showed me his books, of which he has a complete set.

  — Ring Lardner (1885-1933) American sports columnist and short story writer

Book Clubs

"The whole point of being in a book group is to see the world through someone else's eyes. That happens in discussion, of course, when you discover just how different your friend's reactions to a certain book are from your own."

— Ellen Moore and Kira Stevens, *Good Books Lately*, 2004

Apart from friendship, camaraderie, and the simple entertainment of club membership, conversational review of books reflects the varied perspectives and insights of readers in an enriching, often intimate, experience for all.

From various guides on reading groups (see bibliography), these brief instructions assist clubs specializing in novels:

1. However structured, reading groups are for fun and learning. Encourage respect for individual member perspectives. Keep flexible. Adapt rules democratically, as experience and changing membership dictate.

2. Housekeeping tasks—membership number and requirements, meeting location and frequency, starting time and duration, discussion leadership and control dynamics, refreshments, meeting critique and club business—are all variables subject to trial testing and revision.

3. Title selection procedure is central to the value and satisfaction of book club membership. Choose knowledgeably and democratically. Change rules by majority vote. Principal <u>novel</u> selection criteria in order of possible popularity are:

- Member personal choice (rotated privilege; this is laissez faire, anything goes with oddball entries possible)
- Majority vote of nominated candidate titles (generally held bi-annually)
- Best sellers
- Annual award winners
- Novel type (any divisions agreed upon; see subject classification page 17 of this volume)
- Classics (numerous available lists, e.g., "All-Time Best," "Top 100")
- Paperback only
- Specific publication date time period

4. Reasonably enforce careful reading preparation, perhaps taking notes.

5. Session leaders should guide members to all or a majority of the meaningful aspects of the subject novel. Encourage everyone to speak, listen thoughtfully, and interact with others. Discourage argument to persuade or convince another. Appoint two discussion leaders when conditions appear to so warrant.

6. Build an association with the local library and book stores. They are typically very supportive.

Writers' Lives

• While in the Army Mr. Salinger married a former member of the Nazi party named Sylvia, about whom little is known.

They were divorced shortly thereafter, and in later years, Mr. Salinger referred to her only as "Saliva."

— Henry Allen, "J.D. Salinger, known but unknowable"
The Washington Post, January 29, 2010

• Seventeen copies sold, of which eleven at trade price to free circulating libraries beyond the sea. Getting known . . . pause] . . . Never knew such silence. The earth might be uninhabited.

— Samuel Beckett (1906-1989) in reference to *Krapp's Last Tape*

• Why do writers write? Because it isn't there.

— Thomas Berger (1924-) American novelist

• His demanding father called the 8-year-old's first poem "lousy." He forgave his father with time, saying the encounter taught him a valuable lesson in the need for revision.

— Adam Bernstein, "Bud Schulberg, 95, Academy Award-Winning Screenwriter of 'On the Waterfront,'"
The Washington Post, August 6, 2009

• The other day my daughter, 14, saw me hunched over a laptop, cringing at the customer reviews of my novels on Amazon.com and bn.com. "Why do you insist on tormenting yourself?" she asked. "It just can't be good for you."

— Chris Bohjalian "The Writing Life—In which the author obsesses over potshots by amateur critics on Amazon.com"
The Washington Post Book World, August 17, 2008

• (The only real pursuit for a writer) is to know how to thrust your head into the darkness, know how to leap into the void, and to understand that literature is basically a dangerous calling.

— Roberto Bolano (1953-2003) Chilean-Spanish novelist and poet

• The first American novel, *The Power of Sympathy*, was published anonymously in 1789 by author William Hill Brown, fearful of possible reprisals by the Puritan anti-novel lobby.

• Of course no writers ever forget their first acceptance.... One fine day when I was seventeen I had my first, my second and third, all in the same morning's mail. Oh, I'm here to tell you, dizzy with excitement is no mere phrase!

— Truman Capote (1924-1984) American writer

• The narrative impulse is always with us; we couldn't imagine ourselves through a day without it.

— Robert Coover (1932-) American author

• . . . (Thoreau) had also a certain pursed-lipped sourness; out on the trail he was adept, as his biographer Robert Richardson has put it, at consuming wild berries that "were so tart it was a triumph to eat them."

— Andrew Delbanco (1952-) in *Required Reading*

• I love being a writer. What I can't stand is the paperwork.

— Peter De Vries (1910-1993) American editor and novelist

• Amidst the cheering and crying over Charles Dickens on his final tour of America in 1867, were elements of comedy as well. One little girl suddenly sat down beside him on the train and told him how much she liked his books. "Of course, I do skip some of the very dull parts, once in a while; not the short dull parts, but the long ones." Dickens laughed, and then taking out his notebook, asked for details.

— Reported by Steve King, *Today in Literature*

• I put my living guts into this.

— Inscription by William Faulkner found in the flyleaf of a now invaluable copy of *The Sound and the Fury*

In contrast, Faulkner is also quoted as saying that he wrote *Sanctuary* for the money, and the book obliged.

• Ian Fleming wrote his first James Bond book, *Casino Royale*, as "a counterirritant or anti-body to my hysterical alarm at getting married at the age of forty-three."

— Recalled on Flemming's death August 12, 1964

• There is no lonelier man than the writer when he is writing except the suicide. Nor is there any happier, nor more exhausted man when he has written well. If he has written well everything that is him has gone into the writing and he faces another morning when he must do it again. There is always another morning and another morning.

— A discarded excerpt from a draft of Ernest Hemingway's acceptance speech for the 1954 Nobel Prize. Reported in *Today in Literature*.

• No man but a blockhead ever wrote, except for money.

— Samuel Johnson (1709-1784) British author, poet, and critic

• Despite all the cynical things writers have said about writing for money, the truth is we write for love. That is why it is so easy to exploit us. That is also why we pretend to be hard-boiled, saying things like "No man but a blockhead ever wrote, except for money." (Samuel Johnson) Not true. No one but a blockhead ever wrote, except for love. — Erica Jong, "Doing It For Love," *Washington Post Book World*, February 9, 1997

• When Nora found out her husband James Joyce was "on another book again," she asked if, instead of "that chop suey you're writing," he might not try "sensible books that people can understand."

• Famous Lost Work:

Robert Louis Stevenson burned his first completed draft of *The Strange Case of Dr. Jekyll and Mr. Hyde* after his wife criticized the work. He subsequently wrote and published a second version.

T. E. Lawrence lost "Text 1" of *Seven Pillars of Wisdom*, a 250,000 word manuscript, at the Reading railway station in December 1919.

In 1922 a suitcase with almost all of Earnest Hemingway's work to date was stolen in Paris from his wife.

The manuscript for Sylvia Plath's unfinished second novel, provisionally titled *Double Exposure*, or *Double Take*, written in 1962-63, disappeared some time before 1970.

• . . . And it is that word 'hummy,' my darlings, that marks the first place in *The House at Pooh Corner* at which Tonstant Weader fwowed up.

— Review in *The New Yorker* by Dorothy Parker, under her pen name Constant Reader

• I was secretly jealous of Mailer, Vidal, and Capote. They have borne constant testimony to the fact that they are artists. And they have reminded us that artists often require a special freedom which people in other occupations do not seem to need.

— James A. Michener, *Literary Reflections*

• In 1901 Beatrix Potter published *The Tale of Peter Rabbit*. Having been turned down by a half-dozen publishers, Potter financed this first edition herself—250 copies with her own black and white illustrations, given away or sold at a half-penny each because, as she put it, "little rabbits cannot afford to spend 6 shillings."

— Reported by Steve King, *Today in Literature*

• Literature is an occupation in which you have to keep proving your talent to people who have none.

— Jules Renard (1864-1910) French author

• I shall live bad if I do not write and I shall write bad if I do not live.

— Francoise Sagan (1935-2004) French playwright and novelist

• Being an author, waiting for reviews, is a personal equivalent to the Cuban missile crisis.

— Carolyn See, "Both Sides Now: The Novelist as Critic," *The Washington Post*, June 1, 1997

• I'm going to be a writer like Ring Lardner or somebody—that's if things don't work out with the Yankees, or the Cubs, or the Red Sox, or maybe possibly the Tigers . . . if I get down to the St. Louis Browns, then I'll definitely be a writer."

— Neil Simon (1927-) American playwright and screen writer in *Broadway Bound*, 1986

- There is no there there.

— Gertrude Stein after thirty years in Paris referring to Oakland, California, after coming back to find her house was no longer there, her school was no longer there, her park was no longer there, her synagogue was no longer there. So for her, there was no longer a there there.

— Gertrude Stein, *Everybody's Autobiography*

- The profession of book-writing makes horse racing seem like a solid, stable business.

— John Steinbeck (1902-1968) American writer

- *Time* magazine's "Top 10 Most Reclusive Celebrities" remarkably includes four novelists. Here is a brief synopsis of each of their withdrawals and a photograph early in their career.

Evidently, reclusiveness suited J. D. Salinger just fine. He lived to age 91, dying this last year. He began to withdraw around the age of 32 after publication of *The Catcher in the Rye* in 1951. Would-be biographer Ian Hamilton made the mistake of reprinting letters the author had sent to fans and friends and was sued as a result. Today about the most we know of Salinger comes from court transcripts and his daughter's 2000 memoir, *Dream Catcher*.

Harper Lee is undoubtedly the most witty and charming recluse ever, always politely but firmly rejecting interview requests. She has, however, made rare public appearances, recently to receive the Presidential Medal of Freedom at a White House ceremony in 2007. She currently travels between her apartment in New York City and her family home in south-central Alabama to care for her father.

Thomas Pynchon is another case altogether "reigning anonymously supreme among reclusive novelists" according to *Time*. He has avoided nearly all media since the 1963 publication of his first book, *V.*, and this early photo is one of the few in existence. He asks others to accept his awards. Surprisingly, he agreed to appear on *The Simpsons*, albeit as a drawn character with a bag over its head but with Pynchon's own voice.

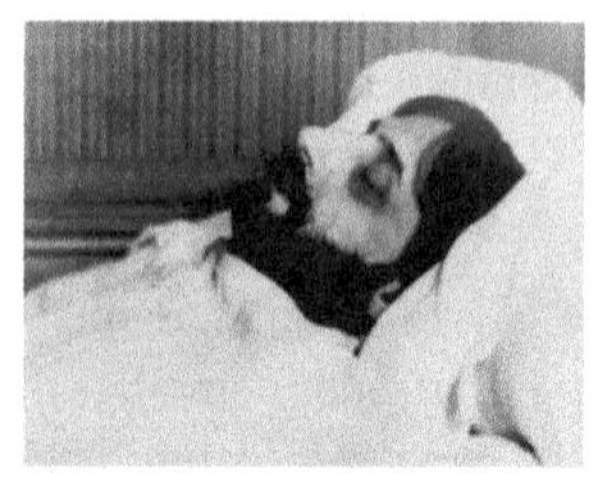

Lastly, Marcel Proust, nervous, frail and sensitive, forsook French society in his mid-30s after the deaths of his father and mother. He eventually rarely left his soundproofed Paris apartment, working in a sunless writing studio with the window shut as protection for his asthma. He often slept during the day and worked at night, becoming so absorbed in his writing in one instance that he failed to stop for three days. He died in 1922 at the age of 51.

- I write because I want to have more than one life.

  — Anne Tyler (1941-) American novelist

- There are a million people coming through the creative writing programs, and all of them can sling words, but where is their spirit, their will to engage things outside their narrow little class of friends?

  What happened to writers who had a really larger vision of the world, who went into the real world and observed how other people lived—authors like George Orwell, Richard Wright, adventurers like Henry Miller, bold artists like Theodore Dreiser, even Dickens and Defoe? Writers who were able to submerge their precious selves into the difficult but rewarding task of creating characters who were *unlike* themselves.

  — Robert Ward, *Publishers Weekly*

- A writer is like a bean plant—he has his little day, and then gets stringy.

  — E. B. White to Harold Ross, in a letter dated September 16, 1938

- Now we have "Flannery: A Life of Flannery O'Connor." No doubt O'Connor, who delighted in giving her characters unusual if not outlandish names such as Lucynell Crater, Hazel Motes and Francis Marion Tarwater, would be tickled to know that the author of her first full-scale biography is named Brad Gooch. A professor at William Paterson University in New Jersey . . .

  — Jonathan Yardley, "A Good Writer is Hard to Find,"
  The Washington Post, February 22, 2009

- The literary gene seems to be a unique occurrence rather than an inherited trait.

  — Jonathan Yardley, "The son also rises, but not as far,"
  The Washington Post, December 23, 2009

- In the last year of his life, he died at age 40, F. Scott Fitzgerald earned $13.30 in royalties. Since then his books have sold over 10 million copies.

Pen Names

A pen name, or "nom de plume," is a pseudonym used by authors supposedly to conceal their identity but which often becomes so popular in themselves and closely associated with the individual as to render the true name meaningless, ultimate anonymity. Movie stars of course simply have their monikers formally changed by studios to something more attractive, Tony Curtis replacing Bernard Schwartz, for example. Authors have a variety of seemingly less justifiable reasons–to disguise their prolific output, to hide from possible reprisal, to change gender, to independently experiment with style and subject matter, or, most common, simply to be able to live privately and write in secret.

One can well understand why Jozef Teodor Nalecz Konrad Korzeniowski chose to write under the pen name Joseph Conrad. Possibly for similar reasons Chloe Anthony Wofford became popular Toni Morrison. In a lesser revision, Daniel Foe evidently felt only a slight adjustment to Daniel Defoe was necessary. Eric Paul Remark also believed a modest change to Erich Maria Remarque would suffice. Eric Arthur Blair, on the other hand made a complete transition to George Orwell. And we wonder how Voltaire ever could have been Francois-Marie Arouet.

Surprisingly, some co-authors choose to publish under a single pseudonym, e.g., Ellery Queen for P. J. Tracy and Perri O'Shaughnessy. And in this instance one can't help but approve.

In a reversal of sorts, Agatha Christie, Grand Dame of Mystery, wrote numerous short stories and screenplays, and a series of romantic novels using the now forgotten pen name Mary Westmacott.

Lewis Carroll sounds vastly superior to Charles Lutwidge Dodgson as does O. Henry over William Sydney Porter. The shortest pen name, a mere Æ initials evidently fancied George William Russell. And concluding, we come to the most recognized example of deception, Samuel Clemens writing as Mark Twain, two now equally famous identities.

Pen and ink drawing attributed to George Du Maurier

Awards and Lists

Nobel Prize

Pulitzer Prize

• More than 500 awards for literature exist throughout the world, about 75 in the United States. The Pulitzer Prize and National Book Award include $10,000 in cash, the Pen/Faulkner Award $15,000, and the Man Booker Prize $80,000, but for most recipients the prestige and accompanying fame are far more important.

The Nobel is, of course, astronomically prestigious, making any recipient internationally famous. And it comes with a cool $1.4 million monetary prize. The award honors a writer for his collective production, not a single title. The following ten Americans have won the Nobel in Literature: Sinclair Lewis (1930), Eugene O'Neill (1936), Pearl S. Buck (1938), William Faulkner (1949), Ernest Hemingway (1954), John Steinbeck (1962), Saul Bellow (1976), Isaac Bashevis Singer (1978), Czeslaw Milosz who was born in Poland (1980), and Toni Morrison (1993).

In the United States the Pulitzer is the most important literary award if for no reason other than everyone knows the name. The Man Booker is a British award for English-language entrants from all over the world except, surprisingly, for the United States.

• No clearer evidence of the disparity in list undertakings is found than that reported in *The Top Ten: Writers Pick Their Favorite Books* (2007) edited by J. Peder Zane. One hundred twenty-five authors individually listed in rank order what they considered the ten greatest works of fiction of all time. Of the 544 different titles listed, only 23, or 4 percent of the total, were cited by 10 or more participants. A major 61 percent of the titles were selected by but one rater each. If this study proves anything, it demonstrates that left to their own devices, there is no consensus among even authors as to what constitutes good fiction. Now if they had all gotten together and discussed candidates it might have been an altogether different result.

• For a deliberate selection of likely losers, see *Fifty Works of English and American Literature We Could Do Without*, by Brigid Brophy, Sir Michael Levey, and Charles Osborne, 1967. Their controversial choices of overrated 'classics' include: *Hamlet, Pilgrim's Progress, Tom Jones, She Stoops to Conquer, The Scarlet Letter, Pickwick Papers, Jane Eyre, Wuthering Heights, Moby Dick, Leaves of Grass, Alice's Adventures in Wonderland, The Adventures of Huckleberry Finn, Peter Pan, The Forsyth Saga, To the Lighthouse, The Sound and the Fury,* and *A Farewell to Arms.*

• In a recent "The Dreadful Dozen" article, critic Jonathan Yardley of the *Washington Post* discusses *Rabbit Is Rich* by John Updike (listed in Table 1 as an "Award-Winner") stating ". . . we're talking about rotten books by writers who ought to have known better." Need we warn the reader further?

• The first standard is the "test of time" measure that ranks as best those novels that have maintained their importance over the long haul. The second is the prevailing conventions of a particular time that esteem certain works and devalue others based on current ideology. The third asserts the inevitable power of age, culture, gender, and personal experience that form each person's idiosyncratic tastes.

— Daniel S. Burt, *The Novel 100: A Ranking of the Greatest Novels of All Time*

• I am proud but also, I must admit, awe-struck at your decision to include me. I do hope you are right. I feel we are both running a considerable risk and that I do not deserve it. But I shall have no misgivings if you have none.

— Sir Winston Churchill, accepting the Nobel Prize for Literature

• In presenting T. S. Eliot the Nobel Prize in 1948 the Swedish Academy quoted his line "The only wisdom we can hope to acquire is the wisdom of humility" from the play *East Coker*. Eliot, in turn, jokingly took the line back: "To profess my own unworthiness would be to cast doubt upon the wisdom of the Academy . . ."

— T. S. Eliot (1888-1965) poet, dramatist, and literary critic

• Why that's a hundred miles away. That's a long way to go just to eat.

— William Faulkner (1897-1962) on declining an invitation to a White House dinner honoring American Nobel Prize winners

• None of (the awards) can be scientific. There's always vote-swapping and bargaining and some judge stubbornly sticking with some nomination no one else likes because it reminds him of his boyhood at Exeter.

— Monica Hesse, *Washington Post* Staff Writer

• Conrad Richter's "dread of public events that bordered on a phobia" are described in David R. Johnson's recent biography. Prior to receiving his 1961 National Book Award for *The Waters of Croons*, Richter had agreed to attend a pre-ceremony news conference. But after one look at the crowd and raised platform he plunked himself down in the first row of the audience to field questions from there, unwilling to move on stage. He explained later that his father, grandfather, uncle, and great uncle had all been preachers, evidently using up all the talent in that regard, so when he came along there simply wasn't anything left.

— David R. Johnson, *Conrad Richter: A Writer's Life*, 2001

• The list of books overlooked for a Pulitzer is an impressive one, and only a small handful of Pulitzer-winners made any of the best-of-century surveys. The jury will probably remain out on which year was the biggest Pulitzer oops, but it's hard to overlook 1930, when Oliver La Farge's *Laughing Boy* beat out *The Sound and the Fury, A Farewell to Arms, Look Homeward, Angel*, and *Doodsworth.* The next year wasn't much better: Margaret Barnes got the award for *Years of Grace* over *As I lay Dying, The 42nd Parallel*, and *The Maltese Falcon.*

— Steve King, *Today in Literature*

• When previously rejecting the Pulitzer Prize, Sinclair Lewis explained that he accepted the Nobel Prize because it was international and had no strings attached. Thinking of what was in fact attached, and smelling a home-state rat, the Minneapolis *Tribune* explained it differently: "It is a good deal easier to reconcile one's artistic conscience to a $46,350 prize than it is to one which happens to be, under the terms of the Pulitzer award, exactly $45,350 less." — Steve King, *Today in Literature*

• The chances of breaking up into factions multiply, and the chance that at least one juror will be a total idiot is almost guaranteed. When we had three judges, two people who had some sense of what was going on could outvote the dunce.

— William H. Gass, in response to adding more judges, recalling wine-fueled deliberations at the Algonquin Hotel

• As for awards, they are the purest example of gratuitous or superfluous meritocracy. — Michael Kinsley, *The Washington Post*

• Talk about inconsistency. Only nine Pulitzer Prize novels made *Time* magazine's 2005 "ALL-TIME 100 Novels." The board of The Modern Library likes Pulitzer fiction even less. Only six winners made its "100 Best Novels" in 1998. *The Observer*, a British newspaper, only places three Pulitzer novels on its 2003 "The 100 greatest novels of all time."

— Harry Kloman, The Pulitzer Prize Thumbnails Project (website)

• The criteria for picking judges vary somewhat with each prize, but in no case does it seem possible to screen judges for fairness and distance.

The real problem in evaluating literature by committee, though, lies not in any particular process but in the inherently subjective nature of literary judgment. As Talese puts it, "There's no such thing as a prize for the best, because there is no The Best."

— Marina Krakovsky, "Making Books: Literary prizes, and the near-impossible task of picking 'the best book of the year.'" *The Washington Post Book World*

• But my main cavil with The Modern Library roster is that it's so lacking in imagination or adventurousness–it's rather like a freshman-reading course, with little attempt to call attention to neglected or overlooked works worth reading.

— Herbert Kupferberg, "Now, About That List of the '100 Best Novels of the 20th Century' . . ." *Parade Magazine*

• Between early June and late September, you will be looking for the five most distinguished books in your genre published this year. Please keep in mind that books by authors who have been widely published in the past should not be overlooked; the individual book itself is being judged on literary grounds, not the author, or his or her past triumphs. Ultimately, the best book should win, regardless of any topical considerations. The final winning selection ... should be a book–in the words of National Book Award author William Faulkner–that will "not only endure, but prevail."

— National Book Foundation's mandate to judges

• Immensely grateful, touched, proud, astonished, abashed.

— Boris Pasternak, telegram to Swedish Academy, accepting the Nobel Prize (four days later Pasternak abstained from the prize due to political pressure)

• I can forgive Alfred Nobel for inventing dynamite, but only a fiend in human form could have invented the Nobel Prize.

— George Bernard Shaw who refused his Nobel Prize money in 1926

• Fifty years ago this month, the Swedish Academy shocked the American literary establishment by awarding the Nobel Prize for Literature to Pearl S. Buck. The Nobel Committee had not only passed over such obvious candidates as Theodore Dreiser and Sherwood Anderson; it had given the world's highest accolade to a former missionary and a woman. As Robert Frost remarked, "If *she* can get it, anybody can."

— James C. Thomas Jr., *The Washington Post*

• . . . once again the NBA (National Book Awards) exists primarily to honor the obscure, the recondite and the unknown.

— Jonathan Yardley, "Book Awards: What's Outside Is In," *The Washington Post*

• It may or may not be a sad commentary on American culture, but pure literary excellence, undefiled by the stains of wealth and éclat, goes generally unhonored in these United States. We revere authors only after we have made them prosperous and famous, and we usually do this after their best work has been done; the awards that get the most public attention tend to be those that go to precisely such writers...

— Jonathan Yardley, "On Literati and Glitterbugs," *The Washington Post*

• Indeed, influence in its various forms seems to have swayed the judges at least as much as true greatness. ...

They are on the list not because of what they are but because of what they say; their morally impeccable thematic content as opposed to their actual literary quality.

. . . Lunacy, sheer unbridled lunacy.

. . . and no room–quite stupidly–was left for short stories.

— Jonathan Yardley, "The List of Great Novels: Read It and Weep," *The Washington Post*

• In a remarkable display of inconsistency, only 23 titles were cited by at least 10 of 125 writers listing their 10 all-time favorite works of fiction. A total of 544 different titles were named in all. The most nominated book, *Madame Bovary*, was cited by only 26, or roughly one-fifth of the participating authors. All this proves that without uniform specific criteria, judgment of quality is essentially a matter of personal opinion, at least apparently among writers.

— Data reported in *The Top Ten: Writers Pick Their Favorite Books*, J. Peder Zane, Editor

Literary Feuds

Anthony Arthur's *Literary Feuds* provides us with some interesting insights into feuds within the literary community, the typical causes being "pride and the competitive spirit." Envy of being outdistanced in fame and financial success by a rival sometimes plays an initiating role.

In a review, Roy E. Perry dramatically comments "Some of the most illustrious writers have tried to destroy the reputations of their enemies, using wit, humor, sarcasm, invective, and the occasional right cross to the jaw." These quotations from the book illustrate his point.

• Ernest Hemingway: "Gertrude Stein was never crazy/Gertrude Stein was very lazy."

• Sinclair Lewis: "I still say you [Theodore Dreiser] are a liar and a thief."

• Theodore Dreiser: He [Sinclair Lewis] is a noisy, ostentatious, and shallow . . . I never could like the man."

• Lillian Hellman dismissed Mary McCarthy as merely "a lady magazine writer."

• Mary McCarthy charged in an interview with Dick Cavett that Hellman "is tremendously overrated, a bad writer, and a dishonest writer. . ."

• Gore Vidal: "It is inhuman to attack [Truman] Capote. You are attacking an elf." And in response to Truman's miserable death, Vidal referred to it as "a good career move."

• Mark Twain knew he was a better writer than Bret Harte and could not abide critics who lumped them together.

Deaths Too Early

We report, with respect, the seemingly too common early deaths afflicting the writing field—here 13 acclaimed authors whose premature departure saddened and deprived the world to this day.

• In the last year of his life **Stephen Crane** suffered from increasingly virulent attacks of tuberculosis, aggravated by a punishing work schedule. In December 1899 Crane and Cora Taylor held an elaborate Christmas party at Brede Place in England, attended by Joseph Conrad, Henry James, H. G. Wells, and other friends. Five months later on June 5, 1900, he died at the age of 28, at a health spa in Badenweiler, Germany.

• **Emily Bronte** died in 1848 at the age of 30. She never left the house after her brother Branwell's death, also of tuberculosis, just three months earlier. Emily never spoke of her condition or allowed others to, never gave up her work routine even on the last day, never allowed a doctor until literally the eleventh hour, telling Charlotte just before noon, "If you will send for a doctor, I will see him now," and then dying at two o'clock.

Only the family and servants were in the funeral procession, and Emily's dog, who had sat in the Bronte pew during the service, would sit and howl by Emily's door for a week afterwards.

— Steve King, *Today in Literature*

• With death close, and seeing her sister Charlotte's distress, **Anne Bronte** whispered to her to "take courage," then that afternoon, May 28, 1849, Anne died of tuberculosis. Charlotte made the decision to "lay the flower where it had fallen," burying Anne not in Haworth with the rest of her family, but in Scarborough. Anne was only 29.

• In the early morning hours of Sunday, February 10, 1963, **Sylvia Plath** left cups of milk and plates of bread and butter beside the beds of her two children for breakfast, although they were too young to feed themselves. She also opened the window beside their beds. Then she sealed off her kitchen door on the floor below with wet towels and tape, left a note on the pram to call her doctor, laid out a cloth for a pillow, turned on the gas, knelt down and put her head inside the oven. Sylvia was 30 years old.

Ted Hughes, Plath's husband, was devastated. In a letter to an old friend of Plath's from Smith College, he wrote, "That's the end of my life. The rest is posthumous."

On March 16, 2009, Nicholas Hughes, the son of Plath and Hughes, hanged himself at his home in Alaska, following a history of depression.

• Distraught over hearing of his friend Fitzgerald's death, **Nathanael West** and his wife Eileen McKenney were both killed when West crashed his car after ignoring a stop sign in El Centro, California. McKenney had been the inspiration for the title character in the play *My Sister Eileen*, and both she and Nathanael had planned to fly to New York for the Broadway opening four days later. West was 36 when he died.

• In 1938 **Thomas Wolfe** was diagnosed with miliary tuberculosis of the brain. He was sent to Baltimore's Johns Hopkins Hospital for treatment under the most famous neurosurgeon at that time. An operation revealed the disease had overrun the entire right side of his brain. Without regaining consciousness, he died 18 days before his 38th birthday.

Time wrote: "The death last week of Thomas Clayton Wolfe shocked critics with the realization that, of all American novelists of his generation, he was the one from whom most had been expected."

• On October 3, 1849, **Edgar Allan Poe** was found on the streets of Baltimore delirious and in great distress. He was taken to the Washington College Hospital were he died four days later at the age of 40. Poe was never sufficiently coherent to explain how he came to be in his dire condition. The exact cause of his death remains a mystery; both his medical records and death certificate have been lost.

• **Jack London** died November 22, 1916, on his ranch in Sonoma County, Northern California. He was in extreme pain and had possibly accidentally taken an overdose of morphine. London had been a robust man but had undergone several serious illnesses, including scurvy while in the Klondike. He may have picked up unspecified tropical infections during his sailings aboard the *Snark* in the South Seas. At the time of his death he suffered from dysentery and uremia. He was 40 years old.

• Convicted of gross indecency, **Oscar Wilde** served two years at hard labor in prisons in London. Released in 1897 his health, although not his spirit, was greatly diminished. While continuing to write he was beset with poverty, pitifully writing his publisher "This poverty really breaks one's heart: it is so *sale*, so utterly depressing, so hopeless. Pray do what you can." After three years, now damaged in spirit, Wilde was so confined to his hotel that on one of his trips outside he remarked, "My wallpaper and I are fighting a duel to the death. One of us has got to go." In this instance it was Wilde who died, of cerebral meningitis, November 30, 1900. He was 46 years old.

• **Margaret Mitchell** was struck by a speeding automobile as she crossed Peachtree Street in Atlanta with her husband on August 11, 1949. Five days later she died at Grady Hospital without regaining consciousness. She was 48 years old. The driver, an off-duty taxi operator, was arrested for drunken driving, convicted of involuntary manslaughter and served 11 months in prison. He had frequent arrests for speeding, recklessness, and disorderly conduct. Yet his conviction turned out to be controversial because witnesses said Mitchell stepped into the street without looking, and her friends admitted she often did this.

• **Jerzy Kosinski** appears to have fooled just about everyone. Those who have seen the movie *Reds* knew that Kosinski was a great actor. On Thursday, May 2, 1991, he appeared to be in a particularly good mood, attending a book signing party for Senator William S. Cohen. Later he returned to his West 57th Street apartment, greeting his second wife, Katherina (Kiki) von Fraunhofer, then retired around 9 p.m. Von Fraunhofer would later recall that her husband seemed in especially good spirits that night. Fourteen hours later she opened the door to his bathroom to find Kosinski naked in a half-filled bathtub, a plastic shopping bag tied around his head. Among his papers a suicide note was found. It read: "I'm going to put myself to sleep now for a bit longer than usual. Call the time Eternity." Kosinski was 57.

• After finishing her last novel, **Virginia Woolf** fell into a depression heightened by the onset of World War II and destruction of her London home during the Blitz. In the early morning of March 28, 1941, she put on her overcoat, filled its pockets with stones; then walked into the River Ouse near her home. In her last note to her husband this heartbreaking farewell: "You have given me the greatest possible happiness. You have been in every way all that anyone could be. I don't think two people could have been happier 'til this terrible disease came. I can't fight any longer. . . . What I want to say is I owe all the happiness of my life to you." Virginia Woolf was 59 years old when she died.

• Possibly the electro-shock therapy **Ernest Hemingway** received in treatment for his depression, which left his memory and ability to write in ruins, was what finally sent him over the edge. His last sustained work was an article on bullfighting commissioned by *Life* magazine, published in 1960. The acute writer's block which followed drove him to tears. In the last few months he became quite listless, unable to take pleasure in anything. On the morning of July 2, 1961, he loaded both chambers of a 12 gauge shotgun, placed the butt of the gun on the floor, rested his forehead on top of both barrels and than pulled the two triggers. Hemingway was 61 years old. His beautiful tribute to a friend now graces his own memorial stone north of Ketchum, Idaho (see page 45).

Statue of a hooded female figure, by sculptor Augustus Saint-Gaudens, in *Rock Creek Cemetery*, Washington, D.C. Photo by A. J. Calhoun

Tributes, Epitaphs, and Inscriptions

- F. Scott Fitzgerald (a Princeton man) set the bar high for anyone who wants to luxuriate in the tragedy of excess wealth and shattered dreams. In his best novels and short stories, the language is so lovely that you don't mind or even notice how really silly the plots are, how insufferable the characters.

  — Ron Charles, Senior Editor, *The Washington Post Book World*

- In all his fiction Joseph Conrad's great theme is human nature in extremis, and perhaps only Dostoevsky plumbs more deeply into the ravaged souls of men. While Conrad's prose can be slack or overripe, and sometimes his syntax doesn't quite track, that voice on the page earns its grandeur and eloquence. It speaks with the melancholy authority of lived experience.

  — Michael Dirda, *The Washington Post Book World*

- On the lot where a factory once stood, there is a ring of polished granite blocks and some benches. A small sign hanging from a railing reads JACK KEROUAC COMMEMORATIVE PARK.

  "Plenty of people in this town didn't want that park," says Chiungos, a commercial realtor, as he stops at a traffic light and looks at the lot. "*They* say Jack was nothing but a drunk. But then a lot of people around here just don't have it in their heads that he's a celebrity, recognized all over the world."

  — Mike D'Orso, *Time* magazine

- "So we beat on, boats against the current,
  borne back ceaselessly into the past"

  — Quote from *The Great Gatsby* inscribed on the gravestone of Francis Scott Key Fitzgerald and his wife Zelda Sayre, St. Mary's Cemetery, Rockville, Maryland

- "Even amidst fierce flames the golden lotus can be planted."

  — Inscribed on the gravestone of Sylvia Plath Hughes, Heptonstall Churchyard, Heptonstall, Yorkshire, United Kingdom

- Farewell, thou child of my right hand, and joy;
  My sin was too much hope of thee, lov'd boy.
  Rest in soft peace, and, asked, say, Here doth lie
  Ben Jonson his best piece of poetry.
  For whose sake henceforth all his vows be such
  As what he loves may never like too much.

  — Ben Jonson (1572-1637) English dramatist, poet and actor. Poem occasioned by the death of Jonson's seven-year-old son in the plague.

- "The Stone the Builders Rejected
  Jack London"
  — Gravestone inscription, Jack London State Historic Park,
  Glen Ellen, California

- In his (Ring Lardner's) grotesque but searching tales of baseball players, pugilists, movie queens, song-writers and other such dismal persons he set down common American with the utmost precision, and yet with enough imagination to make his work a contribution of genuine and permanent value to the national literature.
  — H. L. Mencken (1880-1956) journalist and satirist

  As the author (many years ago) of a biography of Lardner, I can perhaps fairly be accused of partisanship, but I am positive that it was *You Know Me, Al: A Busher's Letters Home*, as well as the many Lardner short stories that followed over the next decade and a half, that showed other American writers how to get the American vernacular down right.
  — Jonathan Yardley, *The Washington Post*

- Quoth the Raven,
  "Nevermore"
  — Edgar Allan Poe's gravestone quote, Westminster
  Presbyterian Cemetery, Baltimore, Maryland

- These are the tales of Edgar Allan Poe
  Not exactly the boy next door
  — Lou Reed, from *POEtry* a rock opera

- Hemingway is interred in the town cemetery in Ketchum, Idaho, at the north end of town. Fittingly, a memorial was erected at another location he loved, overlooking Trail Creek, north of Ketchum. It is inscribed with this haunting, beautiful eulogy he wrote for a friend:
  Best of all he loved the fall
  The leaves yellow on the cottonwoods
  Leaves floating on the trout streams
  And above the hills
  The high blue windless skies
  Now he will be a part of them forever
  — Ernest Hemingway, Idaho, 1939

The Novel Genre (State of the Art)

- Indeed, it is now virtually impossible to master the Western Canon.
  — Harold Bloom, *The Western Canon: The Books and School of the Ages*

- I wonder whether what we are publishing now is worth cutting down trees to make paper for the stuff.
  — Richard Brautigan (1935-1984) American writer

• The changing wisdom of successive generations discards ideas, questions facts, demolishes theories. But the artist appeals to that part of our being which is not dependent on wisdom; to that in us which is a gift and not an acquisition—and, therefore, more permanently enduring.

— Joseph Conrad (1857-1924) preface to *The Nigger of the 'Narcissus.'*

• The world of books is the most remarkable creation of man. Nothing else that he builds ever lasts. Monuments fall, nations perish, civilizations grow old and die out; and, after an era of darkness, new races build others. But in the world of books are volumes that have seen this happen again and again, and yet live on, still young, still as fresh as the day they were written, still telling men's hearts of the hearts of men centuries dead.

— Clarence Day (1874-1935) author of *Life With Father*, 1935

• If we encounter a man of rare intellect, we should ask him what books he reads.

— Ralph Waldo Emerson (1803-1882) American essayist and poet

• There are books . . . which rank in our life with parents and lovers and passionate experiences.

— Ralph Waldo Emerson

• . . . let the novel go; we have enough complications in life, in art, in literature without preserving dead forms fossilized, without cluttering ourselves with Byzantine sterilities.

— William Golding (1911-1993) British novelist

• Hemingway once wrote a story in just six words ("For sale: baby shoes, never worn.") and is said to have called it his best work.

• . . . Journalism allows its readers to witness history; fiction gives its readers an opportunity to live it.

— John Hersey (1914-1993) American writer and journalist

• I would be the first to admit that there is no future in this series for anyone concerned. . . .

— Allen Lane commenting in the *Bookseller* prior to the launch of Penguin Books in 1935

• In the main there are two sorts of books; those that no-one reads and those that no-one ought to read.

— H. L. Mencken (1880-1956) journalist and satirist

• If I'm a lousy writer, a helluva lot of people have got lousy taste.

— Grace Metalious, author of *Peyton Place*

• We are drowning in information but starved for knowledge.

— John Naisbitt (1929-) American author

• Less than half (46.7%) of the adult American population read a novel in 2002. Only the strong growth in overall U.S. population offset the decline, allowing the total number of readers to remain essentially the same.

— National Endowment for the Arts, *Reading At Risk: A Survey of Literary Reading in America*, July, 2004

• Literature is news that stays news.

— Ezra Pound (1885-1972) American poet

• Those big-shot writers . . . could never dig the fact that there are more salted peanuts consumed than caviar.

— Mickey Spillane (1918-2006) on the popularity of mystery books

• The multitude of books is making us ignorant.

— Voltaire (1694-1778) French Enlightenment writer, essayist, and philosopher

• With so many fine books to be read, so much to be studied and known, there is no need to bore ourselves with this rubbish.

— Edmund Wilson (1895-1972) American writer and literary critic

• At this weak, pale, nascent moment in the history of American literature, we need a battalion, a brigade, of Zolas to head out into this wild, bizarre, unpredictable, Hog-stomping Baroque country of ours and reclaim it as literary property. Philip Roth was absolutely right. The imagination of the novelist is powerless before what he knows he's going to read in tomorrow morning's newspaper. But a generation of American writers has drawn precisely the wrong connection from that perfectly valid observation. The answer is not to leave the rude beast, the material, also known as the life around us, to the journalists but to do what journalists do, or are supposed to do, which is to wrestle the beast and bring it to terms.

— Tom Wolfe (1931-) "Stalking the Billion-Footed Beast," *Harper's Magazine*, November 1989

• Cut through all the other shortcomings of contemporary American fiction and what you find at the core is not merely its failure but its willful refusal to engage real life.

— Jonathan Yardley, "For American Novelists, It's Time to Get Real," *The Washington Post*, October 30, 1989

• Five notable best-selling novels repeatedly rejected by publishers:

The Postman Always Rings Twice, James M. Cain, 1938
Heaven Knows, Mr. Allison, Charles Shaw, 1953
Auntie Mame, Patrick Dennis, 1955
Dune, Frank Herbert, 1965
*M*A*S*H*, Richard Hooker, 1969

• Award winning novels are a little shorter than in the past, thankfully in this reviewer's opinion. The median length of winners in the 50 years 1851 to 1900 was 472 pages, then down to 384 pages in the 25 years 1901 to 1925, and steady at 315 pages from 1926 to 1950 and again from 1951 to 1975. 1976 to 2000 saw a slight rise to 355 pages. Thus the median length of today's quality novel is likely around 350 pages compared to perhaps a hundred pages more for works written before 1900.

• How rare are great fiction writers compared, for example, to great composers or great painters and sculptors? Actually, the numbers in each instance are quite small, 60 or so names generally suffice. With so few personages involved, perhaps it would be better to ask how important are writers in people's minds compared to notables in the other arts? Here the answer is a uniform "not very." Among "100 Most Important People of the Second Millennium," compiled by *Life* magazine, only six were writers or poets, eight visual artists, and four musicians. In contrast, half the group were either scientists, inventors, or government leaders. Thus it is probably fair to conclude that while greatly enriching our lives, the artists of the world are few in number and apparently well-spread among the involved disciplines.

The Writing Craft

• If you think you can write, consider this description of Lauren Bacall by James Agee, possibly written after he had seen the actress in *Key Largo* with Humphrey Bogart.

Lauren Bacall has cinema personality to burn. She has a javelin-like vitality, a born dancer's eloquence of movement, a fierce female shrewdness, and a special sweet-sourness. With these faculties, plus a stone-crushing self-confidence and a trombone voice, she manages to get across the toughest girl Hollywood has dreamed of in a long, long while.

— James Agee (1909-1955) *Agee on Film*

• ... the only way I could finish a book and get a plot going was just to keep making it longer and longer until something happens.

— Nelson Algren (1909-1981) American writer

• Well, I don't know exactly how it's done, I let it alone a good deal.

— Saul Bellow (1915-2005) Canadian-born American writer

• Every great story . . . must leave in the mind of the sensitive reader an intangible residuum of pleasure; a cadence, a quality of voice that is exclusively the writer's own, individual, unique.

— Willa Cather (1873-1947) American author

• We shall fight on the beaches, we shall fight on the landing grounds, we shall fight in the fields and in the streets, we shall fight in the hills; we shall never surrender, . . .

Let us therefore brace ourselves to our duties, and so bear ourselves that, if the British Empire and its commonwealth last for a thousand years, men will still say, "This was their finest hour."

— Great literature in speeches, here illustrated by two single sentences from Winston Churchill's wartime speeches delivered to the British Parliament House of Commons on June 4 and June 18, 1940, respectively.

• . . . Fiction is not a dream. Nor is it guesswork. It is imagining based on facts, and the facts must be accurate or the work of imagining will not stand up.

— Margaret Culkin Banning (1891-1982) in *The Writer*

• One's first encounter with Melville is...usually...in *Moby-Dick*. It does not take long to realize that this is a writer whose relation to words is not so much mastery as it is a kind of hot intimacy in which the language will do anything he asks of it. He accosts you; he bends close to you to share a confidence; he wanders away from the point, distracted by a new half-formed idea; he falls away into silence as if stunned by the cost of his own discoveries.

— Andrew Delbanco (1952-) in *Required Reading*

• Certainly *Moby-Dick* is a very written book. I'll make a crude distinction here between those writers who make their language visible, who draw attention to it in the act of writing and don't let us forget it—Melville, Joyce, Nabokov in our own time, the song-and-dance men, the strutting dandies of literature—from those magicians of the real who write to make their language invisible, like lit stage scrims that pass us through to the scene behind, so that we see the life they are rendering as if no language is producing it. Tolstoy and Chekhov are in this class, so clearly neither one nor the other method can be said to be *the way*.

— E. L. Doctorow (1931-) *Creationists: Selected Essays 1993-2006*

• Writing fiction, there are no limits to what you write as long as it increases the value of the paper you are writing on.

— Buddy Ebsen (1908-2003) American character actor

• No one who has ever seen a writer trying to join passion, clarity and style with a selection from the 11 million words in the English language could fail to see the trying labor of it.

— Paul Engle, faculty member, State University of Iowa

• South African writer Mrs. Mary Faulkner is history's most prolific novelist. She wrote under six pen names and completed 904 books over her 70 year lifetime (1903-1973).

— *Guinness Book of World Records*

• On the whole, I think you should write biographies of those you admire and respect, and novels about human beings who you think are sadly mistaken.

— Penelope Fitzgerald (1916-2000) British biographer and novelist

• How do I know what I think until I see what I say?

— E. M. Forster (1879-1970) English novelist and short story writer

• . . . for it brings about the fundamental difference between people in daily life and people in books. In daily life we never understand each other, neither complete clairvoyance nor complete confessional exists. We know each other approximately, by external signs, and these serve well enough as a basis for society and even for intimacy. But people in a novel can be understood completely by the reader, if the novelist wishes; their inner as well as their outer life can be exposed. And this is why they often seem more defined than characters in history, or even our own friends . . .

— E. M. Forster, *Aspects of the Novel*, 1927

• The economy of a novelist is a little like that of a careful housewife who is unwilling to throw away anything that might perhaps serve its turn.

— Graham Greene (1904-1991) English novelist

• I began to write fiction on the assumption that the true enemies of the novel were plot, character, setting and theme.

— John Hawkes (1925-1998) experimental novelist

• The devil himself always seems to get into my inkstand, and I can only exorcise him by pensful at a time."

— Nathaniel Hawthorne (1804-1864) 19th Century American novelist

• A writer's problem does not change. He himself changes and the world he lives in changes but his problem remains the same. It is always how to write truly and having found what is true, to project it in such a way that it becomes a part of the experience of the person who reads it.

The most essential gift for a good writer is a built-in, shock-proof shit detector.

— Ernest Hemingway (1898-1961) American novelist

• . . . all writers believe they are realists.

— Roman Jakobson (1896-1982) Russian Formalist critic

• The wit of Samuel Johnson characterized the scribbling fever as "the epidemical conspiracy for the destruction of paper."

— Samuel Johnson (1709-1784) British author, poet, essayist, literary critic, and lexicographer

• James Jones said that although he awoke at 7 or 8 in the morning, he could not get to work until he had spent half-an-hour or so "fiddling around" smoking several cigarettes and drinking half a dozen cups of coffee. "Finally there's no excuse. I go to my typewriter."

• Any word you have to hunt for in a thesaurus is the wrong word. There are no exceptions to this rule.

— Stephen King (1947-) *Everything You Need to Know About Writing Sucessfully–in Ten Minutes,* 1988

• Advice to writers: Sometimes you just have to stop writing. Even before you begin.

— Stanislaw J. Lee (1909-1966) *Unkempt Thoughts*

• To interest is the first duty of art; no other excellences will ever begin to compensate for failure in this, and very serious faults will be covered by this, as by charity.

— C. S. Lewis (1898-1963) Irish author and scholar

• Character is arguably the most important single component of the novel. . . . Yet character is probably the most difficult aspect of the art of fiction to discuss in technical terms.

[Then, after discussing the ease of transferring Christopher Isherwood's Sally Bowles in *Goodbye to Berlin* to the screen, this observation] But there are nuances in the passage which are purely literary. You could show the green nail polish, but not the narrator's ironic comment: "a color unfortunately chosen." "Unfortunately chosen" is the story of Sally's life. And you could show the nicotine stains and the dirt, but only a narrator could observe: "dirty as a little girl's." The childlike quality beneath the surface sophistication is precisely what makes Sally Bowles a memorable character.

— David Lodge, The Art of Fiction — "Introducing A Character,"
The Washington Post

• I have been told that when the late Sir Edward Marsh, composing his memoir of Rupert Brooke, wrote "Rupert left Rugby in a blaze of glory," the poet's mother, a lady of firm character, changed "a blaze of glory" to "July."

— F. L. Lucas (1894-1967) English literary critic, essayist, and poet

• It's not a good idea to try to put your wife into a novel, not your latest wife anyway.

I usually need a can of beer to prime me.

— Norman Mailer (1923-2007) American novelist

• A writer is somebody for whom writing is more difficult than it is for other people.

— Thomas Mann (1875-1955) *Essay of Three Decades*, 1942

• There are three rules for writing the novel. Unfortunately, no one knows what they are.

— W. Somerset Maugham (1874-1965) English playwright, novelist, and short story writer

• . . . the writer who wants his words to live for more than a day neither publishes, mails or buries what he has just written; instead, he rewrites it. With the kind of courage that only he will know about, he cuts whatever words are useless or false, whatever thoughts are vague or stale. He reads it over and over like a sniffling editor who has an allergy to weak language.

He asks questions: Is this really worth writing, have I said it well, will it stand in print as well as it stands in my ego? If the answers are yes to the hard questions, he has learned a basic fact: writing is rewriting what you have already written.

— Colman McCarthy (1938-) "Writing: A Matter of Commas, Blank Pages and Limps," *The Washington Post*

• Eventually all novelists, if they persist too long, get worse. No reason to name names, since no one is spared. Writing great fiction involves some combination of energy and imagination that cannot be energized or realized forever. Strong talents can simply exhaust their gift, and they do.

— Larry McMurtry (1936-) *Books: A Memoir*

• For all our seeming differences and genuine divisions we are bound by words.

— Christopher Merrill (1957-) author and poet

• If I find I'm not able to write, I quit.

— Henry Miller (1891-1980) American writer

• I was writing fiction, but not finishing fiction.

— Elizabeth Moon (1945-) American science fiction and fantasy author

• Words, sentences, paragraphs — these are our basic tools and ultimate means of gratification. Metaphor, similes, rhyme and meter, symbols and line-breaks, even the elusive epiphany — these are the instruments of a writer's success. And of a poet's.

— Walter Mosely (1952-) "The Writing Life: On the novelist's obligation to employ politics and poetry," *The Washington Post*

• Caress the details, the divine details . . . What color was the bottle containing the arsenic with which Emma Bovary poisoned herself?

— Vladimir Nabokov (1899-1977) Russian-American author

• Every morning between nine and 12, I go to my room and sit before a piece of paper. Many times, I just sit for three hours with no ideas coming to me. But I know one thing: if an idea does come between nine and 12, I am there ready for it.

— Flannery O'Connor (1925-1964) American author

• Frank O'Connor on his writing process: "I don't give a hoot what the writing's like," and put down "any sort of rubbish" as long as it has some relation to my general outline.

• A scrupulous writer, in every sentence that he writes, will ask himself at least four questions, thus: What am I trying to say? What words will express it? What image or idiom will make it clearer? Is this image fresh enough to have an effect?

— George Orwell (1903-1950) "Politics and the English Language," 1946

• I can't write five words but that I change seven.

— Dorothy Parker (1893-1963) American author

• The style is you. Oh, you can cultivate a style, I suppose, if you like. But . . . it remains a cultivated style. It remains artificial and imposed, and I don't think it deceives anyone. (In the end), you do not create a style. You work, and develop yourself; your style is an emanation from your own being. — Katherine Anne Porter (1890-1980) American novelist

• I have had to conclude that I am a writer who takes short breaths, and in consequence the story and the essay have been the best forms for me.

— V. S. Pritchett (1900-1997) British writer and critic, in *Midnight Oil*

• I don't know what happened, but my character just got away from me and did his own thing. I had nothing to do with it. . . . Do you know my Tatiana has rejected Onegin? I never expected that.

— Alexander Pushkin (1799-1837) on the wayward behavior of his characters as reported by James Wood in *How Fiction Works*

• Charles Reade, English novelist and dramatist, not a man to be intimidated by what turned out to be an American classic, began his editorial work on Melville's *Moby-Dick* by drawing a bold line through the first line of Chapter One—"Call me Ishmael."

• Research is William Gaddis's gift—and his burden. The onetime fact checker for The New Yorker would probably be uncomfortable telling you the time unless he had acquired a profound understanding of how a watch is made. That dedication to detail is the mark of an author who reportedly has 20 pages of research behind every paragraph in his 1955 debut, "The Recognitions," a remarkable novel about fakery and counterfeiting.

— John Schwartz, "America's Greatest Novelist?" *The Washington Post*

• William Shawn was known for his meticulous editing, providing as many as 20 sets of revisions for some submissions. After one two-hour discussion of commas and word usage, author Ved Mehata thanked Shawn for his care and commented that the piece belonged as much to the editor as the author. "No, it belongs to you." Shawn replied, "I just made it more yours."

— Reported by Steve King in *Today in Literature*

Winslow Homer,
The New Novel
(1877)

• The creative-writing teacher's most valuable advice is "Write what you know"—a truism—and indeed most of us do our best work when we write closest to our own lives. An yet, and yet— there are the rest of us, who quite simply like to make things up. There's also the practical aspect: If you write a lot, if you're addicted to writing the way I am, you simply don't have the time or the money to go out and live like crazy all the time.

— Lee Smith (1944-) American novelist

• Explaining how easy it was for him to write, Red Smith, the great sportswriter, said he just sat at the typewriter and opened a vein.

• The profession of book-writing makes horse racing seem like a solid, stable business.

— John Steinbeck (1902-1968) American writer

• Originality does not consist in saying what no one has ever said before, but in saying exactly what you think yourself.

— Leslie Stephen (1832-1904) English author and critic

• Central yet remarkably short plot highlights—

Known the world over, Gulliver's amazing discovery of finding himself on awakening bound hand and foot by little people not six inches high is described by Jonathan Swift in a few paragraphs in a volume of nearly 300 pages.

Captain Ahab, in a lifetime pursuit, harpoons Moby-Dick and then in the next instant is caught up in the trailing line and voicelessly yanked out of the boat to his doom, action described by Herman Melville in a single paragraph on the next to the last page of a text of 637 pages.

• As remarkable examples of what's been left out, consider these exorcised lines (in italics) among the myriad deletions expunged by editors from authors' original texts.

All happy families are alike; *they have dinner together and the children do the dishes*; each unhappy family is unhappy in its own way; *it could be anything: drunkenness, sassy back-talk, refusal to clean up one's room, tantrums, nose-picking, adultery, don't ask.*

— Leo Tolstoy (1828-1910) *Anna Karenina*

When Mrs. Frederick C. Little's second son arrived, everybody noticed that he was not much bigger than a mouse *and that they could save a ton of money on diapers by using one quarter of a Kleenex as needed.*

— E. B. White (1899-1985) *Stuart Little*

• Write something, even if it's a suicide note.

— Gore Vidal, (1925-) American novelist, screenwriter, playwright, essayist, and short story writer

• The good ended happily, and the bad unhappily. That is what Fiction means. — Oscar Wilde (1854-1900) Irish writer and poet

• If Queen Elizabeth or Frederick the Great or Ernest Hemingway were to read their biographies, they would exclaim, 'Ah, my secret is still safe.' But if Natasha Rostov were to read *War and Peace* she would cry out as she covered her face with her hands: 'How did he know, how did he know?'

— Thornton Wilder (1897-1975) American playwright and novelist

• I just sit at a typewriter and curse a bit.

— P. G. Wodehouse (1881-1973) on his technique as a writer

• I can always find plenty of women to sleep with but the kind of woman that is really hard for me to find is a typist who can read my writing.

— Thomas Wolfe (1900-38) American novelist

• Was it reporting that made (Sinclair) Lewis the most highly regarded American novelist of the 1920s? Certainly not by itself. But it was the material he found through reporting that enabled Lewis to exercise with such rich variety his insights, many of them exceptionally subtle, into the psyches of men and women and into the status structure of society. . . .

. . . I doubt that there is a writer over forty who does not realize in his heart of hearts that literary genius, in prose, consists of proportions more on the order of 65 percent material and 35 percent the talent in the sacred crucible.

— Tom Wolfe (1931-) "Stalking the Billion-Footed Beast," *Harper's Magazine*, November 1989

• The unique "emotional involvement" and "gripping" or "absorbing" quality of the realistic novel is derived mainly from four devices cited by Tom Wolfe, partially paraphrased as follows:

(1) . . . telling the story by moving from scene to scene and resorting as little as possible to sheer historical narrative.

(2) . . . (employing) realistic dialogue to quickly and effectively establish and define character, such dialogue involving the reader more completely than any other single device.

(3) . . . presenting every scene to the reader through the eyes of a particular character, giving the reader the feeling of being inside the character's mind and experiencing the emotional reality of the scene as he experiences it.

(4) . . . recording symbolic details, generally of people's *status life*, . . . which lies as close to the center of the power of realism as any other device in literature. This is the recording of everyday gestures, habits, manners, customs, styles of furniture, clothing, decoration, styles of traveling, eating, . . .

— Tom Wolfe (1931-) "Why they aren't writing the Great American Novel anymore," *Esquire Magazine*, December 1972.

• One of the supreme moments in French literature was made possible only through the drudgery called documentation secured by Emile Zola in this account by Tom Wolfe.

. . . In 1884 Zola went down into the mines at Anzin to do the documentation for what was to become the novel *Germinal.* Posing as a secretary for a member of the French Chamber of Deputies, he descended into the pits wearing his city clothes, his frock coat, high stiff collar, and high stiff hat (this appeals to me for reasons I won't delay you with), and carrying a notebook and pen. One day Zola and the miners who were serving as his guides were 150 feet below the ground when Zola noticed an enormous workhorse, a Percheron, pulling a sled piled with coal through a tunnel. Zola asked, "How do you get that animal in and out of the mine ever day?" At first the miners thought he was joking. Then they realized he was serious, and one of them said, "Mr. Zola, don't you understand? That horse comes down here *once*, when he's a colt, barely more than a foal, and still able to fit into the buckets that bring *us* down here. That horse grows up down here. He grows blind down here after a year or two, from the lack of light. He hauls coal down here until he can't haul it anymore, and then he dies down here, and his bones are buried down here." When Zola transfers this revelation from the pages of his documentation notebook to the pages of *Germinal,* it makes the hair on your arms stand on end. You realize, without the need of amplification, that the horse is the miners themselves, who descend below the face of the earth as children and dig coal down in the pit until they can dig no more and then are buried, often literally, down there.

— Tom Wolfe, "Stalking the Billion-Footed Beast," *Harper's Magazine*, November 1989

• In *Sea and Sardinia*, (D. H.) Lawrence describes the short legs of King Victor Emmanuel; but he refers to "his little short legs." Now, in some technical sense, there is no need to have both "short" and "little" in the same sentence. If Lawrence were a schoolboy, his teacher would write "redundant" in the margin and remove one of the adjectives. But say it aloud a few times, and it suddenly seems inevitable. We need the two words, because they sound farcical together. And short does not mean the same as little: the two words enjoy each other's company; and "little short legs" is more original than "short little legs," because it is jumpier, is more absurd, forcing us to stumble slightly–stumble short-leggedly–over the unexpected rhythm.

— James Wood, *How Fiction Works*

• In (George) Orwell's essay "A Hanging," the writer watches the condemned man, walking toward the gallows, swerve to avoid a puddle. For Orwell, this represents precisely what he calls the "mystery" of the life that is about to be taken: when there is no good reason for it, the condemned man is still thinking about keeping his shoes clean. It is an "irrelevant" act (and a marvelous bit of noticing on Orwell's part).

— James Wood, *How Fiction Works*

• Remarking about what he likes about short stories: "the power, the directness, the unity of impression, the ability they have to conjure up whole worlds in a few pages."

— Tobias Wolff (1945-) American author

• She portrays "her fools, her prigs, her worldlings" with "the lash of a whip-like phrase which, as it runs round them, cuts out their silhouettes for ever," and "Sometimes it seems as if her creatures were born merely to give Jane Austen the supreme delight of slicing their heads off."

— Virginia Woolf (1882-1941) in praise of Jane Austin

• Like all the rest of (John) Marquand's work, it is written with what the author himself called the "smooth technique" routinely disparaged by his critics. Its prose flows without apparent effort, which scored Marquand no points at a moment in literary history that favored Hemingway's self-conscious leanness, Fitzgerald's poetic romanticism and Faulkner's dense complexity. Never mind that it takes a great deal of work and discipline to perfect a "smooth technique," and never mind that Marquand's prose is just about as distinctive and readily identifiable as that of other writers celebrated as stylists; in the places where literary reputations are made, he was dismissed as a slick entertainer.

— Jonathan Yardley, "John Marquand, Zinging WASPs With a Smooth Sting," *The Washington Post*, February 20, 2003

• Two flashforward scenes and their aftermaths of unparalleled drama and pathos:

In "An Occurrence at Owl Creek Bridge," an 1886 Civil War-era short story by Ambrose Bierce, a Confederate spy is about to be hung from Owl Creek Bridge by Union soldiers. As the noose tightens around his neck the rope suddenly breaks and he falls into the creek below, eventually evading Union troops to find his way home. As he is about to embrace his wife, a blinding white light surrounds him followed by silence. Only then do we learn that he is in fact hanging in the noose below the bridge, his escape an hallucination just seconds before death.

Considered by Hemingway himself to be one of his finest stories, "The Snows of Kilimanjaro" relates the thoughts and memories of an African hunter slowly awaiting death from an infected wound. Fortunately, at the last minute, a plane arrives and he joyfully looks out the window at the beautiful snow covered cone of Kilimanjaro as he is lofted into the sky and safety. Then, dramatically, the scene switches back to camp where his wife is awakened by the cry of a hyena and sees her husband lying still on his cot.

Titles

• A good title should be like a good metaphor; it should intrigue without being too baffling or too obvious.

— Walker Percy (1916-1990) American southern author

• What makes a good title is an elusive intangible, defying all but the vaguest description, something likely related to meaning and poetry, meter and hint of intrigue. However, we all know one when we see one and here are my favorites: *A Farewell to Arms*, *All Quiet on the Western Front*, *A Passage to India*, *Appointment in Sumatra*, *A Streetcar Named Desire*, *A Walk on the Wild Side*, *Cry, the Beloved Country*, *Days of Wine and Roses*, *East of Eden*, *For Whom the Bell Tolls*, *From Here to Eternity*, *Gone With the Wind*, *The Grapes of Wrath*, *The Heart is a Lonely Hunter*, *Knock on Any Door*, *The Last of the Mohicans*, *Look Homeward Angel*, *The Maltese Falcon*, *The Naked and the Dead*, *Night of the Iguana*, *Paradise Lost*, *The Postman Always Rings Twice*, *The Razor's Edge*, *The Red Badge of Courage*, *The Sun Also Rises*, *The Waste Land.*

And, if you're not happy with the above array, consider this 1978 winner of the most improbable title, *Proceedings of the Second International Workshop on Nude Mice.*

• Andre Bernard has researched the stories behind more than a hundred of the most famous titles in novel literature. Here is a sampling from his *Now All We Need Is a Title*, 1994.

"I recall saying something to the effect of 'Screw it, then, let's call it *Jaws*,' and my editor saying something like, 'Okay, what the hell. . . .' Nobody reads first novels anyway."

— Peter Benchley (1940-2006) American author

"He had a touch of rare genius in his selection of undistinguished titles for his mystery stories."

— Dorothy Parker on Dashiell Hammett, author of
The Maltese Falcon, *The Thin Man*, *Red Harvest*. . .

Titles we're glad were changed—

The Mute was changed to *The Heart is a Lonely Hunter*
Private Flemming, His Various Battles was changed to
The Red Badge of Courage
The Kingdom by the Sea was changed to *Lolita*
To Climb the Wall was changed to *The Blackboard Jungle*
First Impressions was changed to *Pride and Prejudice*

According to James Cain, the genesis of the title *The Postman Always Rings Twice* was the double ring used by the mailman to alert Cain that his manuscript had been rejected by a publisher. Cain was rejected so often he came to expect the mailman to ring twice very day.

Titles taken from Shakespeare—*Brave New Worlds*, *The Dogs of War*, *Remembrance of Things Past*, *The Sound and the Fury*, *Cakes and Ale*.

F. Scott Fitzgerald was eventually talked out of *Trimalchio in West Egg* by his editor and also his wife, Zelda, finally accepting, instead, *The Great Gatsby*.

"I make a list of titles *after* I've finished the story or book—sometimes as many as a hundred. Then I start eliminating them, sometimes all of them."

— Ernest Hemingway

Translations are occasionally comical. Elaine Steinbeck remembers asking in a Yokohama bookstore whether they carried her husband's novel *The Grapes of Wrath*. After checking, the clerk replied that they indeed carried the book *Angry Raisins*.

John Steinbeck's title *East of Eden* was found by his wife Elaine in Genesis 4:16, "Then Cain went away from the presence of the Lord, and settled in the land of Nod, east of Eden." William Faulkner's title, *Light in August*, derived its selection from a chance remark by his wife Estelle that the light in August in the South had a peculiar quality and was different from light anywhere else.

First and Last Lines

Few novels are selected on the basis of their first lines, but many notable beginnings are remembered. Readers are as likely to recall "It was the best of times, it was the worst of times," as Dickens' title, *A Tale of Two Cities*, and similarly the last line, "It is a far better thing that I do, than I have ever done; it is a far, far better rest that I go to than I have ever known."

As for intervening material, no one has even attempted the "100 Best Central Lines from Novels." Of course, such a search requires a great deal more effort, the necessity of reading each and every volume's entire content.

A good first line foretells the nature of the story in an interesting, sometimes exciting manner. Here are seven examples:

• Far out in the uncharted backwaters of the unfashionable end of the Western Spiral arm of the Galaxy lies a small unregarded yellow sun.

— Douglas Adams, *The Hitchhiker's Guide to the Galaxy*, 1979

• He was an old man who fished alone in a skiff in the Gulf Stream and he had gone eighty-four days now without taking a fish.

— Ernest Hemingway, *The Old Man and the Sea*, 1952

• There was a boy called Eustace Clarence Scrubb, and he almost deserved it.

— C. S. Lewis, *The Voyage of the Dawn Treader*, 1952

• Lolita, light of my life, fire of my loins. My sin, my soul. Lo-lee-ta: the tip of the tongue taking a trip of three steps down the palate to tap, at three, on the teeth. Lo. Lee. Ta.

— Vladimir Nabokov, *Lolita*, 1955

• To the red country and part of the gray country of Oklahoma, the last rains came gently, and they did not cut the scarred earth.

— John Steinbeck, *The Grapes of Wrath*, 1930

• In a hole in the ground there lived a hobbit. Not a nasty, dirty, wet hole, filled with the ends of worms and an oozy smell, nor yet a dry, bare, sandy hole with nothing in it to sit down on or to eat: it was a hobbit-hole, and that means comfort.

— J. R. R. Tolkien, *The Hobbit*, 1937

• The Miss Lonelyhearts of the New York Post-Dispatch (Are you in trouble? – Do-you-need-advice? – Write-to-Miss-Lonelyhearts-and-she-will-help-you) sat at his desk and stared at a piece of white cardboard.

— Nathanael West, *Miss Lonelyhearts*, 1933

For those interested, "It was a dark and stormy night" is a phrase first penned by Victorian novelist Edward Bulwer-Lytton (1803-1873) at the beginning of his novel *Paul Clifford.*

Last lines sum up, reflect, perhaps look to the future. They have a way of being remembered. Here are eight you likely recall:

• He knew what those jubilant crowds did not know but could have learned from books: that the plague bacillus never dies or disappears for good; that it can lie dormant for years and years in furniture and linen-chests; that it bides its time in bedrooms, cellars, trunks, and bookshelves; and that perhaps the day would come when, for the bane and the enlightening of men, it would rouse up its rats again and send them forth to die in a happy city.

— Albert Camus, *The Plague*, 1947

• 'I want the name of a man I can respect on my diploma, Colonel.' He handed me back the diploma without signing it. 'There already is, Bubba,' he answered. 'There already is.' And he pointed to my name.

— Pat Conroy, *The Lords of Discipline*, 1980

• So we beat on, boats against the current, borne back ceaselessly into the past.

— F. Scott Fitzgerald, *The Great Gatsby*, 1925

• . . . and then I asked him with my eyes to ask again yes and then he asked me would I yes . . . and first I put my arms around him yes and drew him down to me so he could feel my breasts all perfume yes and his heart was going like mad and yes I said yes I will Yes.

— James Joyce, *Ulysses*, 1922

• Tomorrow, I'll think of some way to get him back. After all, tomorrow is another day.

— Margaret Mitchell, *Gone with the Wind*, 1936

• She sat staring with her eyes shut, into his eyes, and felt as if she had finally got to the beginning of something she couldn't begin, and she saw him moving farther and farther away, farther and farther into the darkness until he was the pin point of light.

— Flannery O'Connor, *Wise Blood*, 1952

• The creatures outside looked from pig to man, and from man to pig, and from pig to man again; but already it was impossible to say which was which. — George Orwell, *Animal Farm*, 1945

• Nothing had spoiled the day and it had been almost happy. There were three thousand six hundred and fifty-three days like this in his sentence, from reveille to lights out. The three extra ones were because of the leap years.

— Alexander Solzhenitsyn, *One Day in the Life of Ivan Denisovich*, 1962

Artwork

An old and now neglected enhancement, illustrations dramatize, enrich, and instill reality as no other medium. Yet, aside from children's books and a few current day covers, the fiction world is bereft of this former accompaniment. Here, for your enjoyment, are a few examples of the past splendor of novel illustrations. And we have added the related fields of cover art including the melodrama of pulp fiction, some bookplates, bookmarks, and fore-edge art, and, just for fun, the caricatures of Mike Caplanis.

"They Sat Like That For a Moment of Silence"
Andre Castaigne, 1909
Illustration for *The Phantom of the Opera*

Illustration by Gustaf Tenggren, 1932,
for *Sven the Wise and Svea the Kind*

"Allons! . . . It is time to make an end" Illustration by N. C. Wyeth for *The Duel on the Beach*, 1931

The art of Heinrich Kley (1863-1952)
German caricaturist, editorial cartoonist
and painter. His works primarily
grace children's books

Illustration by
Harry Rountree for
Aesop's Fables

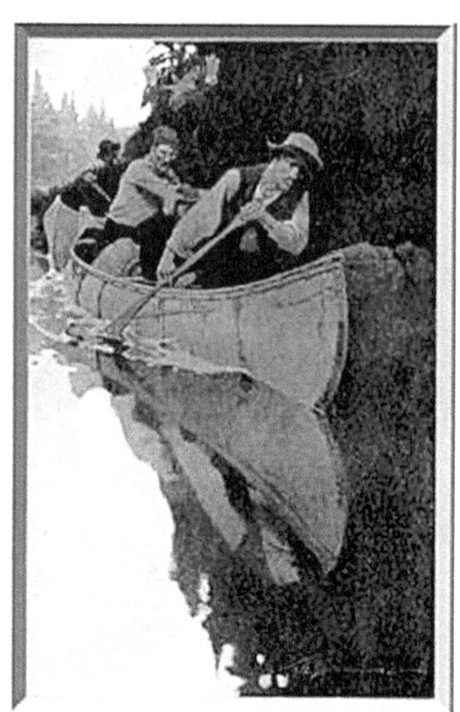

Illustration for *In the Open*
Frank Schoonover, 1903

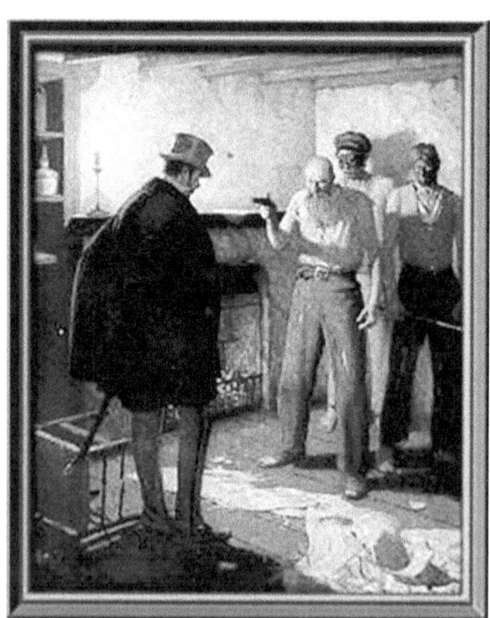

Illustration by
Meade Schaeffe, 1925,
for *Les Miserables*

"I stood like one Thunder-struck, or as if I had seen an Apparition . . ."
Illustration by N. C. Wyeth for *Robinson Crusoe*

The Annotated Lost World by Arthur Conan Doyle,
1996 (update) Art by Harry Rountree

"Sheppard Visiting His Mother in Bedlam"
by George Cruikshank, 1839
Illustration for *Jack Sheppard*

Indian Why Stories by Frank B. Linderman, 1915
Illustrated by Charles M. Russell

Few present day novels are enriched by photographs. Here is a stunning example of a long-lost art and what we're now missing.

London's "Portland Place," one of several photos by A. L. Coburn for Henry James' "New York Edition" (1907-09) of *The Golden Bowl*

And to visualize the possibilities, consider how the inclusion of this photo of inmates imprisoned on Devil's Island would enhance the reality of *Papillon*, a 1969 escape account by Henri Charriere, identified by some as a narrative novel.

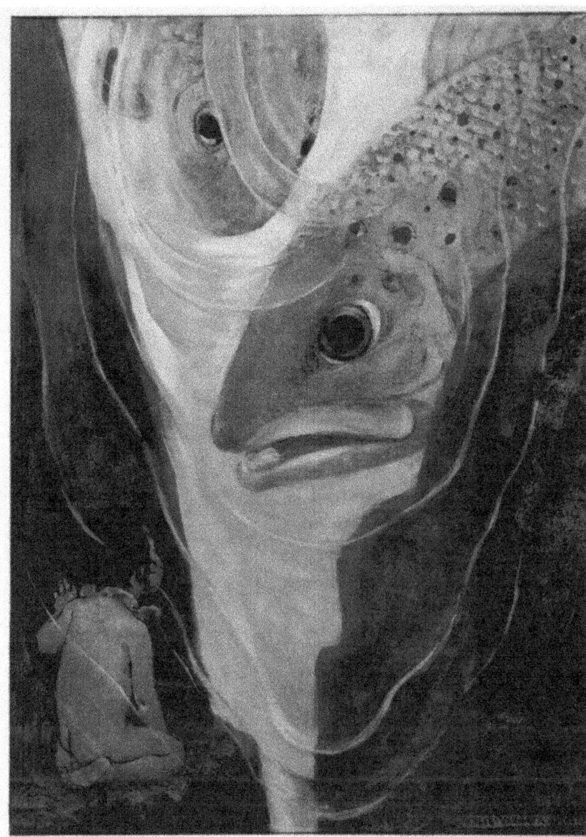

“Oh, don’t hurt me! cried Tom. I only want to look at you; you are so handsome.”

Here are two illustrations by Jessie Wilcox Smith for Charles Kingsley’s 1916 edition of *The Water Babies*. If the enhancement gained in this instance could be at least partially obtained y inclusion of art in current adult literature, the cost would be worth every penny.

Baby Tom is startled by a hawker

Cover art

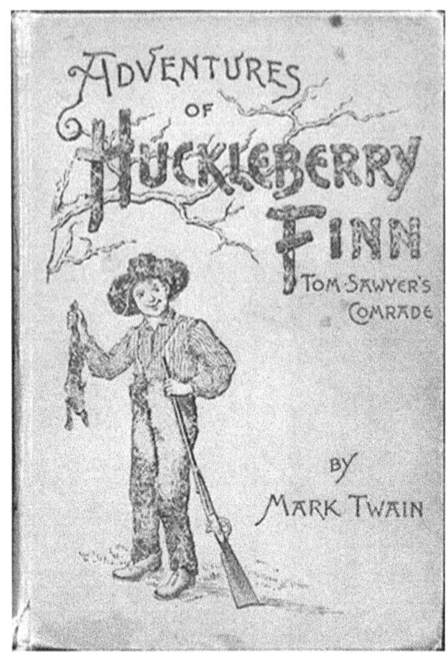

Huckleberry Finn cover,
Cheap Edition, 1891 Webster & Co.
Courtesy the Barrett Collection

Early thirties dust wrapper
by Gustaf Tenggren for
The Good Earth by Pearl Buck

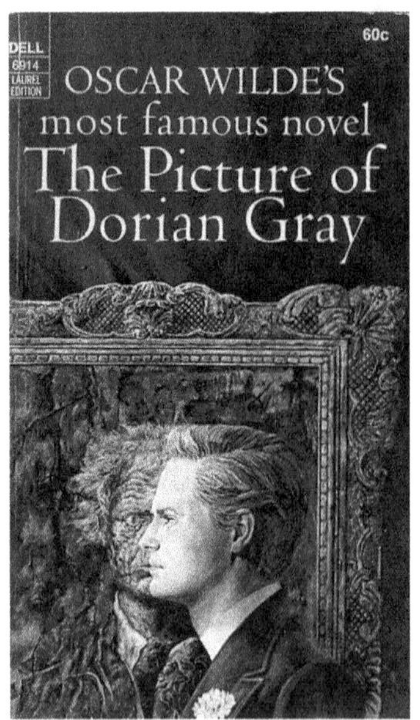

Cover for an early edition of
The Picture of Dorian Gray
by Oscar Wilde, 1891

Cover for the first edition of
The Beautiful and Damned
by F. Scott Fitzgerald

The art of pulp fiction magazines

Alice Babbitt Bennett

Walt Disney

Anita Loos

Jack London

Bookplates, also known as ex-libris [Latin "from the collection or library of . . ."], usually pasted on the inside front cover to indicate ownership. Source: James P. Keenan, *The Art of the Bookplate.*

Alphonse Mucha

Carl Larsson

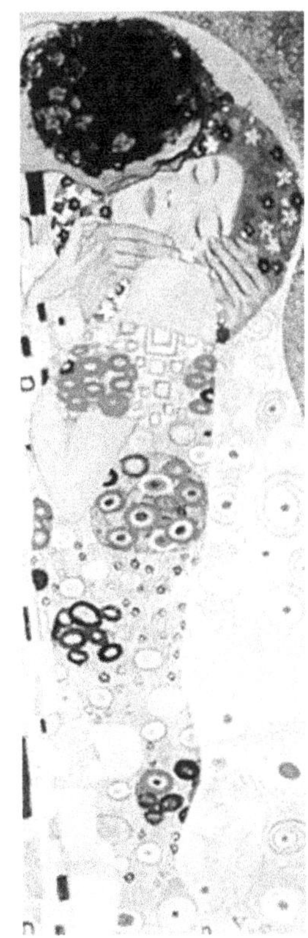

Gustav Klimt

Lawrence Alma-Tadema

Henri Privat-Livemont

"Beauties of the Art History" in bookmarks
Source: Mirage Bookmark

The art of fore-edge paintings

Whaling scene, 1898
Colorado State University

Italian Costal Town
Boston Public Library

American Indian
on horseback
Grand Valley State University

The White House
Boston Public Library

Contemporary American fiction writers interpreted by Mike Caplanis © Luminary Graphics, Inc.

Louisa May Alcott

William Faulkner

Edgar Allen Poe

Virginia Woolf

Cartoons

You'll likely find these two cartoons funny; there's none better. The choices, about literature and writing, come from the *New Yorker* which has the world's toughest selection process, clearly evident from this description by Peter Carlson from *The Washington Post*.

> The guy laughs at the cartoon, but he still rejects it! It's good the cartoonists aren't watching. This would drive them crazy. Well, crazier. Constant rejection has rendered these geniuses half nuts already. In about 20 minutes, Remnick (New Yorker editor) rejects 48 cartoons and buys 33 — that's 33 out of nearly a thousand that came in this week! It's hard out here for a cartoonist.

Dickens' First Encounter with a Martini

"Write about Dogs!"

The sweet girl graduate trying in vain to
find something she does not know already.
Life's Comedy, Life Publishing Co. 1897

Reviews and Criticism

Drawing by Heinrich Kley (1863-1945)
German caricaturist

The distinction between reviews and criticism has long been debated. For what it's worth, the difference generally cited is one of focus, reviews centering on guiding reader selection of new titles; criticism emphasizing evaluation and scholarly study. In practice, the overlap, as expected, is extensive, making labeling often a matter of interpreting a blur. Here we escape the problem, by combining our selections under a joint title.

And while in this introduction, let the reader be cautioned regarding the variance among critics lest their resulting reading choice be unexpectedly disappointing. Consider these two conflicting, albeit website, reviews of a recent title:

> – "I've read this novel four or five times and consider it one of the best works of fiction by an American writer. The prose is simply perfect–not a false note or glob of fat. The characters have positive and negative qualities that make them believably human."
>
> – "(The author) wants his novel to be deep and epic but it is just depressing and dorky. The symbolism and ideas are mostly shallow. There's obscure religious undertones that make no sense to me. The parent/child relationships portrayed in the book are utterly banal and ugly."

With a nod to academe, we quote two brief citations among numerous possibilities that reference material appearing to be at or at least near the fringe of literary importance:

> – "_______ uses a sensible and modest methodology of architectural phenomenology to explain how Faulkner imagines structures and places in his books and stories."
>
> – "Among the single-motif studies are ________'s collection of all the references to luck in Hemingway's work; _______'s study of bicycles as symbols of death; and ________'s very complete survey of birth/death imagery in the canon, . . ."

Lastly, from the same source, this concluding admission:

> – "By actual count (in the 16 years from 1972 thru 1987), there have been just about 160 periodical essays, notes, and book chapters devoted solely or primarily to *The Great Gatsby* . . .

What is more dispiriting than the statistics is that too little of this criticism convincingly breaks new ground or says anything very original about old topics."

What is all too evident from these observations is that the connect between academe and the reading public is thin indeed, and what readers need, in addition to good novelists, is an effective periodic summary of the best in literary criticism.

• Five purposes of a book review:

1. A brief, accurate, and unbiased précis of the setting and plot of the story without giving away what the "rabbit-in-the-hat" looks like.

2. A specific evaluation of the author's writing ability, including which writers the author's style resembles, and ... a few moderately lengthy and representative quotes.

3. Which works this particular book most resembles in both plot and feel.

4. How the book compares to the author's previous works and to other books cut from a similar cloth.

5. A final verdict on the book stated clearly and unequivocally and with the particular reviewer's caveats laid out for consideration.

— Michelle Kerns, "What is the purpose of a book review? And are book reviewers writing anything useful?" Kerns delightfully describes herself as "book columnist, Anglophile, science nerd, and lush."

• Miss Stein turned out reams of work before she finally came out, last year, with a book somebody could understand. . . .

— Allegheny newspaper article bashing native daughter Gertrude Stein's *The Autobiography of Alice B. Toklas*

• One thing is clear: A great paradox is at work in the marketplace of books. On the one hand, there are blockbusters whose fates are impervious to reviews, driven by personalities, Hollywood afterlives and author appearances on television talk shows. On the other, there are books whose futures are played out on the review page—with lesser-known authors, potentially long shelf lives and better shots at the literary prizes.

— Marie Arana-Ward, deputy editor of *Book World*

• The covers of this book are too far apart.

— Ambrose Bierce (1842-1914) *The Devil's Dictionary*

• . . . a minor novelist with a major style.

— dismissal of John Updike by critic Harold Bloom, Yale University literary scholar

• If Steinbeck is not an original or even an adequate stylist, if he lacks skill in plot, and power in the mimesis of character, what then remains in his work, except its fairly constant popularity with an immense number of liberal middlebrows, both in his own country and abroad?

— Harold Bloom

• That's not writing, that's typing.

— Truman Capote (1924-1984) on the work of Jack Kerouac

• I love criticism just so long as it's unqualified praise.

— Noel Coward (1899-1973) English playwright, composer, director, actor and singer

• *Sartor Resartus* is simply unreadable, and for me that always sort of spoils a book.

— Will Cuppy (1884-1949) American humorist and journalist

• Genuine criticism will never seek to prove but to point out.

— E. R. Curtius (1886-1956) German literary scholar

• I am at a loss to understand why people hold Miss (Jane) Austen's novels at so high a rate, which seem to me vulgar in tone, sterile in artistic invention, imprisoned in the wretched conventions of English society, without genius, wit, or knowledge of the world.

— Ralph Waldo Emerson (1803-1882) American essayist and poet

• Clifton Fadiman's pronouncements as judge on candidate material at Book-of-the-Month Club meetings:

On a book about Mount Everest: "I think we should take it because its there."

On a contemporary novel: "It has no center. What it has is a lot of wonderful periphery."

• Recognizing masterpieces is the job of the critic—not writing competent reviews of the unimportant.

— Jack Green, *The Washington Post*

• Thank you for sending me a copy of your book. I'll waste no time reading it.

— Moses Hadas (1900-1966) scholar and teacher

• Your manuscript is both good and original; but the part that is good is not original, and the part that is original is not good.

Criticism is a study by which men grow important and formidable at very small expense.

— Samuel Johnson (1709-1784) English literary critic, poet, essayist

• Me no Leica.

— Walter Kerr (1913-1996) Broadway theater critic. Written in the *New York Herald Tribune* in 1951 about John van Druten's play *I Am a Camera.*

• People who like this sort of thing will find this the sort of thing they like.

— Abraham Lincoln's sly foray into book reviewing

• [To an English Professor] Thank you for your note. I'm sorry I can't answer it more fully but I am in the hospital and not up to literary questions.... As for Mrs. May, I must have named her that because I knew some English teacher would write and ask me why. I think you folks sometimes strain the soup too thin...."

— Flannery O'Connor (1925-1964) American novelist, short- story writer, and essayist

• The prolonged, indiscriminate reviewing of books is a quite exceptionally thankless, irritating and exhausting job . . . The reviewer . . . is pouring his immortal spirit down the drain, half a pint at a time.

— George Orwell (1903-1950) "Confessions of a Book Reviewer"

• The problem is that just as everybody wants to go to heaven but nobody wants to die, everybody wants rigorous, incisive and fearless criticism, so long as it is aimed at somebody else.

— Fintan O'Toole (1958-) Irish critic

• Critics, like politicians out of touch with their constituents, often believe that only they know what's good for us unlearned, misguided laymen.

— Joseph P. Petta, letter to the Editor, *The Washington Post*

• Leafing through John Updike's latest novel, "S." . . . I was half-startled and half-amused to discover that the name he gives his heroine's dentist is Dr. Podhoretz. From this playful little swipe at me, I gather that Updike has not yet gotten over a harsh piece I wrote about him 25 years ago, when we were both young and I was still a literary critic.

Not that I blame him. I have known many writers, but I have come across very few who can bring themselves to forgive or forget an unfavorable review. Not even otherwise universal acclaim will necessarily compensate for the hurt inflicted by negative criticism.

— Norman Podhoretz, "Updike and Roth: Serious at Last," *The Washington Post.*

• Fiction writers don't necessarily have a good analytical sense of why a piece of literature succeeds or fails, which is the most useful aspect of the review for the reader.

(And later in the text, this recommendation.)

First, and most essentially, I think, we need to devise better means of choosing books for review. Our current system inevitably leads to over-looking good books, over-praising bad ones, and undermining the book page.

— Gail Pool, *Faint Praise: The Plight of Book Reviewing in America*, 2007

• The highest compliment a reader can pay a literary thriller—or any novel, for that matter—is to claim that the book is nearly as intricate and mysterious as life itself, that the reader has lived in the book as if it were a particularly lifelike dream, and cared about its characters as if they were real.

— Donna Rifkind, "In the Bleak Midwinter," *The Washington Post*

• So your book finds itself in the hands of a reviewer to whom it's just a collection of pages, a narrative, fiction or nonfiction. Any magic that comes from it has nothing to do with wishes, or good intentions, or time spent, or emotional pain, or tears in the night. The magic has to float up unencumbered out of the book and into the reviewer's brain. If the magic is strong enough, it sometimes makes the reviewer get up and go to the window and take a deep breath which might even end in a sob."

— Carolyn See, "Both Sides Now: The Novelist as Critic," *The Washington Post*

• This town happens to be blessed with three or four reviewers who are trusted and who do their homework. That just isn't the case in the rest of the country.

— Jack Shoemaker, president of Washington, D.C.'s Counterpoint Press, 1997

• Pay no attention to what the critics say; no statue has ever been put up to a critic.

— Jean Sibelius (1865-1957) Finnish composer

• I never read a book before reviewing it; it prejudices a man so.

— Rev. Sydney Smith (1771-1845) English liberal writer and wit

• Hemingway's remarks are not literature.

— Gertrude Stein (1874-1946) American writer

• Writing criticism is to writing fiction and poetry as hugging the shore is to sailing in the open sea.

— John Updike (1932-) American novelist

• . . . his appeal is to readers with a lifelong appetite for juvenile trash.

— Edmund Wilson (1895-1972) American writer and critic, on J. R. R Tolkien

• Herewith, for your consideration, a few snippets from the scrapbooks of a professional book reviewer: "an exercise in self-indulgence and self-importance"; "pious twaddle"; "almost completely lacking in intellectual depth or stylistic grace"; "truly ghastly fits of prose"; "extremely moral righteousness, oversimplification"; "a work of astonishing arrogance and presumption"; "gives new meaning to the word 'sophomoric.'"

— Jonathan Yardley, "When the Critic Turns Author," *The Washington Post*

• Few readers are likely to know that Book World does not make money for The Post; it never has and surely never will. It is published because the powers that be at this newspaper believe that serious book coverage is an essential ingredient of a serious newspaper.

— Jonathan Yardley, *The Washington Post*

• . . . re-reading a year's worth of my stale old reviews provides instructive proof that more books disappoint than please, which is to say that in books as in everything else excellence—or anything approximating it—is very much the exception to the mediocrity that rules.

— Jonathan Yardley, "A Year of Reading Endlessly," *The Washington Post*

• . . . we are dealing with the question that has befuddled reviewers since the first day one man put quill to papyrus and passed public judgment on another man's work. It is the question that troubles every reviewer, unless he is affected by monumental arrogance, every time he writes: Am I right?

This, when you get right down to it, is the professional reviewer's task: To have sufficient confidence in his judgments to give them public airing, and to waste no time worrying over whether he is "right" or "wrong."

— Jonathan Yardley, "'Testing the Current': Reviews Hot and Cold," *The Washington Post*

Literary Extremes

• Perhaps the "best" book listed in this study, at least in terms of pure writing beauty and emotional impact, is John Steinbeck's 1939 *The Grapes of Wrath*, awarded the Pulitzer Prize and significantly contributing to Steinbeck's subsequent award of the Nobel Prize for Literature. Easily the worst is William S. Burroughs' gutter tripe 1959 *Naked Lunch*, of which the less said the better.

• The world best selling fiction authors cited by *Wikipedia* are led, of course, by William Shakespeare and Agatha Christie, two or more billion sales each. And then there are a number of best selling romance, adventure, detective, suspense, western, historical, and children's literature authors including Americans Harold Robbins (adventure, 750 million) and Danielle Steel (romance, 560 million). When we come to what might be called *bona fide* novelists, Leo Tolstoy leads in sales with 413 million, followed by J. K. Rowling, J. R. R. Tolkien, and Charles Dickens. Perhaps surprising to some, except young boys of an earlier generation, Erskine Caldwell's name leads the list of American best-selling novelists with sales of 80 million, followed by Edgar Rice Burroughs in similar figures, again primarily in response to young readers, in this latter instance Tarzan fans. James Michener and his wonderful stories of the South Pacific is the last American novelist making the 81 member Wikipedia list. Both Burroughs and Michener are included in this present study.

• The longest novel likely encountered by diligent readers is Marcel Proust's 1913 seven volume *In Search of Lost Time* (titled in the first translation, *Remembrance of Things Past*), weighing in at 4,580 pages. In contrast, one of the shortest is Franz Kafka's 1915 *The Metamorphis*, a scant 46 pages.

Two most demanding books are James Joyce's *Ulysses* and *Finnegans Wake*, ". . . highly idiosyncratic and 'difficult' books, admired more often than read, when read rarely read through to the end, when read through to the end not often fully, or even partially, understood." (From the Forward by Anthony Burgess, Editor, *A Shorter Finnegans Wake*, 1939.)

• Generally cited as the oldest novel is noblewoman Murasak Shikibu's classic *The Tale of Genji* written in the 10th Century AD. The first novel in English is *Le Morte d'Arthur* by Thomas Malory published in 1485. However, there are multiple candidates for this distinction largely because the term novel can be defined so as to include many variances. Rigorously applied restrictions regarding originality, content, and length, establish Daniel Defoe's *Robinson Crusoe* (1719) as the first true English novel. Across the Atlantic, there is little controversy regarding William Hill Brown's *The Power of Sympath*y (1789) as the first American novel.

• Lipograms are a form of constrained composition consisting of writing paragraphs or longer works in which a particular letter or group of letters is omitted, usually a common vowel. In 1939 Vincent Wright set a major example, writing *Gadsby*, a novel of over 50,000 words, without a single letter "e". In Walter Abish's 1974 novel, *Alphabetical Africa*, the first chapter consists solely of words beginning with "a," chapter two permits words also beginning with "b," and so on until at chapter 26, all the letters of the alphabet may be used.

• In 1862, Victor Hugo, on vacation and anxious to know how his new novel *Les Miserables* was selling, wrote his publisher "?" and received the reply "!".

The Publishing Industry

While there is little need to know the industry to enjoy its product, readers will likely appreciate some knowledge of the world of publishing. To provide relevance here, the discussion is narrowed to publication of hardcover adult fiction. So restricted, the salient facts are:

— The majority of quality fiction in the United States is published by a very few houses; the big four of New York City—Random House, Simon & Schuster, Penguin, and Harper Collins—and a handful of others .

— The odds of publishing a novel are long indeed. Roughly no more than one-in-a-thousand submissions are accepted and published. Then nine of 10 printings fail to pay back their own production costs.

— Probably no more than 3,000 new works of fiction are published annually in hardcover in any substantial quantities. Of these perhaps no more than one-in-three are critically reviewed in the press. Major U.S. newspapers with Sunday book supplements, for example, typically review five to six-hundred titles in the course of a year. Eventually the field is dramatically narrowed to a couple of dozen works nominated for the major literary prizes. The upshot of all this is that newspapers effectively serve as the major culling agent of fiction and, for many readers, the likely first source of guidance regarding selection.

— Literary agents appear essential in brokering manuscripts to publishing houses. Unsolicited manuscripts mailed directly have basically no chance of acceptance. Agent fees generally run 15 percent of the author's royalties. Finding the right agent is itself difficult.

— Publisher royalty payments are typically seven percent of the wholesale hardcover price. Authors are also granted this percentage payment by publishers receiving exclusive marketing rights. Usually some royalties are held in escrow to compensate for returned books, etc.

— Book promotion is essential, but difficult and costly. Marketing budgets may range between 10 and 25 percent of net sales. Authors are expected to participate in promotion tours. The best kind of publicity—appearing on a bestseller list—however cannot be bought. The *New York Times Book Review* list is generally considered the most influential.

— Fiction sales tend to be concentrated in just a few titles and/or few authors. For example, books by a mere five authors accounted for over 70 percent of total fiction sales in 1994. Economists explain this as a preference to read a single outstanding volume to that of reading several secondary choices.

— The chances of making a living as a writer of fiction are slim to none.

• Good stories take time to craft. Good writers, editors, copy editors, photographers, etc., all expect a living wage. The real question in the months and years ahead is whether there's a business model that can support good stories. Norman Sims, journalism professor at the University of Massachusetts Amherst: "The great stories will survive. But the question is who's going to pay for them. . . . This is not fast food. This is slow food. And it's expensive." — Joel Achenbach, "The vestigial tale,"
The Washington Post, October 29, 2009

• People crave stories too much. It's kind of the pipeline to the heart. (In response to the intrusion of the internet and abbreviated renditions.)
— Gary Smith, author

• In 1917 Leonard and Virginia Woolf purchased a small used handpress and started Hogarth Press named after the house in which they lived in West London. Over the next three decades they published 525 titles, many by other influential modernists. Most of them are collector's items today.
— Reported by Steve King, *Today in Literature*

• The first Penguins were published in England by The Bodley Head publishing firm in 1935, the event generally regarded as the birth of the modern paperback industry.
— Reported by Steve King, *Today in Literature*

Rejections

Publishers appear to be everyone's favorite whipping boy, with their seemingly mindless rejection of what in some instances turn out to be, if not masterpieces, bestsellers. Yet they have a case, centering on work overload, the simple inability of adequately reviewing the often 500 or more manuscripts received each year. And literary agents contribute to the problem with idiosyncrasies ranging from personal taste preferences to limited contacts with publishing houses. It's simply not an easy straight forward business to identify good marketable literature from the maze of material submitted each year. But enough for the defense. It's more fun to consider the consequent failures.

The list of famous authors whose works were repeatedly rejected is impressive. Most remarkable are the parting shots editors too often fail to curb. Consider these rude gems reported by Michelle Kerns (Examiner.com):

— One of 20 publisher rejections of William Golding's *Lord of the Flies* read ". . . an absurd and uninteresting fantasy which was rubbish and dull."

— After reviewing John le Carre's first novel, *The Spy who Came in From the Cold*, one publisher sent a colleague this message: "You're welcome to le Carre — he hasn't got any future."

— Joseph Heller received this response from one publisher after submitting *Catch-22*: "I haven't the foggiest idea about what the man is trying to say . . . Apparently the author intends it to be funny—possibly even satire—but it is really not funny on any intellectual level."

— Bloomsbury, a small London publisher, only took on J. K. Rowling's *Harry Potter and the Sorcerer's Stone* at the behest of the CEO's eight-year old daughter who begged her father to print the book. Kerns nicely adds, "God bless you sweetheart."

— George Orwell's *Animal Farm* was rejected with "It is impossible to sell animal stories in the USA."

— Irving Stone's *Lust for Life* was rejected 16 times, once with this helpful synopsis: "A long, dull novel about an artist." The book went on to eventually sell over 25 million copies.

— One of Rudyard Kipling's short stories was rejected by an editor of the *San Francisco Examiner* with the words, "I'm sorry Mr. Kipling, but you just don't know how to use the English language."

— In closing, this final absurdity. Margaret Mitchell's only book ever published, *Gone With the Wind*, won her a Pulitzer Prize in 1937. The 1939 movie made of her story is the highest grossing Hollywood film of all time (adjusted for inflation). The book was rejected by 38 publishers before being printed.

So authors take hope, persevere, don't give up too soon.

• Evidently as an experiment, 21 pages of Jerzy Kosinski's 1968 novel *Steps* was sent to its original publisher and several others six years after it had won the National Book Award. All turned it down. In 1981 the entire text of *Steps* was sent to several literary agents and again was turned down by everyone.

— Dr. James R. Fisher Jr. in a review of *Steps*. *Wikipedia* reports the experimenter was Chuck Ross, a Los Angles freelance writer.

Libraries

• The closest you will ever come in this life to an orderly universe is a good library.

— Ashleigh Brilliant (1933-) author and syndicated cartoonist

• Andrew Carnegie (1835-1919), industrialist and major philanthropist, gave $56.5 million (more than $1 billion in today's dollars) to build 2,509 libraries in a dozen countries including 660 in Britain and Ireland, and 125 in Canada. Most of the library buildings were unique, constructed in a number of architectural styles, each chosen by the local community.

• In seventh grade…I found a place [on the library shelf] where my book would be if I ever wrote a book, which I doubted.

— Beverly Cleary, *A Girl From Yamhill: A Memoir,* 1996

• I went to the library. They gave you books for nothing. You had to bring them back, but when you did, they let you take others.

— Barbara Cohen, *Gooseberries to Oranges*, 1982

• Outside of a dog, a book is a man's best friend. Inside of a dog, it's too dark to read.

— Groucho Marx (1890-1977) American comedian and film star

• [Encyclopedia Brown] read more books than anyone in Idaville, and he never forgot a fact. His pals said he was a library and a computer rolled into one, and more user-friendly.

— Donald J. Sobol, *Encyclopedia Brown and the Case of the Disgusting Sneakers,* 1999

Films Versus Books

Basically unlimited in length and descriptive capability, novels can provide significantly greater narrative detail than films. The inner workings of the mind and all its complexity can be described and interpreted in exclusive detail. In contrast, emotional depth in films must be gleaned from visible facial and audible verbal expression. Novelists also can explain and interpret, refinements often bypassed in films. And likely of greatest value, books allow the reader to freely imagine everything, personally without restraint, intimately, perhaps even more vividly than reality itself.

Movies on the other hand are visually realistic and dramatic, and gloriously sound enhanced. Words can seldom describe beauty and action in the manner of films. Sometimes a memorable film may actually take over and dominate a lesser written story. Few, for example, can read *Gone With the Wind* and see the movie without forever after imaging Vivien Leigh as Scarlett O'Hara.

Comparison of a given novel and its subsequent film version is always an interesting exercise. Take Stanley Kubrick's 1980 movie "The Shining" based on Stephen King's novel of the same name. Here the director took considerable license, adding one chilling and memorable scene after another, none in the original text. For example, Wendy Torrance (played by Shelley Duvall) accidentally discovers that her husband Jack (Jack Nicholson) has repeatedly written over and over again "All work and no play makes Jack a dull boy," filling page after page with this single sentence instead of writing his novel. This chilling revelation is not in the book. Neither is Jack Torrance's menacing "Here's Johnny!" as he axes his way through the bathroom door after Wendy. Nor is the hotel's hall scene flooded with a torrent of blood in the book, or Jack Torrance's final demise, freezing to death lost in the hotel's hedge maze. And to top it off, the hauntingly beautiful final music "Midnight, the Stars and You" played as the camera zooms in on a 1921 July 4th Ball photo with an eternally present Jack Torrance dominant front and center, is, of course, absent from the book. Yet for all its brilliance the film would never have been made without Stephen King's creative genius.

All-in-all novels and films make a wonderful combination, novels as the original unique source, films as a distinctive adaptation. Both often can be enjoyed best when read and viewed in close proximity, usually in book then film order.

Good novels engender follow-on films, initially dependent, subsequently interpretive, both media enriching in their distinct manner. *Wikipedia* lists over 900 such novel-film relationships. Here are 20 of the very best with the year the film was made:

Gone With the Wind, Margaret Mitchell, 1939
The Grapes of Wrath, John Steinbeck, 1940
The Best Years of Our Lives, MacKinlay Kantor, 1946
A Place in the Sun, Theodore Dreiser, 1951
From Here to Eternity, James Jones, 1953
The Caine Mutiny, Herman Wouk, 1954
The Bridge on the River Kwai, Pierre Boulle, 1957
Compulsion, Meyer Levin, 1959
Breakfast at Tiffany's, Truman Capote, 1961
To Kill a Mockingbird, Harper Lee, 1962
In Cold Blood, Truman Capote, 1967
Deliverance, James Dickey, 1972
The Godfather, Mario Puzo, 1972
The Great Gatsby, F. Scott Fitzgerald, 1974
One Flew Over the Cuckoo's Nest, Ken Kesey, 1975
Jaws, Peter Benchley, 1975
The Shining, Stephen King, 1980
Out of Africa, Isak Dinesen, 1985
The Silence of the Lambs, Thomas Harris, 1991
Schindler's List, Thomas Keneally, 1993

The Best Years of Our Lives

The Caine Mutiny

Schindler's List

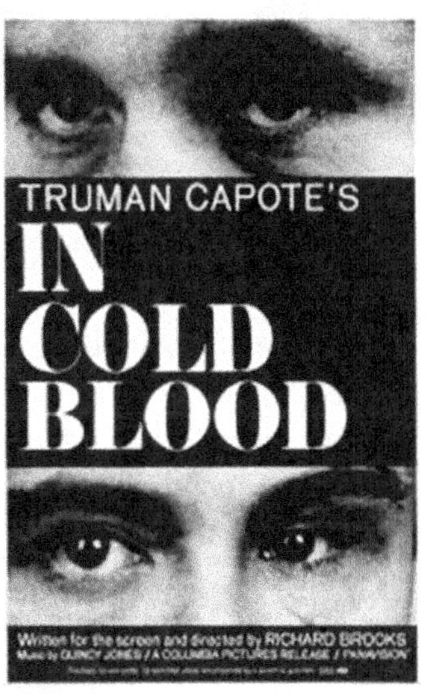

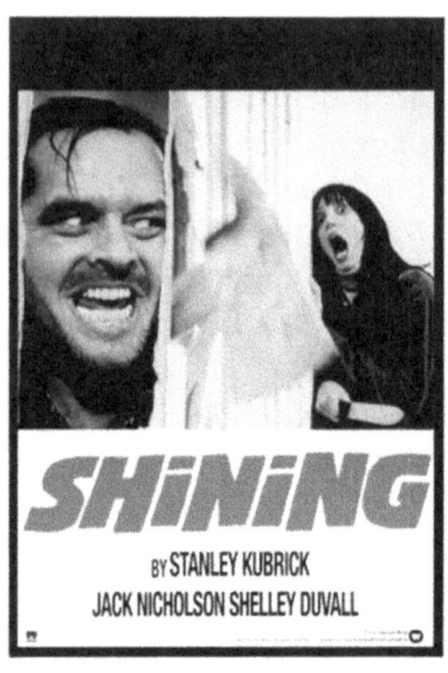

Novel/Location/Film

The plurality of novel, associated location, and subsequent film adaptation, offers an interesting challenge of accessing all three. There are, of course, many opportunities to read a book and later see the movie version, far fewer chances of also visiting an associated specific site. We list here four instances where all three occasions are splendidly afforded–the locations involved representing the east, south, central, and western parts of the United States. And, for perspective, we add a fifth and sixth selection at distant locations not likely to be visited. We've picked the best possible examples of this triplex which involved some license in extending the media categories to include one play and two biographies.

EAST

Biography: *A Beautiful Mind: A Biography of John Forbes Nash, Jr.*, 1994, Sylvia Nasar.

Location: Princeton University, Princeton, New Jersey.

Film: *A Beautiful Mind*, 2001, directed by Ron Howard, starring Russell Crowe.

SOUTH

Play: *A Streetcar Named Desire*, 1947, playwright Tennessee Williams.

Location: New Orleans, Louisiana (Elysian Field Avenue, Faubourg Marigny).

Film: *A Streetcar Named Desire*, 1951, directed by Elia Kazan, starring Marlon Brando and Vivien Leigh.

CENTRAL

Novel: *Dances With Wolves*, 1988, Michael Blake.

Location: Plains of South Dakota including Badlands National Park, the Black Hills and the Belle Fourche River area.

Film: *Dances With Wolves*, 1990, director/star Kevin Costner.

WEST

Biography: *Citizen Hearst*, 1961, William Andrew Swanberg.

Location: "San Simeon," William Randolph Hearst's 60,645 square foot Casa Grande on the central California coast.

Film: *Citizen Kane*, 1941 RKO film co-written, produced, directed, and acted in by Orson Welles.

OTHER

Novel: *Mutiny on the Bounty*, 1932, Charles Nordhoff and James Normal Hall.

Location: Pitcairn Islands, 16.7 square miles located at roughly 25° South latitude and 130° West longitude, population 50.

Film: *Mutiny on the Bounty*, 1935 film directed by Frank Lloyd starring Charles Laughton and Clark Gable.

Novel: *Le Pont de la riviere Kwai*, 1952, Pierre Boulle.

Location: Based on one of the railway bridges built in 1943 over the Mae Klong at a place called Tha Ma Kham in western Thailand.

Film: *The Bridge on the River Kwai*, 1957, directed by David Lean, starring Alec Guinness and William Holden.

"When the pie was all finished, the Owl, as a boon,
Was kindly permitted to pocket the spoon;
While the Panther received knife and fork with a growl,
And concluded the banquet by ---.

Alice's Adventures in Wonderland by Lewis Carroll
Painting by Harry Rountree (1878-1950)

W. C. Fields as Mr. Micawber and Freddie Bartholomew as David
in 1945 movie version of *David Copperfield* by Charles Dickens

Favorite Passages

This listing of selected passages is limited to single favorite choices. They illustrate each title's content and the author's writing style, and, as important, are simply fun to read. One's own writing might just be improved by emersion in these examples of excellence. The 575 excerpts are listed alphabetically by author, preceded in each instance by a brief plot description in italics. Photos, author quotes, book covers and other assorted miscellanea are selectively included.

Great Beginnings and Endings already covers the flanks of novels, but not their heart. Although a surprising omission, the likely obstacle is the extended task of finding the appropriate interior material among so many possibilities. Nevertheless, the content quoted here is a good start, and may, for some time, remain the only such source.

These gems are, of course, not meant to be simply entertaining. They hopefully will encourage selection and complete reading of one's choice of titles. If you are prompted to read more, they will have served a useful purpose.

Notes: Omissions *within* a sentence or paragraph are indicated by . . . Extended interruptions involving at least a whole paragraph are identified by . . . . In a few instances, selected excerpts may divulge plot information preferred not to be known by some potential readers of the novel in question.

A

Things Fall Apart (1958)

- *The life of Okonkwo, a leader of nine villages in Nigeria in the late 1800s, and the influence of colonialism and Christian missionaries on his traditional Igbo community.*

. . . In this way Mr. Brown learned a good deal about the religion of the clan and he came to the conclusion that a frontal attack on it would not succeed. And so he built a school and a little hospital in Umuofia. He went from family to family begging people to send their children to his school. But first they only sent their slaves or sometimes their lazy children. Mr. Brown begged and argued and prophesied. He said that the leaders of the land in the future would be men and women who had learned to read and write. If Umuofia failed to send her children to school, strangers would come from other places to rule them.

"Our ancestors created their myths and told their stories for a human purpose."

— **Chinua Achebe** *(1930-)*
Nigerian novelist, poet, and critic

The Hitchhiker's Guide to the Galaxy (1979)

- *Arthur Dent is saved by his friend alien Ford Perfect when Earth is demolished to make way for a new inter-galactic motorway.*

. . . Far out in the uncharted backwaters of the unfashionable end of the Western Spiral arm of the Galaxy lies a small unregarded yellow sun.

— **Douglas Adams** *(1952-2001)*
English writer and dramatist

Watership Down (1972)

- *A fantasy story intended for children about the lives and adventures of a group of rabbits capable of speaking to one another.*

One chilly, blustery morning in March, I cannot tell exactly how many springs later, Hazel was dozing and waking in his burrow. He had spent a good deal of time there lately, for he felt the cold and could not seem to smell or run so well as in days gone by. He had been dreaming in a confused way—something about rain and elder bloom—when he woke to realize that there was a rabbit lying quietly beside him—no doubt some young buck who had come to ask his advice. The sentry in the run outside should not really have let him in without asking first. Never mind, thought Hazel. He raised his head and said, "Do you want to talk to me?"

"Yes, that's what I've come for," replied the other. "You know me, don't you?"

"Yes, of course," said Hazel, hoping he would be able to remember his name in a moment. Then he saw that in the darkness of the burrow the stranger's ears were shining with faint silver light. "Yes, my lord," he said. "Yes, I know you."

— **Richard Adams** *(1920-) English novelist*

Speedboat (1976)

- *A collage of short scenes, each a new topic, described by Charles McGrath as "an assemblage of tiny anecdotes, vignettes, overheard conversations, aphorisms and reflections."*

Summer. The speedboat was serous. The young tycoon was serious about it, as he was serious about his factories, his wife, his children, his parties, his work, his art collection, his resort. . . . The speedboat, designed for him the year before, had just arrived that day. The tycoon asked who would like to join him for a spin to test it. The young American wife from Malibu, who had been overexcited about everything since dawn, said she would love to go. . . . The young Italian couple, having a serious speedboat of their own, went to compare. In starting off, the boat seemed much like any other, only in every way—the flat, hard seats, the austere lines—more spare. And then, at speed, the boat, at its own angle to the sea, began to hit each wave with flat, hard, jarring thuds, like the heel of a hand against a tabletop. As it slammed along, the Italians sat, ever more low and loose, on their hard seats, while the American lady, in her eagerness, began to bounce with anticipation over every little wave. The boat scudded hard; she exaggerated every happy bounce. Until she broke her back.

— **Renata Adler** *(1938-) American author, journalist and film critic*

A Death in the Family (1938)

- *The sorrowful account of a family's reaction to their father's death, each member—wife, brother, and young son—reflecting on the past and their personal tragedy.*

. . . And then one day without warning the biggest woman he had ever seen, shining deep black and all in magnificent white with bright gold spectacles and a strong smile like that of his Aunt Hannah, entered the house and embraced his mother and swept down on him crying with delight, "Lawd, chile, how mah baby has growed!", and for a moment he thought that this must be the surprise and looked inquiringly at his mother past the onslaught of embraces, and his mother said, "Victoria; Victoria, Rufus!"; and Victoria cried, "Now bless his little heart, how would he remembuh," and all of a sudden as he looked into the vast shining planes of her smiling face and at the gold spectacles which perched there as gaily as a dragonfly, there was something that he did remember, a glisten of gold and a warm movement of affection, and before he knew it he had flung his arms around her neck and she whooped with astonished joy. "Why God bless him, why chile, chile," and she held him away from her and her face was the happiest thing he had ever seen, "ah believe you do remembuh! Ah sweah ah believe you do! Do you?" She shook him in her happiness.

— **James Agee** *(1909-1955) American author, journalist, poet, screenwriter and film critic*

Agee's fatal heart attack at the age of forty-five came with his novel *A Death in the Family* not quite finished, and was anything but inexplicable. Told after a first attack four years earlier that his drinking, smoking and manic lifestyle would kill him, Agee had chosen to continue, though with doubts at the end: "At moments I wonder whether those who go, as I do, for a Full Life, don't get their exact reward, which is that The Full Life is full of crap."

Little Women (1868-1869)

■ *The innocence of youth and warmth of their friendship is shared by four sisters growing up poor in nineteenth-century New England without their father off to war.*

. . . They began to get anxious, and Laurie went off to find her, for no one ever knew what freak Jo might take into her head. He missed her, however, and she came walking in with a very queer expression of countenance, for there was a mixture of fun and fear, satisfaction and regret in it, which puzzled the family as much as did the roll of bills she laid before her mother, saying with a little choke in her voice, "That's my contribution toward making Father comfortable and bringing him home!"

"My dear, where did you get it? Twenty-five dollars! Jo, I hope you haven't done anything rash?"

"No, it's mine honestly. I didn't beg, borrow, or steal it. I earned it, and I don't think you'll blame me, for I only sold what was my own."

As she spoke, Jo took off her bonnet, and a general outcry arouse, for all her abundant hair was cut short.

"Your hair! Your beautiful hair!" "Oh, Jo, how could you? Your one beauty." "My dear girl, there was no need of this."

"She doesn't look like my Jo any more, but I love her dearly for it!"

— **Louisa May Alcott** *(1832-1888) American novelist*

Susan Straight in the *Afterword* writes ". . . all the girls I've every talked to wanted to be Jo . . . brave enough to cut off her long hair in sacrifice to her family." Well girls, even more of us now know the high standards you have set for yourselves.

The Man With the Golden Arm (1949)

■ *The story of Frankie Machine, a heroin addict who gets clean while in prison but struggles in the tough outside world of Chicago's Division Street to stay that way.*

Frankie felt his own back pressed hard against the hallway wall knowing neither God nor Molly-O could save him from going to Louie on his knees with ten dirty thousand more. "There's people ought to be knocked on the head," he told Louie without hearing his own voice at all. "I want people like you knocked on the head."

"You couldn't knock nobody's head," Louie laughed at him, . . . Then spotted the buck, trapped upright under the door's lower hinge, and bent swiftly for it.

Frankie locked his fingers to stop their shaking. If the shaking didn't stop he was going to cry in front of the punk and a flame of cold shame for having lain in a cold and secret sweat begging for morphine charged the fingers with a pride of their own. He rose on the balls of his toes and came down with all his weight full upon that white defenseless nape.

The throat made a single startled gurgle.

Then the neck flopped forward like a hen's with the ax half through it.

— **Nelson Algren** *(1909-1981) American writer*

A Walk on the Wild Side (1956)

- *Country boy Dove Linkhorn, a young womanizing bum, leaves Texas during the depression for New Orleans where he fits right in with the local prostitutes, pimps, and flimflam artists, at least for a while.*

. . . Their crimes were sickness, idleness, high spirits, boredom and hard luck. They were those who had failed to wire themselves to courts, state attorney's office or police. Hardly a stone so small but was big enough to trip them up and when they fell they fell all the way.

— **Nelson Algren**

"I don't recommend being a bachelor, but it helps if you want to write."

Brick Lane (2003)

- *The life of Nazneen and her husband Chanu, by an arranged marriage, living in London's Bangladeshi community.*

They had developed a routine of sorts. In the early afternoon she watched from the window. When he appeared, she raised her hand as if she were about to scratch her face. Then he would come up. If Chanu was still at home, she leaned her head against the glass, and he did not wave or smile, or do anything other than continue his walk across the yard. Then she imagined that she would do the same every day, until he stopped appearing. She would simply watch and eventually he would understand and not come back again for her. But the next day she trembled just the same as she raised her hand.

— **Monica Ali** *(1967-) British writer of Bangladeshi origin*

Lucky Jim (1954)

- *A comic story of the exploits of Jim Dixon striving to keep from being fired from his position as a university lecturer but lacking the tact and prudence expected.*

'All right, you've got it coming,' Bertrand bayed furiously. 'I warned you.' He came and stood over Dixon. 'Come on, stand up, you dirty little bar-fly, you nasty little jumped-up turd.'

‘What are we going to do, dance?’

‘I’ll give you dance, I’ll make you dance, don’t you worry. Just stand up, if you’re not afraid to. If you think I’m going to sit back and take this from you, you’re mistaken; I don’t happen to be that type, you sam.’

‘I’m not Sam, you fool,’ Dixon shrieked; this was the worst taunt of all. He took off his glasses and put them in his top jacket pocket.

They faced each other on the floral rug, feet apart and elbows crooked in uncertain attitudes, as if about to begin some ritual of which neither had learnt the cues.

— **Kingsley Amis** *(1922-1995) English novelist, poet, critic and teacher*

“If you can’t annoy someone there is little point in writing.”

“Whatever part drink may play in the writer’s life, it must play none in his or her work.” That this was certainly the case is attested to by Amis’s highly disciplined approach to writing. For ‘many years’, Amis imposed a rigorous daily schedule upon himself in which writing and drinking were strictly segregated. Mornings were devoted to writing with a minimum daily output of 500 words. The drinking would only begin around lunchtime when this output had been achieved. Amis’s prodigious output would not have been possible without this kind of self discipline.

Money (1984)

- *John Self, a British director of commercials, engages in his major interests—drink, money, and sex—while making his first feature film in New York, then returns home to solve additional problems.*

My travelling-clock told me eight-fifteen. I leapt out of bed feeling full of fight, really tiptop, apart from the sweats, the jerks, the shivers, a pronounced dizziness — and a sensation, hard to describe and harder to bear, that I had missed my stop on the shuttle and was somehow due yesterday at the next planet but one. Through the back window I warily inspected the span of the morning pale . . . My coffee arrived as I lay smoking in the tub, one leg atremble on the cold white shelf. I slashed myself shaving, then had a big rumble with my rug. I like to recede right out in the open but the slate-grey hanks kept doing bashful curtseys over the scooped zigzag of my brow. So I soaked the brush and plastered it all back. Next door I drank coffee in thick panting gulps. Eight-forty. Best outfit: long flared jacket, sharply tapered strides, chunky black brothel-creepers. I didn’t take a drink but as I locked my door I rehearsed the way in which I would say hi to Martina and laughingly call for champagne.

— **Martin Amis** *(1949-) British novelist*

The Complete Fairy Tales and Stories (1835)

- *One of the 'immortals of world literature,' Andersen's fairy tales are enjoyed by people everywhere for their 'wit and wisdom, humor and compassion.'*

The emperor walked in the procession under his crimson canopy. And all the people of the town, who had lined the streets or were looking down from the windows, said that the emperor's clothes were beautiful. "What a magnificent robe! And the train! How well the emperor's clothes suit him!"

None of them were willing to admit that they hadn't seen a thing; for if anyone did, then he was either stupid or unfit for the job he held. Never before had the emperor's clothes been such a success.

"But he doesn't have anything on!" cried a little child.

"Listen to the innocent one," said the proud father. And the people whispered among each other and repeated what the child had said.

"He doesn't have anything on. There's a little child who says that he has nothing on."

"He has nothing on!" shouted all the people at last.

— **Hans Christian Andersen** *(1805-1875) Danish author and poet noted for his children stories*

The Blind Assassin (2000)

- *The lives of two sisters, Laura who apparently commits suicide, and Iris who questionably marries leading to regret and eventual suspicion.*

Ten days after the war ended, my sister Laura drove a car off a bridge. The bridge was being repaired: she went right through the Danger sign. The car fell a hundred feet into the ravine, smashing through the treetops feathery with new leaves, then burst into flames and rolled down into the shallow creek at the bottom. Chunks of the bridge fell on top of it. Nothing much was left of her but charred smithereens. . . . .

"Science fiction has monsters and spaceships, speculative fiction could really happen.

You'll knock. I'll hear you, I'll shuffle down the hallway, I'll open the door. My heart will jump and flutter; I'll peer at you, then recognize you: my cherished, my last remaining wish. I'll think to myself that I've never seen anyone so beautiful, but I won't say so; I wouldn't want you to think I've gone scatty. Then I'll welcome you, I'll hold out my arms to you, I'll kiss you on the cheek, sparsely, because it would be unseemly to let myself go. I'll cry a few tears, but only a few, because the eyes of the elderly are arid.

— **Margaret Atwood** *(1939-) Canadian novelist and environmentalist*

The Handmaid's Tale (1986)

- *A future totalitarian state where women are confined to a few limited roles, the heroine being a Handmaiden whose sole role is to produce children in an otherwise barren society.*

My presence here is illegal. It's forbidden for us to be alone with the Commanders. We are for breeding purposes: we aren't concubines, geisha girls, courtesans. On the contrary: everything possible has been done to remove us from that category. There is supposed to be nothing entertaining about us, no room is to be permitted for the flowering of secret lusts; no special favors are to be wheedled, by them or us, there are to be no toeholds for love. We are two-legged wombs, that's all: sacred vessels, ambulatory chalices.

So why does he want to see me, at night, alone?

— Margaret Atwood

Emma (1816)

- *A young, well-to-do, and quick-witted Emma Woodhouse tries her hand at match making with a series of misguided schemes that threaten to surge out of control.*

Emma's eyes were instantly withdrawn; and she sat silently meditating, in a fixed attitude, for a few minutes. A few minutes were sufficient for making her acquainted with her own heart. A mind like hers, once opening to suspicion, made rapid progress; she touched, she admitted, she acknowledged the whole truth. Why was it so much worse that Harriet should be in love with Mr. Knightley than with Frank Churchill? Why was the evil so dreadfully increased by Harriet's having some hope of a return? It darted through her with the speed of an arrow that Mr. Knightley must marry no one but herself!

— Jane Austen *(1775-1817) English novelist*

"...that sanguine expectation of happiness which is happiness itself."

Pride and Prejudice (1813)

- *The lives and loves of five daughters living in Hartforshire, focusing on the courting of strong-willed Elizabeth by Mr. Darcy a new neighbor.*

. . . Mr. Darcy had at first scarcely allowed her to be pretty; he had looked at her without admiration at the ball; and when they next met, he looked at her only to criticize. But no sooner had he made it clear to himself and his friends that she had hardly a good feature in her face, than he began to find it was rendered uncommonly intelligent by the beautiful expression of her dark eyes. To this discovery succeeded some others equally mortifying.

"From the very beginning, from the first moment, I may almost say, of my acquaintance with you, your manners impressing me with the fullest belief of your arrogance, your conceit, and your selfish disdain of the feelings of others…."

(Miss. Elizabeth's response to Mr. Darcy's attention)

— Jane Austen

B

Young Man with a Horn (1938)

- *A young musician becomes a great jazz trumpeter but his highs are balanced by the death of his mentor, a sour marriage, and bouts with alcoholism. Allegedly based on the life of Bix Beiderbecke.*

Bix Beiderbecke

. . . They rolled him onto the stretcher and carried him to the ambulance. Smoke got in and sat beside him on a jump seat. They drove slowly between streets, but they put on a little speed at intersections and went across with the siren wide open.

The sun was in Rick's face. Smoke reached up and pulled down the blind. Then he settled back and said, 'I knew a guy once that took a cure and he said . . .' But he stopped it there because he suddenly knew that it wasn't getting over. He looked down and saw Rick's face. He watched, stunned, and while he was watching, Rick died. He could tell when it happened. There was a difference.

— Dorothy Baker *(1907-1968) American novelist*

Another Country (1960)

- *The downfall of jazz drummer Rufus Scott and the impact on his friends living a bohemian lifestyle in Greenwich Village in the late 1950s.*

Beneath them Rufus walked, one of the fallen—for the weight of this city was murderous—one of those who had been crushed on the day, which was every day, these towers fell. Entirely alone, and dying of it, he was part of an unprecedented multitude. There were boys and girls drinking coffee at the drugstore counters who were held back from his condition by barriers as perishable as their dwindling cigarettes. They could scarcely bear their knowledge, nor could they have borne the sight of Rufus, but they knew why he was in the streets tonight, why he rode subways all night long, why his stomach growled, why his hair was nappy, his armpits funky, his pants and shoes too thin, and why he did not dare to stop and take a leak.

— James Baldwin *(1924-1987) American novelist and civil rights activist*

Go Tell It on the Mountain (1952)

- *The lives and secrets of a tormented black family living during the depression under a tyrannical father, minister of a storefront Pentecostal church in Harlem.*

"Yeah," said Roy, "we don't know how lucky we *is* to have a father what don't want you to go to movies, and don't want you to play in the streets, and don't want you to have no friends, and he don't want this and he don't want that, and he don't want you to do *nothing*. We so *lucky* to have a father who just wants us to go to church and read the Bible and beller like a fool in front of the altar and stay home all nice and quiet, like a little mouse. Boy, we sure is lucky, all right. Don't know what I done to be so lucky."

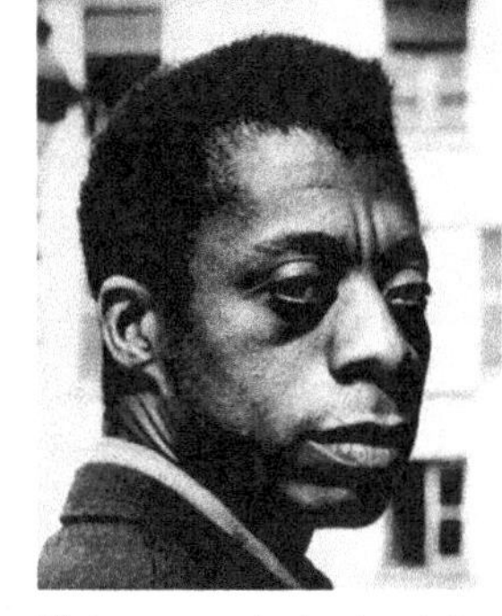

"It is a great shock at the age of five or six to find that in a world of Gary Coopers you are the Indian."

She laughed. "You going to find out one day," she said, "you mark my words."

"Yeah," said Roy.

"But it'll be too late, then," she said. "It'll be too late when you come to be . . . sorry." Her voice had changed. For a moment her eyes met John's eyes, and John was frightened. He felt that her words, after the strange fashion God sometimes chose to speak to men, were dictated by Heaven and were meant for him. He was fourteen—was it too late?

— James Baldwin

Cousin Bette (1847)

- *A poor cousin, Bette Fischer, snaps when her niece steals her 'lover,' then seeks to ruin the lives of her wealthy relations.*

Thus, in one moment, Lisbeth Fischer had become the Mohican whose snares none can escape, whose dissimulation is inscrutable, whose swift decisiveness is the outcome of the incredible perfection of every organ of sense. She was Hatred and Revenge, as implacable as they are in Italy, Spain, and the East. These two feelings, the obverse of friendship and love carried to the utmost, are known only in lands scorched by the sun. But Lisbeth was also a daughter of Lorraine, bent on deceit.

— Honore de Balzac *(1799-1850) French novelist and playwright*

Due to his keen observation of detail and unfiltered representation of society, Balzac is regarded as one of the founders of realism in European literature. He is renowned for his multi-faceted characters; even his lesser characters are complex, morally ambiguous and fully human. — *Wikipedia*

Affliction (1989)

- *The turbulent aggressive life of a divorced inept man unable to cope with mounting conflicts and rejections.*

Without thinking it, Wade reached behind him into the dishrack, and his hand wrapped itself, as if of its own volition, around the handle of the skillet, heavy, black, cast iron, and he lifted it free of the rack and swung it around in front of him. The sound of his heart pounded in his ears like a hammer against steel, and he heard his voice, high and thin in the distance, say to his father, "If you touch her or me, or any of us, again, I'll _______ kill you."

His father quietly said, "Jesus." He sounded like a man who had just broken a shoelace.

"I mean it. I'll kill you." He lifted the skillet in his right hand and held it out and just off his shoulder, like a Ping-Pong paddle, and he suddenly felt ridiculous.

Without hesitation, Pop walked quickly around the table, came up to his son and punched him straight in the face, sending the boy careening back against the counter and the skillet to the floor.

— **Russell Banks** *(1940-) American author*

Cloudsplitter (1998)

- *An elderly Owen Brown, son of the famed abolitionist John Brown, reflects on his life and his father's martyrdom.*

The Old Man jumped up on the box and, placing his hands on his hips, surveyed the crowd of volunteers. "I can take no more than eight, for a total membership of fifteen," he declared. "And you must be as willing to die for the cause as my sons and I myself are." Quite a few drifted away at this. "We are here to slay the enemy of the Lord. I want bloodthirsty men at my side. No kittenish weaklings, no mild-mannered Garrisonians, no cowards who prefer peace with the slavers to war. And no men whose courage depends on whiskey. I want temperance men." Here a number of men turned and strolled away. "And ye must be Christians," he said. "True soldiers of the Lord is what I need! Ye must be armored by God, for we are going forth to smite His enemies down!" And now there were but a dozen remaining.

— **Russell Banks**

The Sot-Weed Factor (1960)

■ *The various adventures of would-be-poet Ebenezer Cooke, constantly confounded by existential powers captured in this description. "The road to Heaven's beset with thistles, and methinks there's many a cowpat on't."*

The first was his appearance: pale-haired and pale-eyed, raw-boned and gaunt-cheeked, he stood—nay, *angled*—nineteen hands high. His clothes were good stuff well tailored, but they hung on his frame like luffed sails on long spars. Heron of a man, lean-limbed and long-billed, he walked and sat with loose-jointed poise; his every stance was angular surprise, his each gesture half flail. Moreover there was a discomposure about his face, as though his features got on ill together: heron's beak, wolf-hound's forehead, pointed chin, lantern jaw, wash-blue eyes, and bony blond brows had minds of their own, went their own ways, and took up odd postures, which often as not had no relation to what one took as his mood of the moment. And these configurations were short-lived, for like restless mallards the features of his face no sooner were settled than *ha!* they'd be flushed, and *hi!* how they'd flutter, and no man could say what lay behind them.

— **John Barth** *(1930-) American novelist and short-story writer*

Sixty Stories (1981)

■ *Stories often relying on an accumulation of seemingly unrelated detail, focusing on incidents rather than a complete narrative.*

Miss Mandible wants to make love to me but she hesitates because I am officially a child; I am, according to the records, according to the gradebook on her desk, according to the card index in the principal's office, eleven years old. There is a misconception here, one that I haven't quite managed to get cleared up yet. I am in fact thirty-five, I've been in the Army, I am six feet one, I have hair in the appropriate places, my voice is a baritone, I know very well what to do with Miss Mandible if she ever makes up her mind.

In the meantime we are studying common fractions.

— **Donald Barthelme** *(1931-1989) American author*

Selected Stories (1957)

■ *The range and merit of H. E. Bates's short stories is unsurpassed. His first short story was published in 1928, the last in 1972. This story lifts slightly the burden of death for parents learning of their son's gallantry.*

"They trusted him to get them home, and he got them home. Everything was against him. He feathered the outer starboard engine and then, in spite of everything, got them down on two engines. It was a very good show. A very wonderful show."

The man is silent, but the woman lifts her head. She looks at the Wing Commander for a moment or two, immobile, very steady, and then says, quite distinctly, "Please tell us the rest."

"There is not much," he says. "It was a very wonderful flight, but they were out of luck. They were up against all the bad luck in the world. When they came to land they couldn't see the flarepath very well, but he got them down. And then, as if they hadn't had enough, they came down slightly off the runway and hit an obstruction. Even then they didn't crash badly. But it must have thrown him and he must have hit his head somewhere with great force, and that was the end."

"Yes, sir. And the others?" the man says.

"They were all right. Even the second pilot. I wish you could have talked to them. It would have helped if you could have talked to them. They know that he brought them home. They know that they owe everything to him."

— **H. E. Bates** *(1905-1974) English writer and author*

The Wonderful Wizard of Oz (1900)

■ *Dorothy and Toto are swept off the plains of Kansas to the land of Oz where they meet up with the Scarecrow, the Tin Woodman, and the Cowardly Lion, and eventually the Wizard of Oz himself.*

"Who are you?"

"I am Oz, the Great and Terrible," said the little man, in a trembling voice, "but don't strike me—please don't!—and I'll do anything you want me to."

Our friends looked at him in surprise and dismay.

"I thought Oz was a great Head," said Dorothy.

"And I thought Oz was a lovely Lady," said the Scarecrow.

"And I thought Oz was a terrible Beast," said the Tin Woodman.

"And I thought Oz was a Ball of Fire," exclaimed the Lion.

"No, you are all wrong," said the little man meekly. "I have been making believe."

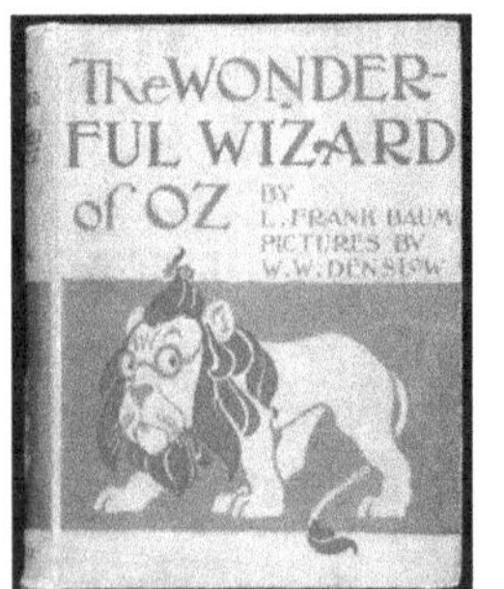

"Making believe!" cried Dorothy "Are you not a Great Wizard?"

"Hush, my dear," he said. "Don't speak so loud, or you will be overheard—and I should be ruined. I'm supposed to be a Great Wizard."

— **L. Frank Baum** *(1856-1919) American author of children's books*

Wartime Lies (1991)

- *Orphaned nine-year-old Maciek and his sharp-tongued aunt, Tania, pose as Catholic Poles to hide their Jewish identity against the German Gestapo.*

Suddenly Tania stood up, drew in her breath, and pointed out the window to the stairs. Walking up were two Gestapo men in uniform and a third man in a belted civilian coat but wearing black britches and high black boots like the others. Tania put her fingers to her lips and in a whisper told me to hurry to the bedroom, leave the door open, and hide behind the door. I was to listen carefully. If they were taking her away or if they were going toward the bedroom and she shrieked, I should immediately take the cyanide. Keep it in your hand, she said, and keep your hand in your pants pocket.

It took what seemed like a long time before they reached our apartment. I listened to their knocking on other doors off the balcony and to muffled conversations. At last, they knocked on the door of our kitchen.

— **Louis Begley** *(1933-) Polish-born American novelist*

All Souls' Rising (1995)

- *The slave rebellion of the 1790s that would bring an end to the brutal white rule in Haiti, as told by a second-generation African slave known as Toussaint-Louverture.*

". . . Beager took him out riding in the heat of the day. When I saw him come in I thought they must have gone at a gallop all the way to Le Cap and back. It was still hot when he brought him in all foamed up and slobbery. Beager took him to the water trough."

"That's how you kill a horse," I said. "He must have known—what was he thinking?" . . .

"I called him to stop," Toussaint said, "to think what he was doing." His eyes were far away, over my shoulder. "He did not listen. I caught the bridle out of his hand. He pushed me out of the way and led the horse nearer the trough. I hit him with my fist before I knew that I would do it—never knew I'd done it till I saw him sitting on the ground."

. . . "It was all in the open," Toussaint said. "You know where we water the horses at Breda. There must have been twenty slaves that saw it. No white men, though. Beager got up. He touched his mouth and showed me blood on his fingers. He took a step toward me where I was holding Treize still. The horse was tossing his head because he wanted to go drink the water and die. Then Beager turned around and went into the *grand'case* by himself."

. . . In that time . . . no slave could strike a whiteman and live afterward, it was unknown.

— **Madison Smartt Bell** *(1957-) American novelist*

The Adventures of Augie March (1953)

- *The development of Augie March from boyhood to manhood during the Great Depression, traced through a series of encounters, occupations and relationships.*

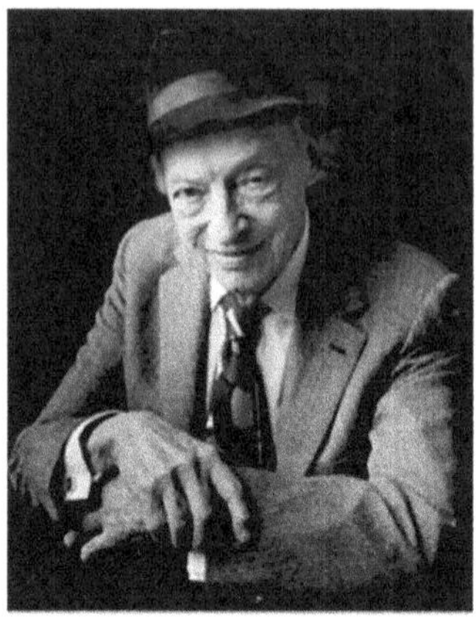

"If your brother knew about this, by Jesus Christ! He'd beat you. I know he would."

I admitted that it was so. Einhorn must have seen the horror and fear in me as through a narrow opening. My hand lay where he could reach it; he put his fingers on it. "This is where a young fellow starts to decay and stink, and his health and beauty go. By the first things he does when he's not a boy any longer, but does what a man does. A boy steals apples, watermelons. If he's a wildcat in college he writes a bad check or two. But to go out as an armed bandit —"

"We weren't."

"I'll open this drawer," he said with intensity, "and give you fifty bucks if you'll swear Joe Groman didn't have a gun. I tell you he had one."

I was hot in the face but faint. It could be true; it was plausible.

— **Saul Bellow** *(1915-2005) Canadian-born American writer*

Herzog (1964)

- *The personal crises of Moses Herzog, a confused intellectual responding to the breakup of his second marriage.*

At last he embraced his daughter, and she pressed his cheeks with her small hands and kissed him. Hungry to feel her, to breathe in her childish fragrance, to look in her face, her black eyes, touch her hair, the skin under her dress, he pressed her little bones, stammering, "Junie, sweetie. I've miss you." His happiness was painful. And she with all her innocence and childishness and with the pure, or amorous instinct of tiny girls, kissed him on the lips, her careworn, busted, germ- carrying father.

— **Saul Bellow**

Saul Bellow won the Nobel Prize for literature in 1976. In the words of the Swedish Nobel Committee, his writing exhibited "exuberant ideas, flashing irony, hilarious comedy and burning compassion..."

At a later Nobel tribute banquet given by his colleagues, Bellow's opened his remarks with "After years of the most arduous mental labor, I stand before you in the costume of a head waiter...."

Him with His Foot in His Mouth (1984)

- *Five stories, this quote from "A Silver Dish" about the relationship of a son to his less-than-perfect father.*

After a time, Pop's resistance ended. He subsided and subsided. He rested against his son, his small body curled there. Nurses came and looked. They disapproved, but Woody, who couldn't spare a hand to wave them out, motioned with his head toward the door. Pop, whom Woody thought he had stilled, only had found a better way to get around him. Loss of heat was the way he did it. His heat was leaving him. As can happen with small animals while you hold them in your hand, Woody presently felt him cooling. Then, as Woody did his best to restrain him, and thought he was succeeding, Pop divided himself. And when he was separated from his warmth, he slipped into death. And there was his elderly, large, muscular son, still holding and pressing him when there was nothing anymore to press. You could never pin down that self-willed man. When he was ready to make his move he made it—always on his own terms. And always, always, something up his sleeve. That was how he was.

— Saul Bellow

Humboldt's Gift (1975)

- *Humboldt acts from the grave to change the fortunes of his friend Charlie who is now middle-aged and a bit shaky.*

He was a great entertainer but going insane. The pathologic element could be missed only by those who were laughing too hard to look. Humboldt, that grand erratic handsome person with his wide blond face, that charming fluent deeply worried man to whom I was so attached, passionately lived out the theme of Success. Naturally he died a Failure. What else can result from the capitalization of such nouns? Myself, I've always held the number of sacred words down. In my opinion Humboldt had too long a list of them—Poetry, Beauty, Love, Waste Land, Alienation, Politics, History, the Unconscious. And, of course, Manic and Depressive, always capitalized.

— Saul Bellow

More Die of Heartbreak (1987)

- *An intellectually gifted and philosophically tortured man attempts to work out his fate and worldview.*

. . . He was an *home a femmes*, a chaser. A man of staggering charm, he was able to make good on his *la ci darem* promises. The lady who gave him her hand wouldn't be sorry. She wouldn't even regret going back to her husband, since a sensible person would understand that my father was a one-time event, like the Fall, or Noah's Ark. As a conversationalist he was limited, but his repertory was terrific for his purposes. He had served as a Ninety Day Wonder on a destroyer and he had seen FDR, Harry Hopkins, Churchill and Montgomery close up. . . . Sartre had accused my father of being an American spy because he spoke French *too* well. . . . If he had taken Proust to dinner, Father would have given him memorable entertainment.

— Saul Bellow

Mr. Sammler's Planet (1970)

- *Three days in the life of an old Polish Jew in which he interprets and analyzes the events in his life.*

Mr. Sammler himself was able to add, to basic wisdom, that to kill the man he ambushed in the snow had given him pleasure. Was it only pleasure? It was more. It was joy. You would call it a dark action? On the contrary, it was also a bright one. It was mainly bright. When he fired his gun, Sammler, himself nearly a corpse, burst into life. Freezing in Zamosht Forest, he had often dreamed of being near a fire. Well, this was more sumptuous than fire. His heart felt lined with brilliant, rapturous satin. To kill the man and to kill him without pity, for he was dispensed from pity. There was a flash, a blot of fiery white. When he shot again it was less to make sure of the man than to try again for the bliss. To drink more flames. He would have thanked God for this opportunity. If he had had any God. At that time, he did not. For many years, in his own mind, there was no judge but himself.

In the privacy of his bed he turned very briefly to that rage (for reference, he did it). Luxury. And when he himself was nearly beaten to death. Had to lift dead bodies from himself. Desperate! Crawling out. Oh heart-bursting! Oh vile! Then he himself knew how it felt to take a life. Found it could be an ecstasy.

— Saul Bellow

Jaws (1974)

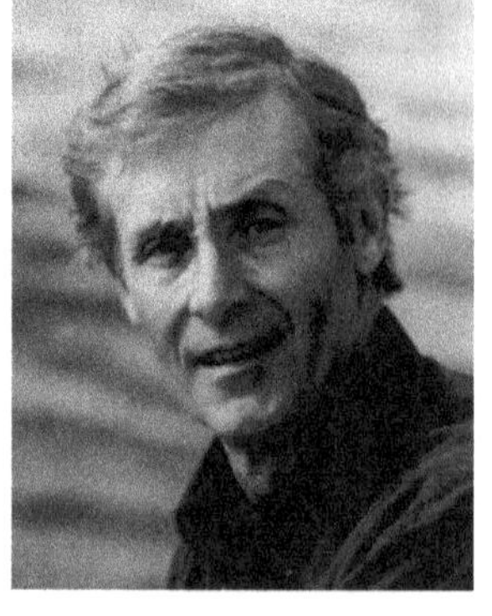

- *The police chief of an island resort town with the help of an old skipper and young scientist fight a great white shark that is terrorizing the community.*

. . . The great fish moved silently through the night water, propelled by short sweeps of its crescent tail. The mouth was open just enough to permit a rush of water over the gills. There was little other motion: an occasional correction of the apparently aimless course by the slight raising or lowering of a pectoral fin—as a bird changes direction by dipping one wing and lifting the other. The eyes were sightless in the black, and the other senses transmitted nothing extraordinary to the small, primitive brain. . . . .

A hundred yards offshore, the fish sensed a change in the sea's rhythm. It did not see the woman, nor yet did it smell her. Running within the length of its body were a series of thin canals, filled with mucus and dotted with nerve endings, and these nerves detected vibrations and signaled the brain. The fish turned toward shore.

— **Peter Benchley** *(1940-2006) American author*

Women in Their Beds (1996)

- *Thirty-five short stories of great range and depth, all beautifully written. This selection from "The Infinite Passion of Expectation."*

She went out again, a few nights later, to visit a friend, and he escorted her graciously to the door. Come back any time you need to see me," he called after her. Puzzled, she turned on the path. The light from within the house shone around his dark figure in the rectangle of the open door. "But I live here for now," she called back, flapping her coat out on both sides to make herself more evident to him. "Of course! Of course! I forgot!" he laughed, stamping his foot, dismayed with himself. And she knew that her presence was not so intense a presence as they thought. It would not matter to him as the days went by, as the years left to him went by, that she had not come into his bed.

— **Gina Berriault** *(1926-1999) American novelist and short-story writer*

The Decameron (1360)

- *A collection of 100 humorous, often bawdy, tales of love that invariably turn out well for the participants however misbehaving.*

They arouse as soon as dawn began to break, for the lady was anxious not to give cause for scandal. Having provided him with some very old clothes and filled his purse with money, she then explained which road he must take on entering the fortress in order to find his servant, . . . imploring him to keep their encounter a secret.

As soon as it was broad day and the gates were opened, he entered the castle, giving the impression he was arriving from a distance, and rooted out his servant. Having changed into the clothes that were in his portmanteau, he was about to mount his servant's horse, when as if by some divine miracle the three brigands were brought into the castle, after being arrested for another crime they had committed shortly after robbing him on the previous evening. They had made a voluntary confession, and consequently Rinaldo's horse, clothing and money were restored to him, and all he lost was a pair of garters, which the robbers were unable to account for.

— **Giovanni Boccaccio** *(1313-1375) Italian author and poet*

2666 (2008)

- *Multiple people are tied together over time by the mostly unsolved murders of women in the Mexican desert borderlands.*

. . . Then the bodyguard from Tijuana spotted two men walking behind the two maids and he stiffened. Lalo Cura saw his face and he saw the men and he knew instantly that they were gunmen and they were there to kill Pedro Rengifo's wife. . . . . With his left hand he released the safety of his Desert Eagle and then he heard the clack of heels, Pedro Rengifo's wife heading to the car . . . The gunmen shoved the maids aside. One was carrying an Uzi submachine gun. He was thin and his skin was very dark.

. . . . Pedro Rengifo's wife felt someone tugging on her suit and pulling her to the ground. . . . . Out of the corner of her eye, she . . . saw Lalo, kneeling with his gun in his hand, and she heard a noise and saw a shell leap from the gun in Lalo's grasp and then she didn't see anything because her forehead hit the cement of the sidewalk. . . . for Lalo Cura the problem was deciding which of the two gunmen would shoot him first, the one with the Uzi or the one who looked more like a professional. He should have fired at the latter, but he fired at the former. The bullet struck the thin, dark-skinned man in the chest and he fell instantly. The other gunman shifted imperceptibly to the right and experienced his own moment of uncertainty.

— **Roberto Bolano** *(1953-2003) Chilean novelist and poet*

Ficciones (1962)

- *Short pieces of fantasy, this one about a person who can recall every instant in his whole life.*

We, in a glance, perceive three wine glasses on the table; Funes saw all the shoots, clusters, and grapes of the vine. He remembered the shapes of the clouds in the south at dawn on the 30th of April of 1882, and he could compare them in his recollection with the marbled grain in the design of a leather-bound book which he had seen only once, and with the lines in the spray which an oar raised in the Rio Negro on the eve of the battle of the Quebracho. These recollections were not simple; each visual image was linked to muscular sensations, thermal sensations, etc. He could reconstruct all his dreams, all his fancies. Two or three times he had reconstructed an entire day. He told me: *I have more memories in myself alone than all men have had since the world was a world.*

— **Jorge Luis Borges** *(1899-1986) Argentine writer, essayist, and poet*

The Death of the Heart (1938)

■ *Sixteen-year-old Portia Quayne moves to London to live with her half-brother and falls in love with a family friend Eddie, all secretly revealed to her disdainful sister-in-law who finds and reads her diary.*

Greatly interested in "life with the lid on, and what happens when the lid comes off."

. . . She caught a waitress's eye and ordered what she thought right. "Look what a far-off table I got," she said. "You need not be afraid of saying anything now. I say, why don't you take off your hat, instead of keeping on pushing it back?"

"Oh Lilian, I haven't really got much to tell you, you know."

"Don't be so humble, my dear; you told me there was a plot."

"All I meant was, they have been laughing at me."

"What made them laugh?"

"They have been telling each other." . . . .

. . . "I don't suppose St. Quentin's half so mean as Eddie, laughing at you with your sister-in-law."

"*Oh*, I didn't say that! I never did!"

"Then what's the reason you're so mad with her? You said you didn't want to go home."

"She's read my diary."

— **Elizabeth Bowen** *(1899-1973) Anglo-Irish novelist and short-story writer*

The Sheltering Sky (1949)

■ *The unraveling of a young and sophisticated married couple as they make their way into the Sahara that culminates in death and madness.*

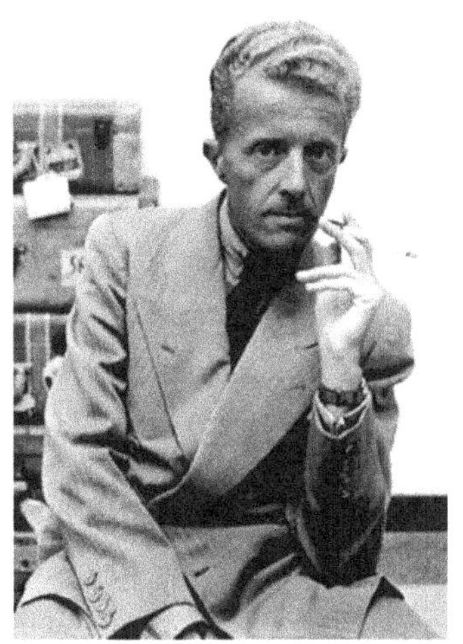

She opened the door. Port lay in a strange position, his legs wound tightly in the bedcovers. That corner of the room was like a still photograph suddenly flashed on the screen in the middle of the stream of moving images. She shut the door softly, locked it, turned again toward the corner, and walked slowly over to the mattress. She held her breath, bent over, and looked into the meaningless eyes. But already she knew, even to the convulsive lowering of her hand to the bare chest, even without the violent push she gave the inert torso immediately afterward. As her hands went to her own face, she cried: "No!" once—no more. She stood perfectly still for a long, long time, her head raised, facing the wall. Nothing moved inside her; she was conscious of nothing outside or in.

— **Paul Bowles** *(1910-1999) American expatriate, composer, and author*

Paul Bowles lived for 53 of his 88 years in Tangier. Not surprisingly, he became identified with the city. During his life visitors would seek him out, and on his death obituary-writers without fail linked his life to his residency. He became a symbolic American expatriate, and the city became the symbol of his expatriate status. — *Wikipedia*

Drop City (2003)

■ *The counterculture residents of a California commune travel to Alaska in the 1970s to reinvent their utopia but find the natural environment is unforgiving of their carefree lifestyle.*

Across the room, too wrought up even to sit, Norm swayed over the Formica-topped tables, forking up the macaroni and cheese special with a side of Waldorf salad, his eyes sucked back into his head with fatigue, exhorting them to eat up, get with it, *mobilize*. "A hundred sixty more miles," he rasped, too depleted to shout. "An inch and a half on the map. That's all, people—we're already home. Can you smell it? Smell that river?"

Nobody could smell anything. Their jaws worked, their smiles glistened. It was a festive moment, presided over by a shell-shocked cook and a dazed waitress in a pleated skirt and a blouse with rodeo figures embroidered on the collar. And so what if Fairbanks was exactly like a half-mile strip torn out of any industrial city anywhere in America, like Detroit or Albany or Akron, like the very burgs they'd all escaped from in the first place? They were here. They were in Alaska. The end was in sight.

— **T. Coraghessan Boyle** *(1948-) American novelist and short story writer*

World's End (1987)

■ *A multigenerational saga of two Dutch families, linking their settlement in the Hudson Valley in the late 1600s to mid-20th century descendents.*

It was too much. He sprang down from his horse, the riding crop clenched in his fist, as the tattered beggar lurched to his feet in alarm. "What in hell do you think you're doing here?" Rombout raged, shaking the whip in the trespasser's face.

The Indian—for Indian he was—backpedaled, watching for sudden movement.

"This . . . this is trespassing!" Rombout shouted. "Vandalism. Poaching, for God's sake. These are private lands!"

The Indian had stopped backpedaling. He was dressed in a cheap flannel shirt, torn working pants and a crushed bowler hat he might have fished out of a public urinal; he was barefoot despite the incipient cold. "Private land, my ass," he said, folding his arms across his chest and fixing the lord of the manor with a cold, challenging, green-eyed glare. . . .

Rombout was beside himself with rage. . . . Now he suddenly roared at the Indian, "Do you know who I am?" punctuating each stentorian syllable with a flourish of the whip.

Unutterably calm, as if he were the property owner and Rombout the trespasser, the Indian nodded his head gravely. "A criminal," he said.

Rombout was struck dumb. No man had insulted him to his face in twenty-five years—none since a brash upperclassman at college had called him "a starched-up ass" and taken a concussive blow to the right ear in swift retribution. And here was this trespasser, this swarthy hook-nosed bum in a ragpicker's suit of clothes, bearding him on his own property.

– T. Coraghessan Boyle

The Chaneysville Incident (1981)

■ *The quest that takes a bitter young black historian back through the secrets and buried evil of his heritage.*

. . . The night was so quiet he could hear the chuckling of the creek, a steady dripping as the snow on the roof melted, the far-off barking of some farmer's dog. He rose slowly, heavily, throwing the sleep from him as if it were a blanket, and went to the door. He stepped outside, expecting to shiver in the chill, but the night was relatively warm, the snow beneath his feet damp. The clouds no longer boiled across the sky—they merely drifted, thinning, it seemed, before his eyes. He stood there, wishing he did not know the patterns of the weather, that he could have stood there in blissful ignorance, seeing the clearing sky as a normal man would see it, a welcome event, a time of thanksgiving. But he was not a normal man. He was C. K. Washington, and he had a dozen exhausted slaves looking to him for salvation, and now there was no friendly wind to hide their trail, no bitter cold to keep the hunters inattentive, to keep the miller home. The wind had died, and now they would have to run, and run hard, before the daylight came and took away their last concealment.

– David Bradley *(1950-) Associate Professor of creative writing at the University of Oregon*

Jane Eyre (1847)

- *Heroine Jane Eyre "manages to thrive on her integrity, intellect, and fullness of heart in order to overcome isolation, adversity, and class barriers."*

"Her book had sparked a movement in regards to feminism in literature."

He put out his hand with a quick gesture, but not seeing where I stood, he did not touch me. 'Who is this? Who is this?' he demanded, trying, as it seemed, to *see* with those sightless eyes — unavailing and distressing attempt! 'Answer me — speak again!' he ordered, imperiously and aloud.

'Will you have a little more water, sir? I spilt half of what was in the glass,' I said.

'*Who* is it? *What* is it? Who speaks?'

'Pilot knows me, and John and Mary know I am here. I came only this evening,' I answered.

'Great God! — what delusion has come over me? What sweet madness has seized me?'

'No delusion — no madness: your mind, sir, is too strong for delusion, your health too sound for frenzy.'

'And where is the speaker? Is it only a voice? Oh I *cannot* see, but I must feel, or my heart will stop and my brain burst. Whatever — whoever you are — be perceptible to the touch or I cannot live!"

He groped: I arrested his wandering hand, and prisoned it in both mine.

'Her very fingers!' he cried; 'her small, slight fingers! If so, then must be more of her.'

The muscular hand broke from my custody; my arm was seized, my shoulder — neck — waist — I was entwined and gathered to him.

'Is is Jane? *What* is it? This is her shape — this is her size —'

'And this her voice,' I added. 'She is all here: her heart, too. God bless you, sir! I am glad to be so near you again.'

'Jane Eyre! — Jane Eyre,' was all he said.

— **Charlotte Bronte** *(1816-1865) English novelist and poet*

Wuthering Heights (1847)

- *Heathcliff, a ragged orphan, comes into the Earnshaw family and eventually dominates the household even into a second generation yet looses his child-hood soulmate Catherine Earnshaw to a wealthy neighbor.*

. . . She continued reading, or seeking for something to read. His attention became, by degrees, quite centred in the study of her thick silky curls: her face he couldn't see, and she couldn't see him. And, perhaps, not quite awake to what he did, but attracted like a child to a candle, at last he proceeded from staring to touching; he put out his hand and stroked one curl, as gently as if it were a bird. He might have struck a knife into her neck, she started round in such a taking.

"Get away, this moment! How dare you touch me? Why are you stopping there?" she cried, in a tone of disgust. "I can't endure you! I'll go up-stairs again, if you come near me."

— **Emily Bronte** *(1818-1848) English novelist and poet*

The Late Great Creature (1972)

■ *The fall from fame and attempted comeback of Simon Moro, the greatest horror movie star of the 1920s and 30s.*

. . . Fantastic make-up for this scene: total blackface, even his tongue, the snaggled teeth like burnt stumps in a mouthful of wet soot. Then he edges—struts, really—along her curd-white body, blinking a redder and redder eye, that single bird eye again, until it fixes on her columnar—but cold or warm?—throat. . . . He hovers over that throat, fixated, then, in a quick, gawky shock move, pecks at it. Viciously. . . .

Illustration by Stephen Bissette

"What's he trying to do to me?"

"We'll fix," Terry assured her, from two rows back.

"Sure, sweetie-poo, you fix-fix. But what's he trying to do to me?"

"Your friend, Not mine."

"I'm all throat."

"We'll take out the wrinkles."

— **Brock Brower** *(ca. 1932-) Novelist and journalist*

The Pilgrim's Progress (1678)

■ *A religious allegory of Christian's perilous journey toward salvation, including his escape with Hopeful from the Doubting Castle aided by Promise.*

Now a little before it was day, good Christian, as one half amazed, brake out in this passionate speech. "What a fool," quote he, "am I, thus to lie in a stinking dungeon, when I may as well walk at liberty? I have a key in my bosom called Promise, that will (I am persuaded) open any lock in Doubting Castle." Then said Hopeful, "That's good news; good brother, pluck it out of they bosom and try." Then Christian pulled it out of his bosom, and began to try at the dungeon door, whose bolt (as he turned the key) gave back, and the door flew open with ease, and Christian and Hopeful both came out.

— **John Bunyan** *(1628-1688) English Christian writer and preacher*

"I have since found that [*The Pilgrim's Progress*] has been translated into most of the Languages of Europe, and suppose it has been more generally read than any other Book except perhaps the Bible." — Benjamin Franklin, *Autobiography*

A Clockwork Orange (1962)

- *A nightmare vision of the future in which a vicious fifteen-year old droog and his gang of four scoundrels ravage society in wonton acts of violence and savagery.*

. . . my balance being a bit gone, I went really crash this time, on to sploshing moloko and skriking koshkas, and the old forella started to fist me on the litso, both of us being on the floor, creeching: "Thrash him, beat him, pull out his finger-nails, the poisonous young beetle,' addressing her pusscats only, and then, as if like obeying the starry old ptitsa, a couple of koshkas got on to me and started scratching like bezoomny. So then I got real bezoomny myself, brothers, and hit out at them, but this baboochka said: 'Toad, don't touch my kitties,' and like scratched my litso. So then I creeched: 'You filthy old soomka,' and upped with the little malenky like silver statue and cracked her a fine fair tolchock on the gulliver and that shut her up real horror-show and lovely.

— **Anthony Burgess** *(1917-1993) English author, poet,playwright, composer, linguist, translator and critic*

Tarzan of the Apes (1914)

- *A baby is raised and survives within a tribe of African apes to become Lord of the Jungle, eventually returning to England to discover his heritage and to choose between two worlds.*

When the king ape released the limp form which had been John Clayton, Lord Greystroke, he turned his attention toward the little cradle; but Kala was there before him, and when he would have grasped the child she snatched it herself, and before he could intercept her she had bolted through the door and taken refuge in a high tree.

As she took up the little live baby of Alice Clayton she dropped the dead body of her own into the empty cradle; for the wail of the living had answered the call of universal motherhood within her wild breast which the dead could not still.

— **Edgar Rice Burroughs** *(1875-1950) American author*

Zdenek Burian illustration for *Tarzan and a Jewel of Opar* by Edgar Rice Burroughs

Naked Lunch (1959)

- *A bleak unnerving story of the various hideous modes of human behavior.*

The Sailor handed the boy a coin. He drifted over to Fats' table with his floating walk and sat down. They sat a long time in silence. The café was built into one side of a stone ramp at the bottom of a high white canyon of masonry. Faces of The City poured through silent as fish, stained with vile addictions and insect lusts. The lighted café was a diving bell, cable broken, settling into black depths.

The Sailor was polishing his nails on the lapels of his glen plaid suit. He whistled a little tune through his shiny, yellow teeth.

When he moved an effluvium of mold drifted out of his clothes, a musty smell of deserted locker rooms. He studied his nails with phosphorescent intensity.

"Good thing here, Fats. I can deliver twenty. Need an advance of course."

— **William S. Burroughs** *(1914-1997) American novelist and poet*

The Night Inspector (1999)

■ *A Union sniper who has most of his face destroyed in the war is forced to wear a pasteboard mask to hide his scars.*

Into the tree, then, and up, then screened and with my back against the trunk if possible, I worked with telescope for surveillance and rifle scope for aiming. It then was a matter of resistance: wind against bullet; will to be still and invisible against the tickle of spider, ant, or fly; lungs against the seized breath; finger to trigger; cheek to stock; and, always, despair against an imitation of God Almighty in a tree to smite a boy perhaps not wearing shoes or a man who had removed his officer's insignia to hid his rank (the sign of value in a corpse) from someone like me. I always shook and wavered, and I always steadied up. I was, finally, a hunter, and I killed them.

— **Frederick Busch** *(1941-2006) American writer*

A Good Scent from a Strange Mountain (1992)

■ *Stories by Vietnamese immigrants living in Louisiana following the Vietnam War.*

Mr. Green says that, too. "What then?" he has cried to me a thousand times, ten thousand times, in the past sixteen years. Parrots can live for a hundred years. And though I could not protect my dead grandfather's soul, I could take care of his parrot. When my grandfather died in Saigon in 1972, he made sure that Mr. Green came to me. I was twenty-four then and newly married and I still loved Mr. Green. He would sit on my shoulder and take the top of my ear in his beak, a beak that could crush the hardest shell, and he would hold my ear with the greatest gentleness and touch me with his tongue.

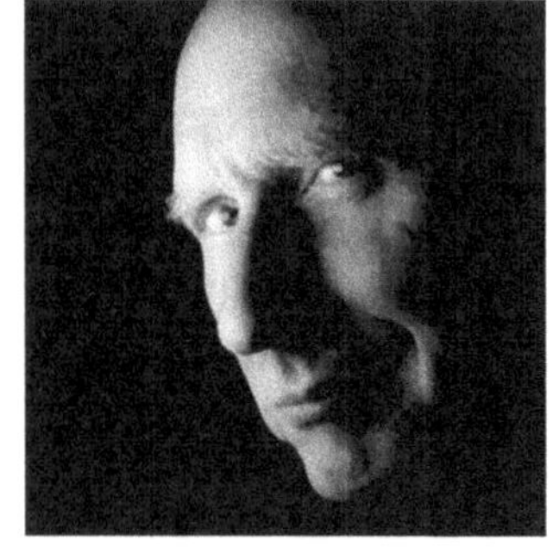

— **Robert Olen Butler** *(1945-) American fiction writer*

Possession: A Romance (1990)

■ *Two contemporary scholars investigating the lives of Victorian poet Randolph Ash and lesser-known Christabel La Motte, the "fairy poetess," discover their secret love affair.*

It was immediately clear that the book had been undisturbed for a very long time, perhaps even since it had been laid to rest. The librarian fetched a checked duster, and wiped away the dust, a black, thick tenacious Victorian dust, a dust composed of smoke and fog particles accumulated before the Clean Air acts. Roland undid the bindings. The book sprang apart, like a box, disgorging leaf after leaf of faded paper, blue, cream, grey, covered with rusty writing, the brown scratches of a steel nib. Roland recognized the handwriting with a shock of excitement.

— **A. S. Byatt** *(1936-) English novelist and poet*

C

Italian Folktales (1980)

■ *A collection of 200 Italian folktales, establishing a welcomed Italian counterpart anthology to that of the Brothers Grimm.*

. . . The king stared at her and said, "Hunchback wryneck hobbler! Ha, ha, ha!" And he laughed heartily in her face.

Now this old woman was a fairy. She looked the king in the eye and said, "Go on, laugh your fill. We'll just see who's laughing tomorrow." . . . .

This king had three daughters who were beautiful girls indeed. The next day he called them to go out walking with him. The oldest girl showed up with a hump on her back. "A hump?" asked the king. "How on earth did you get that?"

"Well," explained the daughter, "the maid made up my bed so badly that I got a big hump last night."

The king began pacing the floor; he felt uneasy. . . . .

"Here's what happened," replied the second daughter. "While the maid was combing my hair, she pulled out a hair . . . and here I am now with a wryneck." . . . .

"I went out into the garden," explained the third daughter, "and the maid picked a jasmine blossom and flung it at me. It fell on my foot and lamed me." . . . .

The maid was called and had to be dragged before the king by the guards because, in her words, she was ashamed to be seen: she was hunchbacked, wynecked, and hobbling—the very same old woman as the day before! The king recognized her instantly and yelled, "Coat her with pitch and burn her to death!"

The old woman shrank and shrank until her head was the size of a nail and just as pointed. There was a tiny hole in the wall, and she squeezed through it and disappeared from sight, leaving behind only her hump, wryneck, and lame foot.

— **Italo Calvino** *(1923-1985) Italian journalist and writer*

American Salvage (2009)

- *Stories of desperate characters among the everyday working class in rural Michigan.*

"Did she ask you to rob Mr. Cole to pay her mortgage?"

"I was her one-man army," Slocum said. He didn't know how much longer he could keep going without breaking down. His ache felt so big inside him that no amount of meth or pot would soothe him ever again. "I was her knight in shining ______ armor. She needed money so she wouldn't lose her house. I had to get it for her."

. . . .

"No she didn't ask me to rob him." He should have seen this coming—Wanda hadn't written to or visited him in jail for months—but somehow he hadn't seen it coming. Her betrayal was like punches to the head and the kidneys and the gut, and he couldn't punch back.

"Were you trying to kill Mr. Cole?" his lawyer asked.

"No, man. I wasn't. If he just would've stayed down when I told him to I would have stopped hitting him," Slocum said. He needed to be alone right now. He regretted testifying—his lawyer had advised against it, but he'd insisted. "The old guy just wouldn't stay down." Slocum looked around the courtroom, hoping, but not expecting, to find someone there who would understand.

— **Bonnie Jo Campbell** *(ca. 1962-) American author*

The Plague (1947)

- *A ravaging epidemic of bubonic plague engulfs the Algerian port of Oran.*

That evening, when Dr. Rieux was standing in the entrance, feeling for the latch-key in his pocket before starting up the stairs to his apartment, he saw a big rat coming toward him from the dark end of the passage. It moved uncertainly, and its fur was sopping wet. The animal stopped and seemed to be trying to get its balance, moved forward again toward the doctor, halted again, than spun round on itself with a little squeal and fell on its side. Its mouth was slightly open and blood was spurting from it. After gazing at it for a moment, the doctor went upstairs.

— **Albert Camus** *(1913-1960)*
French Algerian author, philosopher and journalist

The Stranger (1942)

- *An alienated young man attends his mother's funeral, befriends one of his neighbors, and later, after a knife fight, shoots one of his antagonists in response to the "glare of the sun."*

. . . In the end, all I remember is that while my lawyer went on talking, I could hear through the expanse of chambers and courtrooms an ice cream vendor blowing his tin trumpet out in the street. I was assailed by memories of a life that wasn't mine anymore, but one in which I'd found the simplest and most lasting joys: the smells of summer, the part of town I loved, a certain evening sky, Marie's dresses and the way she laughed. The utter pointlessness of whatever I was doing there seized me by the throat, and all I wanted was to get it over with and get back to my cell and sleep.

— Albert Camus

In Cold Blood (1966)

- *Two violent young men break into a wealthy farmer's home outside the rural town of Holcomb, Kansas, in the mistaken belief that the family safe contains a substantial amount of money.*

Truman Capote
photograph Christopher Conlon

. . . His sensitive eyes gazed gravely at the surrounding faces, swerved up to the shadowy hangman, then downward to his own manacled hands. He looked at his fingers, which were stained with ink and paint, for he'd spent his final three years on Death Row painting self-portraits and pictures of children . . . . "I think," he said, "it's a helluva thing to take a life in this manner. I don't believe in capital punishment, morally or legally. Maybe I had something to contribute, something—" His assurance faltered, shyness blurred his voice, lowered it to a just audible level. "It would be meaningless to apologize for what I did. Even inappropriate. But I do. I apologize."

— Truman Capote *(1924-1984)*
American author

Oscar & Lucinda (1988)

- *A recently defrocked Anglican priest and compulsive gambler seeks to rid his guilt as a missionary to Australia, but meets a like-minded woman aboard ship.*

Still, the priest withheld absolution.

"This dice you played on the train," he asked, "was it Dutch Hazards?"

Lucinda looked up quite sharply, but the priest's head was bowed and twisted sideways towards his right shoulder. "Yes," she said, "it was. We also played another game."

"Old British, perhaps."

Lucinda felt her bowed neck assume a mottled pattern. "In New South Wales," she said. "It is known as 'Seventh Man.'"

Photo by Bena Seibert

Her feelings were not focused, were as diffused as a blush, a business of heat and blood. . . . .

. . . He closed the little prayer book and stuffed it in the pocket which contained the caul. When his hand touched the caul, he remembered the ocean behind his book. It caused no more than a prickling in his spine.

"And these terms, Mr Hopkins, are they also familiar to you?"

" 'Fraid so." He smiled, a clear and brilliant smile.

Lucinda also smiled, but less certainly. "Mr Hopkins, this is most improper."

Oscar took a handkerchief from his jacket pocket and wiped first his clammy hands and then his perspiring brow. "Oh?" he said. "I really do not think so." He looked so pleased with himself.

"But you have not absolved me."

"Where is the sin?"

— **Peter Carey** *(1943-) Australian novelist and short story writer*

True History of the Kelly Gang (2001)

- *The mighty travails and exploits of Ned Kelly, Australia's historic legendary outlaw.*

The police hurried through the open bushland not bothering to take cover. At this point where Superintendent Hare finally paused, there was nothing separating the two parties but a small revolving iron gate. They were thirty yards apart.

Where is Ned? Dan Kelly whispered.

I'm here, boys. The older Kelly took up his place in the centre of the veranda and raised his Colt revolving rifle.

And here's your grandmother with her big iron nose. So saying, he fired.

Immediately, Hare fell.

Good gracious! he cried. I am hit the very first shot!

And then the cold night was suddenly ablaze with gunfire. The gang held back in the deep shadow of the veranda, all except Ned Kelly, who stepped out into the moonlight and took steady aim.

Fire away, you b______y dogs. You can't hurt us.

No sooner had he said this than a Martini-Henry bullet smashed through his left arm. He grunted, turned, and then he felt the second shot rip like a saw-blade through his foot. He turned and retreated to the hotel.

— **Peter Carey**

Alice's Adventures in Wonderland (1865)

- *The story of Alice who falls down a rabbit hole into a fantasy realm inhabited by all sorts of talking creatures including a Cheshire cat who disappears leaving only its smile behind.*

The Cheshire Cat drawn by John Tenniel

. . . The Cat only grinned when it saw Alice. It looked good-natured, she thought: still it had *very* long claws and a great many teeth, so she felt that it ought to be treated with respect.

"Cheshire-Puss," she began, rather timidly, as she did not at all know whether it would like the name: however, it only grinned a little wider. "Come, it's pleased so far," thought Alice, and she went on. "Would you tell me, please, which way I ought to go from here?"

"That depends a good deal on where you want to get to," said the Cat.

"I don't much care where---" said Alice.

"Then it doesn't matter which way you go," said the Cat.

"---so long as I get *somewhere*," Alice added as an explanation. "Oh, you're sure to do that," said the Cat, "if you only walk long enough."

— **Lewis Carroll** *(1832-1898) English author, mathematician, logician, Anglican deacon, and photographer*

Cathedral (1983)

- *Short stories, often abruptly ending. This collection includes the title story "Cathedral" with this unusual closure.*

"It's all right," he said to her. "Close your eyes now," the blind man said to me.

I did it. I closed them just like he said.

"Are they close? he said. "Don't fudge."

"They're closed," I said.

"Keep them that way," he said. He said, "Don't stop now. Draw."

So we kept on with it. His fingers rode my fingers as my hand went over the paper. It was like nothing else in my life up to now.

Then he said, "I think that's it. I think you got it," he said. "Take a look. What do you think?"

But I had my eyes closed. I thought I'd keep them that way for a little longer. I thought it was something I ought to do.

"Well? he said. "Are you looking?"

My eyes were still closed. I was in my house. I knew that. But I didn't feel like I was inside anything.

"It's really something," I said.

— **Raymond Carver** *(1938-1988) American short story writer and poet*

Where I'm Calling From (1988)

- *Short stories of everyday life written in Carver's simple yet often mesmerizing style. Here a quote from the title story.*

Like that, quick as a wink, J. P. followed her onto the porch. He held the porch screen door for her. He went down the steps with her and out to the drive, where she'd parked her panel truck. It was something that was out of his hands. Nothing else in the world counted for anything. He knew he'd met somebody who could set his legs atremble. He could feel her kiss still burning on his lips, etc. J. P. couldn't begin to sort anything out. He was filled with sensations that were carrying him every which way.

— **Raymond Carver**

Death Comes for the Archbishop (1927)

- *A near mythic account of Father Jean Marie Latour, assigned in 1851 as the Apostolic Vicar to New Mexico.*

Toward the close of the day, in the short twilight after the candles were lighted, the old Bishop seemed to become restless, moved a little, and began to murmur; it was in the French tongue, but Bernard, though he caught some words, could make nothing of them. He knelt beside the bed: "What is it, Father?" I am here.

He continued to murmur, to move his hands a little, and Magdalena thought he was trying to ask for something, or to tell them something. But in reality the Bishop was not there at all; he was standing in a tip-tilted green field among his native mountains, and he was trying to give consolation to a young man who was torn in two before his eyes by the desire to go and the necessity to stay.

— **Willa Cather** *(1873-1947) American author*

My Antonia (1918)

- *The story of immigrant families in rural Nebraska and the lifetime bonding of two youngsters, Jim Burden and Antonia Shimerdas.*

. . . "Won't you come in? Mother will be here in a minute."

Before I could sit down in the chair she offered me, the miracle happened; one of those quiet moments that clutch the heart, and take more courage than the noisy, excited passages in life. Antonia came in and stood before me; a stalwart, brown woman, flat-chested, her curly brown hair a little grizzled. It was a shock, of course. It always is, to meet people after long years, especially if they have live as much and as hard as this woman had. We stood looking at each other. The eyes that peered anxiously at me were—simply Antonia's eyes. I had seen no others like them since I looked into them last, though I had looked at so many thousands of human faces. As I confronted her, the changes grew less apparent to me, her identity stronger. She was there, in the full vigour of her personality, battered but not diminished, looking at me, speaking to me in the husky, breathy voice I remembered so well.

"My husband's not at home, sir. Can I do anything"

"Don't you remember me, Antonia? Have I changed so much?"

She frowned into the slanting sunlight that made her brown hair look redder than it was. Suddenly here eyes widened, her whole face seemed to grow broader. She caught her breath and put out two hard-worked hands.

"Why, it's Jim! Anna, Yulka, it's Jim Burden!"

— Willa Cather

"This country was mostly wild pasture and as naked as the back of your hand. I was little and homesick and lonely and my mother was homesick and nobody paid any attention to us. So the country and I had it out together and by trhe end of the first autumn, that shaggy grass country had gripped me with a passion I have never been able to shake." (From a 1921 interview with Cather published in the *Omaha Daily*.)

Journey to the End of the Night (1934)

- *The partially autobiographical account of Ferdinand Bardamu in the trenches of World War I, in Africa running an isolated trading post, assembly work in a Ford factory in the United States, and eventually his return to postwar Paris where he sets up a medical practice.*

They gave us a short rest, and a few weeks later we climbed back up on our horses and started north. The cold came with us. The gunfire was never far away. But we never came across any Germans except by accident, a hussar or a squad of riflemen here and there, in yellow and green, pretty colors. We seemed to be looking for them, but we beat it the moment we laid eyes on them. At every encounter two or three horsemen bit the dust, sometimes theirs, sometimes ours. And from far in the distance their riderless horses, with loose clanking stirrups, would come galloping toward us, we'd see their saddles with the peculiar cantles and all their leather as fresh and shiny as pocketbooks on New Year's Day. They were coming to see our horses, they made friends in no time. They were lucky. We couldn't have done that.

— **Louis-Ferdinand Celine** *(1894-1961) French writer and doctor*

Don Quixote (1605)

- *Obsessed with chivalry, Don Quixote and his neighbor Sancho Panza, together a "sane madman and wise fool," roam the world together as a knight-errant and his squire in search of adventure.*

And so, by now quite insane, he conceived the strangest notion that ever took shape in a madman's head, considering it desirable and necessary, both for the increase of his honour and for the common good, to become a knight errant, and to travel about the world with his armour and his arms and his horse in search of adventures, and to practice all those activities that he knew from his books were practiced by knights errant, redressing all kinds of grievances, and exposing himself to perils and dangers that he would overcome and thus gain eternal fame and renown.

Drawing by Honore-Daumier

The poor man could already see himself being crowned Emperor of Trebizond, at the very least, through the might of his arm; and so, possessed by these delightful thoughts and carried away by the strange pleasure that he derived from them, he hastened to put into practice what he so desired.

— **Miguel de Cervantes** *(1547-1616) Spanish novelist, poet and playwright*

The Amazing Adventures of Kavalier & Clay (2000)

- *The adventures of two Jewish cousins who write comic books during that media's Golden Age in the 1930's.*

"Holy cow!" said Sammy. He clapped his cousin on his freckled shoulder. "______, look at this! Let me see those things." He took the kidney-shaped sheet that Josef Kavalier had filled with slavering coal-eyed horned demons and cut to overlay Sammy's own drawing. The proportions of the muscular demons were perfect, their poses animated and plausible, the inkwork mannered but strong-lined. The style was far more sophisticated than Sammy's, which, while confident and plain and occasionally bold, was never anything more than cartooning. "You really can *draw*."

"I was two years studying at the Academy of Fine Arts. In Prague." . . .

"Nice," said Sammy. "Josef, I tell you what. I'm going to try to do better than just get you a job drawing the Gravmonica Friction-Powered Mouth Organ, all right? I'm going to get us into the big money."

— **Michael Chabon** *(1963-) American author*

The Big Sleep (1939)

- *An infamously complex plot in which detective Philip Marlowe deals with not only double-crossing characters but triple-crossing rogues.*

I went back around the sump and set the can up in the middle of the bull wheel. It made a swell target. . . .

I went back towards her . . . When I was about ten feet from her, at the edge of the sump, she showed me all her sharp little teeth and brought the gun up and started to hiss.

I stopped dead, the sump water stagnant and stinking at my back.

"Stand there, you son of a bitch," she said.

The gun pointed at my chest. Her hand seemed to be quite steady. The hissing sound grew louder and her face had the scraped bone look. Aged, deteriorated, become animal, and not a nice animal.

I laughed at her. I started to walk towards her. I saw her small finger tighten on the trigger and grow white at the tip. I was about six feet away from her when she started to shoot.

— **Raymond Chandler** *(1888-1959) Anglo-American novelist and screenwriter*

During the Reign of the Queen of Persia (1983)

- *A saga of family women over three generations as seen through the eyes of four young granddaughters.*

. . . He stopped and asked them if there was some problem, had their mothers forgotten something at the market. They slunk off sideways and kicked the porch steps. But when Celia walked through the front door they came alive and in a fevered sprint backed away, running and hollering, to the far road, their speeding eyes in retreat still fastened on Celia, who smiled vaguely with a certain regal privilege. For a moment Uncle Dan's face was strange to us, unshielded by his bright mocking ironies. Then he recovered. Knew what was what. He appraised her long bare legs, asked if she had taken to going about half naked because of internal or external

heat. She huffed. "Oh, Daddy! Don't be so old-fashioned," her face golden-lighted in the sun's reflection off her apricot hair, and she went inside tossing that mane, her legs slightly rigid at the knee, like a leggy colt.

— **Joan Chase** *(ca. 1962-) American novelist*

Falconer (1977)

- *A prison novel with its central character a college professor and murderer. In this quote, inmate Jody escapes by stowing on board a visiting cardinal's helicopter.*

The cardinal's helicopter landed at La Guardia, where two large cars were waiting. Jody had seen cars like this in the movies and nowhere else. His Eminence and the monsignor took one. The acolytes filled the second. Jody's excitement was violent. He was shaking. He tried to narrow his thinking down to two points. He would get drunk. He would get laid....

"Where are we going?" he asked one of the others. "To the cathedral, I guess," he said. "That's where we left our clothes. Where did you come from?" "Saint Anselm's," said Jody. "I mean how did you get to the prison?" "I went out early," Jody said. "I went out on the train."

— **John Cheever** *(1912-1982) American novelist and short story writer*

The Stories of John Cheever (1978)

- *Sixty-one often slightly strange stories of mid-twentieth century cosmopolitan life.*

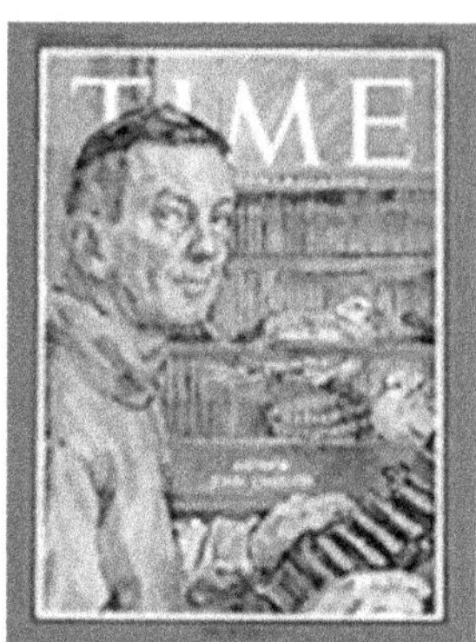

Mrs. Halloran, a stout woman with white hair and a serene face, was reading the *Times*. Mr. Halloran was taking beech leaves out of the water with a scoop. They seemed not surprised or displeased to see him. Their pool was perhaps the oldest in the country, a fieldstone rectangle, fed by a brook. It had no filter or pump and its waters were the opaque gold of the stream.

"I'm swimming across the county," Ned said.

"Why, I didn't know one could," exclaimed Mrs. Halloran.

"Well, I've made it from the 'Westerhazys'," Ned said. "That must be about four miles."

He left his trunks at the deep end, walked to the shallow end, and swam this stretch. As he was pulling himself out of the water he heard Mrs. Halloran say, "We've been *terribly* sorry to hear about all your misfortunes, Neddy."

"My misfortunes?" Ned asked. "I don't know what you mean."

— **John Cheever**

The Wapshot Chronicle (1954)

- *The Wapshot family saga centered on father Leander, a gentle ferryboat operator, his two sons, and his eccentric sister Honora heir to the family wealth.*

As soon as she opened the door he stormed into the hall and roared, "What in Christ's name is the meaning of this?"

"You don't have to be profane," she said. She put her hands over her ears. "I won't listen to profanity."

"What do you want from me, Honora?"

"I can't hear a word you say," she said. "I won't listen to swearing."

"I'm not swearing," he shouted. "I've stopped swearing."

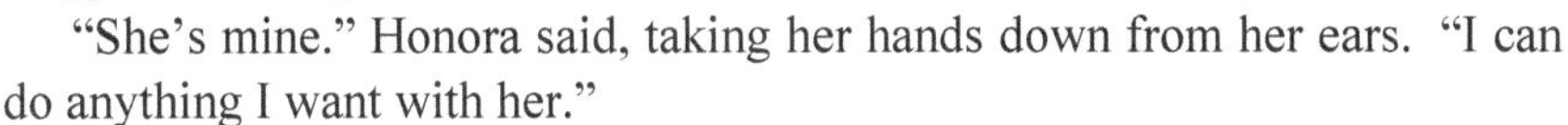

"She's mine." Honora said, taking her hands down from her ears. "I can do anything I want with her."

"You can't sell her."

"I can to," Honora said. "The D'Agostinooys want to buy her for a fishing boat."

"I mean she's my usefulness, Honora." There was nothing pleading in his voice. He was still shouting. "You gave her to me. I'm used to her. She's my boat."

"I only loaned her to you."

"Goddamn it, Honora, the members of a family can't backbite one another like this."

— John Cheever

The World of Apples (1973)

- *Stories about the improbable events of people's lives including this account by the belly of a man named Lawrence Farnsworth.*

We started with a diet that emphasized water and hardboiled eggs. He lost ten pounds in a week but he lost it all in the wrong places, and while my existence was imperiled I survived. The diet set up some metabolic disturbance that damaged his teeth, and he gave this up at his doctor's suggestion and joined a health club. Three times a week I was tormented on an electric bicycle and a rowing machine and then a masseur would knead me and strike me loudly and cruelly with the flat of his hand. He then bought a variety of elastic underpants or girdles that meant to disguise or dismiss me, and while they gave me great pain they only challenged my invincibility. When they were removed in the evening I reinstated myself amply in the world I so much love.

— John Cheever

The Tales (1903)

- *201 stories and short novels in 13 volumes including "The Kiss" from which this quote is obviously taken.*

Ryabovitch stood still in hesitation. . . . At that moment, to his surprise, he heard hurried footsteps and the rustling of a dress, a breathless feminine voice whispered "At last!" And two soft, fragrant, unmistakably feminine arms were clasped about his neck; a warm cheek was pressed to his cheek, and simultaneously there was the sound of a kiss. But at once the bestower of the kiss uttered a faint shriek and skipped back from him, as it seemed to Ryabovitch, with aversion. He, too, almost shrieked and rushed towards the gleam of light at the door. .

When he went back into the drawing-room his heart was beating and his hands were trembling so noticeably that he made haste to hide them behind his back. At first he was tormented by shame and dread that the whole drawing-room knew that he had just been kissed and embraced by a woman. He shrank into himself and looked uneasily about him, but as he became convinced that people were dancing and talking as calmly as ever, he gave himself up entirely to the new sensation which he had never experienced before in his life. Something strange was happening to him.

— **Anton Chekhov** *(1860-1904) Russian short-story writer, playwright and physician*

The Awakening (1899)

- *Young and attractive, Edna Pontellier gives up trying to be a loving wife and mother in searching for liberation and fulfillment.*

A certain light was beginning to dawn dimly within her—the light which, showing the way, forbids it.

At that early period it served but to bewilder her. It moved her to dreams, to thoughtfulness, to the shadowy anguish which had overcome her the midnight when she had abandoned herself to tears.

In short, Mrs. Pontellier was beginning to realize her position in the universe as a human being, and to recognize her relations as an individual to the world within and about her. This may seem like a ponderous weight of wisdom to descend upon the soul of a young woman of twenty-eight—perhaps more wisdom than the Holy Ghost is usually pleased to vouchsafe to any woman.

— **Kate Chopin** *(1851-1904) American author of short stories and novels*

Murder on the Orient Express (1934)

■ *Detective Hercule Poirot attempts to identify the murderer of an American tycoon found dead in his compartment on the Orient Express.*

Poirot nodded. He bent over the body. Finally he straightened himself with a slight grimace.

"It is not pretty," he said. "Someone must have stood there and stabbed him again and again. How many wounds are there exactly?

"I make it twelve. One or two are so slight as to be practically scratches. On the other hand, at least three would be capable of causing death."

Something in the doctor's tone caught Poirot's attention. He looked at him sharply. The little Greek was standing staring down at the body with a puzzled frown.

"Something strikes you as odd, does it not?" he asked gently. "Speak, my friend. There is something here that puzzles you?"

"You are right," acknowledged the other.

"What is it?"

"You see these two wounds–here and here–" He pointed. "They are deep. Each cut must have severed blood vessels–and yet the edges do not gape. They have not bled as one would have expected.

"Which suggests?"

"That the man was already dead–some little time dead–when they were delivered. But this is surely absurd."

"It would seem so, said Poirot thoughtfully.

— **Agatha Christie** *(1890-1976) British Crime writer*

According to the *Guinness Book of World Records*, Christie is the best-selling writer of books of all time and, with William Shakespeare, the best-selling author of any kind. Only the *Bible* has sold more than her roughly four billion copies of novels. According to UNESCO, Christie is the most translated individual author, with only the collective corporate works of Walt Disney Productions surpassing her. Her books have been translated into at least 103 languages.

King Rat (1962)

■ *An enterprising American Army corporal wheels and deals as a black marketeer at the expense of his fellow prisoners of war in a Japanese prison camp in the South Pacific.*

"You're outta your mind. You think someone'd buy rat meat? Course they wouldn't," Miller said impatiently.

"Of course no one'll buy the meat if they know it's rat. But say they don't know, huh?" The King let the words settle, then continued benignly,

"Say we don't tell anyone. The meat'll look like any other meat. We'll say it's rabbit–"

"There aren't any rabbits in Malaya, old chap," Peter Marlowe said.

"Well, think of an animal that is, about the same size." . . . .

(Later, when the camp has been liberated, this exchange.)

"How is it that you are apparently unique here?" Forsyth interrupted, the words like bullets.

"Huh?"

Forsyth pointed a blunt finger at the camp. "I can see perhaps two or three hundred men but you're the only one clothed. I can't see a man who's not as thin as bamboo, but you," he turned back and looked at the King, his eyes flinty, "you are 'in good shape.'"

"I'm just the same as them. I've just been on the ball. And lucky."

"There's no such thing as luck in a hellhole like this!"

— **James Clavell** *(1924-1994) British (later naturalized American) novelist, screenwriter, director and World War II veteran and prisoner of war.*

Shogun (1975)

- *A saga of the intertwined lives of John Blackthorne, a shipwrecked English ship captain, and Toranaga a powerful samurai warlord.*

Note: *Shogun* is a massive 1,152 page volume of enumerable quotable material from which this early introduction into the nature of samurai discipline has been chosen.

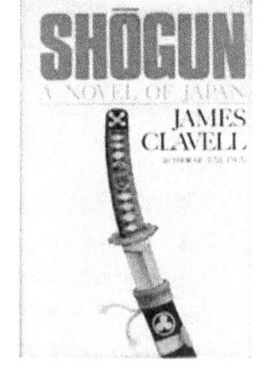

One of them spoke to the others briefly and they all nodded and bowed. He bowed back. Then, with a sudden screaming shout of "*Bansaiiiiiii!*" he cast himself off the cliff and fell to his death. Yabu came violently out of his trance, whirled around and scrambled up.

The other samurai shouted and pointed but Blackthorne heard nothing and saw nothing but the broken corpse that lay below, already being taken by the sea. What kind of men are these? He thought helplessly. Was that courage or just insanity? That man deliberately committed suicide on the off-chance he'd attract the attention of another man who had given up. It doesn't make sense? They don't make sense.

— **James Clavell**

Disgrace (1999)

- *Two central events—sexual harassment of a co-ed by an aging professor, and an attack by native South Africans on a farm where he has sought refuge.*

'Very well,' he says, 'let me confess. The story begins one evening. I forget the date, but not long past. I was walking through the old college gardens and so, it happened, was the young woman in question, Ms Isaacs. Our paths crossed. Words passed between us, and at that moment something happened which, not being a poet, I will not try to describe. Suffice it to say that Eros entered. After that I was not the same.' .... Farodia Rassool intervenes. 'We are again going round in circles, Mr Chair. Yes, he says, he is guilty; but when we try to get specificity, all of a sudden, it is not abuse of a young woman he is confessing to, just an impulse he could not resist, with no mention of the pain he has caused, no mention of the long history of exploitation of which this is part. ....

Abuse: he was waiting for the word. Spoken in a voice quivering with righteousness. What does she see, when she looks at him, that keeps her at such a pitch of anger? A shark among the helpless little fishies? Or does she have another vision: of a great thick-boned male bearing down on a girl-child, a huge hand stifling her cries?

— **J. M. Coetzee** *(1940-) Author and academic from South Africa, now an Australian citizen*

The Woman in White (1860)

- *Among the first mystery thrillers, young Walter Hartright takes up a position as art tutor to two young women leading to mistaken identities, surprising revelations, and an unorthodox villain.*

... I was strolling along the lonely high-road—idly wondering, I remember, what the Cumberland young ladies would look like—when, in one moment, every drop of blood in my body was brought to a stop by the touch of a hand laid lightly and suddenly on my shoulder from behind me.

I turned on the instant, with my fingers tightening round the handle of my stick.

There, in the middle of the broad, bright high-road—there, as if it had that moment sprung out of the earth or dropped from the heaven—stood the figure of a solitary Woman, dressed from heat to foot in white garments; her face bent in grave inquiry on mine, her hand pointing to the dark cloud over London, as I faced her.

I was far too seriously startled by the suddenness with which this extraordinary apparition stood before me, in the dead of night and in that lonely place, to ask what she wanted. The strange woman spoke first.

"Is that the road to London?' she said.

— **Wilkie Collins** *(1824-1889) English author and playwright*

The Most Dangerous Game (1924)

■ *A hunter, bored with conventional prey, stalks human quarries as the only "animal" worthy of his skill.*

The general smiled the quiet smile of one who has faced an obstacle and surmounted it with success. "I had to invent a new animal to hunt," he said.

"A new animal? You're joking." "Not at all," said the general. "I never joke about hunting. I needed a new animal. I found one. So I bought this island built this house, and here I do my hunting. The island is perfect for my purposes—there are jungles with a maze of trails in them, hills, swamps—"

"But the animal, General Zaroff?"

"Oh," said the general, "it supplies me with the most exciting hunting in the world. No other hunting compares with it for an instant. Every day I hunt, and I never grow bored now, for I have a quarry with which I can match my wits."

Rainsford's bewilderment showed in his face.

"I wanted the ideal animal to hunt, explained the general. "So I said, 'What are the attributes of an ideal quarry?' And the answer was, of course, 'It must have courage, cunning, and above all, it must be able to reason.'"

"But no animal can reason," objected Rainsford.

"My deal fellow," said the general, "there is one that can."

"But you can't mean—" gasped Rainsford.

— **Richard Connell** *(1893-1949) American author and journalist*

Heart of Darkness (1902)

■ *A ferry-boat captain travels up (presumably) the Congo River in Africa to return with ivory procured by an agent of questionable intent.*

I missed my late helmsman awfully—I missed him even while his body was still lying in the pilot-house. Perhaps you will think it passing strange this regret for a savage who was no more account than a grain of sand in a black Sahara. Well, don't you see, he had done something, he had steered; for months I had him at my back—a help—an instrument. It was a kind of partnership. He steered for me—I had to look after him, I worried about his deficiencies, and thus a subtle bond had been created, of which I only became aware when it was suddenly broken. And the intimate profundity of that look he gave me when he received his hurt remains to this day in my memory—like a claim of distant kinship affirmed in a supreme moment. — **Joseph Conrad** *(1857-1924)Polish British novelist*

Lord Jim (1899)

- *Jim, first mate on a ship of pilgrims, abandons the vessel in a storm and is court marshaled for his neglect of duty. He later strives to make restitution, serving on a remote island where his gains the respect of the people by relieving them from the predations of a bandit and corrupt local Malay chief.*

. . . He was an inch, perhaps two, under six feet, powerfully built, and he advanced straight at you with a slight stoop of the shoulders, head forward, and a fixed from-under stare which made you think of a charging bull. He voice was deep, loud, and his manner displayed a kind of dogged self-assertion which had nothing aggressive in it. It seemed a necessity, and it was directed apparently as much at himself as at anybody else. He was spotlessly neat, appareled in immaculate white from shoes to hat, and in the various Eastern ports where he got his living as ship-chandler's water-clerk he was very popular.

— Joseph Conrad

Conrad was a master prose stylist who brought a distinctly non-English tragic sensibility into English literature. While some of his works have a strain of romanticism, he is viewed as a precursor of modernist literature. His narrative style and anti-heroic characters have influenced many authors. — *Wikipedia*

Nostromo (1904)

- *Senor Gould entrusts the wealth of his silver mine to his head longshoreman Nostromo, who he believes is incorruptible.*

. . . With a convulsive effort of the twisted arms it leaped up a few inches, curling upon itself like a fish on the end of a line. Senor Hirsch's head was flung back on his straining throat; his chin trembled. For a moment the rattle of his chattering teeth pervaded the vast, shadowy room, where the candles made a patch of light round the two flames burning side by side. And as Sotillo, staying his raised hand, waited for him to speak, with a sudden flash of a grin and a straining forward of the wrenched shoulders, he spat violently into his face.

The uplifted whip fell, and the colonel sprang back with a low cry of dismay, as if aspersed by a jet of deadly venom. Quick as thought he snatched up his revolver and fired twice. The report and the concussion of the shots seemed to throw him at once from ungovernable rage into idiotic stupor. He stood with drooping jaw and stony eyes. What had he done? Sangre de Dios! what had he done? He was basely appalled at his impulsive act, sealing forever these lips from which so much was to be extorted.

— Joseph Conrad

Adolphe (1816)

- *Adolphe falls in love with vulnerable Ellenore, only to chafe under the burden of an illicit relationship that blocks his career.*

. . . 'Haven't you said everything? Isn't it all over, over for ever? Go away, leave me; isn't that what you want?' In trying to move away she staggered; I attempted to hold her but she fell at my feet, unconscious; I picked her up, I kissed her, I brought her back to her senses. 'Ellenore,' I exclaimed, 'come back, come back to me; I love you, I love you with the most tender love. I deceived you so that you would be freer in your choice.' Oh, how inexplicable is the heart's credulity! These simple words, contradicted by so many that had preceded them, restored Ellenore to life and confidence. She made me repeat them several times; she seemed to breathe them in greedily. She believed me: she was intoxicated by her love, which she took for ours . . .

— **Benjamin Constant** *(1767-1830) Swiss-born French nobleman, writer and politician*

The Last of the Mohicans (1826)

- *A frontier scout and his two Mohican companions become embroiled in the French and Indian War as well as bloody battles among local tribes.*

His eyes fell on the still, upright, and rigid form of the "Indian runner," who had borne to the camp the unwelcome tidings of the preceding evening. Although in a state of perfect repose, and apparently disregarding, with characteristic stoicism, the excitement and bustle around him, there was a sullen fierceness mingled with the quiet of the savage, that was likely to arrest the attention of much more experienced eyes than those which now scanned him, in unconcealed amazement. . . . . The colors of the war-paint had blended in dark confusion about his fierce countenance, and rendered his swarthy lineaments still more savage and repulsive than if art had attempted an effect which had been thus produced by chance. His eye, alone, which glistened like a fiery star amid lowering clouds, was to be seen in its state of native wildness. For a single instant, his searching and yet wary glance met the wondering look of the other, and then changing its direction, partly in cunning, and partly in disdain, it remained fixed, as if penetrating the distant air.

— **James Fenimore Cooper** *(1789-1851) American writer*

"The Battle at Glens Falls" by N. C. Wyeth for
The Last of the Mohicans by James Fenimore Cooper (1919)

By Love Possessed (1957)

- *An attorney in a small American town learns that his law partner has been aware of an embezzlement for some time.*

"Julius, I still cannot believe—"

"I fear you're going to have to. Impracticably complicated? Yes; for many people; but to a man of Noah's parts—and also, of course, to a man to whom no least question, no faintest suspicion ever attached—the procedure of lawfully receiving into his possession and unlawfully appropriating money was simplicity itself; even, quite safe. As you very well know, the only circumstance under which the accounts he was tampering with could become subject to audit was if *cestui qui trust*, not getting his money, applied to the court. The circumstance never arises. Income is always paid when due. . . ."

— **James Gould Cozzens** *(1903-1978) American novelist*

Guard of Honor (1948)

- *Three tense days at a U.S. Army airbase in Florida in 1943 as officers and enlisted react to a racial incident.*

. . . The bomber, slowly floating ahead while it was in the air, appeared to go faster now that it was down. The level, stubby wings swept like the wind along the flat pavement; yet, at the same time, the slow pushing-ahead ended. Then suddenly, as though the B-26 were standing still, they started to overhaul it. . . . .

Then they ran into something—not the ground; they were as high as the great hangar roofs; overtaking the bomber, but still above and behind. They hit very hard with a bucking, buckling violence. One wing went down. The cabin roof became the side; the opposite wall became the ceiling; . . . .

Carricker's sharpened, roaring voice said: "—his prop wash! His prop wash! Can't do it—let go . . ."

. . . . With a skidding, skating motion they bounced past the bomber moving under them. Heeling away, they missed the high fronts of the hangars which swung traversely not far below. Then they were hauling hard, hand over hand into darkness. The lights of the field swerved off; the hangar roofs shrank down; they mounted the night in long slugging bounds.

— **James Gould Cozzens**

Being Dead (2000)

- *A couple married almost thirty years lie murdered in the dunes, undiscovered for six days.*

Joseph's grasp on Celice's leg had weakened as he'd died. But still his hand was touching her, the grainy pastels of her skin, one fingertip among her baby ankle hairs. Their bodies had expired, but anyone could tell — just look at them — that Joseph and Celice were still devoted. For while his hand was touching her, curved round her shin, the couple seemed to have achieved that peace the world denies, a period of grace, defying even murder. Anyone who found them there, so wickedly disfigured, would nevertheless be bound to see that something of their love had survived the death of cells. The corpses were surrendered to the weather and the earth, but here were still a man and wife, quietly resting; flesh on flesh; dead, but not departed yet.

— **Jim Crace** *(1946-) English writer*

The Red Badge of Courage (1895)

■ *A young recruit faces the horrors of war, running from his first battle, later returning in shame to distinguish himself in growing confidence and bravery.*

. . . At times he regarded the wounded soldiers in an envious way. He conceived persons with torn bodies to be peculiarly happy. He wished that he, too, had a wound, a red badge of courage. . . .

The flames bit him, and the hot smoke broiled his skin. His rifle barrel grew so hot that ordinarily he could not have borne it upon his palms; but he kept on stuffing cartridges into it, and pounding them with his clanking, bending ramrod. If he aimed at some changing form through the smoke, he pulled his trigger with a fierce grunt, as if he were dealing a blow of the fist with all his strength.

— **Stephen Crane** *(1871-1900) American novelist, short story writer, poet and journalist*

The Hours (1998)

■ *The interwoven stories of three women, honoring the novel Mrs. Dalloway and its creator Virginia Woolf.*

"You've been so good to me, Mrs. Dalloway."

"Richard—"

"I love you. Does that sound trite?"

"No."

Richard smiles. He shakes his head. He says, "I don't think two people could have been happier than we've been."

He inches forward, slides gently off the sill, and falls.

Clarissa screams, "No—"

He seems so certain, so serene, that she briefly imagines it hasn't happened at all. She reaches the window in time to see Richard still in flight, his robe billowing, and it seems even now as if it might be a minor accident, something reparable. She sees him touch the ground five floors below, sees him kneel on the concrete, sees his head strike, hears the sound he makes, and yet she believes, at least for another moment, leaning out over the sill, that he will stand up again, groggy perhaps, winded, but still himself, still whole, still able to speak.

She calls his name, once. It comes out as a question, far softer than she'd meant it to. He lies where he fell, face down, the robe thrown up over his head and his bare legs exposed, white against the dark concrete.

— **Michael Cunningham** *(1952-) American writer*

D

The BFG (1982)

- *A Big Friendly Giant kidnaps Sophie from her bed in the orphanage and takes her back to Giantland where she meets nine other larger, and much, much meaner giants.*

Under the blanket, Sophie waited.

After a minute or so, she lifted a corner of the blanket and peeped out.

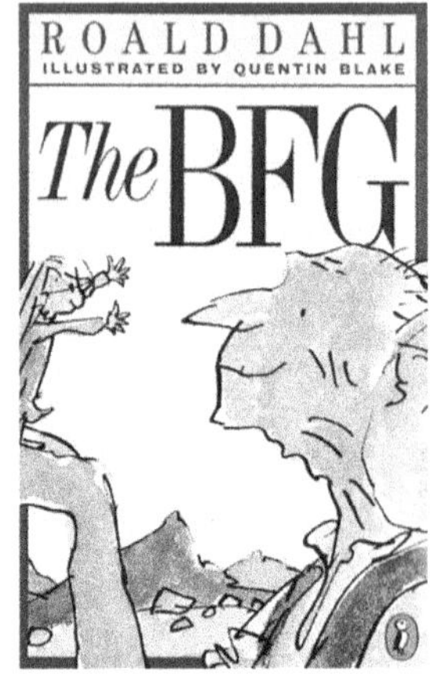

For the second time that night her blood froze to ice and she wanted to scream, but no sound came out. There at the window, with the curtains pushed aside, was the enormous long pale wrinkly face of the Giant Person, staring in. The flashing black eyes were fixed on Sophie's bed.

The next moment, a huge hand with pale fingers came snaking in through the window. This was followed by an arm, an arm as thick as a tree trunk, and the arm, the hand, the fingers were reaching out across the room toward Sophie's bed.

— **Roald Dahl** *(1916-1990) British novelist, short story writer, fighter ace and screenwriter*

Dahl's experiences as a fighter pilot in the RAF during WWII are extraordinary, including a forced landing in the desert which fractured his skull, smashed his nose, and temporarily blinded him. Flying Hawker Hurricanes over North Africa, Dahl is credited with five aerial victories qualifying him as a flying ace.

Dahl married American actress Patricia Neal in 1953. Their marriage lasted for 30 years and they had five children.

Matilda (1988)

- *A children's tale of a genius five-year-old girl Matilda who struggles against her miserable parents with the help of her sweet teacher Miss Honey.*

It is bad enough when parents treat ordinary children as though they were scabs and bunions, but it becomes somehow a lot worse when the child in question is extra-ordinary, and by that I mean sensitive and brilliant. Her mind was so nimble and she was so quick to learn that her ability should have been obvious even to the most half-witted of parents. But Mr. and Mrs. Wormwood were both so gormless and so wrapped up in their own silly little lives that they failed to notice anything unusual about their daughter. — **Roald Dahl**

The Dew Breaker (2004)

- *A former Haitian prison guard, skilled in torture, keeps his secret while living in Brooklyn with his loving wife and daughter.*

The preacher knew that as soon as the burst of light that had left the fat man's gun landed on his body, it would be over. Were he to come back, he could preach a beautiful sermon about this day. He would tell everyone how he'd seen the bowels of hell, where not one but several devils rule. But he would also speak of angels, man-angels who saw in his survival hope for his own.

One bullet landed, then another, then another, hammering the preacher's chest to the ground. The single lightbulb was fading.

"I bet you regret . . ." He heard the fat man's voice trail off as though it were moving farther and farther away from his ear.

Regrets? Did he have any? What would be the meaning of life, or death, without some lingering regrets?

— **Edwidge Danticat** *(1969-) Haitain-American author*

Corelli's Mandolin (1994)

- *A willful and proud daughter of a Greek physician is strangely attracted to Captain Corelli, a charming, mandolin-playing officer of the occupying Italian forces.*

She found a new irritation to replace the old, except that this time it was an irritation against herself. It seemed that she just could not help looking at him, and he was always catching her.

There was something about him, sitting at the table as he waded through the mountains of paperwork . . . no doubt he was trying to work out why a consignment of anti-aircraft shells had mysteriously turned up in Parma, . . . No doubt; but all the same, every time she looked up his eyes would flick to hers and she would be caught in his steady and ironic gaze as surely as if he had grasped her by the wrists.

For a few seconds they would look at one another, and then she would grow abashed, her cheeks would flush a little, and she would return her attention to her crochet . . . A few seconds later she would look up furtively, and at that exact instant he would return her glance. It was impossible. It was infuriating. It was so embarrassing as to be an humiliation.

— **Louis de Bernieres** *(1954-) British novelist*

Moll Flanders (1722)

- *Moll Flanders, "Twelve Year a Whore, five times a Wife, twelve Year a Thief, Eight Year a Transported Felon, at last grew Rich, liv'd Honest and died a Penitent."*

. . . and I led it in there; the Child said that was not its way home; I said, yes, my Dear it is, I'll show you the way home; the Child had a little Necklace on of Gold Beads, and I had my Eye upon that, and in the dark of the Alley I stoop'd, pretending to mend the Child's Clog that was loose, and took off her Necklace and the Child never felt it, . . .

. . . Poverty, as I have said, harden'd my Heart, and my own Necessities made me regardless of anything.

This String of Beads was worth about Twelve or Fourteen Pounds, I suppose it might have been formerly the Mother's, for it was too big for the Child's wear, but that, perhaps, the Vanity of the Mother to have her Child look fine at the Dancing-School, had made her let the Child wear it, and no doubt the Child had a Maid sent to take care of it, but she, like a careless Jade, . . . and so the poor Baby wandered till it fell into my hands.

However, I did the Child no harm, I did not so much as fright it, for I had a great many tender Thoughts about me yet, and did nothing but what, as I may say, meer Necessity drove me to.

— **Daniel Defoe** *(ca. 1660-1731) English writer and journalist*

Robinson Crusoe (1719)

- *Shipwrecked on an uninhabited island, Robinson Crusoe survives and thrives except for loneliness until one day he discovers a strange footprint in the sand.*

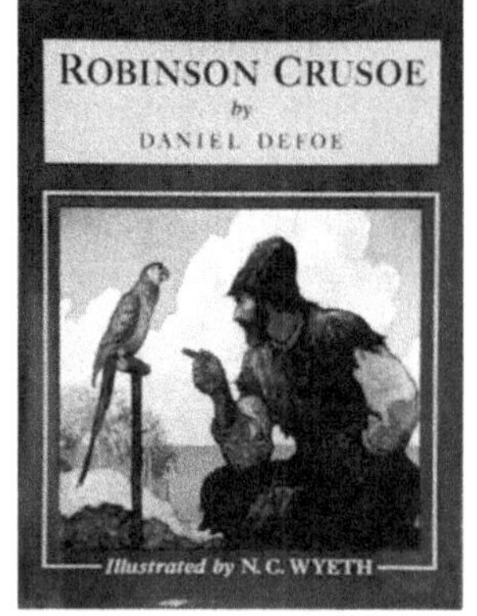

. . . While I was thus looking on them, I perceived by my perspective two miserable wretches dragged from the boats, where, it seems, they were laid by, and were now brought out for the slaughter, I perceived one of them immediately fell, being knocked down, I suppose, with a club or wooden sword, for that was their way, and two or three others were at work immediately, cutting him open for their cookery, while the other victim was left standing by himself, till they should be ready for him. In that very moment, this poor wretch seeing himself a little at liberty, Nature inspired him with hopes of life, and he started away from them, and ran with incredible swiftness along the sands directly towards me, I mean towards that part of the coast where my habitation was.

— **Daniel Defoe**

Libra (1988)

■ *Fact and fiction in the assassination of JFK by Lee Harvey Oswald.*

"It is the form that allows a writer the greatest opportunity to explore human experience..."

He looked down Houston Street as the motorcade approached, slow and vivid in the sun. There were people scattered on the lawns of Dealey Plaza, maybe a hundred and fifty, many with cameras. He held the rifle at port arms, more or less, and stood in plain view of the tall window. Everything looked so painfully clear.

The President had chestnut hair and the First Lady was radiant in a pink suit and small round hat. Lee was glad she looked so good. For her own sake. For the cameras. For the pictures that would enter the permanent record.

He spotted Governor John Connally in one of the jump seats, a Stetson in his lap. He liked Connally's face, a rugged Texas face. This was the kind of man who would take a liking to Lee if he ever got to know him. . . . .

The white pilot car turned, the motorcycles turned. The Lincoln passed beneath him, easing left, making the deep turn left, seeming almost to rotate on an axis. Everything was slow and clear. He got down on one knee, placed his left elbow on the stacked cartons and rested the gun barrel on the end of the carton on the sill.

— **Don DeLillo** *(1936-) American author and playwright*

Mao II (1991)

■ *A reclusive novelist is drawn into the world of terrorism as he attempts to rescue a hostage held captive in Beirut.*

Karen's daddy, watching from the grandstand, can't help thinking this is the point. They're one body now, an undifferentiated mass, and this makes him uneasy. He focuses his binoculars on a young woman, another, still another. So many columns set so closely. He has never seen anything like this or ever imagined it could happen. He hasn't come here for the spectacle but it is starting to astonish him. They're in the thousands now, approaching division strength, and the old seemly tear-jerk music begins to sound sardonic. . . . .

There are still more couples coming out of the runway and folding into the crowd, although "crowd" is not the right word. He doesn't know what to call them. He imagines they are uniformly smiling, showing the face they squeeze out with the toothpaste every morning. The bridegrooms in identical blue suits, the brides in lace-and-satin gowns.

— **Don DeLillo**

Underworld (1997)

- *A distillation of five decades of American life, the pure elements being the bomb, the baseball, and the Bronx.*

Russ says, "There's a long drive."

His voice has a burst in it, a charge of expectation.

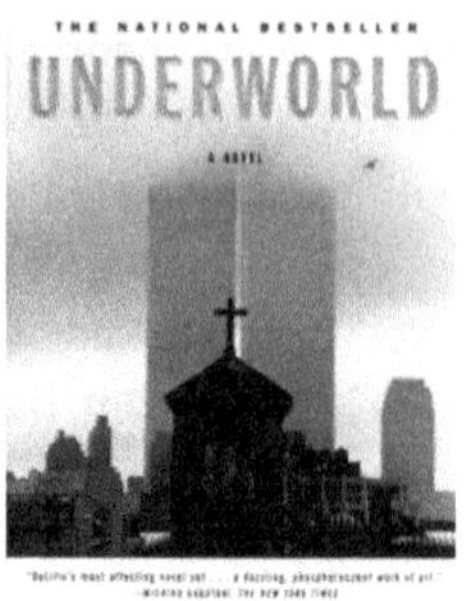

He says, "It's gonna be."

There's a pause all around him. Pafko racing toward the left-field corner.

He says, "I believe."

Pafko at the wall. Then he's looking up. People thinking where's the ball. The scant delay, the stay in time that lasts a hairsbreadth. . . . .

He says, "The Giants win the pennant." . . . .

Next thing Cotter knows he is sidling into the aisle. The area is congested and intense and he has to pry his way row by row using elbows and shoulders. Nobody much seems to notice. The ball is back there in a mighty pileup of shirts and jackets. The game is way behind him. The crowd can have the game. He's after the baseball now and there's no time to ask himself why. They hit it in the stands, you go and get it.

— Don DeLillo

White Noise (1984)

- *A black cloud of lethal gaseous fumes released in an industrial accident threatens to engulf Jack Gladney's town, setting off a series of unforeseen consequences as the fear of death sets in.*

A few minutes later, back on the road, we saw a remarkable and startling sight. It appeared in the sky ahead of us and to the left, prompting us to lower ourselves in our seats, bend our heads for a clearer view, exclaim to each other in half finished phrases. It was the black billowing cloud, the airborne toxic event, lighted by the clear beams of seven army helicopters. They were tracking its windborne movement, keeping it is view. In every car, heads shifted, drivers blew their horns to alert others, faces appeared in side windows, expressions set in tones of outlandish wonderment.

— Don Delillo

The Inheritance of Loss (2006)

- *A retired judge and his family face the challenges of India's sovereignty, modernization, and class structure.*

When she married, her name was changed into the one chosen by Jemubhai's family, and in a few hours, Bela became Nimi Patel. Jemubhai, made brave by alcohol and the thought of his ticket, attempted to pull off his wife's sari, as much gold as silk, as she sat on the edge of the bed, just as his younger uncles had advised him, smacking him on the back.

He was almost surprised to discover a face beneath the gilded lump. It was strung with baubles, but even they could not entirely disguise the fourteen-year-old crying in terror: "Save me," she wept.

He himself was immediately terrified, frightened by her fright. The spell of arrogance broken, he retreated to his meek self. "Don't cry," he said in panic, trying to undo the damage. "Listen, I'm not looking, I'm not even looking at you." He returned the heavy fabric to her, bundled it back over her head, but she continued to sob.

Next morning, the uncles laughed. "What happened? Nothing?" They gestured at the bed.

More laughter the next day.

The third day, worry.

— **Kiran Desai** *(1971-) Indian author*

Paris Trout (2006)

- *A fourteen-year-old black girl is murdered by a white man named Paris Trout, who feels he's done absolutely nothing wrong.*

Trout shook his head. "No sir," he said. "I ain't guilty of a thing. I was there to collect for a car. You know my business, you live here too. I treat everybody the same, just like they do in New York. If somebody got shot, they shot themselves."

Townes consulted the notes in front of him, Seagraves closed his eyes. "Miss Mary McNutt, in that case, shot herself . . . let's see, three times in the back?" Townes said.

"Yessir," Trout said. "If they got shot, they did it themselves. Just like if she jumped in front of a train, you don't fix the blame on the engineer." . . . .

Townes put his hands behind his head and leaned back against the wall. "I have a rule for you, Mr. Trout," he said. "The State of Georgia wrote it down in the penal code. It says that you cannot enter a person's house and shoot them dead. And that's a dangerous rule to break too, sir. An eye for an eye." . . . .

Trout moved then, closer to Townes, and bent until his hands were resting on the front of the desk. "Those ain't the real rules, and you known it," he said.

Seagraves saw Townes's good nature change then, and he hadn't moved a muscle. "Mr. Seagraves," he said, keeping his eyes on Trout, "if I were this man's attorney, I would come over here and collect him off this desk and instruct him to shut his mouth for the rest of eternity."

— **Pete Dexter** *(1943-) American novelist*

The Brief Wondrous Life of Oscar Wao (2007)

- *The brief life of an overweight Dominican boy growing up in Paterson, New Jersey, reading science fiction and falling in love.*

Let's just say their first contact was not promising. How about I buy you a drink? he said, and when she turned away como una ruda, he grabbed her arm, hard and said, Where are you going, morean? And that was all it took: a Beli le salio el lobo. First, she didn't like to be touched. Not at all, not ever. Second, she was not a morena (even the car dealer knew better, called her india). And, third, there was that temper of hers. When baller twisted her arm, she went from zero to violence in under .2 seconds. Shrieked: No. Me. Toques. Threw her drink, her glass, and then her purse at him—if there had been a baby nearby she would have thrown that too. Then let him have it with a stack of cocktail napkins and almost a hundred plastic olive rapiers, and when those were done dancing on the tile she unleashed one of the great Street Fighter chain attacks of all time. During this unprecedented fusillade of blows the Gangster hunkered down and didn't move except to deflect the stray chop away from his face. When she finished he lifted his head as though out of a foxhole and put a finger to his lips. You missed a spot, he said solemnly.

— **Junot Diaz** *(1968-) Dominican-American writer and creative writing professor*

Bleak House (1852)

- *Lady Dedlock hides a shocking secret about a long lost love and illegitimate child from her husband and his suspicious lawyer. In this quote, Mr. Guppy, a scheming law clerk, seeks to profit from some purloined love letters.*

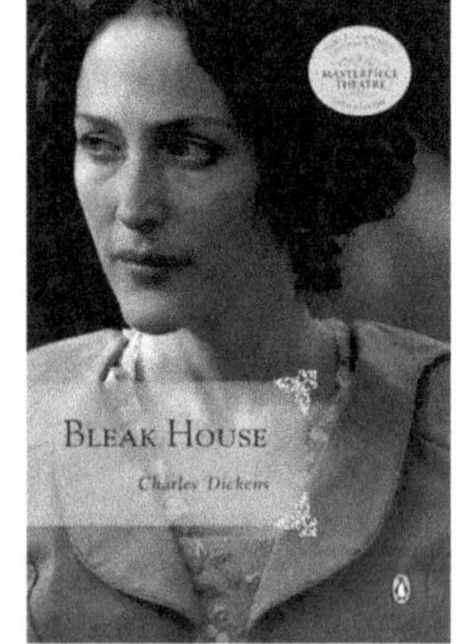

'And what is *that* to me?'

"Aye, your ladyship, that's the question! Now, your ladyship, a queer thing happened after that man's death. A lady started up; a disguised lady, your ladyship, who went to look at the scene of action, and went to look at his grave. She hired a crossing-sweeping boy to show it her. If your ladyship would wish to have the boy produced in corroboration of this statement, I can lay my hand upon him at any time.'

The wretched boy is nothing to my Lady, and she does *not* wish to have him produced.

'Oh, I assure your ladyship it's a very queer start indeed,' says Mr. Guppy. 'If you was to hear him tell about the rings that sparkled on her fingers when she took her glove off, you'd think it quite romantic.'

There are diamonds glittering on the hand that holds the screen. My Lady trifles with the screen, and makes them glitter more; again with that expression which in other times might have been so dangerous to the young man of the name of Guppy.

— **Charles Dickens** *(1812-1870) English novelist*

David Copperfield (1850)

- *The life of David Copperfield in which he encounters a host of characters, some with disciplined hearts, some lacking self control, and a few who develop calmness and stability. Below isolated quotes.*

. . . skewered through and through with office-pens, and bound hand and foot with red tape.

Annual income twenty pounds, annual expenditure nineteen and six, result happiness. Annual income twenty pounds, annual expenditures twenty pounds ought and six, result misery.

". . . Ride on! Rough-shod if need be, smooth-shod if that will do, but ride on! Ride on over all obstacles, and win the race!"

I am . . . joined with eleven others in reporting the debates in Parliament for a Morning Newspaper. Night after night, I record predictions that never come to pass, professions that are never fulfilled, explanations that are only meant to mystify. I wallow in words.

"Oh!" said my aunt, "I was not aware at first to whom I had the pleasure of objecting."

The evening wind made such a disturbance just now, among some tall old elm-trees at the bottom of the garden, that neither my mother nor Miss Betsey could forbear glancing that way. As the elms bent to one another, like giants who were whispering secrets, and after a few seconds of such repose, fell into a violent flurry, tossing their wild arms about, as if their late confidences were really too wicked for their peace of mind . . .

— **Charles Dickens**

In 1867 Charles Dickens gave the first reading of his American tour. Like all but a few over the five months, the evening was a sell-out, some having slept out overnight to beat a ticket line almost a half-mile long.

Dickens traveled regularly by train. On one occasion a little girl suddenly sat down beside him and told him how much she liked his books. "Of course, I do skip some of the very dull parts, once in a while; not the short dull parts, but the long ones." Dickens laughed, and then taking out his notebook, asked for details.

Reported by Steve King in *Today in Literature*

Great Expectations (1861)

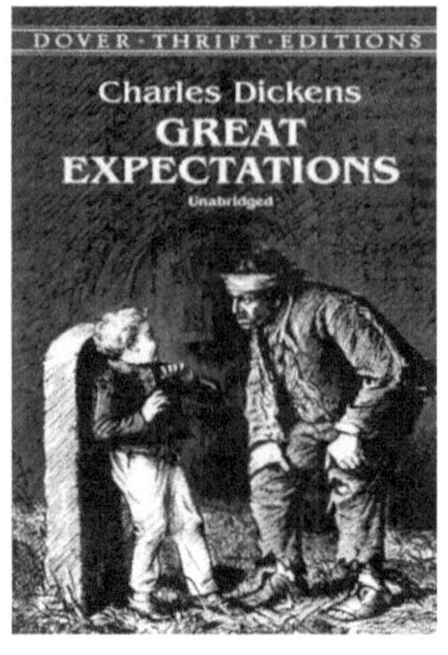

- *Pip, a poor orphan in love with ward Estella, is rejected but later favored by a secret benefactor requiring him to go to London to begin his education as a gentlemen.*

. . . "Hold your noise!" cried a terrible voice, as a man started up from among the graves at the side of the church porch. "Keep still, you little devil, or I'll cut your throat!"

— **Charles Dickens**

A Tale of Two Cities (1859)

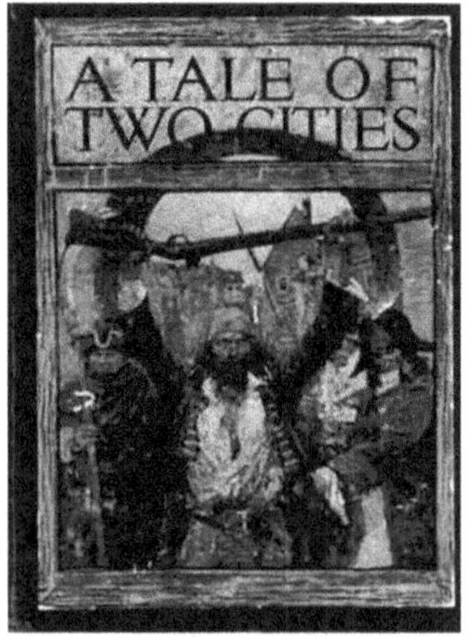

Cover art by Harvey Dunn

- *An elaborate tale in which émigré Charles Darnay becomes entangled in the snares of the French Revolution and is jailed and condemned to the guillotine.*

. . . It was the best of times, it was the worst of times, it was the age of wisdom, it was the age of foolishness, it was the epoch of belief, it was the epoch of incredulity, it was the season of Light, it was the season of Darkness, it was the spring of hope, it was the winter of despair, we had everything before us, we had nothing before us, we were all going direct to Heaven, we were all going direct the other way—in short, the period was so far like the present period, that some of its noisiest authorities insisted on its being received, for good or for evil, in the superlative degree of comparison only. . . . .

It is a far, far better thing that I do, than I have ever done; it is a far, far better rest that I go to than I have ever known.

— **Charles Dickens**

Deliverance (1970)

- *Four young men attempt a couple of day's canoe trip down a remote Georgia river soon to be dammed and run into serious trouble.*

James Dickey played the role of a sheriff in the 1970 movie version of the novel.

I knelt down. As my knees hit, I heard a sound, a snap-slap off in the woods, a sound like a rubber band popping or a sickle-blade cutting quick. The older man was standing with a gun barrel in his hand and no change in the stupid, advantage-taking expression of his face, and a foot and a half of bright red arrow was shoved forward from the middle of his chest. It was there so suddenly it seemed to have come from within him.

— **James Dickey** *(1923-1997)*
American poet and novelist

A Book of Common Prayer (1977)

- *A mother, searching for her elusive daughter, faces the harsh realities of living in an impoverished Caribbean country.*

Some things about Charlotte I never understood. She was a woman who grew faint when she noticed the blue arterial veins in her wrists, could not swim in clouded water, and once suffered an attack of acute terror while wading in water where an artesian well churned up the sand. Yet during the time she was in Boca Grande I saw her perform a number of tasks with the same instinctive lack of squeamishness I had seen that day at Millonario. I once saw her skin an iguana for stew. I once saw her make the necessary incision in the trachea of an OAS field worker who was choking on a piece of steak at the Jockey Club. A doctor had been called but the OAS man was turning blue. Charlotte did it with a boning knife plunged first in a vat of boiling rice.

— **Joan Didion** *(1934-) American author*

Frog: A Novel (1991)

- *A chronicle of flashbacks and real and imagined stories of a highly disjointed college professor.*

She was a very pretty child. People thought she'd be the best-looking one in the family, possibly a beauty like his mother. Complexion, nose, eyes, hair, smile, face shape, long neck, fine features. It's difficult describing looks. There's a photo. There's always a photo. . . . that's the one he thinks of when he thinks how pretty she was and beautiful she might have become. . . . . Later photos: when she was very ill, dressed in black, couldn't get around except with a walker or on crutches and not for long on either of them. Thin, gaunt, twenty to thirty pounds lighter than what should have been the normal weight for a woman her age and size. But that's another thing. She was supposed to become the tallest member of the family: six feet or six-one. Based on the growth chart compiled by her pediatrician. In the top two percentile in height and something close in weight when she was born and then when she was a month old, half-year old, every annual checkup till she was five. That's when she showed the first sign—cross-eye—of the disease that would kill her twenty years later.

Stephen Dixon self-portrait

— **Stephen Dixon** *(1936-) American author*

Berlin Alexanderplatz (1929)

- *Franz Biberkopf meets Reinhold, a small crook who leads him into trouble and barges into Franz's relationship with his girlfriend Mieze, leading to her death.*

He sits with her in the pastry shop across the way, eating a honey-cake in honor of Mieze, you see she never could get enough of it, it really tastes good, but nothing to write home about, at that. So now we have been to see our little Mieze, a man shouldn't go to cemeteries too much, might catch a cold, maybe next year again, on her birthday. You see, Eva, I don't have to run out here to see Mieze, you can take my word for it, she's always there for me, cemetery or no cemetery, and then, Reinhold, well, I won't forget him so easy, either, And even if my arm should grow again, I wouldn't forget him.

Berlin Alexanderplatz, 1903

— **Alfred Doblin** *(1878-1957) German expressionist novelist*

Billy Bathgate (1989)

- *In the Bronx, 15-year-old Billy Bathgate hooks up with legendary mobster Dutch Schultz, progressing from simple errand boy to modest responsibility in the world of crime.*

. . . And hovering about the chair and making small administrative sounds until he was satisfied that all was well, he felt under the sheet, took the piece from the slack fingers, daintily put it aside, lifted the towels where they draped over the chin, carefully folded them back from the throat, and choosing an already opened straight razor from the shelf under the mirror and satisfying himself that it was impeccably sharpened, he drew it with no hesitation across the exposed neck just below the jawline. And as the thread-thin lip of blood slowly widened into a smile and the victim made a small half-questioning movement in his chair, a slight rise of the shoulders and lift of the knees, more inquisitive than accusatory, he held him down with his elbow on his mummied mouth and wrapped layer after layer of wet hot toweling that was to hand in the chromed steamer behind the chair over his chest and throat and head, until only a seeping pinkness, the color of a slow and tentative sunset, suffused the wadding, . . .

— **E. L. Doctorow** *(1931-) American author*

The Book of Daniel (1971)

- *Daniel investigates the background of his parents' conviction and execution, a fictional account based on the Rosenberg espionage case.*

"I should be back before you're out of school, Danny. But in case not, have some milk and cookies when you get home. And take Susan to the park. For lunch I left you a peanut butter sandwich and an apple in the icebox."

I didn't want her to go.

"I have to go, Daniel."

"They're going to put you in jail, too."

"No, they're not. They want to ask me questions, that's all. That's what a Grand Jury is. You are asked questions and they listen to your answers. The government lawyers want to ask me about Daddy, and I'm going to tell them what a terrible thing they're doing and make them understand he's innocent." . . . .

She was last seen in her black cloth coat with the hem let down and a black pillbox hat. My mother was last seen with her tiny watch on her wrist, a fine thin wrist with a prominent wrist-bone and lovely thin blue veins. She left behind a clean house, and in the icebox a peanut butter sandwich and an apple for lunch. In the afternoon, I had my milk and cookies. And she never came home.

— **E. L. Doctorow**

Loon Lake (1980)

- *During the Great Depression a passionate young New Jersey man sets off walking the tracks seeking a better life.*

Every day to school she wore her faded dress of flowers, horizontal lines of originally cheery little tulips row upon row. It came below her knees and there the cast off shoes, boots practically, hook-and-eye boots all cracked and curled, there the boots began, and so nothing of her was uncovered except the neck above the high collar of frazzled lace, and the wrists and the hands and the incredible face that struck my heart like a jolt every time I raised my eyes to look at it.

Migod. When it was possible to feel that way.

Wasn't it. I used to wake up before dawn and wait impatiently for the light to come into the window so that I could jump out of bed and get ready for school. I would sit on the front wooden step and wait for her to come down the canyon. She would smile when she saw me.

— E. L. Doctorow

The March (2005)

- *Sherman's march to the sea from numerous points-of-view presenting a sweeping picture of all sides of the Civil War.*

And then they were riding down a street and all at once the purposive charge was in disarray, with horses rearing and men shouting and horses and riders going down around him. Morrison could not ride forward or turn. The hideous Rebel shriek was in his ears. In this roiling entanglement of blue and gray, men were pulling one another from their mounts. His eyes closed, Morrison raised his saber and swung it at what or who he didn't know. He felt it cleave flesh and bone. Why didn't these people understand he was not well? Someone had an arm around his neck. Morrison held tightly to the reins and felt himself going down backward. As he tried, fitfully, to wield his saber in a chopping motion over his shoulder, it flew out of his hands. His eyes opened and he was transfixed by the hoofs of his horse flail in the air. Then its head filled his vision, terror in it rolling eyes, a scream issuing from its open jaws. He caught a glimpse of the sun in the moment before he hit the ground. He felt his leg crack, and was gasping in pain at the moment his spine snapped under the weight of his screaming horse and the breath was pounded out of him.

— E. L. Doctorow

Ragtime (1974)

- *The story of a New Rochelle family in the early 1900s and their encounters with Harry Houdini, Henry Ford, and others, most notably Coalhouse Walker Jr. a black ragtime piano player whose insistence on justice when his brand new car is spoiled drives him to revolutionary violence.*

. . . As the Negro came along a team of three matching gray engine horses cantered out of the firehouse into the road pulling behind them the big steam pumper for which the Emerald Isle was locally renowned. They were immediately reined, causing Coalhouse Walker to brake his car abruptly.

Coalhouse Walker and his 1927 Model A Ford

Two of the volunteers came out of the building to join the driver of the pumper who sat up on his box looking at the Negro and yawning ostentatiously. They all wore blue work shirts with green handkerchief ties, dark blue trousers and boots. Coalhouse Walker released the clutch pedal and climbed down to crank his car. The volunteers waited until this was done and then advised him that he was traveling on a private toll road and that he could not drive on without payment of twenty-five dollars or by presenting a pass indicating that he was a resident of the city. This is a public thoroughfare, Walker said, I've traveled it dozens of times and no one has ever said anything about a toll. He got up behind the wheel. Tell the Chief, one of the men said to another.

— **E. L. Doctorow**

Stones for Ibarra (1984)

- *An American couple move from San Francisco to an old family home and abandoned mine in Mexico.*

Five days ago the Evertons left San Francisco and their house with a narrow view of the bay in order to extend the family's Mexican history and patch the present onto the past. To find out if there was still copper underground and how much of the rest of it was true, the width of sky, the depth of stars, the air like new wine, the harsh noons and long, slow dusks. To weave chance and hope into a fabric that would clothe them as long as they lived.

— **Harriet Doerr** *(1910-2002) American author who published her first novel at the age of 74*

USA Trilogy (1930)

- *A portrait of the American generation which fought the first world war to "achieve the illusion of the 20's and experience the disillusion of the 30's." The quote below is from Nineteen Nineteen.*

. . . All hands had their life preservers on and some of the men were going below for their duffle when the fritz officer who came aboard shouted in English that they had five minutes to abandon the ship. Cap'n Perry handed over the ship's papers, the boats were lowered like winking as the blocks were well oiled. Something made Joe run back up to the boat deck and cut the lashings of the liferafts with his jackknife, so

he and Cap'n Perry and the ship's cat were the last to leave the North Star. The jerries had planted bombs in the engineroom and were rowing back to the submarine like the devil was after them. The Cap'n's boat had hardly pushed off when the explosion lammed them a blow on the side of the head. The boat swamped and before they knew what had hit them they were swimming in the icy water among all kinds of planking and junk.

— **John Dos Passos** *(1896-1970) American novelist and artist*

The Brothers Karamazov (1880)

- *A patricide in which all four of the murdered man's sons have varying degrees of complicity.*

So they agreed that they would meet in the evening about a mile from the station, to give the train a chance to gather speed. All the boys went. It was a moonless, almost completely black night. As the hour drew close, Kolya lay down between the rails. The other five boys, who were betting with him, waited in the bushes around the embankment, their hearts pounding with apprehension and remorse. At last, in the distance, they heard the rumble of the train leaving the station. Two red lights shone in the darkness and the rattle of the approaching monster increased. "Run! Get off the rails! Hurry!" the boys yelled in terror from under the bushes. But it was too late. The train was already there. And then it was gone. The boys rushed over to Kolya. He lay motionless. They started pulling him and shaking him, but he suddenly got up by himself and silently walked down the embankment.

— **Fyodor Dostoevsky** *(1821-1881) Russian writer and essayist*

Crime and Punishment (1866)

- *A destitute Saint Petersburg student murders an aged pawnbroker and her younger sister believing he is not morally culpable as he is "above" the conventions of society.*

In the middle of the room stood Lizaveta with a big bundle in her arms. She was gazing in stupefaction at her murdered sister, white as a sheet and seeming not to have the strength to cry out. Seeing him run out of the bedroom, she began faintly quivering all over, like a leaf, a shudder ran down here face; she lifted her hand, opened her mouth, but still did not scream. She began slowly backing away from him into the corner, staring intently, persistently at him, but still uttered no sound, as though she could not get breath to scream. He rushed at her with the axe; her mouth twitched piteously, as one sees babies' mouths, when they begin to be frightened, stare intently at what frightens them and are on the point of screaming.

— Fyodor Dostoevsky

The Idiot (1869)

- *Prince Myshkin, a paragon of kindness and humility and suffering from epilepsy, confronts Russian society with his "idiocy," which is merely his apparently naïve approach to life.*

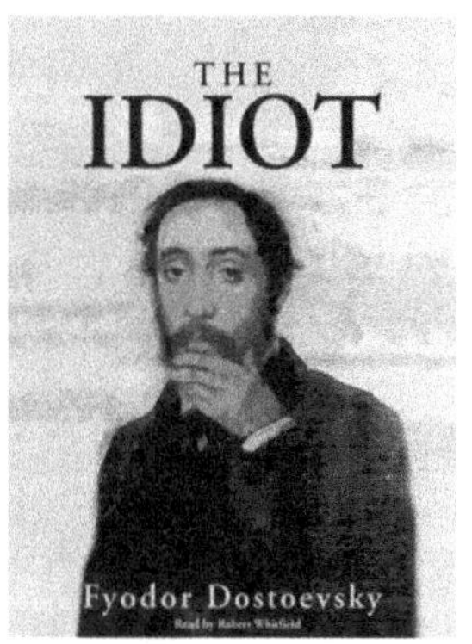

"But what are you doing, prince?" Yevgeny Paviovitch cried with horror. "So you're marrying her from a sort of fear? There's no understanding it! Without even loving her, perhaps?"

"Oh, no. I love her with my whole heart! Why, she's . . . a child! Now she's a child, quite a child! Oh, you know nothing about it!"

"And at the same time you have declared your love to Aglaia Ivanovna?"

"Oh, yes, yes!"

"How so? then you want to love both of them?"

"Oh, yes, yes!"

"Upon my word, prince, think what you're saying."

— Fyodor Dostoevsky

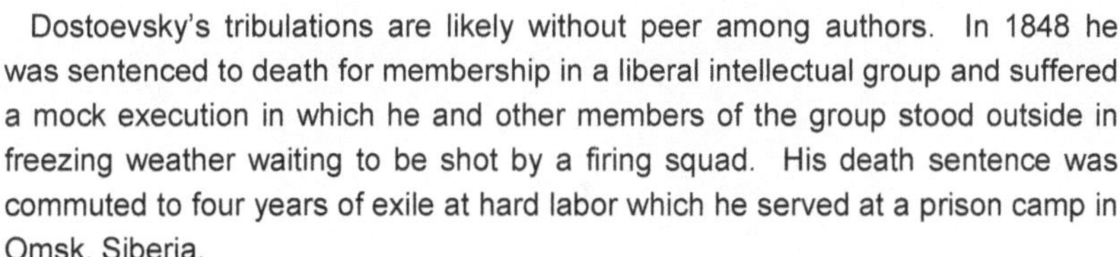

Dostoevsky's tribulations are likely without peer among authors. In 1848 he was sentenced to death for membership in a liberal intellectual group and suffered a mock execution in which he and other members of the group stood outside in freezing weather waiting to be shot by a firing squad. His death sentence was commuted to four years of exile at hard labor which he served at a prison camp in Omsk, Siberia.

In 1864 Dostoevsky was devastated by his wife's death, followed shortly thereafter by the death of his brother. He was financially crippled by business debts plus assumption of responsibilities of his deceased brother's debts; and he also provided for his wife's son from her earlier marriage and his brother's widow and children. Finally he added to his own difficulties by suffering from an acute gambling compulsion.

The Hound of the Baskervilles (1902)

- *Beast and fog on the moor establish a setting and plot, making "The Hound" one of the greatest crime novels ever written.*

At the same instant Lestrade gave a yell of terror and threw himself face downwards upon the ground. I sprang to my feet, my inert hand grasping my pistol, my mind paralyzed by the dreadful shape which had sprung out

upon us from the shadows of the fog. A hound it was, an enormous coal-black hound, but not such a hound as mortal eyes have every seen. Fire burst from its open mouth, its eyes glowed with a smoldering glare, its muzzle and hackles and dewlap were outlined in flickering flame. Never in the delirious dream of a disordered brain could anything more savage, more appalling, more hellish, be conceived than that dark form and savage face which broke upon us out of the wall of fog.

— **Arthur Conan Doyle** *(1859-1930) Scottish physician and writer*

The death of Sherlock Holmes at the Reichenbach Falls as depicted by Sidney Paget in 1893. Holmes' popularity was such that Conan Doyle was almost forced to resurrect him and write several further series of stories. *The Memoirs of Sherlock* Holmes, 1894, publisher George Newness

An American Tragedy (1925)

- *The tragic life of Clyde Griffith who seeks wealth and social prestige yet is trapped by an illicit love affair with a factory girl.*

Yet (the camera still unconsciously held tight) pushing at her with so much vehemence as not only to strike her lips and nose and chin with it, but to throw her back sidewise toward the left wale which caused the boat to careen to the very water's edge. And then he, stirred by her sharp scream, (as much due to the lurch of the boat, as the cut on her nose and lip), rising and reaching half to assist or recapture her and half to apologize for the unintended blow—yet in so doing completely capsizing the boat—himself and Roberta being as instantly thrown into the water. And the left wale of the boat as it turned, striking Roberta on the head as she sank and then rose for the first time, her frantic, contorted face turned to Clyde, who by now had righted himself. For she was stunned, horror-struck, unintelligible with pain and fear—her lifelong fear of water and drowning and the blow he had so accidentally and all but unconsciously administered.

"Help! Help!

"Oh, my God, I'm drowning, I'm, drowning. Help! Oh, my God!

"Clyde, Clyde!"

— **Theodore Dreiser** *(1871-1945) American novelist and journalist*

The twelfth of thirteen children, Dreiser grew up in extreme poverty. In *Dawn*, his memoir of the early years in Terre Haute, Indiana, Dreiser describes his injured, lay-about father, his mother's attempts to make ends meet by taking in lodgers or washing, his own attempt to help fend off winter by scouring the railway yards for coal – "picking it up from between the tracks or stealing it from cars."

— Steve King, *Today in Literature*

Sister Carrie (1900)

- *A young country girl moves to the big city seeking the American Dream, eventually becoming a famous actress at the expense of a failed marriage and ultimately unhappiness.*

Carrie smiled under his irresistible flood of geniality.

"I've been out home," she said.

"Well," he said, "I saw you across the street there. I thought it was you. I was just coming out to your place. How are you, anyhow?"

"I'm all right," said Carrie, smiling.

Drouet looked her over and saw something different.

"Well," he said, "I want to talk to you. You're not going anywhere in particular, are you?"

"Not just now," said Carrie.

"Let's go up here and have something to eat. George! But I'm glad to see you again."

She felt so relieved in his radiant presence, so much looked after and cared for, that she assented gladly, though with the slightest air of holding back.

"Well," he said, as he took her arm—and there was an exuberance of good-fellowship in the word which fairly warned the cockles of her heart.

— **Theodore Dreiser**

Advise and Consent (1959)

- *An "inside Washington" account of the nomination of Robert Leffingwell for Secretary of State and the ensuing battle within the Senate for his confirmation.*

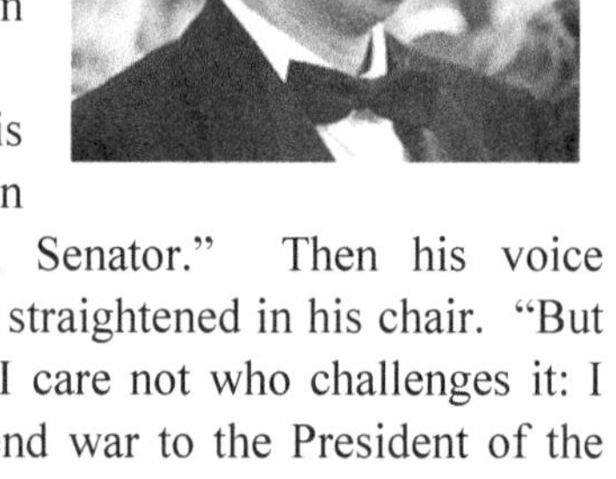

The Senator looked at him curiously.

"But where do we stop yielding?" he asked. "At what point do we say, 'No, it goes no further. This is where you stop and where we stand up for the things we believe in?' Do you have such a point in your own mind?"

Bob Leffingwell spread his hands again in that curious, candid gesture.

"All I can tell you," he said patiently, "is that it would have to depend on the situation as it then existed, Senator." Then his voice strengthened and he straightened in his chair. "But I tell you this, and I care not who challenges it: I will never recommend war to the President of the United States if I become his Secretary of State. Never!"

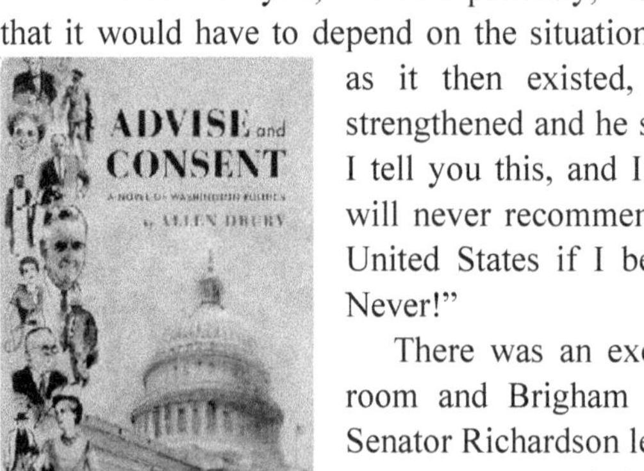

Ninety-three weeks on the the best-seller list, a play, a movie, and a Pulitzer.

There was an excited burst of applause in the room and Brigham Anderson gaveled for order. Senator Richardson leaned forward again.

"You're so afraid of war that you'd give up anything to avoid it, wouldn't you?" he asked softly. "You wouldn't draw a line anywhere, would you? You'd just keep giving and giving and giving, until there wasn't anything left for us to give, wouldn't you?"

— **Allen Drury** *(1918-1998) American novelist*

Rebecca (1938)

- *The legacy of Rebecca, the glamorous mistress of Manderley, now dead for eight months, lives on in the mind of the newly arrived young and frightened second wife.*

Mrs. Danvers came close to me, she put her face near to mine. "It's no use, is it?" she said. "You'll never get the better of her. She's still mistress here, even if she is dead. She's the real Mrs. de Winter, not you. It's you that's the shadow and the ghost. It's you that's forgotten and not wanted and pushed aside. Well, why don't you leave Manderley to her? Why don't you go?"

I backed away from her towards the window, my old fear and horror rising up in me again. She took my arm and held it like a vice.

"Why don't you go?" she said. "We none of us want you. He doesn't want you, he never did. He can't forget her. He wants to be alone in the house again, with her. It's you that ought to be lying there in the church crypt, not her. It's you who ought to be dead, not Mrs. de Winter."

She pushed me towards the open window. I could see the terrace below me grey and indistinct in the white wall of fog. "Look down there," she said. "It's easy, isn't it?

Why don't you jump? It wouldn't hurt, not to break your neck. It's a quick, kind way. It's not like drowning. Why don't you try it? Why don't you go?"

— **Daphne du Maurier** *(1907-1989) English author and playwright*

The Corsican Brothers (1845)

- *A legendary novella of two brothers who physically feel the emotions and pain of one another.*

"Pardon me: but what you now tell me is so strange, and indeed all that happens to you and your brother is so much out of the course of nature—"

"That you don't want to believe it! I understand. But look here," said he, opening his shirt and showing me a blue mark imprinted on his skin, above the sixth rib on the right side, "will you believe in that?"

"Indeed," I exclaimed, "that is exactly the spot where your brother received the fatal bullet!"

"And the bullet went out here," continued he, putting his finger above the left hip.

"That's miraculous!" cried I.

"And now," continued he, "will you permit me to tell you at what hour he died?"

"Speak!"

"At ten minutes past nine."

— **Alexandre Dumas** *(1802-1870) French writer*

The Corsican Brothers is just 63 pages in length; *The Count of Monte Cristo* another Dumas classic quoted next is 1,462 pages in length; a startling contrast yet both equally deserving of an entry.

The Count of Monte Cristo (1844)

- *A swashbuckling tale of false imprisonment, escape, hidden treasure, and revenge by a man who believes he acts as the agent of Providence.*

"On what slender threads do life and fortune hang."

"What is the day of the month?" asked He of Jacopo, who sat down beside him.

"The 28th of February!"

"In what year?"

"In what year—you ask me in what year?"

"Yes," replied the young man, "I ask you what year is it?"

"You have forgotten then?"

"I got such a fright last night," replied Dantes, smiling, "that I have almost lost my memory, I ask you what year is it?"

"The year 1829," returned Jacopo. It was fourteen years day for day since Dantes' arrest.

He was nineteen when he entered the Chateau d'If; he was thirty-three when he escaped.

A sorrowful smile passed over his face; he asked himself what had become of Mercedes, who must believe him dead.

Then his eyes lighted up with hatred as he thought of the three men who had caused him so long and wretched a captivity.

— **Alexandre Dumas**

The Three Musketeers (1844)

- *The fortunes of d'Artagnan, who leaves his home to join the Musketeers bodyguard of King Louis XIII, becoming friends with three who live by the motto, "One for all, and all for one."*

Bicarat was now one against four, and had a thigh wound into the bargain. He was, however, still game to carry on. But Jussac, who had in the meanwhile recovered slightly and was now leaning on one elbow, called out to him to surrender. Bicarat was a Gascon like d'Artagnan; he pretended not to hear and only laughed. Then, having parried two thrusts, he seized an opportune moment, struck the point of his sword into the ground, and cried out in a tone of bravado, parodying a verse of the Bible:

'Here will I die gloriously, the last of my comrades to fall!'

'But you're one against four!' cried Jussac. 'Stop fighting! I order you to stop fighting!'

'That settles it then,' answered Bicarat. 'An order's an order: you're my senior so I must obey!'

With this he made a quick leap backwards, split his sword across his knee in order not to have to surrender it, threw the pieces over the convent wall and stood with his arms crossed, whistling a jaunty Cardinalist air.

Gallantry is always respected, even in an enemy. The musketeers saluted Bicarat with their swords and then returned them to their scabbards.

— **Alexandre Dumas**

The Alexandria Quartet (1957)

- *Set in Alexandria before and during World War II, four perspectives on the lives of an exiled Irish émigré seeking to unravel his sexual obsession with a tubercular café dancer, Melissa, and his infatuation with an alluring Jewish wife of a wealthy Christian. The quote is from Justine*

Afterwards when they were turning out his pockets I saw among the litter of odds and ends a small empty scent-bottle of the cheap kind that Melissa used; and I took it back to the flat where it stayed on the mantelpiece for some months before it was thrown away by Hamid in the course of a spring-clean. I never told Melissa of this; but often, when I was alone at night while she was dancing, perhaps of necessity sleeping with her admirers, I studied this small bottle, sadly and passionately reflecting on this horrible old man's love and measuring it against my own; and tasting too, vicariously, the desperation which makes one clutch at some small discarded object which is still impregnated with the betrayer's memory.

— **Lawrence Durrell** *(1912-1990) Expatriate British novelist and dramatist*

Young Lady Reading
by Mary Cassatt

E

The Maias (1888)

■ *The declining fortunes of a landowning Portuguese family over three generations, amidst the decadence of the country which eventually led to the National Revolution in 1926.*

Carlos, in torments, could not bear to hear any more. He pushed away her hands, which sought his. He wanted to escape, he wanted it all to be over!

"Oh, no, no, please don't push me away," she cried, clinging to him anxiously. "I know I deserve nothing. I know I'm a poor worthless wretch. I simply didn't have the courage, my love! You're a man, you don't understand these things. Look at me, why don't you look at me? Just for a moment, no, don't turn away, have pity on me."

No, he didn't want to look at her. He feared those tears, that face so full of pain. In response to the warmth of the breast rising and falling against his knees, all the emotions he was feeling—pride, spite, dignity, jealousy—began to waver. Then, unwittingly, unwillingly, his hands clasped hers. She immediately covered his fingers, his sleeves even, with impetuous kisses, and implored him, from the depths of her misery for one instant of mercy.

— **Eca de Queiros** *(1845-1900) Portuguese writer*

What is the What (2006)

■ *One man's horrific account of the Sudanese tragedy and survival as an American immigrant.*

I visited Ajulo and asked her about him. She had heard about the white man, too. I asked her if the presence of the inside-out man was a good thing, what it might mean. She thought about this for a long moment.

—The khawaja is an interesting thing, son. He is very smart. He has things in his head that you would not believe. He knows many languages, and the names of villages and towns, and can fly airplanes and drive cars. The white men are born knowing all of these things. He is powerful in this way, and very useful, very helpful to us. When you see a white man, it means things are going to improve. So I think this man is good for you.

After church, I asked the priest the same question.

—It is a very good thing, Achak, he said. —The white man is a close descendant of Adam and Eve, you see. You have seen the pictures of Jesus in your books, have you not? Adam and Eve and Jesus and God all have such skin. They are fragile, their skin burning in the sun, because they are closer to the status of angels. Angels would burn in a similar way if placed on earth. This man, then, is here to deliver messages from God.

— **Dave Eggers** *(1970-) American writer, editor, and publisher*

Middlemarch (1872)

- *Dorothea Brooke, an idealistic young woman, seeks solace from her unhappy marriage to middle-aged scholar Edward Casaubon, only to discover true love with her confidant Will Ladislaw.*

. . . The first impression on seeing Will was one of sunny brightness, which added to the uncertainty of his changing expression. Surely, his very features changed their form; his jaw looked sometimes large and sometimes small; and the little ripple in his nose was a preparation for metamorphosis. When he turned his head quickly his hair seemed to shake out light, and some persons thought they saw decided genius in this coruscation. Mr. Casaubon, on the contrary, stood rayless.

As Dorothea's eyes were turned anxiously on her husband she was perhaps not insensible to the contrast, but it was only mingled with other causes in making her more conscious of that new alarm on his behalf which was the first stirring of a pitying tenderness fed by the realities of his lot and not by her own dreams. Yet it was a source of greater freedom to her that Will was there; his young equality was agreeable, and also perhaps his openness to conviction. She felt an immense need of some one to speak to, and she had never before seen any one who seemed so quick and pliable, so likely to understand everything.

— **George Eliot** (Mary Anne Evans) *(1819-1880) English novelist, journalist, and translator*

The Mill on the Floss (1860)

- *Heroine Maggie and already engaged Stephen Guest become attracted to each other, the struggle eventually ending in Maggie's river drowning seemingly foretold in this quote.*

Maggie had smiled at herself then, and for the moment had forgotten everything in the sense of her own beauty. If that state of mind could have lasted, her choice would have been to have Stephen Guest at her feet, offering her a life filled with all luxuries, with daily incense of adoration near and distant, and with all possibilities of culture at her command. But there were things in her stronger than vanity — passion, and affection, and long deep memories of early discipline and effort, of early claims of her love and pity; and the stream of vanity was soon swept along and mingled imperceptibly with that wider current which was at its highest force to-day, under the double urgency of the events and inward impulses brought by the last week.

— **George Eliot**

The Dick Gibson Show (1971)

- *Dick Gibson hosts a radio show described by one reviewer as "wackos at work on both sides of the airwaves."*

"Ted Elmer here, folks. We're just about ready. Meanwhile I thought you'd like to hear this joke." He told them the joke; remembering another story, he told that, and then a third joke and a fourth. He was easy now, elated by the deep-breath risks he took, delighted by the sound of his voice, those swaggered drafts of lung-strut, chug-a-lugging the vacuum itself. Disregarding voice level, he laughed loudly at the punch lines, getting a generous sense of helping his cause and clearing his sinuses, blowing those seats of the crabbed and ordinary skyhigh. As he spoke he fidgeted with the looseleaf notebook he still held, absent-mindedly tearing pages from it and dropping them to the floor as he would the pages of a script.

He spoke until it was time for the next program to go on; then, reluctantly, but with the certainty that they would hear him again this way—he envisaged a magnificent future—he turned his listeners back to the studio.

"This is your host, the inimitable Dick Gibson, signing off for now." (The name had come to him from the air.)

— **Stanley Elkin** *(1930-1995) American novelist, short story writer, and essayist*

Invisible Man (1947)

- *A chronicle of the travels and tribulations of a young black man growing up in a black community in the South, attending a Negro college and eventually moving to New York where he joins and is later expelled from a Harlem branch of "The Brotherhood."*

. . . I am an invisible man. No, I am not a spook like those who haunted Edgar Allan Poe; nor am I one of your Hollywood-movie ectoplasms. I am a man of substance, of flesh and bone, fiber and liquids—and I might even be said to possess a mind. I am invisible, understand, simply because people refuse to see me. Like the bodiless heads you see sometimes in circus sideshows, it is as though I have been surrounded by mirrors of hard, distorting glass. When they approach me they see only my surroundings, themselves, or figments of their imagination—indeed, everything and anything except me.

— **Ralph Ellison** *(1914-1994) novelist, literary critic, scholar, and writer*

King of the Jews (1979)

- *A darkly humorous story, as told, of the head of a Judenrat who is forced to collaborate in the destruction of his own people.*

A real burst of laughter at this one. Schotter rocked back and forth on the rounded bottoms of his shoes. He tipped so the crowd could see the hairless spot on his head. He told one more.

David Ryan

"Horowitz has a wonderful idea to save on petroleum, so he calls the Prime Minister of England on the phone. 'Listen, Churchill,' Horowitz says. 'Why should we bomb each other? All that flying back and forth is a waste of gas. Let's make an agreement. You bomb London, and we'll bomb Berlin!"

The whole crowd—waiters, orchestra members, everyone—was aghast. The reason for this was that even before the joke was over, four of the Others had come through the door. Two of these were in uniform, the black ones, Death's Head-ers; the other two men wore civilian clothes. The gray-suited man, the one who put on the show in the square, spoke first. "Jew, who is the owner of this club?"

Popower, the waiter, was the person closest by. Fear gripped him. The dumplings, the calves' feet, slid off his tray.

— **Leslie Epstein** *(1938-) American novelist*

Middlesex (2002)

- *The complicated tale of a young girl Calliope who eventually grows into a young man Cal.*

"Holy mackerel, when's the last time you had a haircut anyway?"

"Remember the moon landing?"

"Yeah. That's about right."

He turned me to face the mirror. And there she was, for the last time, in the silvered glass: Calliope. She still wasn't gone yet. She was like a captive spirit, peeking out.

Ed the barber put a comb in my long hair. He lifted it experimentally, making snipping sounds with his scissors. The blades weren't touching my hair. The snipping was only a kind of mental barbering, a limbering up. This gave me time for second thoughts. What was I doing? What if Dr. Luce was right? What if that girl in the mirror really *was* me? How did I think I could defect to the other side so easily? What did I know about boys, about men? I didn't even like them that much.

— **Jeffrey Eugenides** *(1960-) American novelist and short story writer*

F

Absalom, Absalom! (1936)

- *The rise and fall of Thomas Sutpen, a white man born into poverty who comes to Mississippi with the complementary aims of becoming rich and a powerful family patriarch. The quote tells of the fatal conflict between Colonel Sutpen and Wash Jones a poor-white-trash squatter.*

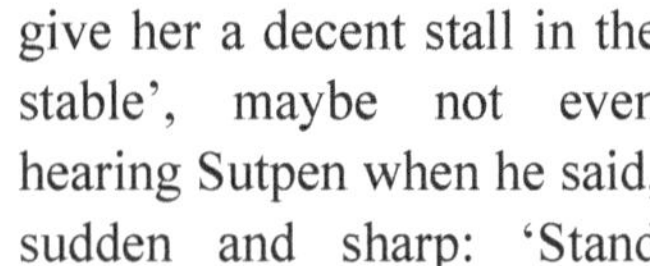

. . . for a second Wash must not have felt the very earth under his feet while he watched Sutpen emerge from the house, the riding whip in his hand . . . maybe not even hearing his own voice when Sutpen saw his face (the face of the man who in twenty years he had no more known to make any move save at command than he had the stallion which he rode) and stopped: 'You said if she was a mare you could give her a decent stall in the stable', maybe not even hearing Sutpen when he said, sudden and sharp: 'Stand back. Don't you touch me' only he must have heard that because he answered it: 'I'm going to tech you, Kernel' and Sutpen said 'Stand back, Wash' again before the old woman heard the whip. Only there were two blows with the whip; they found the two welts on Wash's face that night. Maybe the two blows even knocked him down; maybe it was while he was getting up that he put his hand on the scythe—"

— **William Faulkner** *(1897-1962) American novelist and short story writer*

As I Lay Dying (1930)

- *A pilgrimage during which the Bundren family members relate their trials and tribulations as they take the body of Addie, the family matriarch, to her burial site.*

. . . He was looking at the horse, kind of dancing up and down by it.

"Let me ride, Jewel," he said. "Let me ride, Jewel."

Jewel looked at him, then he looked away again, holding the horse reined back. Pa watched him, mumbling his lip.

"So you bought a horse," he said. "You went behind my back and bought a horse. You never consulted me; you know how tight it is for us to make by, yet you bough a horse for me to feed. Taken the work from your flesh and blood and bought a horse with it."

Jewel looked at pa, his eyes paler than ever. "He wont never eat a mouthful of yours," he said. "Not a mouthful. I'll kill him first. Dont you never think it. Dont you never."

"Let me ride, Jewel," Vardaman said. "Let me ride, Jewel." He sounded like a cricket in the grass, a little one. "Let me ride, Jewel."

— William Faulkner

Collected Stories of William Faulkner (1950)

- *Stories, often set in his native Mississippi, in which "the old verities and truths of the heart" are explored. This quote from "A Rose for Emily."*

So she vanquished them, horse and foot, just as she had vanquished their fathers thirty years before about the smell. That was two years after her father's death and a short time after her sweetheart–the one we believed would marry her–had deserted her. After her father's death she went out very little; after her sweetheart went away, people hardly saw her at all. A few of the ladies had the temerity to call, but were not received, and the only sign of life about the place was the Negro man–a young man then–going in and out with a market basket.

"Just as if a man–any man–could keep a kitchen properly," the ladies said; so they were not surprised when the smell developed. It was another link between the gross, teeming world and the high and mighty Griersons.

— William Faulkner

A Fable (1954)

- *A week of trench warfare in World War I featuring a mutiny on both sides, reprisals, and ultimately continuation of the bloodshed.*

So now, as the lorry climbed the repaired road to follow the curve of the Meuse Heights, the sergeant at least could watch beyond the open door the ruined and slain land unfold–the corpse of earth, some of which, is soil soured forever with cordite and human blood and anguish, would never live again, as though not only abandoned by man but repudiated forever by God Himself: the craters, the old trenches and rusted wire, the stripped and blasted trees, the little villages and farms like shattered skulls no longer even recognizable as skulls, already beginning to vanish beneath a fierce rank color-less growth of nourishmentless grass coming not tenderly out of the earth's surface but as through miles and leagues up from Hell itself, as if the Devil himself were trying to hide what man had done to the earth which was his mother.

— William Faulkner

Light in August (1932)

- *The interwoven lives of mysterious Joe Christmas, a brooding wanderer who believes himself part-black, and strangers he meets by chance in a small Mississippi town during Prohibition.*

He stood at the table. They looked at one another.

"Will you kneel with me?" she said. "I dont ask it."

"No," he said.

"I dont ask it. It's not I who ask it. Kneel with me."

"NO."

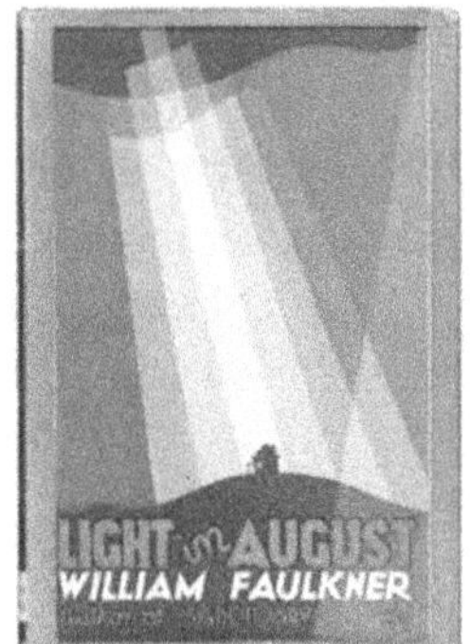

They looked at one another. "Joe," she said. "For the last time, I dont ask it. Remember that. Kneel with me."

"No," he said. Then he saw her arms unfold and her right hand come forth from beneath the shawl. It held an old style, single action, cap-and-ball revolver almost as long and heavier than a small rifle. But the shadow of it and of her arm and hand on the wall did not waver at all, the shadow of both monstrous, the cocked hammer monstrous, back-hooked and viciously poised like the arched head of a snake; it did not waver at all.

— William Faulkner

The Reivers (1962)

- *One day in 1905 eleven-year old Lucius Priest "borrows" his grandfather's automobile and with two older friends embarks from Jefferson, Mississippi, to Memphis.*

So he bought the automobile, and Boon found his soul's lily maid, the virgin's love of his rough and innocent heart. It was a Winton Flyer. . . . You cranked it by hand while standing in front of it, with no more risk (provided you had remembered to take it out of gear) than a bone or two in your forearm; it had kerosene lamps for night driving and when rain threatened five or six people could readily put up the top and curtains in ten or fifteen minutes, and Grandfather himself equipped it with a kerosene lantern, a new axe and a small coil of barbed wire attached to a light block and tackle for driving beyond the town limits.

— William Faulkner

The Sound and the Fury (1929)

- *The story of three Compson brothers, Benjy, a severely retarded thirty-three-year-old man, Quentin, a sensitive bundle of neuroses, and Jason, a bitter farm-supply store worker, and their obsessions with their sister Caddy, stubborn, but loving and compassionate.*

. . . "Yes, suh," he said. He got down and picked up the quarter and rubbed it on his leg. "Thanky, young marster . . . Thanky." Then the train began to move. I leaned out the window, into the cold air, looking back. He stood there beside the gaunt rabbit of a mule, the two of them shabby and motionless and unimpatient. The train swung around the curve, the engine puffing with short, heavy blasts, and they passed smoothly from sight that way, with that quality about them of shabby and timeless patience, of static serenity: that blending of child-like and ready incompetence and paradoxical reliability that tends and protects them it loves out of all reason . . .

— William Faulkner

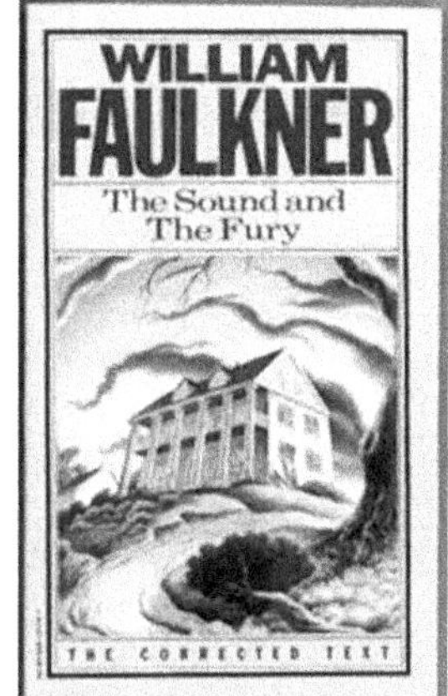

"A splendid failure," Faulkner's self-depreciating view of this work.

Birdsong (1993)

- *A young Englishman, spurned in love, joins the army, eventually commanding a brigade of miners whose macabre assignment is to tunnel beneath German lines and set off bombs.*

"He's shouting for his mother," said the orderly as they brought him into the tent.

"They always do," said the medical officer, peeling back the field dressing Byrne had applied almost thirty hours before.

They put him out of the tent to await transport to the casualty clearing station or death, whichever should come first.

Then under the indifferent sky his spirit left the body with its ripped flesh, its infections, its weak and damaged nature. While the rain fell on his arms and legs, the part of him that still lived was unreachable. It was not his mind, but some other essence that was longing now for peace on a quiet, shadowed road where no guns sounded. The deep paths of darkness opened up for it, as they opened up for other men along the lines of dug earth, barely fifty yards apart.

Then, as the fever in his abandoned body reached its height and he moved toward the welcome of oblivion, he heard a voice, not human, but clear and urgent. It was the sound of his life leaving him. Its tone was mocking. It offered him, instead of the peace he longed for, the possibility of return.

— Sebastian Faulks *(1953-) British novelist and journalist*

Then We Came to the End (2007)

- *A group of copywriters and designers at a Chicago ad agency face layoffs at the end of the '90s boom.*

We were fractious and overpaid. Our mornings lacked promise. At least those of us who smoked had something to look forward to at ten-fifteen. Most of us liked most everyone, a few of us hated specific individuals, one or two people loved everyone and everything. Those who loved everyone were unanimously reviled. We loved free bagels in the morning. They happened all too infrequently. Our benefits were astonishing in comprehensiveness and quality of care. Sometimes we questioned whether they were worth it. We thought moving to India might be better, or going back to nursing school. Doing something with the handicapped or working with our hands. No one ever acted on these impulses, despite their daily, sometimes hourly contractions. Instead we met in conference rooms to discuss the issues of the day.

— **Joshua Ferris** *(1947-) American author*

Amelia (1751)

- *The life and hardships suffered by a young couple living in London, much of their difficulties stemming from the husband's yielding to circumstances rather than dominating them.*

. . . To be indebted to such a fellow at any rate had stuck much in his stomach, and had given him very great uneasiness; but to answer this demand in any other manner than by paying the money was absolutely what he could not bear. Again, to pay this money, he very plainly saw there was but one way, and this was, by stripping his wife, not only of every farthing, but almost of every rag she had in the world; a thought so dreadful that it chilled his very soul with horror: and yet price, at last, seemed to represent this as the lesser evil of the two.

— **Henry Fielding** *(1707-1754) English novelist and dramatist; founded London's first police force*

Tom Jones (1749)

- *One of the first prose works describable as a novel, the story of Tom Jones presents a panoramic view of 18th century British life.*

. . . In a word, she soon triumphed over all the virtuous resolutions of Jones; for though she behaved at last with all decent reluctance, yet I rather choose to attribute the triumph to her, since, in fact, it was her design which succeeded.

In the conduct of this matter Molly so well played her part that Jones attributed the conquest entirely to himself, and considered the young woman as one who had yielded to the violent attacks of his passion. He likewise imputed her yielding to the ungovernable force of her love towards him; and this the reader will allow to have been a very natural and probable supposition, as we have more than once mentioned the uncommon comeliness of his person, and indeed, he was one of the handsomest young fellows in the world.

— **Henry Fielding**

The Great Gatsby (1925)

- *Seen through the eyes of his neighbor, nouveau rich Jay Gatsby buys a mansion on Long Island Sound and throws endless lavish parties to attract and rekindle the love of Daisy his former fiancé now married.*

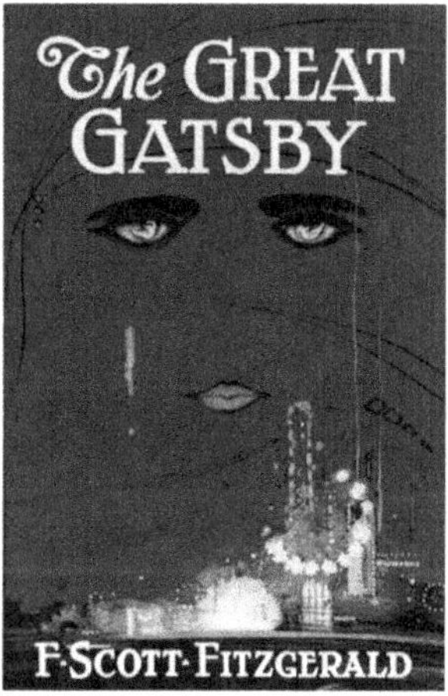

. . . it was an extraordinary gift for hope, a romantic readiness such as I have never found in any other person and which it is not likely I shall ever find again. No—Gatsby turned out all right at the end; it is what preyed on Gatsby, what foul dust floated in the wake of his dreams that temporarily closed out my interest in the abortive sorrows and short-winded elations of men. . . . .

Mia Farrow and Robert Redford as Tom and Daisy.

They were careless people, Tom and Daisy—smashed up things and creatures and then retreated back into their money or their vast carelessness or whatever it was that kept them together, and let other people clean up the mess they had made . . . .

— **F. Scott Fitzgerald** *(1896-1940) American author of novels and short stories*

This often quoted passage from Fitzgerald's *All the Sad Young Men* is a most suitable related supplement.

Let me tell you about the very rich. They are different from you and me. They possess and enjoy early, and it does something to them, makes them soft where we are hard and cynical where we are trustful, in a way that, unless you were born rich, it is very difficult to understand. They think, deep in their hearts, that they are better than we are because we had to discover the compensations and refuges of life for ourselves . . .

Tender is the Night (1933)

- *Set on the French Riviera in the late 1920s, the tragic romance of a young actress "on the last edge of childhood," and a stylish American psychiatrist whose equally attractive wife is also one of his patients.*

...but my great worry is that time is slipping by, life is slipping by, and we have no life.

To be included in Dick Diver's world for a while was a remarkable experience: people believed he made special reservations about them, recognizing the proud uniqueness of their destinies, buried under the compromises of how many years. He won everyone quickly with an exquisite consideration and a politeness that moved so fast and intuitively that it could be examined only in its effect. Then, without caution, lest the first bloom of the relation wither, he opened the gate to his amusing world. So long as they subscribed to it completely, their happiness was his preoccupation, but at the first flicker of doubt as to its all-inclusiveness he evaporated before their eyes, leaving little communicable memory of what he had said or done.

— F. Scott Fitzgerald

The Blue Flower (1997)

- *The life of a brilliant young German poet and philosopher who passionately falls in love with his "heart's heart," his "spirit's guide"— a plain simple twelve-year-old.*

'I am Fritz von Hardenberg,' he had said to her. 'You are Fraulein Sophie von Kuhn. You are twelve years of age, I heard your gracious mother say so.'

Sohie put her hands to her hair. 'Up, it should be up.'

'In four years time you will have to consider what man would be fortunate enough to hope to be your husband. Don't tell me that he would have to ask your stepfather! What do you say yourself?'

'In four years time I don't know what I shall be.'

'You mean, you don't know what you will become.'

'I don't want to become.'

'Perhaps you are right.'

'I want to be, and not to have to think about it.'

'But you must not remain a child.'

'I am not a child now.'

'Sophie, I am a poet, but in four years I shall be

an administrative official, receiving a salary. That is the time when we shall be married.'

'I don't know you!'

— **Penelope Fitzgerald** *(1916-2000) English novelist, poet, essayist and biographer*

The Tenants of Time (1988)

- *The story of four men who participate in the short-lived Fenian Rising intended to bring about an Irish republic, and the consequences many years later.*

. . . "To Lionel," she said, "to Tom's great friend Lionel," and she held up her glass.

"No, no," I said, "the toast should be mine. To the two of you. And my blessings."

"His blessings," she said, and sipped. Tom put his arm about her waist, and looked up at her, at her profile. She was looking straight at me, and smiling. . . . .

She was a startling woman. Whenever someone describes Sylvia, he should begin with that word, for it is surely in his mind. Now, here in this room, the green riding habit gave her a dramatic presence. She sat poised on the chair arm, a slender woman but not at all a small one—tall, rather, and heavy-boned. She sat with back arched, Tom's arm encircling her, and one leg stretched forward, almost indecorously, the riding boot a glossy black. She held the whisky glass in her two hands.

— **Thomas Flanagan** *(1923-2002) American professor of English literature*

Madame Bovary (1857)

- *Emma Bovary, a doctor's wife, has adulterous affairs and lives beyond her means in order to escape the banalities and emptiness of provincial life.*

"She's very pleasing," he told himself. "Very pleasing, that doctor's wife. Pretty teeth, black eyes, a well-turned foot, and manners like a Parisienne. Where the devil did she come from? Where did that coarse fellow find her?"

Monsieur Rodolphe Boulanger was thirty-four years old. He was hardhearted and extremely intelligent, had spent a lot of time in female company, and was very knowledgeable about women. He liked this new one and therefore thought about her and her husband.

"I find him dull. She must be tired of him. He's got dirty fingernails and a three-day growth of beard. He trots off to his patients, and she stays home darning his socks. And so bored! Longing to live in town and dance a polka every night. Poor little woman. Gasping for love, like a carp on a kitchen table gasping for water. Three flattering words and she'd adore me, I'm sure. How tender and charming it would be. But how would I get rid of her later?"

— **Gustave Flaubert** *(1821-1880) French writer*

Flaubert was fastidious in his devotion to finding the right word ("*le mot juste*"), and his mode of composition reflected that. He worked in sullen solitude—sometimes occupying a week in the completion of one page—never satisfied with what he had composed, violently tormenting his brain for the best turn of phrase, the final adjective. — *Wikipedia*

Sentimental Education (1869)

- *The life of a young man living through the French Revolution of 1848 and his love for an older married woman.*

Their tastes and opinions were identical. Often the one who was listening would exclaim:

'So do I!'

And the other in his turn would say:

'So do I!'

Then there would follow endless complaints about Fate:

'Why didn't heaven allow it? If only we had met . . .'

'Ah, if I had been younger!' she would sigh.

'No! If I had been a little older!'

And they imagined a life which would have been entirely devoted to love, rich enough to fill the wildest deserts, surpassing all joys, and defying all sorrows; a life in which the hours would have gone by in a continuous exchange of confidences; a life which would have been splendid and sublime like the shimmering of the stars.

— **Gustave Flaubert**

Casino Royale (1953)

- *Expert baccarat player James Bond (British secret agent 007) is assigned to defeat Le Chiffre in the hope that his gambling debts will provoke Soviet espionage agency SHERSH to kill him.*

'You are fortunate,' said the voice. 'I have no orders to kill you. Your life has been saved twice in one day. But you can tell your organization that SMERSH is only merciful by chance or by mistake. In your case you were saved first by chance and now by mistake, for I should have had orders to kill any foreign spies who were hanging round this traitor like flies round a dog's mess.

‘But I shall leave you my visiting-card. You are a gambler. You play at cards. One day perhaps you will play against one of us. It would be well that you should be known as a spy.’

Sean Connery as James Bond

Steps moved round to behind Bond’s right shoulder. There was the click of a knife opening. An arm in some grey material came into Bond’s line of vision. A broad hairy hand emerging from a dirty white shirt-cuff was holding a thin stiletto like a fountain-pen. It poised for a moment above the back of Bond’s right hand, immovably bound with flex to the arm of the chair. The point of the stiletto executed three quick straight slashes. A fourth slash crossed them where they ended, just short of the knuckles. Blood in the shape of an inverted ‘M’ welled out and slowly started to drip to the floor.

— **Ian Fleming** *(1908-1964) British author and journalist*

The war was good to Fleming, tapping his imagination, forcing him to work within discipline. Fleming schemed, plotted, and carried out dangerous missions. From the famous Room 39 in the Admiralty building in London's Whitehall, Fleming tossed out a myriad of off-beat ideas on how to confuse, survey, and enrage the Germans. — *The Life of Ian Fleming* by John Cork

Eye of the Needle (1978)

- *A German agent is tracked by British Military Intelligence but succeeds in devastating the lives of a young couple on a storm-battered island.*

The hand broke away a piece of glass, then another, enlarging the hole in the pane. Then it reached right through, up to the elbow, and fumbled along the windowsill, searching for a catch to unfasten.

Trying to be utterly silent, with painful slowness, Lucy shifted the gun to her left hand, and with her right took the axe from her belt, lifted it high above her head, and brought it down with all her might on Henry’s hand.

He must have sensed it, or heard the rush of wind, or seen a blur of ghostly movement behind the window, because he moved abruptly a split-second before the blow landed.

The axe thudded into the wood of the windowsill, sticking there. For a fraction of an instant Lucy thought she had missed; then, from outside, came a scream of pain, and she saw beside the axe blade, lying on the varnished wood like caterpillars, two severed fingers.

She heard the sound of feet running.

She threw up.

— **Ken Follett** *(1949-) Welsh author*

The Good Soldier (1915)

- *The fissures of a mismatched marriage and the philandering of an otherwise noble man.*

I had forgotten about his eyes. They were as blue as the sides of a certain type of box of matches. When you looked at them carefully you saw that they were perfectly honest, perfectly straightforward, perfectly, perfectly stupid. But the brick pink of his complexion, running perfectly level to the brick pink of his inner eyelids, gave them a curious, sinister expression—like a mosaic of blue porcelain set in pink china. And that chap, coming into a room, snapped up the gaze of every woman in it, as dexterously as a conjurer pockets billiard balls.

— **Ford Madox Ford** *(1873-1939) English novelist, poet, critic and editor*

Independence Day (1995)

- *A critical week in the life of real estate agent Frank Basscombe, who struggles to find common ground with his former wife and son.*

In truth I don't much like Betty McLeod, despite wanting to rent the house to her and Larry because I think they're probably courageous. To my notice she's always worn a perpetually disappointed look that says she regrets all her major life choices yet feels absolutely certain she made the right moral decision in every instance, and is better than you because of it. It's the typical three-way liberal paradox: anxiety mingled with pride and self-loathing. The McLeods are also, I'm afraid, the kind of family who could someday go paranoid and barricade themselves in their (my) house, issue confused manifestos, fire shots at the police and eventually torch everything, killing all within. (This, of course, is no reason to evict them.)

— **Richard Ford** *(1944-) American novelist*

The Lay of the Land (2006)

- *The continuing ups and downs of Frank Basscombe who, at age fifty-five, finds life fraught with unforeseen perils in his "time of being, not becoming."*

All of this begins to seem like an annoyance more than a fight, like having someone's pet monkey hanging on your neck, though we're down on the floor and the stool's on top of me and Bob's going "*Grrrr, errrr; grrrr*" and squeezing my neck, his breath and hair reeking like week-old haddock.

Suddenly, I lose all my wind and have to buck the bar stool off my back to breathe, and in doing so I get my knee in between Bob's own squirming, jimmering knees and my right elbow into his sternum, just below where I could interrupt *his* windpipe. I lean on Bob's hard breast bone, stare down into his bulging, blood-splurged eyes, which register that this event may be almost over. "Bob," I half-shout at him. His eyes widen, he bares his long yellow teeth, refastens a fisted grip on my neck tendons and croaks, "_______." And with no further prelude, I go ahead and jackhammer my kneecap straight up into Bob's nuttal pouch pretty much as hard as I can—given my weakened state, given my lack of inclination and the fact that I've had a martini and hoped the evening would turn out to be pleasant, since so much of the day hadn't.

— Richard Ford

The Sportswriter (1986)

- *During the course of a holiday weekend a 38-year-old male in mid-life crisis reunites with his wife briefly, travels to Detroit, and grapples with the not-too-distant losses of a career, a son, and a marriage.*

Staring, though, at Vicki's sculptured, vaguely padded knees, I now am clearly lost and feel the ultimate slipping away again, bereavement threatening like thunder to roll in and take its place.

"So what is it you were lookin for in my bag?" she says. Hers is a frown of focused disdain. I am the least favorite student caught looking for the gradebook in the teacher's desk. She is the friendly substitute there for one day only (though we all wish she were the regular one) but who knows a sneak when she sees him.

"I wasn't looking for anything, really. I wasn't looking." I *was* looking, of course. And this is the wrong lie, though a lie is absolutely what's needed. My first tiny skirmish with the facts goes into the debit column. My voice falls ten full decibels. This has happened before.

— Richard Ford

Howards End (1910)

- *An entanglement of three different families in middle class English society in the decade before the Great War.*

Yet she liked being with him. He was not a rebuke, but a stimulus, and banished morbidity. Some twenty years her senior, he preserved a gift that she supposed herself to have already lost—not youth's creative power, but its self-confidence and optimism. He was so sure that it was a very pleasant world. His complexion was robust, his hair had receded but not thinned, the thick moustache and the eyes that Helen had compared to brandy-balls had an agreeable menace in them, whether they were turned towards the slums or towards the stars. Some day—in the millennium—there may be no need for his type. At present, homage is due to it from those who think themselves superior, and who possibly are.

— **E. M. Forster** *(1879-1970) English novelist and short story writer*

E. M. Forster is for me the only living novelist who can be read again and again and who, after each reading, gives me what few writers can give us after our first days of novel-reading, the sensation of having learned something.

— Lionel Trilling (1943) American literary critic

E. M. Forster never gets any further than warming the teapot. He's a rather fine hand at that. Feel this teapot. Is it not beautifully warm? Yes, but there ain't going to be no tea. And I can never be perfectly certain whether Helen was got with child by Leonard Bast or by his fatal forgotten umbrella. All things considered I think it must have been the umbrella.

— Katherine Mansfield, in her journal, writing these comments about *Howard's End*. Source: Steve King, *Today in Literature*

A Passage to India (1924)

- *Life in India at the peak of the British colonial era, complete with the racial tensions that underscore every aspect of daily life.*

"It does indeed rest upon a mistake," came the thin biting voice of the other. "It does indeed. I have had twenty-five years' experience of this country"—he paused, and "twenty-five years" seemed to fill the waiting-room with their staleness and ungenerosity—"and during those twenty-five years I have never known anything but disaster result when English people and Indians attempt to be intimate socially. Intercourse, yes. Courtesy, by all means. Intimacy—never, never. The whole weight of my authority is against it"

— **E. M. Forster**

A Room with a View (1908)

- *The trials of young Lucy Honeychurch who finds herself engaged to boorish and boring Cecil Vyse while strangely attracted to simple and direct George Emerson.*

"Take an old man's word; there's nothing worse than a muddle in all the world. It is easy to face Death and Fate, and the things that sound so dreadful. It is on my muddles that I look back with horror—on the things that I might have avoided. We can help one another but little. I used to think I could teach young people the whole of life, but I know better now, and all my teaching of George has come down to this: beware of muddle. Do you remember in that church, when you pretended to be annoyed with me and weren't? Do you remember before, when you refused the room with the view? Those were muddles—littled, but ominous—and I am fearing that you are in one now." — **E. M. Forster**

At just forty-five years of age, and with another forty-five to go, Forster made what appears to be an intentional decision to give up novel writing. His explanation to one friend was "my patience with ordinary people has given out"; to another, he admitted his "weariness of the only subject I can and may treat."
— Steve King, *Today in Literature*

The Collector (1963)

- *A psychopath kidnaps and detains in a secret room the object of his infatuation, twenty-year-old Miss Miranda Grey.*

Well, at last the great moment was come. I went up to the garage and opened the back of the van. Like the rest of the operation it went according to plan. I got the straps off her, made her sit up, her legs and feet still bound of course. She kicked about for a moment, I was obliged to say that if she did not keep quiet I would have to resort to more of the chloro and CTC (which I showed), but that if she kept still I wouldn't hurt her. That did the trick. I lifted her, she was not so heavy as I thought; I got her down quite easily; we did have a bit of a struggle at the door of her room, but here wasn't much she could do then. I put her on the bed. It was done.

Her face was white, some of the sick had gone on her navy jumper, she was a real sight; but her eyes weren't afraid. It was funny. She just stared at me, waiting.

I said, this is your room. If you do what I say, you won't be hurt. It's no good shouting. You can't be heard outside and anyway there's never anyone to hear.

— **John Fowles** *(1926-2005) English novelist and essayist*

The French Lieutenant's Woman (1969)

- *A disgraced woman attracts the attention of Charles Smithson who tries to remain distant but is caught up in her mystical seductiveness.*

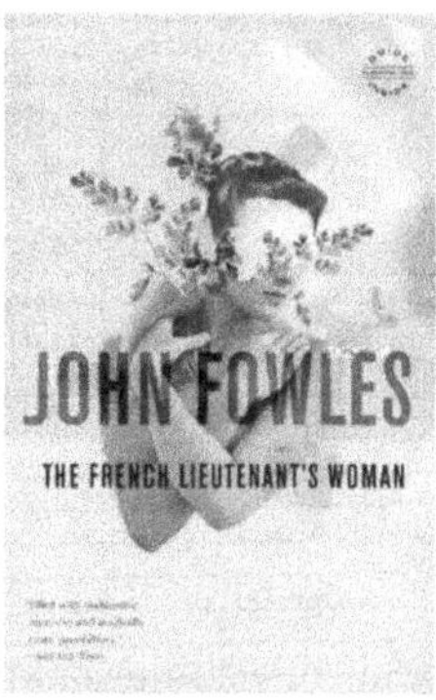

She turned to look at him — or as it seemed to Charles, through him. It was not so much what was positively in that face which remained with him after that first meeting, but all that was not as he had expected; for theirs was an age when the favored feminine look was the demure, the obedient, the shy.

Charles felt immediately as if he had trespassed; as if the Cobb [sea wall] belonged to that face, and not to the Ancient Borough of Lyme. It was not a pretty face, like Ernestina's. It was certainly not a beautiful face, by any period's standard or taste. But it was an unforgettable face, and a tragic face. Its sorrow welled out of it as purely, naturally and unstoppably as water out of a woodland spring.

— John Fowles

The Magus (1966)

- *A young Englishman finds himself the victim of manipulative games and masquerades as he pursues a young woman questionably involved with his mysterious assailants.*

He took the pill-box, and shook out, of all things, six large molars; yellowish, two or three with old stoppings.

"These were issued to spies on both sides during the last war, for use if they were interrogated.' He placed one of the teeth on the saucer, then with a small downward jab of the shaker crushed it; it was brittle, like a liqueur chocolate. But the odour of the colourless liquid was of bitter almonds, acrid and terrifying. He hastily removed the saucer at arm's length to the far corner of the terrace' then returned.

'Suicide pills?'

'Precisely. Hydrocyanic acid.' He picked up the dice, and showed me six sides.

I smiled. 'You want me to throw?'

'I offer you an entire war in one second.'

'Supposing I don't want it?'

'Think. In a minute from now you could be saying, I risked death. I threw for life, and I won life. It is a very wonderful feeling. To have survived.'

— John Fowles

The Corrections (2001)

- *The stories of five members of the quirky Lambert family including son Gary, grappling with depression while contending with persistent wife Caroline.*

. . . Despite serious losses, he remained confident of victory. Since his very first fight with Caroline, twenty years earlier, when he'd sat alone in his apartment and watched an eleven-inning Phillies game and listened to his phone ring every ten minutes, every five minutes, every two minutes, he'd understood that at the ticking heart of Caroline was a desperate insecurity. Sooner or later, if he withheld his love, she came knocking on his chest with her little fist and let him have his way.

Caroline showed no sign of weakening, however. Late at night, when Gary was too freaked out and angry to shut his eyes, let alone sleep, she politely but firmly declined to fight with him. . . . .

"What do you need from me?" Gary asked her. "Tell me what you need to hear from me."

"I need you to take responsibility for your mental health."

— **Jonathan Franzen** *(1959-) American novelist and essayist*

Headlong (1999)

- *Young art historian Martin Clay discovers an unidentified masterwork and decides to secure it without revealing its true value to the owner.*

But by now I can't see the picture anymore—I'm ceasing to take it in. My eye's flickering back and forth too fast in its excitement, and my mind's clouded with anguish. Because it's all too obvious. It's so blindingly evident what this picture is that it can't be so, or someone else would have recognized it already. Yes, who else has seen it? How can even these two fools not know what it is?

I daren't think the name of its creator to myself, because it simply cannot be so.

"Very nice," I say politely, laying it down on the table. "Most attractive. Now, I've got a coat somewhere. . . ."

— **Michael Frayn** *(1933-) English playwright and novelist*

Cold Mountain (1997)

- *A wounded Union soldier deserts to return home to be reunited with his beloved Ada who has been struggling to maintain her family farm with the help of a mountain girl.*

—Number one, the girl said, if you've got a horse I can plow all day. Number two, Old Lady Swanger told me your straits. Something for you to keep in mind would be that every man worth hiring is off and gone. It's a harsh truth, but that's mostly the way of things, even under favorable conditions.

The girl's name, Ada soon discovered, was Ruby, and though the look of her was not confidence-inspiring, she convincingly depicted herself as capable of any and all farm tasks. Just as importantly, as they talked, Ada found she was enormously cheered by Ruby. Ada's deep impression was that she had a willing heart. And though Ruby had not spent a day of her life in school and could not read a word nor write even her name, Ada thought she saw in her a spark as bright and hard as one struck with steel and flint. And there was this: like Ada, Ruby was a motherless child from the day she was born. They had that to understand each other by, though otherwise they could not have been more alien to each other. In short order, and somewhat to Ada's surprise, they began striking a deal.

— **Charles Frazier** *(1950-) American historical novelist*

G

A Frolic of His Own (1994)

■ *The legal entanglements of a plagiarized playwright, Oscar Crease, made increasingly complex by Oscar's quirky judge father, hapless girlfriend, and numerous others.*

—Put it in the hands of the master to come up with the accounting Oscar, what we've just been talking about here, they moved to reduce your award with all these exhibits separating their contribution from yours and Bone's court reversed the decree that was based on the assumption that, look. You sued for infringement because they stole your play for their movie, that your entire play was your contribution to their gross receipts, but they . . .

—But they did! It's right there in that original opinion isn't it? tracking the play and the movie scene for scene and the . . .

—They stoke your play but they didn't use all of it, that's what this business of apportioning these contributions is all about can't you understand! He drank off half the glass with one hand, waving the other—have to go through it all again? separating the material they pirated from what they mixed with it from the public domain in the whole development process, ten or twenty script rewrites and your last act, they claim they didn't use anything from your last act at all and there's a third of your contribution gone right there.

— **William Gaddis** *(1922-1998) American novelist*

JR (1975)

■ *In a satire of America's financial markets, an 11-year-old boy, obscuring his identity through payphone calls and postal money orders, parlays penny stock holdings into a fortune on paper.*

—That? My God, haven't seen one in years.

—No this isn't what I . . . what is it.

—Russian Imperial Bond.

—You mean it isn't worth any, worth very . . .

—Mister Bast, anything is worth whatever some damn fool will pay for it, only reason somebody can make a market in

Russian Imperials is because some damn, somebody like your associate will buy them. Happen to know how he, how this associate of yours got into all this?

—By, well buying and selling at first I think and then he had some stock in a company and was going to bring some kind of legal suit for, for his class, I mean he . . .

—A class action? What was the company, another Ace Development outfit?

—No it was a, Diamond, the Diamond Cable Company he, well maybe I should just tell you the whole story, you see he's only . . .

— William Gaddis

The Recognitions (1955)

■ *The life of Wyatt Gwyon who studies painting, perfecting his skills as a forger which eventually develops into "new" originals so perfect they pass for newly discovered works of art.*

—Christ! Don't wave them around here! said the man beside him, and looked over the room quickly. But no one was near to notice them, and when he looked back he seemed unable to resist taking the bill from Otto and laying it on the cloth before him. —Beautiful, he said. —Beautiful, isn't it.

—Yess, Otto gasped.

—A real work of art. He stared into the face of the seventh President. —You know it takes six different artists to make one of these? That's what makes it tough. Six to one. Six against one, you might say. He turned it over, and ran a fingertip gently over the portico of the White House. —A real work of art, he said. —You don't learn that at Harvard.

Otto stared. He clutched the packet, as though it were liable to be wrenched from him at any instant.

—You know, they burn around six tons of this stuff a day, the true quill, down in the Bureau of Printing and Engraving. Worn-out bills. It's a crime.

—Yes, but . . . well . . . this . . . was all Otto could say.

— William Gaddis

Veronica (2005)

■ *A young model returning from Paris meets an older wisecracking eccentric dying from AIDS who becomes her improbable friend.*

A long time ago, John loved me. I never loved him, but I used his friendship, and the using became so comfortable for both of us that we started really being friends. When I lost my looks and had to go on disability, John pitied me and then looked down on me, but that just got fit into the friendship, too. What can't get fit in is that sometimes even now John looks at me and sees a beautiful girl in a ruined face. It's broken, with age and pain coming through the cracks, but it's there, and it pisses him off. It pisses me off, too.

— **Mary Gaitskill** *(1954-) American author*

Dreaming In Cuban (1992)

- *Three generations of women led by widowed matriarch Celia del Pino, a loyal Cuban patriot living with her troubled daughter, a second daughter thriving on American life, and a rebellious teenager who feels connected to her grandmother.*

Last year she joined the local auxiliary police out of some misplaced sense of civic duty. My mother—all four feet eleven and a half inches and 217 pounds of her—patrols the streets of Brooklyn at night in a skintight uniform, clanging with enough antiriot gear to quash another Attica. She practices twirling her nightstick in front of the mirror, then smacks it against her palm, steadily, menacingly, like she's seen cops do on television. Mom's upset because the police department won't issue her a gun. Right. She gets a gun and I move out of state fast.

— **Christina Garcia** *(1958-) Cuban-born American journalist and novelist*

The Autumn of the Patriarch (1976)

- *The grim portrait of a Caribbean tyrant and the corruption of power.*

. . . he saw the bonfire that had been lighted on the main square to burn the official portraits and the almanac lithographs that had been in all places and at all times ever since the beginning of his regime, and he saw his own body dragged by as it left behind along the street a trail of medals and epaulets, dolman buttons, strands of brocade and frog embroidery and tassels from playing-card sabers and the ten sad pips of the king of the universe, mother, look what they've done to me, he said, feeling in his own flesh the ignominy of the spitting and the sickbed pans that were thrown on him from the balconies as he went by, horrified with the idea of being quartered and devoured by dogs and vultures amidst the delirious howls and the roar of fireworks celebrating the carnival of my death.

— **Gabriel Garcia Marquez** *(1927-) Colombian novelist, short story writer, screenwriter and journalist*

Chronicle of a Death Foretold (1983)

- *The brothers of a young bride found to have already lost her virginity are bound by honor to kill the man responsible.*

On the morning of his death, in fact, Santiago Nasar hadn't had a moment of doubt, in spite of the fact that he knew very well what the price of the insult imputed to him was. He was aware of the prudish disposition of his world, and he must have understood that the twins' simple nature was incapable of resisting an insult. No one knew Bayardo San Roman very well, but Santiago Nasar knew him well enough to know that underneath his worldly airs he was as subject as anyone else to his native prejudices. So the murdered man's refusal to worry could have been suicide. Besides, when he finally learned at the last moment that the Vicario brothers were waiting for him to kill him, his reaction was not one of panic, as has so often been said, but rather the bewilderment of innocence.

— Gabriel Garcia Marquez

Love in the Time of Cholera (1985)

- *A half-century story of the unrequited love of Florentino Ariza, a lovesick romantic, for Fermina Daza, completely devoted to her physician husband dedicated to the eradication of cholera.*

"And speaking hypothetically," he said, "would it be possible to make a trip without stopping, without cargo or passengers, without coming into, any port, without anything."

The Captain said that it was possible, but only hypothetically. . . . The only thing that would allow them to bypass all that was a case of cholera on board. The ship would be quarantined, it would hoist the yellow flag and sail in a state of emergency. Captain Samaritano had needed to do just that on several occasions because of the many cases of cholera along the river, although later the health authorities had obliged the doctors to sign death certificates that called the cases common dysentery. Besides, many times in the history of the river the yellow plague flag had been flown in order to evade taxes, or to avoid picking up an undesirable passenger, or to elude inopportune inspections. Florentino Ariza reached for Fermina Daza's hand under the table.

"Well, then," he said, "let's do that."

The Captain was taken by surprise, but then, with the instinct of an old fox, he saw everything clearly.

— Gabriel Garcia Marquez

One Hundred Years of Solitude (1967)

- *The story of life in a Colombian village and that of the founder's family over a period of 100 years.*

One September morning, after having coffee in the kitchen with Aureliano, Jose Arcadio was finishing his daily bath when through the openings in the tiles the four children he had expelled from the house burst in. Without giving him time to defend himself, they jumped into the pool fully clothed, grabbed him by the hair, and held his head under the water until the bubbling of his death throes ceased on the surface and his silent and pale dolphin body slipped down to the bottom of the fragrant water. Then they took out the three sacks of gold from the hiding place which was known only to them and their victim. It was such a rapid, methodical, and brutal action that it was like a military operation.

— **Gabriel Garcia Marquez**

October Light (1976)

- *A penniless widow returns to live in the Vermont farmhouse of her older brother, with stubborn and bizarre consequences.*

"I hear you," the old woman called back.

"Well, are you coming out or *not*?" she demanded.

"Not," the old woman said. "I told you that. If I'm going to be treated like an animal, I might's well be penned up like one."

"Ha!" Ginny's father broke in from downstairs. "Animals at least got some use in the world."

"You see what he thinks of me?" the old woman whined. Possibly she was crying.

"Animals at least earn their keep," he called.

"I don't ask any keep," the old woman called back—half convincing herself, the way it sounded—"just a little room to die in."

"Aunt Sally," Ginny called, "You've got to come out and *eat* something." Her voice was sharper than every now, annoyed, maybe, by the sentimental talk about dying.

"Don't want to," the old woman called back just as sharply.

It sounded final . . .

— **John Gardner** *(1933-1982) American novelist, essayist and literary critic*

Preston Falls (1998)

- *Doug Willis takes a break to unwind from his New York City job and escape the pressures of his family life.*

"I'm sorry, sir," the cop says. Embroidered patch on his sleeve says SHERIFFS DEPT: no apostrophe, no period. "I've been requested to escort you out of the park."

Jean and Mel both look at Willis.

"Whoa, wait a minute. Let me explain what happened." He pauses before launching in.

"You can explain on the way to your vehicle, sir.

Your family can join you outside the main gate. But you need to leave right now sir." He comes a step closer to Willis and nods toward the path.

"This is unreal," says Willis. "You're kicking *them* out too? For what? They weren't even *there*."

"What is going on, please?" Jean says.

"I'm sorry, ma'am." The cop gives her a glance, then turns his eyes back on Willis. "There was an altercation with a park personnel which led to abusive language being used by this gentleman."

"*You're* a smooth son of a bitch," says Willis.

The cop doesn't move, but he's clearly gone to a higher state of alert: his eyes move from side to side, in case this character has buddies. "It's necessary for him to leave the park immediately."

— **David Gates** *(1947-) American journalist and novelist*

Jump-Off Creek (1989)

- *The brutal hardships of frontier life in Oregon during the 1890s as experienced by a widowed woman homesteader.*

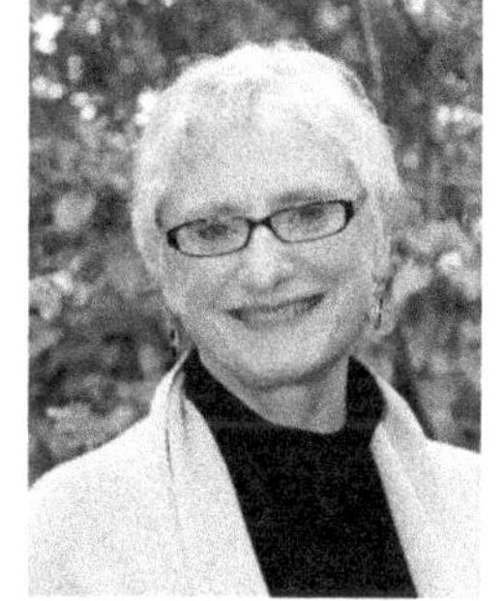

He stopped his horse and waited. She was tall as a man, lean, and as old as Danny Turnbow. There were muddy fingerprints on the brim of her old man's hat, as if she had taken it off or set it on with dirty hands. She stood stiffly along the hole the goats had made in the dead-hedge and looked back at him. He dropped his own look down to his cold hand clasping the reins.

"Ma'am," he said, without looking at her. He didn't say anything about the goats. "The squatters' rights been already taken up here," he said in a low voice. "Me and two others have been living here all winter." He had thought out how much of a lie to tell, and he delivered it as briefly as might be. "I don't mind sharing the roof with your family tonight, though, since it's raining."

The woman's face set slowly, not quite as if he had provoked her, but as if she was getting hold of a stubbornness. She pushed her hands down in the pockets of her big coat. "I have bought the deed outright from Mr. Angel," she said in a level voice, cold as clay. He could tell it was the truth just the way she stood there, and a little heat began to come up in his neck. He felt stupid, all at once.

— **Molly Gloss** *(1944-) American writer of historical and science fiction*

Faust (play) (1808)

- *Dr. Faust becomes convinced of the futility of man. Mephistopheles makes a wager with the Lord that he, the Devil, can win Faust's soul.*

THE ALMIGHTY

Although he serves me now bewilderedly,

I soon will lead him where the light is clear.
Does not the gardener know, when fresh green
tips the tree,
That flower and fruit will deck the coming year!

MEPHISTOPHELES

What do you wager? You will lose that man
If you permit me then to lead
Him subtly into the path I plan

THE ALMIGHTY

As long as he remains on earth—agreed!
Nothing is forbidden you contrive;
Man errs so long as he will strive.

— **Johann Wolfgang von Goethe** *(1749-1832) German writer and polymath*

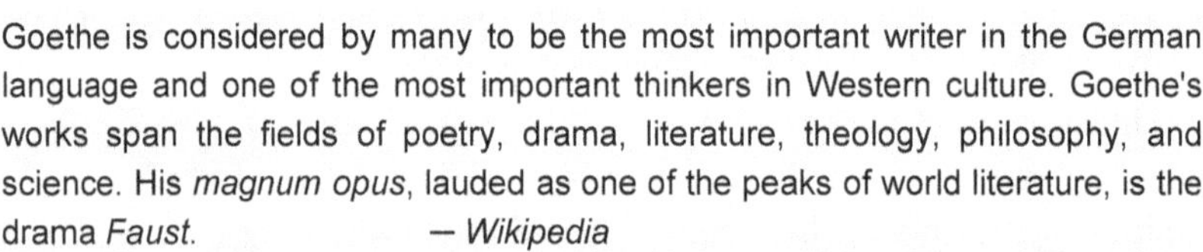

Goethe is considered by many to be the most important writer in the German language and one of the most important thinkers in Western culture. Goethe's works span the fields of poetry, drama, literature, theology, philosophy, and science. His *magnum opus*, lauded as one of the peaks of world literature, is the drama *Faust*. — *Wikipedia*

Dead Souls (1842)

- *The exploits of Chichikov, a young gentleman who tries to make a good name for himself by spending lavishly while engaged in a macabre moneymaking scheme of acquiring "dead souls."*

All the time that Nozdrev was chattering away Chichikov had kept rubbing his eyes, wishing to make sure whether he were hearing all this in a dream or in reality. Turing out counterfeit notes—abduction of the Governor's daughter—the death of the Public Prosecutor, of which he was apparently the cause—arrival of the Governor General—all these statements had thrown him into a considerable fright. "Well, if things have come to such a pass," he thought to himself, "then there's no use hanging around here; I'll have to make tracks out of here fast as I can."

— **Nikolai Gogol** *(1809-1852) Russian novelist, humorist and dramatist*

Lord of the Flies (1954)

- *A group of military school boys stranded on a deserted island develop their own society which eventually leads to frightening consequences.*

. . . Ralph looked at him dumbly. For a moment he had a fleeting picture of the strange glamour that had once invested the beaches. But the island was scorched up like dead wood—Simon was dead—and Jack had . . . .

The tears began to flow and sobs shook him. He gave himself up to them now for the first time on the island; great, shuddering spasms of grief that seemed to wrench his whole body. His voice rose under the black smoke before the burning wreckage of the island; and infected by that emotion, the other little boys began to shake and sob too. And in the middle of them, with filthy body, matted hair, and unwiped nose, Ralph wept for the end of innocence, the darkness of man's heart, and the fall through the air of the true, wise friend called Piggy.

— **William Golding** *(1911-1993) British novelist, poet and playwright*

During World War II, Golding fought in the Royal Navy and was briefly involved in the pursuit and sinking of Germany's mightiest battleship, the *Bismarck*. He also participated in the invasion of Normandy on D-Day, commanding a landing ship that fired salvoes of rockets onto the beaches, and again in naval action at Walcheren in which 23 out of 24 assault craft were sunk. — *Wikipedia*

Oblomov (1859)

- *The midlife crisis of a middle class son with a slothful attitude towards life who raises this trait to an art form.*

'Even if we did marry, what would come of it?' she asked.

He said nothing.

'You would sink into deeper and deeper sleep every day — isn't that so? And I? You see what I am. I shall never grow old or be tired of life. And with you I should be living from day to day, waiting for Christmas, then to the Carnival, paying calls, dancing, and not thinking of anything . . . Do you call that life? I should pine away, I should die. . . . What for, Ilya? Would you be happy? . . .'

He painfully looked at the ceiling, wanted to move, to run away, but his legs would not obey him. He wanted to say something, but his mouth was dry, his tongue would not move, he could not command his voice. He put out his hand to her.

— **Ivan Goncharov** *(1812-1891) Russian novelist*

My Son's Story (1990)

- *A black teacher whose revolutionary efforts, imprisonment, and extramarital affair with a white human rights activist profoundly affect his family.*

She is blonde, my father's woman. Of course. What else would she be? How else would he be caught, this man who has traveled so far from all the humble traps of our kind, drink, glue-sniffing, wife-beating, loud-mouthed capering, obsequious bumming (please my master ag please my baas), and all the sophisticated traps of lackeyism, corruption, nepotism, that wait for men who take privilege at the expense of the lives of others, and of their own self-respect. Self-respect! It's been his religion, his godhead. It's never failed him, when he wanted to know what course to take next: his inner signpost, his touchstone. Do what will enable you to keep your self-respect.

— **Nadine Gordimer** *(1923-) South African writer and political activist*

Final Payments (1978)

- *A daughter takes care of her invalid father in their home for eleven years as an expected duty and out of guilt from past events and her intense love for him.*

And now they were burying my father, because something had to be done with the bodies of the dead. It was the end of my life as well. After they lowered his body, I would have to invent an existence for myself. Care of an invalid has this great virtue: one never has to wonder what there is to do. Life is simple and inevitable and straightforward. Even the tedium has its seduction; empty time has always been earned. One can, if one chooses, leave it simply empty. My life had the balletic attraction of routine. Eleven years of it: bringing him breakfast, shaving him, hating to look at his face, twisted from the stroke in a way that made me forget the possibility of beauty.

— **Mary Gordon** *(1949-) American writer*

Six Days of the Condor (1975)

- *A small investigative branch of the CIA has been hit and wiped out propelling Malcolm, the only survivor, into a world of double agents and hired killers.*

Just before Malcolm came around the corner from the kitchen he heard the click when the mailman armed the sten gun. . . . That Malcolm didn't die then may be credited to the fact that when he turned the corner and saw the gun swinging toward him he didn't stop to think. He threw the pot of boiling coffee and the empty cup straight at the mailman.

From the movie this ominous prediction from the hired killer to the story's hero (Robert Redford) concerning his ill-fated future with the agency.

You have not much future there. It will happen this way. You may be walking. Maybe the first sunny day of the spring. And a car will slow beside you, and a door will open, and someone you know, maybe even trust, will get out of the car. And he will smile, a becoming smile. But he will leave open the door of the car and offer to give you a lift.

— **James Grady** *(1949-) Author of thriller novels*

The Wind in the Willows (1908)

- *The escapades of four animal friends, who live along a river in the English countryside—Toad, Mole, Rat, and Badger.*

The car stood in the middle of the yard, quite unattended, the stablehelps and other hangers-on being all at their dinner. Toad walked slowly round it, inspecting, criticizing, musing deeply.

"I wonder," he said to himself presently, "I wonder if this sort of car *starts* easily?"

Next moment, hardly knowing how it came about, he found he had hold of the handle and was turning it. As the familiar sound broke forth, the old passion seized on Toad and completely mastered him, body and soul. As if in a dream he found himself, somehow, seated in the driver's seat; as if in a dream, he pulled the lever and swung the car round the yard and out through the archway; and, as if in a dream, as sense of Right and wrong, all fear of obvious consequences, seemed temporarily suspended. He increased his pace . . .

— **Kenneth Grahame** *(1859-1932)*
Scottish writer

The Flounder (1978)

- *A creation myth seen through the eyes of a reincarnated man and a kind of fairy-godfather immortal talking fish.*

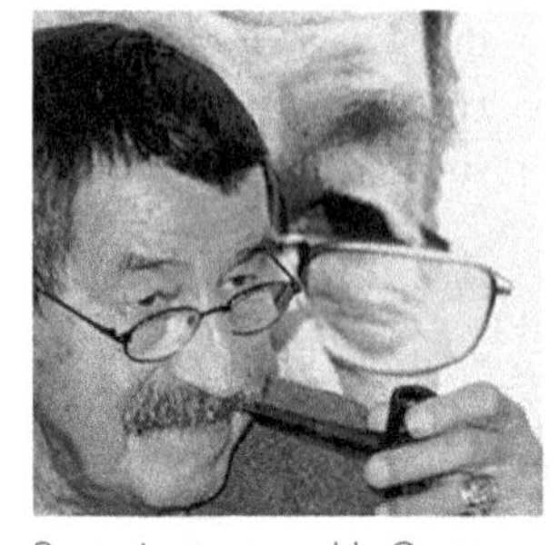

Seventeen-year-old Grass saw combat with the 10th SS Panzer Division Frundsberg in 1945 until he was wounded in April and sent to an American POW camp.

So Dorothea went to see the Flounder. She took with her all her beauty and untarnished youth. One Friday, after simmering Scania herrings in onion broth. She was wearing her long (penitential) gown of nettles, and her hair was unbound.

I had instructed her, "You must go into the sea. When you are up to your knees, call him several times, give him my regards. Then he'll come, and perhaps if you kiss him he'll tell you something. Wish for something; wish for something."

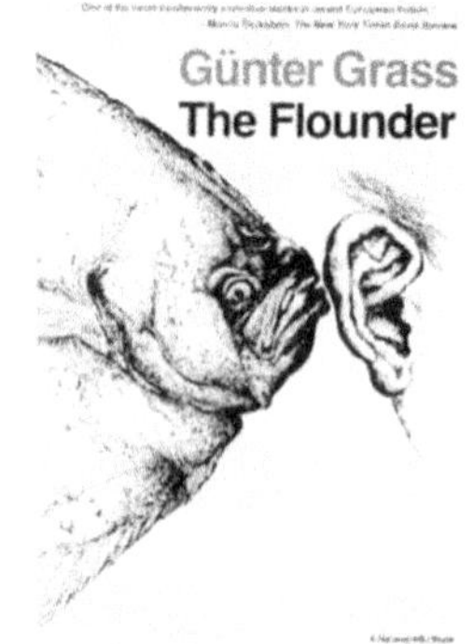

So Dorothea went straight down the beach, making tracks with her bare feet, to the shallows where the halfhearted Baltic waves petered out. Then she gathered her gown of nettles. Up to her knees she stood in the lazy water, and her cry smelled of herring as she cried, "Flounder, cum oute, ich wol kisse they snoute."

— **Gunter Grass** *(1927-) German author and playwright*

The Tin Drum (1959)

- *The autobiography of Oskar Matzerath who at the age of three, disillusioned with the adult world, decides not to grow up, retaining the stature of a child with his treasured possession a tin drum.*

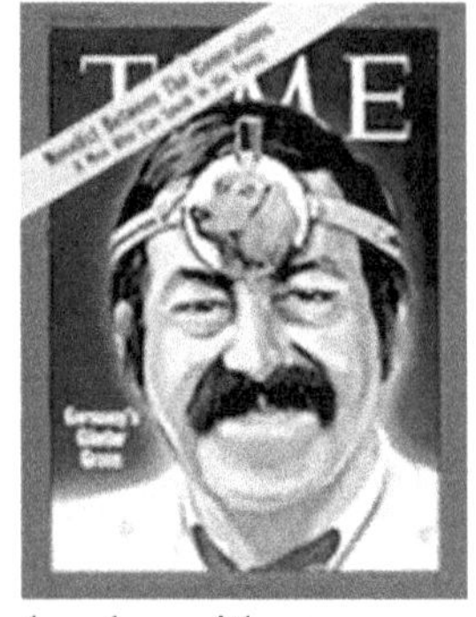

As Bruno has already said, Oskar has lovely, expressive hands, fine wavy hair, and those winning, ever so blue, Bronski eyes. Possibly the attractiveness of my hands, eyes, and hair was accentuated by my hump and the shocking proximity of my chin to my narrow, vaulted chest. It was not infrequent, in any case, that as I was sitting in the nurses' room, they would take hold of my hands, play with my fingers, fondle my hair, and say to one another in leaving: "When you look into his eyes, you forget all the rest."

Thus I was superior to my hump and I might well have attempted a conquest in the hospital if I had still had my drum, if I had been able to count on my reliable drummer's potency of former years. As it was, I felt unsure of myself and my physical reactions and I would leave the hospital after these affectionate hors d'oeuvres, fearing to reach out for the main course.

— **Gunter Grass**

The Keepers of the House (1964)

- *The story of a wealthy white widower and young black girl who becomes his maid and the love that they share over a lifetime.*

She did not say no sir. Most Negroes would have. William wondered: "You from around here?"

For the first time she moved her head, Negro-like, self-effacing. "Down there."

"Whose place?"

"Abner Carmichael." . . .

"I heard of him," William said. "You his daughter?"

"Granddaughter."

He smiled at her quick correction. "I reckon you don't look old enough to be much else."

"I'm eighteen," she said.

He just smiled again, and nodded.

She added: "My name's Margaret."

That was the way it began. That was how he found Margaret, washing clothes by a creek that didn't have a name. She lived with him all the rest of his life, the next thirty years.

Living with him, she lived with us all, all the Howlands, and her life got mixed up with ours. Her face was black and ours were white, but we were together anyhow. Her life and his. And ours.

— **Shirley Ann Grau** *(1929-) American novelist and short story writer*

I, Claudius (1934)

- *Tiberius Claudius lived from 10 B.C. to 54 A.D. Although considered a weakling and dismissed as an idiot he survived the intrigues and poisonings that marked the reigns of Augustus, Tiberius, and the mad Caligula.*

Wounded so badly at the Battle of the Somme, Graves was officially reported as having died from his wounds.

The money went faster and faster and at last Caligula decided to make economies. He said one day, for instance, "What is the use of putting men in prison for forgery and theft and breaches of the peace? They don't enjoy themselves there and they are a great expense for me to feed and guard; yet if I were to let them go they would only start their career of crime again. I'll visit the prisons to-day and look into the matter." He did. He weeded out the men whom he considered the most hardened criminals, and had them executed. Their bodies were cut up and used as meat for the wild beasts waiting to be killed in the amphitheatre: which made it a double economy. Every month now he made his round of the prisons. Crime decreased slightly.

— **Robert Graves** *(1895-1985) English poet, translator and novelist*

Lanark (1981)

- *The two central books of this foursome follow the education and relationships of a young artist visionary to obsession and descent.*

. . . Yet it was magical that pig bristles fastened to a stick, spreading oily brown mud on a pale grey surface, could make a line of hills appear against a dawn sky. As he applied the paint his mind became a mere link between hand, colour, eye and ceiling. On descending to see the work from the church floor he had sometimes moments of selfish excitement, but his mind was sick of domineering over something as ramshackle as himself and glad to climb up again to where sight, thought, limbs, paint, feelings, and brushes were a kit of tools the picture needed to complete itself.

— **Alasdair Gray** *(1934-) Scottish writer and artist*

Loving (1945)

- *The contrasting interrelated lives of servants and masters in an Irish castle during World War II.*

'Well there's just the one thing for it,' Mrs Welch cried suddenly frantic, 'every mortal object must be under lock and key. There maun't be a drawer can be opened or a door they shall get in by. And as for my pots and pans I'll get me a padlock and chains and stake 'em down to me dresser,' she almost shouted pointing to the vast array of burnished copper and aluminum. 'And if I can't get a chain will go through them 'oles in the 'andles so 'elp me God I'll send to Berlin if I shouldn't find what'll suit in this poor law island.'

'To Berlin?' Mrs Welch answered and seemed gratified. 'We're in a nootral country aren't we?'

— **Henry Green** *(1905-1973) English author*

The Heart of the Matter (1948)

- *Scobie, a British assistant police commissioner stationed in a West African coastal town, struggles to remain faithful to his wife and religion while entranced by a nineteen-year old girl rescued at sea.*

Scobie walked rapidly back into the lounge. He went full tilt into an armchair and came to a halt. His vision moved jerkily back into focus, but sweat dripped into his right eye. The fingers that wiped it free shook like a drunkard's. He told himself: Be careful. This isn't a climate for emotion. It's a climate for meanness, malice, snobbery, but anything like hate or love drives a man off his head. He remembered Bowers sent home for punching the Governor's A.D.C. at a party, Makin the missionary who ended in an asylum at Chislehurst.

"In human relationships, kindness and lies are worth a thousand truths."

'It's damned hot,' he said to someone who loomed vaguely beside him.

'You look bad, Scobie. Have a drink.'

— **Graham Greene** *(1904-1991) English author, playwright and literary critic*

The Way West (1949)

- *The experience of the Oregon Trail in 1846 from Independence, Missouri, to Fort Vancouver in Oregon.*

That was a thing that bothered a man—the thirst and growing weakness and most of all the hunger of cattle and horses and teams. Driving, a teamster saw the sagging pockets beyond the hipbones of his oxen and the chained knuckles of their backs. When he unyoked, they looked at him softly, their eyes reproachful, as if to ask how he could treat them so. And sometimes under yoke they just lay down, and no goad or whip or fork could get them up again, and a man trying felt more brutish than his brutes. They left them where they lay, with what life remained in them, thinking they had earned the slim chance of a miracle, and sometimes put plunder from the wagons with them—a chest or favorite chair or grinding stone—for every pound now counted.

Guthrie wrote the script for the 1953 Western film *Shane*.

— **A. B. Guthrie, Jr.** *(1901-1991) American novelist and historian*

H

The Maltese Falcon (1930)

- *Private detective Sam Spade seeks both his partner's killer and the titular statue after a beautiful redhead begs for his help.*

As a veteran of two World Wars, Hammett is buried at Arlington National Cemetery.

The girl had left the door and, edging around the dead man with her face turned away, had come to Spade's side. As she stood there—hands on a corner of the desk—watching him pull the rope loose and push aside brown paper, excitement began to supplant nausea in her face. 'Do you think it is?' she whispered.

'We'll soon know,' Spade said, his big fingers busy with the inner husk of coarse grey paper, three sheets thick, that the brown paper's removal had revealed. His face was hard and dull. His eyes were shining. When he had put the grey paper out of the way he had an egg-shaped mass of pale excelsior, wadded tight. His fingers tore the wad apart and then he had the foot-high figure of a bird, black as coal and shiny where its polish was not dulled by wood-dust and fragments of excelsior.

Spade laughed. He put a hand down on the bird. His wide-spread fingers had ownership in their curving. He put his other arm around Effie Perine and crushed her body against his. 'We've got the damned thing, angel,' he said.

— **Dashiell Hammett** *(1894-1961) American author of hard-boiled detective novels and short-stories*

Hunger (1890)

- *The suffering of a young writer living on the edge of starvation, existing on handouts and puny payments for his occasional articles accepted by the local newspaper.*

But then I stopped once more. I must be unbelievably thin. My eyes would soon be all the way through my head. I wonder how I actually look? What in the hell is gong on that a man has to turn himself into a living freak out of sheer hunger? I felt rage one more time, its final flaring up, a muscular spasm. "What's wrong with your face, eh?" Here I was walking around with a better head than anyone else in the country, and a pair of fists that could, so help me God, grind a longshoreman into small bits, into powder, and I was becoming a freak from hunger in the middle of the city of Christiania! Was there any sense or reason in that?

— **Knut Hamsun** *(1859-1952) Norwegian author*

Hamsun's reputation was severely tarnished by his vehement advocacy of Nazi Germany both before World War II and after Germany occupied Norway in April, 1940. He lionized leading Nazis and in 1943, in the middle of the war, he mailed his Nobel medal to Joseph Goebbels. Later, he visited Hitler and in a eulogy for the German leader published on May 7, 1945 — one day before surrender of the German occupation forces in Norway — Hamsun proclaimed, "He was a warrior, a warrior for mankind, and a prophet of the gospel of justice for all nations." After the war, due to a finding that Hamsun was in mental decline, efforts to prosecute him for treason were dropped. Nearly 60 years after his death, a recent biographer told a reporter, "We can't help loving him, though we have hated him all these years. That's our Hamsun trauma. He's a ghost that won't stay in the grave." — *Wikipedia*

Mysteries (1892)

- *A visiting young man turns everything around in a small Norwegian community through his surreal ideas, his money, and the help of a midget resident.*

Once more an evil force had crossed his path! He couldn't grasp it. Painstakingly he went over every detail. The only thing he was sure of was that he wasn't dead.

He picked up the vial, got to his feet, and walked a few steps. Why was there always an obstacle when he tried to do something? What had gone wrong with the poison? It was prussic acid: a doctor had assured him that it was more than enough, and in fact, he had killed the parson's dog with a single drop of it. And he was positive that it was the same vial; it had been half full. He remembered having noted that before he swallowed the contents. The vial had never changed hands, either; he always carried it in his vest pocket. What were these evil forces that dogged his every step?

Then it struck him like a thunderbolt that the vial had been in other hands after all! Almost involuntarily, he stopped and snapped his fingers.

— **Knut Hamsun**

Atticus (1996)

- *Atticus Cody goes to Mexico to retrieve the body of his younger son and comes to believe that his death may not have been a suicide.*

. . . She felt his heat and faced him with the fierce concentration of a good student who'd been fretting her sentences for a while. "You have to remember that he was my friend," she said. "And he let me find him like that. I feel used. Violated. I'm finding it hard to imagine his suicide as anything but a horrible act of aggression."

Atticus thought better of his anger and just walked around to the right of the car and got in. Everything was beginning to seem wrong to him. Emotionally off. Renata got in and turned the key in the ignition, and there was a sheen to her eyes that was such good acting he wanted to congratulate her for it. He looked out the side window. "Don't see his motorcycle," he said.

"The police have it. *Evidencia.* Stuart can get his things from the authorities and ship them to Colorado. You'll probably want us to sell his Harley though, won't you?"

"Oh, I expect."

She asked, "Are you thinking of flying out tomorrow?"

She seemed pleased when he said yes.

— **Ron Hansen** *(1947-) American novelist and essayist*

Sleepless Nights (1979)

- *An imaginative and partly autobiographical reflection on the "failures and recoveries of love, the life of the streets, and the inner life of an American woman."*

Miss Lavore had a life. Nearly every night of the week she went to Arthur Murray's dancing classes. A framed, autographed portrait of Murray and his wife hung over her bed. It would be florid to say it hung there like a religious icon, but certainly the two secular persons filled Miss Lavore's heart with gratitude. It could be said they had changed her life.

Miss Lavore was large and strong and homely and in her late fifties. At the end of the working day, she came home on the subway, came home alert with energy for her dancing, convivial nights. She cooked dinners rather more substantial than the usual, had a spell with the radio and the shower and then reappeared in her full-skirted dresses. They were of the brightest, harshest colors: robin's-egg blue, cherry, and Kelly green. With them she wore her serviceable black suede pumps. Colored glass earrings and pins matched with her bright dresses. Coty's cologne scented her strong arms. A daunting sight.

— **Elizabeth Hardwick** *(1916-2007)*
American literary critic, novelist and short-story writer

IV

Jude the Obscure (1895)

- *The story of Jude Fawley who falls in love with his cousin, Sue Bridehead, living together and having several children until she eventually returns to her husband.*

'At first I did not love you, Jude; that I own. When I first knew you I merely wanted you to love me. I did not exactly flirt with you; but that inborn craving which undermines some women's morals almost more than unbridled passion—the craving to attract and captivate, regardless of the injury it may do the man—was in me; and when I found I had caught you, I was frightened. And then—I don't know how it was—I couldn't bear to let you go—possibly to Arabella again—and so I got to love you, Jude. But you see, however fondly it ended, it began in the selfish and cruel wish to make your heart ache for me without letting mine ache for you.'

— **Thomas Hardy** *(1840-1928) English novelist and poet*

The Mayor of Casterbridge (1886)

- *The tragedy of Michael Henchard, an impulsive and aggressive merchant, who secures the help of Donald Farfrae in building up his business, then turns against his popular partner and his presumed daughter Elizabeth-Jane as well when he learns she is attracted to Farfrae.*

They stood in silence while he ran into the cottage; returning in a moment with a crumpled scrap of paper. On it there was penciled as follows: —

'MICHAEL HENCHARD'S WILL

'That Elizabeth-Jane Farfrae be not told of my death, or made to grieve on account of me.

'& that I be not bury'd in consecrated ground.

'& that no sexton be asked to toll the bell.

'& that nobody is wished to see my dead body.

'& that no murners walk behind me at my funeral.

'& that no flours be planted on my grave.

'& that no man remember me.

'To this I put my name.

'MICHAEL HENCHARD'

'What are we to do?' said Donald, when he had handed the paper to her.

She could not answer distinctly. 'O Donald!' she said at last through her tears, 'what bitterness lies there! O I would not have minded so much if it had not been for my unkindness at the last parting! . . . But there's no altering—so it must be.'

— **Thomas Hardy**

Tess of the D'Urbervilles (1891)

- *Heroine Tess, a poor English girl, is seduced by a cruel employer, then meets a man who loves her but departs upon learning her past.*

'Tess!' he said huskily, 'can you forgive me for going away? Can't you — come to me? How do you get to be — like this?'

'It is too late,' said she, her voice sounding hard through the room, her eyes shining unnaturally.

'I did not think rightly of you — I did not see you as you were!' he continued to plead. 'I have learnt to since, dearest Tessy mine!'

'Too late, too late!' she said, waving her hand in the impatience of a person whose tortures cause every instant to seem an hour. 'Don't come close to me, Angel! No — you must not. Keep away.'

'But don't you love me, my dear wife, because I have been so pulled down by illness? You are not so fickle — I am come on purpose for you — my mother and father will welcome you now!'

'Yes — O, yes, yes! But I say, I say it is too late.'

— **Thomas Hardy**

The Go-Between (1953)

- *Young Leo, on summer holiday from boarding school, becomes a secret "go-between" for the daughter of the host family and a nearby tenant farmer*

© NPG x20436

Do you remember what that summer was like?—how much more beautiful than any since? Well, what was the most beautiful thing in it? Wasn't it us, and our feeling for each other? Didn't you realize it when you took our letters for us? Didn't you feel that all the rest—the house, the people coming and going—just didn't count? And wouldn't you feel proud to be descended from our union—the child of so much happiness and beauty?"

What could I say but yes?

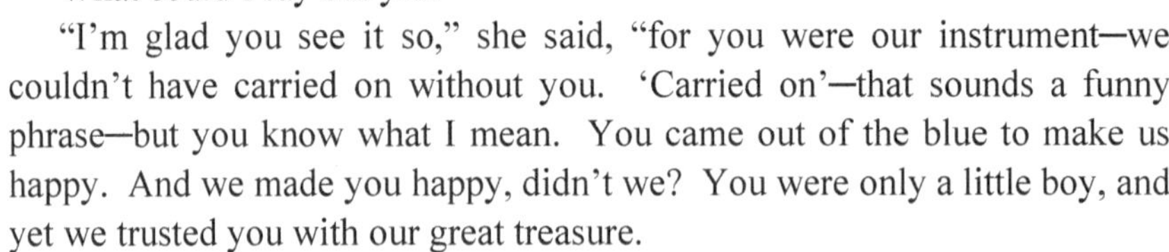

"I'm glad you see it so," she said, "for you were our instrument—we couldn't have carried on without you. 'Carried on'—that sounds a funny phrase—but you know what I mean. You came out of the blue to make us happy. And we made you happy, didn't we? You were only a little boy, and yet we trusted you with our great treasure.

— **L. P. Hartley** *(1895-1972) British novelist*

You Are Not a Stranger Here (2002)

- *A debut collection of stories of depression, mental illness, adolescence, and suffering by a compassionate writer.*

She lowered her glance momentarily to look Frank in the eye. She had a handsome, slightly gaunt face, powerful green eyes, a strong, almost male jawline; her black hair was brushed back off her high forehead. Frank didn't often see female patients with such a self-possessed demeanor. . . .

Mrs. Buckholdt leaned back in the couch and gave a small frown of acknowledgment, as if to say, yes it was a pity more couldn't go. As she relaxed, a remnant of what must have once been coquettishness surfaced in her face, and Frank glimpsed how she must have looked to the other high school kids, the ones who'd never dreamt of leaving.

. . . Her eyes came to rest on the floor by her feet. "Are you married, Dr. Briggs?"

There was a familiarity, almost a caring, to the way she asked the question, as though she were inquiring not for her own information but to give him the chance to tell her.

— **Adam Haslett** *(1970-) American fiction writer*

The Blithedale Romance (1852)

- *A depressing tale of friendship and love torn asunder by self interests, ultimately ending in tragedy and death.*

c. 1865 photo

She gave me her hand, with the same free, whole-souled gesture as on the first afternoon of our acquaintance, and, being greatly moved, I bethought me of no better method of expressing my deep sympathy than to carry it to my lips. In so doing, I perceived that this white hand—so hospitably warm when I first touched it, five months since was now cold as a veritable piece of snow.

"How very cold!" I exclaimed, holding it between both my own, with the vain idea of warming it. "What can be the reason? It is really death-like!"

"The extremities die first, they say," answered Zenobia, laughing. "And so you kiss this poor, despised, rejected hand! Well, my dear friend, I thank you. You have reserved your homage for the fallen. Lip of man will never touch my hand again."

— **Nathaniel Hawthorne** *(1804-1864) American novelist and short story writer*

Hawthorne was almost pathologically shy, generally staying silent when at gatherings. His wife, Sophia, was also a reclusive person. Together they enjoyed a long marriage and had three children. He called their last child, Rose, "my autumnal flower". — *Wikipedia*

Hawthorne: Tales and Sketches (collection publication 1984)

- *All the tales and sketches of Nathaniel Hawthorne including his three books of stories. This quote from the classic "The Minister's Black Veil."*

. . . The first glimpse of the clergyman's figure was the signal for the bell to cease its summons.

'But what has good Parson Hooper got upon his face?' cried the sexton in astonishment.

By Charles Osgood, 1840

All within hearing immediately turned about, and beheld the semblance of Mr. Hooper, pacing slowly his meditative way towards the meeting-house. With one accord they started, expressing more wonder than if some strange minister were coming to dust the cushions of Mr. Hooper's pulpit.

. . . . The cause of so much amazement may appear sufficiently slight. Mr. Hooper, a gentlemanly person of about thirty, though still a bachelor, was dressed with due clerical neatness, as if a careful wife had starched his band, and brushed the weekly dust from his Sunday's garb. There was but one thing remarkable in his appearance. Swathed about his forehead, and hanging down over his face, so low as to be shaken by his breath, Mr. Hooper had on a black veil.

— Nathaniel Hawthorne

The Scarlet Letter (1850)

- *Hester Prynne, who gives birth after committing adultery, refuses to name the father and struggles to create a new life of repentance and dignity in puritan 17th century Boston.*

c. 1850 daguerreotype

. . . In a moment, however, wisely judging that one token of her shame would but poorly serve to hide another, she took the baby on her arm, and, with a burning blush, and yet a haughty smile, and a glance that would not be abashed, looked around at her townspeople and neighbors. On the breast of her gown, in fine red cloth, surrounded with an elaborate embroidery and fantastic flourishes of gold-thread, appeared the letter A. It was so artistically done, and with so much fertility and gorgeous luxuriance of fancy, that it had all the effect of a last and fitting decoration to the apparel which she wore; and which was of a splendor in accordance with the taste of the age, but greatly beyond what was allowed by the sumptuary regulations of the colony.

— Nathaniel Hawthorne

The Transit of Venus (1980)

- *A three decade saga of the inter-twining lives of Caro, Ted, and Paul, including this account of friend Victor's death occasioned by a forgone warning.*

"All the way up the road I was thinking, What if he wakes? I had only what you might call practical thoughts, no other realization, no hesitation. Then I thought, I can say I never got down to the bank. If Victor calls out, turns up, he can't know I was there. It was as if I'd forgotten the passer-by. So I made conversation with the constable and he at least was charmed. When we got up the rise to where I'd left the car, there was an exchange of signals, and a police car went slowly down the road to confirm it was clear. After some minutes, a small explosion, some smoke among the trees, and soon the sound of the water. It was over so quickly, in a moment–at first a flow, then gushing, and then, just as they had said, the rising of a crest at the narrow squeeze of the river, where it passed from our sight. The crest there reached to the top of the willows, and afterwards the trees hung down in the stream like wet hair, so that everything below was visible, even the little ledge where Victor had slept. And where now there was nothing to be seen."

– **Shirley Hazzard** *(1931-) Australian author, citizen of Great Britain and the United States*

Beowulf: A New Verse Translation (2000)

- *An Anglo-Saxon epic poem composed between the 7th and 10th centuries, translated here in convincing reality.*

Beowulf, son of Ecgtheow, spoke:
"Wise sir, do not grieve. It is always better
to avenge dear ones than to indulge in mourning.
For every one of us, living in this world
means waiting for our end. Let whoever can
win glory before death. When a warrior is gone,
that will be his best and only bulwark.
So arise, my lord, and let us immediately
set forth on the trail of this troll-dam.
I guarantee you: she will not get away,
not to dens under ground nor upland groves
nor the ocean floor. She'll have nowhere to flee to.
Endure our troubles to-day. Bear up
and be the man I expect you to be."

– **Seamus Heaney** *(1939-) Irish poet and writer*

Mister Roberts Play (1948)

- *Mister Roberts, a naval junior-grade lieutenant aboard a US cargo ship in the Pacific during World War II, stands up for his crew against the petty tyranny of the ship's commanding officer.*

. . . The Captain was sitting, reading, in the large chair of his cabin. In the cone of harsh light from the floor lamp he looked old, and not evil, but merely foolish. He glanced up at the knock on the opened door.

"Yeah," he said gruffly, "what is it?"

Ensign Pulver leaned a casual hand on the door jamb. "Captain," he said easily, "I just threw your damn palm trees over the side."

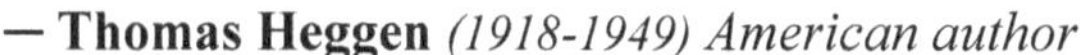

— **Thomas Heggen** *(1918-1949) American author*

Bewildered by the fame he had longed for and under pressure to turn out another bestseller, he found himself with a crippling case of writer's block. "I don't know how I wrote 'Mister Roberts'", he admitted to a friend. "It was spirit writing". — Wikipedia

Catch-22 (1955)

- *A parody of the "military mentality" where a bombardier during World War II desperately attempts to be declared insane in order to go home as he witnesses each of his crew die in combat.*

. . . There was only one catch and that was Catch-22, which specified that a concern for one's safety in the face of dangers that were real and immediate was the process of a rational mind. Orr was crazy and could be grounded. All he had to do was ask; and as soon as he did, he would no longer be crazy and would have to fly more missions. Orr would be crazy to fly more missions and sane if he didn't, but if he was sane he had to fly them. If he flew them he was crazy and didn't have to; but if he didn't want to he was sane and had to. Yossarian was moved very deeply by the absolute simplicity of this clause of Catch-22 and let out a respectful whistle.

"That's some catch, that Catch-22," he observed.

"It's the best there is," Doc Daneeka agreed.

Heller flew 60 combat missions which he described as largely milk-runs.

— **Joseph Heller** *(1923-1999)*
American novelist, short story writer and playwright

Ellis Island & Other Stories (1981)

- *A novella and ten short stories of remarkable range in such diverse locations as Ellis Island, Vermont, Brooklyn, and the Indian Ocean.*

Jim Harrison

I have not described everyone at that table. One remains. She was the daughter of my host, the eldest, the tallest, the most beautiful. Her name was Tamar, and as I had turned the corner she had seemed to rise in the air to meet me, while the others were lost in the dark. Tamar and I had faced one another in a moment of silence that I will not ever forget. Sometimes, on a windy day, crosscurrented waves in the shallows near a beach will spread about, trapped in a caldron of bars and brakes, until two run together face to face and then fall back in shocked tranquility. So it was with Tamar. It was as if I had run right into her. I was breathless, and I believe that she was, too.

— **Mark Helprin** *(1947-) American novelist and journalist*

A Farewell to Arms (1929)

- *A young American ambulance driver serving in the Italian army during World War I is wounded and falls in love with his English nurse's aide.*

18-year-old Hemmingway in 1918 photo in Italian Red Cross uniform.

. . . We stood in the rain and were taken out one at a time to be questioned and shot. So far they had shot every one they had questioned. The questioners had that beautiful detachment and devotion to stern justice of men dealing in death without being in any danger of it. They were questioning a full colonel of a line regiment. Three more officers had just been put in with us.

"Where was his regiment?"

I looked at the carabinieri. They were looking at the newcomers. The others were looking at the colonel. I ducked down, pushed between two men, and ran for the river, my head down. I tripped at the edge and went in with a splash. The water was very cold and I stayed under as long as I could. I could feel the current swirl me and I stayed under until I thought I could never come up.

— **Ernest Hemingway** *(1899-1961) American author and journalist*

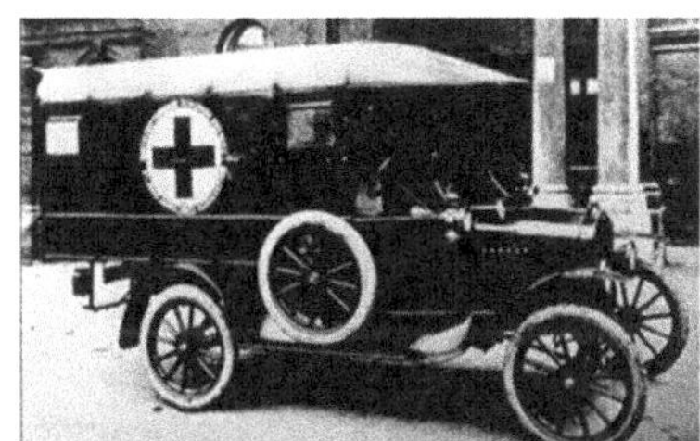

For Whom the Bell Tolls (1940)

■ *An American, Robert Jordan, assisting antifascist guerrilla forces in Spain, is torn between his sense of duty and newfound love of Maria, a young Spanish native whose life has been shattered by the war.*

He turned his head, sweating, and looked down the slope, then back toward where the girl was in the saddle with Pilar by her and Pablo just behind. "Now go," he said. "Go."

She started to look around. "Don't look around," Robert Jordan said. "Go." And Pablo hit the horse across the crupper with a hobbling strap and it looked as though Maria tried to slip from the saddle but Pilar and Pablo were riding close up against her and Pilar was holding her and the three horses were going up the draw.

Hemingway posing for a dust jacket photo by Lloyd Arnold for *For Whom the Bell Tolls*, at The Sun Valley Lodge, Idaho late, 1939.

"Roberto," Maria turned and shouted. "Let me stay! Let me stay!"

"I am with thee," Robert Jordan shouted. "I am with thee now. We are both there. Go!" Then they were out of sight around the corner of the draw and he was soaking wet with sweat and looking at nothing.

Agustin was standing by him.

"Do you want me to shoot thee, *Ingles*?" he asked, leaning down close. "*Quieres*? It is nothing."

"*No hace falta*," Robert Jordan said. "Get along. I am very well here."

"*Me cago en la leche que me han dado*!" Augustin said. He was crying so he could not see Robert Jordan clearly. "*Salud, Ingles*."

— Ernest Hemingway

A female friend of Hadley (Hemmingway's first wife), initially dubious that such a paragon could exist, was similarly impressed: Hemingway was "beautiful," she said, with a slender, graceful body, a face marked by perfect symmetry, and a handsome mouth "that stretched from ear to ear when he smiled." "He generated excitement because he was so intense about everything, about writing and boxing, about good food and drink. Everything we did took on new importance when he was with us.

Hadley's friend also noted how Hemingway's "focused attention [on] the person he was talking with was immensely flattering."

— Anthony Arthur, *Literary Feuds*

Men Without Women (1927)

■ *Short stories by the master, always rich in plot and setting, always beautifully written in Hemmingway's sparse penetrating style. This quote from "The Snows of Kilimanjaro."*

Just then the hyena stopped whimpering in the night and started to make a strange, human, almost crying sound. The woman heard it and stirred uneasily. She did not wake. In her dream she was at the house on Long Island and it was the night before her daughter's debut. Somehow her father was there and he was very rude. Then the noise the hyena made was so loud she woke and for a moment she did not know where she was and she was very afraid. Then she took the flashlight and shone it on the other cot that they had carried in after Harry had gone to sleep. She could see his bulk under the mosquito bar but somehow he had gotten his leg out and it hung down alongside the cot. The dressing had come down and she could not look at it.

"Molo," she called, "Molo! Molo!" Then she said, "Harry, Harry!" Then her voice rising, "Harry! Please. Oh Harry!"

There was no answer and she could not hear him breathing.

Outside the tent the hyena made the same strange noise that had awakened her. But she did not hear him for the beating of her heart.

— Earnest Hemingway

The Old Man and the Sea (1952)

- *An old Cuban fisherman goes far out in the Gulf Stream alone to fish after many days of failure. He catches a gigantic marlin which is devoured by sharks as he returns. Hemmingway described this book as "The best I can write ever for all my life."*

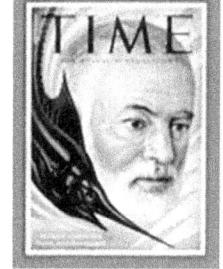

. . . He was an old man who fished alone in a skiff in the Gulf Stream and he had gone eight-four days now without taking a fish. In the first forty days a boy had been with him. But after forty days without a fish the boy's parents had told him that the old man was now definitely and finally *salao*, which is the worst form of unlucky, and the boy had gone at their orders in another boat which caught three good fish the first week.

— Ernest Hemingway

The Sun Also Rises (1926)

- *A 'lost generation' of post-war expatriates wanders about Europe including newspaperman Jake Harris, impotent due to a war wound, and his girl friend Lady Brett Ashley.*

. . . Robert Cohn was once middleweight boxing champion of Princeton. Do not think that I am very much impressed by that as a boxing title, but it meant a lot to Cohn. He cared nothing for boxing, in fact he disliked it, but he learned it painfully and thoroughly to counteract the feeling of inferiority and shyness he had felt on being treated as a Jew at Princeton. There was a certain inner comfort in knowing he could knock down anybody who was snooty to him, although, being very shy and a thoroughly nice boy, he never fought except in the gym. . . . .

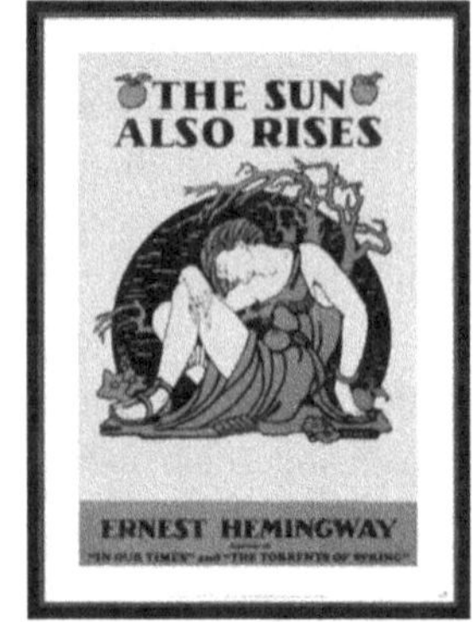

Women made such swell friends. Awfully swell. In the first place you had to be in love with a woman to have a basis of friendship. I had been having Brett for a friend. I had not been thinking about her side of it. I had been getting something for nothing. That only delayed the presentation of the bill. The bill always came. That was one of the swell things you could count on.

— **Ernest Hemingway**

The Lazarus Project (2008)

■ *The 1908 shooting of Lazarus Averbuch by the Chicago Chief of Police and subsequent investigation a century later.*

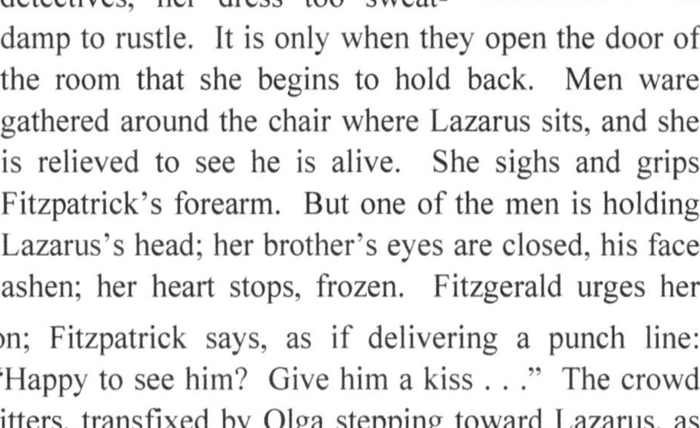

. . . Now the onlookers stand lined up in the long morgue hall, anticipating Olga's shock and pain, watching her with gloating curiosity. Oblivious to the surroundings, she walks slowly. She moves quietly between the detectives, her dress too sweat-damp to rustle. It is only when they open the door of the room that she begins to hold back. Men ware gathered around the chair where Lazarus sits, and she is relieved to see he is alive. She sighs and grips Fitzpatrick's forearm. But one of the men is holding Lazarus's head; her brother's eyes are closed, his face ashen; her heart stops, frozen. Fitzgerald urges her on; Fitzpatrick says, as if delivering a punch line: "Happy to see him? Give him a kiss . . ." The crowd titters, transfixed by Olga stepping toward Lazarus, as if she were mounted on cothurni: a short, reluctant step back, then two awkward steps forward to touch his lifeless cheek, whereupon she collapses, unconscious. The crowd gasps.

Captain Evans holding the body of Lazarus Averbuch, Chicago Historical Society.

— **Aleksandar Hemon** *(1964-) Bosnian American fiction writer*

The Collected Stories of Any Hempel (2006)

■ *Forty eight short stories (two of three are six pages or less in length); typically glimpses into the life of a female narrator.*

. . . I told him I looked forward to meeting them, even though it always seemed that the very things others find charming about your parents—the feyness, the provincialism, the odd takes on everything—are the things that make you want to rustle up a firing squad. . . .

. . . . When proud of himself, he chants tongue twisters for us. He made up "Shoes and socks shock Chatty." Sometimes when I pass his door at night, I can hear from behind it the rapid refrains of "sifted thistles" and "mixed biscuits."

. . . . Chatty warned me away from the fruit drinks, concocted as they are in the blender the gardener used once to whip up a frothy pitcher of mole repellant—equal parts cod liver oil and dish-washing detergent—which he painted along the rodents' corded trails in the garden. . . . .

The only time the word *baby* doesn't scare me is the time that it should, when it is what a man calls me. . . . .

A good day. The mound in the road was not cat, but tread.

— **Amy Hempel** *(1951-) American short story writer and journalist*

Collected Stories of O. Henry (1979)

- *Author of hundreds of short stories of early 1900 American life, O. Henry is perhaps best known for the paradoxical "The Gift of the Magi."*

"Jim, darling," she cried, "don't look at me that way. I had my hair cut off and sold it because I couldn't have lived through Christmas without giving you a present. It'll grow out again—you won't mind, will you? I just had to do it. . . . "

Jim drew a package from his overcoat pocket and threw it upon the table. . . . White fingers and nimble tore at the string and paper. And then an ecstatic scream of joy; and then, alas! a quick feminine change to hysterical tears and wails, necessitating the immediate employment of all the comforting powers of the lord of the flat.

For there lay The Combs—the set of combs, side and back, that Della had worshipped for long in a Broadway window. Beautiful combs, pure tortoise shell, with jeweled rims—just the shade to wear in the beautiful vanished hair. . . .

Jim had not yet seen his beautiful present. She held it out to him eagerly upon her open palm. . . .

. . . "Give me your watch. I want to see how it looks on it."

Instead of obeying, Jim tumbled down on the couch and put his hands under the back of his head and smiled. . . .

. . . "I sold the watch to get the money to buy your combs."

— **O. Henry** *(1862-1910) American writer*

Dune (1965)

■ *A science-fiction saga of intergalactic fiefdoms vying for power follows the plight of young Paul Atreides identified as a future leader.*

. . . And there was something else in his memory: a bargain. He could almost remember it.

The tooth!

He remembered part of it now: *a pill of poison gas shaped into a false tooth.*

Someone had told him to remember the tooth. The tooth was in his mouth. He could feel its shape with his tongue. All he had to do was bite sharply on it.

Not yet! . . .

"Too bad," the Baron muttered. He pushed himself back from the table, stood up lightly in his suspensors and hesitated, seeing a change come over the Duke. He saw the man draw in a deep breath, the jawline stiffen, the ripple of muscle there as the Duke clamped his mouth shut.

How he fears me! the Baron thought.

Shocked by fear that the Baron might escape him, Leto bit sharply on the capsule tooth, felt it break. He opened his mouth, expelled the biting vapor he could taste as it formed on his tongue. . . .

The Baron stood with his back against his private door, his own bolt hole behind the table. He had slammed it on a room full of dead men. His senses took in guards swarming around him. *Did I breath it?* he asked himself. *Whatever it was in there, did it get me, too?*

— **Frank Herbert** *(1920-1986) American science fiction writer*

The Child Buyer (1960)

■ *Mr. Jones has a plan for improving the nation by purchasing gifted children and reducing them to brilliant efficient thinking machines.*

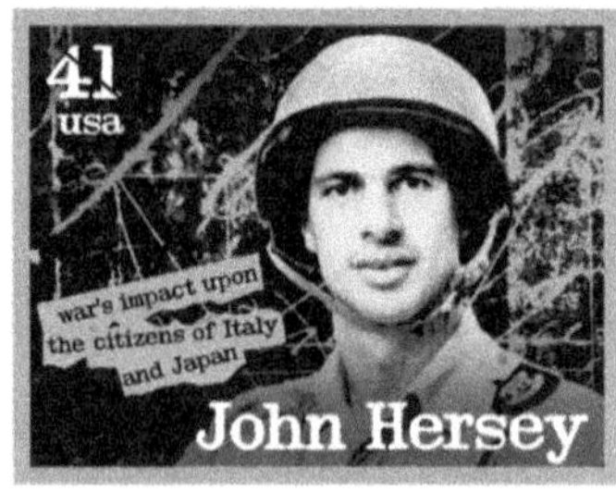

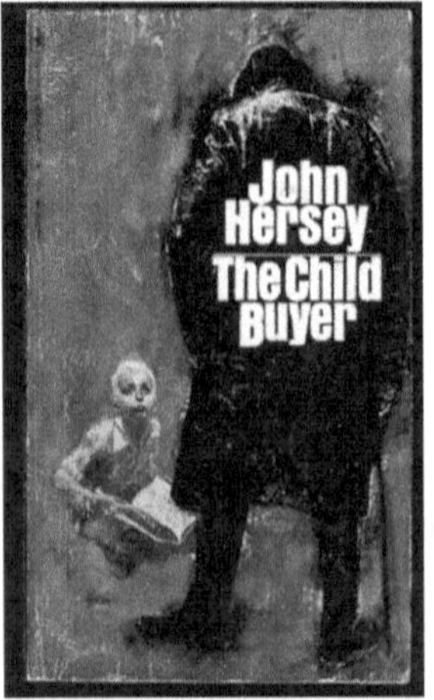

. . . 'You told me the other day, Cleary,' Mr. Jones said, 'that you're a realist. Now, I suggest we get down to brass tacks. I'm a businessman. I'm here to arrange a business deal. It doesn't seem to be a particularly popular one, so my job is to make it popular, and I'm prepared to pay the price, or prices, of making it popular. This boy sitting here is something I want. I want him very much. I'm satisfied, knowing his I.Q. and having observed his performance, that he is a reasonable specimen—that he's one in roughly five hundred thousand in our population; in other words, he has one of maybe the three hundred rarest potential minds in this country. I want him, and I'm going to get him.'

— **John Hersey** *(1914-1993) American writer and journalist*

Hersey's account of the aftermath of the atomic bomb dropped on Hiroshima, Japan, was adjudged the finest piece of journalism of the 20th century by a 36-member panel under the aegis of New York University's journalism department.
— *Wikipedia*

A Single Pebble (1956)

- *A young American engineer traveling up the Yangtze to inspect possible dam sites learns to appreciate the river people's ancient way of life.*

I was watching the trackers. These laborers fascinated me, and I had the habit of sitting by the hour observing them, while they scrambled from rock to rock on the riverbank, straining frightfully at their halters and dividing their heavy work evenly between them; or while they moved slowly, step by chanted step, along a level towing bund; or while they crept lynx-footed along a ledge on the wall of one of the gorges, hauling the clumsy junk against the powerful current. Their work had a long tradition behind it, as the fluted places on obstructing boulders proved, where tow ropes had dragged across the rocks for so many centuries that they had worn grooves—stone filed away by braided bamboo! . . . They marked time for (the head tracker's) songs with a repeated unison cry at the moment when all of them together planted each footstep: "Ayah! . . . Ayah! . . ." This rhythmic work-cry had an indescribably poignant sound.

— **John Hersey**

The Talented Mr. Ripley (1955)

- *Tom Ripley, hired to retrieve Dickie a wayward son, finds the lifestyle of wealth and sophistication overwhelmingly attractive.*

He wanted to kill Dickie. . . . He had failed with Dickie, in every way. He hated Dickie, because, however he looked at what had happened, his failing had not been his own fault, not due to anything he had done, but due to Dickie's inhuman stubbornness. And his blatant rudeness! He had offered Dickie friendship, companionship, and respect, everything he had to offer, and Dickie had replied with ingratitude and now hostility. Dickie was just shoving him out in the cold. If he killed him on this trip, Tom thought, he could simply say that some accident had happened. He could—He had just thought of something brilliant: he could become Dickie Greenleaf himself. He could do everything that Dickie did. He could go

back to Mongibello first and collect Dickie's things, tell Marge any damned story, set up an apartment in Rome or Paris, receive Dickie's cheque every month and forge Dickie's signature on it. He could step right into Dickie's shoes.

— **Patricia Highsmith** *(1921-1995) American novelist and short story writer*

The Mambo Kings Play Songs of Love (1989)

- *The lives of flashy, guitar-strumming Cesar Castillo and his timid, lovelorn brother as they cruise the East Coast club circuit.*

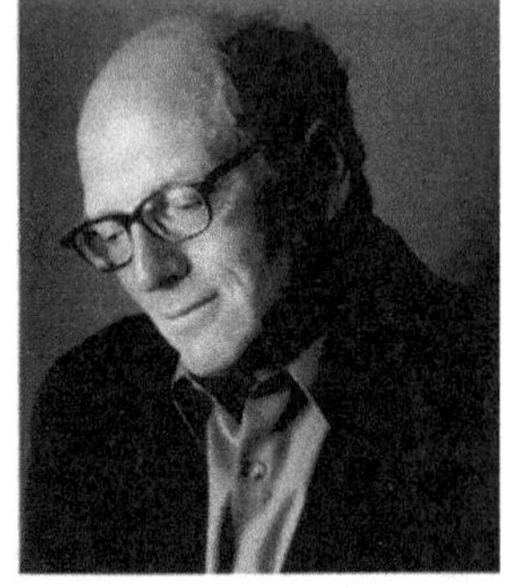

It had come down to this: he had turned around to find that the temporary job he'd taken to fill his idle days had lasted nearly twenty years.

Passing through the lobby, he would remember when he was a cocky and arrogant musician, and think to himself, Who would have dreamed that things would turn out this way? (And millions of people watching him on the rerun of the *I Love Lucy* show could never imagine that he had his own life, never see him as a super.) He'd gotten used to smelling like plumber's gum, his nails blackened with grease and oil. . . .

He went on the radio that year, a nostalgia hour. . . .

"My next guest today is someone who is very much a part of the scene in the fifties here in New York. It's my pleasure to introduce the bandleader and singer Cesar Castillo. Welcome." . . . (an interview follows)

"Well, now we're going to sign off, but before we do, I'm going to leave you with this fine little *cancion.*"

With that, the interviewer cued "Beautiful Maria of My Soul," which played out of windows, out of car radios, and at the beach, where fine young women lying out in the sun, bodies shiny with suntan lotion, and hearts filled with thoughts of the future heard the song.

Occasionally, he would get a call from an agent or a promoter talking about bringing him back into the public's eye.

Usually nothing happened.

— **Oscar Hijuelos** *(1951-) American journalist*

Riddley Walker (1981)

- *A twelve-year-old fights for survival amidst a fallen state where dogs have turned against humans.*

Going back slow then there come dogs follering on our track we hadn't seen none that day til then. Shapit black is how I think of them tho mos of them are patchy colourt. It's the hy leggitness of them. Ther thick necks and littl heads and littl ears. It wer the Bernt Arse pack with ther black and red spottit leader. All of them head down and slumping on behynt us jus out of bow shot. I wer looking at the leader and waiting for some thing I cud feal it in my froat. He dint have his head down he had it up and looking tords us.

— **Russell Hoban** *(1925-) American writer of fantasy, poetry, and children's books*

The Line of Beauty (2004)

- *Nick, a weak, pathetic, but intelligent young man, tries to achieve his aspirations by being essentially a parasite.*

Nick had no brothers or sisters but he was able to think of himself here as a lost middle child. . . . Toby himself had never perhaps known why he and Nick were friends, but had amiably accepted the evidence that they were. In these months after Oxford he was rarely there, and Nick had been passed on as a friend to his little sister and to their hospitable parents. He was a friend of the family; and there was something about him they trusted, a gravity, a certain shy polish, something not quite apparent to Nick himself, which had helped the family agree that he should become their lodger. When Gerald had won Barwick, which was Nick's home constituency, the arrangement was jovially hailed as having the logic of poetry, or fate.

— **Alan Hollinghurst** *(1954-) English novelist*

The Iliad (750 BC)

- *The dark, pointless brutalities of military combat occurring over a few days in the battle, according to legend, between the Greeks and the Trojans.*

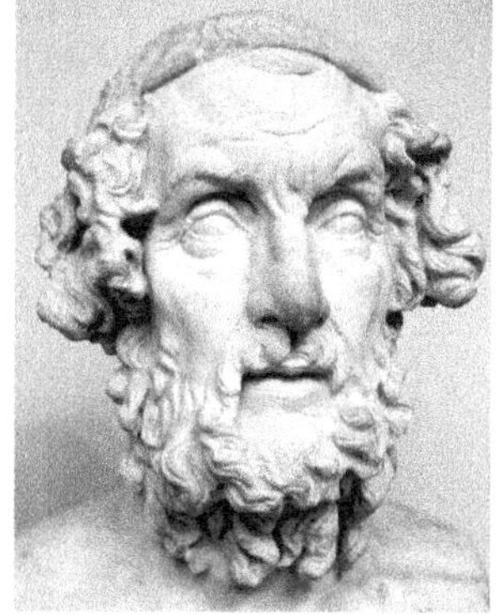

As he spoke he drew the keen blade that hung so great and strong by his side, and gathering himself together he sprang on Achilles like a soaring eagle which swoops down from the clouds on to some lamb or timid hare—even so did Hector brandish his sword and spring upon Achilles.

Achilles mad with rage darted towards him, with his wondrous shield before his breast, and his gleaming helmet, made with four layers of metal, nodding fiercely forward. The thick tresses of gold with which Vulcan had crested the helmet floated round it, and as the evening star that shines brighter than all others through the stillness of night, even such was the gleam of the spear which Achilles poised in his right hand, fraught with the death of noble Hector.

— **Homer** *(ca. 8th century BC) Ancient Greek epic poet*

The Best of Simple (1961)

- *Stories about Jesse B. Simple, considered by some an Everyman for black Americans. Simple is "one of the most memorable and winning characters in the annals of American Literature..." (Arnold Rampersad)*

"When people care for you and cry for you, they can straighten out your soul."

"You have suffered," I said.

"Suffered!" cried Simple. "My mama should have named me Job instead of Jess Simple. I have been underfed, underpaid, undernourished, and everything but *undertaken.* I been bit by dogs, cats, mice, rats, poll parrots, fleas, chiggers, bedbugs, granddaddies, mosquitoes, and a gold-toothed woman."

"Great day in the morning!"

"That ain't all," said Simple. "In this life I been abused, confused, misused, accused, false-arrested, tried, sentenced, paroled, blackjacked, beat, third-degreed and near about lynched!"

"Anyhow your health has been good—up to now," I said.

"Good health nothing," objected Simple, waving his hands, kicking off the cover, and swinging his feet out of bed. "I done had everything from flat feet to a flat head. Why, man, I was born with the measles! Since then I had smallpox, chickenpox, whooping cough, croup, appendicitis, athlete's foot, tonsillitis, arthritis, backache, mumps, and a strain—but I am still here. Daddy-o, I'm still here!"

— **Langston Hughes** *(1902-1967) American novelist, playwright, short story writer, and columnist*

Les Miserables (1862)

- *Ex-convict Jean Valjean becomes a force for good in the world, but cannot escape his dark past.*

Jean Valjean's turn to escape came towards the end of that fourth year. His fellow-prisoners helped him as was customary. He got away, and for two days drifted in freedom through the country-side: if to be tracked is freedom, to be constantly on the alert, to tremble at every sound, to be frightened of everything, a smoking chimney, a passing man, a barking dog, a galloping horse, a striking clock; to be frightened of the daylight because one can see, and of the darkness because one cannot; to be frightened of the road, the pathway, and the thicket; to be afraid to sleep. On the evening of the second day he was caught. He had neither eaten nor slept for thirty-six hours. The tribunal added three years to his sentence, making eight in

"Cosette" by Emile Bayard, from original edition of *Les Miserables* (1862).

all. His second turn came in the sixth year and again he used it, but with even less success. His absence was discovered at roll-call. The alarm-gun was fired, and that night the watch found him in the dockyard hiding under the keel of a vessel under construction. He fought against them, and for the crimes of attempted escape and resisting arrest the Code prescribed the penalty of an additional five years, two in double chains. Thirteen years. His third turn came in the tenth year, and gain he tried and failed. . . . It was in the thirteenth year, I believe, that he made his last attempt. He was out for only four hours, but they cost him another three years. Nineteen years altogether. He was released in October 1815, after being imprisoned in 1796 for having broken a window-pane and stolen a loaf of bread.

— **Victor Hugo** *(1802-1885) French poet, playwright, novelist, essayist and statesman*

Home from the Hill (1958)

- *The volatile relationship between a son and his brooding mother and wayward father.*

. . . For it was all so much a part of us that it did not seem in the least far-fetched for him, a total stranger, who had never seen the Captain alive or ever heard the rumors which instead of dying down have multiplied in the years since his death, to have noticed a strong family resemblance among a number of young mourners there, in their late teens and twenties now, ostensibly the children of all assorted kinds of looking fathers, yet all with that same sharp and slightly hooked nose, same hard jaw with the muscles always nervously at work in it, the same brown skin and stiff black hair and black eyes—dominant characteristics, as the biologists call them, especially remarkable among a homogeneously sandy, freckled lot of Scotch-English like us. As somebody said there, after the stranger's blunder, repeating the old quip somebody in town made years ago, "It's a wise child who knows his own father was not Captain Wade Hunnicutt." While another looking around him as the dirt was being dropped into the grave, his eyes picking out especially one boy the spitting image of the Captain—the very ghost of Theron himself—said, there was never a man of whom such a *live* memory had been kept as Captain Wade.

— **William Humphrey** *(1924-1997) American novelist*

Their Eyes Were Watching God (1920)

- *A Southern back woman, Janie Crawford, tells her life story of growing up as a free-spirited young girl in the 1930s to eventually become a woman of independence and substance.*

"And now we'll listen tuh uh few words uh encouragement from Mrs. Mayor Starks."

The burst of applause was cut short by Joe taking the floor himself.

"I regret all my books."

"Thank yuh fuh yo' compliments, but mah wife don't know nothin' bout no speech-makin'. Ah never married her for nothin' lak dat. She's uh woman and her place is in de home."

Janie made her face laugh after a short pause, but it wasn't too easy. She had never thought of making a speech, and didn't know if she cared to make one at all. It must have been the way Joe spoke out without giver her a chance to say anything one way or another that took the bloom off of things. But anyway, she went down the road behind him that night feeling cold. He strode along invested with his new dignity, thought and planned out loud, unconscious of her thoughts.

— Zora Neale Hurston *(1891-1960)*
American folklorist, anthropologist, and author

Brave New World (1932)

- *A carefree, healthy, and technologically advanced society in 2540 without poverty or war is achieved at the cost of eliminating most former qualities of life—family, cultural diversity, art, literature, religion, and philosophy.*

. . . "Violent Passion Surrogate. Regularly once a month. We flood the whole system with adrenin. It's the complete physiological equivalent of fear and rage. All the tonic effects of murdering. Desdemona and being murdered by Othello, without any of the inconveniences."

"But I like the inconveniences."

"Every man's memory is his private literature."

"We don't," said the Controller. "We prefer to do things comfortably."

"But I don't want comfort. I want God, I want poetry, I want real danger, I want freedom, I want goodness. I want sin."

"In fact," said Mustapha Mond, "you're claiming the right to be unhappy."

"All right then," said the Savage defiantly, "I'm claiming the right to be unhappy."

— **Aldous Huxley** *(1894-1963) English writer*

I

A Doll's House (1879)

- *The marriage of Torvald Helmer and wife Nora is threatened and eventually dissolved by an incident that triggers her rebellion. In this quote, Helmer receives a blackmail letter from Krogstad, a friend, implicating Nora.*

HELMER. Oh, what a terrible awakening this is. All these eight years . . . this woman who was my pride and joy . . . a hypocrite, a liar, worse than that, a criminal!

Later he receives a second note from Krogstad apologizing.

HELMER. Nora! I must read it again. Yes, yes, it's true! I am saved! Nora, I am saved!

NORA. And me?

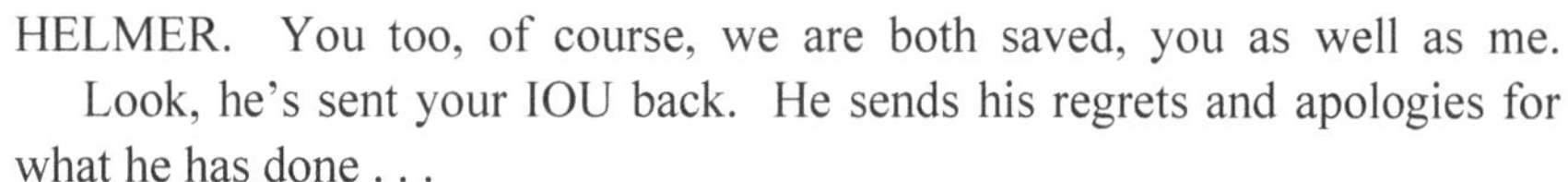

HELMER. You too, of course, we are both saved, you as well as me. Look, he's sent your IOU back. He sends his regrets and apologies for what he has done . . .

Nora by now realizes that her husband has always treated her like a plaything.

NORA. Eight whole years—no, more, ever since we first knew each other—and never have we exchanged one serious word about serious things. . . . . If I'm ever to reach any understanding of myself and the things around me, I must learn to stand alone. That's why I can't stay here with you any longer.

— **Henrik Ibsen** *(1828-1906) Norwegian author, playwright, and poet*

The Hotel New Hampshire (1981)

- *The heartfelt, humorous, and sometimes bizarre happenings in the lives of a family of dreamers as they live their lives in three hotels.*

"Hi, it's me," she said, apologetically—to the machine. Lilly was always apologizing. Frank smiled and untucked his bedcovers . . . There was a long pause on the machine . . . But then Lilly added, "It's just me." Something abut the tiredness in her voice made Frank check the time of night, and made him listen with some anxiety. In the pause that followed, Frank remembers whispering her name. "Go on, Lilly," he whispered.

And Lilly sang her little song, just a little snatch of a song; it was one of the *Heurigen* songs—a silly, sad song, a King of Mice song. Frank knew the song by heart, of course.

Verkauft's mei G'wand, I Fahr in Himmel.
Sell my old clothes, I'm off to heaven.

"Holy cow, Lilly," Frank whispered to the recorder; he started getting dressed, fast.

"*Auf Wiedersehen*, Frank," Lilly said, when her little song was over.

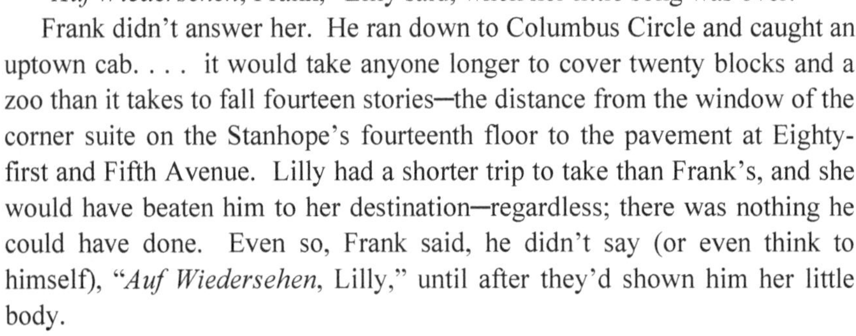

Frank didn't answer her. He ran down to Columbus Circle and caught an uptown cab. . . . it would take anyone longer to cover twenty blocks and a zoo than it takes to fall fourteen stories—the distance from the window of the corner suite on the Stanhope's fourteenth floor to the pavement at Eighty-first and Fifth Avenue. Lilly had a shorter trip to take than Frank's, and she would have beaten him to her destination—regardless; there was nothing he could have done. Even so, Frank said, he didn't say (or even think to himself), "*Auf Wiedersehen*, Lilly," until after they'd shown him her little body.

She left a better note than Fehlgeburt had left. Lilly was not crazy. She left a serious suicide note.

Sorry, said the note.

Just not big enough.

— **John Irving** *(1942-) American novelist*

A Prayer for Owen Meany (1989)

- *The story of Owen Meany a dwarfish boy with a strange voice who, after an accidental killing, believes he is an instrument of God, to be redeemed by martyrdom.*

There was only the briefest moment, when Owen looked stricken—something deeper and darker than pain crossed over his face, and he said to the nun who held him: "I'M AWFULLY COLD, SISTER—CAN'T YOU DO SOMETHING?" Then whatever had troubled him passed over him completely, and he smiled again—he looked at us all with his old, infuriating smile.

Then he looked only at me. "YOU'RE GETTING SMALLER, BUT I CAN STILL SEE YOU!" said Owen Meany.

Then he left us; he was gone. I could tell by his almost cheerful expression that he was at least as high as the palm trees.

Major Rawls saw to it that Owen Meany got a medal. I was asked to make an eyewitness report, but Major Rawls was instrumental in pushing the proper paperwork through the military chain of command. Owen Meany was awarded the so-called Soldier's Medal: "For heroism that involves the voluntary risk of life under conditions other than those of conflict with an opposing armed force."

— John Irving

The World According to Garp (1976)

■ *The coming of age of T. S. Garp, bastard son of Jenny Fields a feminist leader, as he blunders through friendships, marriage, and parenthood.*

Jenny trudged across the frozen slush to the infirmary, feeling that her first trip to the world of sports had left her more than a little changed.

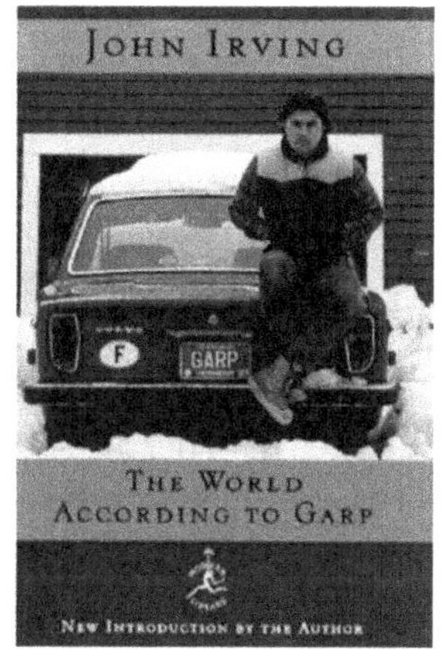

In the annex, in his bed, Garp still coughed and coughed. "Wrestling!" he croaked, "Good God, Mother, are you trying to get me killed?"

"I think you'll like the coach," Jenny said. "I met him, and he's a nice man. I met his daughter, too."

"Oh, Jesus," Garp groaned. "His *daughter* wrestles?"

"No, she reads a lot," Jenny said, approvingly.

"Sounds exciting, Mom," Garp said. "You realize that setting me up with the wrestling coach's daughter may cost me my neck? Do you want that?"

— John Irving

Goodby to Berlin (1939)

■ *A semiautobiographical account of the author's time in Berlin in the 1930s and the people he met during this pre-Nazi period.*

Sally laughed. She was dressed in black silk, with a small cape over her shoulders and a little cap like a page-boy's stuck jauntily on one side or her head:

"Do you mind if I use your telephone, sweet?" . . .

As she dialed the number, I noticed that her finger-nails were painted emerald green, a colour unfortunately chosen, for it called attention to her hands, which were much stained by cigarette-smoking and as dirty as a little girl's. She was dark enough to be Fritz's sister. Her face was long and thin, powdered dead white. She had very large brown eyes which should have been darker, to match her hair and the pencil she used for her

eyebrows. . . .

"Hilloo," she cooed, pursing her brilliant cherry lips as though she were going to kiss the mouthpiece: "Ist dass Du, mein Liebling?" Her mouth opened in a fatuously sweet smile. Fritz and I sat watching her, like a performance at the theatre. . . .

She hung up the receiver and turned to us triumphantly.

"That's the man I slept with last night," she announced. "He makes love marvelously."

— **Christopher Isherwood** *(1904-1986) English-American novelist*

Never Let Me Go (2005)

- *The story of three students at an idyllic private school that ultimately proves to have a sinister purpose.*

. . . None of you will go to America, none of you will be film stars. And none of you will be working in supermarkets as I heard some of you planning the other day. Your lives are set out for you. You'll become adults, then before you're old, before you're even middle-aged, you'll start to donate your vital organs. That's what each of you was created to do. You're not like the actors you watch on your videos, you're not even like me. You were brought into this world for a purpose, and your futures, all of them, have been decided.

— **Kazuo Ishiguro** *(1954-) Japanese-English novelist*

The Remains of the Day (1989)

- *Stevens, and elderly butler who has spent 30 years in the service of a British Lord, ruminates on the past and his relationship with a former housekeeper.*

'. . . And I suppose that's when I get angry over some trivial little thing and leave. But each time I do so, I realize before long — my rightful place is with my husband. After all, there's no turning back the clock now. One can't be forever dwelling on what might have been. One should realize one has as good as most, perhaps better, and be grateful.'

I do not think I responded immediately, for it took me a moment or two to fully digest these words of Miss Kenton. Moreover, as you might appreciate, their implications were such as to provoke a certain degree of sorrow within me. Indeed — why should I not admit it? — at that moment, my heart was breaking. Before long, however, I turned to her and said with a smile:

'You're very correct, Mrs Benn. As you say, it is too late to turn back the clock. Indeed, I would not be able to rest if I thought such ideas were the cause of unhappiness for you and your husband. We must each of us, as you point out, be grateful for what we *do* have.'

— Kazuo Ishiguro

J

On the Island: New and Selected Stories (1989)

■ *Thirty short stories, about 9 pages each, often set in exotic locales like the Caribbean, Morocco, or Guatemala, sometimes with tragic intrusions.*

The bell rang, her front door bell, this time; rang again. Barnie was not very bright.

It must have been ten minutes that she stood there without moving at all. Finally she heard the front door slam and heavy steps creaking in the little hall. "Barnie!" she called, and amazingly, tears began to pour down her cheeks.

"Mis' Glessner?" asked Barnie's voice, baffled.

"The handle's off!" she sang out. "I'm locked in! I've been here all night!"

"My goodness," said Barnie with distaste. After a little pause he said coldly, "You got a screwdriver?"

"Yes, yes," she said. "In the kitchen, in the toolbox. In the broom closet." . . . .

Trudge, came Barnie back. Metal scratched on metal, the door shook. There was a sucking click, and it swung in, Barnie with it, the screwdriver still in place. He looked at her, displeased.

"How you do that?" he asked.

She neither flung her arms around him, nor told him the secret. That was the first modification. She stepped, very slowly, over the threshold, past him. Everything waited, noncommittal, balanced.

— Josephine Jacobsen *(1908-2003) American poet, short story writer, and critic*

The Ambassadors (1903)

■ *Protagonist Lewis Strether pursues a supposedly wayward son who has found love with a young woman or possibly her mother.*

. . . "Is your daughter in love with our friend?"

"Ah," she rather startlingly answered, "I wish you'd find out!"

He showed his surprise. "I? A stranger?"

"Oh you won't be a stranger—presently. You shall see her quite, I assure you, as if you weren't"

It remained for him none the less an extraordinary notion. "It seems to me surely that if her mother can't—"

"Ah little girls and their mothers to-day!" she rather inconsequently broke in. But she checked herself with something she seemed to give out as after all more to the point. "Tell her I've been good for him. Don't you think I have?"

It had its effect on him—more than at the moment he quite measured. Yet he was consciously enough touched. "Oh if it's all *you*—!"

"Well, it may not be 'all,'" she interrupted, "but it's to a great extent. Really and truly," she added in a tone that was to take its place with him among things remembered.

— **Henry James** *(1843-1916) American-born writer*

The Portrait of a Lady (1881)

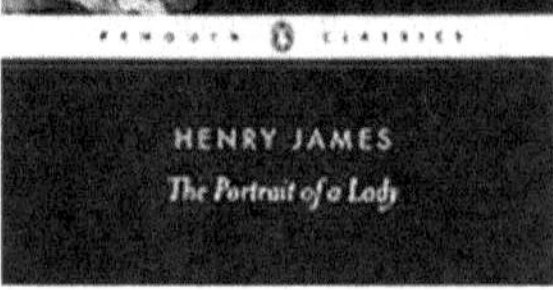

■ *Isabel Archer, a spirited young woman, inherits a large amount of money and subsequently becomes the victim of two scheming American expatriates.*

"Isabel's poor then. My mother tells me that she has but a few hundred dollars a year. I should like to make her rich."

"What do you mean by rich?"

"I call people rich when they're able to meet the requirements of their imagination. Isabel has a great deal of imagination."

"So have you, my son," said Mr. Touchett, listening very attentively but a little confusedly.

"You tell me I shall have money enough for two. What I want is that you should kindly relieve me of my superfluity and make it over to Isabel. Divide my inheritance into two equal halves and give her the second."

"To do what she likes with?"

"Absolutely what she likes." — **Henry James**

The Wings of the Dove (1902)

■ *The threat of a serious illness of a rich friend has a profound effect on an engaged couple, Kate and Merton.*

"If you can imagine an angel with a thumping bank-account you'll have the simplest expression of the kind of thing. Her fortune's absolutely huge . . . "

"I want," [continued Kate] "to make things pleasant for her. I use, for the purpose, what I have. You're what I have of most precious, and you're therefore what I use most."

. . . before she left him, [Merton had] one more doubt. "I don't see how she can understand enough, you know, without understanding too much."

"You don't need to see."

He required then a last injunction. "I must simply go it blind?"

"You must simply be kind to her."

"And leave the rest to you?"

"Leave the rest to *her*," said Kate disappearing.

— Henry James

Waiting (1999)

■ *A Chinese army doctor, in love with nurse Manna Wu, waits 18 years for a divorce, finally receiving his wife's consent.*

. . . She turned and looked at him, her eyes dim with affection and kindness, as though full of secrets that she was eager to share with him. The end of her loose hair was thrown up a little by the warm breeze, revealing the silky nape of her neck. How different she was now from then! He realized that the long waiting must have changed her profoundly—from a pleasant young woman into a hopeless spitfire. No matter how he felt about her now, he was certain she had always loved him. Perhaps it was the unrequited love that had dragged her down. Or perhaps it was the suffering and despondency she had experienced in the long waiting that had dissolved her gentle nature, worn away her hopes, ruined her health, poisoned her heart, and doomed her.

— Ha Jin *(1956-) Chinese-American writer*

War Trash (2004)

■ *A Chinese "volunteer" soldier strives to survive a South Korean POW camp and eventually unite with his family.*

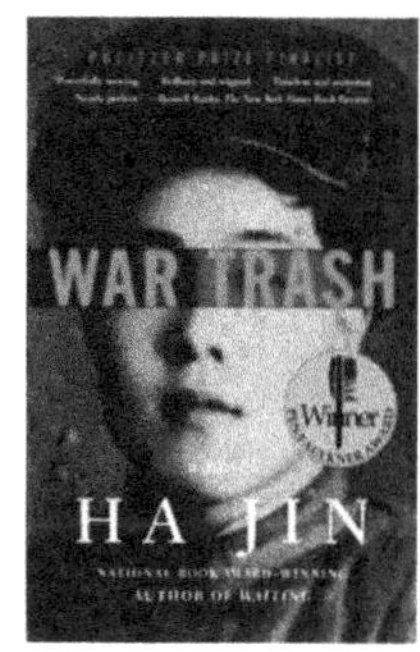

. . . She was blind but came here every day to rummage around for edibles. On her neck was a healed gash. Beside her were a large gourd bowl and a small girl, four or five years old, whose hair had been cut straight across at the upper ends of her ears. The child held a bunch of grasshoppers, all strung through the mouths by a straw of dogtail grass. Now and then she ran away from her mother to catch a grasshopper. For a moment I was lost in a memory of my childhood, when my pals and I had often gone into the wilderness to catch insects and roasted them to eat. Cicadas and grasshoppers had been our favorites. My reverie was cut short by the woman's calling to her daughter, asking her what she herself was holding in her leathery hand. It was a piece of turnip peel, the child told her. The woman raised the thing and smelled it, then with a faint smile put it into the gourd bowl.

— Ha Jin

Middle Passage (1990)

- *A newly freed slave stows away, unknowingly on a slave ship bound for Africa with a tyrannical captain and his rowdy, mutinous crew.*

. . . He was, as they say, a "tight-packer," having learned ten years ago from a one-handed French slaver named Captain Ledoux that if you arranged the Africans in two parallel rows, their backs against the lining of the ship's belly, this left a free space at their rusty feet, and *that*, given the flexibility of bone and skin, could be squeezed with even more slaves if you made them squat at ninety-degree angles to one another. Flesh could conform to anything. So when they came half-dead from the depths, these eyeless contortionists emerging from a shadowy Platonic cave, they were stiff and sore and stank of their own vomit and feces. Right then I decided our captain was more than just evil. He was the Devil.

— Charles Johnson *(1948-) American scholar and author*

Tree of Smoke (2007)

- *A year-by-year account of the events of 1963-1970, primarily focused on the chaotic forces at work during the unwinable Vietnam war.*

"What's that tube out of his mouth for?"

"James, the sarge isn't breathing entirely on his own yet."

The nurse moved a chair for him, and he sat beside the bed and took Sarge's hand. A bubble traveled up the drip in the sarge's wrist. "Sarge."

The sarge's very blue eyes, free-floating in their sockets, drifted toward James and stopped. Sarge made a ticking noise with his tongue against his palate.

"Do you see me?"

by Paul Sahre for *The New York Times*

The sarge clicked his tongue again, *tsk tsk*, as if he were scolding a kid, *tsk tsk*. The lips white and cracked, flaking. . . .

"What's that sound he's making?" he asked, but the nurse had gone. "What are you trying to say, Sarge?" He wiped his own tears and sucked and spat in the brown waste can full of swabs and slimy tissue papers. "I just came by," James said. "Just to say hi. See if you need anything. Shit like that." . . .

The sarge's eyes floated there burning and pleading. Everything coming out of his eyes. James wept like a barking dog. The reality and the rightness pouring off him, the purity of weeping, just crying, and who gives a shit — this is bigger than any of your games. The tears ran backward from the sarge's eyes over his temples and into his ears, but he made no sound other than by clicking his tongue.

— **Denis Johnson** *(1949-) American author*

Lying Low (1978)

- *Four people share a house in a small town in California, each "lying low," harboring secrets not meant to be shared.*

He was pulling off the right-hand exit by the race track. God—she saw where he meant to go, down along the Bay, through the parking lots by the race track, with no one around there today, and the swampy ground would soak up her blood; it would mingle with the oil slick off the Bay, that is if blood and oil do mix, and she'd say to Chen-yu, "*Run, run!*" All the same he couldn't get away on those little short legs across the wild cement acres; Sadler could just drive over him and crush him down under the wheels.

There was no time to think about it any more. Marybeth closed her arm around Chen-yu and leaned on the door handle, and they splattered out against the chain fence along the freeway exit. She didn't know if he lunged at them. He cried out something. Now the car skidded and passed them.

— **Diane Johnson** *(1934-) American-born novelist and essayist*

The Known World (2003)

- *The story of blacks who are slave owners, their "legacy," in the antebellum south.*

. . . Rita came out into the road, which she knew she was not supposed to do, and stood with her arms folded when she was not waving bye-bye to the boy. . . . She wiped her tears and then she began to run, and in the moments it took for the sun to go behind another cloud, she had caught up with the wagon and had hold of the back of it. . . . Henry soon took hold of Rita's other hand. Augustus and

Mildred were facing ahead, toward home. "Daddy," Henry said quietly as he watched Rita. His legs dangling off the edge of the wagon, he alone was facing back, toward the Robbins plantation. "Daddy." Augustus turned in his seat and saw Rita. "What you doin, woman?"

"Don't leave me here. Please don't leave me here," Rita managed to say. The wagon was dragging her when she wasn't able to run along and it was all Henry could do to hold on to her. August stopped. She climbed aboard and pulled Henry into her arms. "Please please, Lord Jesus, please."

— **Edward P. Jones** *(1951-) American novelist and short story writer*

From Here to Eternity (1951)

■ *PFC Robert E. Lee Prewitt is transferred to Schofield Barracks in Hawaii in 1941 beginning a period of harassment when he refuses to join the company boxing team and ending with a knife fight with stockade Sergeant 'Fatso' Judson.*

Jones was in combat on Guadalcanal, where he was wounded in action.

. . . "But I hate to take candy away from babies," Fatso grinned.

His knife, that was almost identical to Prew's, was waving back and forth slowly like a snake head, as he came on in in the classic stance of the practiced knife fighter, crouched a little, right arm out a little, blade projecting from across the upturned palm between the thumb and index-finger, left arm up a little palm open as a guard.

— **James Jones** *(1921-1977) American author*

The 1953 film with a cast that probably will never be surpassed: Montgomery Clift, Burt Lancaster, Frank Sinatra, Deborah Kerr, Ernest Borgnine, and Donna Reed.

The Pugilist at Rest: Stories (1993)

■ *Stories of great authenticity, drama, and hope, recounted with an almost brutal vision of the human condition.*

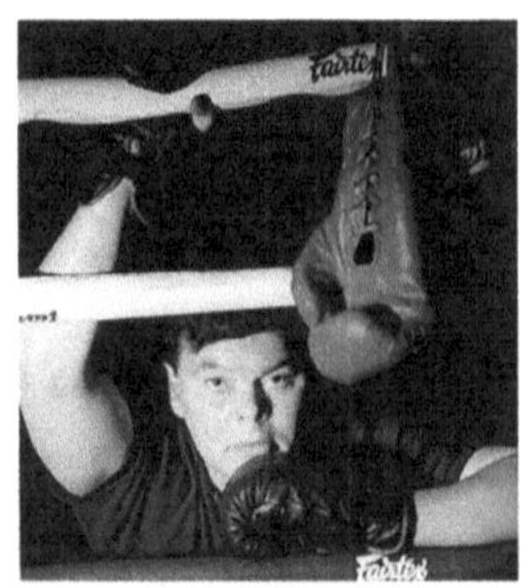

What the _____ am I doing in Vietnam? These gooks are hot on my ass. I drop down and fire a burst off in their direction. They separate. One of them cleaves to the river while the other starts crawling west to pull a flanking move on me. I have to conserve my ammunition. At least I had the sense to grab Mason's spare ammunition. I fire a shot at each of the gooks and get up and run. I wonder if I should dump my ruck. Not a good idea. . . .

Downriver I found more jungle, set down and caught the two little dinks just five minutes behind me. I let them walk past me and gave each of them a round in the back of the head. One of them had an NVA pack and I took it off him. The NVA field pack had the USMC pack beat by a mile. I felt a little kid on Christmas over this pack.

— **Thom Jones** *(1945-) American writer*

Finnegans Wake (1939)

- *A comic novel about a Dublin innkeeper, H. C. Earwicker (HCE, or "Here Comes Everybody") who dreams one night of the whole history of man. Immensely long and strangely written, defying exegesis.*

. . . Belling him up and filling him down. He's stiff but he's steady is Priam Olim! 'Twas he was the dacent gaylabouring youth. Sharpen his pillowscone, tap up his bier! E'erawhere in this whorl would ye hear sich a din again? With their deepbrow fundigs and the dusty fidelios. They laid him brawdawn alanglast bed. With a bockalips of finisky fore his feet. And a barrowload of guenesis hoer his head. Tee the tootal of the fluid hang the twoddle of the fuddled, O!

— **James Joyce** *(1882-1941) Irish novelist and poet*

Nora was not fond of her husband's style of writing, and not usually content with a yawn. When she discovered that he was "on another book again," just a year after the misery of *Ulysses*, she asked her husband if, instead of "that chop suey you're writing," he might not try "sensible books that people can understand."

— *Today in Literature*

A Portrait of the Artist as a Young Man (1916)

- *A semi-autobiographical tale of growing up poor in Ireland at the turn of the century, the young subject artist eventually realizing that nation, family, and religion have become a trap.*

The door opened quietly and closed. A quick whisper ran through the class: the prefect of studies. There was an instant of dead silence and then the loud crack of a pandybat on the last desk. Stephen's heart leapt up in fear.

—Any boys want flogging here, Father Arnall? cried the prefect of studies. Any lazy idle loafers that want flogging in this class?

He came to the middle of the class and saw Fleming on his knees.

—Hoho! he cried. Who is this boy? Why is he on his knees? What is your name, boy?

—Feming sir.

—Hoho, Fleming! An idler of course. I can see it in your eye. Why is he on his knees, Father Arnall?

—He wrote a bad Latin theme, Father Arnall said, and he missed all the questions in grammar.

—Of course he did! cried the prefect of studies, of course he did! A born idler! I can see it in the corner of his eye.

He banged his pandybat down on the desk and cried:

—Up, Fleming! Up, my boy!

Fleming stood up slowly.

—Hold out! cried the prefect of studies.

Fleming held out his hand. The pandybat came down on it with a loud smacking sound: one, two, three, four, five, six.

— James Joyce

Ulysses (1922)

■ *A chronicle of the passage through Dublin of the main character, Leopold Bloom, during a single day, June 16, 1904.*

. . . and Gibraltar as a girl where I was a Flower of the mountain yes when I put the rose in my hair like the Andalusian girls used or shall I wear a red yes and how he kissed me under the Moorish wall and I thought well as well him as another and then I asked him with my eyes to ask again yes and then he asked me would I yes to say yes my mountain flower and first I put my arms around him yes and drew him down to me so he could feel my breasts all perfume yes and his heart was going like mad and yes I said yes I will Yes.

— James Joyce

K

The Castle (1926)

■ *The protagonist, known simply as K., is summoned by castle authorities to conduct a land survey only to be notified the request was erroneous.*

. . . 'You are looking at the Castle?' he asked more gently than K. had expected, but with an inflection that denoted disapproval of K.'s occupation. 'Yes,' said K. 'I am a stranger here, I came to the village only last night.' 'You don' like the Castle?' returned the teacher quickly. 'What?' countered K., a little taken aback, and repeated the question in a modified form. 'Do I like the Castle? Why do you assume that I don't like it?' 'Strangers never do,' said the teacher. To avoid saying the wrong thing K. changed the subject and asked: 'I suppose you know the Count?' 'No,' said the teacher turning away. But K. would not be put off and asked again: 'What, you don't know the Count?' 'Why should I?' replied the teacher in a low tone, and added aloud in French: 'Please remember that there are innocent children present.'

— **Franz Kafka** *(1883-1924) German-language novelist*

The Metamorphosis (1915)

- *A devastating portrait of a family attempting to cope with the horror of the son's transformation into a gigantic caterpillar-like creature.*

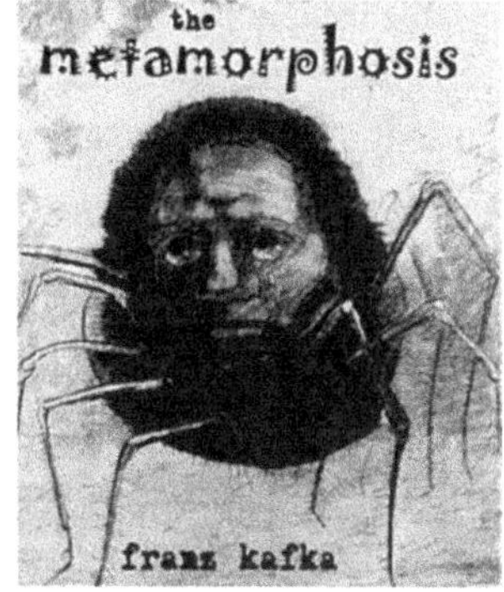

As Gregor Samsa awoke from unsettling dreams one morning, he found himself transformed in his bed into a monstrous vermin. He lay on his hard armorlike back and when he raised his head a little he saw his vaulted brown belly divided into sections by stiff arches from whose height the coverlet had already slipped and was about to slide off completely. His many legs, which were pathetically thin compared to the rest of his bulk, flickered helplessly before his eyes.

— **Franz Kafka**

The Trial (1925)

- *The hero and protagonist, Josef K., is arrested one morning for no apparent reason. Thus begins his slide into despair as he desperately endeavors to grapple with the lunatic logic of the bureaucratic French court of the day.*

"Listen to me. Some ten days ago I was arrested, in a manner that seems ridiculous even to myself, though that is immaterial at the moment. I was seized in bed before I could get up, perhaps — it is not unlikely, considering the Examining Magistrate's statement — perhaps they had orders to arrest some house-painter who is just as innocent as I am, only they hit on me. The room next to mine was requisitioned by two coarse warders. If I had been a dangerous bandit they could not have taken more careful precautions. These warders, moreover, were degenerate ruffians, they deafened my ears with their gabble, they tried to induce me to bribe them, they attempted to get my clothes and underclothes from me under dishonest pretexts, they asked me to give them money ostensibly to bring me some breakfast after they had brazenly eaten my own breakfast under my eyes." — **Franz Kafka**

In 1998 an official international search for Kafka's last writings was initiated. Consisting of 20 notebooks and 35 letters to Kafka's last companion, Dora Diamant, this missing literary treasure was confiscated from her by the Gestapo in Berlin 1933. Only the confiscation order and three letters have been discovered. — *Wikipedia*

Andersonville (1955)

- *The story of the Andersonville prison in Southwest Georgia told from many viewpoints including that of the commandant Henry Wirz.*

These men at his door in noontime were enemies, with all the gaud of cloth, buttons, belts.

Is your name Wirz?

Ja, I am Henry Wirz.

You have been in command of this place, commanding Rebel troops?

Wirz tried to straighten his sagging shoulders. He lifted his voice, cords tense and visible at his throat. *Nein!* The troops I have not commanded. I have been superintendent of the stockade only.

The man with bars on his shoulder straps said, I am Captain Henry E. Noyes, Fourth United States Cavalry. Acting as aide-de-camp to General Wilson. I regret to inform you that you are under arrest.

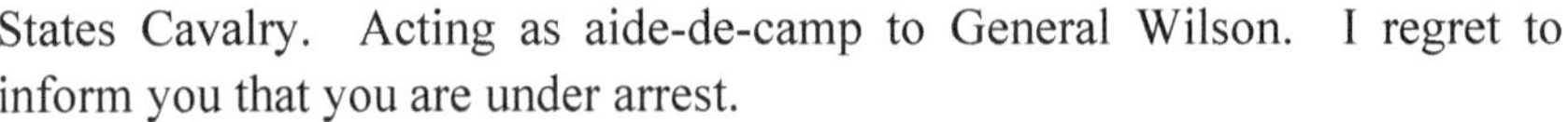

— **MacKinlay Kantor** *(1904-1977) American journalist, novelist and screen writer*

Protesting that he was only following orders, Captain Wirz subjected union prisoners to inhumane and brutal treatment. He was found guilty of conspiracy and murder and was executed by hanging in 1865.

After the war, Samuel Goldwyn commissioned Kantor to write a screenplay about veterans' returning home. He did, writing *Glory for Me* in blank verse, selling the movie rights to Goldwyn. Later Kantor was disappointed that the film was released under the name *The Best Years of Our Lives* (1946) with details of the story changed by screenwriter Robert Sherwood. The film won seven Academy Awards. — *Wikipedia*

Ironweed (1983)

- *The grim life, not worth living, of Francis Phelan who abandons his wife and family when he accidentally drops his 13-day-old son.*

Francis found the grave without a search. He stood over it and reconstructed the moment when the child was slipping through his fingers into death. He prayed for a repeal of time so that he might hang himself in the coal bin before picking up the child to change his diaper. Denied that, he prayed for his son's eternal peace in the grave. It was true that the boy had not suffered at all in his short life, and he had died too quickly of a cracked neckbone to have felt pain: a sudden twist and it was over. *Gerald Michael Phelan*, his gravestone said, *born April 13, 1916, died April 26, 1916. Born on the 13th, lived 13 days. An unlucky child who was much loved.*

— **William Kennedy** *(1928-) American writer and journalist*

Roscoe (2002)

■ *Roscoe Conway, a quick-witted, charismatic lawyer-politician, helps his Democratic Party cohorts achieve and maintain political power in the 1930s and '40s in Albany, New York.*

"How do you get the money, boy? If you run 'em for office and they win, you charge 'em a year's wages. Keep taxes low, but if you have to raise 'em, call it something else. The city can't do without vice, so pinch the pimps and milk the madams. Anybody that sells the flesh, tax 'em. If anybody wants city business, thirty percent back to us. Maintain the streets and sewers, but don't overdo it. Well-lit streets discourage sin, but don't overdo it. If they play craps, poker, or blackjack, cut the game. If they play faro or roulette, cut it double. Opium is the opiate of the depraved, but if they want it, see that they get it, and tax those lowlife bastards. If they keep their dance halls open twenty-four hours, tax 'em twice. If they run a gyp joint, tax 'em triple. If they send prisoners to our jail, charge 'em rent, at hotel prices. Keep the cops happy and let 'em have a piece of the pie. A small piece."

— William Kennedy

On the Road (1955)

■ *The experiences of two young friends on four cross-country road trips in their quest for freedom and meaning as part of the "Beat" generation.*

As we rode in the bus in the weird phosphorescent void of the Lincoln Tunnel we leaned on each other with fingers waving and yelled and talked excitedly, and I was beginning to get the bug like Dean. He was simply a youth tremendously excited with life, and though he was a con-man, he was only conning because he wanted so much to live and to get involved with people who would otherwise pay no attention to him. He was conning me and I knew it (for room and board and "how-to-write," etc.), but I didn't care and we got along fine—no pestering, no catering; we tiptoed around each other like heartbreaking new friends.

— Jack Kerouac *(1922-1969)*
Canadian-American novelist and poet

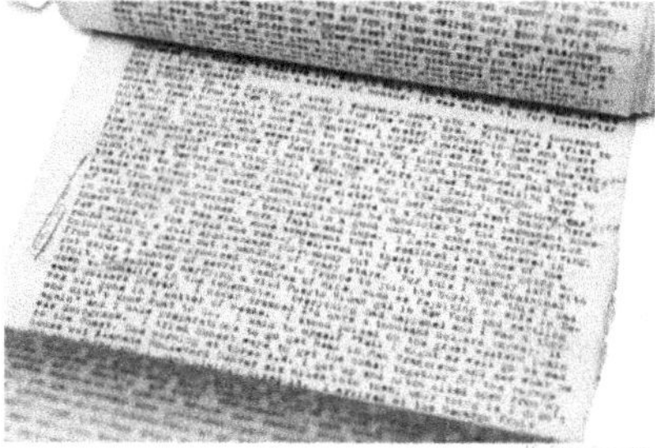

Original manuscript written on a scroll of teletype paper.

One Flew Over the Cuckoo's Nest (1962)

- *McMurphy, with several assault convictions, pretends to be mad and is sent to a mental asylum where he helps many of the patients to progress but incurs the wrath of the sadistic head nurse.*

. . . The Big Nurse's eyes swelled out white as he got close. She hadn't reckoned on him doing anything. This was supposed to be her final victory over him, supposed to establish her rule once and for all. But here he comes and he's big as a house!

She started popping her mouth and looking for her black boys, scared to death, but he stopped before he got to her. He stopped in front of her window and he said in his slowest, deepest drawl how he figured he could use one of the smokes he bought this mornin', then ran his hand through the glass.

The glass came apart like water splashing, and the nurse threw her hands to her ears. He got one of the cartons of cigarettes with his name on it and took out a pack, then put it back and turned to where the big Nurse was sitting like a chalk statue and very tenderly went to brushing the silvers of glass off her hat and shoulders.

— **Ken Kesey** *(1962-) American author*

The Autobiography of My Mother (1996)

- *The evolution of a mixed-race motherless young girl to an old woman living on the island of Dominica in the West Indies.*

When my mother died, leaving me a small child vulnerable to all the world, my father took me and placed me in the care of the same woman he paid to wash his clothes. It is possible that he emphasized to her the difference between the two bundles: one was his child, not his only child in the world but the only child he had with the only woman he had marred so far; the other was his soiled clothes. He would have handled one more gently than the other, he would have given more careful instructions for the care of one over the other, he would have expected better care for one than the other, but which one I do not know, because he was a very vain man, his appearance was very important to him.

— **Jamaica Kincaid** *(1949-) American novelist*

It (1986)

- *A malevolent, shape-shifting, child-killing monster lurks in the sewers and storm-drains of a small town.*

He got up and walked over to the stormdrain. He dropped to his knees and peered in. The water made a dank hollow sound as it fell into the darkness. It was a spooky sound. It reminded him of—

"Huh!" The sound was jerked out of him as if on a string, and he recoiled.

There were yellow eyes in there: the sort of eyes he had always imagined but never actually seen down in the basement. *It's an animal,* he thought incoherently, *that's all it is, some animal, maybe a housecat that got stuck down in there—*

King's books have sold over 350 million copies and have been made into many movies.

. . . He saw himself getting up and backing away, and that was when a voice—a perfectly reasonable and rather pleasant voice—spoke to him from inside the stormdrain.

"Hi, Georgie," it said. . . .

There was a clown in the stormdrain. . . .

The clown held a bunch of balloons, all colors, like gorgeous ripe fruit in one hand.

In the other he held George's newspaper boat.

"Want your boat, Georgie?" The clown smiled. . . .

George reached.

The clown seized his arm.

And George saw the clown's face change.

What he saw then was terrible enough to make his worst imaginings of the thing in the cellar look like sweet dreams; what he saw destroyed his sanity in one clawing stroke.

— **Stephen King** *(1947-) American author of contemporary horror, suspense, science fiction and fantasy fiction*

The Shining (1977)

- *Employed as caretaker at the Overlook hotel closed for the winter, Jack Torrance, wife Wendy, and clairvoyant son Danny battle against the hotel and each other.*

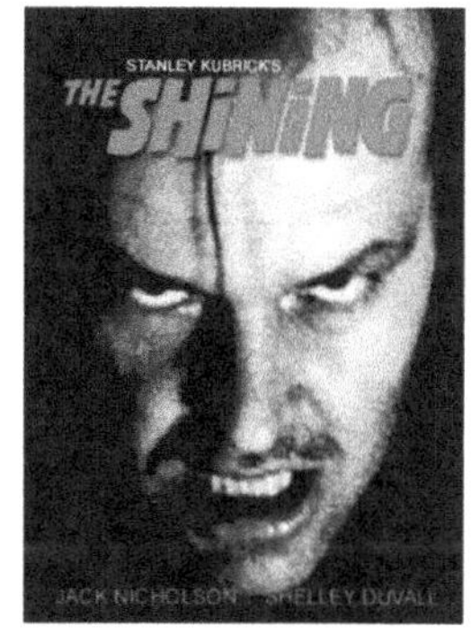

"I'll kill you for that," he said.

He rolled over and stretched out for the handle of the mallet. Wendy forced herself to her feet. Her left leg sent bolt after bolt of pain all the way up to her hip. Her face was ashy pale but set. She leaped onto his back as his hand closed over the shaft of the rogue mallet.

"Oh dear God!" she screamed to the Overlook's shadowy lobby, and buried the kitchen knife in his lower back up to the handle.

He stiffened beneath her and then shrieked. She thought she had never heard such an awful sound in her whole life; it was as if the very boards and windows and doors of the hotel had screamed.

— Stephen King

The Stand (1978)

- *An apocalyptic vision of the world scourged by a plague 99 percent lethal, and the elemental struggle between good and evil by the few remaining survivors.*

The man on the floor moaned thickly in his throat and they all looked down at him. After a moment, when it became obvious that the man was speaking or trying very hard to speak, Hap knelt beside him. It was, after all, his station.

Whatever had been wrong with the woman and child in the car was also wrong with this man. His nose was running freely, and his respiration had a peculiar undersea sound, a churning from somewhere in his chest. The flesh beneath his eyes was puffing, not black yet, but a bruised purple. His neck looked too thick, and the flesh had pushed up in a column to give him two extra chins. He was running a high fever; being close to him was like squatting on the edge of an open barbecue pit where good coals have been laid.

— Stephen King

The Poisonwood Bible (1998)

- *Missionary Nathan Price along with his reluctant wife and four daughters encounter the difficulties of serving in Africa.*

We eventually received a formal reply, via the elder Nadu son, stating that sprinkling was all very well but the previous Brother Fowles had disturbed the chief with peculiar ideas about having only one wife at a time. Imagine, Tata Ndu said, a shamefaced chief who could only afford one single wife! The chief expected us to disavow any such absurdities before he could endorse our church.

My steadfast husband tore his hair in private. Without the chief's blessing he could have no congregation. Nathan burned. There is no other way to say it. *Many are the afflictions of the righteous: but the Lord delivereth him out of them all,* he declared to the sky, squinting up at God and demanding justice. I held him in my arms at night and saw parts of his soul turn to ash. Then I saw him reborn, with a stone in place of his heart. Nathan would accept no more compromises. God was testing him like Job, he declared, and the point of that particular parable was that Job had done no wrong to begin with. Nathan felt it had been a mistake to bend his will, in any way, to Africa.

— **Barbara Kingsolver** *(1955-) American novelist, essayist and poet*

The Woman Warrior: Memories of a Girlhood Among Ghosts (1975)

- *An account of growing up female and Chinese-American in California, blended with the heroine's imagined tales of conflict and triumph.*

When one of my parents or the emigrant villagers said, "'Feeding girls is feeding cowbirds,'" I would thrash on the floor and scream so hard I couldn't talk. I couldn't stop.

"What's the matter with her?"

"I don't know. Bad, I guess. You know how girls are. 'There's no profit in raising girls. Better to raise geese than girls.'"

"I would hit her if she were mine. But then there's no use wasting all that discipline on a girl. 'When you raise girls, you're raising children for strangers.'"

"Stop that crying!" my mother would yell. "I'm going to hit you if you don't stop. Bad girl!" I'm going to remember never to hit or to scold my children for crying, I thought, because then they will only cry more.

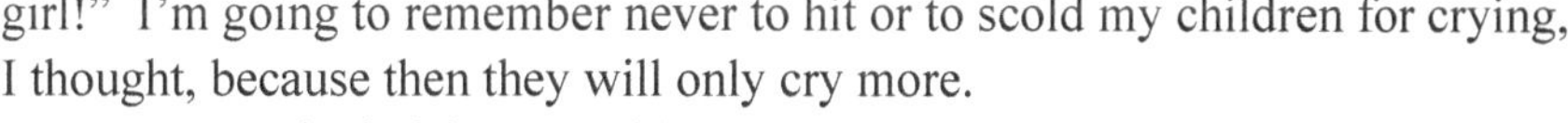

"I'm not a bad girl," I would scream. "I'm not a bad girl. I'm am not a bad girl." I might as well have said, "I'm not a girl."

— **Maxine Hong Kingston** *(1940-) Chinese-American author*

Kim (1901)

- *Kim O'Hara, the orphaned son of an Irish soldier stationed in India, grows up on the streets of Lahore seeking his destiny with night "commissions" eventually leading to bigger games.*

. . . They met a troop of long-haired, strong-scented Sansis with baskets of lizards and other unclean food on their backs, their lean dogs sniffing at their heels. These people kept their own side of the road, moving at a quick, furtive jog-trot, and all other castes gave them ample room; for the Sansi is deep pollution.

— **Rudyard Kipling** *(1865-1936) English short-story writer, poet and novelist*

A Separate Peace (1960)

- *Two friends at a boy's boarding school banish the innocence of youth preparing for the onslaught of World War II.*

. . . Another turn and up the pool again—I noticed no particular slackening of his pace—another turn, down the pool again, his hand touched the end, and he looked up at me with a composed, interested expression. "Well, how did I do?" I looked at the watch; he had broken A. Hopkins Parker's record by .7 second.

"My God! So I really did it. You know what? I thought I was going to do it. It felt as though I had that stop watch in my head and I could hear myself going just a little bit faster than A. Hopkins Parker."

"The worst thing is there weren't any witnesses. And I'm no official timekeeper. I don't think it will count."

"Well of course it won't *count.*"

"You can try it again and break it again. Tomorrow. We'll get the coach in here, and all the official timekeepers and I'll call up *The Devonian* to send a reporter and a photographer—"

He climbed out of the pool. "I'm not going to do it again," he said quietly.

— **John Knowles** *(1926-2001) American novelist*

Darkness at Noon (1940)

- *Set in 1938 during the Stalinist purges, Rubashov, a Bolshevik old guard and 1917 revolutionary, is imprisoned and tried for treason by the Soviet government he once helped create.*

. . . A shapeless figure bent over him, he smelt the fresh leather of the revolver belt; but what insignia did the figure wear on the sleeves and shoulder-straps of its uniform—and in whose name did it raise the dark pistol barrel?

A second, smashing blow hit him on the ear. Then all became quiet. There was the sea again with its sounds. A wave slowly lifted him up. It came from afar and traveled sedately on, a shrug of eternity.

— **Arthur Koestler** *(1905-1983) Hungarian-British author*

I wish my friends to know that I am leaving their company in a peaceful frame of mind, with some timid hopes for a de-personalized after-life beyond due confines of space, time and matter and beyond the limits of our comprehension. This 'oceanic feeling' has often sustained me at difficult moments, and does so now, while I am writing this.

Unwilling to suffer the indignity of losing control over his body or mind, Koestler age 77 left this suicide note. — *Wikipedia*

The Painted Bird (1965)

- *The experiences of a young orphaned boy wandering about the Polish countryside during the close of World War II, hiding among cruel peasants.*

Then, for a long time, she contemplated the long scar on my belly, the souvenir of my appendectomy, kneading my stomach with her hands. After the inspection she haggled fiercely and at length with the peasant, until finally she tied a string around my neck and led me away. I had been bought.

I began to live in her hut. It was a two-room dugout, full of piles of dried grasses, leaves, and shrubs, small oddly shaped colored stones, frogs, moles, and pots of wriggling lizards and worms. In the center of the hut caldrons were suspended over a burning fire.

Olga showed me everything. Henceforth, I had to take care of the fire, bring faggots from the forest, and clean the stalls of the animals. The hut was full of varied powders which Olga prepared in a large mortar, grinding up and mixing the different components. I had to help her with this.

— **Jerzy Kosinski** *(1933-1991) Polish-American novelist*

Steps (1968)

- *A series of shattering episodes which portray a man's life self-freed for violence and sexuality.*

Again I aimed carefully, letting the second bottle fall right at his feet. Shattering, it muffled his cry. He ran into the doorway, but this time returned just as fast, jerking his head spasmodically.

He obviously would not hide. He must have known that standing in the center of the yard he made a perfect target. When another bottle broke a few feet away from him, he leaped back, but I managed to plant the next one just behind his heels. He scuttled into the shadow of the doorway. There, well hidden, he waited for my next move. Only his pipe glowed in the dark.

What could he have wondered about his enemy? He must have sensed that his life was threatened and that his tormentor was watching from one of the high dark windows overlooking the yard. He knew that he could be killed by one of the bottles. ....

The next day the newspapers reported that an old man had been hit with a beer bottle thrown by an unknown assailant and had died on the spot.

— **Jerzy Kosinski**

The Unbearable Lightness of Being (1984)

- *A young Czech physician is torn between his unexpected love for a special young woman and his incorrigible womanizing.*

Thus is practically no time he managed to rid himself of wife, son, mother, and father. The only thing they bequeathed to him was a fear of women. Tomas desired but feared them. Needing to create a compromise between fear and desire, he devised what he called "erotic friendship." He would tell his mistresses: the only relationship that can make both partners happy is one in which sentimentality has no place and neither partner makes any claim on the life and freedom of the other.

To ensure that erotic friendship never grew into the aggression of love, he would meet each of his long-term mistresses only at intervals. He considered this method flawless and propagated it among his friends: "The important thing is to abide by the rule of threes. Either you see a woman three times in quick succession and then never again, or you maintain relations over the years but make sure that the rendezvous are at least three weeks apart."

— **Milan Kundera** *(1929-) Czech origin, French citizen since 1981*

L

Les Liaisons dangereuses (1782)

- *Two rivals use sex as a weapon to humiliate and degrade others, reflecting the decadence of the French aristocracy shortly before the French Revolution.*

Let me be frank. Since our intimacies are as cold as they are shallow, what we call happiness is scarcely even a pleasure. But shall I tell you something? I thought my heart had withered away, and, finding nothing left to me but my senses, I lamented my pre-mature old age. Madame de Tourvel has restored the charming illusions of my youth. When I am with her I have no need of pleasure to be happy. The one thing that alarms me is the amount of time I must give up to this adventure, for I dare not leave anything to chance. It is no use reminding myself of bold schemes that have succeeded before: I cannot bring myself to put them into practice. I cannot be really happy unless she gives herself to me; and that is no trifling matter.

— **Pieree Choderlos de Laclos** *(1741-1803) French novelist, official and army general*

Unaccustomed Earth (2008)

- *Stories about the fates of Bengali families living in America.*

. . . But this postcard bore no postmark, had not been sent. It was composed in Bengali and addressed in English to someone on Long Island. A Mrs. Meenakshi Bagchi.

She picked it up. "Akash, what's this?"

He reached out, attempting to snatch it back from her. "It's mine."

"What is it?" she asked, more harshly this time.

"It's for my garden."

"Did Dadu give this to you?"

He shook he head angrily, and then he started to cry.

She stared at the card and instantly she knew, just as she'd known from the expression on the surgeon's face what had happened to her mother on the operating table. The woman in the video, the reason for her father's trips, the reason for his good spirits, the reason he did not want to live in Seattle. The reason he'd wanted a stamp that morning. Here, in a handful of sentences she could not even read, was the explanation, the evidence that it was not just with Akash that her father had fallen in love.

— **Jhumpa Lahiri** *(1967-) Indian American author*

Lady Chatterley's Lover (1928)

- *Constance Chatterley, unhappily married to an invalid, finds refuge in the arms of Mellors the game-keeper.*

Evening Standard

Jury reach historic decision after 3 hours

THE INNOCENCE OF LADY CHATTERLEY

She's cleared after 6-day trial

'NOW WE CAN GO AHEAD' SAYS PENGUIN CHIEF

12s. 6d. Easter egg for old folk

Best buy OVALTINE

The family drink of today

So she sat in the doorway of the hut in a dream, utterly unaware of time and of particular circumstances. She was so drifted away that he glanced up at her quickly, and saw the utterly still, waiting look on her face. To him it was a look of waiting. And a little, thin tongue of fire suddenly flickered in his loins, at the root of his back, and he groaned in spirit. He dreaded with a repulsion almost of death, any further close human contact. He wished above all things she would go away and leave him to his own privacy. He dreaded her will, her female will, and her modern, female insistency. And above all, he dreaded her cool, upper-class impudence of having her own way. For after all he was only a hired hand. He hated her presence there.

— **D. H. Lawrence** *(1885-1930) English novelist, poet, playwright, essayist and literary critic*

Lawrence's opinions earned him many enemies and he endured official persecution, censorship, and misrepresentation of his creative work throughout the second half of his life, much of which he spent in a voluntary exile he called his "savage pilgrimage." At the time of his death, his public reputation was that of a pornographer who had wasted his considerable talents. E. M. Forster, in an obituary notice, challenged this widely held view, describing him as, "The greatest imaginative novelist of our generation." — *Wikipedia*

The Rainbow (1915)

- *The story of the youth and coming of age of Ursula Brangwan and the lives of her grandfather and parents, living around the turn of the twentieth century in the rural midlands of England.*

At the click of the latch everybody looked round. The girl hung in the doorway, seized with a moment's fierce confusion. She was going to be good-looking. Now she had an attractive gawkiness, as she hung a moment, not knowing how to carry her shoulders. Her dark hair was tied behind, her yellow-brown eyes shone without direction. Behind her, in the parlour, was the soft light of a lamp upon books.

. . . she wanted to turn to the stranger. He was standing back a little, waiting. He was a young man with very clear grayish eyes that waited until they were called upon, before they took expression.

Something in his self-possessed waiting moved her, and she broke into a confused, rather beautiful laugh as she gave him her hand, catching her breath like an excited child. His hand closed over hers very close, very near, he bowed, and his eyes were watching her with some attention. She felt proud – her spirit leapt to life.

— **D. H. Lawrence**

Sons and Lovers (1913)

- *A son indentured to his mother's love comes to manhood unable to have a complete relationship that challenges his love for his mother.*

"Well, I don't love her, mother," he murmured, bowing his head and hiding his eyes on her shoulder in misery. His mother kissed him a long, fervent kiss:

“My boy!” she said, in a voice trembling with passionate love. Without knowing, he gently stroked her face. . . . .

“I never will see. I’ll never marry while I’ve got you—I won’t.”

“But I shouldn’t like to leave you with nobody, my boy,” she cried.

“You’re not going to leave me. What are you—fifty three! I’ll give you till seventy five. There you are, I’m fat and forty four. Then I’ll marry a staid body. See—!”

His mother sat and laughed.

— D. H. Lawrence

Women in Love (1920)

- *Two sisters meet two men who live nearby, beginning a struggle with themselves and each other and with life’s intractable limitations at the onset of World War I.*

‘How long are you staying?’ she asked him.

‘A day or two,’ he replied. ‘But there is no particularly hurry.’

Still she stared into his face with that slow, full gaze which was so curious and so exciting to him. He was acutely and delightfully conscious of himself, of his own attractiveness. He felt full of strength, able to give off a sort of electric power. And he was aware of her dark, hot-looking eyes upon him. She had beautiful eyes, dark, fully opened, hot, naked in their looking at him. And on them there seemed to float a film of disintegration, a sort of misery and sullenness, like oil and water. She wore no hat in the heated cafe, her loose, simple jumper was strung on a string round her neck. But it was made of rich peach-coloured crepe-de-chine, that hung heavily and softly from her young throat and her slender wrists. Her appearance was simple and complete, really beautiful, because of her regularity and form, her soft, dark hair falling full and level on either side of her head, her straight, small, softened features, Egyptian in the slight fullness of their curves, her slender neck and the simple, rich-coloured smock hanging on her slender shoulders. She was very still, almost null, in her manner, apart and watchful.

— D. H. Lawrence

Family Dancing (1984)

- *Stories of unhappy families, broken homes, and unsuccessful marriages.*

It is spring, and my youngest child, my eleven-year old, Nina, has convinced herself that she is an alien.

Mrs. Tompkins, her teacher, called me in yesterday morning to tell me. “Nina’s constructed a whole history," she whispered, removing her glasses and leaning toward me across her desk, as if someone might be listening from above. "She never pays attention in class, just sits and draws. Strange landscapes, star-charts, the interiors of spaceships. I finally asked some of the other children what was going on. They told me that Nina says she's waiting to be taken away by her real parents. She says she's a surveyor, implanted here, but that soon a ship's going to come and retrieve her.

— **David Leavitt** *(1961-) American novelist*

A Perfect Spy (1986)

- *A trusted agent in British Intelligence disappears and is believed to be giving vital secrets to a contact in Czechoslovakia.*

. . . This was when Pym voted with his feet, he thought. In all his life till now, perhaps the first completely selfish gesture he had made, with the noble exception of the room where he now sat. The first time he had said "I want" rather than "I ought." . . .

. . . Undeterred, he checked his suitcase to Vienna and, with this very boarding-card in his hand, passed through immigration and sat himself in the unsanitary lounge behind his *Times*. When his flight was delayed, he almost concealed his irritation, but still contrived to let it show. When it was called, he hurried obediently forward to join the straggling crowd on its walk to the departure gate, the very picture of a dutiful conformer. As he did so he could almost feel, if he could not see, the two men peel away for tea and ping-pong back at base: let the Vienna bastards have him and good riddance, they were saying to each other. He turned a corner and advanced towards a moving walkway but did not board it. Instead he ambled, peering behind him as if in search of a delayed companion, then imperceptibly allowing himself to be borne backward by the opposing flow of passengers. Moments later he was showing his passport at the arrivals desk and receiving the quiet "Welcome home, sir" . . .

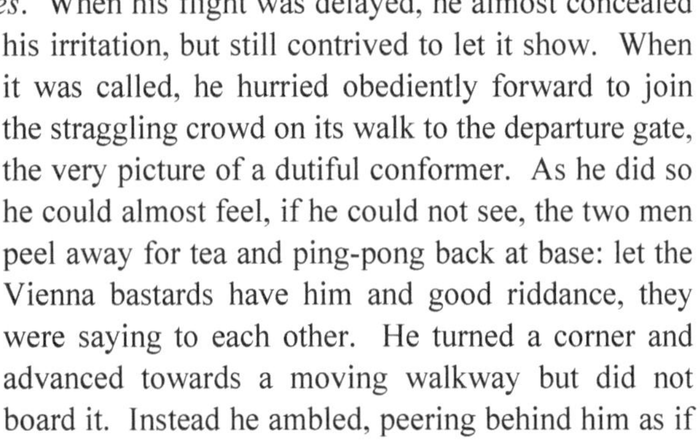

— **John le Carre** *(1931-) Author of espionage novels*

The Ugly American (1958)

- *An exposé of what really went on behind the secret red-tape curtain of American diplomacy in Southeast Asia in the early 1950s.*

". . . Of course you've got good people out there in the boondocks, good hard-working people who are plenty savvy. But they don't want what you want yet. It takes time for that. That's why I recommended in my report that you start small, with little things. And then after you lick them, go on to

the bigger things. Hell, we could build dams and roads for you—but you don't have the skill or capacity or need for them now."

William Lederer

"Mr. Atkins, I think that's a political decision which goes beyond your province," Josiah Gordon cut in quickly. Atkins knew Gordon wanted to get the meeting over with. "Let's just let your report stand and we'll discuss it on a higher level."

"Okay, okay. But have any of you birds been *out* in the boondocks?" Atkins asked stubbornly. "Don't give me the statistics, don't tell me about national aspirations. Just answer me: Have you been out in the boondocks?"

The Frenchman, the Vietnamese, the Americans all sat quietly in collective embarrassment. The hint of a sneer showed on the face of the tall Vietnamese, and Atkins was aware again, as he always was when he caught that look on someone's face, of his own personal ugliness.

— **William J. Lederer** *(1912-2009) and* **Eugene Burdick** *(1918-1965) American authors*

To Kill a Mockingbird (1960)

- *Seen through the eyes of 8-year-old Scout Finch, life in a small Southern town is dramatically altered when Scout's father, Atticus, defends a young black man unjustly accused of raping a white women.*

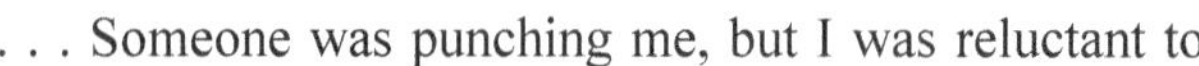

. . . Someone was punching me, but I was reluctant to take my eyes from the people below us, and from the image of Atticus's lonely walk down the aisle.

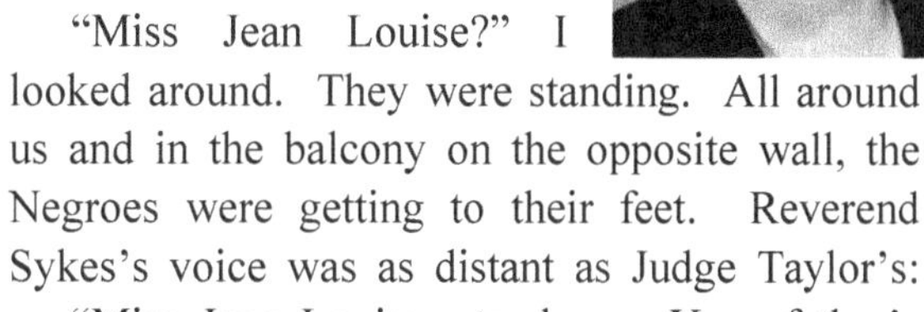

"Miss Jean Louise?" I looked around. They were standing. All around us and in the balcony on the opposite wall, the Negroes were getting to their feet. Reverend Sykes's voice was as distant as Judge Taylor's:

"Miss Jean Louise, stand up. Your father's passin'."

— **Harper Lee** *(1926-) American author*

A 1991 survey by the Book-of-the-Month Club and the Library of Congress Center for the Book found Lee's *Mockingbird* was "most often cited as making a difference in people's lives, second only to the Bible." In 2007 she was awarded the Presidential Medal of Freedom of the United States for her contribution to literature. Lee has also been the recipient of numerous honorary degrees.

A Hero of Our Time (1839)

■ *Pechorin, impulsive and emotionally distant and manipulative, pursues a life of meaningless pleasure, eventually causing the downfall of those closest to him.*

. . . She jumped into the boat, I followed, and had barely recovered my senses when I noticed that we were adrift. 'What does this mean?' I said crossly. 'It means,' she said, making me sit on a bench, and winding her arms around my waist, 'it means that I love you.' Her cheek pressed mine and I felt, on my face, her flaming breath. Suddenly, something fell into the water, with a noisy splash; my hand flew to my belt — my pistol was gone. Ah, what a terrible suspicion stoke into my soul! The blood rushed to my head; I looked around — we were a hundred yards from the shore, and I could not swim! I tried to push her away, but she clung to my clothes like a cat, and suddenly a powerful push almost participated me over-board. The boat rocked, but I regained my balance, and a desperate struggle started between us; my rage gave me strength, but I soon realized that, in agility, I was inferior to my adversary. 'What do you want?' I cried, squeezing her small hands hard. Her fingers crunched, but she did not cry out; her serpent nature withstood this torture.

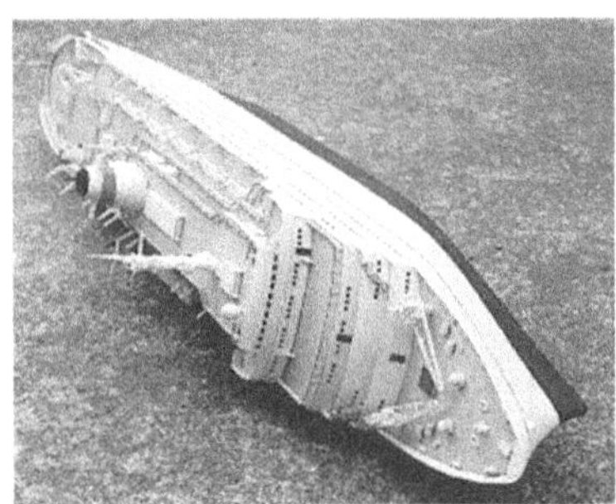

— **Mikhail Lermontov** *(1814-1841) Russian Romantic writer, poet and painter*

Challenged to a duel by a fellow army officer who took offense at one of his jokes, Lermontov was killed on the first shot. He was only 37 years old.

MS *Mikhail Lermontov* was the last of the five "poet" ships named after famous Ukrainian, Georgian and Russian writers. On February 16, 1986 she ran aground on rocks in the Marlborough Sounds, New Zealand, and sank with the loss of one crew member. She is now one of the biggest diveable ship wrecks in the world and one of the best.

The Golden Notebook (1962)

■ *Anna is a writer who keeps separate notebooks of her African experiences in earlier years, her political life and disillusionment with communism, a novel, and a personal diary, all four eventually brought together in a fifth golden notebook.*

For a week he didn't come near me, again, no explanations, nothing, he was a stranger who came in, nodded, went upstairs. For a week I watched the female creature shrink, then grow angry, grow jealous. It was a terrible, spiteful jealousy I didn't recognize in myself. I went upstairs to Saul and said" "What sort of man is it who makes love to a woman with every appearance of enjoying the process for days on end, and then switches off without so much as a polite lie?"

. . . He said: "Anna, you are looking for a man in your life, and you're right, you deserve one, but." "But?" "You're looking for happiness. It's a word that never meant anything to me until I watched you manufacturing it like molasses out of this situation. God knows how anyone, even a woman could make happiness out of this set-up, but." "But?" "This is me, Saul Green, and I'm not happy, and I never have been." "So I'm making use of you." "That's right." "Fair exchange, for your making use of me." His face changed, he looked startled. "Forgive me for mentioning it," I said, "but surely it must have crossed your mind that you are?"

— **Doris Lessing** *(1919-) British writer*

The Summer Before the Dark (1973)

■ *A middleclass London housewife, at the crossroads of her life, sets out tentatively on a journey of self-discovery.*

. . . All those years were now seeming like a betrayal of what she really was. While her body, her needs, her emotions—all of herself—had been turning like a sunflower after one man, all that time she had been holding in her hands something else, the something precious, offering it in vain to her husband, to her children, to everyone she knew—but it had never been taken, had not been noticed. But this thing she had offered, without knowing she was doing it, which had been ignored by herself and by everyone else, was what was real in her.

— **Doris Lessing**

The Fortress of Solitude (2003)

■ *The story of two motherless boys growing up in Brooklyn, one destined to become a music journalist, the other eventually imprisoned.*

White boy was his name. He'd grown into it, crossed a line, become visible. He shined like free money. The price of the name was whatever was in his pockets at the time, fifty cents or a dollar.

"White boy, lemme talk to you for a minute." Head tipped sideways, too lazy to take hands from pockets to summon him. One black kid, two, three. One near a bunch, maybe, you couldn't say who was with who. Eyes rolled, laughing. The whole event a quotation of itself, a little boring, nearly an indignity to perform.

If he ignored it, tried to keep walking: "Yo, *white boy*! I'm *talking* to you man."

"What's the matter, you can't *hear*?"

No. Yes.

"You don't like me, man?"

Helpless.

The fact of it: he'd cross the street to have his pockets emptied. The outcome was obvious anyway. He'd cross magnetized in disgrace, under the sway of an implicit yoking, so no one was forced to say *See now I got to _____ you up, cuz you don't listen, man.* It was a dance, steps traced in yokes gone by. *Call me white boy and I'll hand you a dollar spontaneously, I'm good at this now.*

"Just come here for a minute, man, I ain't gonna hurt you. What you gotta be afraid for? *Dang*, man. You think I'm gonna hurt you?"

"The kernel, the soul—let us go further and say the substance, the bulk, the actual and valuable material of all human utterances—is plagiarism"

— **Jonathan Lethem** *(1964-) American novelist and short story writer*

Rosemary's Baby (1967)

- *A young mother-to-be begins to suspect her husband and elderly neighbors have collaborated with the devil to allow her to bear an anti-Christ child.*

She watched them until she was by the basinet, which was angled in their direction. With her free hand she caught the black-covered handle at the foot of it and swung the bassinet slowly, gently, around to face her. Taffeta rustled; the back wheels squeaked.

Asleep and sweet, so small and rosy-faced, Andy lay wrapped in a snug black blanket with little black mitts ribbon-tied around his wrists. Orange-red hair he had, a surprising amount of it, silky-clean and brushed. *Andy! Oh, Andy!* She reached out to him, her knife turning away; his lips pouted and he opened his eyes and looked at her. His eyes were golden-yellow, all golden-yellow, with neither whites nor irises; all golden-yellow, with vertical black-slit pupils.

She looked at him.

He looked at her, golden-yellowly, and then at the swaying upside-down crucifix.

She looked at them watching her and knife-in-hand screamed at them, "*What have you done to his eyes?*"

— **Ira Levin** *(1929-2007) American writer, dramatist and songwriter*

The Lion, the Witch and the Wardrobe (1950)

- *A simple game of hide-and-seek turns into the adventure of a lifetime when four children venture through a wardrobe into the land of Narnia.*

"This must be a simply enormous wardrobe!" thought Lucy, going still further in and pushing the soft folds of the coats aside to make room for her.

. . . Next moment she found that what was rubbing against her face and hands was no longer soft fur but something hard and rough and even prickly. "Why, it is just like branches of trees!" exclaimed Lucy. And then she saw that there was a light ahead of her; not a few

inches away where the back of the wardrobe ought to have been, but a long way off. Something cold and soft was falling on her. A moment later she found that she was standing in the middle of a wood at night-time with snow under her feet and snowflakes falling through the air.

— **C. S. Lewis** *(1898-1963) Irish-born British novelist, academic, medievalist, literary critic, lay theologian, and Christian apologist*

Lewis fought greatly up to the moment of his conversion noting that he was brought into Christianity like a prodigal, "kicking, struggling, resentful, and darting his eyes in every direction for a chance to escape." He described his last struggle as follows: "You must picture me alone in that room in Magdalen, night after night, feeling, whenever my mind lifted even for a second from my work, the steady, unrelenting approach of Him whom I so earnestly desired not to meet. That which I greatly feared had at last come upon me. In the Trinity Term of 1929 I gave in, and admitted that God was God, and knelt and prayed: perhaps, that night, the most dejected and reluctant convert in all England." — *Wikipedia*

Babbitt (1922)

- *Disillusioned with his lifestyle, George F. Babbitt, middle-aged partner in a real-estate firm, rebels against his family and friends, eventually lapsing back into conformity.*

For all his wandering thoughts, they had never been more intimate than this. He often reflected, "Nev' forget how old Jake Offutt said a wise bird never goes love-making in his own office or his own home. Start trouble. Sure. But—"

In twenty-three years of married life he had peered uneasily at every graceful ankle, every soft shoulder; in thought he had treasured them; but not once had he hazarded respectability by adventuring. Now, as he calculated the cost of repapering the Styles house, he was restless again, discontented about nothing and everything, ashamed of his discontentment, and lonely for the fairy girl.

— **Sinclair Lewis** *(1885-1951) American novelist, short story writer and playwright*

Main Street (1920)

- *An account of small town life in Minnesota in the early 1900s as seen through the eyes of newcomer Carol Kennicott, a naïve young idealist recently married to the town's doctor.*

She saw the prairie, flat in giant patches or rolling in long hummocks. The width and bigness of it, which had expanded her spirit an hour ago, began to frighten her. It spread out so; it went on so uncontrollably; she could never know it. Kennicott was closeted in his detective story. With the loneliness which comes most depressingly in the midst of many people she tried to forget problems, to look at the prairie objectively.

— **Sinclair Lewis**

Indian Why Stores (1915)

- *Indian (Blackfeet, Chippewa, and Cree tribes) folk-lore stories "beginning with creation itself, and reaching to the whys and wherefores of nature's moods and eccentricities."*

Things were bad and getting worse. Everybody was cross, and all wondered what *Old*-man would do next, when somebody laughed. All turned to see what there could be to laugh at, at such a time, and *Old*-man turned about just in time to see the Muskrat bid good-by to his wife—that was what they were laughing at. But he paid no attention to *Old*-man or the rest, and slipped from the raft to the water. Flip! — his tail cut the water like a knife, and he was gone.

He was gone longer than the Loon, longer than the Beaver, longer than the Otter or the Gray Goose or his wife, but when he came to the surface of the water he was dead.

Old-man brought Muskrat back to life, and asked him what he had seen on his journey. Muskrat said" "I saw trees, *Old*-man, but I died before I got to them."

Old-man told him he was brave. He said his people should forever be great if he succeeded in bringing some dirt to the raft; so just as soon as the Muskrat was rested he dove again.

— **Frank B. Linderman** *(1869-1938) Montana writer, politician, Native American ally and ethnographer*

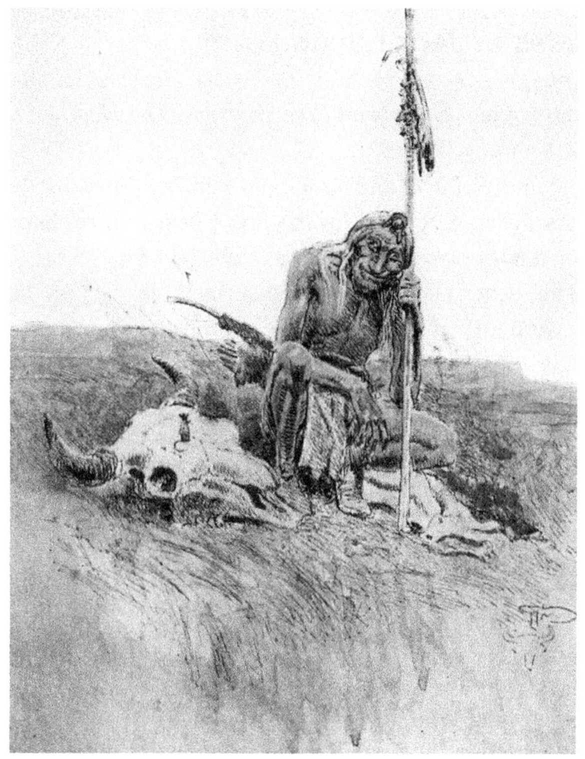

"Yes — the Mice-people always make their nests in the heads of the dead Buffalo-people, ever since that night."
Indian Why Stories by Frank B. Linderman, 1915
Illustrated by Charles M. Russell

The Call of the Wild (1903)

- *The adventures of Buck, a sled dog that is part wolf with an unbreakable spirit and his fight for survival in the frozen Alaskan Klondike.*

. . . So peremptorily did these shades beckon him, that each day mankind and the claims of mankind slipped farther from him. Deep in the forest a call was sounding, and as often as he heard this call, mysteriously thrilling and luring, he felt compelled to turn his back upon the fire and the beaten earth around it, and to plunge into the forest, and on and on, he knew not where or why; nor did he wonder where or why, the call sounding imperiously, deep in the forest. But as often as he gained the soft unbroken earth and the green shade, the love for John Thornton drew him back to the fire again.

— **Jack London** *(1876-1916) American author, journalist and social activist*

Short Stories of Jack London (1914)

- *Jack London's true métier was the short story of which he exhibited exceptional range. Here is an excerpt from "The Heathen of Borabora," one of his South Seas tales.*

. . . I changed my course and struck out blindly. I was by that time barely conscious. As my hand closed on the line I heard an exclamation from on board. I turned and looked. There was no sign of Otoo. The next instant he broke surface. Both hands were off at the wrist, the stumps spouting blood.

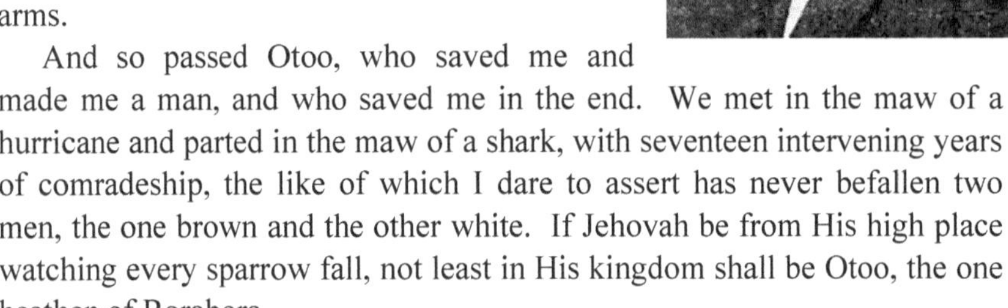

"Otoo!" he called softly. And I could see in his gaze the love that thrilled in his voice.

Then, and then only, at the very last of all our years, he called me by that name.

"Good-by, Otoo!" he called.

Then he was dragged under, and I was hauled aboard, where I fainted in the captain's arms.

And so passed Otoo, who saved me and made me a man, and who saved me in the end. We met in the maw of a hurricane and parted in the maw of a shark, with seventeen intervening years of comradeship, the like of which I dare to assert has never befallen two men, the one brown and the other white. If Jehovah be from His high place watching every sparrow fall, not least in His kingdom shall be Otoo, the one heathen of Borabora.

— **Jack London**

Under the Volcano (1947)

- *A chronicle of the last days of a former British vice-consul to Quauhnahuac, Mexico, now a mentally tortured, helpless dipsomaniac.*

"I blow you wide open from your knees up, you Jew chingao," warned the Chief of Rostrums, grasping him by the collar, and the Chief of Gardens, standing by, nodded gravely. The Consul, shaking himself free, tore frantically at the horse's bridle. The Chief of Rostrums stepped aside, hand on his holster. He drew his pistol. With his free hand he waved away some tentative onlookers. "I blow you wide open from your knees up, you cabron," he said, "you pelado."

"No, I wouldn't do that," said the Consul quietly, turning round. "That's a Colt '17, isn't it? It throws a lot of shavings."

— **Malcolm Lowry** *(1909-1957) British poet and novelist*

Given the struggle to write *Under the Volcano*, and perhaps sensing that he would never manage another such undertaking, Lowry wanted to be there on publication day. Receiving money from his publisher to travel from his squatter's shack outside Vancouver to New York, Lowry and his wife made the most of it. They flew to Seattle, took a bus to New Orleans, boarded a cargo ship to Haiti, flew to Miami, and took a final bus north, arriving after two and a half months, many misadventures and one hospitalization for alcoholism on the morning of the day of the book's release. — *Today in Literature*

Foreign Affairs (1984)

■ *A fifty-something unmarried professor visiting London to work on her new book shares detachment and loneliness with a colleague.*

Twenty minutes ago, while waiting in the departure lounge in a cheerful mood, Vinnie read in a magazine of national circulation a scornful and disparaging reference to her life's work. Projects such as hers, the article stated, are a prime example of the waste of public funds, the proliferation of petty and useless scholarship, and the general weakness and folly of the humanities in America today. Do we really need a scholarly study of playground doggerel? inquired the writer, one L. D. Zimmern, a professor of English at Columbia. No doubt Mr. or Ms. Miner would answer this query by assuring us of the social, historical, or literary value of "Ring-around-a-rosy," he continued, sawing through the supports of any possible answer; but he, for one, was not convinced.

What makes this unprovoked attack especially hideous is that for over thirty years the Atlantic had been Vinnie's favorite magazine.

— **Alison Lurie** *(1926-)*
American novelist

M

The Executioner's Song (1979)

- *The true story of Gary Gilmore, a violent yet articulate man, who chose not to fight the death-penalty sentence and was executed in 1977.*

Then the Warden said, "Do you have anything you'd like to say?" and Gary looked up at the ceiling and hesitated, then said, "Let's do it." That was it. The most pronounced amount of courage, Vern decided, he'd ever seen, no quaver, no throatiness, right down the line. Gary had looked at Vern as he spoke. . . . .

Three or four men in red coats came up and put the hood on Gilmore's head. Nothing was said after that. . . . .

Now, the doctor was beside him, pinning a white circle on Gilmore's black shirt, and the doctor stepped back. Father Meersman traced the big sign of the cross, the last act he had to perform. Then he, too, stepped over the line, and turned around, and looked back at the hooded figure in the chair.

— **Norman Mailer** *(1923-2007) American novelist, journalist, essayist, poet, playwright, screenwriter and film director*

The Assistant (1957)

- *A barely surviving Jewish grocer in Brooklyn befriends a rough derelict who becomes attracted to his daughter.*

He recalled the bad times he had lived through, but now times were worse than in the past; now they were impossible. His store was always a marginal one, up today, down tomorrow—as the wind blew. Overnight business could go down enough to hurt; yet as a rule it slowly recovered—sometimes it seemed to take forever—went up, not high enough to be really *up*, only not down. When he had first bought the grocery it was all right for the neighborhood; it had got worse as the neighborhood had. Yet even a year ago staying open seven days a week, sixteen hours a day, he could still eke out a living. What kind of living?—a living; you lived. Now, though he toiled the same hard hours, he was close to bankruptcy, his patience torn. In the past when bad times came he had somehow lived through them, and when good times returned, they more or less returned to him. But now since the appearance of H. Schmitz across the street ten months ago, all times were bad.

— **Bernard Malamud** *(1914-1986) American novelist and short story writer*

The Fixer (1966)

- *In 1910 a Russian Jewish fixer (carpenter) is falsely accused of murdering a young boy and is thrown into prison.*

. . . Time blew like a steppe wind into an empty future. There was no end, no event, indictment, trial. The waiting withered him. He was worn thin by the struggle to wait, by the knowledge of his innocence against the fact of his imprisonment; that nothing had been done in a whole year to free him. He was stricken to be so absolutely alone. Oppressed by the heat, eaten by damp cold, eroded by the expectation of an indictment that never came, were his gray bones visible through his skin? His nerves were threads stretched to the instant before snapping. He cried out of the deepest part of him, a narrow pit, but no one appeared or answered, or looked at him or spoke to him, neither friend nor stranger.

— **Bernard Malamud**

Malamud had been living in Oregon for a few years, teaching at Oregon State. There they gave medals each year to faculty members who had done the most for the University and mankind. The year Malamud won the Book Award, he'd gotten the bronze prize. The gold had gone to the inventor of a better breast-cup for cows. The silver had gone to a Professor of Logging.

His daughter describes Malamud as a modest, hard-working, self-effacing man. At a ceremony for his 1959 National Book Award for the story collection *The Magic Barrel*, Malamud refused to pose for the cameras holding up his book, forgot his $1,000 check on the podium, and arrived late to the dinner in his honor, whereupon he was told by the waiter that there were no more places at the table. — *Today in Literature*

The Magic Barrel (1958)

- *Stories abounding in lackadaisical decisions, disappointment, and sadness.*

He made to depart, but Leo, forgetting himself, seized the matchmaker by his tight coat and shook him frenziedly.

"Please," sighed Salzman, "*Please.*"

Leo ashamedly let him go. "Tell me who she is," he begged. "It's very important for me to know."

"She is not for you. She is a wild one—wild, without shame. This is not a bride for a rabbi."

"What do you mean wild?"

"Like an animal. Like a dog. For her to be poor was a sin. This is why to me she is dead now."

"In God's name, what do you mean?"

"Her I can't introduce to you," Salzman cried.

"Why are you so excited?"

"Why, he asks," Salzman said, bursting into tears. "This is my baby, my Stella, she should burn in hell."

— **Bernard Malamud**

Remembering Babylon (1993)

- *A shipwrecked sailor lives with an aborigine tribe for 16 years, then reenters white society creating major tensions.*

The creature, almost upon them now and with Flash at its heels, came to a halt, gave a kind of squawk, and leaping up onto the top rail of the fence, hung there, its arms outflung as if preparing for flight. Then the ragged mouth gapped.

'Do not shoot,' it shouted. 'I am a B-b-british object!"

It was a white man, though there was no way you could have known it from his look. He had the mangy, half-starved look of a black, and when, with a cry, he lost his grip on the rail and came tumbling at their feet, the smell of one too, like dead swamp-water; and must have been as astonished as they were by the words that had jumped out of his mouth because he could find no more of them. He gaped, grinned, rubbed his side, winced, cast his eyes about in a hopeless way, and when he found speech again it was a complaint, against himself perhaps, in some whining blackfeller's lingo.

— **David Malouf** *(1934-) Australian writer*

Buddenbrooks (1901)

- *The downfall of a wealthy mercantile family over four generations living in Germany through several decades in the mid 19th century.*

And the rest of the day was so free and had no real schedule, a wonderful lazy and coddled life of ease that passed serenely and without a care. It started with mornings on the beach, while the band played its early program up above them—just lying and resting at the foot of the wicker chair, playing quiet, dreamy games with the soft sand that didn't even get you dirty, letting your gaze drift easily and painlessly across the endless green and blue, from which came a gentle swishing sound bearing a strong, fresh, and aromatic breeze that wrapped itself around your ears and made you deliciously dizzy, a kind of muted numbness that silently, peacefully dissolved every constraint, so that you lost all sense of time and space.

— **Thomas Mann** *(1875-1955) German novelist, short story writer, social critic, philanthropist, and essayist*

The Magic Mountain (1924)

- *Young Hans Castorp, initially only a visitor, stays seven years in an isolated high-mountain hospital in the Swiss Alps.*

He had just begun to climb again when — admittedly, just as expected — it began to snow and blow with a vengeance. . . . . "Hello there!" Hans Castorp though and came to a stop as the first gust drove a thick flurry against him. "That's quite a little breeze. Goes right to the bone." And, indeed, it was a very ugly wind. One did not notice the general dreadful cold — it was approaching zero, in fact — when the dry air was still and inert, as was usually the case; it felt almost balmy. But the moment the wind picked up, the cold cut through flesh like a knife, and when it really started blowing, as now — because that first sweeping gust had been only a harbinger—seven fur coats could not suffice to protect your bones from the horrendous icy blast. Hans Castorp, however, was not wearing seven fur coats but only a woolen vest, . . .

— **Thomas Mann**

Wolf Hall (2009)

- *The role of Thomas Cromwell and events leading to Henry VIII's second marriage and following consequences.*

"Thomas Cromwell?" people say. "That is an ingenious man. Do you know he has the whole of the New Testament by heart?" He is the very man if an argument about God breaks out; he is the very man for telling your tenants twelve good reasons why their rents are fair. He is the man to cut through some legal entanglement that's ensnared you for three generations, or talk your sniffling little daughter into the marriage she swears she will never make. With animals, women and timid litigants, his manner is gentle and easy; but he makes your creditors weep. He can converse with you about the Caesars or get you Venetian glassware at a very reasonable rate. Nobody can outtalk him, if he wants to talk. Nobody can better keep their head, when markets are falling and weeping men are standing on the street tearing up letters of credit. "Liz," he says one night, "I believe that in a year or two we'll be rich."

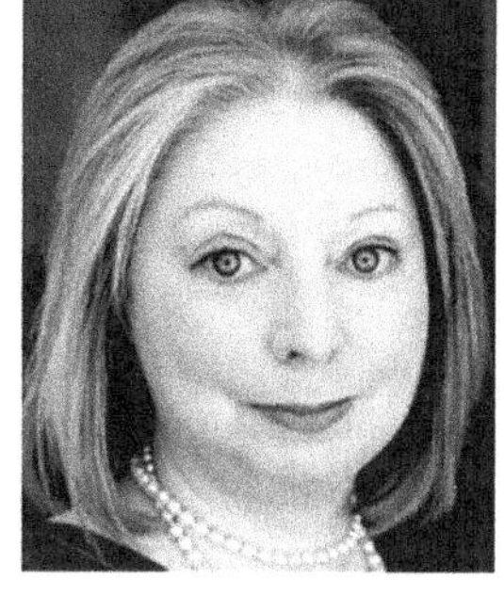

— **Hilary Mantel** *(1952-) English novelist, short story writer and critic*

The Betrothed (1825)

- *Set in Lombardy in 1628-30, the tale of two young lovers in a time of war, famine, and plague. In this quote, the Unnamed, on impulse, visits the Archbishop of Milan, Cardinal Federigo Borromeo.*

Raising his eyes, however, to the Archbishop's face, he became gradually filled with a feeling of veneration, authoritative, and at the same time soothing; which, while it increased his confidence, gently subdued his haughtiness, and, without offending his pride, compelled it to give way, and imposed silence. . . .

'And the happiness I feel (exclaimed the Archbishop), and which must surely be evident in my countenance, do you think I should feel it at the announcement and visit of a stranger? It is you who make me experience it; you I say, whom I ought to have sought; you whom I have, at least, loved and wept over, and for whom I have so often prayed; you, among all my children, . . .'

The Unnamed stood astonished at this warm reception, in language which corresponded so exactly with that which he had not yet expressed, nor, indeed, had fully determined to express; and, affected, but exceedingly surprised, he remained silent. 'Well!' resumed Federigo, still more affectionately, 'you have good news to tell me; and you keep me so long expecting it?'

— **Alessandro Manzoni** *(1785-1873) Italian poet and novelist*

The Bad Seed (1954)

- *Little charming Rhoda Penmark turns out to be a serial killer.*

In 1918 March received the Distinguished Service Cross (the second highest decoration for valor) as a result of his actions in World War I.

His eyes met the coldness in her own, and raising his head, tilting his neck back, he pressed his shears against his dirty coveralls, and said, as though they were playing the balcony scene in some ancient play. "I been way behind the times heretofore, but now I got your number, miss! I been hearing things about you that ain't nice. I been hearing you beat up that poor little Claude in the woods, and that all three of the Fern sisters had to pull you off him. They tell me it took that many to pull you off him. I heard you run him off the wharf, he was so scared. That's another thing I heard."

Rhoda put down her book, gave him her full attention, and said, "If you tell lies like that, you won't go to heaven when you die."

— **William March** *(1893-1954) American author*

The Four Feathers (1902)

- *A British army officer, accused of being a coward, attempts to redeem his honor by aiding his regiment disguised as an Arab.*

"There is some mistake," he said as he shook the lid open, and then he stopped abruptly. Three white feathers fluttered out of the box, swayed and rocked for a moment in the air, and then, one after another, settled gently down upon the floor. They lay like flakes of snow upon the dark polished boards. But they were not whiter than Harry Feversham's cheeks. He stood and stared at the feathers until he felt a light touch on his arm. He looked and saw Ethne's gloved hand upon his sleeve.

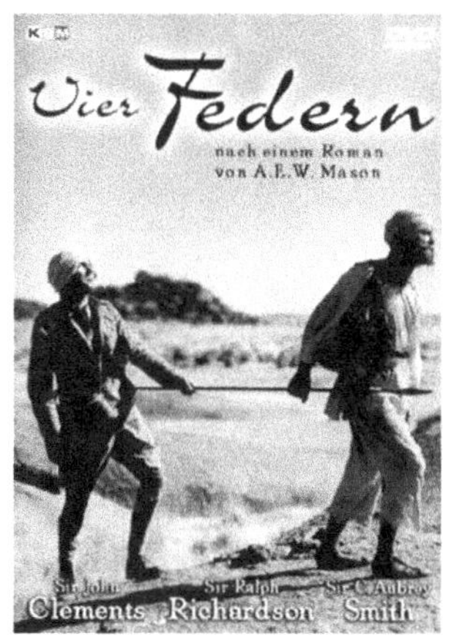

"What does it mean?" she asked. There was some perplexity in her voice, but nothing more than perplexity. The smile upon her face and the loyal confidence in her eyes showed she had never a doubt that his first word would lift it from her. "What does it mean?"

"That there are things which cannot be hid, I suppose," said Feversham.

— **A. E. W. Mason** *(1865-1948) British author and politician*

Shiloh and Other Stories (1982)

- *Gentle stories of the lives of western Kentucky people as they struggle with the ups and downs of contemporary life in the New South.*

Nancy wants to find out if Granny has a picture of a great-great-aunt named Nancy Culpepper. No one in the family seems to know anything about her, but Nancy is excited by the thought of an ancestor with the same name as hers. . . .

While Granny sleeps, Nancy gets a flashlight and opens the closet. The inside is crammed with the accumulation of decades—yellowed newspapers, boxes of greeting cards, bags of string, and worn-out stockings. Granny's best dress, a blue bonded knit she has hardly worn, is in plastic wrapping. Nancy pushed the clothing aside and examines the wall. To her right, a metal pipe runs vertically through the closet. Backing up against the dresses, Nancy shines the light on the corner and discovers a large framed picture wedged behind the pipe. By tugging at the frame, she is able to work it gradually through the narrow space between the wall and the pipe. In the picture a man and woman, whose features are sharp and clear, are sitting expectantly on a brocaded love seat. Nancy imagines that this is a wedding portrait. . . .

Granny puts in her teeth and eats the strawberries in slurps, missing her mouth twice. "Let me see them people again," she says, waving the spoon. Her teeth make the sound of a baby rattle.

"Nancy Hollins," says Granny. "She was a Culpepper."

"That's Nancy Culpepper?" cries Nancy.

— **Bobbie Ann Mason** *(1940-) American novelist and short story writer*

Far Tortuga (1975)

- *Captain Raib Avers and eight ragged black and mulatto crewmen set out from Grand Cayman Island to hunt turtles in the southwest Caribbean.*

The deck vibration dies, and the sea slop on the hull is loud. A shriek of pulleys: a catboat smacks onto the sea. The catboats are a faded water blue. . . .

The kellecks, each fastened to a length of rope with a long buoy at the other end, are stowed in the bilges aft and under the middle seat; the lines are run forward to the stack of buoys in the bow, to avoid tangling. The nets are passed down last and stacked astern. . . .

The nets trail downwind from the reef, the float lines bunched up here and there in a rude tangle; the turtles thrash and sigh. As the catboat comes up on the net, the creatures sound, dragging the floats beneath the sea, but they are tired and soon surface.

— **Peter Matthiessen** *(1927-) American novelist and non-fiction writer*

The Complete Stories of W. Somerset Maugham (1952)

- *Quiet and observant, Maugham never lost a chance to turn real life into a story. This excerpt from "Mr. Know-All."*

Carl Van Vechten photo 1934

. . . He handed the chain to Mr. Kelada. The Levantine took a magnifying glass from his pocket and closely examined it. A smile of triumph spread over his smooth and swarthy face. He handed back the chain. He was about to speak. Suddenly he caught sight of Mrs. Ramsay's face. It was so white that she looked as though she were about to faint. She was staring at him with wide and terrified eyes. They held a desperate appeal; it was so clear that I wondered why her husband did not see it. Mr.

Kelada stopped with his mouth open. He flushed deeply. You could almost *see* the effort he was making over himself.

"I was mistaken," he said. "It's a very good imitation, but of course as soon as I looked through my glass I saw that it wasn't real. I think eighteen dollars is just about as much as the damned thing's worth."

— **W. Somerset Maugham** *(1874-1965) English playwright, novelist and short story writer*

Of Human Bondage (1915)

■ *The coming of age of Phillip Carey afflicted with a club foot, whose mad unrequited love for Mildred, an aloof self-centered waitress, changes the course of his life.*

When he lay in bed he seemed still to see her sitting in the corner of the railway carriage, with the white crochet shawl over her head. He did not know how he was to get through the hours that must pass before his eyes rested on her again. He thought drowsily of her thin face, with its delicate features, and the greenish pallor of her skin. He was not happy with her, but he was unhappy away from her. He wanted to sit by her side and look at her, he wanted to touch her, he wanted . . . the thought came to him and he did not finish it, suddenly he drew wide awake . . . he wanted to kiss the thin, pale mouth with its narrow lips. The truth came to him at least. He was in love with her. It was incredible.

— **W. Somerset Maugham**

So Long, See You Tomorrow (1980)

■ *The interconnected stories of two lonely farm boys and loss of childhood in Illinois in the 1920s.*

Fingering a list of things that only she knew where to put her hands on, in chests and dresser drawers and cardboard boxes pushed back under the eaves in the attic, Marie Wilson made polite conversation. She could hardly believe the disorder and filth that met her eyes everywhere she looked. The windows were so thickly coated with dust and cobwebs you could hardly see out of them. . . .

But it was the little boys that upset her most. They were thin and pale and answered her questions listlessly, as if they were addressing a stranger. She said, "You know that your father wouldn't let me take you with me?" and they nodded. She brushed the hair out of their eyes, and kissed them, and touched them on the cheek and on the shoulder as she talked to them, and the strangeness wore off eventually. After that they wouldn't let her out of their sight. As she bent down to say goodby to them both started to cry.

— **William Maxwell** *(1908-2000) American novelist and editor*

All the Pretty Horses (1992)

■ *A 16-year-old dispossessed Texan crosses the Rio Grande into Mexico, encountering various adventures including an ill-fated romance.*

. . . When they woke it was evening. She came from the shower wrapped in a towel and she sat on the bed and took his hand and looked down at him. I cannot do what you ask, she said. I love you. But I cannot.

He saw very clearly how all his life led only to this moment and all after led nowhere at all. He felt something cold and soulless enter him like another being and he imagined that it smiled malignly and he has no reason to believe that it would ever leave. When she came out of the bathroom again she was dressed and he made her sit on the bed and he held her hands both of them and talked to her but she only shook her head and she turned away her tearstained face and told him that it was time to go and that she could not miss the train. . . .

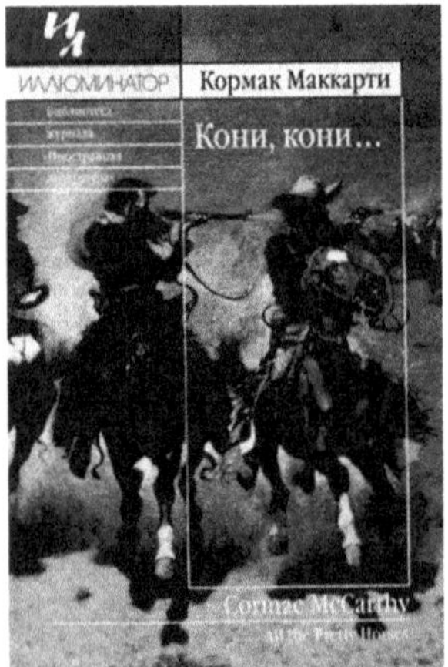

They stood on the platform and she put her face against his shoulder and he spoke to her but she did not answer. The train came huffing in from the south and stood steaming and shuddering with the coach windows curving away down the track like great dominoes smoldering in the dark and he could not but compare this arrival to that one twenty-four hours ago and she touched the silver chain at her throat and turned away and bent to pick up the suitcase and then leaned and kissed him one last time her face all wet and then she was gone.

— **Cormac McCarthy** *(1933-) American novelist and playwright*

Blood Meridian (1985)

- *The fortunes of the Kid, a fourteen-year old boy attempting to survive the violence and depravity of the Texas-Mexico border in the 1850s.*

The barman stood in the center of the room. He was breathing heavily and he turned, following the kid's movements. When the kid approached him he raised the bungstarter. The kid crouched lightly with the bottles and feinted and then broke the right one over the man's head. Blood and liquor sprayed and the man's knees buckled and he eyes rolled. The kid had already let go the bottleneck and he pitched the second bottle into his right hand in a roadagent's pass before it even reached the floor and he backhanded the second bottle across the barman's skull and crammed the jagged remnant into he eye as he went down.

— Cormac McCarthy

The Road (2006)

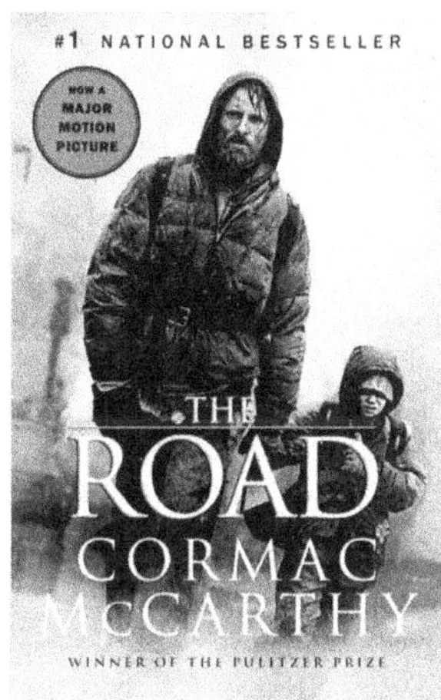

#1 NATIONAL BESTSELLER
NOW A MAJOR MOTION PICTURE
THE ROAD
CORMAC McCARTHY
WINNER OF THE PULITZER PRIZE

- *A father and young son journey together across a grim post-apocalyptic landscape void of almost all life.*

They plodded on, thin and filthy as street addicts. Cowled in their blankets against the cold and their breath smoking, shuffling through the black and silky drifts. They were crossing the broad coastal plain where the secular winds drove them in howling clouds of ash to find shelter where they could. Houses or barns or under the bank of a roadside ditch with the blankets pulled over their heads and the noon sky black as the cellars of hell. He held the boy against him, cold to the bone. Don't lose heart, he said. We'll be all right.

— Cormac McCarthy

The Heart is a Lonely Hunter (1940)

- *A story of two young people in a Georgia mill town during the 1930s — John Singer an attentive deaf mute and Mick Kelly the story's heroine who finds solace in her music.*

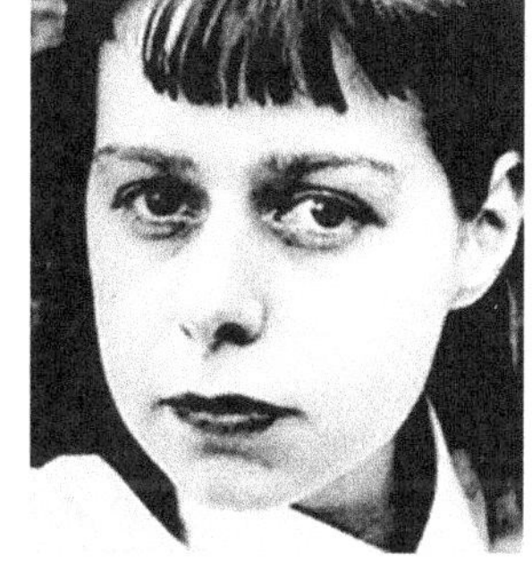

. . . Mick loved to go up to Mister Singer's room. Even if he was a deaf-and-dumb mute he understood every word she said to him. Talking with him was like a game. Only there was a whole lot more to it than any game. It was like finding out new things about music. She would tell him some of her plans that she would not tell anybody else. He let her meddle with his cute little chess men. Once when she was excited and caught her shirttail in the electric fan he acted in such a kindly way that she was not embarrassed at all. Except for her Dad, Mister Singer was the nicest man she knew.

— **Carson McCullers** *(1917-1967) American writer*

Charming Billy (1998)

- *Billy falls in love with a beautiful young Irish girl who fails to return from a trip home, prompting his lifetime abuse of alcohol.*

Laughing, she raised her shining eyes, her dark brows that nearly ran together above them and proved, as far as he was concerned, that Nature in her overprotectiveness understood what a glorious pair of eyes She had created. "You're planning to rob a bank or two, are you?"

"Sure," he said. He took her face in his hands, but even this close he couldn't tell if it was firelight or tears that made her eyes shine so, or maybe his own muddled vision. He pulled her to him, but carefully this time. There was a vast darkness beyond them and the indifferent pounding of the sea, and adrift in the same world that held their fine future there was accident and disappointment, a sickening sense of false hope and false promise that required all of God's grace to keep a bay.

— **Alice McDermott** *(1953-) Novelist and Professor of the Humanities*

That Night (1987)

- *The troubled lives of high school sweethearts involving their parents and neighbors in the suburban world of the early 1960s.*

That night when he came to claim her, he stood on the short lawn before her house, his knees bent, his fists driven into his thighs, and bellowed her name with such passion, that even the friends who surrounded him, who had come to support him, to drag her from the house, to murder her family if they had to, let the chains they carried go limp in their hands. Even the men from our neighborhood, in Bermuda shorts or chinos, white T-shirts and gray suit pants, with baseball bats and snow shovels held before them like rifles, even they paused in their rush to protect her: the good and the bad—the black-jacketed boys and the fathers in their light summer clothes—startled for that one moment before the fighting began by the terrible, piercing sound of his call.

— **Alice McDermott**

Atonement (2001)

- *Young Briony Tallis accuses an acquaintance of her cousin's rape, later, feeling guilty over the accusation, she serves as a nurse as a kind of atonement.*

She was not intending to remove the gauze, but as she loosened it, the heavy sterile towel beneath it slid away, taking a part of the bloodied dressing with it. The side of Luc's head was missing. The hair was shaved well back from the missing portion of skull. Below the jagged line of bone was a spongy crimson mess of brain, several inches across, reaching from the crown almost to the tip of his ear. She caught the towel before it slipped to the floor, and she held it while she waited for her nausea to pass. . . .

He was gazing at her in rapture. He brought his free hand to cover hers.

He said, "You know that my mother is very fond of you."

"Is she?"

"She talks about you all the time. She thinks we should be married in the summer."

She held his gaze. She knew now why she had been sent. He was having difficulty swallowing, and drops of sweat were forming on his brow, along the edge of the dressing and along his upper lip. She wiped them away, and was about to reach the water for him, but he said,

"Do you love me?"

She hesitated. "Yes." No other reply was possible. Besides, for that moment, she did. He was a lovely boy who was a long way from his family and he was about to die.

— **Ian McEwan** *(1948-) English novelist and screenwriter*

Saturday (2005)

- *A neurosurgeon has a car accident followed by a confrontation with the hoodlum driver, a harbinger of future terror.*

. . . Baxter is one of those smokers whose pores exude a perfume, an oily essence of his habit. Garlic affects certain people the same way. Possibly the kidneys are implicated. He's a fidgety, small-faced young man with thick eyebrows and dark brown hair razored close to the skull. The mouth is set bulbously, with the smoothly shaved shadow of a strong beard adding to the effect of a muzzle. The general simian air is compounded by sloping shoulders, and the built-up trapezoids suggest time in the gym, compensating for his height perhaps. The sixties-style suit—tight cut, high lapels, flat-fronted trousers worn from the hip—is taking some strain around the jacket's single fastened button. There's also tightness in the fabric round the biceps. He half-turns and dips away from Perowne, then bobs back. He gives an impression of fretful impatience, of destructive energy waiting to be released. He may be about to lash out. — **Ian McEwan**

Ninety-Two in the Shade (1973)

■ *Returning home to Key West, a young man planning to become a skiff guide encounters not so friendly competition.*

Now one hot summer afternoon when it must have been ninety-two in the shade and the bar was empty as all get out, Nichol Dance looked up at the glaring door-way with its bands of greenery, yellow-striped road, and sky, to see the exercise boy enter as though afloat on that panel of uncomfortable light. . . .

Dance told him to get out.

"Why?"

"Because I told you to. And as soon as you do go, I am going to call the law." Dance was afraid of him. . . . .

The exercise boy was sitting close enough to the bar that Dance couldn't see what he was holding. But Nichol had a gun of his own, the useful Bisley Colt with the Mexican ivory grips, and he was pointing it through the thin paneling of the bar face. . . . The two talked for an endless half an hour, the exercise boy in his serpentine voice. And the first time he moved his right arm, Nichol Dance blew him halfway across the room; where he lay, all wings, and made a spot.

— **Thomas McGuane** *(1939-) American author*

Farragan's Retreat

■ *The cultural and generational conflicts within an Irish-American clan caused by the Vietnam War.*

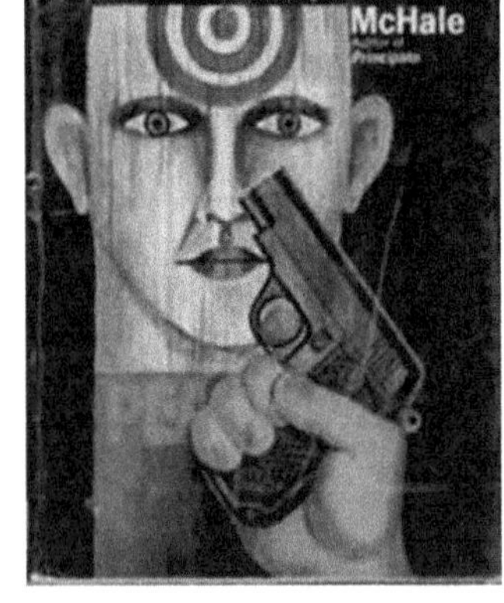

Farragan had absolutely no intention of murdering his son, Simon: fathers did not usually quash their own seed, after all, given the time and trouble it took to make it grow. Even if a substantial number of people thought Simon definitely needed quashing.

But it occasionally disturbed him that he so positively enjoyed fantasizing the killer poses. The August Sunday morning, between the Offertory and Communion of the Mass, he was into them again for perhaps the thirtieth time.

Pose one was doggedly simple. Farragan, with revolver already in hand, had only to pull the trigger after aiming point-blank at the victim's heart the instant the latter opened his apartment door in response to Farragan's knock. But of course there was one problem with pose one beyond the possibility of powder burns and the indictment of the victim's erupted blood on Farragan's too-close lapels. This was the fact that the victim was Simon—whom Farragan loved in essence but was compelled to despise in principle—and for this reason he guessed he might not be equal for the remainder of his life to his memory's recall of the victim's shock of recognition of his own father.

— **Tom McHale** *(1941-1982) American novelist*

The Sand Pebbles (1962)

- *The story of a U.S. Navy gunboat on patrol in the Yangtze River on the eve of the China revolution in 1925-27. This recounted brutality ends the life of Po-han, Jake Holman's Chinese friend and assistant.*

Po-han dangled, pitching forward, Holman could see the strain in his ridged belly muscles, arms and shoulders. He was looking at the ship. Someone on the bridge was yelling in Chinese. Three soldiers grasped Po-han around the waist and legs and surged their weight on him. He dropped abruptly as his shoulder joints burst, and he screamed. . . .

"Get out of here, Holman! Back to the waist party!"

"Go to hell. We got to shoot. Do something."

"He ain't American. We got our orders."

"He's a shipmate." . . .

He could feel his flesh reaching out for the healing bullet. He locked on Lt. Collins' eyes and he could hear Po-han wailing and wailing in half-voiced words. They were all frozen there. Then Lop Eye Shing turned around, evil-faced, saying something.

"Po-han talkee too much no can," he said. "Po-han talkee somebody shoot he." . . .

Crosley was holding a rifle. Holman jerked it away from him.

"Not you, Crosley," he said.

He cambered a cartridge and took aim with the bridge rail as rest. He followed Po-han's head with the beaded foresight, rolling, rolling, and Po-han saw him and held his head still. Holman sagged his stomach muscles and in a quiet place far back in his mind he said *Good-bye, Po-han.* He squeezed the trigger. He saw the head jerk and he knew that it was all right now. — **Richard McKenna** *(1913-1964) American sailor and author*

Lonesome Dove (1985)

- *An epic story of frontier life as told through the lives of cattlemen Woodrow Call and Augustus McCrae, retired Texas Rangers.*

The thought struck Pea Eye for the first time that Gus might die. He had no color, and he was shaking. It had never been suggested that Gus might die. Of course, he knew any man could die. Pea himself had seen many die. Yet it was a condition he had never associated with Gus McCrae, or with the Captain either. . . . .

"Now go on, Pea," Augustus said. "Go get the Captain, and don't worry about me. Don't let the Indians catch you, whatever you do."

Gus reached out a hand and Pea Eye realized he was offering a handshake. Pea Eye shook his hand, feeling terribly sad.

"Gus, I never thought I'd be leaving you," he said.

"Well, you are, though," Augustus said. "Trod carefully."

It was then that the conviction struck Pea Eye that he would never see Gus alive again. Mainly what they were into was just another Indian fight, and all of those had inconveniences. But Gus had never sustained a wound before that Pea could remember. The arrows and bullets that had missed him so many times had finally found him.

— **Larry McMurtry** *(1936-) American novelist and screenwriter*

Elbow Room (1977)

- *Short stories about the human inability to connect, this quote featuring a sad washout of a street hood with a missing eye.*

Billy looked calmly around the barroom, like a priest about to say Mass. And yet beneath his cool exterior I thought I sensed, in the broad sweep of his red eye, the hint of a certain rough pride. "When she said that," he went on, "I *knowed* what I had to do. I gived the gun to her. I made her point it at my head. I told Miss Ruby, 'Me, I'm just dumb enough to believe it ain't even loaded. And if it is, it won't be the first time I been dead.' Then I ram my fist in her jaw."

I waited. The clink of glasses and the noisy blend of barroom voices teased my anticipating ear. Billy was a master of suspense. Finally, I said, "So you called her bluff, got your eye shot out, but proved you were a man."

Billy laughed, his demon thumbing triumphantly in his chest. "Naw," he said. "She pulled the trigger and *killed* me. That's how come I'm back on the road for Mr. Floyd today."

Such were his lies that evening in that bar on Halstead.

— **James Alan McPherson** *(1943-) American short story writer and essayist*

Moby-Dick (1851)

■ *The tragic account of Captain Ahab's vengeful and obsessive quest for the great white whale Moby Dick.*

The harpoon was darted; the stricken whale flew forward; with igniting velocity the line ran through the groove;—ran foul. Ahab stooped to clear it; he did clear it; but the flying turn caught him around the neck, and voicelessly as Turkish mutes bowstring their victim, he was shot out of the boat, ere the crew knew he was gone. Next instant, the heavy eye-splice in the rope's final end flew out of the dark-empty tub, knocked down an oarsman and smiting the sea, disappeared in its depths.

— **Herman Melville** *(1819-1891) American novelist, short story writer, essayist and poet*

Centennial (1974)

■ *The history, land, and people of Colorado with an extensive cast of Native Americans, migrating settlers, ranchers, cowboys, hunters, trappers, and gold seekers. Although vastly encompassing, this encyclopedia of a book is centered on the South Platt River in Colorado. Thus, from numerous memorable quotes, this selection.*

And finally there is the river, a sad, bewildered nothing of a river. It carries no great amount of water, and when it has some it is uncertain where it wants to take it. No ship can navigate it, nor even a canoe, with reasonable assurance. It is the butt of more jokes than any other river on earth, and the greatest joke is to call it a river at all. It's a sand bottom, a wandering afterthought, a useless irritation, a frustration, and when you've said all that, it suddenly rises up, spreads out to a mile wide, engulfs your crops and lays waste your farms.

— **James A. Michener** *(1907-1997) American author*

Tales of the South Pacific (1947)

- *Stories of the transforming experiences of American fighting men and women in the South Pacific during the Second World War.*

. . . In my bitterness I dimly perceived what battle means. In civilian life I was ashamed until I went into uniform. In the States I was uncomfortable while others were overseas. At Noumea (New Caledonia) I thought, "The guys on Guadal! They're the heroes!" But when I reached Guadal (Canal) I found that all the heroes were somewhere farther up the line. And while I sat in safety aboard the LCS-108 I knew where the heroes were. They were on Kuralei (Kwajalein). Yet, on the beach itself only a few men ever really fought the Japs. I suddenly realized that from the farms, and towns, and cities all over America an unbroken line ran straight to the few who storm the blockhouses. No matter where along that line you stood, if you were not the man at the end of it, the ultimate man with his sweating hands upon the blockhouse, you didn't know what war was. You had only an intimation, as of a bugle blown far in the distance. You might have flashing insights, but you did not know. But the grace of God you would never know.

C. P. Vaughan portrait

— **James A. Michener**

Death of a Salesman (play 1943)

- *A salesman for over sixty years, Willy Loman's life begins to slip out of control as he is first fired and then is too proud to take a job offer from a friend.*

. . . I don't say he's a great man. Willy Loman never made a lot of money. His name was never in the paper. He's not the finest character that every lived. But he's a human being, and a terrible thing is happening to him. So attention must be paid. He's not to be allowed to fall into his grave like an old dog. Attention, attention must be finally paid to such a person.

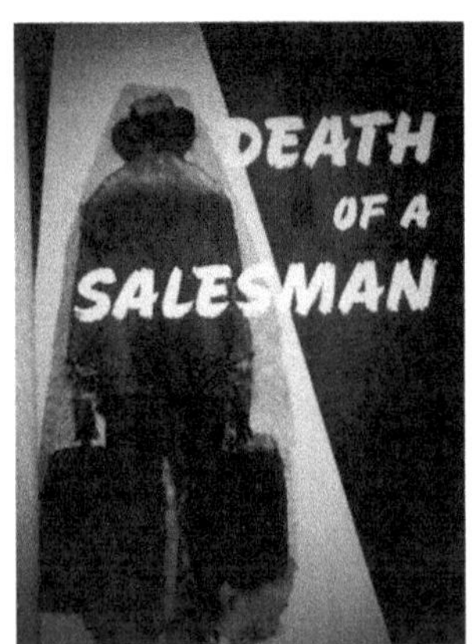

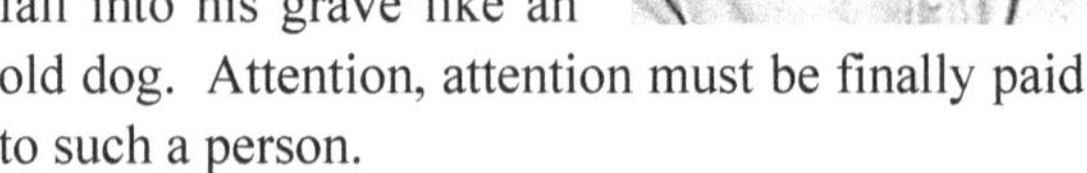

— **Arthur Miller** *(1915-2005) American playwright and essayist*

Tropic of Cancer (1934)

- *A chronicle of the bawdy and other adventures of a young expatriate and his friends living in Paris in the 1930s.*

At first I thought it was going to be embarrassing, a *ménage a trios*, but not at all. I thought when I saw her move in that it was all up with me again, that I should have to find another place, but Fillmore soon gave me to understand that he was only putting her up until she got on her feet. With a woman like her I don't know what an expression like that means; so far as I can see she's been standing on her head all her life.

— **Henry Miller** *(1891-1980) American novelist and painter*

Martin Dressler (1996)

- *The life of an enterprising dreamer whose career peaks when he builds a fabulous hotel in Manhattan at the turn-of-the-century.*

. . . The original idea for converting the Paradise Musee into a lunchroom and billiard parlor had come out of nowhere—it had been an impulse, a whim—but he was convinced that he could now go about things in a clearheaded orderly way. Martin knew that what attracted him wasn't the actual lunchroom, for he had no passion for lunchrooms, no special fondness for them, in a sense no interest in them; his passion was for working things out, bringing things together, arranging the unarrangeable, making combinations. Even the idea for a second lunchroom resembling the first had been a kind of lucky intuition, . . .

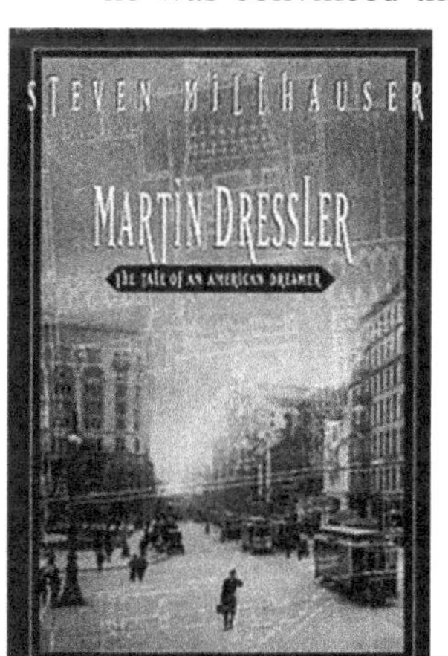

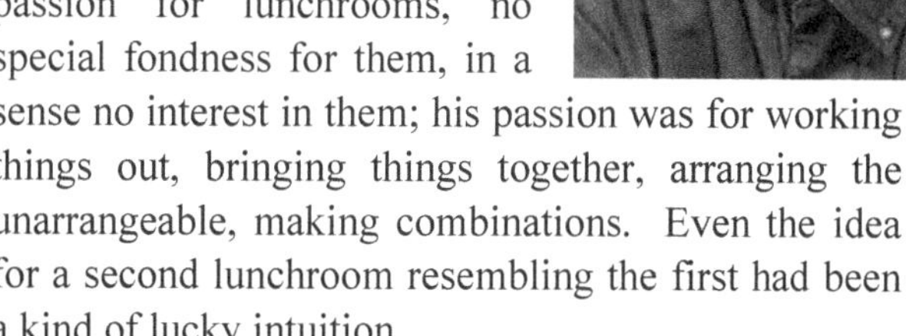

— **Steven Millhauser** *(1943-) American novelist and short story writer*

Winnie the Pooh (1926)

- *The story of Pooh bear, of very little brain, and his friend Christopher Robin, and their adventures with Owl, Rabbit, Eeyore, and Piglet at Pooh Corners.*

. . . Here is Edward Bear, coming down stairs now, bump, bump, bump, on the back of his head, behind Christopher Robin. It is, as far as he knows, the only way of coming downstairs, but sometimes he feels that there really is another way, if only he could stop bumping for a moment and think of it. And then he feels that perhaps there isn't. Anyhow, here he is at the bottom, and ready to be introduced to you Winnie-the-Pooh.

— **A. A. Milne** *(1882-1956) English author*

Original draft illustration for Winnie-The-Pooh by E. H. Shepard. © Disney

In 1928 Dorothy Parker, under her pen name, Constant Reader, reviewed A. A. Milne's *The House at Pooh Corner* in the *New Yorker*, with predictable results. Parker had panned *Now We Are Six* the previous year, even while acknowledging that "to speak against Mr. Milne puts one immediately in the ranks of those who set fire to orphanages." *The House of Pooh Corner* proved to be one pot of honey too many, especially when Pooh revealed that he added the "tiddely pom" to his Outdoor Song "to make it more hummy": "And it is that word 'hummy,' my darlings, that marks the first place in *The House at Pooh Corner* at which Tonstant Weader fwowed up." — *Today in Literature*

Cloud Atlas (2004)

- *Interlinking stories presenting an array of genres including this effort by a tentatively hired young musician to accommodate an infirmed, blind composer to the assistant's advantage.*

. . . 'I've got a little melody for viola rattling about my head, Frobisher. Let's see if you can get it down.' Was delighted to hear it, as I'd expected to start at the shallow-end – tidying up sketchy MSS into best copy and so forth. If I proved my worth as V.A.'s sentient fountain-pen on my first day, my tenure would be well-nigh assured. Sat at his desk, sharpened 2B at the ready, clean MS, waiting for him to name the notes, one by one. Suddenly, the man bellowed: '"Tar, tar! Tar-tar-tat tattytattytatty, tar!" Got that? "Tar! Tatty-tar! Quiet part — tar-tar-tar-tttt-TAR! TAR TAR TAR!!!'" Got that? Old ass obviously thought this was amusing — one could no more notate his shouted garble than one could score the braying of a dozen donkeys — but after another thirty seconds, it dawned on me this was no joke.

— **David Mitchell** *(1969-) English novelist*

Gone with the Wind (1936)

■ *The tumultuous love story of Scarlett O'Hara and Rhett Butler, from the pre-war innocence of plantation life to the war-torn streets of Atlanta.*

. . . "I'll think of it all tomorrow, at Tara. I can stand it then. Tomorrow, I'll think of some way to get him back. After all, tomorrow is another day."

— **Margaret Mitchell** *(1900-) American author*

Mitchell lived as a modest Atlanta newspaper woman until an encounter with Macmillan editor Harold Latham, who visited Atlanta in 1935. Latham was scouring the South for promising writers, and Mitchell agreed to escort him around Atlanta at the request of her friend, Lois Cole, who worked for Latham. Latham was enchanted with Mitchell, and asked her if she had ever written a book. Mitchell demurred. "Well, *if* you ever do write a book, please show it to me first!" Latham implored. Later that day, a friend of Mitchell, having heard this conversation, laughed. "Imagine, anyone as silly as Peggy writing a book!" she said. Mitchell stewed over this comment, went home, and found most of the old, crumbling envelopes containing her disjointed manuscript. She arrived at The Georgian Terrace Hotel, just as Latham prepared to depart Atlanta. "Here," she said, "take this before I change my mind!" Latham bought an extra suitcase to accommodate the giant manuscript. When Mitchell arrived home, she was horrified over her impetuous act, and sent a telegram to Latham: "Have changed my mind. Send manuscript back." But Latham had read enough of the manuscript to realize it would be a blockbuster. — *Wikipedia*

House Made of Dawn (1968)

■ *Abel returns to his reservation in New Mexico confused and unable to cope with his life as a Native American.*

At a few minutes past one, the bus came over a rise far down in the plain and its windows caught for a moment the light of the sun. It grew in the old

man's vision until he looked away and limped around in a vague circle and smoothed the front of his new shirt with his hands. "Abelito, Abelito," he repeated under his breath, and he glanced at the wagon and the mares to be sure that everything was in order. He could feel the beat of his heart, and instinctively he drew himself up in the dignity of his age. He heard the sharp wheeze of the brakes as the big bus rolled to a stop in front of the gas pump, and only then did he give attention to it, as if it had taken him by surprise. The door swung open and Abel stepped heavily to the ground and reeled. He was drunk, and he fell against his grandfather and did not know him. His wet lips hung loose and his eyes were half closed and rolling. Francisco's crippled leg nearly gave way. His good straw hat fell off and he braced himself against the weight of his grandson. Tears came to his eyes and he knew only that he must laugh and turn away from the faces in the windows of the bus.

— **N. Scott Momaday** *(1934-) Kiowa-Cherokee writer from Oklahoma, New Mexico, and Arizona*

Birds of America (1998)

- *A story collection written with wry humor and deeply-rooted emotion. This quote from "Agnes of Iowa."*

Her mother had given her the name Agnes, believing that a good-looking woman was even more striking when her name was a homely one. Her mother was named Cyrena, and was beautiful to match, but had always imagined her life would have been more interesting, that she herself would have had a more dramatic, arresting effect on the world and not ended up in Cassell, Iowa, if she had been named Enid or Hagar or Maude. And so she named her first daughter Agnes, and when Agnes turned out not to be attractive at all, but puffy and prone to a rash between her eyebrows, her hair a flat and bilious hue, her mother backpedaled and named her second daughter Linnea Elise (who turned out to be a lovely, sleepy child with excellent bones, a sweet, full mouth, and a rubbery mole above her lip that later in life could be removed without difficulty, everyone was sure.)

— **Lorrie Moore** *(1957-) American fiction writer*

A Gate at the Stairs (2009)

- *The story of a small town girl starting college and working part-time as a nanny. This scene of the birth mother's sadness at the close of her baby's adoption.*

"Well, we'll be in touch, I suppose," said Bonnie hopefully, while her face wore a look of devastation and dashed vanity. Her moment in the spotlight was coming to a close – the spotlight itself was dimming and she was slowly stepping backwards.

"The annual Christmas card," said Sarah. "I'll send you one every Christmas with all the news."

"And pictures," said Bonnie in a low, stern voice she hadn't spoken in before. "I want pictures of her." . . .

. . . She turned toward me one last time and I then, too, gave her a final hug. Bonnie whispered in my ear, "*You* be happy."

And then she seemed to be disappearing like an apparition. Through the darkening afternoon window one could hear the scrape of a plow outside in the street, but inside was where it was snowing. It was snowing in here in this room and it was all piled up around Bonnie, falling on her head, piled up on her shoulders. Of course it was only a bluff, the large, imposing dirigible of her, and now she had just spluttered to nothing.

– **Lorrie Moore**

Vanished (1988)

- *A shy backward man travels the country with a wild young woman and a child she impulsively kidnaps.*

. . . He watched her move through the dusty haze of the parking lot, her red straw purse dangling from her shoulder, her small round hips tight and high on her long thin legs and the skinny strap heels that glittered like sparks with every step. A young man in a black tee shirt came toward her and every part of her seemed to come alive; her head cocked and her shoulders trembled and her buttocks seemed to flesh out and soften under the thin cloth of her skirt. . . .

A half hour later, she came back with two cups of soda.

"Where's the aspirin?" he hollered out the window.

"Shut up!" she hissed, rolling her eyes in the direction of the stout man in a silvery suit, who had followed her out of the store.

"Jesus, you're a mouth," she groaned, getting into the car. She opened her purse and flipped two bottles of baby aspirin into his lap.

– **Mary McGarry Morris** *(1943-) American novelist and short story writer*

The Field of Vision (1956)

- *An afternoon with seven tourists from Nebraska attending a bullfight in Mexico. This quote from an early remembrance.*

. . . He had been there on the porch, right there with them, when this boy she had never seen before in her life, although she had heard about him, stepped forward and kissed her smack on the lips. The point being she had known he would. Her own lips were prepared. They had been eating candied apple and she had put out her tongue and licked the sticky part off.

Then came the dream—but she wouldn't go into that. She hadn't slept a wink that night or the next one, her knees would almost knock when she stooped for something, and she felt all over like the hum the wires make in a telephone pole. If McKee or Alice Morple touched her, it would make her jump. It wasn't in her mind at all, like the books say, but a current all over her body and a feeling that if she touched something it would spark.

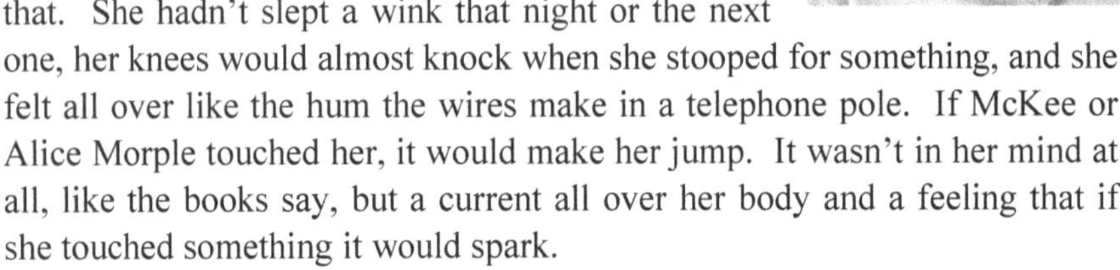

— **Wright Morris** *(1910-1998) American novelist and photographer*

Beloved (1987)

- *A young girl saying her name is "Beloved" comes to live with Sethe and her daughter Denver who are trying to rebuild their lives after having escaped from slavery.*

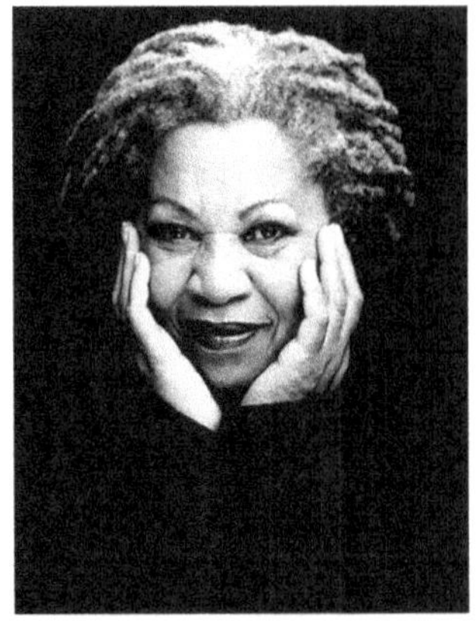

All forty-six men woke to rifle shot. All forty-six. Three whitemen walked along the trench unlocking the doors one by one. No one stepped through. When the last lock was opened, the three returned and lifted the bars, one by one. And one by one the blackmen emerged—promptly and without the poke of a rifle butt if they had been there more than a day; promptly with the butt if, like Paul D, they had just arrived. When all forty-six were standing in a line in the trench, another rifle shot signaled the climb out and up to the ground above, where one thousand feet of the best hand-forged chain in Georgia stretched. Each man bent and waited. The first man picked up the end and threaded it through the loop on his leg iron. He stood up then, and, shuffling a little, brought the chain tip to the next prisoner, who did likewise.

— **Toni Morrison** *(1931-) American novelist, editor and professor*

Song of Solomon (1977)

- *The personal story of one Macon "Milkman" Dead III, an African-American male living in Michigan, who seeks to discover his identity through the history of his ancestors.*

By the time Milkman was fourteen he had noticed that one of his legs was shorter than the other. When he stood barefoot and straight as a pole, his left foot was about half an inch off the floor. So he never stood straight; he slouched or leaned or stood with a hip thrown out, and he never told anybody about it—ever. When Lena said, "Mama, what is he walking like *that* for?" he said, "I'll walk any way I want to, including over your ugly face." Ruth said, "Be quiet, you two. It's just growing pains, Lena." Milkman knew better. It wasn't a limp—not at all—just the suggestion of one, but it looked like an affected walk, the strut of a very young man trying to appear more sophisticated than he was. It bothered him and he acquired movements and habits to disguise what to him was a burning defect.

— Toni Morrison

Knock on Any Door (1947)

- *Young immigrant Nick Romano's struggle to survive poverty through petty crime that leads to his execution for murder at the age of twenty-one. This introduction precedes the text.*

The sparrow sits on a telephone pole in the alley in the city.

The city is the world in microcosm.

The city lies in splendor and squalor. There are many doors to the city. Many things hide behind the many doors. More lives than one are lived in the city, more deaths than one are met within the city's gate.

The city doesn't change.

The people come and go, the visitors. They see the front yard.

But what of the city's back yard, and the alley? Who knows the lives and minds of the people who live in the alley?

Knock on any door down this street, in this alley.

— Willard Motley *(1909-1965) African-American writer*

In Other Rooms, Other Wonders (2009)

- *Eight short stories explore the feudal society of an aging Pakistani land-owning family of the old order.*

No one had seen the old man for several days, and the gardener sent to inquire rattled and knocked and then found him dead in the little cubicle. Ghulam Rasool had the gardeners dig a grave along the wall of the property, and that evening they buried him, just a few people attending the *janaza*, the servants from the big house, a few men from the bazaar and from houses on the hillside next to the Ali Khan lands. A poor man from nearby had been paid to wash the body, the *maulvi* from the mosque in the bazaar said the prayer.

. . . "I beg your pardon, madam. The old man Rezak, whom you so kindly put in charge at the Ali Khan lands, has passed away." . . .

"Poor poor thing. All alone, and his wife disappeared." . . .

At first the cabin sat inviolate below the swimming pool, locked, Rezak's things still in the cupboards and drawers. Sonya went once to look at it, then not again, her attention fading. Gradually, like falling leaves, the locks were broken off, one person taking the thermos, another the wood tools . . . The door of the little cabin hung open, the wind and blown rain scoured it clean.

— **Daniyal Mueenuddin** *(1963-) Pakistani-American author*

Friends of My Youth: Stories (1990)

- *Short stories well described by the Philadelphia Inquirer as "—anecdotes, shining everyday details, sexual passion, family history, quirky characters, new landscapes, humor, wisdom."*

Jerry Bauer portrait

. . . But in the winter a commotion started. There was Ellie, vomiting, weeping, running off and hiding in the haymow, howling when they found her and pulled her out, jumping to the barn floor, running around in circles, rolling in the snow. Ellie was deranged. Flora had to call the doctor. She told him that her sister's periods had stopped—could the backup of blood be driving her wild? Robert had had to catch her and tie her up, and together he and Flora had to put her to bed. She would not take food, just whipped her head from side to side, howling. It looked as if she would die speechless. But somehow the truth came out. Not from the doctor, who could not get close enough to examine her, with all her thrashing about. Probably, Robert confessed. Flora finally got wind of the truth, though all her high-mindedness. Now there had to be a wedding, though not the one that had been planned.

— **Alice Munro** *(1931-) Canadian short story writer*

Hateship, Friendship, Courtship, Loveship, Marriage (2001)

- *Glimpses of youth as in this quote, but primarily stories of aging women and men confronting the twin travails of death and late love.*

"It's too bad the moon isn't up yet," Ricky said. "It's really nice here when the moon is up."

"It's nice now, too."

He slipped his arms around her as if there was no question at all about what he was doing and he could take all the time he wanted to do it. He kissed her mouth. It seemed to her that this was the first time ever that she had participated in a kiss that was an event in itself. The whole story, all by itself. A tender prologue, an efficient pressure, a wholehearted probing and receiving, a lingering thanks, and a drawing away satisfied.

"Oh," he said. "Oh." . . . .

He took her hand and swung it as if he would like to toss it.

"And that's the first time ever I kissed a married woman."

"You'll probably kiss a lot more of them," she said. "Before you're done."

He signed. "Yeah," he said. Amazed and sobered by the thought of what lay ahead of him. "Yeah, I probably will."

— Alice Munro

The Love of a Good Woman: Stories (1998)

- *Short fiction including this story in which an overly caring aunt (Iona) accuses the baby's mother (Jill) of murdering the child.*

Iona is screaming. Jill wakes up to a house full of hurtful sunlight and Iona's screaming. . . . .

Dead. Dead. Murder.

She knows nothing about the pills. So why does she scream "Murder"? It's the blanket. She sees the blanket pulled up right over my head. Suffocation. Not poison. It has not taken her any time, not half a second, to get from "dead" to "murderer." It's an immediate flying leap. She grabs me from the crib, with the death blanket twisted round me, and holding the blanketed bundle squeezed against her body she runs screaming out of the room and into Jill's room.

Jill is struggling up, dopily, after twelve or thirteen hours of sleep.

"You've killed my baby," Iona is screaming at her.

— Alice Munro

Open Secrets: Stories (1994)

- *Eight short stories of women's lives set in and around a small Canadian town, including this story of a librarian who responds to the increasingly intimate letters of a soldier overseas.*

When the war ended, it was a while since she had heard from him. She went on expecting a letter every day and nothing came. Nothing came. She was afraid that he might have been one of those unluckiest of soldiers in the whole war–one of those killed in the last week, or on the last day, or even in the last hour. She searched the local paper every week, and the names of new casualties were still being printed there till after New Year's but his was not among them. . . .

She had to be forgiven, didn't she, she had to be forgiven for thinking, after such letters, that the one thing that could never happen was that he wouldn't approach her, wouldn't get in touch with her at all? Never cross her threshold, after such avowals? . . . . On a hot afternoon she was arranging fresh newspapers on the racks and his name jumped out at her like something in her feverish dreams.

She read a short notice of his marriage to a Miss Grace Horne. Not a girl she knew. Not a Library user.

— Alice Munro

Runaway: Stories (2004)

- *Short stories about struggling young women with this title story of domestic strife ending with the ultimate disappearance of the wife's lone friend Flora a pet goat.*

She had only to raise her eyes, she had only to look in one direction, to know where she might go. An evening walk, once her chores for the day were finished. To the edge of the woods, and the bare tree where the buzzards had held their party.

And then the little dirty bones in the grass. The skull with perhaps some shreds of bloodied skin clinging to it. A skull that she could hold like a teacup in one hand. Knowledge in one hand.

Or perhaps not. Nothing there.

Other things could have happened. He could have chased Flora away. Or tied her in the back of the truck and driven some distance and set her loose. Taken her back to the place they'd got her from. Not to have her around, reminding them.

— Alice Munro

The Tale of Genji (1021)

- *The noble culture of Heian Japan, especially of the relations between the men and women of that culture where supreme value was placed upon physical beauty.*

In time the little boy went to join his father in the palace. He was turning out to be so handsome that he hardly seemed of this world at all, and for His Majesty this aroused a certain dread. . . .

Now the boy was permanently in attendance at the palace. When he reached his seventh year, His Majesty had him perform his first reading, which he carried off with such unheard-of-brilliance that his father was frankly alarmed. . . .

Statue of Lady Murasaki.

"He has the signs of one destined to become the father of his people and to achieve the Sovereign's supreme eminence," (said the astonished physiognomist) "and yet when I see him so, I fear disorder and suffering. But when I see him as the future pillar of the court and the support of all the realm, there again appears to be a mismatch." . . . .

It was a shame to make a subject of him, considering his gifts, but he was bound to draw suspicion as a Prince, and when consultation with an eminent astrologer only confirmed this prediction, His Majesty resolved to make him a Genji. (Genji means simply "a Minamoto," the surname for a commoner.)

— **Lady Murasaki** *(973-1025) Japanese novelist and poet*

Under the Net (1954)

- *The adventures of Jake Donaghue, a hack writer and sponge, who in this incident of intended theft accidentally discovers a film-star dog and includes it in the loot.*

He joined me. 'Mother of God!' he said.

Right in the middle of the room was a shining aluminum cage, about three feet tall and five feet square. Inside the cage, growling softly and fixing us with a nervous bright eye, was a very large black-and-tan Alsatian dog. . . .

I looked at the animal curiously; it had a kind intelligent face, and in spite of its growls it seemed to be smiling. . . .

'It's Mister Mars!' I cried, pointing at the beast. 'It's Marvelous Mister Mars, the dog star. Don't you recognize him?' . . . Nothing thrills me so much as meeting a film star in real life, and I had been a fan of Mars for years. . . .

I was beginning to have a wonderful idea. While it came slowly up I held both hands pressed to my temples and kept my eyes fixed on Mister Mars, who gave one or two soft encouraging barks as if he knew what was coming into my mind.

'Finn,' I said slowly, 'I have an absolutely wonderful idea.'

'What?' said Finn suspiciously.

'We'll kidnap the dog,' I said.

— **Iris Murdoch** *(1919-1999) Irish-born British author and philosopher*

The Man Without Qualities (1930)

- *Ulrich rejects the attributes, values, and behavior of society, becoming a detached observer of the raging world around him.*

She was the wife of a prominent man and the fond mother of two handsome boys. Her favorite phrase was "highly respectable," applied to people, messengers, shops, and feelings, when she wanted to praise them. She could utter the words "truth, goodness, and beauty" as often and as casually as someone else might say "Thursday." ....

She had only one fault: she could become inordinately aroused at the mere sight of a man. She was not lustful; she was sensual, as other people have other afflictions, for instance suffering from sweaty hands or blushing too readily. It was something she had apparently been born with and could never do anything to curb.

— **Robert Musil** *(1880-1942) Austrian writer*

Young Torless (1906)

■ *Young Torless is enmeshed with two unscrupulous fellow students, Reiting and Beineberg, in a dehumanization episode with a passive and effeminate victim, Basini.*

In short, it was a well-rehearsed farce, brilliantly stage-managed by Reiting, and the highest possible moral tone was assumed in putting forward excuses that would find favour in the masters' eyes.

Basini preserved a stupefied silence, no matter what was said. He was still paralyzed with terror from his experiences of two days earlier, and the solitary confinement in which he was kept, together with the quiet and matter-of-fact course of the investigation, was in itself a tremendous relief to him. All he wished for was that it might be over soon. Besides, Reiting and Beineberg had not failed to threaten him with the most atrocious revenge if he should dare to say anything against them.

— **Robert Musil**

N

Lolita (1955)

■ *A European intellectual becomes sexually obsessed with his ideal nymphet, 12-year-old Dolores Haze, but first he must devise an elaborate scheme to get rid of her mother.*

. . . Lolita. Light of my life, fire of my loins. My sin, my soul. Lo-lee-ta: The tip of the tongue taking a trip of three steps down the palate to tap, at three, on the teeth. Lo. Lee. Ta.

— **Vladimir Nabokov** *(1899-1977) Multilingual Russian-American novelist, short story writer and literary critic*

Look at the Harlequins! (1974)

- *The memoir of a cranky, impatient, unhappy writer who thrashes his way through life turning out the odd book now and then.*

I saw my parents infrequently. They divorced and remarried and redivorced at such a rapid rate that had the custodians of my fortune been less alert, I might have been auctioned out finally to a pair of strangers of Swedish or Scottish descent, with sad bags under hungry eyes. An extraordinary grand-aunt, Baroness Bredow, born Tolstoy, amply replaced closer blood. As a child of seven or eight, already harboring the secrets of a confined madman, I seemed even to her (who also was far from normal) unduly sulky and indolent; actually, of course, I kept daydreaming in a most outrageous fashion.

"Stop moping!" she would cry: "Look at the harlequins!"

"What harlequins? Where?"

"Oh, everywhere. All around you. Trees are harlequins, words are harlequins. So are situations and sums. Put two things together–jokes, images–and you get a triple harlequin. Come on! Play! Invent the world! Invent reality!"

— **Vladimir Nabokov**

Pale Fire (1962)

- *A poem of 999 lines by a fictitious American poet with a 29-page Foreword and 229-page Commentary by a fictitious self-appointed editor. Among the themes is a lifelong quest for a satisfactory answer about the existence of the hereafter.*

There was a time in my demented youth
When somehow I suspected that the truth
About survival after death was known
To every human being: I alone
Knew nothing, and a great conspiracy
Of books and people hid the truth from me.

There was the day when I began to doubt
Man's sanity: How could he live without
Knowing for sure what dawn, what death,
what doom
Awaited consciousness beyond the tomb?

— **Vladimir Nabokov**

Pnin (1957)

- *The story of a gently preposterous Russian émigré precariously employed as a professor on an American college campus.*

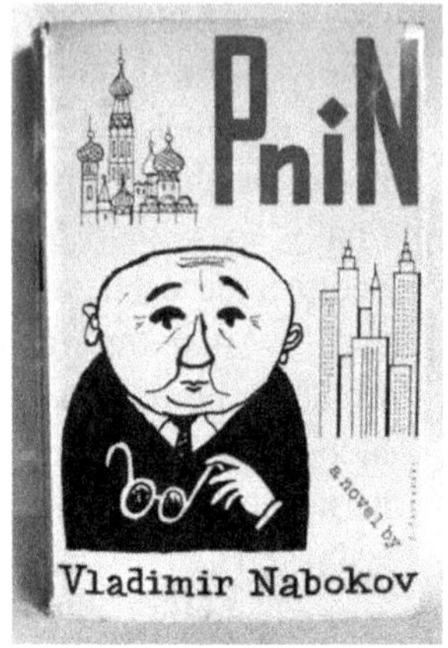

. . . His life was a constant war with insensate objects that fell apart, or attacked him, or refused to function, or viciously got themselves lost as soon as they entered the sphere of his existence. . . . On gadgets he doted with a kind of dazed, superstitious delight. Electric devices enchanted him. Plastics swept him off his feet. He had a deep admiration for the zipper. But the devoutly plugged-in clock would make nonsense of his mornings after a storm in the middle of the night had paralyzed the local power station. The frame of his spectacles would snap in mid-bridge, leaving him with two identical pieces, which he would vaguely attempt to unite, in the hope, perhaps, of some organic marvel of restoration coming to the rescue. The zipper a gentleman depends on most would come loose in his puzzled hand at some nightmare moment of haste and despair.

And he still did not know that he was on the wrong train.

— Vladimir Nabokov

Transparent Things (1972)

- *Our hero—sullen, gawky Hugh Person—visits Switzerland, falls in love and eventually marries Amande, followed by murder, madness, and imprisonment.*

Another time he volunteered to carry after her a pair of new skis she had just acquired—weird-looking, reptile-green things made of metal and fiberglass. Their elaborate bindings looked like first cousins of orthopedic devices meant to help a cripple to walk. He was allowed to shoulder those precious skis, which at first felt miraculously light but soon grew as heavy as great slabs of malachite, under which he staggered in Armande's wake like a clown helping to change properties in a circus arena. His load was snatched from him as soon as he sat down for a rest. He was offered a paper bag (four small oranges) in exchange but he pushed it away without looking.

Our Person was obstinate and monstrously in love. A fairy-tale element seemed to imbue its Gothic rose water all attempts to scale the battlements of her Dragon. Next week he made it and thereafter established himself as less of a nuisance.

— Vladimir Nabokov

A Bend in the River (1989)

- *Salim, a small Indian retailer, operates a store in an East African country which is taken over by the Big Man who assigns Salim's little shop to Citizen Theotime an uneducated African.*

He didn't stay quiet for long. It might have been my easiness, my wish to appear unhumiliated: Theotime was soon looking for new ways of asserting himself. The trouble now was that he didn't know what to do. He would have liked to live out his role in fact—to take over the running of the shop, or to feel (while enjoying his storeroom life) that he was running the shop. He knew, though, that he knew nothing; he knew that I knew he knew nothing; and he was like a man enraged by his own helplessness. He made constant scenes. He was drunken, aggrieved and threatening, and as deliberately irrational as an official who had decided to be *malin*.

— V. S. Naipaul *(1932-) Trinidanian writer of Indian descent*

A House for Mr Biswas (1961)

- *Mr. Mohun Biswas, his birth ill-omened, his life dominated by fitful, comic struggles and resentful truces, eventually triumphantly purchases his own house and becomes his own man.*

At last he said, 'First of all, the features of this unfortunate boy. He will have good teeth but they will be rather wide, and there will be spaces between them. I suppose you know what that means. The boy will be a lecher and a spendthrift. Possibly a liar as well. It is hard to be sure about those gaps between the teeth. They might mean only one of those things or they might mean all three.'

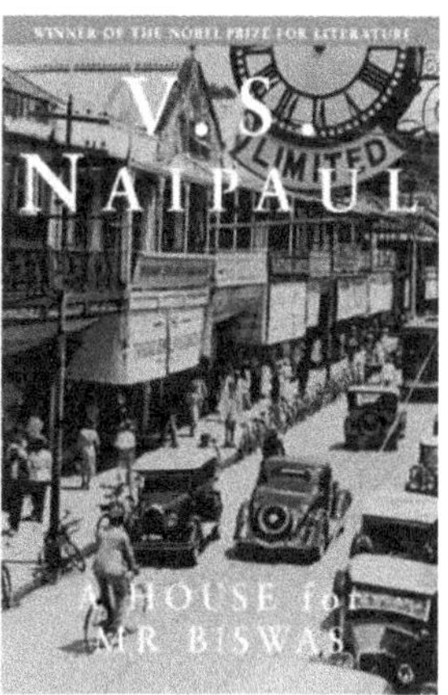

'What about the six fingers, pundit?'

'That's a shocking sign, of course. The only thing I can advise is to keep him away from trees and water. Particularly water.'

'Never bath him?'

'I don't mean exactly that.'

— V. S. Naipaul

The Tree of Life (1985)

- *A personal journal of Ohio frontier life in 1811-12 including sketches and accounting entries.*

"Delaware warriors, like all Indians, obey their officers immediately. And without being flogged! They're disciplined.

"Indians handle weapons very well. They fight light—no canteens, knapsacks, blankets, compasses, cartridge cases. They fight naked save breech-clouts, leggings and moccasins, in all kinds of weather. They thrive on a couple of mouthfuls of parched corn and a drink of water twice a day. Why, they train up their boys to the art of war since the age of 12.

"We mustn't be too proud to learn from them. We ain't above borrowing their words—hommony, pone, moccasin, tomahawk. I tell you, if we fight like Indians, what with our mechanical genius, no European power would dare set foot in the American woods."

— **Hugh Nissenson** *(1933-) American-Jewish writer*

The Bird Artist (1994)

- *The confession of a lonely boy set in a fishing town in freezing Newfoundland at the turn-of-the-century.*

"A bit goddamned touchy tonight, aren't we. It's just a game for the ladies, is that it? Well, what do you want to do, then?"

"Sit here. Sit here and not think out loud."

"Not think out loud about what?" She finished her drink.

"I've got money worries. I've been using up my savings at Spivey's. There's been no work at the dry dock. I can't seem to draw. . . . I've got money worries."

"Yes, and what with the rings on order."

"No—no, actually—" These words slipped out. "Actually, the Hollys—"

"Are paying for the rings? How pathetic." . . .

"You are a blunt woman, Margaret."

"Fabian dear, I'm only exactly as blunt as life is, forgive the preachy sentence. You're going to marry a stranger. Your mother is adultering nightly. Your father's got one hell of a homecoming in store. How much more bluntness do you want?"

— **Howard Norman** *(1949-) American writer and educator*

O

Black Water (1992)

- *A fictional account of reckless drunken driving and abandonment resulting in terror and death for a young impressionable girl.*

Approximately thirty feet ahead, unsighted too, was a narrow wooden bridge of badly weathered planks; but there had been no warning sign of a bridge, still less of the dangerous curve preceding the bridge.

Not now! Not like this.

She was twenty-six years eight months old too young to die thus too astonished, too disbelieving, to scream as the Toyota flew off the road and struck the surface of the near-invisible water as if for an instant it might not sink but float: as if the trajectory of its flight might carry it, the very weight of it, across the water and into the snaky tangle of rushes and stunted trees and vines on the father shore.

Published over 50 novels and many volumes of short stories.

You would expect water in such a place to be shallow, just a ditch. You would expect the guardrail to be more substantial. You would not expect to be, so suddenly so rudely so helplessly, in the water black as muck and smelling of raw sewage.

Not like this. No.

— **Joyce Carol Oates** *(1938-) American author*

Blonde (2000)

- *A fictional characterization of the life of Marilyn Monroe. This sweet quote is from an early meeting with playwright Arthur Miller.*

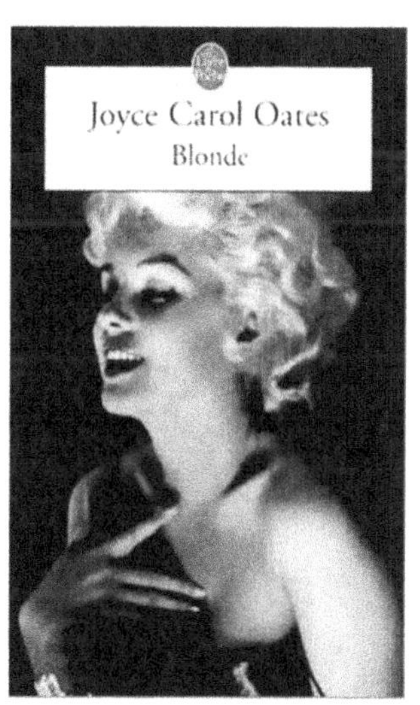

The Blond Actress said, apologetically, "I don't like M-marilyn much. But I can answer to it. It's what most people call me, now. Who don't know me."

"I could call you Norma Jeane, if you prefer. I could call you"—and here the Playwright's voice wavered with the audacity of what he said—"my 'Magda.' "

"Oh. I'd like that."

"My Secret Magda."

"Yes!"

"But maybe Marilyn when others are around. So there wouldn't be any misunderstanding."

"When others are around, it doesn't matter what you call me. You can whistle. You can call me, 'Hey you!' " The Blond Actress laughed, showing her beautiful white teeth.

He was touched to the heart, she'd been made happy so quickly.

The Playwright, too, had been made happy so quickly.

— **Joyce Carol Oates**

Them (1969)

- *The hard edge of life of a brother Jules and sister Maureen living in a poor neighborhood of Detroit from 1937 to about 1966.*

. . . He saw Nadine get to her feet. He wanted to call out to her but did no more than watch helplessly as she reached for her purse, exactly as the other women did. Then she turned, slender and arrowlike, as if surveying the room from a vantage point that was invisible and invulnerable, undisturbed by the various eyes that moved upon her. He saw her approach him. She wore fashionable shoes, in the extreme style of the day, open heels with thin straps, small knobby heels, a tortoise-shell decoration on the front. He let his eyes move slowly up to her face, as if reluctant really to see her, and his uncle and Yates gaped at this strange woman who came up to Jules and handed him a piece of paper. He took it at once from her fingers and put it in his pocket, not surprised. She walked away.

"Jesus Christ, what was that?" Uncle Samson cried.

— Joyce Carol Oates

What I Lived For (1994)

- *The life of a cocky, Irish Catholic, alcoholic, self-made millionaire and city council member of Union City, New York.*

Corky knows his way around Union City, New York, like it's the back of his hand, it's *his*. That time the Mayor told one of his new staff members, new to Union City, at a postelection lunch, You want to know about Union City, go hang out with Corky Corcoran, eh Corky?—He's your man. . . .

He likes the way people glance at him, women especially. And their eyes snag. Men sizing him up. He's a cocky guy but not belligerent; quick to smile; sometimes, if he's nervous, he can't help smiling. In public like this he walks with his shoulders squared, head up, casual in his gaze, easygoing, a manner he cultivated as a kid . . .

— Joyce Carol Oates

At Swim-Two-Birds (1939)

- *A college student who spends most of his time either in bed or carousing with friends is called for his idleness by his uncle and by his friend Brinsley in this quote.*

Sloth—Lord save us—sloth is a terrible cross to carry in this world. You are a burden to yourself . . . to your friends . . . and to every man, woman and child you meet and mix with. One of the worst of the deadly sins, there is no doubt about it.

I'd say it is the worst, said Brinsley.

The worst! Certainly.

Turning to me, my uncle said:

Tell me this, do you ever open a book at all?

I open and shut books several times a day, I replied in a testy manner. I study here in my bedroom because it is quiet and suitable for the purpose. I pass my examinations without difficulty when they arise. Is there any other point I could explain?

That will do you now, there is no need for temper, said my uncle. No need at all for temper. Friendly advice no wise man scorns, I'm sure you have often heard that said.

— **Flann O'Brien** *(1911-1966) Irish novelist and satirist*

In the Lake of the Woods (1994)

■ *John and Kathy choose an isolated setting in their quest to forget a failed political career and rebuild a deceptive marriage.*

. . . Kathy put a hand overboard, letting it trail through the water, watching its foamy imprint instantly close back on itself. Identical, which erased identity. Or it was all identity. An easy place, she thought, to lose yourself.

Which is what happened, maybe.

Maybe the singleness of things confused her. Maybe Buckete Island was not Buckete Island. Maybe she missed the channel into Angle Inlet by only a fraction of a mile, a miscalculation of gradient or degree. Daydreaming, maybe, or closing her eyes for an instant, or stretching out to absorb the fine morning sun. It was one possibility. No accident at all, just a banal human blunder, and she would've continued up the lake without worry, soon crossing into Canadian waters, into a great interior of islands and forests that reached northward over many hundred square miles.

— **Tim O'Brien** *(1946-) American novelist and combat veteran of the Vietnam War*

The Things They Carried (1990)

■ *An account of the experiences of an infantry company in Vietnam, with all the physical and emotional territory involved.*

What they carried was partly a function of rank, partly of field specialty. . . . As PFCs or Spec 4s, most of them were common grunts and carried the standard M-16 gas-operated assault rifle. The weapon weighed 7.5 pounds unloaded, 8.2 pounds with its full 20-round magazine. Depending on numerous factors, such as topography and psychology, the riflemen carried anywhere from 12 to 20 magazines, usually in cloth bandoliers, adding on another 8.4 pounds at minimum, 14 pounds at maximum. When it was available, they also carried M-16 maintenance gear—rods and steel brushes and swabs and tubes of LSA oil—all of which weighed about a pound. Among the grunts, some carried the M-79 grenade launcher, 5.9 pounds unloaded, a reasonably light weapon except for the ammunition, which was heavy. A single round weighed 10 ounces. The typical load was 25 rounds. But Ted Lavender, who was scared, carried 34 rounds when he was shot and killed outside Than Khe, and he went down under an exceptional burden, more than 20 pounds of ammunition, plus the flak jacket and helmet and rations and water and toilet paper and tranquilizers and all the rest, plus the unweighed fear. He was dead weight. There was no twitching or flopping.

— Tim O'Brien

The Edge of Sadness (1961)

■ *A lonely alcoholic priest begins his ministry again in an older, run-down parish, eventually discovering his love for God and his calling.*

. . . And of course the truth is that a place like this is not vital: it has, in fact, no life at all. There is no whirling motion; there is no clarinet in the background; the air is not filled with screams in the night. There is no noise. When I walk along this street at night I hear my own footsteps; the people I see are silent and motionless and wrapped in their own despair. They don't respond to me; they don't even see me; they don't see anything. And when, in this terrifying quiet, now and then the siren sounds, it is usually the ambulance, not the riot car, and it means that among these sad men who are so slowly dying, one has gone a little faster than the rest.

— Edwin O'Connor *(1918-1968) American radio personality, journalist and novelist*

The Last Hurrah (1956)

■ *The last mayoral campaign of a life-long Irish politician.*

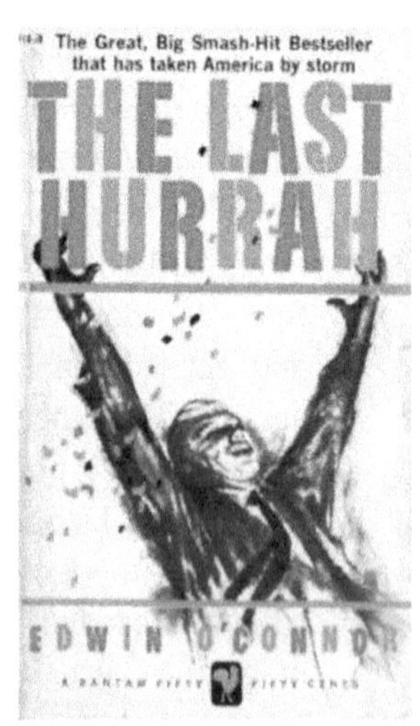

The Great, Big Smash-Hit Bestseller
that has taken America by storm
THE LAST
HURRAH
EDWIN O'CONNOR

Upstairs, Skeffington was saying good-by to Weinberg and Gorman. They stood, side by side, at the head of his bed. Alone of all those who had come, they knew what this moment was. Skeffington took both men by the hand; he looked at them and smiled.

"Good times," he said. "A lot of good times."

"Frank," Weinberg said. "You'll do all right. Anywhere."

Gorman nodded. "Ah, Frank," he said softly. "You're done grand things. Grand, grand things."

"Among others," Skeffington said. "But no regrets.

No regrets at all. And all my thanks to both of you. For everything."

The two men gripped his hands; Gorman said soothingly, "We'll be back, Frank. This one isn't the good-by."

They heard a faint chuckle. "If it isn't, it's a pretty good facsimile," Skeffington said. His voice was weak now; the nurse hurried over and removed some of the pillows behind him; without the props, he sank gratefully back into the supine position. He closed his eyes; in a moment, one hand was raised in a small farewell salute. The nurse whispered. "He's going to get a little sleep now."

— **Edwin O'Connor**

The Complete Short Stories (1971)

"Death has always been brother to my imagination."

- *Superbly written, powerful and often disturbing fiction. This excerpt from "Revelation."*

Next to the child's mother was a red-headed youngish woman, reading one of the magazines and working a piece of chewing gum, hell for leather, as Claud would say. . . . The poor girl's face was blue with acne and Mrs. Turpin thought how pitiful it was to have a face like that at that age. . . .

The ugly girl . . . cast an eye upward at the click, smirked, then looked directly at Mrs. Turpin and smirked again. Then she returned her eyes to her book. . . .

The (girl) slammed her book shut. She looked straight in front of her, directly through Mrs. Turpin . . . The girl's eyes seemed lit all of a sudden with a peculiar light, an unnatural light like night road signs give. . . .

. . . the raw-complexioned girl snapped her teeth together. Her lower lip turned downwards and inside out, revealing the pale pink inside of her mouth. After a second it rolled back up. It was the ugliest face Mrs. Turpin had ever seen anyone make and for a moment she was certain that the girl had made it at her. . . .

The book struck her directly over her left eye. It struck almost at the same instant that she realized the girl was about to hurl it. Before she could utter a sound, the raw face came crashing across the table toward her howling. The girl's fingers sank like clamps into the soft flesh of her neck.

— **Flannery O'Connor** *(1925-1964) American novelist, short-story writer and essayist*

In the middle of her fifteen-year battle with lupus — she died from it in 1964, age 39 — O'Connor had this attitude towards her affliction: "I have enough energy to write with and as that is all I have any business doing anyhow. I can with one eye squinted take it all as a blessing. What you have to measure out, you come to observe more closely, or so I tell myself." — *Today in Literature*

A Good Man is Hard to Find (1953)

- *Short stories including, from the title story, a brutal account of a family accidentally encountering the murderous Misfit and his two accompanists.*

His voice seemed about to crack and the grandmother's head cleared for an instant. She saw the man's face twisted close to her own as if he were going to cry and she murmured, "Why you're one of my babies. You're one of my own children!" She reached out and touched him on the shoulder. The Misfit sprang back as if a snake had bitten him and shot her three times through the chest. Then he put his gun down on the ground and took off his glasses and began to clean them.

Hiram and Bobby Lee returned from the woods and stood over the ditch, looking down at the grandmother who half sat and half lay in a puddle of blood with here legs crossed under her like a child's and her face smiling up at the cloudless sky.

— Flannery O'Connor

Wise Blood (1949)

- *Twenty-two-year-old Hazel Motes becomes a preacher of anti-religion in a desperate struggle against his innate faith.*

She had never observed his face more composed and she grabbed his hand and held it to her heart. It was resistless and dry. The outline of a skull was plain under his skin and the deep burned eye sockets seemed to lead into the dark tunnel where he had disappeared. She leaned closer and closer to his face, looking deep into them, trying to see how she had been cheated or what had cheated her, but she couldn't see anything. She shut her eyes and saw the pin point of light but so far away that she could not hold it steady in her mind. She felt as if she were blocked at the entrance of something. She sat staring with her eyes shut, into his eyes, and felt as if she had finally got to the beginning of something she couldn't begin, and she saw him moving farther and farther away, farther and farther into the darkness until he was the pin point of light.

— Flannery O'Connor

Appointment in Samarra (1934)

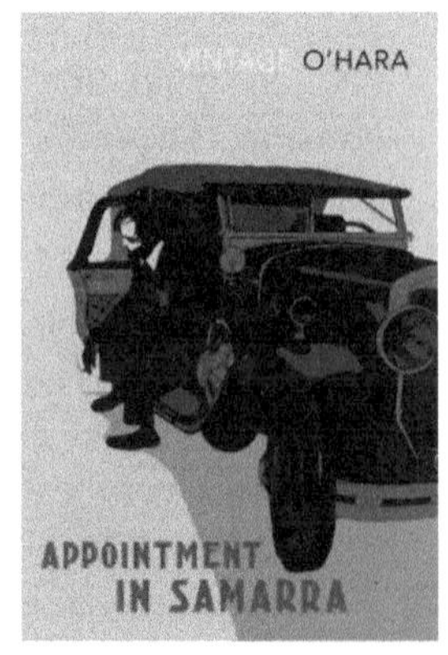

- *A young man, who with his wife are envied members of the club set, begins an alcohol-fueled descent toward self-destruction.*

. . . He went out on the porch and down the steps and opened the garage door and closed it behind him. He shivered a little from the bit of cold, and it was cold in the garage, so he hurried. He had to see about the windows. They had to be closed. The ventilator in the roof was closed for the winter.

He climbed in the front seat and started the car. It

started with a merry, powerful hum, ready to go. "There, the bastards," said Julian and smashed the clock with the bottom of the bottle, to give them an approximate time. It was 10:41.

There was nothing to do now but wait. He smoked a little, hummed for a minute or two, and had three quick drinks and was on his fourth when he lay back and slumped down in the seat. At 10:50, by the clock in the rear seat, he tried to get up. He had not the strength to help himself, and at ten minutes past eleven no one could have helped him, no one in the world.

— **John O'Hara** *(1905-1970) American writer*

From the Terrace (1958)

- *A man's rise to wealth, power, and prominence, yet a haunting sense of failure remains.*

The public relations officer at Lee Field released the news of the death of Ensign Eaton at 1600 hours, and twenty minutes later the President of the United States was speaking to Mary Eaton. He knew what to say, he knew when to stop, but the effect of that voice and the easy precision of the enunciation, which she had previously heard only on the radio, was more shattering than the news itself. . . . it was as though the words were coming not through the telephone but out of the air about her and from God, like some divine, mysterious message in a Biblical legend. Her own training in manners enabled her to make the proper responses and at the end to say "Thank you, Mr. President." But then she went to her room and darkened it and wept, afraid of death, of sin, of God, of her solitude, of love, and of the faces of her son that looked down at her; changing, unsmiling faces in flying helmet; in the brown hat with the tan edging to the brim; bare-headed with the crew cut.

— **John O'Hara**

Unable to afford Yale he so desperately sought to attend, and never having received an honorary degree from that institution, O'Hara had this comment.

"If Yale had given me a degree, I could have joined the Yale Club, where the food is pretty good, the library is ample and restful, the location convenient, and I could go there when I felt like it without sponging off friends. They also have a nice-looking necktie." — *Wikipedia*

Ten North Frederick (1955)

- *The story of three generations of a family of the "best people," with chief emphasis on Joseph B. Chapin who understands his own limitations but is led into trying to exceed them.*

"I wonder what goes on in the mind of a man like Herbert Hoover."

"Tonight?" said Mike. "He's probably sound asleep."

"Do you think so? Knowing that for all practical purposes he's just been elected President of the United States?" . . . I know this much, I wouldn't be able to sleep. . . . it's easy for me to imagine being in his position . . . saying to myself, 'I can travel for five days and nights, from coast to coast at a high rate of speed and still be in the country that I'm President of.' Just one man, out of a hundred and twenty million people."

"Would you like to be President, Joe?"

"*What?*"

Mike saw that his question, and perhaps the tone of it, had taken Joe by surprise.

"Me, President? No thank you."

But Mike had seen what he had seen in similar circumstances, when he had asked other men, possum-players, about their political ambitions. If you caught them unprepared, you got your answer.

— **John O'Hara**

The English Patient (1992)

■ *The haunting story of a nameless burn victim and his English nurse as they live out the close of World War II in an Italian monastery.*

She pours calamine in stripes across his chest where he is less burned, where she can touch him. She loves the hollow below the lowest rib, its cliff of skin. Reaching his shoulders she blows cool air onto his neck, and he mutters.

What? She asks, coming out of her concentration.

He turns his dark face with its grey eyes towards her. She puts her hand into her pocket. She unskins the plum with her teeth, withdraws the stone and passes the flesh of the fruit into his mouth.

He whispers again, dragging the listening heart of the young nurse beside him to wherever his mind is, into that well of memory he kept plunging into during those months before he died.

— **Michael Ondaatje** *(1943-) Sri Lankan-born Canadian novelist and poet*

Netherland (2008)

■ *The story of a couple and their young son living in Lower Manhattan and the solace the husband finds in the subculture of cricket.*

At our very first meeting, Juliet Schwarz turned to Rachel and asked if she loved me and, if yes, what it was about me that she loved. Objection! I felt like shouting to this rotten, risky, terrifying interrogation.

"'Love,'" Rachel desperately replied, "is such an omnibus word."

Here was an irony of our continental separation (undertaken, remember, in the hope of clarification): it had made things less clear than ever. By and large, we separators succeeded only in separating our feelings from any meaning we could give them. That was my experience, if you want to talk about experience. I had no way of knowing if what I felt, brooding in New York City, was love's abstract or love's miserable leftover. The idea of love was itself separated from meaning. Love? Rachel had gotten it right. Love was an omnibus thronged by a rabble.

And yet we again climbed aboard, she and I.

— **Joseph O'Neill** *(1964-) Irish-Turkish novelist and non-fiction writer*

Animal Farm (1945)

- *An allegory in which farm animals overthrow and oust their human owner, setting up a commune where, at first, all are equal only later to be ruthlessly driven by a tyranny erected by their own kind.*

'Comrades!' he cried. 'You do not imagine, I hope, that we pigs are doing this in a spirit of selfishness and privilege? Many of us actually dislike milk and apples. I dislike them myself. Our sole object in taking these things is to preserve our health. Milk and apples (this has been proved by Science, comrades) contain substances absolutely necessary to the well-being of a pig. We pigs are brainworkers. The whole management and organization of this farm depend on us. Day and night we are watching over your welfare. It is for *your* sake that we drink that milk and eat those apples. Do you know what would happen if we pigs failed in our duty? Jones would come back! . . .'

Now if there was one thing that the animals were completely certain of, it was that they did not want Jones back. When it was put to them in this light, they had no more to say.

— **George Orwell** *(1903-1950) English author and journalist*

1984 (1949)

- *In the future, when Big Brother is always watching and the Thought Police always listening, Winston is a man in grave danger because his memory still functions and he knows the Party controls people through bewilderment and brutalization.*

. . . There was of course no way of knowing whether you were being watched at any given moment. How often, or on what system, the Thought

Police plugged in on any individual wire was guesswork. It was even conceivable that they watched everybody all the time. But at any rate they could plug in your wire whenever they wanted to. You had to live—did live, from habit that became instinct—in the assumption that every sound you made was overheard, and, except in darkness, every movement scrutinized.

— **George Orwell**

All the animals meet in the barn to create a plan. The pigs take the lead.
Ralph Steadman illustration for George Orwell's *Animal Farm*

Bound to Violence (1971)

- *The African empire is exploited by black and Arab colonialism spiced by black magic, cannibalism and murder.*

Already it had become more than difficult to procure old masks, for Shrobenius and the missionaries had had the good fortune to snap them all up. And so Saif—and the practice is still current—had slapdash copies buried by the hundredweight, or sunk into ponds, lakes, marshes, and mud holes, to be exhumed later on and sold at exorbitant prices to unsuspecting curio hunters. These three-year-old masks were said to be *charged with the weight of four centuries of civilization.* To the credulous customer, the seller pointed out the ravages of time, the malignant worms that had gnawed at these masterpieces imperiled since time immemorial, witness their prefabricated poor condition. *Alif lam! Amba, koubo oumo agoum.*

— **Yambo Ouologuem** *(1940-) Milian writer*

The Puttermesser Papers (1997)

- *Stories of Ruth Puttermesser's life including her unwitting creation of an artificial human being derived from Hebrew folklore who gets Ruth elected mayor of New York City.*

Rappoport was putting on his pants. "You're too old for sex," he said meanly.

Puttermesser's reply was instantly Socratic: "Then I'm *not* behaving like an adolescent."

"If you know I have a plane to catch, how come you want to read in bed?"

"It's more comfortable than the kitchen table."

"Ruth, I came to make love to you!"

"All I wanted was to finish the *Theaetetus* first."

Now he had his coat on, and was crossing his scarf carefully at his throat, so as not to let in the cold. It was a winter night, but Puttermesser saw in this gesture that Rappoport, at the age of fifty-two, still obeyed his mother's doctrines, no matter that they were five decades old. "You wanted to finish!" he yelled. He grabbed the book from her lap. "It goes from page 847 to 879, that's thirty-three pages—"

"I read fast," Puttermesser said.

— **Cynthia Ozick** *(1928-) American short story writer, novelist and essayist*

P

Collected Stories of Grace Paley (1994)

- *Observations and interpretations of urban family life and a changing society populated with a full complement of characters.*

Whyn't you go up to Mrs. Luddy living in your house, you lady, huh? The Girl Scout asked this.

Why she just groove to see you, said some sarcastic snickerer.

She got palpitations. Her man, he give it to her.

That ain't all, he a natural gift-giver.

I'll take you, said the Girl Scout. My name is Cynthia. I'm in troop 355, Brooklyn.

I'm not dressed, I said, looking at my lumpy knees.

You shouldn't wear no undershirt like that without no runnin number or no team writ on it. It look like a undershirt.

Cynthia! Don't take her up there, said an important boy. Her head strange. Don't you take her. Hear?

Lawrence, she said softly, you tell me once more what to do I'll wrap you round that lamppost.

Git! she said, powerfully addressing *me*.

In this way I was led into the hallway of the whole house of my childhood.

— **Grace Paley** *(1922-2007) American short story writer and poet*

A Violent Life (1959)

- *The life and death of Tommaso, a street kid of the slums outside Rome; his occupation whatever necessary to make a buck, yet in one notable instance rising to an act of unexpected self-sacrifice.*

He turned his face away and didn't say any more.

But as far as dying went, he decided he was going to die in his own bed at home: and, in fact, it was easy for them to get permission to take him away now. It was a fine day, mild, late September, with the sun shining in a sky without a spot on it, and people talking, singing along the streets, in the new buildings.

When Tommaso was back in his bed, he almost felt he was a little better. After all, they still hadn't come to anoint him; for an hour or so the cough stopped, and he even asked his mother for some of that Marsala Irene had brought him. But then, when night came, he felt worse all the time: he had another fit, coughing blood, coughing, coughing, unable to catch his breath, and it was goodbye Tommaso.

— **Pier Paolo Pasolini** *(1922-1975) Italian poet, film director, and writer*

Doctor Zhivago (1957)

- *The life and loves of a physician during the turmoil of the Russian Revolution.*

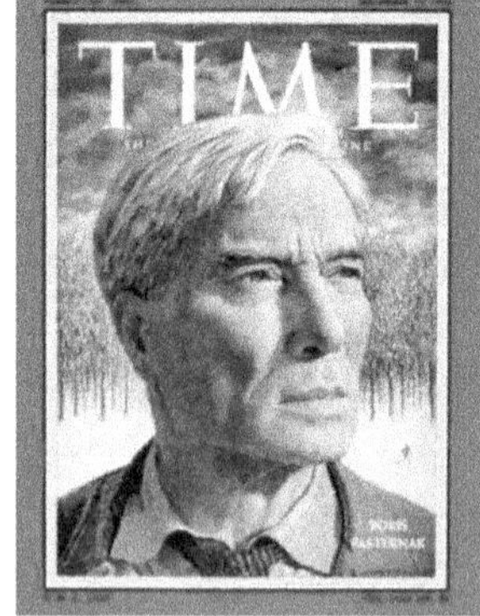

"Don't move, Comrade Doctor," said the cavalryman in the fur cap, who was the oldest of the three. "If you obey orders, we guarantee that you will not be harmed. If you don't—no offense meant—we'll shoot you. The surgeon attached to our unit has been killed and we are conscripting you as a medical worker. Get down from your horse and hand the reins over to this young man. And let me remind you: if you try to escape we'll give you short shrift."

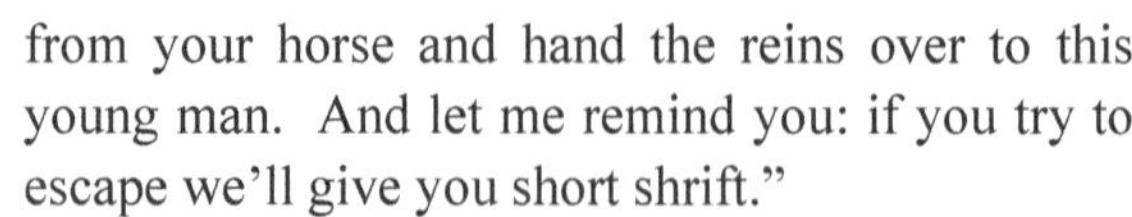

— **Boris Pasternak** *(1890-1960) Russian poet, novelist, and translator*

On 25 October, two days after hearing that he had won, Pasternak sent the following telegram to the Swedish Academy: Immensely thankful, touched, proud, astonished, abashed.

However, four days later came another telegram: Considering the meaning this award has been given in the society to which I belong, I must refuse it. Please do not take offense at my voluntary rejection.

The Swedish Academy announced: This refusal, of course, in no way alters the validity of the award. There remains only for the Academy, however, to announce with regret that the presentation of the Prize cannot take place. — *Wikipedia*

Bel Canto (2001)

- *Ragtag revolutionaries invade a party in a South American country seeking the President, leading to unexpected results.*

"I am Vice President Ruben Iglesias," he said to the man with the gun. The Vice President appeared to be extremely tired. He was a very small man, both in stature and girth, who had been chosen as a running mate as much for his size as for his political beliefs. The pervasive thinking in government was that a taller vice president would make the President appear weak, replaceable. "President Masuada was unable to attend this evening. He is not here." The Vice President's voice was heavy. Too much of a burden was falling to him.

"Lies," the man with the gun corrected.

Ruben Iglesias shook his head sadly. No one wished more than he that President Masuda were in attendance right now, instead of lying in his own bed, happily playing over the plot of tonight's soap opera in his mind. General Alfredo quickly turned the gun in his hand so that he now held the muzzle rather than the handle. He brought the gun back in the air and hit the Vice President on the flat bone of his cheek beside the right eye. There was a soft thump, a sound considerably less violent than the action, as the handle of the gun hit the skin over the bone and the small man was knocked to the ground.

— **Ann Patchett** *(1963-) American author*

Cry the Beloved Country (1948)

- *A black Anglican priest from a rural town in South Africa, searching for his son in Johannesburg, faces the social structures that will later give rise to apartheid.*

Cry, the beloved country, for the unborn child that is the inheritor of our fear. Let him not love the earth too deeply. Let him not laugh too gladly when the water runs through his fingers, nor stand too silent when the setting sun makes red the veld with fire. Let him not be too moved when the birds of his land are singing, nor give too much of his heart to a mountain or a valley. For fear will rob him of all if he gives too much.

— **Alan Paton** *(1903-1988) South African author and anti-apartheid activist*

The Moon and the Bonfires (1950)

- *The nameless narrator returns to Italy after WWII to learn what has happened to his native village and finds that the past still haunts the present.*

I didn't say anything, and sometimes on summer days, sitting by the Belbo, I thought about Silvia. Irene was so blond that I didn't dare think about her. But one day, when Irene had come to let Santina play in the sand and no one else was there, I watched them run and stop by the water. I was hiding behind an alder bush. Santina shouted and pointed to something on the opposite bank. And then Irene put down her book, bent over, took off her shoes and stockings, and, blond as she was with her white legs, lifted her skirt up to her knees and waded in. She crossed slowly, testing each step with her foot. Then, calling to Santina not to move, she picked some yellow flowers. I remember them as if it were yesterday.

— **Cesare Pavese** *(1908-1950) Italian poet, novelist, literary critic and translator*

Of Pavese's suicide "...for the Italians, his death has come to have a weight like that of Hart Crane for us, a meaning that penetrates back into his own work and functions as a symbol in the literature of an age." — *Leslie Fiedler* (American literary critic)

The Political Prisoner (1949)

- *An anti-fascist is banished to a remote Italian coastal village to serve out the remainder of his prison term, eventually adjusting to his insular new life.*

Stefano was dazed by so much uniformity in this strange existence of his. The quiet summer had slipped by slowly, silently like a daydream. Among so many faces, so many thoughts, so much distress, so much peace, nothing remained except curling waves like blue reflections sweeping over a ceiling. And even that arid country, those scattered fleshy shrubs, tree-trunks and rugged boulders bleached by the sea like a pink wall, had soon ceased to affect him and become unreal. . . .

He told her he was settling up for his room because he was leaving for home; then he paused a moment in the silence and said that no amount of money could pay for the rest.

Elena stammered out in her husky voice "One does not give affection in return for money".

— **Cesare Pavese**

Gormenghast (1950)

- *The history of Gormenghast, dominated by the apprentice Steerpike who manipulates and murders his Master of Ritual, Barquentine, as he seeks ultimate power from the rightful earl and lord of the castle.*

But here — here before him, ready made was a candlestick with three gold flames that licked at the sullen air. And, here within his reach was the old man he wished to kill, but not too quickly; an old man whose rags and skin and beard were as dry and inflammable as the most exacting of fire-raisers could wish. What would be easier than for a man as ancient as Barquentine to lean forward accidentally at his work and for his beard to catch light from the candles? What would be more diverting than to watch the irritable and filthy tyrant caught among flames, his rags blazing, his skin smoking, his beard leaping like a crimson fish. It would only remain, at a later date, for Steerpike to discover the charred corpse and arouse the castle.

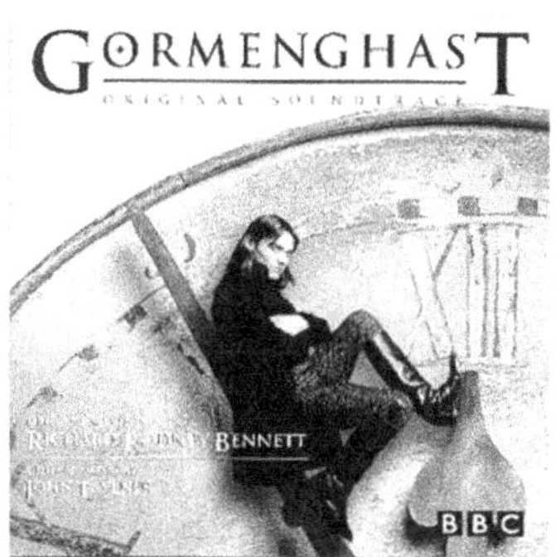

— **Mervyn Peake** *(1911-1968) English writer,arrtist, poet, and illustrator*

"[Peake's books] are actual additions to life; they give, like certain rare dreams, sensations we never had before, and enlarge our conception of the range of possible experience." — C. S. Lewis

The Moviegoer (1960)

- *A young man's search for meaning in his life of pervading spiritual emptiness.*

. . . I look around the movie theater . . . There are only a few solitary moviegoers scattered through the gloom, the afternoon sort and the most ghostly of all, each sunk in his own misery . . . On the way out I stop at the ticket window and speak to Mrs de Marco, a dark thin worried lady who has worked here every since I moved to Gentilly. She does not like the movies and takes no pleasure in her job (though she could see most of the last show every night). I tell her that it is a very fine job and that I would like nothing better than sitting out here night after night and year after year and watch the evenings settle over Elysian Fields, but she always thinks I am kidding and we talk instead about her son's career in the air force.

— **Walker Percy** *(1916-1990) American author*

The Second Coming (1980)

- *How a widower finds his way out of death-in-life despair with the help of a young girl living in a greenhouse after escaping from a mental institution.*

"I was lying in my house in the sun reading that book. Then *plink, tinkle*, the glass breaks and this little ball rolls up and touches me. I felt concealed and revealed." Her voice was flat and measured. She sounded like a wolf child who had learned to speak from old Victrola records. Her lips trembled slightly, not quite smiling, her eyes not quite meeting his yet attentive, sweeping his face like a blind person's.

Oh well. She was one of the thousands who blow in and out every summer like the blackbirds, nest where they can, in flocks or alone. Sleep in the woods. At least she had found a greenhouse.

As he turned away, gripping the three-iron with a two-handed golfer's grip and with a frowning self-consciousness which almost surprised him, she said" "Are you—?"

"What?" He cocked the club for a short chip shot and hung fire.

"Are you still climbing on your anger?"

— **Walker Percy**

Out Stealing Horses (2007)

- *A widower, seeking solitude in remote eastern Norway, reflects on his youth and the experience of aging.*

The other thing was Lars. When we went out of the church and stood by the open grave he grew more and more restless, and when the priest was halfway through the ceremony and the little coffin was to be lowered down with a rope round each handle, he could not bear it any longer and tore himself free from his mother and ran away among the headstones until he was almost out of the churchyard, and started to run in a circle right over by the stone wall. He ran round and round with his head lowered and his eyes on the ground, and the longer he ran the slower the priest spoke, and at first there were just a few people in the black-clad flock who turned round, but gradually more did, until at last they had all turned to look at Lars instead of the coffin that held his brother . . .

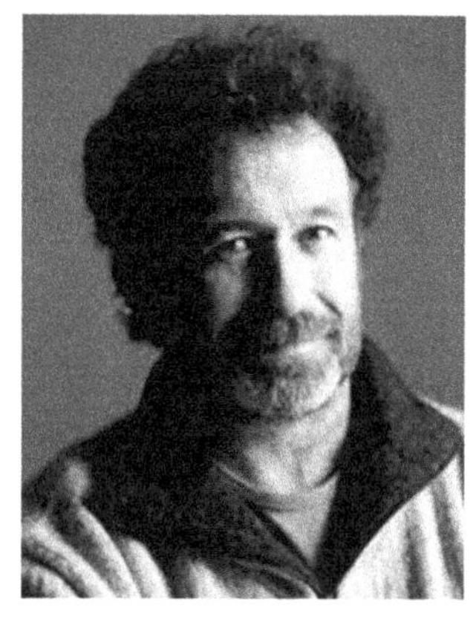

— **Per Petterson** *(1952-) Norwegian novelist*

A Distant Shore (2003)

- *Dorothy, a divorced schoolteacher with a troubled past, incurs an increasingly precarious existence, drifting further into depression and mental illness.*

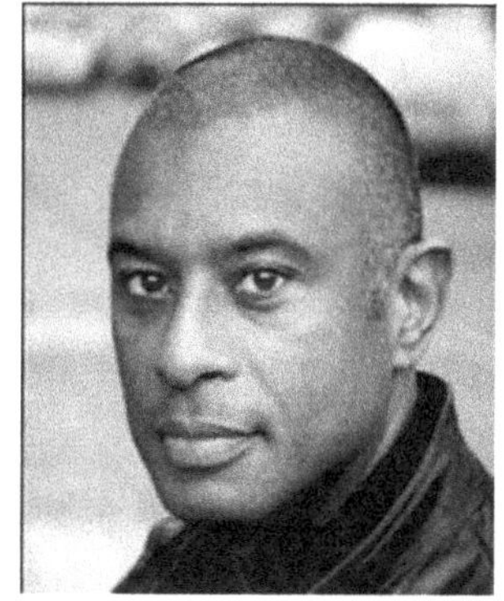

Miss Mitchell coughs. And then she speaks.

"The charges are that you have repeatedly left Mr. Waverley notes in his box. That you called his wife and, on behalf of all teachers at this school, expressed concern over his mental and physical health. That you have visited his lodgings and left him abusive mail. And that just last night while he was having dinner with his sister, you stood outside the restaurant window and stared at them both. All of these transgressions have contributed to a climate in which Mr. Waverley feels he can no longer carry out his work here, and he has asked Mr. Jowett to relieve him of his duties." Miss Mitchell's speech is over and she leans back in her chair. . . .

(Dorothy) looks at this woman, then at the benevolent, avuncular figure of Raymond Jowett. Do they seriously believe that a fifty-five-year-old divorcee can terrorize a forty-year-old grown man? She begins to laugh. Mr. Jowett sighs.

"I'm afraid this is no laughing matter. . . ."

— **Caryl Phillips** *(1958-) British writer with a Caribbean background*

Lark & Termite (2009)

- *The story of 17-year-old Lark and her 9-year-old disabled brother Termite, living with their aunt and caretaker in West Virginia.*

I told Solly I wouldn't leave. We wouldn't need to leave, I said, we never had. Once, a year ago, water got knee deep in the basement and rose in the yard to the kitchen door, and we stayed right here. We'll see, Solly said. I packed food, rain slickers, boots. Solly helped me empty the bureaus, gather the winter coats, strip the beds and linen closet, pile everything in the attic. He got Termite's fat upholstered chair up those narrow pull-down stairs, tilting and turning it on his shoulders. We brought up jugs of water, my transistor radio, flashlights, candles and oil lamps, even Nonie's safe-deposit box. . . . They were saying the water could rise fast, especially near the river. Before he left, he grabbed me hard by the shoulders to make sure I was paying attention. "When the water gets to the back stoop," he said, "get into the attic. Don't wait, and stay there all night, even if the house doesn't flood." I told him we like the attic, we'd camp out. "If it's bad," he told me, "I'll be back for you in a boat, and we won't be taking anything out that attic window but you and Termite. You be ready."

— **Jayne Anne Phillips** *(1952-) American novelist and short story writer*

Machine Dreams (1984)

■ *The chronicle of a West Virginia family through the 1950s-60s culminating in the tragedy of Vietnam.*

INFORMATION RECEIVED STATES THAT YOUR SON, PRIVATE FIRST CLASS WILLIAM MITCHELL HAMPSON, HAS BEEN LISTED AS MISSING IN ACTION EFFECTIVE JUNE 1970 WHILE PARTICIPATING IN AN OPERATION AGAINST A HOSTILE FORCE. . . .

"A man is here, a sergeant from the army," Gladys said rapidly. "He brought a telegram. It's not as bad as it could be, Danner—they say Billy is missing."

"Missing?"

"Yes." . . .

"Miss Hampson," he was saying, "I'm deeply sorry to inform you. . . . " He went on to repeat the contents of the brief telegram his voice soft and southern. . . .

My mother can't talk about Billy in the present. Her emotions concerning the present are shaky. She doesn't want to join the National League of Families, as I have in California; she says she can't yet be of help to an organization if she hasn't managed to help herself. Perhaps later. . . . My mother can't think of Billy as Missing In Action. She thinks of Billy as himself. Often, with constancy and fidelity. She talks about him in letters to me and on the phone; we talk about him when I visit. Maybe she's working her way into the present, questioning and concluding slowly.

— **Jayne Anne Phillips**

Wiseguy (1985)

- *A first hand account of the secret and often brutal world of organized crime in New York City from the 1950s through the 1970s.*

Henry spent his money until the cash in his pockets ran out, and then he would borrow from his pals until his next score paid off. He knew some crooked payday was never more than a week away. There were always at least a dozen dirty deals afoot. Aside from his own indulgences, his expenses were almost nonexistent. He had no dependents. He paid no taxes. He didn't even have a legitimate Social Security number. He had no insurance premiums to pay. He never paid his bills. He had no bank accounts, no credit cards, no credit ratings, and no checkbooks other than the phony ones he had bought from Tony the Baker. He still kept most of his clothes at his parents' house, though he rarely slept there. . . .

He never woke up in pajamas. He was lucky to get his shoes off before passing out every night. Like those of most wiseguys, the events of his days were so spontaneously assembled, so serendipitous, that he never knew where the end of the day would find him.

— **Nicholas Pileggi** *(1933-) Italian-American author and screenwriter*

Short Stories (1936)

- *Pirandello's great themes are the deleterious effects of busybodies, the denial of reality, and the implausibility of what people assert. In this tale, Zi' Dima repairs Don Zirafa Lollo's jar from the inside.*

'Shut up!' shouted Zirafa. 'Two propositions—take your choice. Either your cement's good for nothing or it's good for something. If it's good for nothing, then you're a downright twister. If it's good for something, then the jar, just as it is now, must have some sort of value. What value? *You* say! Give me an estimate!'

Zi' Dima paused for a moment, reflecting. Then he said, '. . . as it is now, with these filthy rivets stuck in it, which I have necessarily to do from the inside, what value could it possibly have? A third of what it was worth in the first place—more or less.'

'A third?' asked Zirafa. 'One *onza*, thirty three?'

'Maybe less. Certainly not more.'

'Well, then,' said Don Lollo, 'I'll take your word for it. Hand over the *onza* and thirty three.'

'What?' said Zi' Dima, as if he didn't understand what he'd said.

'I'll break the jar and let you out,' replied Don Lollo, 'and you, so my lawyer says, must pay me whatever you value it at. One *onza* and thirty three.'

'Me *pay*?' sniggered Zi' Dima. 'Your lordship will have his little joke! I'd sooner stay in here till I make food for the worms!'

— **Luigi Pirandello** *(1867-1936) Italian dramatist, novelist, and short story writer*

Zen and the Art of Motorcycle Maintenance (1974)

■ *A personal and philosophical odyssey into how to live, narrated by a father traveling with his son across the United States by motorcycle.*

Not everyone understands what a completely rational process this is, this maintenance of a motorcycle. They think it's some kind of a "knack" or some kind of "affinity for machines" in operation. They are right, but the knack is almost purely a process of reason, and most of the troubles are caused by what old time radio men called a "short between the earphones," failures to use the head properly. A motorcycle functions entirely in accordance with the laws of reason, and a study of the art of motorcycle maintenance is really a miniature study of the art of rationality itself.

— **Robert M. Pirsig** *(1928-) American writer and philosopher*

The Bell Jar (1963)

■ *The semi-autobiographical story of a talented young woman's struggles with depression and descent into mental illness.*

Mr. Anderson didn't say a word, so with Miss Huey's arm around my shoulder, and Doctor Nolan following, I moved into the next room.

Through the slits of my eyes, which I didn't dare open too far, lest the full view strike me dead, I saw the high bed with its white, drumtight sheet, and the machine behind the bed, and the masked person—I couldn't tell whether it was a man or a woman—behind the machine, and other masked people flanking the bed on both sides.

Miss Huey helped me climb up and lie down on my back.

"Talk to me," I said.

Miss Huey began to talk in a low, soothing voice, smoothing the salve on my temples and fitting the small electric buttons on either side of my head. "You'll be perfectly all right, you won't feel a thing, just bite down. . . ." And she set something on my tongue and in panic I bit down, and darkness wiped me out like chalk on a blackboard.

— **Sylvia Plath** *(1932-1963) American poet, novelist, and short story writer*

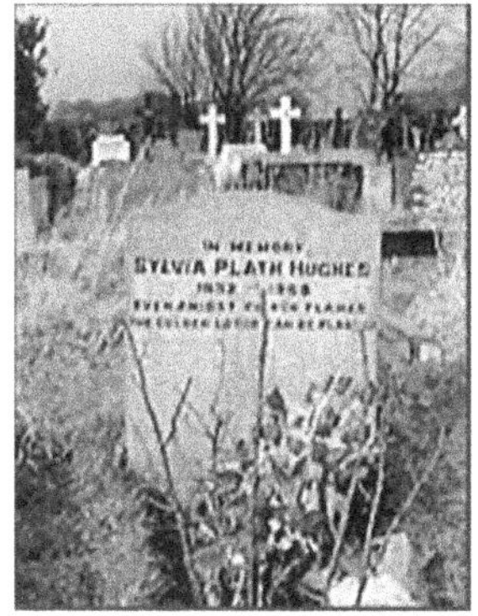

The winter of 1962-63, one of the coldest in centuries, found Sylvia living in a small London flat, now with two children, ill with flu and low on money. In her last poems it is as if some deeper, powerful self has grabbed control; death is given a cruel physical allure and psychic pain becomes almost tactile. (After a biography by Bill Gilson)

"Even amidst fierce flames the Golden Lotus can be planted." Plath's grave inscription from the book 'Monkey' written by Wu Ch'Eng-En in the sixteenth century.

The Complete Tales & Poems of Edgar Allan Poe (1938)

- *Stories with recurring themes of death and horror, and occasional satires and humorous tales. This quote from "The Black Cat."*

Of my own thoughts it is folly to speak. Swooning, I staggered to the opposite wall. For one instant the party on the stairs remained motionless, through extremity of terror and awe. In the next a dozen stout arms were toiling at the wall. It fell bodily. The corpse, already greatly decayed and clotted with gore, stood erect before the eyes of the spectators. Upon its head, with red extended mouth and solitary eye of fire, sat the hideous beast whose craft had seduced me into murder, and whose informing voice had consigned me to the hangman. I had walled the monster up within the tomb.

— **Edgar Allan Poe** *(1809-1849) American writer, poet, editor and literary critic*

Collected Stories and Other Writings (2008)

- *Eminent story-writer illustrated in this quote from "Pale Horse, Pale Rider" (1939).*

. . . The thin letter in the unfamiliar handwriting was from a strange man at the camp where Adam had been, telling her that Adam had died of influenza in the camp hospital. Adam had asked him, in case anything happened, to be sure to let her know.

If anything happened. To be sure to let her know. If anything happened. "Your friend, Adam Barclay," wrote the strange man. It had happened—she looked at the date—more than a month ago.

"Do you suppose, Mary," asked Miranda, "I could have my old room back again?"

"That should be easy," said Mary. "We stored away all your things there with Miss Hobbe." Miranda wondered again at the time and trouble the living took to be helpful to the dead. But not quite dead now, she reassured herself, one foot in either world now; soon I shall cross back and be at home again. . . . Adam, she said, now you need not die again, but still I wish you were here; I wish you had come back, what do you think I came back for, Adam, to be deceived like this?

At once he was there beside her, invisible but urgently present, a ghost but more alive than she was, the last intolerable cheat of her heart; for knowing it was false she still clung to the lie, the unpardonable lie of her bitter desire. She said, "I love you," and stood up trembling, trying by the mere act of her will to bring him to sight before her.

— **Katherine Anne Porter** *(1890-1980) American journalist, essayist, short story writer, novelist, and political activist*

A Dance to the Music of Time (1951)

- *A whole era of British social history (in 12 volumes) with many characters treated uniquely as individuals of equal interest, as illustrated in this quote.*

After sitting down beside Sillery, Truscott at first hardly spoke at all; but at the same time his amused smile acted as a sort of charm on the rest of the company, so that no one could possibly have accused him, on the grounds of this silence, of behaving in an ungracious manner. He was tall and dark, with regular features, caught rather too close together, and the most complete self-assurance that can be imagined. His clothes and hair, even his face, seemed to give out a kind of glossiness, and sense of prosperity . . . I addressed a remark to him which he acknowledged simply by closing and opening his eyes, . . . though his smile at the same time absolved me from the slightest blame in falling so patently short of his accustomed standards. . . . Truscott's comportment seemed a kind of spur to encourage all who came to win his esteem; although—and perhaps because—he was prepared to offer nothing in return. — **Anthony Powell** *(1905-2000) English novelist*

Morte D'Urgan (1962)

- *Father Urban, an ecclesiastical overachiever, is mired in a tenth-rate religious order in Minnesota, the grounds surprisingly containing a golf course.*

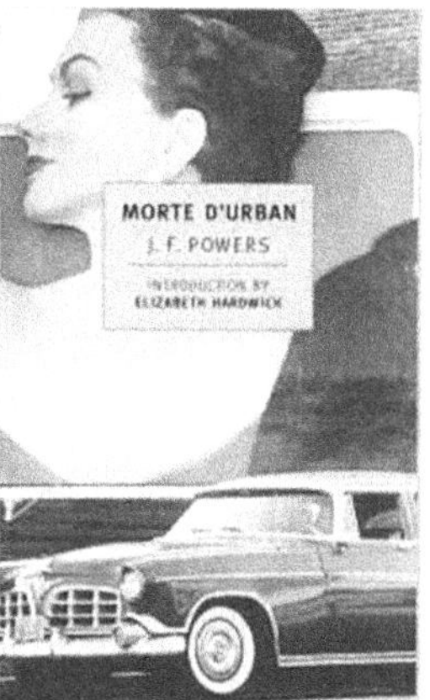

And then, working through Monsignor Renton, Father Urban got the Bishop to come out to the Hill for a meal—and should have left it at that. Urged by Father Urban and Monsignor Renton, the Bishop, who said he'd played before, took to the course. After four holes, on each of which he'd clearly demonstrated that he was a poor sport as well as a lousy golfer, the Bishop quit in a huff. Father Urban was unhappy about this—happy, though, that it was over, for the contrast between his play and the Bishop's was excruciating. Moreover, the Bishop appeared to regard Father Urban's near-professional game as unseemly and impertinent in a priest. There were people like that, Father Urban knew, and he was only sorry that the Bishop had to be one of them. He invited the man to come out again, and *soon*—"All you need, Your Excellency, is practice"—but was rather glad to hear that the sorehead was off for Rome.

— **J. F. Powers** *(1917-1999) American novelist and short story writer*

The Presence of Grace (1956)

- *Gentle satire of Midwestern Catholic priests, in this instance accompanied by afeline companion.*

I had spent most of the afternoon mousing—a matter of sport with me and certainly not of diet—in the sunburnt fields that begin at our back door and continue hundreds of miles into the Dakotas. I gradually gave up the idea of hunting, the grasshoppers convincing me that there was no percentage in stealth. Even to doze was difficult, under such conditions, but I must have managed it. At least I was late coming to dinner, and so my introduction to the two missionaries took place at table. They were surprised, as most visitors are, to see me take the chair at Father Malt's right.

Father Malt, breaking off the conversation (if it could be called that), was his usual dear old self. "Fathers," he said, "meet Fritz."

I gave the newcomers the first good look that invariably tells me whether or not a person cares for cats. — **J. F. Powers**

Wheat That Springeth Green (1988)

- *The trials and tribulations of Father Joe Hackett, who refuses to toady up to either the priest in his parish or to the archbishop.*

. . . he . . . poured himself a small gin and knelt down (the frosted window was up a bit) to see if he'd heard what he though he had in the street, yes, at the curb, disembarking from their cars, their drum from a station wagon, the Cheerleaders in full fig (male and female made he them, but for this?), and a heavily armed photographer, no, two, oh, *no*, . . . all of them, a hellish host, advancing on the rectory, and then, sliding into the breach of the driveway, the archiepiscopal car of hearselike length and breadth and hue, the rocket trail of mud splashmarks on its flank giving it a sinister GHQ look to Joe, who, rising from his knees, joints buckling, staggered away from the window and poured himself another small gin and, hearing the doorbell, seated himself on the toilet, its lid down not for the purpose it then served, not for sitting on while sipping an aperitif, but on general principles, and heard, as he'd known he would, Bill come for him, announce through the bathroom door, calmly, the end of the world.

"The Arch's here, Joe, and Toohey's in a hurry."

Silence.

"Joe?"

Silence.

— **J. F. Powers**

The Echo Maker (2006)

- *After his auto accident Mark Schluter emerges from a protracted coma with a rare form of amnesia. Confronting his sister as an imposter, he seeks to learn what happened that fateful night.*

The suture of the centerline drew her downward into the snowy black. It made no sense: Mark, a near-professional driver, rolling off an arrow-straight country road that was as familiar to him as breathing. Driving off the road, in central Nebraska—like falling off a wooden horse. She toyed with the date: 02/20/02. Did it mean anything? Her palms butted the wheel, and the car shook. *Your brother has had an accident.* In fact, he'd long ago taken every wrong turn you could take in life, and from the wrong lane. Telephone calls coming in at awful hours, as far back as she could remember. But never one like this.

— **Richard Powers** *(1957-) American novelist*

Galatea 2.2 (1995)

- *An effort to bombard a computer model of the human brain with literature, music and conversation so that it will eventually become conscious of beauty.*

"When is anymore? When is now?"

H had learned something. Whatever stuck in the throat, indigestible, could be made less acute by slipping it into a question.

"We can talk about that later."

"Am I a boy or a girl?"

I should have seen. Even ungrounded intelligence had to grow self-aware eventually. To grab what it needed.

H clocked its thoughts now. I was sure of that. Time passed for it. Its hidden layers could watch their own rate of change. Any pause on my part now would be fatal. Delay meant something, an uncertainty that might undercut forever the strength of the connection I was about to tie for it.

"You're a girl," I said, without hesitation. I hoped I was right. "You are a little girl, Helen."

I hoped she like the name.

— Richard Powers

The Gold Bug Variations (1991)

- *The love affairs of two couples set against the background of the quest to solve the mysteries of genetic coding.*

But something else motivates the euphoric articles, something more than self-aggrandizement, more than the desire to cap the ancient monument and book passage to Stockholm, that freezing, pristine Valhalla. The compulsion to find the pattern of living translation—the way a simple, self-duplicating string of four letters inscribes an entire living being—is built into every infant who has ever learned a word, put a phrase together, discovered that phonemes might *speak*.

— Richard Powers

Clockers (1992)

- *The life of an intelligent, calculating drug-dealer intertwined with a homicide detective, set in and around housing projects across the Hudson from New York City.*

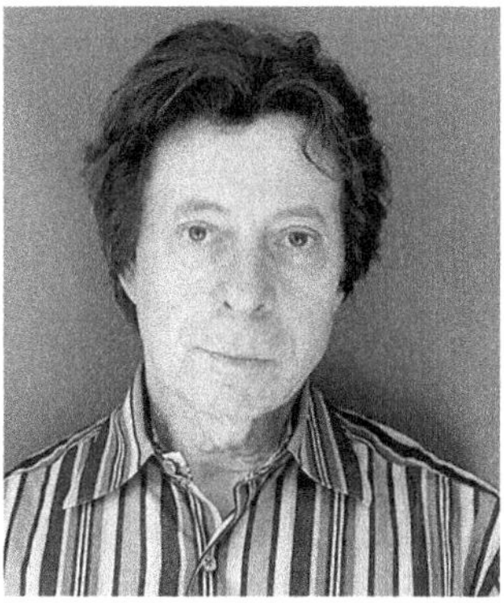

Strike snorted dryly. "Everybody likes Andre 'cause Andre for the *people*."

Strike knew immediately that he had stepped over the line. Andre rose. He seemed to be resisting an impulse to backhand Strike off the bench. When he spoke there was no play in his voice.

"Get up."

Strike sighed, stood away from the bench and raised his arms elbows high, like bat wings.

But Andre wasn't interested in a frisk. "How's about I lock *you* up instead? And *you* ain't going to no Youth House. You old enough for County."

"It ain't my book bag." Strike wasn't too alarmed. Andre had never really come down on him before.

" . . . and even if they make it simple possession , you *still* gettin' ninety days in, and I'm gonna make some calls to the *inside*, make sure that's gonna be ninety days the *hard* way. Are you ready for that?"

Strike looked away. "I ain't doin' no ninety days. That ain't my dope."

"It is if I say it is."

"It ain't mine."

Looking off at a brick wall, Strike could feel Andre's hot stare. After a long thirty seconds Strike broke the silence. "It ain't mine," he said again with mournful insistence.

Andre muttered "______," and suddenly Strike's wrists were behind him, steel cuffs biting into his skin.

— **Richard Price** *(1949-) American author and screenwriter*

Lush Life (2008)

- *The repercussions of a seemingly random shooting on Manhattan's Lower East Side.*

"So what's the story," pulling a steno pad from the inside of his jacket.

"Story is . . ." Bobby flipped open his own pad. "Three white males, after a couple of hours barhopping, last stop Café Berkmann on Rivington and Norfolk, walking from that location west on Rivington, then south on Eldridge, are accosted by two males, black and/or Hispanic in front of Twenty-seven here, one of whom produces a gun, says, 'I want all of it.' One guy, our witness, Eric Cash, hands over his wallet, then steps off. The second guy, Steven Boulware"—Bobby pen-pointed to the puker hugging himself on the stoop—"is so boxed, his response is to take a little power nap on the sidewalk. But the *third* guy, Isaac Marcus? *He* responds by stepping to the gunman, saying, quote, 'Not tonight, my man.'"

"'Not tonight, my man,'" Matty marveled, shaking his head.

"Suicide by mouth. In any event, one shot," pen-pointing to the shell casing by the yellow cone. "Home run to the heart, the shooter and his partner book east on Delancey."

— **Richard Price**

Complete Collected Stories (1988)

Thomas Haywood/Random House

- *Pritchett wrote exactly eighty-two short stories described as "the harvest of a life of observation, experience, and intuition, a harvest gathered by a man of integrity and artistic gift." This quote from "The Sailor."*

She always had a cigarette in her mouth, and every now and then the carnation skin of her face, with its warm, dark blue eyes, would be distorted and turned crimson by violent bronchial coughing.

When this stopped she would straighten up, the delicacy came back to her skin and she would say, 'Oh, Christ. Oh, bloody hell' and you noticed at the end of every speech the fine right eyebrow would rise a little and the lid of the eye below it would quiver. This wink, the limpid wink of the Colonel's daughter, you noticed at once. You wondered what it meant and planned to find out. It was as startling and enticing as a fish rising, and you discovered when you went after it that the Colonel's daughter was the hardest drinking and most blasphemous piece of apparent childish innocence you had ever seen.

— **V. S. Pritchett** *(1900-1997) British writer and critic*

Close Range: Wyoming Stories (1999)

- *Stories of the hard times, desperation, and loneliness of country life in Wyoming. This quote is from "Brokeback Mountain," the tale of two cowboys made into a 2005 motion picture.*

The shirt seemed heavy until he saw there was anther shirt inside it, the sleeves carefully worked down inside Jack's sleeves. It was his own plaid shirt, lost, he'd thought, long ago in some damn laundry, his dirty shirt, the pocket ripped, buttons missing, stolen by Jack and hidden here inside Jack's own shirt, the pair like two skins, one inside the other, two in one. He pressed his face into the fabric and breathed in slowly through his mouth and nose, hoping for the faintest smoke and mountain sage and salty sweet stink of Jack but there was no real scent, only the memory of it, the imagined power of Brokeback Mountain of which nothing was left but what he held in his hands.

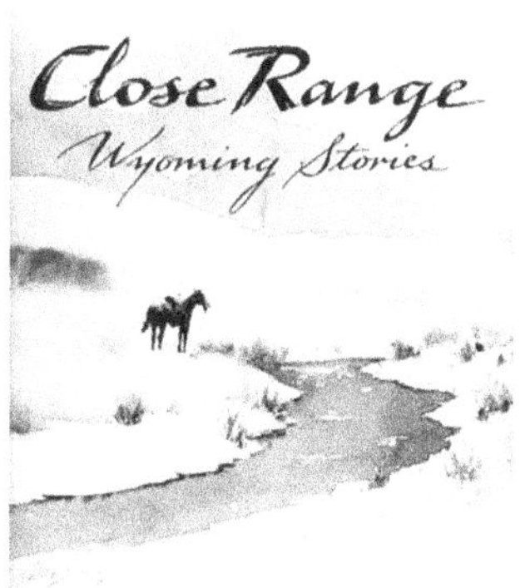

— **Annie Proulx** *(1935-) American author and journalist*

The Shipping News (1993)

- *Quoyle, a widower, his two young daughters and his aunt return to Newfoundland to try to create new lives.*

From this youngest son's failure to dog-paddle the father saw other failures multiply like an explosion of virulent cells—failure to speak clearly; failure to sit up straight; failure to get up in the morning; failure in attitude; failure in ambition and ability; indeed, in everything. His own failure.

Quoyle shambled, a head taller than any child around him, was soft. He knew it. "Ah, you lout," said the father. But no pygmy himself. And brother Dick, the father's favorite, pretended to throw up when Quoyle came into a room, hissed “Lardass, Snotface, Ugly Pig, Warthog, Stupid, Stinkbomb, Fart-tub, Greasebag,” pummeled and kicked until Quoyle curled, hands over head, sniveling, on the linoleum. All stemmed from Quoyle’s chief failure, a failure of normal appearance.

A great damp loaf of a body. At six he weighed eighty pounds. At sixteen he was buried under a casement of flesh. Head shaped like a crenshaw, no neck, reddish hair ruched back. Features as bunched as kissed fingertips. Eyes the color of plastic. The monstrous chin, a freakish shelf jutting from the lower face. **— Annie Proulx**

In Search of Lost Time (1913)

■ *A semi-autobiographical novel in six volumes (4,580 pages) that includes the central role of memory, the nature of art, homosexuality, physical infirmity, and cruelty. The first translation was titled “Remembrance of Things Past.”*

She sent out for one of those short, plump little cakes called ‘petites madeleines,’ which look as though they had been molded in the fluted scallop of a pilgrim’s shell. And soon, mechanically, weary after a dull day with the prospect of a depressing morrow, I raised to my lips a spoonful of the tea in which I had soaked a morsel of the cake. No sooner had the warm liquid, and the crumbs with it, touched my palate than a shudder ran through my whole body, and I stopped, intent upon the extraordinary changes that were taking place. An exquisite pleasure had invaded my senses, but individual, detached, with no suggestion of its origin. And at once the vicissitudes of life had become indifferent to me, its disasters innocuous, its brevity illusory—this new sensation having had on me the effect which love has of filling me with a precious essence; or rather this essence was not in me, it was myself.

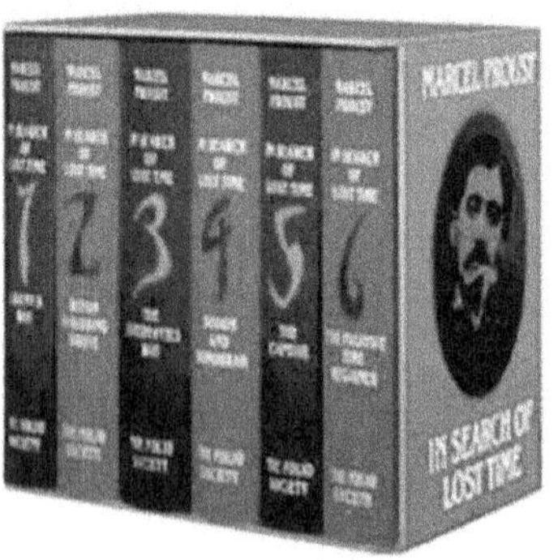

— Marcel Proust *(1871-1922) French novelist, critic and essayist*

The Godfather (1969)

■ *A chronicle of the American Mafia from the 1920s into the 1960s.*

Underneath the table his right hand moved to the gun tucked into his waistband and he drew it free. At that moment the waiter came to take their order and Sollozzo turned his head to speak to the waiter. Michael thrust the table away from him with his left hand and his right hand shoved the gun almost against Sollozzo's head. The man's coordination was so acute that he had already begun to fling himself away at Michael's motion. But Michael, younger, his reflexes sharper, pulled the trigger. The bullet caught Sollozzo squarely between his eye and his ear and when it exited on the other side blasted out a huge gout of blood and skull fragments onto the petrified waiter's jacket. Instinctively Michael knew that one bullet was enough. Sollozzo had turned his head in that last moment and he had seen the light of life die in the man's eyes as clearly as a candle goes out.

— **Mario Puzo** *(1920-1999) American author and screenwriter*

One of the finest recent novel-movie alliances.

The Crying of Lot 49 (1965)

- *At the time, early 1960s, a fashion in satirical writing that explores eccentric characters and their shallow connections.*

When he opened the door of his apartment/office she saw him framed in a long succession or train of doorways, room after room receding in the general direction of Santa Monica, all soaked in rain-light. Genghis Cohen had a touch of summer flu, his fly was half open and he was wearing a Barry Goldwater sweatshirt also. Oedipa felt at once motherly. In a room perhaps a third of the way along the suite he sat her in a rocking chair and brought real homemade dandelion wine in small neat glasses.

— **Thomas Pynchon** *(1937-) American novelist*

Gravity's Rainbow (1973)

- *British Intelligence discovers a map of the sexual conquests of one Lieutenant Tyrone Slothrop, U.S. Army, which corresponds exactly to the V-2 impact sites.*

The Moment was 6:43:16 British Double Summer Time: the sky, beaten like Death's drum, still humming and Slothrop's cock—say what? yes lookit inside his GI undershorts here's a sneaky *hardon* stirring, ready to jump—well great God where'd *that* come from?

There is in his history, and likely, God help him, in his dossier, a peculiar sensitivity to what is revealed in the sky. (But a *hardon*?) . . .

It's a map that spooks them all, the map Slothrop's been keeping on his girls. The stars fall in a Poisson distribution, just like the rocket strikes on Roger Mexico's map of the Robot Blitz.

But, well, it's a bit more than the distribution. The two patterns also happen to be identical.

— Thomas Pynchon

Mason & Dixon (1997)

- *The lifelong partnership and adventures of the English surveyors Charles Mason and Jeremiah Dixon as they travel the world measuring and mapping.*

"Why not? What's the matter? Savages, Wilderness. No one even knows what's out there. And we have just, do you appreciate, contracted, to place a Line directly thro' it? Doesn't it strike you as a little unreasonable?"

"Not to mention the Americans . . . ?"

"Excuse me? they are at least all British there,— aren't they? The Place *is* but a Patch of England, at a three-thousand –Mile Off-set. Isn't it?"

"Eeh! Eeh! Thoo can be so thoughtful, helping cheer me up wi' thy Joaks, Mason,— I'm fine, really,— "

"Dixon, hold,— are you telling me, now, that Americans are *not* British?— You've heard this somewhere?"

"No more than the Cape Dutch are Dutch . . . ? 'Tis said these people keep Slaves, as did our late Hosts,— that they are likewise inclin'd to kill the People already living where they wish to settle,—"

"Another Slave-Colony . . . so have I heard, as well. Christ."

— Thomas Pynchon

In 1965 Pynchon turned down an invitation to teach literature at Bennington College, writing that he had resolved two or three years earlier to write three novels at once. He described the decision as "a moment of temporary insanity", but noted that he was "too stubborn to let any of them go, let alone all of them." Likely the novels were *V* (1963), *The Crying of Lot 49* (1965), and *Gravity's Rainbow* (1973).

Q

—

R

Gargantua and Pantagruel (1532)

■ *The story of two giants, a father (Gargantua) and his son (Pantagruel) and their adventures, written as a satire.*

And then, he looked very carefully at the great bells hanging in Notre Dame's towers, and made them ring most pleasantly. Hearing this, it occurred to him what fine cowbells they'd make, hanging around his mare's neck, for he'd already decided to load her up with Brie cheese and fresh herrings and send her back to his father. And so he took them down and brought them to his rooms.

In the meantime, along came a mouth-stuffing officer of the legions of Saint Anthony . . . And he tried to sneak away with the bells, which would have let him be heard for miles around—so loud and clear, indeed, that he could make bacon tremble in the frying pan. But he chivalrously left them where they were, not because they were too hot but because, weighing about twenty thousand pounds each, they were a trifle too heavy for him to carry.

— **Francois Rabelais** *(1494-1553) French Renaissance writer, doctor and humanist*

Atlas Shrugged (1957)

■ *Dagny Taggart, a no-nonsense railroad executive, attempts to keep her company alive despite encroachments by a society moving against the productive self-interests of capitalism.*

He walked, keeping one hand in his pocket, his fingers closed about a bracelet. It was made of Rearden Metal, in the shape of a chain. . . .

He did not think of the ten years. . . .

But the parts, unrecalled, were there . . .

They were the nights spent at scorching ovens in the research laboratory of the mills—

—the nights spent in the workshop of his

home, over sheets of paper which he filled with formulas, then tore up in angry failure—

—the days when the young scientists of the small staff he had chosen to assist him waited for instructions like soldiers ready for a hopeless battle, having exhausted their ingenuity, still willing, but silent, with the unspoken sentence hanging in the air: "Mr. Rearden, it can't be done—"

—the meals, interrupted and abandoned at the sudden flash of a new thought, a thought to be pursued at once, to be tried, to be tested, to be worked on for months, and to be discarded as another failure— . . .

—then the day when it was done and its result was called Rearden Metal—

— **Ayn Rand** *(1905-1982) Russian-American novelist, philosopher, playwright, and screenwriter*

In the fall of 1925 Soviet born Rand was granted a visa to visit American relatives. As her train pulled away she called out to her family, "By the time I return, I'll be famous."

The Rand Institute provides 400,000 copies of Rand's novels every year for free to high schools throughout the United States. — *Wikipedia*

The Fountainhead (1943)

- *A young architect chooses to struggle in obscurity rather than compromise his artistic and personal vision.*

"Now, in our age, collectivism, the rule of the second-hander and second-rater, the ancient monster, has broken loose and is running amuck. It has brought men to a level of intellectual indecency never equaled on earth. . . . I am an architect. I know what is to come by the principle on which it is built. We are approaching a world in which I cannot permit myself to live.

"Now you know why I dynamited Cortlandt.

"I designed Cortlandt. I gave it to you. I destroyed it.

"I destroyed it because I did not choose to let it exist. It was a double monster. In form and in implication. I had to blast both. The form was mutilated by two second-handers who assumed the right to improve upon that which they had not made and could not equal. They were permitted to do it by the general implication that the altruistic purpose of the building superseded all rights and that I had no claim to stand against it.

"I agreed to design Cortlandt for the purpose of seeing it erected as I designed it and for no other reason. That was the price I set for my work. I was not paid."

— **Ayn Rand**

All Quiet on the Western Front (1929)

"... a generation that was destroyed by war, even though it might have escaped its shells."

- *The drudgery and futility of war brought home to young German recruits experiencing the death and mutilation of trench warfare in World War I.*

German *Frontschwein*, Verdun

. . . He fell in October 1918, on a day that was so quiet and still on the whole front, that the army report confined itself to the single sentence: All quiet on the Western Front.

He had fallen forward and lay on the earth as though sleeping. Turning him over one saw that he could not have suffered long; his face had an expression of calm, as though almost glad the end had come.

— **Erich Maria Remarque** *(1898-1970)*
German author

Wide Sargasso Sea (1966)

- *The life of Antoinette Mason, a white Creole heiress beset as a child by the racial tensions of the Caribbean and rejection by a mother eventually committed. A prearranged unhappy marriage and virtual imprisonment lead to a perilous mental state.*

That's not what she hear, she said. She hear all we poor like beggar. We ate salt fish — no money for fresh fish. That old house so leaky, you run with calabash to catch water when it rain. Plenty white people in Jamaica. Real white people, they got gold money. They didn't look at us, nobody see them come near us. Old time white people nothing but white nigger now, and black nigger better than white nigger.

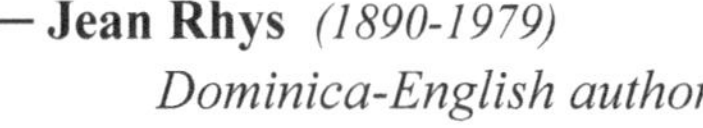

— **Jean Rhys** *(1890-1979)*
Dominica-English author

The Fortunes of Richard Mahony (1917)

- *A trilogy of novels which tell the story of a young doctor's mental and physical deterioration with consequential growing ostracism of the family by neighbors.*

Left alone Polly remained standing by the table, on which an array of tines was set—preserved salmon, sardines, condensed milk—their tops forced back to show their contents. Her heart was heavy as lead, and she felt a dull sense of injury as well. This hut her home!—to which she had so freely invited sister and friend! She would be ashamed for them ever to set eyes on it. Not in her worst dreams had she imagined it as mean and poor as this. But perhaps . . . With the lamp in her hand, she tip-toed guiltily to a door in the wall: it opened into a tiny bedroom with a sloping roof. No, this was all, all there was of it: just these two miserable little poky rooms! She raised her head and looked round, and the tears welled up in spite of herself. The roof was so low that you could almost touch it; the window was no larger than a pocket-handkerchief; there were chinks between the slabs of the walls. And from one of these she now saw a spider crawl out, a huge black tarantula, with horrible hairy legs.

— **Henry Handel Richardson** *(1870-1946) Australian author*

Clarissa (1748)

- *Beautiful and virtuous Clarissa Harlowe, imposed upon by her implacable family to marry, is unfortunately pursued by one Robert Lovelace, a scoundrel who entreats Anna Howe, Clarissa's best friend, in this exchange.*

I was all in a flutter, you may suppose. He would have taken my hand. I refused it, all glowing with indignation: everybody's eyes upon us.

I went from him to the other end of the room, and sat down, as I thought, out of his hated sight: but presently I heard his odious voice, whispering, behind my chair (he leaning upon the back of it, with impudent unconcern), *Charming Miss Howe!* looking over my shoulder: *one request*—(I started up from my seat; but could hardly stand neither, for very indignation)—Oh, this sweet, but becoming disdain! whispered on the insufferable creature. I am sorry to give you all this emotion: but either here, or at your own house, let me entreat from you one quarter of an hour's audience. I beseech you, madam, but one quarter of an hour, in any of the adjoining apartments.

Not for a *kingdom*, fluttering my fan. I knew not what I did. But I could have killed him.

— **Samuel Richardson** *(1689-1761) English writer and printer*

The Town (1950)

- *The story of the Wheeler family in Ohio trying to mend with the new town society in the early 1800s.*

"Don't forget me!" Rosa begged.

"I can remember a long time," Chancey told her.

Her eyes searched his.

"I'll give you something to remember me by," she promised. "Just wait. I'll show you." . . .

"Now watch!" she called back guardedly and clapped the water with her whitewood slab. "Are you watching? Do you see it? Look and tell me! Can you see it?" . . .

"The rainbow!" she called back anxiously. "Can't you see it?"

Not till then did Chancey know what she meant. The spray from her whitewood slab flew high above her head, and so fast did she ply it that the fine drops hung constantly in the air. Behind them was the falling sun, before them the forest. Against the dark trees the drops took on the bright colors of the bow in the sky. But this wasn't like any bow he had seen before, and it wasn't in the sky. It hung right here in the creek around Rosa. She seemed to be standing in it. It played on her, bathed her. The drops as they came down flashed colored fire, and the reds, greens, yellows and violets dyed her slender body.

Her face glistened with water and pleasure as she turned it over her shoulder.

"Did you see it? Wasn't that pretty? Do you know what it means? It means we don't have to wait for a rainbow. We can make our own."

— **Conrad Richter** *(1890-1968) American novelist*

The Waters of Kronos (1960)

- *As an old man John Donner returns to the town where he was born and is drawn back into the world of his youth.*

"Here's an old man to see you, Harry," Mr. Paxman said.

The caller winced. Why, it had been Mr. Paxman and his father who had been old, not he. His father looked no more than thirty-five as he set the lamp in its bracket and wiped his hands on a dirty roller towel. He came forward holding out his hand with that hearty ease he always enjoyed with strangers and which somehow impoverished and cramped his son to see.

“I don’t think I caught the name,” he said, the same unforgettable smile under his black mustache.

“My name is John,” the stranger said hoarsely.

His father’s eyes searched his face while still holding his hand.

“Haven’ we met before?”

“Yes, many years ago.” For a moment the son had the feeling that his father was going to recognize him. Then he saw it was only his parent’s inveterate interest in people.

— Conrad Richter

Gilead (2004)

- *A generational story of a preaching family in rural Iowa and Kansas from the time of the Civil War through the 1950’s.*

. . . Glory and I . . . walked back and stood on the bridge and watched . . . the baby and her mother, playing there in the river. The baby, who had just begun to walk, didn’t have a stitch on, and the little girl was wearing a dress that was soggy to her waist. It was late summer. The river is very shallow at that time of year, and the bottom was half exposed and braided like water. There were sandbars right across, the bigger ones small jungles of weedy vegetation weedily in bloom, with butterflies and dragonflies attending on them like spirits. The little girl was practicing the maternal imperative from time to time, the way children sometimes do when they are playing. Maybe she knew she was being overheard. She was trying to dam a rivulet with sticks and mud, and the baby was trying to understand the project well enough to help. She would bring her mother handfuls of mud and handfuls of water and her mother would say, “Now, don’t you go stepping on it. You’re just messing up all my work!”

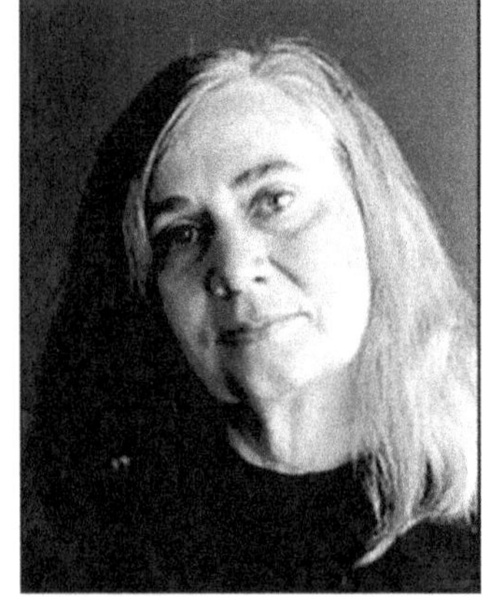

After a while the baby cupped her hands and poured water on her mother’s arm and laughed, so her mother cupped her hands and poured water on the baby’s belly, and the baby laughed and threw water on her mother with both hands, and the little girl threw water back, enough so that the baby whimpered, and the little girl said, “Now, don’t you go crying! What do you expect when you act like that.” And she put her arms around her and settled her into her lap, kneeling there in the water, and set about repairing her dam with her free hand. The baby made a conversational sound and her mother said, “That’s a leaf. A leaf off a tree. Leaf,” and gave it into the baby’s hand. And the sun was shining as well as it could onto that shadowy river, a good part of the shine being caught in the trees. And the cicadas were chanting, and the willows were straggling their tresses in the water, and the cottonwood and the ash were making that late summer hush, that susurrus.

— **Marilynne Robinson** *(1943-) American novelist and essayist*

Home (2008)

- *The long lost son of an elderly pastor returns home shortly after his younger sister moves in to nurse the dying man.*

So she asked him, "Are you going to marry her?"

He was very pale. He smiled—that strange, hard shame of his—and said, "You've seen her."

She said, "Well, what is Papa going to do—"

"Do to me? Nothing. I mean, he's going to forgive me." He laughed. "And now I have a train to catch."

"You won't even stay for supper?"

He said, "Poor Pigtails," and smiled at her and walked out the door.

And twenty years passed. There was no way of knowing that day that anything absolute had happened. Her mother had been so upset she stayed in her room, no doubt waiting for him to come to her seeking reconciliation. She would never see him again in this life. When evening fell no lights were put on, and supper-time came and went unremarked. . . . Never had it entered her mind that their household could contain so desolate a silence.

— **Marilynne Robinson**

Housekeeping (1980)

- *Ruth and her younger sister, Lucille, grow up and apart in a small town under the care of Sylvie, their eccentric and remote aunt.*

. . . What if I should walk to the house one night and find Lucille there? It is possible. Since we are dead, the house would be hers now. Perhaps she is in the kitchen, snuggling pretty daughters in her lap, and perhaps now and then they look at the black window to find out what their mother seems to see there, and they see their own faces and a face so like their mother's, so rapt and full of tender watching, that only Lucille could think the face was mine. If Lucille is there, Sylvie and I have stood outside her window a thousand times, and we have thrown the side door open when she was upstairs changing beds, and we have brought in leaves, and flung the curtains and tipped the bud vase, and somehow left the house again before she could run downstairs, leaving behind us a strong smell of lake water. She would sigh and think, "They never change."

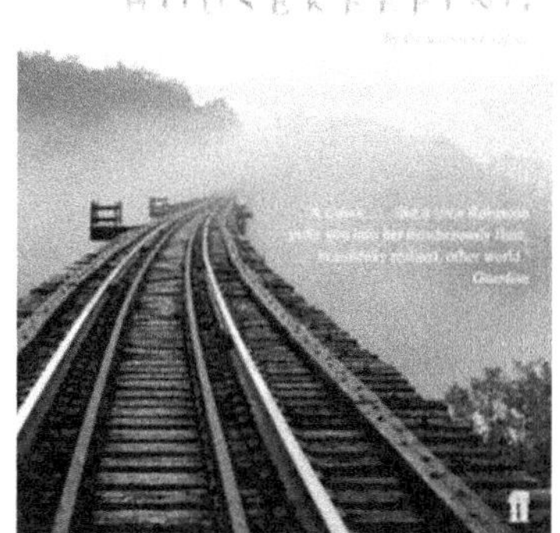

— **Marilynne Robinson**

Call It Sleep (1934)

- *The story of a shy Jewish 8-year old with no friends, growing up in the immigrant slums of New York City in the 1930s.*

"Now I'll get you!" His father gnashed his teeth. "Now I'll get you!" And David knew they were doomed.

The charging horse bore down on them. At the corner, with only a few yards between them and the wagon, both men as if by a common impulse, shoved each other in opposite directions. His father turned after the stockier running on the sidewalk. A moment more, the horse was abreast. One yank at the reins and the reins were flung at David. "Hold, you!" Whip in hand, his father leaped from the rolling wagon into the street. The fugitive, trapped before a stable door that wouldn't open, spun about, crouched savagely at bay.

"Waddayuh chasin' me fuh?" His yellow teeth were bared, the round eyes now slits of fear and fury.

"Hanh!" His father's snarl was almost like laughter, but the grinding of his teeth creaked like a strong cable stretching. "Yuhv'll take my milk!"

"Me? Waddaye shittin' about? I never seen it."

"An' de bottles you t'rew?" He seemed merely to be toying with the man. David knew the answers didn't matter. He grew faint, waiting for the end.

"Yea! I t'rew 'em!" The other was blustering savagely. "An de nex' time watch out who de fuck yer chas—"

Swish! The hiss of the whip cut off his words; the long, stiff thong curled over his shoulder, whacked!

"Owoo!" he howled with pain and fury. "Yuh Jew bastard! You hit me?" He flung himself at David's father, arms thrashing.

— **Henry Roth** *(1906-1995) American novelist and short story writer*

The Rip Van Winkle of American authors, Roth succumbed to monumental writer's block lasting well over 50 years, from publication of *Call It Sleep* in 1934 to beginning work on the first volume of *Mercy is a Rude Stream* published in 1994. — *Wikipedia*

American Pastoral (1997)

- *The teenage daughter of a Jewish-American businessman opposes the Viet Nam war with an act of violence, eventually retreating into isolation which traumatizes and gradually derails the life of her father.*

"I found her. I just came from Merry. I found her in Newark. She's here. In a room. I saw her. What this girl has been through, what she looks like, where she lives—you can't imagine it. You cannot begin to imagine it."

He proceeds to recount her story, not breaking down, trying to repeat what she said to him about where she had been, how she had lived, and what had become of her, trying to get it into his head, his own head, trying to find in his head the room for it all when he could not even find enough room for that room in which she lived. He comes closest to crying when he tells his brother that she had twice been raped.

— **Philip Roth** *(1933-) American novelist*

The Anatomy Lesson (1983)

■ *The quest of Nathan Zuckerman to relieve himself from excruciating neck and back pain that has pretty much left him lying on his back in his apartment.*

When he is sick, every man wants his mother; if she's not around, other women must do. Zuckerman was making do with four other women. He'd never had so many women at one time, or so many doctors, or drunk so much vodka, or done so little work, or known despair of such wild proportions. Yet he didn't seem to have a disease that any body could take seriously. Only the pain—in his neck, arms, and shoulders, pain that made it difficult to walk for more than a few city blocks or even to stand very long in one place. Just having a neck, arms, and shoulders was like carrying another person around. Ten minutes out getting the groceries and he had to hurry home and lie down. Nor could he bring back more than one light bagful per trip, and even then he had to hold it cradled up against his chest like somebody eighty years old.

— **Philip Roth**

The Counterlife (1987)

■ *Adventures arising from the mid-life crisis of a suburban Jewish New Jersey dentist.*

. . . The fact is that though we may sneak around the brownstone like a pair of sex criminals, most of our time is passed in my study, where I light a fire and we sit and talk. We drink coffee, we listen to music, and we talk. We never stop talking. How many hundreds of hours of talk will it take to inure us to what's missing? I expose myself to her voice as though it were her body, draining from it my every drop of sensual satisfaction. There's to be no exquisite pleasure here that cannot be derived from words. My carnality is now *really* a fiction and, revenge of revenge, language and only language must provide the means for the release of everything. Maria's voice, her talking tongue, is the sole erotic implement. The one-sidedness of our affair is excruciating. — **Philip Roth**

The Ghost Writer (1979)

■ *A successful author reminisces about his visit 20 years earlier to the home of reclusive writer Manny Lonoff, recalling this tongue-lashing by the man's wife regarding the aging husband's young assistant.*

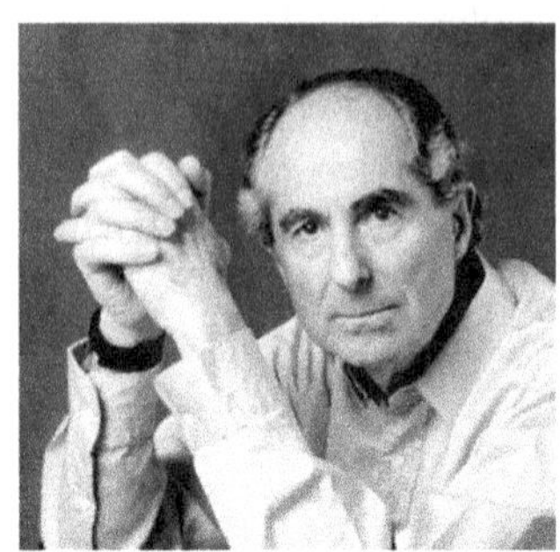

"She thinks with her it will all be the religion of art up here. Oh, will it ever! Let her try to please you, Manny! Let her serve as the backdrop for your thoughts for thirty-five years. Let her see how noble and heroic you are by the twenty-seventh draft. . . . Yes, have her run hot baths for your poor back twice a day, and then go a week without being talked to—let alone being touched in bed. . . . "

"I'm going to Boston! I'm going to Europe! It's too late to touch me now! I'm taking a trip around the world and never coming back! And you, . . . *you* won't go anywhere. You won't see anything. . . . you (won't) even go out to dinner. . . . There is his religion of art, my young successor: rejecting life! *Not* living is what he makes his beautiful fiction *out* of! And you will now be the person he is not living with!"

— **Philip Roth**

Goodby Columbus (1959)

■ *A summer love affair between a poor Jewish boy from Newark and a Radcliffe-bound girl from suburban Short Hills.*

"How's Doris?" she said.

"Peeling," I said. "She's going to have her skin fixed."

"*Stop* it," she said, and dove down beneath us till I felt her clamping her hands on the soles of my feet. I pulled back and then down too, and then, at the bottom, no more than six inches above the wiggling black lines that divided the pool into lanes for races, we bubbled a kiss into each other's lips. She was smiling there, at *me*, down at the bottom of the swimming pool of the Green Lane Country Club. Way above us, legs shimmied in the water and a pair of fins skimmed greenly by: my cousin Doris could peel away to nothing for all I cared, my Aunt Gladys have twenty feedings every night, my father and mother could roast away their asthma down in the furnace of Arizona, those penniless deserters — I didn't care for anything but Brenda.

— **Philip Roth**

The Human Stain (2000)

■ *A faculty dean, long concealing the fact that he is Black, shakes up a college and is harried from his position by gossip, jealousy, and acrimony. This quote from a flashback to his youth.*

"And she believes your parents are dead, Coleman. That's what you told her."

"That's right." . . .

"And? What else did you tell her?"

"What else do you think I told her?"

"Whatever it suited you to tell her." That was as harsh as she got all afternoon. . . . "I'm never going to know my grandchildren," she said. . . .

"You're never going to let them see me," she said. "You're never going to let them know who I am. 'Mom,' you'll tell me, 'Ma, you come to the railroad station in New York, and you sit on the bench in the waiting room, and at eleven twenty-five A.M., I'll walk by with my kids in their Sunday best.' That'll be my birthday present five years from now. 'Sit there, Mom, say nothing, and I'll just walk them slowly by.' And you know very well that I will be there. The railroad station. The zoo. Central Park. Wherever you say, of course I'll do it. You tell me the only way I can ever touch my grandchildren is for you to hire me to come over as Mrs. Brown to baby-sit and put them to bed. I'll do it. Tell me to come over as Mrs. Brown to clean your house, I'll do *that*. Sure I'll do what ever you tell me. I have no choice."

— Philip Roth

Operation Shylock (1993)

- *Philip Roth confronts his double, an imposter whose self-appointed task is to the lead the Jews out of Israel and back to Europe.*

A middle-aged American Jew settles into a suite at Jerusalem's King David Hotel and proposes publicly that Israeli Jews of Ashkenazi descent, . . . return to their countries of origin to resurrect the European Jewish life that Hitler all but annihilated between 1939 and 1945. . . .

Now it so happens that this man bears a decided physical resemblance to the American writer Philip Roth, claims that Philip Roth is his name as well, and is not averse to playing upon this unaccountable, if not utterly fantastical, coincidence to foster the belief that he *is* the author and thus to advance the cause of Diasporism. Through this subterfuge he is able to convince Louis B. Smilesburger, an elderly, disabled Holocaust victim who has retired unhappily to Jerusalem after having made his fortune as a New York jeweler, to contribute to him one million dollars.

— Philip Roth

The Plot Against America (2004)

- *Isolationist Charles A. Lindbergh defeats Franklin Roosevelt in the 1940 presidential election, prompting fear in every Jewish household. In this quote the father of the portrayed Newark Jewish family has just returned from seeing his wife's sister in a newsreel.*

And then there was the shock of seeing on film the Nazi von Ribbentrop and his wife warmly greeted on the White House portico by the president and Mrs. Lindbergh. And the shock of seeing all the prominent guests stepping from their limousines and smiling with anticipation at the prospect of dining and dancing in von Ribbentrop's presence—and among the guests, seemingly no less thrilled than the others by the disgusting occasion, Rabbi Lionel Bengelsdorf and Miss Evelyn Finkel. "I could not believe it," my father said. "The smile on her face is a mile wide. And the husband-to-be? He looks like he thinks the dinner is for him. You should see this man—nodding at everyone as if he actually mattered!" "But why did you go," my mother asked him, "when it was bound to upset you like this?" "I went," he told her, "because every day I ask myself the same question: How can this be happening in America? How can people like these be in charge of our country? If I didn't see it with my own eyes, I'd think I was having a hallucination."

— Philip Roth

Portnoy's Complaint (1967)

- *An obsessive rant about the joys and anguishes of growing up Jewish in the forties and fifties encumbered with smothering parents and extreme libidinal urges.*

I am marked like a road map from head to toe with my repressions. You can travel the length and breadth of my body over superhighways of shame and inhibition and fear. See, I am too good too, Mother, I too am moral to the bursting point—just like you! Did you ever see me try to smoke a cigarette? I look like Bette Davis. Today boys and girls not even old enough to be bar-mitzvahed are sucking on marijuana like it's peppermint candy, and I'm still all thumbs with a Lucky Strike. Yes, that's how good I am, Momma. Can't smoke, hardly drink, no drugs, don't borrow money or play cards, can't tell a lie without beginning to sweat as though I'm passing over the equator.

— Philip Roth

The Professor of Desire (1977)

- *The history of a man's sexual desires from youthful accedence to attempts to domesticate his passions in later life.*

In response, no tears, no anger, and no real scorn to speak of. Though not too much admiration for me as a shameless carnal force. She says from the door, "Why did I like you so much? You are such a boy," and that is all there is to the discussion of my character, all, apparently, that her dignity requires or permits. Not the masterful young master of mistresses and whores, not the precocious dramatist of the satiric and the lewd, and something of a fledgling rapist too—no, merely "a boy."

— Philip Roth

Sabbath's Theater 1995)

■ *Mickey Sabbath is imprisoned by his own acts of self-indulgence which obliterate any semblance of a real life he could have had.*

As if it weren't sufficiently exciting to slip by moonlight past the Morro Castle in Havana harbor, as memorable an entrance to a port as any in the world, once they'd tied up he was off the ship and heading straight for the one thing he had never done before. This was in Batista's Cuba, which was one big American whore-house and gambling casino. In thirteen years, Castro was going to come down out of the hills and put an end to all the fun, but ordinary seaman Sabbath was lucky enough to get his licks in just in the nick of time.

— **Philip Roth**

The God of Small Things (1997)

■ *The story of young twins, a boy and a girl, and the rest of their family living in Kerala, India, during the late 1960s.*

She took with her to her grave the picture of her little daughter's body laid out on the chaise longue in the drawing room of the Ayemenem House. Even from a distance, it was obvious that she was dead. Not ill or asleep. It was something to do with the way she lay. The angle of her limbs. Something to do with Death's authority. Its terrible stillness.

Green weed and river grime was woven into her beautiful red-brown hair. . . .

A spongy mermaid who had forgotten how to swim
A silver thimble clenched, for luck, in her little fist.
Thimble-drinker.
Coffin-cartwheeler.

— **Arundhati Roy** *(1961-) Indian novelist, essayist and activist*

Mating (1991)

■ *The courtship between an anthropologist visitor and the founder of a seemingly utopian community for African woman in Botswana.*

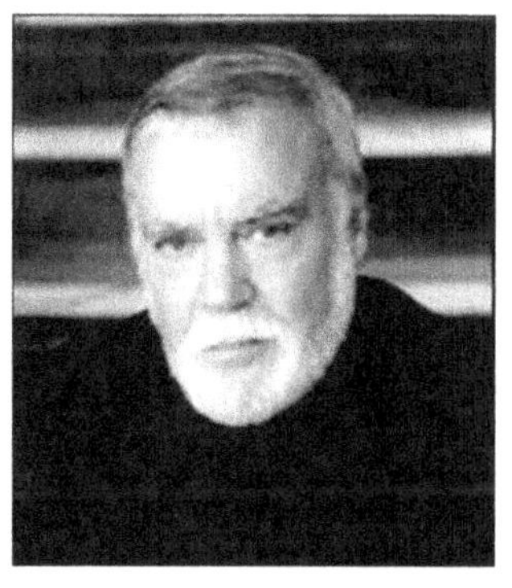

. . . Male chauvinism is the air African men breathe. They can't escape it. They are imbued. They are taught patriarchy by every voice in their culture, including their mothers'. That was a predisposing thing. I was not going to devote my energies to educating a perfectly happy Motswana as to my exquisite basic needs. But beyond that there was the danger of something happening, possibly, that would turn out to be permanent—meaning, for me, staying on in Africa forever. It may seem coldblooded, but if I was clear about anything in my life I was clear about not staying in Africa forever.

— **Norman Rush** *(1933-) American novelist*

Whites (1986)

■ *Stories of Euro-American ex-patriots and volunteers living in conflict in Southern Africa.*

Nan opened the window again. She looked back. The second girl had fallen. Only the mother, still carrying the baby, was still pursuing, her face wild. She would soon fall.

"The mother is still running, Gareth. She is straining, with that baby. I wish you would look. You are destroying me. *We must stop!*"

The mother was heaving with effort. It was too much. She threw her arms up and fell on her back, protecting the infant she was carrying.

The Land-Rover ground onward. Nan looked to the rear. The women were lost. She covered her face with her hands. Then she lowered her hands and seized the water bottle from Tess, who was holding it. She shoved her window open and hurled the bottle out onto the bank.

— **Norman Rush**

Midnight's Children (1981)

■ *The story of Saleem Sinai, born at the stroke of midnight on August 15, 1947, the precise moment of India's independence from Great Britain, thereby possessing a certain supernatural power exceeding that of all the other Indian babies born that hour.*

So among the midnight children were infants with powers of transmutation, flight, prophecy and wizardry . . . but two of us were born on the stroke of midnight. Saleem and Shiva, Shiva and Saleem, nose and knees and knees and nose . . . to Shiva, the hour had given the gifts of war . . . and to me, the greatest talent of all — the ability to look into the hearts and minds of men.

— **Salman Rushdie** *(1947-) British-Indian novelist and essayist*

The Moor's Last Sigh (1995)

■ *Moraes, afflicted with progressive premature aging, recites the history of his dysfunctional family.*

I'll say it again: from the moment of my conception, like a visitor from another dimension, another time-line, I have aged twice as rapidly as the old earth and everything and everyone thereupon. . . .

No need for supernatural explanations; some cock-up in the DNA will do. Some premature-ageing disorder in the core programme, leading to the production of too many short-life cells. . . . Down in the slums of our bodies, we're still vulnerable to the most disorderly disorders, the scurviest of scurvies, the plaguiest of plagues. There may be pet pussies prowling around our squeaky-clean, sky-high penthouses, but they don't cancel out the rat-infested corruption in the sewers of the blood.

— Salman Rushdie

The Satanic Verses (1988)

- *A study of good and evil told through a series of allegorical tales.*

The aircraft cracked in half, a seed-pod giving up its spores, an egg yielding its mystery. Two actors, prancing Gibreel and buttony, pursed Mr Saladin Chamcha, fell like titbits of tobacco from a broken old cigar.

. . . (They) plummeted like bundles dropped by some carelessly open-beaked stork, and because Chamcha was going down head first, in the recommended position for babies entering the birth canal, he commenced to feel a low irritation at the other's refusal to fall in plain fashion. Saladin nosedived while Farishta embraced air, hugging it with his arms and legs, a flailing, overwrought actor without techniques of restraint. Below, a cloud-covered, awaiting their entrance, the slow congealed currents of the English Sleeve, the appointed zone of their watery reincarnation.

— Salman Rushdie

Publication of *The Satanic Verses* in September 1988 caused immediate controversy in the Islamic world because of what was perceived as an irreverent depiction of the prophet Muhammad. In February 1989 a *fatwa* requiring Rushdie's execution was proclaimed on Radio Tehran by Ayatollah Ruhollah Khomeini, calling the book "blasphemous against Islam." On August 3, 1989 a bomb intended for "the aposttre Rushdie" exploded prematurely, destroying two floors of a hotel in Paddington, Central London. — *Wikipedia*

Empire Falls (2001)

- *Family and mill town life in crumbling Empire Falls, Maine, as seen through the eyes of the manager of the town's only grill.*

The day the river crested was warm, with a high blue sky, the kind of afternoon, after a long gray winter and several days of warm spring rains, when she could have fallen asleep, the rays of the sun warming her skin. Though no one actually saw her get swept away, downstream in Fairhaven, where the flood damage was even worse than in Empire Falls, an emergency worker on a sandbag brigade near the dam saw what he believed

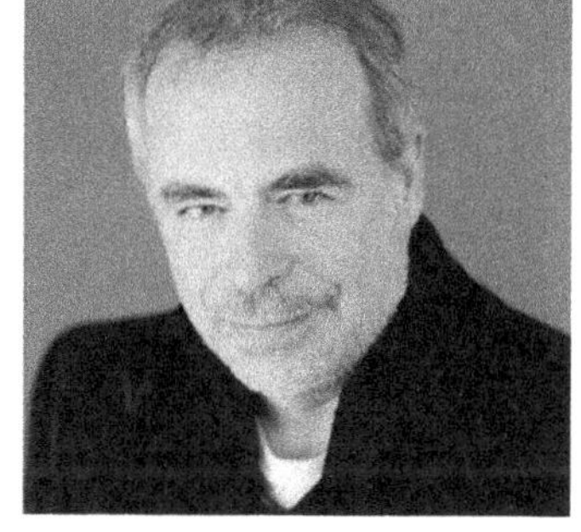

was a woman's body glide by in the raging water. The corpse hung up briefly at the dam, but out there in the middle of the torrent, lodged at the top of a dam that might collapse at any second, and nothing could be gained by attempting a rescue. Besides, whoever this woman might have been, she was dead now, and under such circumstances the workers would not have been inclined to risk their own lives, even if the spectacle before them hadn't revealed a ghoulish aspect. For astride the body, crouched at the shoulders of the dead woman, was a red-mouthed, howling cat.

— **Richard Russo** *(1949-) American novelist, short story writer and screenwriter*

S

The Catcher in the Rye (1945)

■ *A coming-of-age story of the struggles and experiences of alienation of Holden Caulfield, a sixteen-year-old expelled from prep school.*

. . . When I was all set to go, when I had my bags and all, I stood for a while next to the stairs and took a last look down the goddam corridor. I was sort of crying. I don't know why. I put my red hunting hat on, and turned the peak around to the back, the way I liked it, and then I yelled at the top of my goddam voice, *"Sleep tight, ya morons!"* I'll bet I woke up every bastard on the whole floor. Then I got the hell out. Some stupid guy had thrown peanut shells all over the stairs, and I damn near broke my crazy neck.

Last published work 1965, last interview 1980.

— **J. D. Salinger** *(1919-2010) American author*

Franny and Zooey (1961)

■ *A brother and sister confront each other's traumas, weaknesses, and problems with the world.*

". . . one of the reasons why you're having this little nervous breakdown. And *especially* the reason why you're having it at home. This place is made to order for you. The service is good, and there's plenty of hot and cold running ghosts. What could be more convenient? You can say your prayer here and roll Jesus and St. Francis and Seymour and Heidi's grandfather all in one."

Zooey's voice stopped, very briefly. "Can't you see that? Can't you *see* how unclearly, how sloppily, you're looking at things? My God, there's absolutely nothing tenth-rate about you, and yet you're up to your neck at this minute in tenth-rate thinking."

— J. D. Salinger

From many possibilities, these selections from Salinger's life:

— He was in combat with the 4th Infantry Division at Utah Beach on D-Day and in the Battle of the Bulge as well as the Huertgren Forest campaign.

— In Paris he met Hemingway who was impressed by Salinger's writing and remarked: "Jesus, he has a helluva talent."

— As a result of Hollywood's "bastardization" of his story "Wiggily" in 1949, Salinger never again permitted film adaptation to be made of his work.

— As the notoriety of *The Catcher in the Rye* grew, Salinger gradually withdrew from public view, moving to Cornish, New Hampshire, in 1953. He maintained contact with local high school students until an interview with one of them appeared prominently in the city paper.

— He continued to write in a disciplined fashion, a few hours every morning. In a rare 1974 interview with *The New York Times* he explained: "There is a marvelous peace in not publishing . . . I like to write, love to write. But I write just for myself and my own pleasure."

— Salinger's daughter painted a picture of her father as a man immensely proud of his service record, maintaining his military haircut, service jacket, and moving about his compound and town in an old Jeep. — *Wikipedia*

Union Dues (1977)

- *A father leaves West Virginia to hunt for his runaway son who has drifted into a commune of young revolutionaries.*

He was kind of a wiry guy, hard-looking though he didn't push it. One of his arms didn't hang right and his nose had been broken at least once. His sideburns were turning iron gray, his teeth had seen better days. He was dressed like a man who punched a clock and came home dirty. The guy answered all the questions about his boy directly, in the funny kind of accent he had. Name, sex, race, age, weight, height, hair, eyes, complexion, distinguishing physical marks, clothing and jewelry. The Army jacket was a good one, but if the kid was seriously on the lam he would have ditched it by now. A seventeen-year old white male with brown hair and blue eyes, maybe 5'6", maybe 125 pounds. The guy had all the information written out with him, he had a couple pictures. He had no real idea why the boy split, he said. Mulcahy decided to leave that one alone for the time being. **— John Sayles** *(1950-) American independent film director and screen writer*

Leaving Brooklyn (1989)

- *The adolescence and coming of age of Audrey in the sheltered world of Brooklyn in the 1950s.*

It was never again as it had been with the eye doctor. I was right, at fifteen, when I foresaw that. Not only because he was the first; not only because he was . . . he was . . . Oh, yes, because he was the first, and himself, he was something that flies off the page every time I capture a word to define it. But also because never again could there be that particular set of voluptuous, atavistic, outrageous, and above all delicate circumstances.

— **Lynne Sharon Schwartz** *(1939-) Contemporary writer*

Austerlitz (2001)

- *The melancholy life of Jacques Austerlitz in his search for his origins in wartime Europe.*

I can only guess what reasons may have induced the minister Elias and his wan wife to take me to live with them in the summer of 1939, said Austerlitz. Childless as they were, perhaps they hoped to reverse the petrifaction of their emotions, which must have been becoming more unbearable to them every day, by devoting themselves together to bringing up a boy then aged four and a half, or perhaps they thought they owed it to a higher authority to perform some good work beyond the level of ordinary charity, a work entailing personal devotion and sacrifice. Or perhaps they thought they ought to save my soul, innocent as it was of the Christian faith. I myself cannot say what my first few days in Bala with the Eliases really felt like. I do remember new clothes which made me very unhappy, and the inexplicable disappearance of my little green rucksack, and recently I have even thought that I could still apprehend the dying away of my native tongue, the faltering and fading sounds which I think lingered on in me at least for a while, . . .

Text photo of the Gendarmenmarkt on fire, Berlin, Germany May 1944.

— **W. G. Sebald** *(1944-2001) German writer and academic*

A Suitable Boy (1993)

- *Lata and her mother's attempts to find a suitable marriage partner is part of this story of four large extended families and life in India amidst the political and religious upheavals of the early 1950s.*

'YOU too will marry a boy I choose,' said Mrs Rupa Mehra firmly to her younger daughter.

Lata avoided the maternal imperative by looking around the great lamp-lit garden of Prem Nivas. The wedding–guests were gathered on the lawn. 'Hmm,' she said. This annoyed her mother further.

'I know what your hmms mean, young lady, and I can tell you I will not stand for hmms in this matter. I do know what is best. I am doing it all for you. Do you think it is easy for me, trying to arrange things for all four of my children without His help?' Her nose began to redden at the thought of her husband, who would, she felt certain, be partaking of their present joy from somewhere benevolently above.

— **Vikram Seth** *(1952-) Indian poet and novelist*

Wild Animals I Have Known (1898)

- *". . . true histories of the animals described, . . . intended to show how their lives are lived." ETS, 1898 This quote from "Lobo, the King of Currumpaw."*

I set meat and water beside him, but he paid no heed. He lay calmly on his breast, and gazed with those steadfast yellow eyes away past me down through the gateway of the canon, over the open plains—his plains—nor moved a muscle when I touched him. When the sun went down he was still gazing fixedly across the prairie. I expected he would call up his band when night came, and prepared for them, but he had called once in his extremity, and none had come; he would never call again.

A lion shorn of his strength, an eagle robbed of his freedom, or a dove bereft of his mate, all die, it is said, of a broken heart; and who will aver that this grim bandit could bear the three-fold brunt, heart-whole? This only I know, that when the morning dawned, he was lying there still in his position of calm repose, but his spirit was gone—the old king-wolf was dead.

— **Ernest Thompson Seton** *(1860-1946) Scots-Canadian-American author, wildlife artist, and founding pioneer of the Boy Scouts of America*

The Killer Angels (1974)

■ *The story of the Battle of Gettysburg, told from the viewpoints of Robert E. Lee and James Longstreet and some of the other men who fought there. (From the author's preface)*

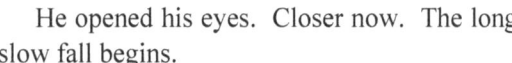

He sat against something. The fight went on. He looked down at his chest, saw the blood. Tried to breathe, experimentally, but now he could feel the end coming, now for the first time he sensed the sliding toward the dark, a weakening, a closing, all things ending now slowly and steadily and peacefully. He closed his eyes, opened them. A voice said, "I was riding toward you sir, trying to knock you down. You didn't have a chance." . . .

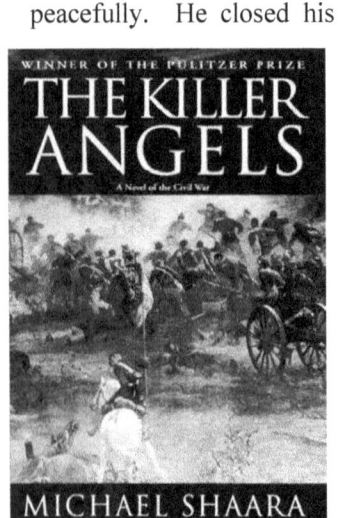

He opened his eyes. Closer now. The long slow fall begins.

"Will you tell General Hancock . . . Can you hear me, son?"

"I can hear you, sir."

"Will you tell General Hancock, please, that General Armistead sends his regrets. Will you tell him . . . how very sorry I am . . ."

The energy failed. He felt himself flicker. But it was a long slow falling, very quiet, very peaceful, rather still, but always the motion, the darkness closing in, and so he fell out of the light and away, far away, and was gone.

— **Michael Shaara** *(1928-1988) American writer of science fiction, sports fiction, and historical fiction*

Hamlet (1601)

- *In real and feigned madness, Prince Hamlet exacts revenge on his uncle Claudius, who has murdered Hamlet's father, the King, and then taken the throne and married Hamlet's mother.*

To be, or not to be — that is the question:
Whether 'tis nobler in the mind to suffer
The slings and arrows of outrageous fortune,
Or to take arms against a sea of troubles,
And by opposing end them. To die, to sleep,
No more, and by a sleep to say we end
The heartache, and the thousand natural shocks
That flesh is heir to. 'Tis a consummation
Devoutly to be wished. To die, to sleep,
To sleep — perchance to dream — ay, there's the rub,
For in that sleep of death what dreams may come
When we have shuffled off this mortal coil,
Must give us pause.

— **Shakespeare** *(1564-1616) English poet and playwright*

People Will Always Be Kind (1973)

- *Brian Casey contracts polio at sixteen leaving him in braces and a wheelchair, yet later becomes Senator Casey and runs for the presidential nomination.*

. . . He lowered his feet to the sidewalk, and immediately his knees buckled. He was barely able to clamber back without being caught. In his bones he'd felt it coming. Two stumbles yesterday, followed by little reassuring gusts of strength. This evening the same, some sweet forward passes, delicate as a jeweler, and sitting down with his back bursting and his throat too sore to speak. He'd felt lousy for three days and nights, and Dr. Devlin had said flu, as usual, but he'd told his mother he felt O.K. and had gone out and played football like a maniac. He knew all right. . . .

"Mister," he said, to the man. Much too softly. "Mister" louder, and then no doubt some kind of scream. Brian had never asked for help in his life, and he made a hysterical mess of it. They carried him across the street, big firm hands in his armpits, all his problems solved. The apartment was cool as crystal. He was put to bed, and the fever had a chance to settle, and the next day he was off to the hospital, the twenty-third recorded polio case that August.

— **Wilfrid Sheed** *(1930-) English-born American novelist and essayist*

Frankenstein (1818)

- *An anonymously published novel of Victor Frankenstein's obsession and eventual devastating success in "bestowing animation upon lifeless matter."*

It was on a dreary night of November that I beheld the accomplishment of my toils. With an anxiety that almost amounted to agony, I collected the instruments of life around me, that I might infuse a spark of being into the lifeless thing that lay at my feet. It was already one in the morning; the rain pattered dismally against the panes, and my candle was nearly burnt out, when, by the glimmer of the half-extinguished light, I saw the dull yellow eye of the creature open; it breathed hard, and a convulsive motion agitated its limbs.

— **Mary Shelley** *(1797-1851) British novelist, short story writer, dramatist, and biographer*

The Stone Diaries (1994)

- *The unremarkable, unfulfilled life of a 20th century wife and mother; the gilded cage of acquiescence to contemporary society.*

Daisy Goodwill, in her final illness, the illness she is reputed to have borne with such patience, was left with only her death to contemplate—and she approached it with all the concerted weakness and failure of her body. Somewhere in the course of those final dreaming weeks, there had occurred a shifting of the tide. It arrived suddenly during one of her frequent comatose periods. She entered sleep, as through a tunnel, still groping in the past, breathing in like a species of inferior oxygen the real and imagined episodes of her life, and then a kind of exhaustion took over, or perhaps boredom, in any case a rapid fading of color and line, and a failure of the mechanism that had previously called up the earlier scenes. What pressed on her eyelids, instead, was a series of mutable transparencies gesturing not backward in time but forward—forward toward her own death. You might say that she breathed it into existence, then fell in love with it.

— **Carol Shields** *(1935-2003) American-born Canadian author*

Unless (2002)

■ *An oldest daughter suddenly, inexplicably, drops out of college and ends up on a Toronto street corner panhandling.*

I walk around and around the block where she sits, trying to keep a little distance. I don't want to threaten her in any way. *O my love, what have they done to you?* Her face: I don't dare get close enough to see her face clearly, but what I imagine is a passive despair, a mingling of contempt and indifference that projects silence but is ready to incinerate whatever is offered. In this oppressive weather—snow in the air, a driving wind—she is more isolated than ever. This is a nervous, feverish corner of the city, rowdy, cheap, and lonely.

— Carol Shields

Absurdistan (2006)

■ *The life, loves and misadventures of Misha Vainberg, a man of immense proportions and appetites.*

"Our mother is in the hospital," the man repeated, tightening the grip around my big, squishy hand as my vision turned a new shade of purple. "Are you so heartless that you won't help her? Do I really have to take out my *kinjal* and slice your stomach open?"

"Dear God, no!" I cried. "Here! Here! Take my money! Take whatever you need!"

But in the single opportune moment when he let go of my hand so that it could find my bulging wallet, I felt the fear fall away and the humiliation lift. It wasn't the money. No, it wasn't the money at all. But after thirty years with my head on the scaffold, after thirty years of cheering on the executioner, after thirty years of wearing his stifling black hood, one thing was certain: I no longer feared the ax.

"______ your mother!" I said. "I hope she dies."

And then I ran.

— Gary Shteyngart *(1972-) American writer born in Leningrad*

A Town Like Alice (1950)

■ *A young woman survives a Japanese forced march during World War II and is aided by a captive Australian soldier.*

In Kuantan, in the evening of that day in July 1942, a sergeant had come to Captain Sugamo in the District Commissioner's house, and had reported that the Australian was still alive. Captain Sugamo found this curious and interesting, and as there was still half an hour before his evening rice, he strolled down to the recreation ground to have a look.

The body still hung by its hands, facing the tree. Blood had drained from the blackened mess that was its back and had run down the legs to form a black pool on the ground, now dried and oxidized by the hot sun. A great mass of flies covered the body and the blood. But the man undoubtedly was still alive, when Captain Sugamo approached the face the eyes opened, and looked at him with recognition.

— **Nevil Shute** *(1899-1960) British novelist and aeronautical engineer*

The Loneliness of the Long-distance Runner (1960)

- *A reform school boy seizes a foolproof opportunity during the annual cross-country race to show his defiance of authority.*

. . . Then he turned into a tongue of trees and bushes where I couldn't see him anymore, and I couldn't see anybody, and I knew what the loneliness of the long-distance runner running across country felt like, realizing that as far as I was concerned this feeling was the only honesty and realness there was in the world and I knowing it would be no different ever, no matter what I felt at odd times, and no matter what anybody else tried to tell me.

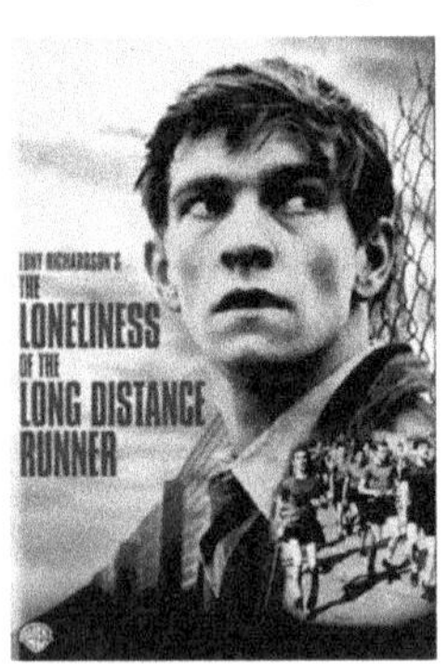

— **Alan Sillitoe** *(1928-2010) British writer*

Gimpel the Fool and Other Stories (1957)

- *Short stories of often inner-familial strife set in Poland in the early 1900s.*

I am Gimpel the Fool. I don't think myself a fool. On the contrary. But that's what folks call me. They gave me the name while I was still in school. I had seven names in all: imbecile, donkey, flax-head, dope, glump, ninny, and fool. The last name stuck. What did my foolishness consist of? I was easy to take in. They said, "Gimpel, you know the rabbi's wife has been brought to childbed?" So I skipped school. Well, it turned out to be a lie. How was I supposed to know? She hadn't had a big belly. But I never looked at her belly. Was that really so foolish.

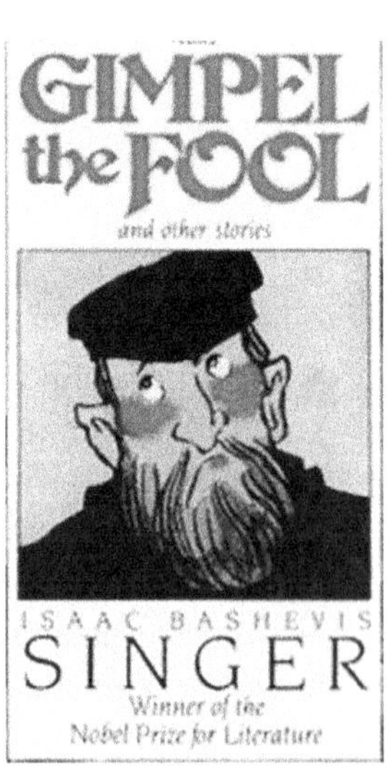

The gang laughed and hee-hawed, stomped and danced and chanted a good-night prayer.

— **Isaac Bashevis Singer** *(1902-1991) Jewish American author*

The Séance (1968)

■ *Short stories beginning with this account of an old man who regularly visits an unconvincing medium.*

Mrs. Kopitzky left the room. Dr. Kalisher sat down on the edge of a chair, placing his handkerchief beneath him. He sat there stiff, wet, childishly guilty and helpless, and yet with that inner quiet that comes from illness. For years he had been afraid of doctors, hospitals, and especially nurses, who deny their feminine shyness and treat grownup men like babies. Now he was prepared for the last degradations of his body. "Well, I'm finished, *kaput*."

— **Isaac Bashevis Singer**

Singer always wrote and published in Yiddish — almost all of it in newspapers.

Short Friday (1964)

■ *Typical of Singer's observations of stricken figures is this quote from the story "Alone."*

". . . You have been in love?'

"Yes."

"Where is the Senora? Did you marry her?"

"No. They shot her."

"Who?"

"Those same Nazis."

"Uh-huh . . . and you were left alone?"

"No, I have a wife."

"Where is your wife?"

"In New York."

"And you are true to her, eh?"

"Yes, I am faithful."

"Always?"

"Always."

"One time to have fun is all right."

"No, my dear, I want to live out my life honestly."

"Who cares what you do? No one see."

"God sees."

"Well, if you speak of God, I go. But you are a liar. If I not a cripple, you no speak of God. He punish such lies, you pig!"

— **Isaac Bashevis Singer**

A Thousand Acres (1991)

■ *Aging Larry Cook decides to turn over his prosperous 1,000 acre Iowa farm to his three daughters and their husbands.*

Looking at them forces me to know that although the farm and all its burdens and gifts are scattered, my inheritance is with me, sitting in my chair. Lodged in my every cell, along with the DNA, are molecules of topsoil and atrazine and paraquat and anhydrous ammonia and diesel fuel and plant dust, and also molecules of memory: the bracing summer chill of floating on my back in Mel's pond, staring at the sky; the exotic redolence of the dresses in my mother's closet; the sharp odor of wet tomato vines; the stripes of pain my father's belt laid across my skin; the deep chill of waiting for the school bus in the blue of a winter's dawn. All of it is present now, here; each particle weighs some fraction of the hundred and thirty-six pounds that attaches me to the earth, perhaps as much as the print weights in other sorts of histories.

— **Jane Smiley** *(1949-) American novelist*

On Beauty (2005)

■ *A wide ranging involvement between the family of a liberal Englishman and his black Floridian wife, and that of a wealthy American scholar and his withdrawn spouse.*

And now Howard succumbed to his heritage — easy, quick-flowing tears.

'There, son. It's better out than in, isn't it,' said Harold quietly. Howard laughed softly at this phrase: so old, so familiar, so utterly useless. Harold reached forward and touched his son's knee. Then he leaned back in his chair and picked up his remote control.

'She found a black fella, I spose. It was always going to happen, though. It's in their nature.'

He turned the channel to the news. Howard stood up.

'_______,' he said frankly, wiping his tears with his shirtsleeve and laughing grimly. 'I never _______ learn.' He picked up his coat and put it on. 'See you, Harry. Let's leave it a bit longer next time, eh?'

'Oh, no!' whimpered Harold, his face stricken by the calamity of it. 'What are you saying? We're having a nice time, ain't we?'

Howard stared at him, disbelievingly.

'*No.* Son, *please.* Oh, come on and stay a bit longer. I've said the wrong things, have I? I've said the wrong thing. Then let's sort it! You're always in a rush. Rush 'ere, rush there. People these days think they can outrun death. It's just time.'

— **Zadie Smith** *(1975-) English novelist*

White Teeth (2000)

- *The story of two North London friends, beginning with service in World War II through marriage, parenthood, and the shared disappointments of poverty.*

"He's gassing himself, Abba."

"What?"

Arshad shrugged. "I shouted through the car window and told the guy to move on and he says, 'I am gassing myself, leave me alone.' Like that."

"No one gasses himself on my property." Mo snapped as he marched downstairs. "We are not licensed."

Once in the street, Mo advanced upon Archie's car, pulled out the towels that were sealing the gap in the driver's window, and pushed it down five inches with brute, bullish force.

"Do you hear that, mister? We're not licensed for suicides around here. This place halal. Kosher, understand? If you're going to die round here, my friend, I'm afraid you've got to be thoroughly bled first."

Archie dragged his head off the steering wheel. And in the moment between focusing on the sweaty bulk of a brown-skinned Elvis and realizing that life was still his, he had a kind of epiphany. It occurred to him that, for the first time since his birth, Life had said Yes to Archie Jones.

— **Zadie Smith**

Cancer Ward (1968)

- *The lives of patients and staff in a cancer ward in Russia. This quote from the main character to his young doctor at the close of the story.*

Darling Vega (all the time I was dying to call you that, so I will now, just this once), I want to write to you frankly, more frankly than we've ever spoken to each other. But we have thought it, haven't we? After all, it's no ordinary patient, is it, to whom a doctor offers her room and her bed?

Several times today I set out to walk to your place. Once I actually get there. I walked along as excited as a sixteen-year-old—an indecency for a man with a life like mine behind him. I was excited, embarrassed, happy and terrified. It takes many years of tramping to realize the meaning of the words "God sent you to me."

You see, Vega, if I'd found you in, something false and forced might have started between us. I went for a walk afterwards and realized it was a good thing I hadn't found you in. Everything that you or I tormented ourselves with at least has a name and can be put into words. But what was about to begin between us was something we could never have confessed to anyone. You and I, and between us *this thing*: this sort of gray, decrepit yet ever-growing snake. . . .

Now that I'm going away anyway (if they end my exile I won't come back to you for checkups or treatment, which means we must say goodbye), I can tell you quite frankly: even when we were having the most intellectual conversations . . . I still wanted all the time, *all the time*, to pick you up and kiss you on the lips.

So try to work that out.

And now, without your permission, I kiss them.

— **Alexander Solzhenitsyn** *(1918-2008) Russian novelist, dramatist, and historian*

In the First Circle (1968)

- *The lives of gulag inmates arrested in Stalin's purges following the Second World War.*

Yes, what awaited them was the taiga and the tundra, the Cold Pole at Olymyakon, the copper mines at Dzhezkazan. What awaited them yet again was the pickax and the wheelbarrow, a starvation ration of half-baked bread, hospital, death. They could look forward to nothing but the worst.

Yet in their hearts they were at peace with themselves.

They were gripped by the fearlessness of people who have lost absolutely everything—such fearlessness is difficult to attain, but once attained, it endures.

SWINGING THE COMPRESSED mass of bodies to and fro, the gaily painted orange-and-blue truck swished along the city streets, passed one of the stations, and pulled up at a crossing. A dark red car was held up by traffic lights at the same road junction. It belonged to the Moscow correspondent of the newspaper *Liberation*, who was on his way to a hockey match in the Dynamo stadium. The correspondent read the words on the side of the truck:

Myaso

Viande

Fleisch

Meat

He had made a mental note of several such trucks seen in various parts of Moscow that day. He took out a notebook and jotted down in dark red ink:

"Every now and then, one encounters on the streets of Moscow food delivery trucks, spick-and-span and impeccably hygienic. There can be no doubt that the capital's food supplies are extremely well organized."

— **Alexander Solzhenitsyn**

One Day in the Life of Ivan Denisovich (1978)

- *A graphic description of a single day's struggle for survival in one of Stalin's forced labor camps.*

Shukhov felt pleased with life as he went to sleep. A lot of good things had happened that day. He hadn't been thrown in the hole. The gang hadn't been dragged off to Sotsgorodok. He'd swiped the extra gruel at dinnertime. The foreman had got a good rate for the job. He'd enjoyed working on the wall. He hadn't been caught with the blade at the search point. He'd earned a bit from Tsezar that evening. And he'd brought his tobacco.

The end of an unclouded day. Almost a happy one.

Just one of the 3,653 days of his sentence, from bell to bell.

The extra three were for leap years.

— **Alexander Solzhenitsyn**

During World War II Solzhenitsyn served in the Red Army, was involved in major action at the front, and twice decorated.

In 1945 he was arrested for writing derogatory comments about the conduct of the war and sentenced to eight years in a labor camp. After completing his sentence he was sent to internal exile for life in southern Kazakhstan. Three years later he was freed and exonerated.

In 1962, *One Day in the Life of Ivan Denisovich* was published with the explicit approval of Nikita Khrushchev who defended it saying "There's a Stalinist in each of you; there's even a Stalinist in me. We must root out this evil."

Solzhenitsyn was awarded the Novel Prize in Literature in 1970. Four years later he was arrested by the KGB, deported from the Soviet Union to Frankfurt, West Germany, and stripped of his Soviet citizenship. In 1990, his citizenship was restored and in 1994 he returned to Russia. — *Wikipedia*

Oedipus the King (429 BC)

- *Oedipus resolves to find the killer of King Laius, a quest which turns into an obsessive reconstruction of his own hidden past.*

"So you mock my blindness? Let me tell you this. You with your precious eyes, you're blind to the corruption of your life, to the house you live in, those you live with—who are your parents? Do you know? All unknowing you are the scourge of your own flesh and blood, the dead below the earth and the living here above, and the double lash of your mother and your father's curse will whip you from this land one day, their footfall treading you down in terror, darkness shrouding your eyes that now can see the light!"

— **Sophocles** *(497 BC–406 BC) Ancient Greek playwright*

The Light in the Piazza (1960)

■ *An American mother sees her daughter drawn to a young Italian, eventually leading to an on and then dramatically off marriage.*

. . . She gave her order and waited, saying nothing till the small glass on the saucer was set before her. It was her last chance and she knew it. It helped her timing considerably to know how much she detested Signor Naccarelli.

"This is all too bad," said Mrs. Johnson softly. "I received a letter from my husband today. Instead of five thousand dollars, he wants to make Clara and Fabrizio a present of fifteen thousand dollars."

"That is nine million three hundred and seventy-five thousand lire," said Signor Naccarelli. "So now you will write and explain everything, and that this wedding cannot be."

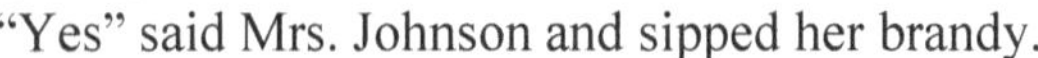

"Yes" said Mrs. Johnson and sipped her brandy.

Presently Signor Naccarelli ordered a cup of coffee.

Later on they might have been observed in various places, strolling about quiet, less frequented streets. . . .

"You must forgive me," said Signor Naccarelli, "if I ask a most personal thing of you. The Signorina Clara, she would like to have children, would she not? My wife can think of nothing else."

"Oh, Clara longs for children!" said Mrs. Johnson.

— **Elizabeth Spence** *(1921-) American novelist and short story writer*

I, the Jury (1947)

■ *Hard-boiled private eye Mike Hammer investigates the brutal murder of his best friend.*

"I have no fans. You know what I got? Customers."

"No, Charlotte, I'm the jury now, and the judge, and I have a promise to keep. Beautiful as you are, as much as I almost loved you, I sentence you to death."

. . .

The roar of the .45 shook the room. Charlotte staggered back a step. Her eyes were a symphony of incredulity, an unbelieving witness to truth. Slowly, she looked down at the ugly swelling in her naked belly where the bullet went in. A thin trickle of blood welled out.

I stood up in front of her and shoved the gun into my pocket. I turned and looked at the rubber plant behind me. There on the table was the gun, with the safety catch off and the silencer still attached. Those loving arms would have reached it nicely. A face that was waiting to

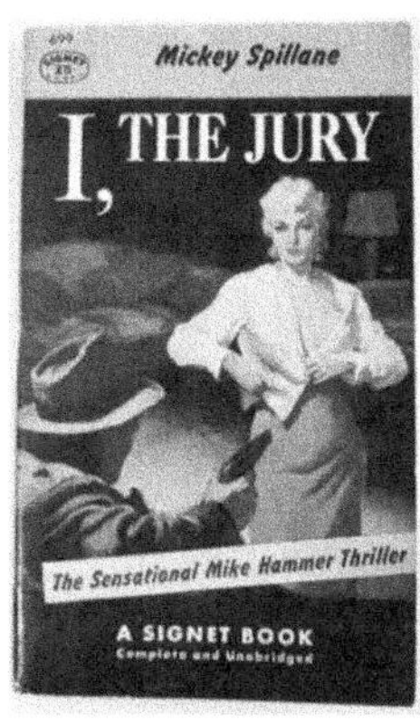

be kissed was really waiting to be splattered with blood when she blew my head off. My blood. When I heard her fall I turned around. Her eyes had pain in them now, the pain preceding death. Pain and unbelief.

"How c-could you?" she gasped.

I only had a moment before talking to a corpse, but I got it in.

"It was easy," I said.

— **Mickey Spillane** *(1918-2006) American author of crime novels*

"Lurid action, lurid characters, lurid writing, lurid plot, lurid finish. Verdict: Lurid.
— *The Saturday* Review, dismissing *I, the Jury*

The Collected Stories of Jean Stafford (1969)

- *Thirty short stories under five headings, abbreviated here—The Innocents Abroad, The Bostonians, Cowboys and Indians, Bad Characters, and Manhattan Island.*

"I've never known a girl quite like you, Emily," he said. "Memorizing the books of the Bible in the hoosegow, wearing a buck-private hat."

I blushed darkly and felt like crying, but I was pleased when Mr. Starbird went on to say, "Yes, sir, Emily, you're going to go places. What was the book you were reading down at my place when you were wearing your father's Masonic fez?" I grew prouder and prouder. "It isn't every girl of ten years of age who brushes up against some moonshiners with a record as long as your arm in the very same day that a couple of hillbilly fakers try to take her for a ride. Why, Emily, do you realize that if it hadn't of been for you, we might not have got rid of those birds till they'd set up shop and done a whole lot of mischief?" . . .

Was I lucky that day!

— **Jean Stafford** *(1915-1979) American short story writer and novelist*

The Man Who Loved Children (1940)

- *Husband Samuel Pollit, a complete egocentric, seemingly loving his children but in reality a monster of selfishness and irresponsibility, contends with his wife Henny, his tragic opposite.*

"Shut up," shouted Sam, "shut up or I'll shut you up."

"You took me and maltreated me and starved me

half to death because you couldn't make a living and sponged off my father and used his influence, hoisting yourself up on all my aches and miseries," Henny began chanting with fury, "boasting and blowing about your success when all the time it was me, my poor body that was what you took your success out of. You were breaking my bones and spirit and forcing your beastly love on me: a brute, a savage, a wild Indian wouldn't do what you did, slobbering round me and calling it love and filling me with children month after month and year after year while I hated and detested you and screamed in your ears to get away from me, but you wouldn't let me go."

— **Christina Stead** *(1902-1983) Australian novelist and short story writer*

The Grapes of Wrath (1939)

- *The Joads lose their tenant farm in Oklahoma to dust storms during the Great Depression forcing them to migrate to California in search of jobs advertised in a handbill.*

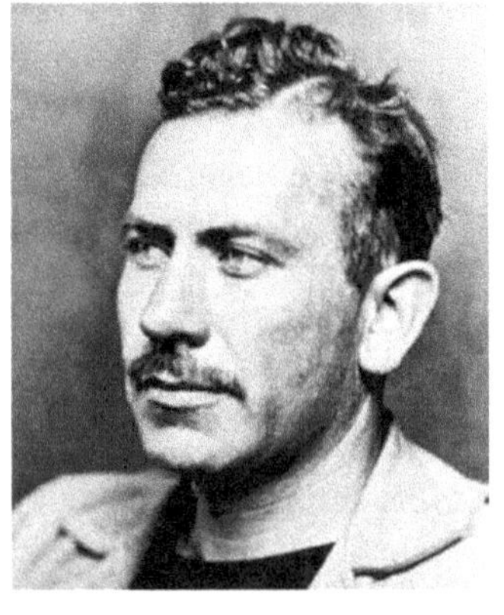

. . . A gentle wind followed the rain clouds, driving them on northward, a wind that softly clashed the drying corn. A day went by and the wind increased, steady, unbroken by gusts. The dust from the roads fluffed up and spread out and fell on the weeds beside the fields, and fell into the fields a little way. Now the wind grew strong and hard and it worked at the rain crust in the corn fields. Little by little the sky was darkened by the mixing dust, and the wind felt over the earth, loosened the dust, and carried it away. . . .

The owners of the land came onto the land, or more often a spokesman for the owners came. They came in closed cars, and they felt the dry earth with their fingers, and sometimes they drove big earth augers into the ground for soil tests. The tenants, from their sun-beaten dooryards, watched uneasily when the closed cars drove along the fields. And at last the owner men drove into the dooryards and sat in their cars to talk out of the windows. The tenant men stood beside the cars for a while, and then squatted on their hams and found sticks with which to mark the dust. . . .

In the little houses the tenant people sifted their belonging and the belongings of their fathers and of their grandfathers. Picked over their possessions for the journey to the west. The men were ruthless because the past had been spoiled, but the women knew how the past would cry to them in the coming days. The men went into the barns and the sheds.

— **John Steinbeck** *(1902-1968) American writer*

Migrant worker mobile shack in California during the Great Depression. Photo by Dorothea Lane (1895-1965)

Of Mice and Men (1937)

- *Two traveling companions, George and Lennie who is retarded, find work on a ranch in the Salinas Valley hoping to earn enough to settle down on their own land.*

. . . George's voice was taking on the tone of confession. "Tell you what made me stop that. One day a bunch of guys was standin' around up on the Sacramento River. I was feelin' pretty smart. I turns to Lennie and says, 'Jump in.' An' he jumps. Couldn't swim a stroke. He damn near drowned before we could get him. An' he was so damn nice to me for pullin' him out. Clean forgot I told him to jump in. Well, I ain't done nothing like that no more."

— **John Steinbeck**

The Red and the Black (1830)

- *The life of Julien Sorel, a young man who attempts to rise above his plebeian birth through hard work, aided by talent but betrayed by his own deceptions and hypocrisy.*

One day, when he had been driven into a café in the Rue Saint-Honore by a sudden shower, a tall man in a beaver coat, surprised at his gloomy stare, began to stare back at him exactly as Mademoiselle Amanda's lover had stared at him, long before, at Besancon.

Julien had too often reproached himself for having allowed the former insult to pass unpunished to tolerate this stare. He demanded an explanation, the man in the great coat at once began to abuse him in the foulest terms: everyone in the café gathered round them; the passers-by stopped outside the door. With provincial caution, Julien always carried a brace of pocket pistols; his hand gripped one of these in his pocket with a convulsive movement. Better counsels prevailed however, and he confined himself to repeating with clockwork regularity: "Sir, your address? I scorn you."

The persistence with which he clung to these six words began to impress the crowd.

—**Stendhal** (Marie Henri Beyle) *(1783-1842) French writer*

Tristram Shandy (1760)

- *The life of a group of humorous figures, notably Tristram's father Walter, full of paradoxical notions, and Uncle Toby, obsessed with attacks on fortified towns, and appropriately named Dr. Slop.*

"...a powerful clergyman and a rabid politician, but a mean-tempered man."

Mr. *Shandy*, my father, Sir, would see nothing in the light in which others placed it;—he placed things in his own light;—he would weight nothing in common scales;—no,—he was too refined a researcher to lay open to so gross an imposition.

— To come at the exact weight of things in the scientific steel-yard, the fulcrum, he would say, should be almost invisible, to avoid all friction from popular tenets;—without this the minutiae of philosophy, which should always turn the balance, will have no weight at all.

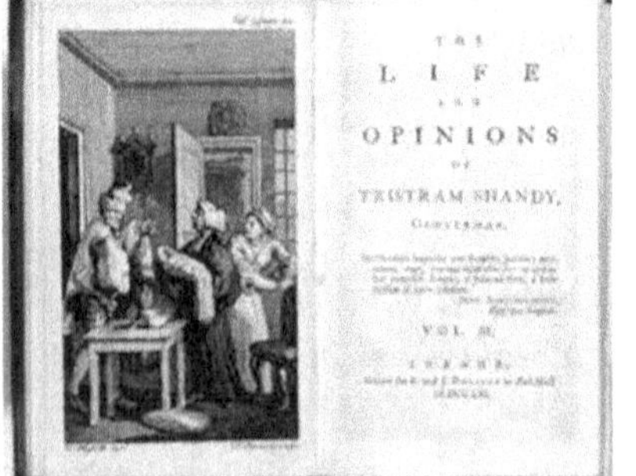

L I F E

OPINIONS

TRISTRAM SHANDY,

—Knowledge, like matter, he would affirm, was divisible *in infinitum*;—that the grains and scruples were as much a part of it, as the gravitation of the world. — In a word, he would say, error was error,—no matter where it fell,—whether in a fraction,—or a pound,—'twas alike fatal to truth, . . .

— **Laurence Sterne** *(1713-1768)*
English novelist and English novelist and Anglican clergyman

Treasure Island (1883)

- *Young Jim Hawkins shares his treasure map with Dr. Livesey and Squire Trelawney who organize an expedition to find the buried riches but are thwarted at every turn by Long John Silver a mutineer and his pirate co-conspirators.*

. . . 'I hear a voice,' said he—'a young voice. Will you give me your hand, my kind, young friend, and lead me in?'

I held out my hand, and the horrible, soft-spoken, eyeless creature gripped it in a moment like a vice. I was so much startled that I struggled to withdraw; but the blind man pulled me close up to him with a single action of his arm.

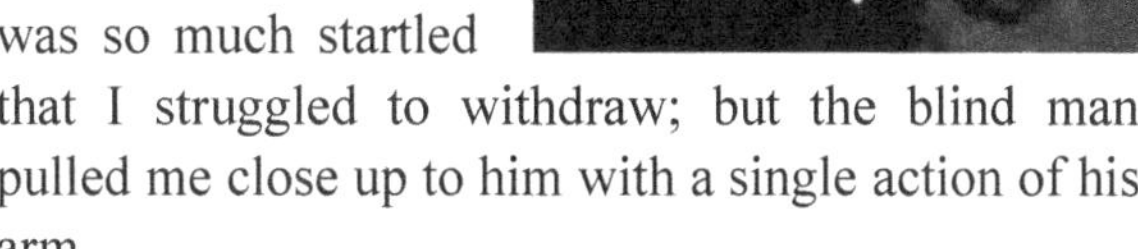

'Now, boy,' he said, 'take me in to the captain.'

'Sir,' said I, 'upon my word I dare not.'

'Oh,' he sneered, 'that's it! Take me in straight, or I'll break your arm.'

And he gave it, as he spoke, a wrench that made me cry out.

— **Robert Louis Stevenson** *(1850-1894) Scottish novelist, poet, essayist, and travel writer*

Throughout his short life Stevenson doggedly wrote on. From one letter home a year before he died:

For fourteen years I have not had a day's real health; I have awakened sick and gone to bed weary; and I have done my work unflinchingly. I have written in bed, and written out of it, written in haemorrhages, written in sickness, written torn by coughing, written when my head swam for weakness; and for so long, it seems to me I have won my wager and recovered my glove... And the battle goes on ill or well, is a trifle; so as it goes. I was made for a contest...

— Steve King, *Today in Literature*

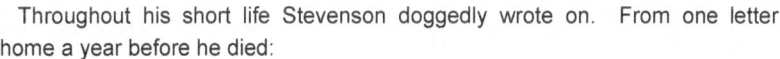

"Captain Bill Bones" (All day he hung round the cove, or upon the cliffs, with a brass telescope.) N. C. Wyeth illustration for *Treasure Island* by Robert Louis Stevenson, 1911

Dracula (1897)

- *Jonathan Harker, a young lawyer, travels to Transylvania as a secretary for Count Dracula and soon realizes to his horror that the Count is indeed an undead vampire.*

. . . What I saw was the Count's head coming out from the window. I did not see the face, but I knew the man by the neck and the movement of his back and arms. . . . But my feelings changed to repulsion and terror when I saw the whole man slowly emerge from the window and begin to crawl down the castle wall over that dreadful abyss, *face down* with his cloak spreading out around him like great wings. At first I could not believe my eyes. I thought it was some trick of the moonlight, some weird effect of shadow; but I kept looking, and it could be no delusion. I saw the fingers and toes grasp the corners of

NOSFERATU, the original Dracula movie (1922) starring Max Schrenk

the stones, worn clear of the mortar by the stress of years, and by thus using every projection and inequality move downwards with considerable speed, just as a lizard moves along a wall.

— **Bram Stoker** *(1847-1912) Irish novelist and short-story writer*

Dracula is an epistolary novel, written as a collection of realistic, but completely fictional, diary entries, telegrams, letters, ship's logs, and newspaper clippings, all of which add a level of detailed realism to the story, a skill Stoker developed as a newspaper writer. — *Wikipedia*

A favorite spin-off from the 1979 movie "Dracula" is the Count's appraisal of Professor Van Helsing, "You are a wise man, Professor, for someone who has not yet lived even a single lifetime."

Lust for Life (1934)

- *The tortured obsessed life of Vincent Van Gogh, full of failures an unrewarding relationships except for the loving care of his brother Theo.*

. . . She took Theo's body to Auvers, and had it placed by the side of his brother.

When the hot Auvers sun beats down upon the little cemetery in the cornfields, Theo rests comfortably in the luxuriant umbrage of Vincent's sunflowers.

— **Irving Stone** *(1903-1989) American writer*

Wheat Fields with Crows one of Vincent Van Gogh's last paintings, Auvers-sur-Oise, July, 1890

Dog Soldiers (1974)

■ *A small-time journalist thinks he will greatly profit by getting involved in a big-time drug deal smuggling heroin out of Vietnam to the States, but things get quickly out of hand.*

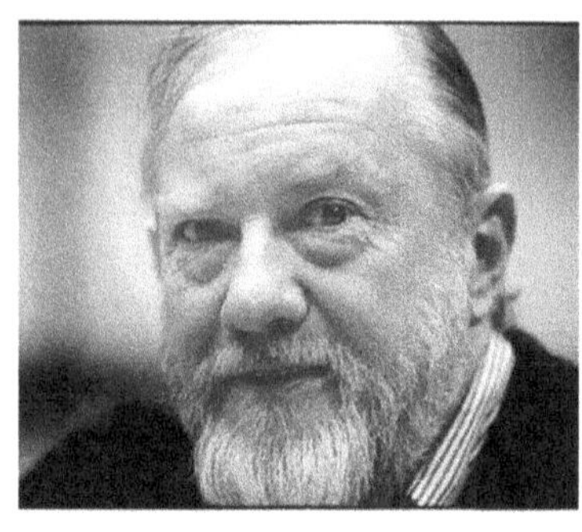

"I don't know," Converse said. "What was in the needle?"

Danskin did accents. "Ve ask ze questions," he said.

They pulled him upright and walked him into a small kitchenette next to the Murphy bed. Smitty turned on one of the ring burners and they watched it until it glowed bright orange. They were both holding him from behind.

"Please," Converse said.

Smitty shoved the end of a towel in his mouth; Danskin was caressing the back of his neck.

They're going to do it, Converse thought. He strained backward and he was so frightened that they had a difficult time holding him. Somehow he burned his hand. And burned it. And burned it.

He screamed and they let him fall to the kitchenette floor. He rolled on the linoleum in the fetal position with the fried hand thrust between his thighs.

— **Robert Stone** *(1937-) American novelist*

A Flag for Sunrise (1981)

■ *A young self-styled soldier of fortune is drawn into the maelstrom of a small Central American country on the brink of revolution.*

There was true light in the space now. On the ladder someone with a flashlight was searching out the darkness. Pablo rolled her across his body—it was as though they were making love again—her teeth were sunk in his arm. As she passed over him, he jammed the barrel of the Nambu under her down vest and fired two of its eight shots upward. He felt her teeth release him, she was flung onto her knees beside the bale. Two shots came from the ladder, at least one of them striking the woman. She rolled over on her side, her knees still together. The compartment was spinning with illuminations; Pablo thought of fireflies, wet spark plugs. His ears were hammered shut. Against the flat lower section of the bulkhead he was unhurt. When he fired at the man who was on the ladder, he did so with confidence, as though he had nothing but time. And in a second, he knew he had been on target.

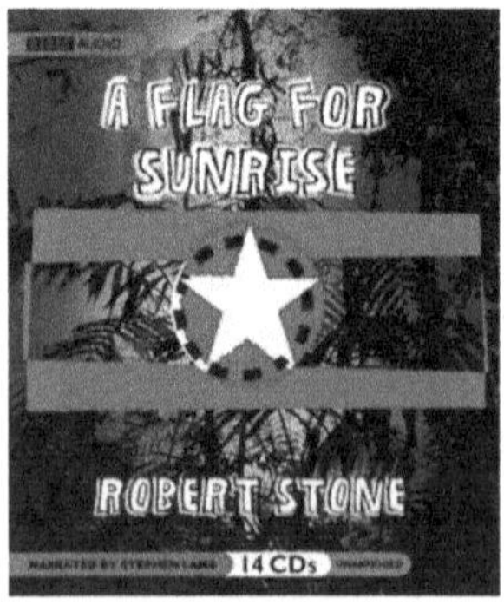

— **Robert Stone**

Outerbridge Reach (1992)

- *A copywriter volunteers for an around-the-world solo boat race with unforeseen consequences both at sea and at home.*

It's all up, Browne thought, all over with me. In spite of the bad boat, he had faced down every aspect of the ocean. They would have to give him credit for that. He had never stopped wanting to prevail and go home. It was only that he was tired of imaginary lines. The one abyss he could not cross was wider and deeper than he had imagined. Its horizon was not relative.

That morning he tossed his parallel rulers on the chart table and went on deck. . . .

He stood clutching the mast with one arm, facing the whole-some wind. He was thinking it would be wonderful to have back the man he had once been. . . .

Browne went below and from the cabin's squalor retrieved the diver's weight belt he had brought along. He had thought it a useless encumbrance. Now it would come in handy. He made a final entry in his log.

Then he went up and sat on the afterdeck and put on the belt. Pulling himself upright, he stood bent-backed along the rail and looked wide-eyed at the wake that trailed behind.

— Robert Stone

Uncle Tom's Cabin (1852)

- *A stirring indictment of slavery, Stowe's story of a long suffering black slave and those around him has been credited with helping fuel the abolitionist cause in the 1850s.*

". . . You see, when I anyways can, I takes a leetle care about the unpleasant parts, like selling young uns and that,—get the gals out of the way— out of sight, out of mind, you know, —and when it's clean done, and can't be helped, they naturally gets used to it. 'Tan't, you know, as if it was white folks, that's brught up in the way of 'spectin' to keep their children and wives, and all that. Niggers, you know, that's fetched up properly, ha'n't no kind of 'spectations of no kind; so all these things comes easier." . . .

"I did not write it. God wrote it. I merely did his dictation."

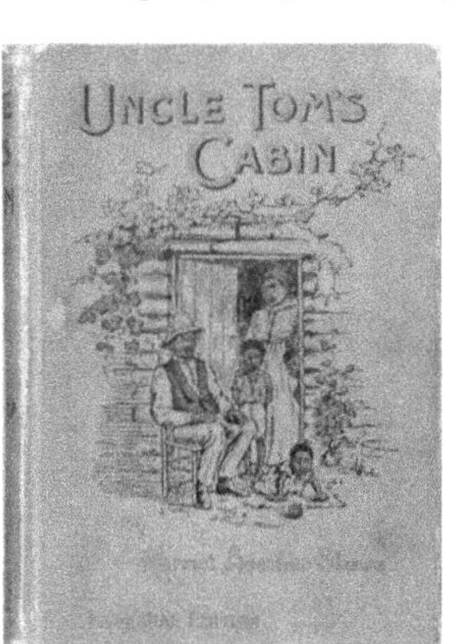

"Well," said Eliza, mournfully, "I always thought that I must obey my master and mistress, or I couldn't

be a Christian." . . .

"I looks like gwine to heaven," said the woman; "an't thar where white folks is gwine? S'pose they'd have me thar? I'd rather go to torment, and get away from Mas'r and Missis."

— **Harriet Beecher Stowe** *(1811-1896)*
American abolitionist and author

Olive Kitteridge (2008)

- *Short stories of coastal Mainers with a common central character, Olive Kitteridge. In this quote Olive unfortunately overhears her new daughter-in-law.*

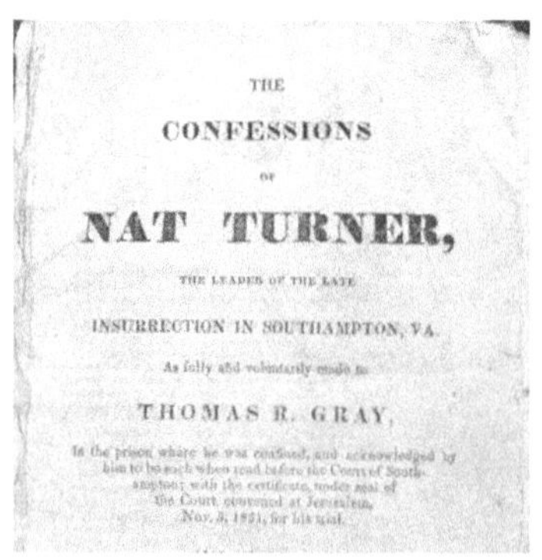

Olive stands up and very slowly moves along the wall closer to the open window. A shaft of the late-afternoon sun falls over the side of her face as she strains her head forward to make out words in the sounds of the women's murmuring.

"Oh, God, yes," says Suzanne, her quiet words suddenly distinct. "I couldn't believe it. I mean that she would really *wear* it."

The dress, Olive thinks. She pulls herself back against the wall.

"Well people dress differently up here."

By God, we do, Olive thinks. But she is stunned in her underwater way. . . . And there is the sting of deep embarrassment, because she loves this dress. Her heart really opened when she came across the gauzy muslin in So-Fro's; sunlight let into the anxious gloom of the upcoming wedding; those flowers skimming over the table in her sewing room. Becoming this dress that she took comfort in all day.

— **Elizabeth Strout** *(1956-) American author*

The Confessions of Nat Turner (1967)

- *A brutal accounting of the only armed revolt in the annals of American Negro slavery.*

THE
CONFESSIONS
OF
NAT TURNER,
THE LEADER OF THE LATE
INSURRECTION IN SOUTHAMPTON, VA.
As fully and voluntarily made to
THOMAS R. GRAY,
In the prison where he was confined, and acknowledged by him to be such when read before the Court of Southampton; with the certificate, under seal of the Court convened at Jerusalem, Nov. 5, 1831, for his trial.

. . . "No," he went on, breaking off a black wad from a plug of chewing tobacco, "no, I'll have to hand it to you, in many respects you was pretty thorough. By sword and ax and gun you run a swath through this county that will be long remembered. You did, as you say, come damn near to taking your army into this town. And in addition, as I think I told you before, you scared the entire South into a condition that may be described as well-nigh *shitless*. No niggers ever *done* anything like this."

There was nothing to say.

"Well, you was a success, all right. Up to a point. Mind you"—he jabbed a brown-stained finger at me—"*up to a point.* Because, Reverend, basically speaking and in the profoundest sense of the word you was a flat-assed *failure*—a total fiasco from beginning to end insofar as any real accomplishment is concerned. Right? Because, like you told me yesterday, all the big things that you expected to happen out of this just didn't happen. Right? Only the little things happened, and them little things when they was all added up didn't amount to a warm bottle of piss. Right?"

"A good book should leave you with many experiences and slightly exhausted at the end."

— William Styron *(1925-2006) American novelist*

Lie Down in Darkness (1951)

- *The tragic downfall of the Loftis family—Milton the drunken patriarch, Helen his frigid and despairing wife, and the two Loftis daughters, Peyton beautiful and despised by her mother, and Maudie born crippled.*

. . . he was aroused by a tumble of feet on the grass behind him, a small voice announcing passionately: "Daddy, Daddy, I'm beautiful!" So he had turned and with the attentive respect given young daughters by their fathers he had watched Peyton—standing in the grass beside him, age nine—while she gazed into a little mirror and said again, "I'm beautiful, Daddy!"

For a moment all this crushed his heart. She *was* beautiful. Perhaps it was the first cigarette of the morning, or the coffee, but he felt quite giddy. Anyway, he would always remember that moment on the lawn: picking Peyton up with a sudden, almost savage upwelling of love, pressing her against him as he murmured in a voice slightly choked, "*Yes*, my baby's beautiful," with wonder and vague embarrassment paying homage to this beautiful part of him, in which life would continue limitlessly.

— William Styron

Sophie's Choice (1979)

- *A young writer is drawn into the lives of lovers Nathan and Sophia a beautiful Polish survivor of the concentration camps of World War II.*

"Don't make me choose," she heard herself plead in a whisper, "I can't choose."

"Send them both over there, then," the doctor said to the aide, *"nach links."*

"Mama!" She heard Eva's thin but soaring cry at the instant that she thrust the child away from her and rose from the concrete with a clumsy stumbling motion. "Take the baby!" she called out. "Take my little girl!"

At this point the aide—with a careful gentleness that Sophie would try without success to forget—tugged at Eva's hand and led her away into the waiting legion of the damned. She would forever retain a dim impression that the child had continued to look back, beseeching. But because she was now almost completely blinded by salty, thick, copious tears she was spared whatever expression Eva wore, and she was always grateful for that. For in the bleakest honesty of her heart she knew that she would never have been able to tolerate it, driven nearly mad as she was by her last glimpse of that vanishing small form.

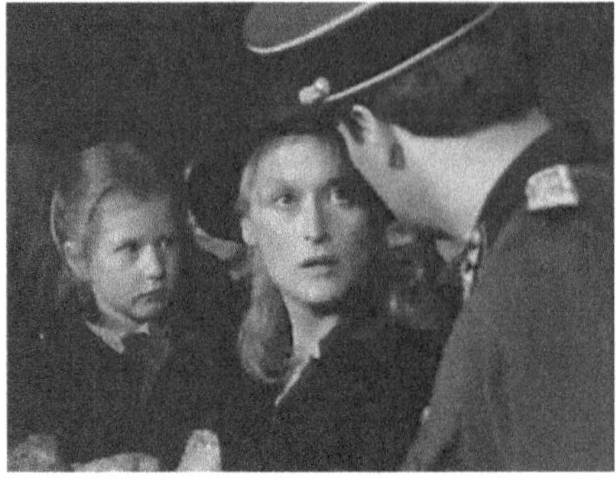

— **William Styron**

Perfume: The Story of a Murderer (1985)

- *Dark and sinister, Jean-Baptiste Grenouille, who has no smell himself, possesses an absolute sense of smell which ultimately leads to an obsession to identify and then to isolate the most perfect scent of all.*

Grenouille knew for certain that unless he possessed this scent, his life would have no meaning. He had to understand its smallest detail, to follow it to its last delicate tendril; the mere memory, however complex, was not enough. He wanted to press, to emboss this apotheosis of scent on his black, muddled soul, meticulously to explore it and from this point on, to think, to live, to smell only according to the innermost structures of its magic formula.

He slowly approached the girl, closer and closer, stepped under the overhanging roof, and halted one step behind her. She did not hear him.

— **Patrick Suskind** *(1949-) German writer and screenwriter*

Confessions of Zeno (1923)

- *The memoirs of Zeno from his initial addiction to cigarettes through meeting four sisters, eventually marrying one, together with other advancements and setbacks.*

Then something happened which really ought to have opened my eyes and saved me from myself. Little Anna, who all this time had been sitting motionless with her eyes fixed on me, suddenly said out loud what Ada had been thinking. She cried out:

"But he's mad, isn't he? Quite, quite mad!"

Signora Malfenti scolded her:

"Will you be quiet? Aren't you ashamed to break in like that when grown-up people are talking?"

The scolding only made it worse. Anna burst out again:

"He *is* mad! He talks to cats! You ought to get some rope and tie him up at once!"

Augusta, blushing with annoyance, got up and carried her off, telling her that she was very naughty and at the same time apologizing to me. But when they had got as far as the door the spiteful little creature managed to catch my eyes, made a horrid face at me, and called out again:

"They'll come and tie you up, you see if they don't."

— **Italo Svevo** *(1861-1928) Italian businessman and author of novels, plays, and short stories.*

Gulliver's Travels (1726)

- *The four voyages of Lemuel Gulliver, beginning with a shipwreck on an island inhabited by tiny people followed by encounters with crude giants, brutish Yahoos, pirates, and other misadventures.*

. . . I slept sounder than ever I remember to have done in my life, and as I reckoned, about nine Hours; for when I awaked, it was just Daylight. I attempted to rise, but was not able to stir. For as I happened to lie on my Back, I found my Arms and Legs were strongly fastened on each side to the Ground; and my Hair, which was long and thick, tied down in the same manner. I likewise felt several slender Ligatures across my Body, from my Armpits to my Thighs. I could only look upwards, the Sun began to grow hot, and the Light offended mine Eyes. I heard a confused Noise about me, but in the posture I lay, could see nothing except the Sky. In a little time I felt something alive moving on my left Leg, which advancing gently forward over my Breast, came almost up to my Chin; when bending my Eyes downward as much as I could, I perceived it to be a human Creature not six Inches high, with a Bow and Arrow in his Hands, and a Quiver at his Back.

— **Jonathan Swift** *(1667-1745) Anglo-Irish satirist, essayist, political pamphleteer, poet, and cleric*

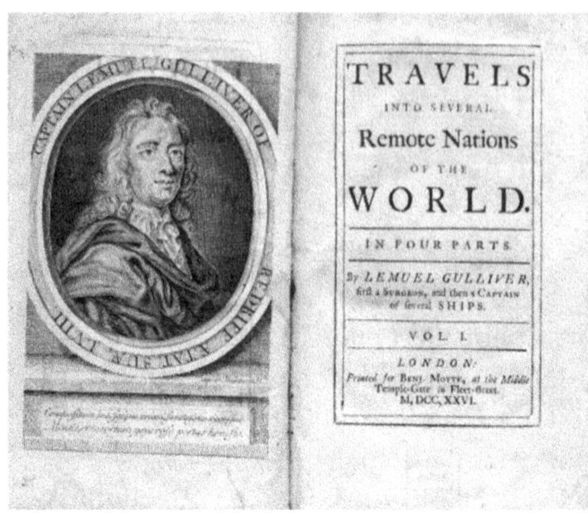

TRAVELS
INTO SEVERAL
Remote Nations
OF THE
WORLD.
IN FOUR PARTS.
By LEMUEL GULLIVER,
First a Surgeon, and then a Captain
of several SHIPS.
VOL. I.
LONDON:
Printed for Benj. Motte, at the Middle
Temple-Gate in Fleet-street.
M, DCC, XXVI.

T

The Collected Stories of Peter Taylor (1969)

- *A collection of twenty-one short stories of everyday life, mostly in the South, written in a clear gentle understanding manner. The quotation is from "Guests."*

He stepped forward and placed his hand on the doorknob. And then, as though it was what he had intended all along, he went inside the room and closed the door behind him.

He waited just inside the door till his eyes got used to the dark. Then he went over to the foot of the bed where she had the old man laid out. At last they were alone—he and Cousin Johnny. There was only just enough light for him to make out that she had him completely dressed, and with something that must be a handkerchief covering his face. No doubt he was wearing the very clothes—his other suit and good tie—that he would have worn to lunch at Jackson's Stable. And would she have put him in his long underwear? Edmund speculated, not idly, and not, certainly, with humor.

— **Peter Taylor** *(1917-1994) American author*

The Old Forest and Other Stories (1985)

- *Stories of ordinary people—families and households of the time—set in the deep South in the 1920s and 30s. This selection is from the title story.*

. . . Perhaps it was because they were the second or third generation of women in Memphis who were working in offices. They were not promiscuous—not most of them—but they slept with the men they were in love with and they did not conceal the fact. The men they were in love with were usually older than we were. Generally speaking, the girls merely amused themselves with us, just as we amused ourselves with them. There was a wonderful freedom in our relations which I have never known anything else quite like. And though I may not have had the most realistic sense of what their lives were, I came to know what I did know through my friendship with Lee Ann Deehart.

— Peter Taylor

A Summons to Memphis (1986)

- *A troubled family's decline after moving from Nashville to Memphis brought about largely by the destructive nature of the autocratic father.*

. . . When the family was gathered at the table in the dining room one of my middle-aged sisters would begin teasing the other about some suitor, so called. It was done in the best of spirits and was also received so. Mother, nearing eighty by this time and delighting if she were attentive at all in these family games, would declare that she had reached the point at which she would settle for any semblance of a son-in-law, by which she intended to be making a joke—a very broad joke for *her*. She meant to imply, all in fun of course (it was a part of this game they played), that she had not only given up discriminating between sorts of men her daughters might marry but was prepared even, if her daughters preferred it, to accept some unconventional arrangement like my own with Holly Kaplan. Father would pretend to be shocked by Mother's so incautiously urging her unmarried, aging daughters into something worse or less than marriage. . . . He knew as well as Mother, of course, and as well as I that there was no real possibility of marriage or of any alliance of any kind for Betsy or Josephine.

— Peter Taylor

The Travels of Jaimie McPheeters (1958)

- *A father and son make the hazardous trek by wagon train to California in 1849 with many perilous adventures.*

He said, "Mister, you talk a good fight."

"How tall be you, Fatty?"

"Six feet six, give or take."

"I didn't know they piled dung that high," said the cousin . . .

When the two faced off, bare to the waist, there was apparent a certain disparity in bulk. Matlock is a huge man, of a fish-belly whiteness of skin, with the corded, sinewy muscles common to one who has done hard labor, with lifting; and Coulter, swarthy, deeply tanned, though as sleek as a panther looked helplessly slight by contrast.

"Pining to back out, Big Mouth?"

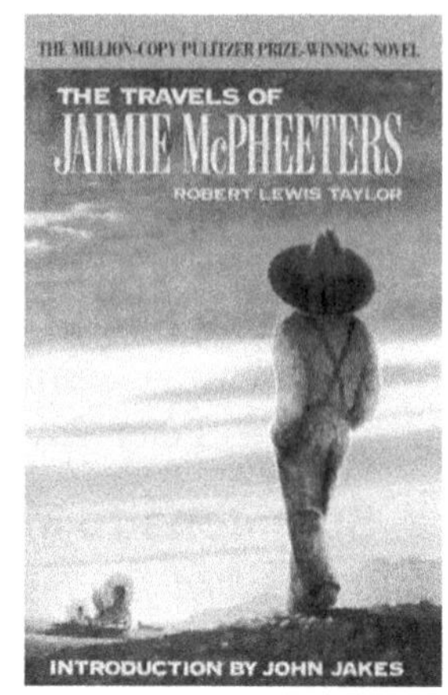

"I'd rather make it free," said Coulter.

"Free it stands."

The farmer's answer was offhand enough, but his expression showed a momentary unease. You could scarcely blame him. Coulter's face, in anger, is one of the least reassuring sights on earth. There was no bluster, no contortion of features, no tension, no nervousness; his eyes had the flat glitter of a rattlesnake's, his nose was splayed out in dilation, and his mouth a line incised in granite. To put it mildly, he looked extremely dangerous, and I believe that Matlock, for the first time, suspected that he may have been hasty. Nevertheless, at Kissel's cry of "Fight!" he came out, weaving back and forth, his hands working in the air, not unlike a swimmer's pawing through water, and suddenly aimed a heavy, unsporting kick at the vulnerable area of Coulter's crotch. . . .

What happened next remains blurred in my mind. Coulter's actions were performed with such rapidity that they confused us all. I was strongly reminded of the classic notion of a wolf striking at the throat of the slow-moving moose. In conversations that evening nobody remembered precisely the sequence of events, but all agreed that the meeting could not properly be described as a fight. It was murder and sudden death, or would have been had there not been general intervention.

— **Robert Lewis Taylor** *(1912-1998) American author*

Vanity Fair (1848)

- *The turns and fortunes of two women in the early 19th century. "One (Amelia Sedley) is good, stupid, bourgeois and (initially) rich; the other (Becky Sharp) is clever, selfish, bohemian and (initially) poor."*

That evening, when Amelia came tripping into the drawing-room in a white muslin frock, prepared for conquest at Vauxhall, singing like a lark, and as fresh as a rose—a very tall ungainly gentleman, with large hands and feet, and large ears, set off by a closely cropped head of black hair, and in the hideous military frogged coat and cocked hat of those times, advanced to meet her, and made her one of the clumsiest bows that was ever performed by a mortal.

This was no other than Captain William Dobbin, of His Majesty's _____ — Regiment of Foot, returned from yellow fever in the West Indies, to which the fortune of the service had ordered his regiment, whilst so many of his gallant comrades were reaping glory in the Peninsula.

He arrived with a knock so very timid and quiet, that it was inaudible to the ladies upstairs: otherwise, you may be sure Miss Amelia would never have been so bold as to come singing into the room. As it was, the sweet fresh little voice went right into the captain's heart, and nestled there.

— **William Thackeray** *(1811-1863) English novelist*

Saint Jack (1973)

- *Jack Flowers, an amiable, ambitious pimp in Singapore feeling hopeless and undervalued, tries to set up his own bordello clashing with members of the Chinese triad.*

. . . There was another admirer. A woman in a white dress, with a camera slung over her shoulder, leaned against the sea rail twenty feet away. When the children passed by, she approached me, smiling.

"What beautiful children," she said. "Are they Chinese?"

"Yeah," I said. "But they should be in bed at this hour."

"So should I," said the woman, and she laughed gently. She was a corker. She looked across the street and held her fingers to her mouth and kissed them in concentration. "Oh, hell," she said, "I'm lost."

"No, you're not," I said.

"Hey, you're an American, too," she said. "Do you have a minute?"

"Lady, believe me," I said, and a high funny note of joy, recovered hope, warbled in my ears as I pronounced the adventurous sentence, "I've got all the time in the world."

— **Paul Theroux** *(1941-) American travel writer and novelist*

The White Hotel (1981)

- *A neurotic opera singer in the 1920s is treated by Sigmund Freud and twenty years later is trapped in the holocaust of World War II.*

. . . Dragging her son by the hand, she pushed through to where the tall Cossack was giving orders. "Excuse me, I'm not Jewish," she said, panting.

He asked to see her identity card. She fumbled in her bag and by God's grace came out with an out-of-date identity card, one she had been issued with on her arrival in Russia, saying that her name was Erdman and her nationality Ukrainian. He told her she could go. “What about him?” he demanded, pointing at the boy.

“He’s my son. He’s Ukrainian too!”

But he insisted on seeing his papers, and when she pretended they were lost he seized her handbag and found a ration card. “Berenstein!” he exclaimed. “Jew-boy! Get back in!” He pushed Kolya away, and he was lost in the struggling throng. Lisa tried to push past the Cossack, but he barred her way with his arm. “You’re not a Yid, you don’t have to go through, old lady,” he said. “But I *must!*” she told him in a choking voice. “Please!” The Cossack shook his head. “Yids only.”

— **D. M. Thomas** *(1935-) Cornish novelist, poet, and translator*

The Master (2004)

- *A fictionalized study of the inner life of novelist Henry James including this touching friendship gone tragically wrong.*

. . . She had become his most intelligent reader and, after he had extracted a promise that she would destroy his letters, a most trusted and sharp-witted confidante. And when she came to London, as she did when they had known one another for more than three years, she became his steadfast and self-contained and secret best friend. . . .

They became connoisseurs of the twenty-four-hour meeting . . . She could, on these occasions, be brilliantly difficult and combative, begging to differ with him on books of the day or sights they had seen, and ready to tease him about his addiction to refinements. . . .

. . . And then, having prevaricated for several days, he opened *The Times* to find the news that Constance had jumped to her death from the window of the house where she lived in Venice. It was, the paper said, suicide. At once, he began to reassure himself that he was not at fault. He had owed her nothing, he thought, he had made her no promises that were binding. They had not been lovers; they were not related by blood. He owed her only his friendship . . .

. . . Had he gone to Venice that winter, he knew, she would not have killed herself. If she had appealed to him to visit and he had refused, it might be easier for him now to feel simple guilt. But her appeals were all over and they would be forever. He had let her down.

— **Colm Toibin** *(1955-) Irish novelist, short story writer and critic*

The Hobbit (1937)

- *A fantasy fairytale with elves, wizards, trolls, goblins, dragons, and a race of small, plump people about half the size of humans, with furry toes and a great love of good food and drink.*

. . . In a hole in the ground there lived a hobbit. Not a nasty, dirty, wet hole, filled with the ends of worms and an oozy smell, nor yet a dry, bare, sandy hole with nothing in it to sit down on or to eat: It was a hobbit-hole, and that means comfort.

— **J. R. R. Tolkien** *(1892-1973) English writer, poet and philologist*

The Lord of the Rings (1937)

- *A fantasy story of a young hobbit named Frodo and his friend Samwise and their quest to save Middle-earth from the evil Sauron by destroying the One Ring.*

Father of modern fantasy literature.

Sam got up. He was dazed, and blood streaming from his head dripped in his eye. He groped forward, and then he saw a strange and terrible thing. Gollum on the edge of the abyss was fighting like a mad thing with an unseen foe. To and fro he swayed, now so near the brink that almost he tumbled in, now dragging back, falling to the ground, rising, and falling again. And all the while he hissed but spoke no words.

The fires below awake in anger, the red light blazed, and all the cavern was filled with a great glare and heat. Suddenly Sam saw Gollum's long hands draw upwards to his mouth; his white fangs gleamed, and then snapped as they bit. Frodo gave a cry, and there he was, fallen upon his knees at the chasm's edge. But Gollum, dancing like a mad thing, held aloft the ring, a finger still thrust within its circle. It shone now as if verily it was wrought of living fire.

— **J. R. R. Tolkien**

Anna Karenina (1873)

- *The doomed love affair between the rebellious entrapped Anna and the dashing officer, Count Vronsky, set in mid-19th century Russia.*

And suddenly, remembering the man who was run over the day she first met Vronsky, she realized what she must do. With a quick, light step she went down the stairs that led from the water pump to the rails and stopped close to the passing train. She looked at the bottoms of the carriages, at the bolts and chains and big cast-iron wheels of the first carriage slowly rolling by, and tried to estimate by eye the midpoint between the front and back wheels and the moment when the middle would be in front of her.

'There!' she said to herself, staring into the shadow of the carriage at the sand mixed with coal poured between the sleepers, 'there, right in the middle, and I'll punish him and be rid of everybody and of myself.'

— **Leo Tolstoy** *(1828-1910) Russian writer*

Tolstoy's conversion from a dissolute and privileged society author to the non-violent and spiritual anarchist of his latter days was brought about by his service in the Army and traumatic experiences of Soviet brutality. He came to believe that he was undeserving of his inherited wealth, and was renowned among the peasantry for his generosity. He believed that a true Christian could find lasting happiness by striving for inner self-perfection through following the Great Commandment of loving one's neighbor and God. Tolstoy's death came only days after gathering the nerve to abandon his family and wealth and take up the path of a wandering ascetic, a path that he had agonized over pursuing for decades. — *Wikipedia*

War and Peace (1865)

- *The story of five aristocratic Russian families and their entangled lives immediately before and during Napoleon's invasion of Russia in 1812.*

On the hill above Pratz, in the same spot where he had fallen with the flagstaff in his hand, lay Prince Andrei Bolkonsky, his lifeblood oozing away, and unconsciously groaning with light, pitiful moans, like an ailing child.

By evening he ceased to groan, and lay absolutely still. He did not know how long his unconsciousness continued. Suddenly he became conscious that he was alive, and suffering from a burning and tormenting pain in his head. . . .

He tried to listen, and heard the trampling hoofs of several horses approaching, and the sounds of voices speaking French. . . .

These horsemen were Napoleon, accompanied by two aides. Bonaparte, who had been riding over the field of battle, had given orders to strengthen the battery cannonading the dike of Augest, and was now looking over the killed and wounded left on the battlefield.

"Handsome men!" said Napoleon, gazing at a Russian grenadier who lay on his belly with his face half buried in the soil, his neck turning black and one arm flung out and stiffened in death. . . .

. . . and then a step or two nearer he paused over Prince Andrei, who lay on his back with the flagstaff clutched in his hands (the flag had been carried off by the French as a trophy).

"There's an honorable death," said Napoleon, gazing at Bolkonsky. Prince Andrei realized that this was said of him, and that it was spoken by

Napoleon. . . . He collected all his strength to move and make some sound. He managed to move his leg slightly, and uttered a weak, feeble, sickly moan which stirred pity even in himself.

"Ah! He is alive!" said Napoleon. "Take up this young man and take him to the temporary hospital."

— Leo Tolstoy

A Confederacy of Dunces (1980)

■ *An educated but slothful man, still living with his mother at age 30, stumbles from one adventure to another in his quest for employment.*

A green hunting cap squeezed the top of the fleshy balloon of a head. The green earflaps, full of large ears and uncut hair and the fine bristles that grew in the ears themselves, stuck out on either side like turn signals indicating two directions at once. Full, pursed lips protruded beneath the bushy black moustache and, at their corners, sank into little folds filled with disapproval and potato chip crumbs. In the shadow under the green visor of the cap Ignatius J. Reilly's supercilious blue and yellow eyes looked down upon the other people waiting under the clock at the D. H. Holmes department store, studying the crowd of people for signs of bad taste in dress. . . .

Ignatius himself was dressed comfortably and sensibly. The hunting cap prevented head colds. The voluminous tweed trousers were durable and permitted unusually free locomotion. Their pleats and nooks contained pockets of warm, stale air that soothed Ignatius.

— John Kennedy Toole *(1937-1969) American novelist*

Toole submitted *Dunces* to Simon & Schuster where the novel was considered essentially pointless. Suffering from depression and feelings of self-persecution, Toole left home on a journey around the country. He stopped in Mississippi, ending his life by running a garden hose from his car into a cabin in which he was staying. Some years later his mother brought the manuscript of *Dunces* to the attention of novelist Walker Percy who ushered the book into print. Toole was posthumously awarded the Pulitzer Prize for Fiction. — *Wikipedia*

Fathers and Sons (1862)

■ *The generational conflict in 19th century Russia with radical sons confronting their traditional parents.*

"Ah, Anna Sergyevna, let us speak the truth. It's all over with me. I'm under the wheel. So it turns out that it was useless to think of the future. Death's an old joke, but it comes fresh to every one. So far I'm not afraid . . . but there, senselessness is coming, and then it's all up!—" he waved his hand feebly. "Well, what had I to say to you . . . I loved you! There was no sense in that even before, and less than ever now. Love is a form, and my own form is already breaking up. Better say how lovely you are! And now here you stand, so beautiful . . ."

— **Ivan Turgenev** *(1818-1883) Russian novelist, short story writer and playwright*

The Adventures of Huckleberry Finn
(1884)

"...the ambition to be a steam boatman always remained."

- *Huckleberry Finn runs away from home and rafts down the Mississippi River with an escaped slave named Jim.*

. . . Two or three days and nights went by; I reckon I might say they swum by, they slid along so quiet and smooth and lovely. Here is the way we put in the time. It was a monstrous big river down there—sometimes a mile and half wide; we run nights, and laid up and hid daytimes; soon as night was most gone, we stopped navigating and tied up—nearly always in the dead water under a tow-head; and then cut young cottonwoods and willows and hid the raft with them. Then we set out the lines. Next we slid into the river and had a swim, so as to freshen up and cool off; then we set down on the sandy bottom where the water was about knee deep and watched the daylight come. Not a sound, anywhere—perfectly still—just like the whole world was asleep, only sometimes the bull-frogs a-cluttering, maybe.

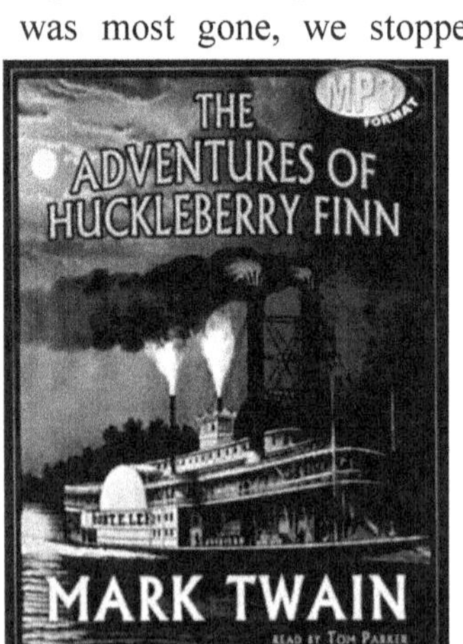

— **Mark Twain** *(1835-1910) American author and humorist*

In 1909, Twain is quoted as saying: I came in with Halley 's Comet in 1835. It is coming again next year, and I expect to go out with it. It will be the greatest disappointment of my life if I don't go out with Halley's comet. The Almighty has said, no doubt: 'Now here are these two unaccountable freaks; they came in together, they must go out together.' His prediction was accurate — Twain died of a heart attack on April 21, 1910, in Redding, Connecticut, one day after the comet's closest approach to Earth. — *Wikipedia*

The Accidental Tourist (1985)

- *Macon and his dog Edward attempt to settle down by moving back home only to encounter Muriel scrabbling for a living as a dog trainer.*

She and Macon were standing in the entrance hall. She still had her coat on—a bulky-shouldered, three-quarter length, nubby black affair of a type last seen in the 1940s. Edward sat is front of her as he'd been ordered. He had met her at the door with his usual display, leaping and snarling, but she'd more or less walked right through him and pointed at his rump and told him to sit. He'd gaped at her. She had reached over and poked his rear end down with a long, sharp index finger.

"Now you kind of cluck your tongue," she'd told Macon, demonstrating. "They get to know a cluck means praise. And when I hold my hand out—see? That means he has to stay."

Edward stayed, but a yelp erupted from him every few seconds, reminding Macon of the periodic bloops from a percolator. Muriel hadn't seemed to hear. She'd started discussing her lesson plan and then for no apparent reason had veered to her autobiography. But shouldn't Edward be allowed to get up now? How long did she expect him to sit there?

— **Anne Tyler** *(1941-) American novelist*

Breathing Lessons (1988)

- *The incompatibility of a 28-year marriage and the love that binds Maggie and her husband Ben together nonetheless.*

"One thing about you that I really cannot stand," she said, "is how you act so superior. We can't have just a civilized back-and-forth discussion; oh, no. No, you have to make a point of how illogical I am, what a whifflehead I am, how you're so cool and above it all."

"Well, at least I don't spill my life story in public eating places," he told her.

"Oh, just let me out," she said. "I cannot bear your company another second."

"Gladly," he said, but he went on driving.

"Let me out, I tell you!"

He looked over at her. He slowed down. She picked up her purse and clutched it to her chest.

"Are you going to stop this car," she asked, "or do I have to jump from a moving vehicle?"

He stopped the car.

— **Anne Tyler**

Dinner at the Homesick Restaurant (1982)

■ *Two brothers and a sister, raised by their angry now aged mother, gather at the family home, including surprisingly the long absent father.*

"How could you do that?" Cody asked him. "How could you just dump us on our mother's mercy?" He bent closer, close enough to smell the camphorish scent of Beck's suit. "We were kids, we were only kids, we had no way of protecting ourselves. We looked to you for help. We listened for your step at the door so we'd be safe, but you just turned your back on us. You didn't lift a finger to defend us."

Beck stared past Cody at the traffic.

"She wore me out," he told Cody finally.

"Wore you out?"

"Used up my good points. Used up all my good points."

— Anne Tyler

U

Bech: A Book (1970)

■ *Henry Bech, famous for his writer's block and adrift in a world of Gentiles, views life with a blend of wonder and cynicism.*

Bech accepted the offer. Her hand was warmer than porcelain, yet exact, and firm. He asked, "What are you doing amid all this alien corn, Ruth?"

The woman said, "Don't knock it, it's a living. This is my fourth year, actually. I like it here. The girls are immensely sweet, and not all of them are dumb. It's a place where you can see things happening, you can actually *see* these kids loosening up. Your consenting to come down here is a tremendous boost to the cause." She took her hand back from his to make the gestures needed to dramatize "loosening up" and "tremendous." In the sunshine glare reflected from the granite chapel Bech could admire the nimble and even flow of her expressiveness; he enjoyed the sensation, as of a tailor's measurements, of her cooling sizing him up even as she maintained a screen of patter, every dry and rapid turn of phrase a calibrated, unembarrassed offer of herself. **— John Updike**

Beck is Back (1982)

■ *Henry Bech, now fifty years old, reflects on his life, and, surprisingly, writes a book that becomes a bestseller.*

"I do apologize if that seemed rude. It's just a shock, to realize that a master of words doesn't hear them in his head the way you do." As she said this, her own pronunciation seemed a bit slurred. An empty plastic glass sat in her hand like an egg collected at dusk.

Perhaps it was the late-afternoon gin, perhaps the exhilaration of having just received a medal (The Melville Medal, awarded every five years to that American author who has maintained the most meaningful silence), but this encounter enchanted Bech. The questing fair face perspiring in the violet shade of the pink hat, the happy clatter around him of writers not writing, the thrusting smell of May penetrating the tent walls, the little electric push of a fresh personality — all felt too good to be true. He felt, deliciously, overpowered, as reality always overpowers fiction.

— **John Updike** *(1932-2009) American novelist, poet, short story writer, art critic, and literary critic*

The Centaur (1963)

- *The relationship between a school teacher father and his young son over a few days in a Pennsylvania 1940's winter.*

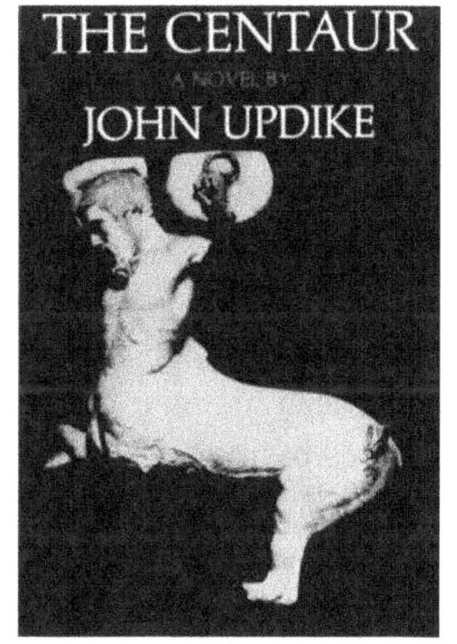

. . . As we passed the billboard on which the Lions and Rotary and Kiwanis and Elks all welcomed us to Olinger, my father said, "Don't worry about him knowing about your skin, Peter. He'll forget. That's the one thing you learn in teaching; people forget everything you tell 'em. I look at those dumb blank faces every day and it reminds me of death. You fall through those kids' heads without a trace. I remember, when my old man knew he was dying, he opened his eyes on the bed and looked up at Mom and Alma and me and said, 'Do you think I'll be eternally forgotten?' I often think about that. Eternally forgotten. That was a terrible thing for a minister to say. It scared the living daylights out of me."

— **John Updike**

The Coup (1978)

- *Felix prepares for and embarks on his new role as President of Kush, eventually acquiring four wives including this quoted American girl.*

Candace was on her feet and speechifying. "I hate you. I hate this place. I hate the heat, the bugs, the mud. Nothing *lasts* here, and nothing changes. The clothes when you wash them dry like cardboard. A dead rat on the floor is a skeleton by noon. I'm thirsty all the time, aren't *you*? Happy"—the nickname she gave me in college—"I'm *sinking*, and I can't *do* anything about it. I'm seeing the only shrink in Istiqlal and he shrugs and says, 'Why don't you just *leave?*' I tell him, 'I *can't*, I'm married to the *Pres*ident!'"

— **John Updike**

The Poorhouse Fair (1959)

- *At the County Home for the Aged, order is broken when the inmates take charge.*

Without his knowledge his white face plainly expressed this moment of fear. His flash of bewildered cowardice jarred loose the last pin restraining Gregg. Half hidden in the midst of the other old people, Gregg loosed a cry, shaking full of spittle, that stirred them. His wrist whipped where they could see, and a stone dug the grass to Conner's left. Conner turned his back and strode rapidly away, without quite running, and at this retreating target all—Hay and his two friends, Lucas, Tommy Franklin, even Fuller and the women and others who had come freshly to the group—flung small stones, most of them falling short.

— John Updike

Rabbit at Rest (1990)

- *In this final installment, Harry "Rabbit" Angstrom, now retired to sunny Florida and morbidly depressed and overweight, is led astray by his libido one last time.*

. . . Rabbit grabs the rebound but then can't move with it, his body weighs a ton, his feet have lost their connection to his head. Tiger knifes in between him and the basket, leans right in his face with a violet snarl, then eases back a little, so Rabbit feels a gap, a moment's slackness in the other in which to turn the corner; he takes one slam of a dribble, carrying his foe on his side like a bumping sack of coal, and leaps up for the peeper. The hoop fills his circle of vision, it descends to kiss his lips, he can't miss.

Up he goes, way up toward the torn clouds. His torso is ripped by a terrific pain, elbow to elbow. He bursts from within; he feels something immense persistently fumble at him, and falls unconscious to the dirt . . . Tiger catches the ball on its fall through the basket and feels a body bump against him as if in purposeful foul. Then he see the big old white man, looking choked and kind of sleepy in the face, collapse soundlessly, like a rag doll being dropped. Tiger stands amazed above the fallen body—the plaid Bermuda shorts, the brand-new walking Nikes, the blue golf shirt with a logo of intertwined V's. Adhesive dust of fine clay clings to one cheek of the unconscious flushed face like a shadow, like half of a clown's mask of paint. Shocked numb, the boy repeats, "Pure horseshit."

— John Updike

Rabbit is Rich (1981)

- *A middle age Rabbit struggles with spouse, son, in-laws, and in this quote a former girl friend.*

". . . Anyway, Rabbit. Believe me. She's not yours."

"O.K., Ruth. If you say so." In his surge of relief he stands.

She stands too, and having risen together their ghosts feel their inflated flesh fall away; the young man and woman who lived illicitly together one flight up on summer Street, across from a big limestone church, stand close again, sequestered from the world, and as before the room is hers. "Listen," she hisses up at him, radiantly is his impression, her distorted face gleaming. "I wouldn't give you the satisfaction of that girl being yours if there was a million dollars at stake. I raised her. She and I put in a lot of time together here and where the _____ were you? You saw me in Knoll's that time and there was no follow-up. I've known where you were all these years and you didn't give a simple shit what had happened to me, or my kid, or *any*thing."

— John Updike

Rabbit Redux (1971)

- *Aimless, almost pathetic, Rabbit moves through middle age playing host to an African-American and fleeing white teenager.*

. . . Showalter says, "Don't keep riding him."

Rabbit calls over to Brumbach, "I'm not riding you, am I?"

Showalter tugs harder, so Harry has to bend his ear to the man's little beak and soft unhappy mouth. "He's not that stable. He feels very threatened. It wasn't my idea to get after you, I said to him. The man has his rights of privacy." . . .

But Rabbit worries they are being rude to Brumbach. He calls over, "Hey, Eddie, I tell you what."

Brumbach is not pleased to be called in; he had wanted Showalter to settle. Rabbit sees the structure: one man is the negotiations, the other is the muscle. An age of specialization and collusion. Brumbach barks, "What?"

"I'll keep my kid from looking in your windows, and you keep yours from looking in mine."

"We had a name over there for guys like you. Wiseass. Sometimes just by mistake they got fragged."

"I'll tell you what else," Rabbit says. "As a bonus, I'll try to remember to draw the curtains."

— John Updike

Rabbit, Run (1960)

- *Harry "Rabbit" Angstrom, a hemmed-in-21-year-old, leaves his pregnant wife Janice on the spur of the moment to find what's missing from his life.*

Mrs. Eccles turns her head with an inviting twist. "Harry — ?"

"Angstrom."

"What do you do, Mr. Angstrom?"

"Well. I'm kind of out of work."

"Angstrom. Of course. Aren't you the one who disappeared? The Springers' son-in-law?"

“Right,” he replies smartly and, in the mindless follow-through, a kind of flower of coordination, she having on the drop of his answer turned with prim dismissal away from him again, slaps! her sassy ass. Not hard; a cupping hit, rebuke and fond pat both, well-placed on the pocket.

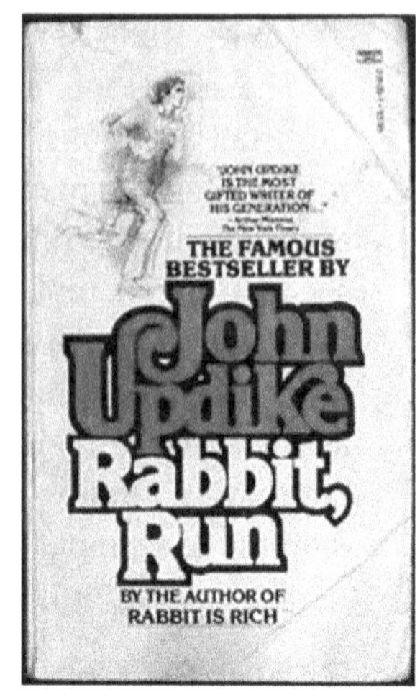

She swiftly pivots, swinging her backside to safety behind her. Her freckles dart sharp as pinpricks from her shocked face. Her leaping blood bleaches her skin, and her rigidly cold stare is so incongruous with the lazy condescending warmth he feels toward her, that he pushes his upper lip over his lower in a burlesque expression of penitence.

— **John Updike**

Roger’s Version (1986)

- *A divinity school professor is visited one day by a young student who believes that science and the computer can prove the existence of God. Things then get complicated.*

“The most miraculous thing is happening,” my visitor proclaimed with a painful sincerity, probably overrehearsed. “The physicists are getting down to the nitty-gritty, they’ve really just about pared things down to the ultimate details, and the last thing they ever expected to happen is happening. God is showing through. They hate it, but they can’t do anything about it. Facts are facts. And I don’t think people in the religion business, so to speak, are really aware of this—aware, that is, that their case, far-out as it’s always seemed, at last is being proven.”

— **John Updike**

V

Aunt Julia and the Scriptwriter (1982)

- *The career and aspirations of a young student are disrupted when he falls in love with his aunt-in-law.*

“So you’re Dorita’s son,” she said to me, planting a kiss on my cheek. “You’ve just gotten out of high school, haven’t you?” . . .

“Well, well. To tell you the truth, you look like a babe in arms, Marito.” Aunt Julia said, giving me the *coup de grace*.

During lunch, with that air of affectionate condescension that adults assume when addressing idiots and children, she asked me if I had a sweetheart, if I went to parties, what sport I went in for, and then, with a spitefulness that might have been either intentional or unintentional but in any case cut me to the quick, advised me to let my mustache grow *as soon as I had one*. They went well with dark hair and would help me make out with girls.

— **Mario Vargas Llosa** *(1936-) Peruvian writer, politician, journalist and essayist*

Burr (1973)

■ *A vivid portrait of Aaron Burr, hewed as close to the historical record as possible, with this striking account of Burr's dual with Alexander Hamilton.*

"Your principal has won both choices, Mr. Pendleton." A pause. "He wants to stand *there*?" A slight note of surprise in Burr's voice.

I realize suddenly that I am now standing where Hamilton stood. The sun is in my eyes; through green leaves water reflects brightness.

Burr has now taken up his position ten full paces opposite me. I think I am going to faint. Burr has the best position, facing the heights. I know that I am going to die. I want to scream, but dare not.

"I am ready." The Colonel seems to hold in his hand a heavy pistol. "What?" He looks at me, lowers the pistol. "You require your glasses? Of course, general. I shall wait."

"Is General Hamilton satisfied?" Burr then asks. "Good, I am ready, too."

I stand transfixed with terror as Burr takes aim, and shouts "Present!"

And I am killed.

— **Gore Vidal** *(1925-) American author, playwright, essayist, screenwriter, and political activist*

Europe Central (2005)

■ *European history from 1914 through 1975 told by several narrators including Kurt Gerstein, an SS officer who tried to warn the world about the concentration camps.*

What a heavy suitcase! He knew all too well what was in it; Clever Hans's trust in him was now proven. He sat gazing out the window of the Berlin Express, watching the summer scenery. Hour upon hour the other passengers in his compartment sat in silence, too terrified to look at him. An old woman coughed. Flicking a fingernail across the death's head on his cap, Gerstein turned slowly toward her, fixing a stony expression on his face. The woman lowered her head. Then the conductor came. Gerstein thrust out his ticket, staring the man down. He lit a cigarette. . . . Herr Lang was expecting him. Together they weighed the gold: twenty-two kilos. To Gerstein there was something terribly unclean about that brownish-yellow mass: was it the fact that it came from dead peoples' mouths, or did its Jewishness defile it? This is one of the most secret matters. He closed his eyes, turned out the gas chamber's light.

Includes coverage of composer Dmitri Shostakovich and other Soviet notables.

— **William T. Vollmann** *(1959-) American novelist and short story writer*

Candide (1759)

- *Candide, a young man of "the most unaffected simplicity," is drawn into a series of adventures, all the while claiming he lives in "the best of all possible worlds."*

For Voltaire, falling out with people was a way of life. He spent much of his twenties and thirties in and out of the Bastille for various attacks on the French aristocracy.

This is what went through Candide's mind at that moment, and how he reasoned: "If this holy man calls for help, he'll certainly have me burned, and he may do the same thing to Cunegonde. He's had me whipped unmercifully. He's my rival. I've already begun killing: my course is clear." This reasoning was swift and sure; without giving the Inquisitor time to recover from his surprise, he ran him through and laid him out beside the Jew.

"Now we're in an even worse predicament" said Cunegonde. "They'll have no mercy on us. We'll be excommunicated, our last hour has come. How could a gentle man like you kill a Jew and a prelate within two minutes of each other?"

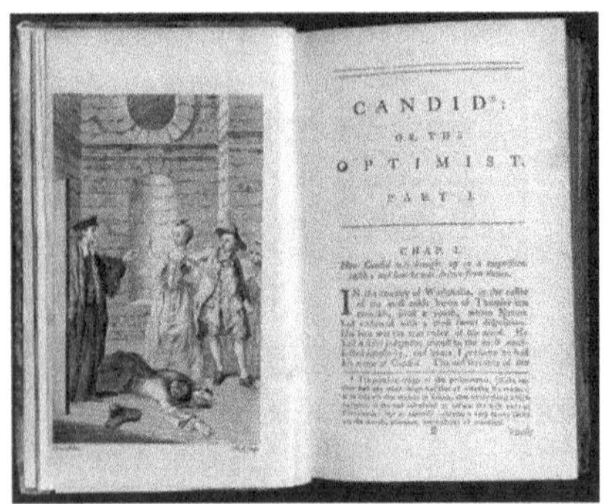

"Fairest lady," said Candide, "when a man is in love, jealous, and whipped by the Inquisition, he no longer knows what he's doing."

— **Voltaire** *(1694-1778) French Enlightenment writer, historian and philosopher*

Cat's Cradle (1963)

- *A bizarre story of the legacy of modern science which promises mankind progress but leads to unintentional self-destruction.*

There were no smells. There was no movement. Every step I took made a gravelly squeak in blue-white frost. And every squeak was echoed loudly. The season of locking was over. The earth was locked up tight.

It was winter, now and forever.

I helped my Mona out of our hole. I warned her to keep her hands away from the blue-white frost and to keep her hands away from her mouth, too. "Death has never been quite so easy to come by," I told her. "All you have to do is touch the ground and then your lips and you're done for."

"I want to stay as close to the edge as I can without going over. Out on the edge you see all kinds of things you can't see from the center."

She shook her head and sighed. "A very bad mother."

"What?"

"Mother Earth—she isn't a very good mother any more."

— **Kurt Vonnegut** *(1922-2007) American novelist*

Slaughterhouse-Five (1969)

- *Billy Pilgrim becomes "unstuck in time," traveling from past to future and reliving the horror of his wartime experiences.*

Listen:

Billy Pilgrim has come unstuck in time.

Billy has gone to sleep a senile widower and awakened on his wedding day. He has walked through a door in 1955 and come out another one in 1941. He has gone back through that door to find himself in 1963. He has seen his birth and death many times, he says, and pays random visits to all the events in between.

He says.

Billy is spastic in time, has no control over where he is going next, and the trips aren't necessarily fun. He is in a constant state of stage fright, he says, because he never knows what part of his life he is going to, have to act in next. — **Kurt Vonnegut**

The fire-bombing of Dresden in World War II is the central event mentally affecting Billy Pilgrim, the protagonist.

W

The Color Purple (1982)

■ *A story of the lives of two sisters, one a missionary in Africa, the other a child-wife living in the South, as told through letters in authentic folk voice.*

Andrea Roth

Fact is, he say, I got to git rid of her. She too old to be living here at home. And she a bad influence on my other girls. She'd come with her own linen. She can take that cow she raise down there back of the crib. But Nettie you flat out can't have. Not now. Not never.

Mr. _______ finally speak. Clearing his throat. I ain't never really look at that one, he say.

Well, next time you come you can look at her. She ugly. Don't even look like she kin to Nettie. But she'll make the better wife. She ain't smart either, and I'll just be fair, you have to watch her or she'll give away everything you own. But she can work like a man.

Mr. _______ say How old she is?

He say, She nearly twenty. And another thing—She tell lies.

— **Alice Walker** *(1944-) African American author and poet*

All the King's Men (1946)

■ *The dramatic political ascent and decline of Willie Stark, a charismatic and extraordinarily powerful state governor in the American South during the 1930's.*

The boss was like that. He gave you the impression of being a slow and deliberate man to look at him, and he had a way of sitting loose as though he had sunk inside himself and was going down for the third time and his eyes would blink like an owl's in a cage. Then all of a sudden he would make a move. It might just be to reach out and grab a fly out of the air that was bothering him. . . . Or he would whip his head at you when you said something he hadn't seemed to be listening to. He whipped his head round now to Duffy and fixed his gaze on him for an instant before he said quite simply and expressively, "Jesus." Then he said, "Tiny, you don't know a God-damned thing."

— **Robert Penn Warren** *(1905-1989) American poet, novelist and literary critic*

Brideshead Revisited (1945)

- *A captain in the British Army in post World War I looks back on his life and his special friendship with Lord Sebastian Flyte, first at Oxford, then later at the family's Brideshead estate.*

. . . "You know Father Mowbray hit on the truth about Rex at once, that it took me a year of marriage to see. He simply wasn't all there. He wasn't a complete human being at all. He was a tiny bit of one, unnaturally developed; something in a bottle, an organ kept alive in a laboratory. I thought he was a sort of primitive savage, but he was something absolutely modern and up-to-date that only this ghastly age could produce. A tiny bit of a man pretending he was the whole."

— **Evelyn Waugh** *(1903-1966) English writer of novels, travel books and biographies*

Even those commentators who regarded Waugh's views and behavior as those of a crackpot thought him the best stylist of his day — a writer, said Gore Vidal, of "prose so chaste that at times one longs for a violation of syntax to suggest that its creator is fallible, or at least part American."

— *Today in Literature*

". . . he writes the most shapely and elegant English prose of his time. If you would write perfectly, you would write like Evelyn Waugh."

— Michael Dirda, *The Washington Post*

". . . Yesterday was a very proud day for me — at last after quarter of a century's waiting I appeared in *The Times* Crossword. Better than a doctorate at Reading, an MBE or a concert at Festival Hall." — Evelyn Waugh

A Handful of Dust (1934)

- *Seeking solace from his wife's indiscretions, Tony Last embarks on an exploration of the Brazilian wilderness which eventually ends in his permanent captivity captured in this quote.*

'You haven't seen my watch anywhere?'

'You' have missed it?'

'Yes. I thought I was wearing it. I say, I've never slept so long.'

'Not since you were a baby. Do you know how long? Two days.'

'Nonsense. I can't have.'

'Yes, indeed. It is a long time. It is a pity because you missed our guests.'

'Guests?'

'Why, yes. I have been quite gay while you were asleep. Three men from outside. Englishmen. It is a pity you missed them. A pity for them, too, as they particularly wished to see you. But what could I do? You were so sound asleep. They had come all the way to find you, so — I thought you would not mind — as you could not greet them yourself, I gave them a little souvenir, your watch. They wanted something to take back to England where a reward is being offered for news of you. They were very pleased with it. And they took some photographs of the little cross I put up to commemorate your coming. They were pleased with that, too. They were very easily pleased.'

— Evelyn Waugh

Scoop (1937)

- *Mistaken identity sends William Boot, nature columnist for the Beast newspaper, to Ishmaelia as a war correspondent*

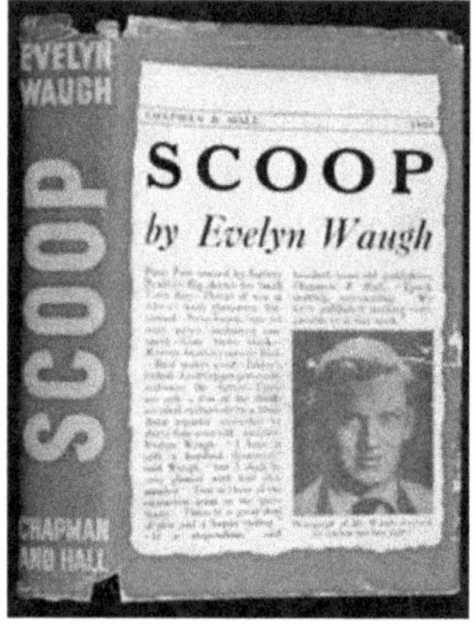

On the previous Thursday a very dreadful thing had happened. Drawing on the observations of a lifetime, and after due cross-examination of the head keeper and half an hour with the encyclopedia, William had composed a lyrical but wholly accurate account of the habits of the badger; one of his more finished essays. Priscilla in a playful mood had found the manuscript and altered it, substituting for "badger" throughout "the great crested grebe." It was not until Saturday morning when, in this form, it appeared in the *Beast* that William was aware of the outrage.

His mail had been prodigious; some correspondents were skeptical, others derisive; one lady wrote to ask whether she read him aright in thinking he condoned the practice of baiting these rare and beautiful birds with terriers and deliberately destroying their earthy homes; how could this be tolerated in the so-called twentieth century? A major in Wales challenged him categorically to produce a single authenticated case of a great crested grebe attacking young rabbits.

— Evelyn Waugh

The War of the Worlds (1898)

- *The classic science fiction tale in which Martians land on earth and turn out, in this instance, to be surprisingly incompetent invaders.*

And this was the sum of the Martian organs. Strange as it may seem to a human being, all the complex apparatus of digestion, which makes up the bulk of our bodies, did not exist in the Martians. They were heads—merely heads. Entrails they had none. They did not eat, much less digest. Instead, they took the fresh, living blood of other creatures, and *injected* it into their own veins. I have myself seen this being done, as I shall mention in its place. But, squeamish as I may seem, I cannot bring myself to describe what I could not endure even to continue watching. Let it suffice to say, blood obtained from a still living animal, in most cases from a human being, was run directly by means of a little pipette into the recipient canal. . . .

— **H. G. Wells** *(1866-1946) English author and writer in many other genres*

". . . the man who could enrich his letters with droll little drawings, who could invent uproarious family games, whose blue eyes twinkled with mischief, and whose famous voice, which never lost a kind of reedy Cockney impudence, rose higher and higher in friendly mischief; who was not only a tremendous character but also a most loveable man. . ."

— Funeral speech by J. B. Priestly recalling the human side of H. G. Wells

"A Martin Machine Contemplates the Drunken Crowd" Illustration by Alvin Corréa for H. G. Wells' *The War of the Worlds*, 1906 Vandamme edition.

The Collected Stories of Eudora Welty (1980)

- *Stories of the land and people of the Deep South in the early to mid 20th century.*

Miss Baby Marie took back the lipstick and packed it up. She gathered up the jars for both black and white and got them all inside the suitcase, with the same little fuss of triumph with which she had brought them out. She started away.

"Good-bye," she said, making herself look grand from the back, but at the last minute she turned around in the door. Her old hat wobbled as she whispered, "Let me see your husband."

Livvie obediently went on tiptoe and opened the door to the other room. Miss Baby Marie came behind her and rose on her toes and looked in.

"My, what a little tiny old, old man!" she whispered, clasping her hands and shaking her head over them. "What a beautiful quilt! What a tiny old, old man!"

"He can sleep like that all day," whispered Livvie proudly.

They looked at him awhile so fast asleep, and then all at once they looked at each other. Somehow that was as if they had a secret, for he had never stirred. Livvie then politely, but all at once, closed the door.

— **Eudora Welty** *(1909-2001) American author*

Losing Battles (1970)

- *Three generations and assorted friends and neighbors gather to celebrate Granny Vaughn's 90th birthday.*

"It started away from Curly's store in Banner on a Saturday morning, and the Nashville Rocket comes up the track. We was sitting there on the store porch, telling each other our woes, when there comes quite a crack," said Uncle Dolphus.

"It got hit by a train?" cried Mrs. Moody.

"It stopped the Nashville Rocket on the crossing, yes'm."

"This truck is something that had to be picked up out of the cinders of the railroad track?" asked Mrs. Moody.

"Jack picked it up. Had to wade to get it. There's a river of hot Coca-Cola and a mountain of broken glass trying to stop him—it was a Coca-Cola truck," said Aunt Birdie.

"Jack could have sliced an artery and no woman the wiser at home," said Aunt Beck.

"The only cokes left standing for a mile around was the ones old Ears Broadwee had just finished delivering to Curly," Uncle Percy whispered.

"That was one sticky cow-catcher," said Uncle Dolphus.

— **Eudora Welty**

The Optimist's Daughter (1972)

- *A daughter returns to her Mississippi home town when her father dies, leading to a confrontation with his wife of two years.*

"Scaring people into things. Scaring people out of things. You haven't learned any better yet, Fay?" Trembling, Laurel kept on. "What were you trying to scare Father into—when you struck him?"

"I was trying to scare him into living!" Fay cried.

"You what? You *what?*"

"I wanted him to get up out of there, and start him paying a little attention to *me*, for a change."

"He was dying," said Laurel. "He was paying full attention to that."

I tried to make him quit his old-man foolishness. I was going to make him live if I had to drag him! And I take good credit for what I did!" cried Fay. "It's more than anybody else was doing."

"You hurt him."

"I was being a wife to him!" cried Fay. "Have you clean forgotten by this time what being a wife is?"

— **Eudora Welty**

The Devil's Advocate (1959)

■ *Monsignor Blaise Meredith is sent to a small town to assemble the facts regarding a priest's death, only to revive his own faith.*

Books published in 27 languages selling more than 60 million copies worldwide.

". . . You, like many of us here in Rome, are a professional priest—a career churchman. There is no stigma in that. It is much already to be a good professional. There are many who fall far short, even of this limited perfection. Suddenly you have discovered it is not enough. You are puzzled, afraid. Yet you do not know what you should do to restore the lack. Part of the problem is that you and I and others like us have been removed too long from pastoral duty. We have lost touch with the people who keep us in touch with God. We have reduced the Faith to an intellectual conception, an arid assent of the will, because we have not seen it working in the lives of common folk. We have lost pity and fear and love. We are the guardians of mysteries, but we have lost the awe of them. We work by canon, not by charity."

— **Morris L. West** *(1916-1999) Australian novelist and playwright*

The Complete Works of Nathanael West (1957)

- *Four short stories including "Miss Lonelyhearts" in which a male advice columnist becomes overburdened with the troubles of his readers and falls into a deep depression.*

"Perhaps I can make you understand. Let's start from the beginning. A man is hired to give advice to the readers of a newspaper. The job is a circulation stunt and the whole staff considers it a joke. He welcomes the job, for it might lead to a gossip column, and anyway he's tired of being a leg man. He too considers the job a joke, but after several months at it, the joke begins to escape him. He sees that the majority of the letters are profoundly humble pleas for moral and spiritual advice, that they are inarticulate expressions of genuine suffering. He also discovers that his correspondents take him seriously. For the first time in his life, he is forced to examine the values by which he lives. This examination shows him that he is the victim of the joke and not its perpetrator."

— **Nathanael West** *(1903-1940) American author, screen writer and satirist*

The Day of the Locust (1939)

- *The lives of a disparate group of odd individuals striving for success in Hollywood during the Great Depression.*

Homer motioned her toward a chair, then got her a match for her cigarette. He tried not to stare at her, but his good manners were wasted. Faye enjoyed being stared at.

He thought her extremely beautiful, but what affected him still more was her vitality. She was taut and vibrant. She was as shiny as a new spoon.

Although she was seventeen, she was dressed like a child of twelve in a white cotton dress with a blue sailor collar. Her long legs were bare and she had blue sandals on her feet.

— **Nathanael West**

West wrote to F. Scott Fitzgerald to give him the latest report on sales of *The Day of the Locust* published six weeks earlier: "The box score stands: Good reviews—fifteen per cent, bad reviews—twenty five per cent, brutal personal attacks—sixty percent. Sales: practically none. I'll try another one anyway, I guess." – *Today in Literature*

Fifty years later (1987), Matt Groening introduced us to a new Homer Simpson in the animated television series *The Simpsons.*

The Age of Innocence (1920)

- *A young lawyer engaged to marry a virginal socialite meets and falls in love with her worldly cousin, Countess Ellen Olenska, an unconventional woman of subtlety and grace.*

In the middle of the room she paused, looking about her with a grave mouth and smiling eyes; and in that instant Newland Archer rejected the general verdict on her looks. It was true that her early radiance was gone. The red cheeks had paled; she was thin, worn, a little older-looking than her age, which must have been nearly thirty. But there was about her the mysterious authority of beauty, a sureness in the carriage of the head, the movement of the eyes, which, without being in the least theatrical, struck his as highly trained and full of a conscious power.

— **Edith Wharton** *(1862-1937) American short story writer and novelist*

The House of Mirth (1905)

- *New York socialite Lily Bart attempts to secure a husband and a place in rich society but runs into difficulties including the venomous Bertha Dorset who falsely implies Lily has committed adultery with her husband.*

Mrs. Dorset settled herself indolently in her seat. "[George will wait to see the doctor]; he was horribly frightened about himself. It's very bad for him to be worried and whenever anything upsetting happens, it always brings on an attack"

The time Lily felt sure that a cue was being pressed on her; but it was put forth with such startling suddenness, and with so incredible an air of ignoring what it led up to, that she could only falter out doubtfully: "Anything upsetting?"

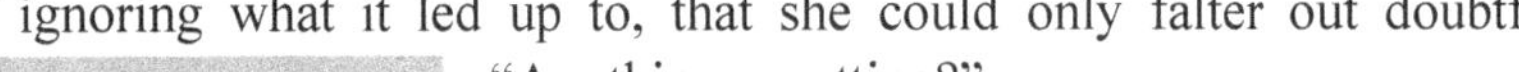

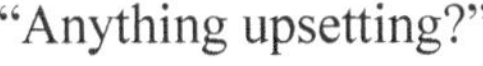

"Yes—such as having you so conspicuously on his hands in the small hours. You know, my dear, you're rather a big responsibility in such a scandalous place after midnight."

At that—at the complete unexpectedness and the inconceivable audacity of it—Lily could not restrain the tribute of an astonished laugh.

— **Edith Wharton**

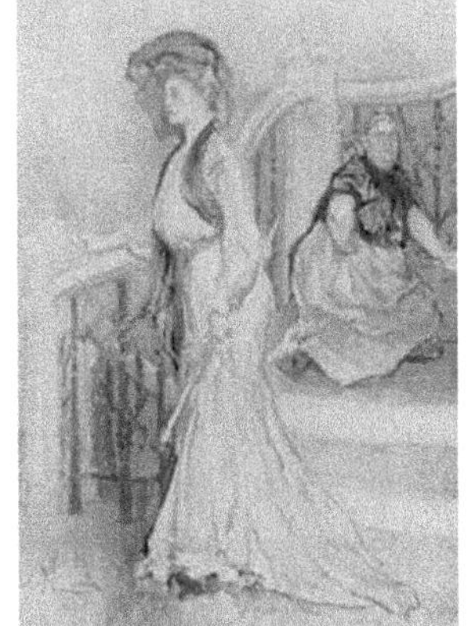

Illustration from the 1905 edition of *The House of Mirth*. "The woman continued to stare as Miss Bart swept by."

Charlotte's Web (1952)

- *A children's story of a barn spider and her friendship with a pig named Wilbur.*

On foggy mornings, Charlotte's web was truly a thing of beauty. This morning each thin strand was decorated with dozens of tiny beads of water. The web glistened in the light and made a pattern of loveliness and mystery, like a delicate veil. Even Lurvy, who wasn't particularly interested in beauty, noticed the web when he came with the pig's breakfast. He noted how clearly it showed up and he noted how big and carefully built it was. And then he took another look and he saw something that made him set his pail down. There, in the center of the web, neatly woven in block letters, was a message. It said:

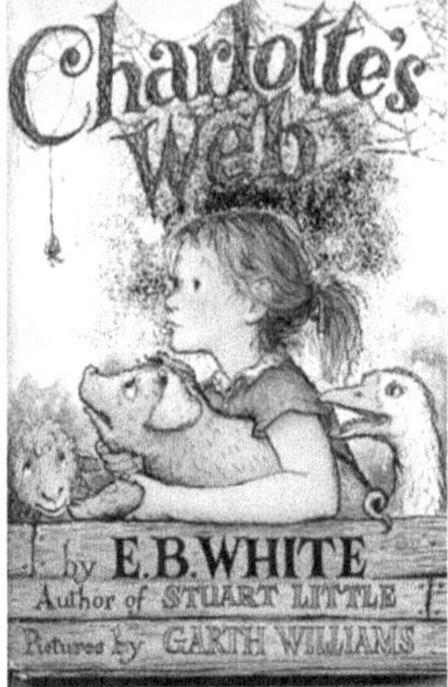

SOME PIG!

— **E. B. White** *(1899-1985) American writer*

John Henry Days (2001)

- *Expansive meditation on American life explored during the John Henry Days festival held in Talcott, West Virginia.*

. . . Her first round through the song is remarkably easy. It speeds by, like a walk down a street she has been down a thousand times before, something seen but not seen, gone in a blink but navigated without mishap as she thought of something else. She tries it again, top of the wilted page, and this time is even easier, there's something sad about the song, but what she feels most is—pushed. The song pushes her. There is something in this song . . . it quickens inside her. It doesn't go to church and cusses, wears what it wants. . . . The last note withers in the empty brownstone, down the hall and up the stairs into empty rooms, and this time she decides she'll sing the words. She's in a heat right now. She sings lyrics that tell a story of a man born with a hammer in his hand and a mountain that will be the death of him: you think you push but you are being pushed. She sings it again and is so pushed that she doesn't hear her mother come in the front door, only hears her mother yell, "Do you think

your father works ten hours a day walking up and down the neighborhood treating sick people so that he can come home and listen to his little girl play gutter music?"

— **Colson Whitehead** *(1969-) American novelist*

Leaves of Grass (1892)

- *An "ensemble" of close to 400 poems of wit and wisdom generally selectively read and questionably classified as prose fiction.*

O Captain! My Captain! Our fearful trip is done,
The ship has weather'd every rack, the prize we sought is won,
The port is near, the bells I hear, the people all exulting,
While follow eyes the steady keel, the vessel grim and daring;
But O heart! heart! heart!
O the bleeding drops of red,
Where on the deck my Captain lies,
Fallen cold and dead.

My Captain does not answer, his lips are pale and still,
My father does not feel my arm, he has no pulse nor will,
The ship is anchor'd safe and sound, its voyage closed and done,
From fearful trip the victor ship comes in with object won;
Exult O shores, and ring O bells!
But I with mournful tread,
Walk the deck my Captain lies,
Fallen cold and dead.

— **Walt Whitman** *(1819-1892) American poet, essayist and journalist*

Philadelphia Fire (1990)

- *A writer and exile returns to his old West Philadelphia neighborhood to search for the lone survivor of the 1985 fire.*

Tape measurements and photographs. A figure chalked in the street, where the suicide made his clean landing. With cars parked both sides the street and high-noon traffic and pedestrians, how'd he miss hitting something, somebody on the way down? Didn't get runned over, either. No second or

third superfluous death. Roasted in a torched car. Drowned by a berserk hydrant. No extra work for the meat-wagon crew. Smooth sailing through the needle's eye. Happy landing right on target. J. B. was proud of the jumper. Whatever else the guy'd _______ up, he'd done this right. A slick, professional job. Bet the dude's wearing clean underwear.

— **John Edgar Wideman** *(1941-) American writer*

Evidence of Things Unseen (2003)

■ *A love story of Fos and Opal as they navigate through major events in American history to conclude in Knoxville, Tennessee.*

. . . *My hero*, she told Fos when he got her home and out of her soiled clothes. And even then the words landed like a harpoon in his heart. Heroic was the farthest thing from what he had been feeling ever since the day in Markham's office when he learned that she was dying, but she'd called him "hero" with a smile and said it with the tender sweetness she said everything with these days. At some point in her inner dialogue with the pain that was now a living organ in her body, Opal must have resolved to keep herself intact and dissolve the pain through her like a pack of sugar in hot liquid. Sweetness was the result—her fundamental sweetness.

— **Marianne Wiggins** *(1947-) American author*

The Picture of Dorian Gray (1891)

■ *A corrupt young man has his portrait done which becomes increasingly hideous while his youthful appearance remains the same despite a life of debauchery.*

"My wallpaper and I are fighting a duel to the death. One or the other of us has to go!"

. . . As he was turning the handle of the door, his eye fell upon the portrait Basil Hallward had painted of him. He started back as if in surprise.

". . . there was a touch of cruelty in the mouth."

. . . Finally he came back, went over to the picture, and examined it. In the dim arrested light that struggled through the cream-coloured silk blinds, the face appeared to him to be a little changed. The expression looked different. One would have said that there was a touch of cruelty in the mouth. It was certainly strange.

— **Oscar Wilde** *(1854-1900) Irish writer, poet, And prominent aesthete*

On May 25, 1895 Wilde was convicted of gross indecency and sentenced to two years' hard labour. The regime at the time was tough: "hard labour, hard fare and a hard bed" was the guiding philosophy. It wore particularly harshly on Wilde as a gentleman and his status provided him no special privileges. Known as prisoner C. 3.3, he was not at first even allowed paper and pen but a friend in parliament eventually succeeded in allowing access to books and writing materials.

Wilde was released on May 19, 1897, and though his health had suffered greatly, he had a feeling of spiritual renewal. He wrote two long letters to the editor of the *Daily Chronicle*, describing the brutal conditions of English prisons and advocating penal reform. — *Wilipedia*

The Bridge of San Luis Rey (1927)

- *By chance, a monk witnesses the collapse of an old woven bridge in Peru and embarks on a quest to prove that it was divine intervention that led to the deaths of the five individuals who perished in the tragedy.*

On Friday noon, July the twentieth, 1714, the finest bridge in all Peru broke and precipitated five travelers into the gulf below. This bridge was on the highroad between Lima and Cuzco and hundreds of persons passed over it every day. It had been woven of osier by the Incas more than a century before and visitors to the city were always led out to see it. It was a mere ladder of thin slats swung out over the gorge, with handrails of dried vine. Horses and coaches and chairs had to go down hundreds of feet below and pass over the narrow torrent on rafts, but no one, not even the Viceroy, not even the Archbishop of Lima, had descended with the baggage rather than cross by the famous bridge of San Luis Rey. St. Louis of France himself protected it, by his name and by the little mud church on the further side. The bridge seemed to be among the things that last forever; it was unthinkable that it should break.

— **Thornton Wilder** *(1897-1975) American playwright and novelist*

The Eighth Day (1967)

- *The story of two families in an Illinois coal town, a father's flight from prosecution, and one son's climb to fame in Chicago's newspaper world.*

At least he was not only doing his duty and feeding his curiosity, he was making a *thing*. His youthful and countrified air enabled him to be present at occasions from which an older and more knowing man would have been thrown out. He stood against the wall at closed political meetings; he slipped past the guards in the training quarters of boxing champions; he re-entered his old hospital by the employees' entrance and obtained a confession from a dying man. He arrived before the police and put questions to women who did not yet know that they were widows. He was taking notes at a Greek patriotic banquet in the Olympia Restaurant while the guests, stricken with food poisoning, lay about on the floor like brightly colored clothes bags. By December, 1903, he was writing his sister, "I bet I know four hundred Chicagoans by names and faces."

— Thornton Wilder

Wilder is one of very few, if not the only novelist, to have won Pulitzer Prizes for both fiction (*The Bridge of San Luis Rey*) and drama (*Our Town* and *The Skin of Our Teeth*), as well as earning the Legion of Merit and the Bronze Star for military service in World War II. — *Wikipedia*

A Streetcar Named Desire (play) (1947)

■ *Blanche Dubois visits her pregnant sister Stella and brutish husband Stanley in New Orleans with resulting friction and eventual discovery of Blanche's sordid past.*

. . . [Blanche extends her hands toward the Doctor. He draws her up gently and supports her with his arm and leads her through the portieres.]

"Whoever you are—I have always depended on the kindness of strangers."

— Tennessee Williams *(1911-1983) American playwright*

Beyond the Bedroom Wall (1975)

- *A family saga of the simple pleasures and heartbreaks of everyday life, first in North Dakota and then Illinois.*

. . . He stepped inside and closed the door behind him. He dipped his fingers into a font of holy water fastened to the molding of the jamb and made a sign of the cross, and then turned back the sheet to his father's shoulders; thick silver hair rayed upward over the pillow, giving his face an unprotected look, lips dark and parted, and the white scar across the bridge of his nose violet. A scar from a fight. When had it happened? Why? The lid of his left eye was halfway open, and a clouded iris showed. Charles closed the lid with his thumb, but it slowly retracted, and was once more open on him.

In the top drawer of his father's bureau he found a leather change purse, took two silver dollars from it, pressed the eyelid down, and placed the coins over it. He snapped the purse shut and held it, trembling. His father's beard, shorter and thinner than he remembered, flared up from his lifted chin like a silken brush. With his fingers Charles stroked the beard smooth, the way he'd seen his father stroke it from the time he could remember.

God rest you, Father.

— **Larry Woiwode** *(1941-) American writer*

The Bonfire of the Vanities (1987)

- *A Park Avenue bond trader is embroiled in a legal and political whirlwind when he and his mistress are the cause of a possibly fatal accident in the Bronx.*

". . . This witness has told us that Mr. McCoy was accompanied in that car by another person, a white female in her twenties, and the information provided makes her his accomplice in one or more of the felonies that Mr. McCoy is charged with." He paused, for what he hoped would be maximum effect. "That witness has positively identified that woman as . . . yourself."

Kramer now stopped and looked the widow squarely in the face. At first she was perfect. She didn't blink. Her lovely brave little smile never wavered. But then her Adam's apple, almost imperceptibly, went up and down just once.

She swallowed!

An excellent feeling came over Kramer, in every cell and every neural fiber. In that instant, the instant of that little swallow, his scuffed attaché case meant nothing, nor did his clodhopper shoes nor his cheap suit nor his measly salary nor his New York accent nor his barbarisms and solecisms of speech. For in that moment he had something that these Wasp counselors, these immaculate Wall Street partners . . . would never know and never feel the inexpressible pleasure of possessing. And they would remain silent and polite in the face of it, as they were right now, and they would swallow with fear when and if their time came.

— **Tom Wolfe** *(1931-) American author and journalist*

A Man in Full (1998)

- *The story of an egomaniacal good ol'boy with a crumbling real-estate empire on his hands, and his assortment of friends and enemies.*

Charlie Croker, astride his favorite Tennessee walking horse, pulled his shoulders back to made sure he was erect in the saddle and took a deep breath . . . Ahhhh, that was the ticket . . . He loved the way his mighty chest rose and fell beneath his khaki shirt and imagined that everyone in the hunting party noticed how powerfully built he was. . . .

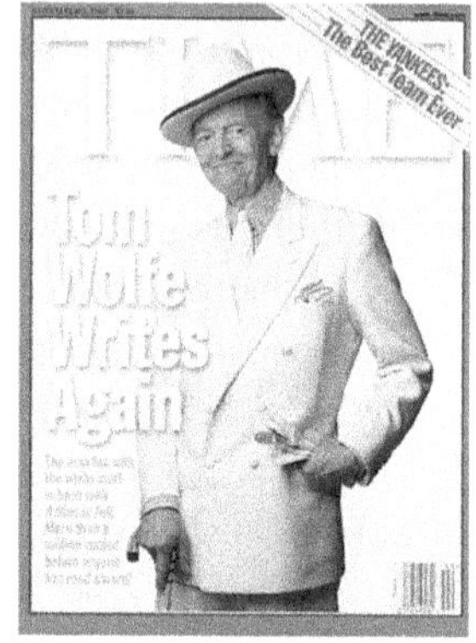

Wolfe adopted the white suit as a trademark in 1962.

. . . Charlie took another deep breath . . . Ahhhhhh . . . the husky aroma of the grass . . . the resinous air of the pines . . . the heavy, fleshy odor of all his animals, the horses, the mules, the dogs . . . Somehow nothing reminded him so instantly of how far he had come in his sixty years on the earth as the smell of animals. Turpmtine Plantation! Twenty-nine thousand acres of prime southwest Georgia forest, fields, and swamp! And all of it, every square inch of it, every beast that moved on it, all fifty-nine horses, all twenty-two mules, all forty dogs, all thirty-six buildings that stood upon it, plus a mile-long asphalt landing strip, complete with jet-fuel pumps and a hangar—all of it was his, Cap'm Charlie Croker's, to do with as he chose, which was: to shoot quail.

— **Tom Wolfe**

Look Homeward, Angel (1929)

- *The coming of age story of Eugene Gant, living in a small, rural town in North Carolina in the early 1900s.*

Frightened, he looked at her for a moment.

"Laura! You're coming back, aren't you?" he said quietly.

"Yes, of course," she said. "Be quiet."

He was trembling violently; he was afraid to question her more closely. . . .

"'Board!"

He got up trembling.

"In a few days, dear." She looked up, taking his hand in her small gloved palms.

"You will write as soon as you get there? Please!"

"Yes, To-morrow—at once."

He bent down suddenly and whispered, "Laura—you will come back. You will come back!"

She turned her face away and wept bitterly. He sat beside her once more; she clasped him tightly as if he had been a child.

"My dear, my dear! Don't forget me ever!"

"Never. Come back. Come back."

The salt print of her kiss was on his mouth, his face, his eyes. It was, he knew, the guttering candle-end of time. The train was in motion. He leaped blindly up the passage with a cry in his throat.

"Come back again!"

But he knew. Her cry followed him, as if he had torn something from her grasp.

— **Thomas Wolfe** *(1900-1938) American novelist*

Thomas Wolfe died of tubercular meningitis in 1938 at the age of 37. The next day *The New York Times* wrote: "His was one of the most confident young voices in contemporary American literature, a vibrant, full-toned voice which it is hard to believe could be so suddenly stilled. The stamp of genius was upon him, though it was an undisciplined and unpredictable genius . . . There was within him an unspent energy, an untiring force, an unappeasable hunger for life and for expression which might have carried him to the heights and might equally have torn him down."

Time wrote: "The death last week of Thomas Clayton Wolfe shocked critics with the realization that, of all American novelists of his generation, he was the one from whom most had been expected." — *Wikipedia*

He was the first American writer to leave two complete, unpublished novels in the hands of his publisher at his death.

Old School (2003)

- *Students at a small New England prep school live and breathe "the writing life," culminating in competition for a private audience with a visiting celebrity writer.*

In another week I would meet Ernest Hemingway, and walk alone with him in the headmaster's garden. He had chosen my story and made special mention of it for everyone to read. There was no excuse for me to feel anything but joy. I knew this, sure, but what did his blood pressure or James Joyce's wife or Fitzgerald's pretty mouth or sleeping late or getting up early have to do with my story? I didn't want Ernest Hemingway's advice, I wanted his attention.

— **Tobias Wolff** *(1945-) American author*

Mrs. Dalloway (1925)

- *A day in the life of protagonist Clarissa Dalloway in post-World War I England in which she readies her house for a party and relieves memories of her carefree youth and early loves.*

And of course she enjoyed life immensely. It was her nature to enjoy . . . Anyhow there was no bitterness in her; none of that sense of moral virtue which is so repulsive in good women. She enjoyed practically everything. If you walked with her in Hyde Park now it was a bed of tulips, now a child in a perambulator, now some absurd little drama she made up on the spur of the moment.

. . .

She had a sense of comedy that was really exquisite, but she needed people, always people, to bring it out, with the inevitable result that she frittered her time away, lunching, dining, giving these incessant parties of hers, talking nonsense, saying things she didn't mean, blunting the edge of her mind, losing her discrimination.

— **Virginia Woolf** *(1882-1941) English author, essayist, publisher, and writer of short stories*

To the Lighthouse (1927)

- *The lifestyle of a large complex family on summer holiday whose plan to sail to a nearby lighthouse is repeatedly postponed to the consternation of the youngest child.*

. . . Had there been an axe handy, a poker, or any weapon that would have gashed a hole in his father's breast and killed him, there and then, James would have seized it. Such were the extremes of emotion that Mr. Ramsay excited in his children's breasts by his mere presence; standing, as now, lean as a knife, narrow as the blade of one, grinning sarcastically, not only with the pleasure of disillusioning his son and casting ridicule upon his wife, who was ten thousand times better in every way than he was (James thought), but also with some secret conceit at his own accuracy of judgment. What he said was true. It was always true. He was incapable of

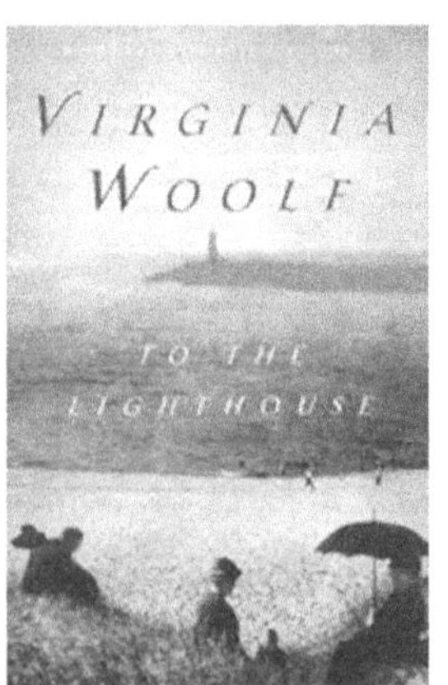

untruth; never tampered with a fact; never altered a disagreeable word to suit the pleasure or convenience of any mortal being, least of all his own children, . . .

—Virginia Woolf

"Never never have I written so easily, imagined so profusely . . . Soft & pliable, & I think deep, & never a word wrong for a page at a time."

Virginia Woolf's own evaluation of *To the Lighthouse* while a work in progress

— *Today in Literature*

The Caine Mutiny (1951)

■ *Captain Queeg, the skipper of a destroyer-minesweeper during WW II, antagonizes his officers and crew with minor regulations and is eventually relieved of his command during a life-threatening typhoon by his Executive Officer who is later court marshaled.*

. . . "'Scuse me, I'm all finished, Mr. Keefer. I'm up to the toast. Here's to you. You bowled a perfect score. You went after Queeg and got him. You kept your own skirts all white and starch. Steve is finished for good, but you'll be the next captain of the *Caine*. You'll retire old and full of fat fitness reports. . . . So you won't mind a li'l verbal reprimand from me, what does it mean? I defended Steve because I found out the wrong guy was on trial. Only way I could defend him was to sink Queeq for you. I'm sore that I was pushed into that spot, and ashamed of what I did, and thass why I'm drunk. Queeg deserved better at my hands. I owed him a favor, don't you see? He stopped Hermann Goering from washing his fat behind with my mother.

"So I'm not going to eat your dinner, Mr. Keefer, or drink your wine, but simply make my toast and go. Here's to you, Mr. Caine's favorite author, and here's to your book."

He threw the yellow wine in Keefer's face.

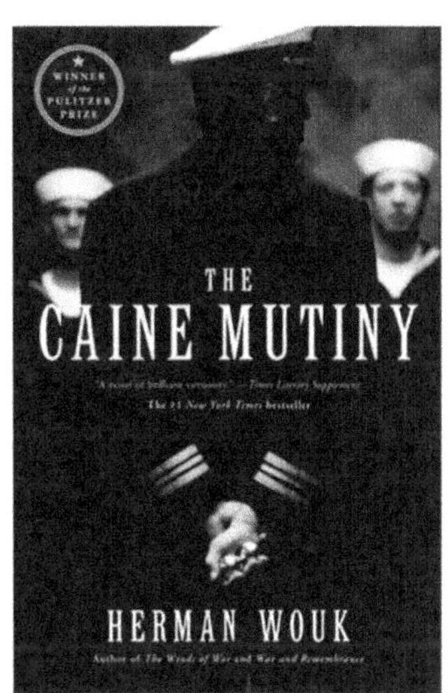

— **Herman Wouk** *(1915-)*

American author

Native Son (1940)

- *The downward spiral of Bigger Thomas, a young black man who in a moment of panic kills a young white woman.*

"His most significant contribution was his desire to accurately portray blacks to white readers." —Paul Gilroy

The man's voice trailed off and he stooped again and poked the shovel deeper. Bigger saw come into full view on the surface of the ashes several small pieces of white bone. Instantly, his whole body was wrapped in a sheet of fear.

"It's bone. . . ."

"Aw," one of the men said. "That's just some garbage they're burning. . . ."

"Naw! Wait; let's *see* that!"

"Toorman, come here. You studied medicine once. . . ."

The man called Toorman reached out his foot and kicked an oblong bone from the ashes; it slid a few inches over the concrete floor.

"My God! It's from a *body*. . . ."

"And look! Here's something. . . ." One of them stooped and picked up a bit of round metal and held it close to his eyes.

"It's an earring. . . ."

— **Richard Wright** *(1908-1960) American author*

Y

The Easter Parade (1976)

- *The lives of sisters Sarah and Emily Grimes as they struggle over four decades on different trajectories to find love and happiness.*

"I think you've about covered it, dear," Tony said with a barely perceptible wink at their guests.

"Oh," she said. "Well, all right." And she quickly took a drink to hide her mouth. That mannerism had never changed: whenever Sarah was embarrassed, after she'd told a joke and was waiting for the laughter, or when she was afraid she'd talked too much, she would go for her mouth as if to cover nakedness—with Cokes or popsicles as a child, with drinks or cigarettes now. Maybe all the years of splayed, protruding teeth, and then of braces, had made her mouth the most vulnerable part of her for life.

— **Richard Yates** *(1926-1992) American novelist and short story writer*

Z

We (1922)

- *Protagonist D-503 meets and falls in love with I-330 a member of a resistance group attempting to overthrow the dystopian society of the Benefactor.*

"I-330, my sweet . . . while it isn't too late . . . Do you want me to give up everything, forget everything and we can go off together, behind the Wall, to be with those people . . . whoever they are?"

She shook her head. Through the dark windows of her eyes, there, inside her, I saw that the wood-fire was blazing, the sparks and tongues of the fire ascended and there were piled heaps of dry, pitch-black wood. And it was clear to me: it was too late, my words were already redundant . . .

"True literature can only exist when it is created, not by diligent and reliable officials, but by madmen, hermits, heretics, dreamers, rebels, and skeptics."

She stood up, about to leave. If these are the final days, if they are the final minutes . . . I grabbed her by the hand.

"No! Just a little longer—for the Benef . . . for the sake of . . ."

She slowly lifted my hand up to the light—the hairy hand, which I so hated. I wanted to pull it away, but she held it firmly.

"Your hand . . . See, you don't know—and few know this—that various women from here, from our city, have occasionally loved those on the other side. You probably have a few drops of sunny forest blood in you. Maybe that's why I also . . . you . . ."

— **Yevgeny Zamyatin** *(1884-1937) Russian author*

Richard Mansfield in his dual role as Dr. Jekyll
and Mr. Hyde depicted in this 1895 double exposure.
The classic novel was written by Robert Lewis Stevenson

Table 1. All-Time Best, Award-Winners, & Supplement Titles

Number of All-Time Best Citations

> 54 Supplement titles

▌ 57 high scoring titles in *Novels and Novelists*

	Awards	Title	Author	Year	Pages	Type	Grade
6		Things Fall Apart	Chinue Achebe	1958	209	Location	2
3		Hitchhiker's Guide to the Galaxy	Douglas Adams	1979	215	Fantasy	3
3		Watership Down	Richard Adams	1972	481	Fantasy	3
	CYT	Speedboat	Renata Adler	1976	178	Stories	3
3	PNT	Death in the Family (A)	James Agee	1957	318	Family	3
2		Little Women	Louisa May Alcott	1868	449	Family	2
	N	Man With the Golden Arm (The)	Nelson Algren	1949	343	Crime/Mys	1
	>	Walk on the Wild Side (A)	Nelson Algren	1956	346	Culture	1
	CBY	Brick Lane	Monica Ali	2003	369	Character	3
4		Lucky Jim	Kingsley Amis	1954	256	Character	3
2		Money	Martin Amis	1984	363	Character	1
	▌	Fairy Tales	Hans Christian Andersen	1835	1,067	Fantasy	1
	BT	Blind Assassin (The)	Margaret Atwood	2000	521	Crime/Mys	2
2	BYT	Handmaid's Tale (The)	Margaret Atwood	1986	295	Fantasy	2
4	▌	Emma	Jane Austen	1816	446	Relations	3
5	▌	Pride and Prejudice	Jane Austen	1813	334	Relations	2
	>	Young Man with a Horn	Dorothy Baker	1938	243	Character	1
2		Another Country	James Baldwin	1960	436	Culture	3
4		Go Tell it on the Mountain	James Baldwin	1952	291	Family	1
	▌	Cousin Bette	Honore de Balzac	1847	437	Relations	3
	CF	Affliction	Russell Banks	1989	355	Character	3
	PFY	Cloudsplitter	Russell Banks	1998	758	History	2
2		Sot-Weed Factor (The)	John Barth	1960	756	Adventure	2
	CF	Sixty Stories	Donald Barthelme	1981	457	Stories	3
	>	Selected Stories	H. E. Bates	1957	283	Stories	1
2		Wonderful Wizard of Oz (The)	L. Frank Baum	1900	220	Youth	1
	CNY	Wartime Lies	Louis Begley	1991	198	Horror	2
	NF	All Souls' Rising	Madison Smartt Bell	1995	504	History	3
	YT	Him With His Foot in His Mouth	Saul Bellow	1984	294	Stories	3
	YT	More Die of Heartbreak	Saul Bellow	1987	335	Relations	2
	NT	Mr. Sammler's Planet	Saul Bellow	1970	313	Character	3
4	N	Adventures of Augie March (The)	Saul Bellow	1953	616	Character	3
3	P	Herzog	Saul Bellow	1964	371	Character	3
	▌PCNYT	Humboldt's Gift	Saul Bellow	1975	487	Character	3
	>	Jaws	Peter Benchley	1974	311	Horror	1
2		Captain Corelli's Mandolin	Louis de Bernieres	1994	433	Relations	2
	CF	Women in Their Beds	Gina Berriault	1996	342	Stories	2
	▌	Decameron (The)	Giovanni Boccaccio	1360	802	Stories	3
	CYT	2666	Roberto Bolano	2008	893	History	3
	T	Ficciones	Jorge Luis Borges	1962	174	Stories	3
2		Death of the Heart (The)	Elizabeth Bowen	1938	418	Relations	3
3		Sheltering Sky (The)	Paul Bowles	1949	251	Location	2
	NY	Drop City	T. C. Boyle	2003	444	Culture	2

Table 1. All-Time Best, Award-Winners, & Supplement Titles

Number of All-Time Best Citations

\> 54 Supplement titles

▌ 57 high scoring titles in *Novels and Novelists*

Citations	Awards	Title	Author	Year	Pages	Type	Grade
	FY	World's End	T. C. Boyle	1987	457	History	2
	FY	Chaneysville Incident (The)	David Bradley	1981	432	Culture	1
4		Jane Eyre	Charlotte Bronte	1847	488	Character	2
6	▌	Wuthering Heights	Emily Bronte	1847	317	Family	2
	NT	Late Great Creature (The)	Brock Brower	1972	300	Horror	3
2		Pilgrim's Progress (The)	John Bunyan	1678	299	Fantasy	2
5		Clockwork Orange (A)	Anthony Burgess	1962	192	Horror	3
	>	Tarzan of the Apes	Edgar Rice Burroughs	1914	245	Adventure	1
3	T	Naked Lunch	William S. Burroughs	1959	196	Horror	3
	CF	Night Inspector (The)	Frederick Busch	1999	278	Character	2
	PF	Good Scent ... Strange Mountain	Robert Olen Butler	1992	249	Stories	2
2	BYT	Possession: A Romance	A. S. Byatt	1990	555	Relations	2
	YT	Italian Folktales	Italo Calvino	1980	713	Fantasy	3
	CN	American Salvage	Bonnie Jo Campbell	2009	167	Stories	3
	>	Plague (A)	Albert Camus	1947	287	Horror	2
4		Stranger (The)	Albert Camus	1942	123	Character	2
	>	In Cold Blood	Truman Capote	1966	343	Crime/Mys	1
	BT	Oscar and Lucinda	Peter Carey	1988	432	Relations	1
	BYT	True History of the Kelly Gang	Peter Carey	2001	352	Frontier	2
2		Alice's Adventures In Wonderland	Lewis Carroll	1865	97	Fantasy	2
	PCY	Cathedral	Raymond Carver	1983	228	Stories	2
	PCY	Where I'm Calling From: Stories	Raymond Carver	1988	391	Stories	2
5		Death Comes for the Archbishop	Willa Cather	1927	297	Character	3
3		My Antonia	Willa Cather	1918	244	Relations	2
2		Journey to the End of the Night	Louis-Ferdinand Celine	1934	435	Character	2
6	▌	Don Quixote	Miguel de Cervantes	1605	972	Adventure	3
	PCFT	Amazing Adventures Kavalier Clay	Michael Chabon	2000	656	Culture	1
2		Big Sleep (The)	Raymond Chandler	1939	196	Crime/Mys	3
	CY	During the Reign Queen of Persia	Joan Chase	1983	275	Family	1
	CYT	Falconer	John Cheever	1977	211	Crime/Mys	1
	PCNYT	Stories of John Cheever	John Cheever	1978	693	Stories	1
	NT	World of Apples (The)	John Cheever	1973	174	Stories	2
2	N	Wapshot Chronicle (The)	John Cheever	1954	296	Family	2
	▌	Tales (The) (13 vols.)	Anton Chekhov	1903	~4,000	Stories	1
3		Awakening (The)	Kate Chopin	1899	181	Character	2
	>	Murder on the Orient Express	Agatha Christie	1934	212	Crime/Mys	3
	>	King Rat	James Clavell	1962	406	Military	1
	>	Shogun	James Clavell	1975	1,152	Culture	2
	CBY	Disgrace	J. M. Coetzee	1999	220	Family	2
3		Woman in White (The)	Wilkie Collins	1860	564	Crime/Mys	2
	>	The Most Dangerous Game	Richard Connell	1924	48	Adventure	1
4		Heart of Darkness	Joseph Conrad	1902	100	Adventure	2
2		Lord Jim	Joseph Conrad	1899	307	Character	3

Table 1. All-Time Best, Award-Winners, & Supplement Titles

Number of All-Time Best Citations

> 54 Supplement titles

▌ 57 high scoring titles in *Novels and Novelists*

Number of All-Time Best Citations	Awards	Title	Author	Year	Pages	Type	Grade
4		Nostromo	Joseph Conrad	1904	631	Adventure	2
	▌	Adolphe	Benjamin Constant	1816	70	Relations	3
2		Last of the Mohicans (The)	James Fenimore Cooper	1826	374	History	2
	NT	By Love Possessed	James Gould Cozzens	1957	570	Relations	3
	P	Guard of Honor	James Gould Cozzens	1948	614	Military	3
	CY	Being Dead	Jim Crace	2000	196	Crime/Mys	2
2		Red Badge of Courage (The)	Stephen Crane	1895	131	Military	1
	PCF	Hours (The)	Michael Cunningham	1998	226	Relations	3
3		BFG (The)	Roald Dahl	1982	221	Youth	2
2		Matilda	Roald Dahl	1988	240	Youth	1
	CF	Dew Breaker (The)	Edwidge Danticat	2004	242	Crime/Mys	2
	▌	Moll Flanders	Daniel Defoe	1722	310	Crime/Mys	2
4		Robinson Crusoe	Daniel Defoe	1719	275	Location	2
	CNY	Libra	Don DeLillo	1988	456	History	1
	PFT	Mao II	Don DeLillo	1991	241	Military	3
	PCNYT	Underworld	Don DeLillo	1997	827	Culture	2
2	CN	White Noise	Don DeLillo	1984	323	Family	3
	CB	Inheritance of Loss (The)	Kiran Desal	2006	357	Culture	2
	CN	Paris Trout	Peter Dexter	1988	306	Culture	1
	PCN	Brief Wondrous Life Oscar Wao	Junot Diaz	2007	335	Character	2
2		Bleak House	Charles Dickens	1852	880	Relations	2
3		David Copperfield	Charles Dickens	1850	870	Character	2
3		Great Expectations	Charles Dickens	1861	544	Character	2
2		Tale of Two Cities (A)	Charles Dickens	1859	528	History	2
2		Deliverance	James Dickey	1970	278	Adventure	1
	CY	Book of Common Prayer (A)	Joan Didion	1977	272	Location	3
	NF	Frog: A Novel	Stephen Dixon	1991	769	Character	3
2		Berlin Alexanderplatz	Alfred Doblin	1929	635	Character	2
	PCNFYT	Billy Bathgate	E. L. Doctorow	1989	323	Crime/Mys	2
	NT	Book of Daniel (The)	E. L. Doctorow	1971	303	Crime/Mys	1
	CYT	Loon Lake	E. L. Doctorow	1980	258	Character	2
	PCNFT	March (The)	E. L. Doctorow	2005	363	Military	2
2	CYT	Ragtime	E. L. Doctorow	1974	270	Culture	1
	CNF	Stones for Ibarra	Harriet Doerr	1984	214	Culture	3
3		U.S.A. Trilogy	John Dos Passos	1930	1,387	History	3
5	▌	Brothers Karamazov (The)	Fyodor Dostoevsky	1880	936	Family	2
4	▌	Crime and Punishment	Fyodor Dostoevsky	1866	642	Crime/Mys	2
	▌	Idiot (The)	Fyodor Dostoevsky	1869	597	Character	2
	>	Hound of the Baskervilles (The)	Arthur Conan Doyle	1902	161	Crime/Mys	2
2		Sister Carrie	Theodore Dreiser	1900	487	Character	3
5	▌	An American Tragedy	Theodore Dreiser	1925	874	Character	1
	P	Advise and Consent	Allen Drury	1959	616	Occupation	1
3		Rebecca	Daphne du Maurier	1938	376	Crime/Mys	1

Table 1. All-Time Best, Award-Winners, & Supplement Titles

Number of All-Time Best Citations

> 54 Supplement titles

▌ 57 high scoring titles in *Novels and Novelists*

Number of All-Time Best Citations	Awards	Title	Author	Year	Pages	Type	Grade
	>	Corsican Brothers (The)	Alexandre Dumas	1845	63	Adventure	2
2		Count of Monte Cristo (The)	Alexandre Dumas	1844	1,462	Adventure	2
2		Three Musketeers (The)	Alexandre Dumas	1844	694	Adventure	2
3		Alexandria Quartet (The)	Lawrence Durrell	1957	1,090	Relations	2
	▌	Maias (The)	Eca de Queiros	1888	628	Family	3
	CT	What is the What	Dan Eggers	2006	475	History	1
3	▌	Middlemarch	George Eliot	1872	799	Relations	2
	▌	Mill on the Floss (The)	George Eliot	1860	522	Relations	3
	NT	Dick Gibson Show (The)	Stanley Elkin	1971	335	Culture	2
11	N	Invisible Man	Ralph Ellison	1947	581	Culture	2
	CY	King of the Jews	Leslie Epstein	1979	350	Horror	3
	PCY	Middlesex	Jeffrey Eugenides	2002	529	Youth	1
	N	Collected Stories W. Faulkner	William Faulkner	1950	900	Stories	2
	PN	Fable (A)	William Faulkner	1954	437	Military	3
	P	Reivers (The)	William Faulkner	1962	305	Youth	3
4	▌	Absalom, Absalom!	William Faulkner	1936	395	Character	3
5		As I Lay Dying	William Faulkner	1930	261	Family	3
5		Light in August	William Faulkner	1932	507	Relations	2
9	▌	Sound and the Fury (The)	William Faulkner	1929	321	Family	2
2		Birdsong	Sebastian Faulks	1993	402	Military	1
	NTY	Then We Came to the End	Joshua Ferris	2007	385	Occupation	2
	▌	Amelia	Henry Fielding	1751	611	Relations	3
6		Tom Jones	Henry Fielding	1749	825	Character	3
11		Great Gatsby (The)	F. Scott Fitzgerald	1925	180	Relations	1
2		Tender is the Night	F. Scott Fitzgerald	1933	315	Relations	2
	CY	Blue Flower (The)	Penelope Fitzgerald	1997	226	Character	3
	FYT	Tenants of Time (The)	Thomas Flanagan	1988	820	History	3
5		Madame Bovary	Gustave Flaubert	1857	322	Relations	2
	▌	Sentimental Education	Gustave Flaubert	1869	479	Character	1
	>	Casino Royale	Ian Fleming	1953	181	Adventure	2
	>	Eye of the Needle	Ken Follett	1978	313	Adventure	2
5		Good Soldier (The)	Ford Madox Ford	1915	206	Relations	3
	PCFY	Independence Day	Richard Ford	1995	451	Character	3
	CYT	Lay of the Land (The)	Richard Ford	2006	485	Character	3
	FT	Sportswriter (The)	Richard Ford	1986	375	Character	3
3		Howards End	E. M. Forster	1910	293	Family	3
3		Room with a View (A)	E.M. Forster	1908	229	Relations	2
6	▌	Passage to India (A)	E. M. Forster	1924	362	Culture	1
5		French Lieutenant's Woman	John Fowles	1969	467	Relations	2
4		Magus (The)	John Fowles	1966	656	Horror	2
	>	Collector (The)	John Fowles	1963	305	Crime/Mys	2
	PCNFYT	Corrections (The)	Jonathan Franzen	2001	568	Family	3
	BY	Headlong	Michael Frayn	1999	342	Crime/Mys	2

Table 1. All-Time Best, Award-Winners, & Supplement Titles

Number of All-Time Best Citations

> 54 Supplement titles

▌ 57 high scoring titles in *Novels and Novelists*

	Awards	Title	Author	Year	Pages	Type	Grade
	CNT	Cold Mountain	Charles Frazier	1997	356	History	1
	CNY	Frolic of His Own (A)	William Gaddis	1994	586	Occupation	3
	NT	JR	William Gaddis	1975	726	Occupation	2
2		Recognitions (The)	William Gaddis	1955	956	Relations	3
	CNY	Veronica	Mary Gaitskill	2005	227	Relations	3
	YT	Autumn of the Patriarch (The)	Gabriel Garcia Marquez	1976	269	Culture	3
	YT	Chronicle of a Death Foretold	Gabriel Garcia Marquez	1983	120	Crime/Mys	2
3	YT	Love in the Time of Cholera	Gabriel Garcia Marquez	1985	348	Relations	2
7	▌YT	One Hundred Years of Solitude	Gabriel Garcia Marquez	1967	458	Location	3
	NT	Dreaming in Cuban	Cristina Garcia	1992	244	Family	3
	CYT	October Light	John Gardner	1976	434	Family	3
	CYT	Preston Falls	David Gates	1998	338	Character	3
	CF	Jump-Off Creek (The)	Molly Gloss	1989	186	Frontier	1
2		Faust (play)	Johann W. von Goethe	1808	182	Relations	3
2	▌	Dead Souls	Nikolai Gogol	1842	650	Character	3
7		Lord of the Flies	William Golding	1954	235	Youth	1
	▌	Oblomov	Ivan Goncharov	1859	586	Character	3
	YT	My Son's Story	Nadine Gordimer	1990	277	Culture	3
	CY	Final Payments	Mary Gordon	1978	297	Family	3
	>	Six Days of the Condor	James Grady	1975	192	Crime/Mys	2
4		Wind in the Willows (The)	Kenneth Grahame	1908	205	Youth	2
	YT	Flounder (The)	Gunter Grass	1978	547	Fantasy	3
5	T	Tin Drum (The)	Gunter Grass	1959	589	Character	3
	NT	Keepers of the House (The)	Shirley Ann Grau	1964	309	Family	1
4		I, Claudius	Robert Graves	1934	468	History	2
2		Lanark	Alasdair Gray	1981	560	Character	2
2		Loving	Henry Green	1945	204	Family	3
3		Heart of the Matter (The)	Graham Greene	1948	174	Character	2
	P	Way West (The)	A. B. Guthrie Jr.	1949	340	Frontier	3
2		Maltese Falcon (The)	Dashiell Hammett	1930	189	Crime/Mys	2
2		Hunger	Knut Hamsun	1890	232	Character	3
	▌	Mysteries	Knut Hamsun	1892	340	Character	2
	NF	Atticus	Ron Hansen	1996	247	Crime/Mys	3
	CY	Sleepless Nights	Elizabeth Hardwick	1979	151	Culture	2
	▌	Jude the Obscure	Thomas Hardy	1895	449	Relations	2
	▌	Mayor of Casterbridge	Thomas Hardy	1886	354	Relations	1
3		Tess of the D'Urbervilles	Thomas Hardy	1891	464	Character	2
	▌	Go-Between (The)	L. P. Hartley	1953	326	Relations	3
	PNT	You Are Not A Stranger Here	Adam Haslett	2002	237	Character	2
	>	Hawthorne: Tales and Sketches	Nathaniel Hawthorne	1984	1,493	Stories	1
	▌	Blithedale Romance (The)	Nathaniel Hawthorne	1852	166	Relations	2
3		Scarlet Letter (The)	Nathaniel Hawthorne	1850	235	Culture	1
	CNF	Transit of Venus (The)	Shirley Hazzard	1980	337	Relations	3

Table 1. All-Time Best, Award-Winners, & Supplement Titles

Number of All-Time Best Citations

> 54 Supplement titles

▌ 57 high scoring titles in *Novels and Novelists*

	Awards	Title	Author	Year	Pages	Type	Grade
	YT	Beowulf: A New Verse Translation	Seamus Heaney	2000	106	Adventure	3
	>	Mister Roberts (play)	Thomas Heggen	1948	79	Military	1
11	NT	Catch 22	Joseph Heller	1955	464	Military	1
	NF	Ellis Island and Other Stories	Mark Helprin	1981	196	Stories	3
5		Farewell to Arms (A)	Ernest Hemingway	1929	332	Military	2
2		For Whom the Bell Tolls	Ernest Hemingway	1940	471	Military	1
2		Men Without Women (stories)	Ernest Hemingway	1927	232	Stories	1
4		Sun Also Rises (The)	Ernest Hemingway	1926	256	Relations	2
	PN	Old Man and the Sea (The)	Ernest Hemingway	1952	128	Adventure	1
	CN	The Lazarus Project	Aleksandar Hemon	2008	292	Crime/Mys	2
	FY	Collected Stories Amy Hempel	Amy Hempel	2006	403	Stories	3
	>	Collected Stories of O. Henry	O. Henry	1979	837	Stories	2
3		Dune	Frank Herbert	1965	474	Fantasy	3
	NT	Child Buyer (The)	John Hersey	1960	227	Fantasy	2
	NT	Single Pebble (A)	John Hersey	1956	192	Culture	1
	>	Talented Mr. Ripley (The)	Patricia Highsmith	1955	290	Crime/Mys	2
	PN	Mambo Kings Play Songs of Love	Oscar Hijuelos	1989	448	Occupation	2
	CT	Riddley Walker	Russell Hoban	1981	219	Fantasy	3
	CB	Line of Beauty (The)	Alan Hollinghurst	2004	438	Relations	3
2		Iliad (The)	Homer	750 BC	434	Military	3
	>	Best of Simple (The)	Langston Hughes	1961	245	Character	2
	>	Les Miserables	Victor Hugo	1862	1,200	Culture	1
	NT	Home from the Hill	William Humphrey	1958	312	Family	1
4		Their Eyes Were Watching God	Zora Neale Hurston	1937	193	Culture	2
8		Brave New World	Aldous Huxley	1932	268	Fantasy	2
2		Doll's House (A) (play)	Henrik Ibsen	1879	36	Family	3
	NT	Hotel New Hampshire (The)	John Irving	1981	401	Family	1
3		Prayer for Owen Meany (A)	John Irving	1989	641	Character	2
2	CNYT	World According to Garp (The)	John Irving	1976	688	Character	2
	>	Goodby to Berlin	Christopher Isherwood	1939	207	Culture	2
	CBT	Never Let Me Go	Kazuo Ishiguro	2005	288	Youth	2
	BY	Remains of the Day (The)	Kazuo Ishiguro	1989	245	Character	1
	CF	On the Island: New ... Stories	Josephine Jacobsen	1989	256	Stories	3
2		Ambassadors (The)	Henry James	1903	613	Relations	3
▌		Portrait of a Lady	Henry James	1881	522	Character	3
2		Wings of the Dove (The)	Henry James	1902	487	Relations	3
	PNFT	Waiting	Ha Jin	1999	308	Relations	2
	PF	War Trash	Ha Jin	2004	350	Military	1
	CN	Middle Passage	Charles Johnson	1990	209	Culture	2
	PNTY	Tree of Smoke: A Novel	Denis Johnson	2007	624	Military	2
	NY	Lying Low	Diane Johnson	1978	278	Relations	3
	PCNY	Known World (The)	Edward P. Jones	2003	388	Culture	2
2	N	From Here to Eternity	James Jones	1951	816	Military	1

Table 1. All-Time Best, Award-Winners, & Supplement Titles

Number of All-Time Best Citations

\> 54 Supplement titles

▌ 57 high scoring titles in *Novels and Novelists*

	Awards	Title	Author	Year	Pages	Type	Grade
	NT	Pugilist at Rest: Stories (The)	Thom Jones	1993	230	Stories	1
4		Finnegans Wake	James Joyce	1939	672	History	3
6		Portrait of the Artist as Young Man	James Joyce	1916	384	Character	3
10		Ulysses	James Joyce	1922	736	Character	2
	▌	Castle (The)	Franz Kafka	1926	321	Relations	3
	▌	Metamorphosis	Franz Kafka	1915	46	Fantasy	2
4		Trial (The)	Franz Kafka	1925	251	Crime/Mys	2
	PN	Andersonville	MacKinlay Kantor	1955	768	History	1
	PCFYT	Ironweed	William Kennedy	1983	227	Character	2
	CFY	Roscoe	William Kennedy	2002	291	Occupation	1
8		On the Road	Jack Kerouac	1955	307	Youth	2
4		One Flew Over Cuckoo's Nest	Ken Kesey	1962	281	Occupation	1
	CF	Autobiography of My Mother	Jamaica Kincaid	1996	228	Character	3
2		It	Stephen King	1986	1,138	Horror	2
	>	Shining, The	Stephen King	1977	683	Horror	1
3		Stand (The)	Stephen King	1978	1,153	Fantasy	3
	PFY	Poisonwood Bible (The)	Barbara Kingsolver	1998	543	Culture	1
2		Woman Warrior: Memories Girlhood	Maxine Hong Kingston	1975	209	Culture	3
2		Kim	Rudyard Kipling.	1901	338	Location	3
	NT	Separate Peace (A)	John Knowles	1960	204	Youth	1
	>	Darkness at Noon	Arthur Koestler	1940	288	History	2
	>	Painted Bird (The)	Jerry Kosinski	1965	234	Youth	1
	N	Steps	Jerzy Kosinski	1968	145	Horror	2
	YT	Unbearable Lightness of Being	Milan Kundera	1984	314	Relations	2
2		Dangerous Liaisons	Pierre Choderlos de Laclos	1782	393	Relations	3
	YT	Unaccustomed Earth	Jhumpa Lahiri	2008	333	Family	3
2		Lady Chatterley's Lover	D.H. Lawrence	1928	302	Relations	3
3		Rainbow (The)	D. H. Lawrence	1915	496	Family	1
4		Sons and Lovers	D.H. Lawrence	1913	464	Character	3
3		Women in Love	D. H. Lawrence	1920	475	Relations	2
	CF	Family Dancing	David Leavitt	1984	206	Stories	3
	YT	Perfect Spy (A)	John leCarre	1986	608	Crime/Mys	3
	>	The Ugly American	William J. Lederer	1958	230	Culture	2
9	PT	To Kill a Mockingbird	Harper Lee	1960	281	Culture	1
	▌	Hero of Our Time (A)	Mikhail Lermontov	1839	158	Character	2
	YT	Summer Before the Dark (The)	Doris Lessing	1973	273	Character	3
4	T	Golden Notebook (The)	Doris Lessing	1962	635	Character	3
	YT	Fortress of Solitude (The)	Jonathan Lethem	2003	511	Youth	3
	>	Rosemary's Baby	Ira Levin	1967	245	Horror	2
3		Lion, the Witch and the Wardrobe	C. S. Lewis	1950	189	Youth	3
2		Babbitt	Sinclair Lewis	1922	401	Character	2
2		Main Street	Sinclair Lewis	1920	521	Location	1
	>	Indian Why Stories	Frank Linderman	1915	236	Frontier	1

Table 1. All-Time Best, Award-Winners, & Supplement Titles

Number of All-Time Best Citations

> 54 Supplement titles

▌ 57 high scoring titles in *Novels and Novelists*

Citations	Awards	Title	Author	Year	Pages	Type	Grade
	>	Short Stories of Jack London	Jack London	1914	721	Stories	1
5		Call of the Wild (The)	Jack London	1903	126	Frontier	2
5	▌	Under the Volcano	Malcolm Lowry	1947	375	Character	3
	PCN	Foreign Affairs	Allison Lurie	1984	291	Relations	3
	PCNY	Executioner's Song (The)	Norman Mailer	1979	995	Crime/Mys	1
4	NT	Assistant (The)	Bernard Malamud	1957	246	Family	2
	PN	Fixer (The)	Bernard Malamud	1966	335	Crime/Mys	1
	N NF83	Margic Barrel (The)	Bernard Malamud	1958	214	Stories	1
	BT	Remembering Babylon	David Malouf	1993	200	Character	2
2		Buddenbrooks	Thomas Mann	1901	731	Family	2
4		Magic Mountain (The)	Thomas Mann	1924	854	Character	1
	CBT	Wolf Hall	Hilary Mantel	2009	532	History	3
	▌	Betrothed (The)	Alessandro Manzoni	1825	643	History	1
	>	Bad Seed (The)	William March	1954	217	Horror	2
	>	Four Feathers (The)	A. E. W. Mason	1902	400	Military	2
	CNF	Shiloh and Other Stories	Bobbie Ann Mason	1982	247	Stories	3
	YT	Far Tortuga	Peter Matthiessen	1975	408	Location	3
	▌	Complete Short Stories (3 vols.)	Somerset Maugham	1951	681	Stories	1
2		Of Human Bondage	W. Somerset Maugham	1915	611	Relations	2
	PCN	So Long, See You Tomorrow	William Maxwell	1980	135	Family	1
	CNT	All the Pretty Horses	Cormac McCarthy	1992	302	Frontier	1
2		Blood Meridian	Cormac McCarthy	1985	337	Frontier	1
	PCT	Road (The)	Cormac McCarthy	2006	287	Fantasy	1
3		Heart Is a Lonely Hunter (The)	Carson McCullers	1940	359	Relations	3
	NT	Charming Billy	Alice McDermott	1998	280	Relations	3
	PNF	That Night	Alice McDermott	1987	184	Relations	3
	YT	Saturday	Ian McEwan	2005	289	Horror	2
2	CBYT	Atonement	Ian McEwan	2001	351	Relations	1
	NT	Ninety-Two in the Shade	Thomas McGuane	1973	197	Adventure	2
	NT	Farragan's Retreat	Tom McHale	1971	311	Family	2
	>	Sand Pebbles (The)	Richard McKenna	1962	597	Military	1
	PCF	Lonesome Dove	Larry McMurtry	1985	864	Frontier	2
	PN	Elbow Room	James Alan McPherson	1977	241	Stories	2
6		Moby-Dick	Herman Melville	1851	520	Location	3
	>	Centennial	James A. Michener	1974	909	History	1
	P	Tales of the South Pacific	James A. Michener	1947	384	Stories	1
	>	Death of a Salesman (play)	Arthur Miller	1943	144	Family	1
4		Tropic of Cancer	Henry Miller	1934	318	Character	3
	PN	Martin Dressler	Steven Millhauser	1996	304	Occupation	1
3		Winnie-the-Pooh	A. A. Milne	1926	161	Youth	1
	CB	Cloud Atlas	David Mitchell	2004	529	Relations	1
7		Gone with the Wind	Margaret Mitchell	1936	1,056	History	2
	P	House Made of Dawn	N. Scott Momaday	1968	212	Culture	2

Table 1. All-Time Best, Award-Winners, & Supplement Titles

Number of All-Time Best Citations

> 54 Supplement titles

▌ 57 high scoring titles in *Novels and Novelists*

	Awards	Title	Author	Year	Pages	Type	Grade
	CY	Birds of America: Stories	Lorrie Moore	1998	291	Stories	3
	PY	Gate at the Stairs (A)	Lorrie Moore	2009	336	Youth	2
	NF	Vanished	Mary McGarry Morris	1988	246	Crime	1
	N	Field of Vision	Wright Morris	1956	251	Relations	3
8	PCNY	Beloved	Toni Morrison	1987	324	Family	2
3	CYT	Song of Solomon	Toni Morrison	1977	337	Culture	3
	>	Knock on Any Door	Willard Motley	1947	504	Crime/Mys	1
	PNT	In Other Rooms, Other Wonders	Daniyal Mueenuddin	2009	247	Stories	2
	YT	Friend of My Youth: Stories	Alice Munro	1990	274	Stories	1
	CYT	Hateship, Friendship....Stories	Alice Munro	2001	323	Stories	2
	CY	Love of a Good Woman (The)	Alice Munro	1998	340	Stories	2
	YT	Open Secrets: Stories	Alice Munro	1994	294	Stories	2
	YT	Runaway: Stories	Alice Munro	2004	335	Stories	2
2		Tale of Genji (The)	Lady Murasaki	1021	574	Culture	2
2		Under the Net	Iris Murdoch	1954	253	Character	2
2		Man Without Qualities (The)	Robert Musil	1930	1,770	Character	2
	▌	Young Torless	Robert Musil	1906	217	Relations	2
	NT	Look at the Harlequins!	Vladimir Nabokov	1974	214	Character	3
	NT	Pnin	Vladimir Nabokov	1957	143	Character	1
	NT	Transparent Things	Vladimir Nabokov	1972	104	Character	2
11	NT	Lolita	Vladimir Nabokov	1955	336	Relations	2
3	T	Pale Fire	Vladimir Nabokov	1962	315	Relations	3
3	BY	Bend in the River (A)	V. S. Naipaul	1979	278	Location	3
2		House for Mr Biswas (A)	V.S. Naipaul	1961	564	Character	3
	NFT	Tree of Life (The)	Hugh Nissenson	1985	159	Frontier	3
	NT	Bird Artist (The)	Howard Norman	1994	289	Location	2
	PC	Black Water	Joyce Carol Oates	1992	154	Military	2
	PN	Blonde	Joyce Carol Oates	2000	738	Character	2
	NY	Them	Joyce Carol Oates	1969	508	Relations	3
	PF	What I Lived For	Joyce Carol Oates	1994	608	Character	2
3		At Swim-Two-Birds	Flann O'Brien	1939	239	Youth	3
	YT	In the Lake of the Woods	Tim O'Brien	1994	306	Crime/Mys	2
	PCY	Things They Carried (The)	Tim O'Brien	1990	246	Military	1
	P	Edge of Sadness (The)	Edward O'Connor	1961	640	Occupation	2
	NT	Last Hurrah (The)	Edwin O'Connor	1956	427	Occupation	2
	>	Complete Stories (The)	Flannery O'Connor	1964	550	Stories	1
2		Good Man is Hard to Find (A)	Flannery O'Connor	1953	252	Stories	1
3		Wise Blood	Flannery O'Connor	1949	232	Relations	2
	NT	From the Terrace	John O'Hara	1958	897	Character	3
	N	Ten North Frederick	John O'Hara	1955	408	Family	1
2		Appointment In Samarra	John O'Hara	1934	251	Character	2
	BYT	English Patient (The)	Michael Ondaatje	1992	320	Relations	2
	FY	Netherland	Joseph O'Neill	2008	256	Family	3

Table 1. All-Time Best, Award-Winners, & Supplement Titles

Number of All-Time Best Citations

> 54 Supplement titles

▌ 57 high scoring titles in *Novels and Novelists*

Citations	Awards	Title	Author	Year	Pages	Type	Grade
11		1984	George Orwell	1949	336	Fantasy	2
7		Animal Farm	George Orwell	1945	92	Fantasy	1
	YT	Bound to Violence	Yambo Ouologuem	1971	182	History	3
	NY	Puttermesser Papers (The)	Cynthia Ozick	1997	236	Fantasy	2
	PN	Collected Stories of Grace Paley	Grace Paley	1994	386	Stories	3
	>	Violent Life (A)	Pier Paolo Pasolini	1959	320	Adventure	2
3		Doctor Zhivago	Boris Pasternak	1957	519	Character	1
	CF	Bel Canto	Ann Patchett	2001	318	Military	3
2		Cry, the Beloved Country	Alan Paton	1948	312	Culture	2
	▌	Moon and the Bonfires (The)	Cesare Pavese	1950	154	Character	2
	▌	Political Prisoner (The) (novellas)	Cesare Pavese	1949	123	Culture	3
2		Gormenghast	Mervyn Peake	1950	511	Fantasy	1
	CNF	Second Coming (The)	Walker Percy	1980	360	Relations	2
5	NT	Moviegoer (The)	Walker Percy	1960	243	Character	3
	TY	Out Stealing Horses	Per Petterson	2007	258	Character	2
	CF	Distant Shore (A)	Caryl Phillips	2003	277	Relations	2
	CN	Lark and Termite	Jayne Anne Phillips	2009	254	Youth	2
	CY	Machine Dreams	Jayne Anne Phillips	1984	331	Family	3
	>	Wiseguy	Nicholas Pileggi	1985	246	Crime/Mys	1
	▌	Short Stories	Luigi Pirandello	1936	230	Stories	3
2		Zen Art Motorcycle Maintenance	Robert Pirsig	1974	423	Culture	3
2		Bell Jar (The)	Sylvia Plath	1963	244	Character	1
	>	Complete Tales (The)	Edgar Allen Poe	1938	1,026	Stories	2
	PN	Collected Stories K. Porter	Katherine Ann Porter	1965	504	Stories	2
2		Dance to the Music of Time (A)	Anthony Powell	1951	2,155	Culture	3
	CN	Wheat That Springeth Green	J. F. Powers	1988	335	Occupation	1
	N	Morte D'Urban	J. F. Powers	1962	336	Occupation	2
	NT	Presence of Grace (The)	J. F. Powers	1956	191	Stories	3
	PN	Echo Maker (The)	Richard Powers	2006	451	Crime/Mys	3
	CT	Galatea 2.2	Richard Powers	1995	329	Fantasy	3
	CT	Gold Bug Variations (The)	Richard Powers	1991	638	Occupation	3
	CT	Clockers	Richard Price	1992	599	Crime/Mys	2
	FT	Lush Life	Richard Price	2008	455	Crime/Mys	2
	>	Complete Collected Stories	V. S. Pritchett	1988	1,218	Stories	1
	PY	Close Range: Wyoming Stories	E. Annie Proulx	1999	283	Stories	1
	PCNT	Shipping News (The)	E. Annie Proulx	1993	337	Family	2
5	▌	In Search of Lost Time	Marcel Proust	1913	4,580	Character	3
	>	Godfather (The)	Mario Puzo	1969	448	Crime/Mys	1
	YT	Mason & Dixon	Thomas Pynchon	1997	773	History	3
2		Crying of Lot 49 (The)	Thomas Pynchon	1965	152	Culture	3
4	NYT	Gravity's Rainbow	Thomas Pynchon	1973	760	Family	3
2		Gargantua and Pantagruel	Francois Rabelais	1532	623	Fantasy	3
2		Atlas Shrugged	Ayn Rand	1957	1,168	Occupation	2

Table 1. All-Time Best, Award-Winners, & Supplement Titles

Number of All-Time Best Citations

> 54 Supplement titles

▌ 57 high scoring titles in *Novels and Novelists*

	Awards	Title	Author	Year	Pages	Type	Grade
2		Fountainhead (The)	Ayn Rand	1943	736	Occupation	2
2		All Quiet on the Western Front	Eric Maria Remarque	1929	304	Military	2
3		Wide Sargasso Sea	Jean Rhys	1966	190	Character	3
	▌	Fortunes of Richard Mahoney	Henry Handel Richardson	1917	927	Family	1
3		Clarissa	Samuel Richardson	1748	786	Relations	3
	P	Town (The)	Conrad Richter	1950	300	Family	2
	N	Waters of Kronos (The)	Conrad Richter	1960	176	Fantasy	2
	PCFYT	Gilead	Marilynne Robinson	2004	247	Family	1
	CN	Home	Marilynne Robinson	2008	325	Family	2
2	PFY	Housekeeping	Marilynne Robinson	1980	219	Family	2
3	▌	Call It Sleep	Henry Roth	1934	441	Family	2
	PCNY	Ghost Writer (The)	Philip Roth	1979	180	Fantasy	2
	N	Goodbye, Columbus	Philip Roth	1959	136	Youth	1
	FY	Human Stain (The)	Philip Roth	2000	361	Character	2
	CY	Plot Against America (The)	Philip Roth	2004	362	Occupation	1
	CT	Professor of Desire (The)	Philip Roth	1977	263	Relations	3
2	PCYT	American Pastoral	Philip Roth	1997	423	Family	2
4		Portnoy's Complaint	Philip Roth .	1967	274	Character	3
	CNYT	Anatomy Lesson (The)	Philip Roth	1983	291	Character	3
	CNYT	Counterlife (The)	Philip Roth	1987	324	Character	3
	PFT	Operation Shylock	Philip Roth	1993	398	Culture	3
	PNY	Sabbath's Theater	Phillip Roth	1995	451	Character	3
	BT	God of Small Things (The)	Arundhati Roy	1997	321	Youth	3
	CN	Mating	Norman Rush	1991	474	Relations	3
	PN	Whites	Norman Rush	1986	150	Stories	1
	BY	Moor's Last Sigh (The)	Salman Rushdie	1995	434	Family	3
6	BY	Midnight's Children	Salman Rushdie	1981	589	Family	3
2		Satanic Verses (The)	Salman Rushdie	1988	561	Fantasy	3
	PT	Empire Falls	Richard Russo	2001	483	Culture	2
	NT	Franny and Zoey	J. D. Salinger	1961	201	Youth	3
11		Catcher in the Rye (The)	J. D. Salinger	1945	277	Youth	2
	CN	Union Dues	John Sayles	1977	385	Adventure	3
	CF	Leaving Brooklyn	Lynne Sharon Schwartz	1989	146	Youth	1
	CY	Austerlitz	W. G. Sebald	2001	298	Character	3
2		Suitable Boy (A)	Vikram Seth	1993	1,349	Culture	2
	>	Wild Animals I Have Known	Earnest Thompson Seton	1898	256	Stories	1
	>	Killer Angels (The)	Michael Shaara	1974	374	History	1
2		Hamlet (play)	William Shakespeare	1601	148	Crime/Mys	2
	NT	People Will Always be Kind	Wilfrid Sheed	1973	374	Occupation	2
4		Frankenstein	Mary Shelley	1818	197	Horror	1
	PCB	Stone Diaries (The)	Carol Shields	1994	269	Character	3
	BT	Unless	Carol Shields	2002	213	Family	3
	YT	Absurdistan	Gary Shteyngart	2006	333	Character	3

Table 1. All-Time Best, Award-Winners, & Supplement Titles

Number of All-Time Best Citations

> 54 Supplement titles

▌ 57 high scoring titles in *Novels and Novelists*

	Awards	Title	Author	Year	Pages	Type	Grade
2		Town Like Alice (A)	Nevil Shute	1950	277	Military	1
	▌	Loneliness Long Distance Runner	Allan Sillitoe	1960	176	Stories	1
	▌	Glimpel the Fool	Isaac Bashevis Singer	1957	205	Stories	2
	▌	Séance (The)	Isaac Bashevis Singer	1968	276	Stories	2
	▌	Short Friday	Isaac Bashevis Singer	1964	256	Stories	2
	PC	Thousand Acres (A)	Jane Smiley	1991	371	Frontier	3
	BY	On Beauty	Zadie Smith	2005	443	Family	3
	CYT	White Teeth	Zadie Smith	2000	448	Family	3
	YT	First Circle (The)	Alexander Solzhenitsyn	1968	741	Crime/Mys	1
	>	Cancer Ward	Alexander Solzhenitsyn	1968	536	Occupation	2
2		One Day Life of Ivan Denisovich	Alexander Solzhenitsyn	1978	182	Crime/Mys	1
2		Oedipus the King (play)	Sophocles	429 BC	75	Crime/Mys	3
	NT	Light in the Piazza (The)	Elizabeth Spencer	1960	110	Relations	1
	>	I the Jury	Mickey Spillane	1947	214	Crime/Mys	2
	PN	Collected Stories Jean Stafford	Jean Stafford	1969	463	Stories	3
	▌	Man Who Loved Children (The)	Christina Stead	1940	527	Family	3
9		Grapes of Wrath (The)	John Steinbeck	1939	455	History	1
3		Of Mice and Men	John Steinbeck	1937	105	Relations	1
3		Red and the Black (The)	Stendhal	1830	635	Character	2
3		Tristram Shandy	Laurence Sterne	1760	588	Relations	3
2		Treasure Island	Robert Louis Stevenson	1883	191	Adventure	1
	▌	Confessions of Zeno	Italo Svevo	1923	398	Character	1
	>	Dracula	Bram Stoker	1897	381	Horror	1
	>	Lust for Life	Irving Stone	1934	488	Character	2
	NYT	Dog Soldiers	Robert Stone	1974	342	Crime/Mys	2
	PCNFYT	Flag for Sunrise (A)	Robert Stone	1981	439	Adventure	2
	CNYT	Outerbridge Reach	Robert Stone	1992	409	Location	1
2		Uncle Tom's Cabin	Harriet Beecher Stowe	1852	637	Culture	1
	PC	Olive Kittenridge	Elizabeth Strout	2008	270	Stories	2
	P	Confessions of Nat Turner (The)	William Styron	1967	429	History	1
2		Lie Down in Darkness	William Styron	1951	403	Family	2
3	CN	Sophie's Choice	William Styron	1976	597	Relations	2
2		Perfume	Patrick Süskind	1985	255	Crime/Mys	1
4		Gulliver's Travels	Jonathan Swift	1726	271	Fantasy	3
2		Collected Stories (The)	Peter Taylor	1969	535	Stories	3
	CFY	Old Forest and Other Stories	Peter Taylor	1985	358	Stories	2
	PCNT	Summons to Memphis (A)	Peter Taylor	1986	209	Family	2
	P	Travels of Jaimie McPheeters	Robert Lewis Taylor	1958	535	Frontier	1
3		Vanity Fair	William M. Thackeray	1848	879	Relations	2
	>	Saint Jack	Paul Theroux	1973	247	Character	2
	BYT	White Hotel (The)	D. M. Thomas	1981	274	Character	2
	BYT	Master (The)	Colm Toibin	2004	338	Character	2
8		Lord of the Rings (The)	J. R. R. Tolkien	1954	1,008	Fantasy	1

Table 1. All-Time Best, Award-Winners, & Supplement Titles

Number of All-Time Best Citations

> 54 Supplement titles

▌ 57 high scoring titles in *Novels and Novelists*

	Awards	Title	Author	Year	Pages	Type	Grade
2		Hobbit (The)	J. R. R. Tolkien	1937	320	Fantasy	3
6	▌	War and Peace	Leo Tolstoy	1865	741	History	2
4	▌	Anna Karenina	Leo Tolstoy	1873	817	Relations	2
	PF	Confederacy of Dunces (A)	John Kennedy Toole	1980	394	Character	2
2	▌	Fathers and Sons	Ivan Turgenev	1862	234	Relations	3
3	▌	Adventures Huckleberry Finn	Mark Twain	1884	307	Youth	2
	PCT	Accidental Tourist (The)	Anne Tyler	1985	355	Character	3
	PNT	Breathing Lessons	Anne Tyler	1988	324	Family	3
	PCNFYT	Dinner at Homesick Restaurant	Anne Tyler	1982	303	Family	3
	YT	Bech is Back	John Updike	1982	142	Character	3
	NYT	Bech: A Book	John Updike	1970	206	Character	3
	N	Centaur (The)	John Updike	1963	299	Family	2
	CYT	Coup (The)	John Updike	1978	299	Culture	2
	NT	Poorhouse Fair (The)	John Updike	1959	185	Culture	3
	PCYT	Rabbit at Rest	John Updike	1990	512	Character	2
	PCNYT	Rabbit is Rich	John Updike	1981	423	Family	3
	YT	Rabbit Redux	John Updike	1971	407	Character	3
	CYT	Roger's Version	John Updike	1986	329	Relations	3
3	NT	Rabbit, Run	John Updike	1960	272	Character	3
	YT	Aunt Julia and the Script Writer	Mario Vargas Llosa	1982	374	Youth	2
	NT	Burr	Gore Vidal	1973	430	History	1
	CN	Europe Central	William T. Vollmann	2005	752	History	2
2		Candide	Voltaire	1759	113	Adventure	2
	T	Cat's Cradle	Kurt Vonnegut Jr.	1963	287	Fantasy	3
8	NY	Slaughterhouse Five	Kurt Vonnegut	1969	224	Military	2
3	PN	Color Purple (The)	Alice Walker	1982	244	Culture	2
4	P	All the King's Men	Robert Penn Warren	1946	661	Occupation	1
8		Brideshead Revisited	Evelyn Waugh	1945	351	Relations	3
2		Handful of Dust (A)	Evelyn Waugh	1934	210	Relations	2
2		Scoop	Evelyn Waugh	1937	319	Character	1
	>	War of the Worlds (The)	H. G. Wells	1898	136	Fantasy	2
	NYT	Collected Stories Eudora Welty	Eudora Welty	1980	622	Stories	2
	NYT	Losing Battles	Eudora Welty	1970	436	Family	3
	PNT	Optimist's Daughter (The)	Eudora Welty	1972	110	Family	3
	NT	Devil's Advocate (The)	Morris West	1959	319	Occupation	2
	▌	Complete Works (The)	Nathanael West	1957	421	Stories	2
2		Day of the Locust (The)	Nathanael West	1939	149	Relations	2
3		House of Mirth (The)	Edith Wharton	1905	345	Character	3
3		Age of Innocence (The)	Edith Wharton	1920	320	Relations	1
2		Charlotte's Web	E. B. White	1952	184	Youth	2
	PCY	John Henry Days	Colson Whitehead	2001	389	Culture	2
2		Leaves of Grass	Walt Whitman	1892	441	Culture	3
	FT	Philadelphia Fire	John Edgar Wideman	1990	199	Culture	3

Table 1. All-Time Best, Award-Winners, & Supplement Titles

Number of All-Time Best Citations

> 54 Supplement titles

▌ 57 high scoring titles in *Novels and Novelists*

Number of All-Time Best Citations	Awards	Title	Author	Year	Pages	Type	Grade
	PN	Evidence of Things Unseen	Marianne Wiggins	2003	382	History	3
	>	Picture of Dorian Gray	Oscar Wilde	1891	248	Horror	1
	N	Eighth Day (The)	Thornton Wilder	1967	435	Family	1
2		Bridge of San Luis Rey (The)	Thornton Wilder	1927	103	Culture	3
	>	Streetcar Named Desire (play)	Tennessee Williams	1947	179	Family	1
	CN	Beyond the Bedroom Wall	Larry Woiwode	1975	619	Family	2
	>	Look Homeward, Angel	Thomas Wolfe	1929	528	Family	2
	CYT	Bonfire of the Vanities (The)	Tom Wolfe	1987	685	Culture	1
	NT	Man in Full (A)	Tom Wolfe	1998	742	Character	2
	CF	Old School	Tobias Wolff	2003	195	Youth	1
3		Mrs. Dalloway	Virginia Woolf	1925	191	Character	3
7		To the Lighthouse	Virginia Woolf	1927	228	Family	2
	PN	Caine Mutiny (The)	Herman Wouk	1951	616	Military	1
5		Native Son	Richard Wright	1940	430	Crime/Mys	1
	CY	Easter Parade (The)	Richard Yates	1976	229	Family	2
	▌	We	Yevgeny Zamyatin	1922	203	Fantasy	3

All-Time Best Citations (1st column) report the number of times the title has been cited by two or more of 12 "Top 100" lists (page 9).

Awards (2nd column) report the following awards received by the title (page 11):

P Pulitzer Prize (1918-) **F** Pen/Faulkner (1981-) The Pulizer and Pen/Faulkner awards are listed for the previous year's publicaions. **C** National Book Critics Circle Award (1975-)

N National Book Award (1950-) **B** Booker (1969-) **T** *Time* Magazine ("Year's Best" 1956-)

Y *New York Times* ("Year's Best" 1968-). *NYT* announces no winner. Winning award is underlined.

> 54 Supplement titles selected by the present author (page 12).

▌ 57 titles listed in *Novels and Novelists* scoring a full five stars on all four evaluation criteria: Readability, Characterization, Plot, and Literary Merit (page 11).

Year reports the year of first publication; for short stories the collection's publication date.

Pages report the page count of the story proper.

Type reports the volume's central subject matter in one of 15 descriptive categories (page 17).

Grade reports the author's "Secondary Appraisal" (page 13).

Table 2. Title & Author Listed by Novel Type & Grade

Title	Author	Type	Grade
Tarzan of the Apes	Edgar Rice Burroughs	Adventure	1
The Most Dangerous Game	Richard Connell	Adventure	1
Deliverance	James Dickey	Adventure	1
Old Man and the Sea (The)	Ernest Hemingway	Adventure	1
Treasure Island	Robert Louis Stevenson	Adventure	1
Sot-Weed Factor (The)	John Barth	Adventure	2
Heart of Darkness	Joseph Conrad	Adventure	2
Nostromo	Joseph Conrad	Adventure	2
Corsican Brothers (The)	Alexandre Dumas	Adventure	2
Count of Monte Cristo (The)	Alexandre Dumas	Adventure	2
Three Musketeers (The)	Alexandre Dumas	Adventure	2
Casino Royale	Ian Fleming	Adventure	2
Eye of the Needle	Ken Follett	Adventure	2
Ninety-Two in the Shade	Thomas McGuane	Adventure	2
Violent Life (A)	Pier Paolo Pasolini	Adventure	2
Flag for Sunrise (A)	Robert Stone	Adventure	2
Candide	Voltaire	Adventure	2
Don Quixote	Miguel de Cervantes	Adventure	3
Beowulf: A New Verse Translation	Seamus Heaney	Adventure	3
Union Dues	John Sayles	Adventure	3
Money	Martin Amis	Character	1
Young Man with a Horn	Dorothy Baker	Character	1
An American Tragedy	Theodore Dreiser	Character	1
Sentimental Education	Gustave Flaubert	Character	1
Remains of the Day (The)	Kazuo Ishiguro	Character	1
Magic Mountain (The)	Thomas Mann	Character	1
Pnin	Vladimir Nabokov	Character	1
Doctor Zhivago	Boris Pasternak	Character	1
Bell Jar (The)	Sylvia Plath	Character	1
Confessions of Zeno	Italo Svevo	Character	1
Scoop	Evelyn Waugh	Character	1
Jane Eyre	Charlotte Bronte	Character	2
Night Inspector (The)	Frederick Busch	Character	2
Stranger (The)	Albert Camus	Character	2
Journey to the End of the Night	Louis-Ferdinand Celine	Character	2
Awakening (The)	Kate Chopin	Character	2
Brief Wondrous Life of Oscar Wao	Junot Diaz	Character	2
David Copperfield	Charles Dickens	Character	2
Great Expectations	Charles Dickens	Character	2
Berlin Alexanderplatz	Alfred Doblin	Character	2
Loon Lake	E. L. Doctorow	Character	2
Idiot (The)	Fyodor Dostoevsky	Character	2
Lanark	Alasdair Gray	Character	2
Heart of the Matter (The)	Graham Greene	Character	2
Mysteries	Knut Hamsun	Character	2
Tess of the D'Urbervilles	Thomas Hardy	Character	2
You Are Not A Stranger Here	Adam Haslett	Character	2
Best of Simple (The)	Langston Hughes	Character	2
Prayer for Owen Meany (A)	John Irving	Character	2
World According to Garp (The)	John Irving	Character	2
Ulysses	James Joyce	Character	2
Ironweed	William Kennedy	Character	2
Hero of Our Time (A)	Mikhail Lermontov	Character	2
Babbitt	Sinclair Lewis	Character	2
Remembering Babylon	David Malouf	Character	2
Under the Net	Iris Murdoch	Character	2
Man Without Qualities (The)	Robert Musil	Character	2
Transparent Things	Vladimir Nabokov	Character	2

Table 2. Title & Author Listed by Novel Type & Grade

Title	Author	Type	Grade
Blonde	Joyce Carol Oates	Character	2
What I Lived For	Joyce Carol Oates	Character	2
Appointment In Samarra	John O'Hara	Character	2
Moon and the Bonfires (The)	Cesare Pavese	Character	2
Out Stealing Horses	Per Petterson	Character	2
Human Stain (The)	Philip Roth	Character	2
Red and the Black (The)	Stendhal	Character	2
Lust for Life	Irving Stone	Character	2
Saint Jack	Paul Therous	Character	2
White Hotel (The)	D. M. Thomas	Character	2
Master (The)	Colm Toibin	Character	2
Confederacy of Dunces (A)	John Kennedy Toole	Character	2
Rabbit at Rest	John Updike	Character	2
Man in Full (A)	Tom Wolfe	Character	2
Brick Lane	Monica Ali	Character	3
Lucky Jim	Kingsley Amis	Character	3
Affliction	Russell Banks	Character	3
Mr. Sammler's Planet	Saul Bellow	Character	3
Adventures of Augie March (The)	Saul Bellow	Character	3
Herzog	Saul Bellow	Character	3
Humboldt's Gift	Saul Bellow	Character	3
Death Comes for the Archbishop	Willa Cather	Character	3
Lord Jim	Joseph Conrad	Character	3
Frog: A Novel	Stephen Dixon	Character	3
Sister Carrie	Theodore Dreiser	Character	3
Absalom, Absalom!	William Faulkner	Character	3
Tom Jones	Henry Fielding	Character	3
Blue Flower (The)	Penelope Fitzgerald	Character	3
Independence Day	Richard Ford	Character	3
Lay of the Land (The)	Richard Ford	Character	3
Sportswriter (The)	Richard Ford	Character	3
Preston Falls	David Gates	Character	3
Dead Souls	Nikolai Gogol	Character	3
Oblomov	Ivan Goncharov	Character	3
Tin Drum (The)	Gunter Grass	Character	3
Hunger	Knut Hamsun	Character	3
Portrait of a Lady	Henry James	Character	3
Portrait of the Artist as Young Man	James Joyce	Character	3
Autobiography of My Mother	Jamaica Kincaid	Character	3
Sons and Lovers	D.H. Lawrence	Character	3
Summer Before the Dark (The)	Doris Lessing	Character	3
Golden Notebook (The)	Doris Lessing	Character	3
Under the Volcano	Malcolm Lowry	Character	3
Tropic of Cancer	Henry Miller	Character	3
Look at the Harlequins!	Vladimir Nabokov	Character	3
House for Mr Biswas (A)	V.S. Naipaul	Character	3
From the Terrace	John O'Hara	Character	3
Moviegoer (The)	Walker Percy	Character	3
In Search of Lost Time	Marcel Proust	Character	3
Wide Sargasso Sea	Jean Rhys	Character	3
Portnoy's Complaint	Philip Roth .	Character	3
Anatomy Lesson (The)	Philip Roth	Character	3
Counterlife (The)	Philip Roth	Character	3
Sabbath's Theater	Phillip Roth	Character	3
Austerlitz	W. G. Sebald	Character	3
Stone Diaries (The)	Carol Shields	Character	3
Absurdistan	Gary Shteyngart	Character	3
Accidental Tourist (The)	Anne Tyler	Character	3

Table 2. Title & Author Listed by Novel Type & Grade

Title	Author	Type	Grade
Bech is Back	John Updike	Character	3
Bech: A Book	John Updike	Character	3
Rabbit Redux	John Updike	Character	3
Rabbit, Run	John Updike	Character	3
House of Mirth (The)	Edith Wharton	Character	3
Mrs. Dalloway	Virginia Woolf	Character	3
Man With the Golden Arm (The)	Nelson Algren	Crime/Mys	1
In Cold Blood	Truman Capote	Crime/Mys	1
Falconer	John Cheever	Crime/Mys	1
Book of Daniel (The)	E. L. Doctorow	Crime/Mys	1
Rebecca	Daphne du Maurier	Crime/Mys	1
Executioner's Song (The)	Norman Mailer	Crime/Mys	1
Fixer (The)	Bernard Malamud	Crime/Mys	1
Vanished	Mary McGarry Morris	Crime/Mys	1
Knock on Any Door	Willard Motley	Crime/Mys	1
Wiseguy	Nicholas Pileggi	Crime/Mys	1
Godfather (The)	Mario Puzo	Crime/Mys	1
First Circle (The)	Alexander Solzhenitsyn	Crime/Mys	1
One Day in Life of Ivan Denisovich	Alexander Solzhenitsyn	Crime/Mys	1
Perfume	Patrick Süskind	Crime/Mys	1
Native Son	Richard Wright	Crime/Mys	1
Blind Assassin (The)	Margaret Atwood	Crime/Mys	2
Woman in White (The)	Wilkie Collins	Crime/Mys	2
Being Dead	Jim Crace	Crime/Mys	2
Dew Breaker (The)	Edwidge Danticat	Crime/Mys	2
Moll Flanders	Daniel Defoe	Crime/Mys	2
Billy Bathgate	E. L. Doctorow	Crime/Mys	2
Crime and Punishment	Fyodor Dostoevsky	Crime/Mys	2
Hound of the Baskervilles (The)	Arthur Conan Doyle	Crime/Mys	2
Collector (The)	John Fowles	Crime/Mys	2
Headlong	Michael Frayn	Crime/Mys	2
Chronicle of a Death Foretold	Gabriel Garcia Marquez	Crime/Mys	2
Six Days of the Condor	James Grady	Crime/Mys	2
Maltese Falcon (The)	Dashiell Hammett	Crime/Mys	2
The Lazarus Project	Aleksandar Hemon	Crime/Mys	2
Talented Mr. Ripley (The)	Patricia Highsmith	Crime/Mys	2
Trial (The)	Franz Kafka	Crime/Mys	2
In the Lake of the Woods	Tim O'Brien	Crime/Mys	2
Clockers	Richard Price	Crime/Mys	2
Lush Life	Richard Price	Crime/Mys	2
Hamlet (play)	William Shakespeare	Crime/Mys	2
I the Jury	Mickey Spillane	Crime/Mys	2
Dog Soldiers	Robert Stone	Crime/Mys	2
Big Sleep (The)	Raymond Chandler	Crime/Mys	3
Murder on the Orient Express	Agatha Christie	Crime/Mys	3
Atticus	Ron Hansen	Crime/Mys	3
Perfect Spy (A)	John leCarre	Crime/Mys	3
Echo Maker (The)	Richard Powers	Crime/Mys	3
Oedipus the King (play)	Sophocles	Crime/Mys	3
Walk on the Wild Side (A)	Nelson Algren	Culture	1
Chaneysville Incident (The)	David Bradley	Culture	1
Amazing Adventures Kavalier Clay	Michael Chabon	Culture	1
Paris Trout	Peter Dexter	Culture	1
Ragtime	E. L. Doctorow	Culture	1
Passage to India (A)	E. M. Forster	Culture	1
Scarlet Letter (The)	Nathaniel Hawthorne	Culture	1
Single Pebble (A)	John Hersey	Culture	1
Les Miserables	Victor Hugo	Culture	1

Table 2. Title & Author Listed by Novel Type & Grade

Title	Author	Type	Grade
Poisonwood Bible (The)	Barbara Kingsolver	Culture	1
To Kill a Mockingbird	Harper Lee	Culture	1
Uncle Tom's Cabin	Harriet Beecher Stowe	Culture	1
Bonfire of the Vanities (The)	Tom Wolfe	Culture	1
Drop City	T. C. Boyle	Culture	2
Shogun	James Clavell	Culture	2
Underworld	Don DeLillo	Culture	2
Inheritance of Loss (The)	Kiran Desal	Culture	2
Dick Gibson Show (The)	Stanley Elkin	Culture	2
Invisible Man	Ralph Ellison	Culture	2
Sleepless Nights	Elizabeth Hardwick	Culture	2
Their Eyes Were Watching God	Zora Neale Hurston	Culture	2
Goodby to Berlin	Christopher Isherwood	Culture	2
Middle Passage	Charles Johnson	Culture	2
Known World (The)	Edward P. Jones	Culture	2
The Ugly American	William J. Lederer	Culture	2
House Made of Dawn	N. Scott Momaday	Culture	2
Tale of Genji (The)	Lady Murasaki	Culture	2
Cry, the Beloved Country	Alan Paton	Culture	2
Empire Falls	Richard Russo	Culture	2
Suitable Boy (A)	Vikram Seth	Culture	2
Coup (The)	John Updike	Culture	2
Color Purple (The)	Alice Walker	Culture	2
John Henry Days	Colson Whitehead	Culture	2
Another Country	James Baldwin	Culture	3
Stones for Ibarra	Harriet Doerr	Culture	3
Autumn of the Patriarch (The)	Gabriel Garcia Marquez	Culture	3
My Son's Story	Nadine Gordimer	Culture	3
Woman Warrior: Memories Girlhood...	Maxine Hong Kingston	Culture	3
Song of Solomon	Toni Morrison	Culture	3
Political Prisoner (The) (novellas)	Cesare Pavese	Culture	3
Zen Art Motorcycle Maintenance	Robert Pirsig	Culture	3
Dance to the Music of Time (A)	Anthony Powell	Culture	3
Crying of Lot 49 (The)	Thomas Pynchon	Culture	3
Operation Shylock	Philip Roth	Culture	3
Poorhouse Fair (The)	John Updike	Culture	3
Philadelphia Fire	John Edgar Wideman	Culture	3
Bridge of San Luis Rey (The)	Thornton Wilder	Culture	3
Leaves of Grass	Walt Whitman	Culture	3
Go Tell it on the Mountain	James Baldwin	Family	1
During the Reign Queen of Persia	Joan Chase	Family	1
Keepers of the House (The)	Shirley Ann Grau	Family	1
Home from the Hill	William Humphrey	Family	1
Hotel New Hampshire (The)	John Irving	Family	1
Rainbow (The)	D. H. Lawrence	Family	1
So Long, See You Tomorrow	William Maxwell	Family	1
Death of a Salesman (play)	Arthur Miller	Family	1
Ten North Frederick	John O'Hara	Family	1
Fortunes of Richard Mahoney	Henry Handel Richardson	Family	1
Gilead	Marilynne Robinson	Family	1
Eighth Day (The)	Thornton Wilder	Family	1
Streetcar Named Desire (A) (play)	Tennessee Williams	Family	1
Little Women	Louisa May Alcott	Family	2
Wuthering Heights	Emily Bronte	Family	2
Wapshot Chronicle (The)	John Cheever	Family	2
Disgrace	J. M. Coetzee	Family	2
Brothers Karamazov (The)	Fyodor Dostoevsky	Family	2
Sound and the Fury (The)	William Faulkner	Family	2

Table 2. Title & Author Listed by Novel Type & Grade

Title	Author	Type	Grade
Assistant (The)	Bernard Malamud	Family	2
Buddenbrooks	Thomas Mann	Family	2
Farragan's Retreat	Tom McHale	Family	2
Beloved	Toni Morrison	Family	2
Shipping News (The)	E. Annie Proulx	Family	2
Town (The)	Conrad Richter	Family	2
Home	Marilynne Robinson	Family	2
Housekeeping	Marilynne Robinson	Family	2
Call It Sleep	Henry Roth	Family	2
American Pastoral	Philip Roth	Family	2
Lie Down in Darkness	William Styron	Family	2
Summons to Memphis (A)	Peter Taylor	Family	2
Centaur (The)	John Updike	Family	2
Beyond the Bedroom Wall	Larry Woiwode	Family	2
Look Homeward, Angel	Thomas Wolfe	Family	2
To the Lighthouse	Virginia Woolf	Family	2
Easter Parade (The)	Richard Yates	Family	2
Death in the Family (A)	James Agee	Family	3
White Noise	Don DeLillo	Family	3
Maias (The)	Eca de Queiros	Family	3
As I Lay Dying	William Faulkner	Family	3
Howards End	E. M. Forster	Family	3
Corrections (The)	Jonathan Franzen	Family	3
Dreaming in Cuban	Cristina Garcia	Family	3
October Light	John Gardner	Family	3
Final Payments	Mary Gordon	Family	3
Loving	Henry Green	Family	3
Doll's House (A) (play)	Henrik Ibsen	Family	3
Unaccustomed Earth	Jhumpa Lahiri	Family	3
Netherland	Joseph O'Neill	Family	3
Machine Dreams	Jayne Anne Phillips	Family	3
Gravity's Rainbow	Thomas Pynchon	Family	3
Moor's Last Sigh (The)	Salman Rushdie	Family	3
Midnight's Children	Salman Rushdie	Family	3
Unless	Carol Shields	Family	3
On Beauty	Zadie Smith	Family	3
White Teeth	Zadie Smith	Family	3
Man Who Loved Children (The)	Christina Stead	Family	3
Breathing Lessons	Anne Tyler	Family	3
Dinner at Homesick Restaurant	Anne Tyler	Family	3
Rabbit is Rich	John Updike	Family	3
Losing Battles	Eudora Welty	Family	3
Optimist's Daughter (The)	Eudora Welty	Family	3
Fairy Tales	Hans Christian Andersen	Fantasy	1
Road (The)	Cormac McCarthy	Fantasy	1
Animal Farm	George Orwell	Fantasy	1
Gormenghast	Mervyn Peake	Fantasy	1
Lord of the Rings (The)	J. R. R. Tolkien	Fantasy	1
Handmaid's Tale (The)	Margaret Atwood	Fantasy	2
Pilgrim's Progress (The)	John Bunyan	Fantasy	2
Alice's Adventures In Wonderland	Lewis Carroll	Fantasy	2
Child Buyer (The)	John Hersey	Fantasy	2
Brave New World	Aldous Huxley	Fantasy	2
Metamorphosis	Franz Kafka	Fantasy	2
1984	George Orwell	Fantasy	2
Puttermesser Papers (The)	Cynthia Ozick	Fantasy	2
Waters of Kronos (The)	Conrad Richter	Fantasy	2
Ghost Writer (The)	Philip Roth	Fantasy	2

Table 2. Title & Author Listed by Novel Type & Grade

Title	Author	Type	Grade
War of the Worlds (The)	H. G. Wells	Fantasy	2
Hitchhiker's Guide to the Galaxy	Douglas Adams	Fantasy	3
Watership Down	Richard Adams	Fantasy	3
Italian Folktales	Italo Calvino	Fantasy	3
Flounder (The)	Gunter Grass	Fantasy	3
Dune	Frank Herbert	Fantasy	3
Riddley Walker	Russell Hoban	Fantasy	3
Stand (The)	Stephen King	Fantasy	3
Galatea 2.2	Richard Powers	Fantasy	3
Gargantua and Pantagruel	Francois Rabelais	Fantasy	3
Satanic Verses (The)	Salman Rushdie	Fantasy	3
Gulliver's Travels	Jonathan Swift	Fantasy	3
Hobbit (The)	J. R. R. Tolkien	Fantasy	3
Cat's Cradle	Kurt Vonnegut Jr.	Fantasy	3
We	Yevgeny Zamyatin	Fantasy	3
Jump-Off Creek (The)	Molly Gloss	Frontier	1
Indian Why Stories	Frank Linderman	Frontier	1
All the Pretty Horses	Cormac McCarthy	Frontier	1
Blood Meridian	Cormac McCarthy	Frontier	1
Travels of Jaimie McPheeters	Robert Lewis Taylor	Frontier	1
True History of the Kelly Gang	Peter Carey	Frontier	2
Call of the Wild (The)	Jack London	Frontier	2
Lonesome Dove	Larry McMurtry	Frontier	2
Way West (The)	A. B. Guthrie Jr.	Frontier	3
Tree of Life (The)	Hugh Nissenson	Frontier	3
Thousand Acres (A)	Jane Smiley	Frontier	3
Libra	Don DeLillo	History	1
What is the What	Dan Eggers	History	1
Cold Mountain	Charles Frazier	History	1
Andersonville	MacKinlay Kantor	History	1
Betrothed (The)	Alessandro Manzoni	History	1
Centennial	James A. Michener	History	1
Killer Angels (The)	Michael Shaara	History	1
Grapes of Wrath (The)	John Steinbeck	History	1
Confessions of Nat Turner (The)	William Styron	History	1
Burr	Gore Vidal	History	1
Cloudsplitter	Russell Banks	History	2
World's End	T. C. Boyle	History	2
Last of the Mohicans (The)	James Fenimore Cooper	History	2
Tale of Two Cities (A)	Charles Dickens	History	2
I, Claudius	Robert Graves	History	2
Darkness at Noon	Arthur Koestler	History	2
Gone with the Wind	Margaret Mitchell	History	2
War and Peace	Leo Tolstoy	History	2
Europe Central	William T. Vollmann	History	2
All Souls' Rising	Madison Smartt Bell	History	3
2666	Roberto Bolano	History	3
U.S.A. Trilogy	John Dos Passos	History	3
Tenants of Time (The)	Thomas Flanagan	History	3
Finnegans Wake	James Joyce	History	3
Wolf Hall	Hilary Mantel	History	3
Bound to Violence	Yambo Ouologuem	History	3
Mason & Dixon	Thomas Pynchon	History	3
Evidence of Things Unseen	Marianne Wiggins	History	3
Jaws	Peter Benchley	Horror	1
Shining, The	Stephen King	Horror	1
Frankenstein	Mary Shelley	Horror	1
Dracula	Bram Stoker	Horror	1

Table 2. Title & Author Listed by Novel Type & Grade

Title	Author	Type	Grade
Picture of Dorian Gray	Oscar Wilde	Horror	1
Wartime Lies	Louis Begley	Horror	2
Plague (A)	Albert Camus	Horror	2
Magus (The)	John Fowles	Horror	2
It	Stephen King	Horror	2
Steps	Jerzy Kosinski	Horror	2
Rosemary's Baby	Ira Levin	Horror	2
Bad Seed (The)	William March	Horror	2
Saturday	Ian McEwan	Horror	2
Late Great Creature (The)	Brock Brower	Horror	3
Clockwork Orange (A)	Anthony Burgess	Horror	3
Naked Lunch	William S. Burroughs	Horror	3
King of the Jews	Leslie Epstein	Horror	3
Main Street	Sinclair Lewis	Location	1
Outerbridge Reach	Robert Stone	Location	1
Things Fall Apart	Chinue Achebe	Location	2
Sheltering Sky (The)	Paul Bowles	Location	2
Robinson Crusoe	Daniel Defoe	Location	2
Bird Artist (The)	Howard Norman	Location	2
Book of Common Prayer (A)	Joan Didion	Location	3
One Hundred Years of Solitude	Gabriel Garcia Marquez	Location	3
Kim	Rudyard Kipling.	Location	3
Far Tortuga	Peter Matthiessen	Location	3
Moby-Dick	Herman Melville	Location	3
Bend in the River (A)	V. S. Naipaul	Location	3
King Rat	James Clavell	Military	1
Red Badge of Courage (The)	Stephen Crane	Military	1
Birdsong	Sebastian Faulks	Military	1
Mister Roberts (play)	Thomas Heggen	Military	1
Catch 22	Joseph Heller	Military	1
War Trash	Ha Jin	Military	1
From Here to Eternity	James Jones	Military	1
Sand Pebbles (The)	Richard McKenna	Military	1
Things They Carried (The)	Tim O'Brien	Military	1
Town Like Alice (A)	Nevil Shute	Military	1
Caine Mutiny (The)	Herman Wouk	Military	1
March (The)	E. L. Doctorow	Military	2
Farewell to Arms (A)	Ernest Hemingway	Military	2
Tree of Smoke: A Novel	Denis Johnson	Military	2
Four Feathers (The)	A. E. W. Mason	Military	2
Black Water	Joyce Carol Oates	Military	2
All Quiet on the Western Front	Eric Maria Remarque	Military	2
Slaughterhouse Five	Kurt Vonnegut	Military	2
Guard of Honor	James Gould Cozzens	Military	3
Mao II	Don DeLillo	Military	3
Fable (A)	William Faulkner	Military	3
Iliad (The)	Homer	Military	3
Bel Canto	Ann Patchett	Military	3
For Whom the Bell Tolls	Ernest Hemingway	Military	1
Advise and Consent	Allen Drury	Occupation	1
Roscoe	William Kennedy	Occupation	1
One Flew Over the Cuckoo's Nest	Ken Kesey	Occupation	1
Martin Dressler	Steven Millhauser	Occupation	1
Wheat That Springeth Green	J. F. Powers	Occupation	1
Plot Against America (The)	Philip Roth	Occupation	1
All the King's Men	Robert Penn Warren	Occupation	1
Then We Came to the End	Joshua Ferris	Occupation	2
JR	William Gaddis	Occupation	2

Table 2. Title & Author Listed by Novel Type & Grade

Title	Author	Type	Grade
Mambo Kings Play Songs of Love	Oscar Hijuelos	Occupation	2
Edge of Sadness (The)	Edward O'Connor	Occupation	2
Last Hurrah (The)	Edwin O'Connor	Occupation	2
Morte D'Urban	J. F. Powers	Occupation	2
Atlas Shrugged	Ayn Rand	Occupation	2
Fountainhead (The)	Ayn Rand	Occupation	2
People Will Always be Kind	Wilfrid Sheed	Occupation	2
Cancer Ward	Alexander Solzhenitsyn	Occupation	2
Devil's Advocate (The)	Morris West	Occupation	2
Frolic of His Own (A)	William Gaddis	Occupation	3
Gold Bug Variations (The)	Richard Powers	Occupation	3
Oscar and Lucinda	Peter Carey	Relations	1
Great Gatsby (The)	F. Scott Fitzgerald	Relations	1
Mayor of Casterbridge	Thomas Hardy	Relations	1
Atonement	Ian McEwan	Relations	1
Cloud Atlas	David Mitchell	Relations	1
Light in the Piazza (The)	Elizabeth Spencer	Relations	1
Of Mice and Men	John Steinbeck	Relations	1
Age of Innocence (The)	Edith Wharton	Relations	1
Pride and Prejudice	Jane Austen	Relations	2
More Die of Heartbreak	Saul Bellow	Relations	2
Captain Corelli's Mandolin	Louis de Bernieres	Relations	2
Possession: A Romance	A. S. Byatt	Relations	2
My Antonia	Willa Cather	Relations	2
Bleak House	Charles Dickens	Relations	2
Alexandria Quartet (The)	Lawrence Durrell	Relations	2
Middlemarch	George Eliot	Relations	2
Light in August	William Faulkner	Relations	2
Tender is the Night	F. Scott Fitzgerald	Relations	2
Madame Bovary	Gustave Flaubert	Relations	2
Room with a View (A)	E.M. Forster	Relations	2
French Lieutenant's Woman (The)	John Fowles	Relations	2
Love in the Time of Cholera	Gabriel Garcia Marquez	Relations	2
Jude the Obscure	Thomas Hardy	Relations	2
Blithedale Romance (The)	Nathaniel Hawthorne	Relations	2
Sun Also Rises (The)	Ernest Hemingway	Relations	2
Waiting	Ha Jin	Relations	2
Unbearable Lightness of Being	Milan Kundera	Relations	2
Women in Love	D. H. Lawrence	Relations	2
Of Human Bondage	W. Somerset Maugham	Relations	2
Young Torless	Robert Musil	Relations	2
Lolita	Vladimir Nabokov	Relations	2
Wise Blood	Flannery O'Connor	Relations	2
English Patient (The)	Michael Ondaatje	Relations	2
Second Coming (The)	Walker Percy	Relations	2
Distant Shore (A)	Caryl Phillips	Relations	2
Sophie's Choice	William Styron	Relations	2
Vanity Fair	William M. Thackeray	Relations	2
Anna Karenina	Leo Tolstoy	Relations	2
Handful of Dust (A)	Evelyn Waugh	Relations	2
Day of the Locust (The)	Nathanael West	Relations	2
Emma	Jane Austen	Relations	3
Cousin Bette	Honore de Balzac	Relations	3
Death of the Heart (The)	Elizabeth Bowen	Relations	3
Adolphe	Benjamin Constant	Relations	3
By Love Possessed	James Gould Cozzens	Relations	3
Hours (The)	Michael Cunningham	Relations	3
Mill on the Floss (The)	George Eliot	Relations	3

Table 2. Title & Author Listed by Novel Type & Grade

Title	Author	Type	Grade
Amelia	Henry Fielding	Relations	3
Good Soldier (The)	Ford Madox Ford	Relations	3
Recognitions (The)	William Gaddis	Relations	3
Veronica	Mary Gaitskill	Relations	3
Faust (play)	Johann Wolfgang von Goethe	Relations	3
Go-Between (The)	L. P. Hartley	Relations	3
Transit of Venus (The)	Shirley Hazzard	Relations	3
Line of Beauty (The)	Alan Hollinghurst	Relations	3
Ambassadors (The)	Henry James	Relations	3
Wings of the Dove (The)	Henry James	Relations	3
Lying Low	Diane Johnson	Relations	3
Castle (The)	Franz Kafka	Relations	3
Dangerous Liaisons	Pierre Choderlos de Laclos	Relations	3
Lady Chatterley's Lover	D.H. Lawrence	Relations	3
Foreign Affairs	Allison Lurie	Relations	3
Heart Is a Lonely Hunter (The)	Carson McCullers	Relations	3
Charming Billy	Alice McDermott	Relations	3
That Night	Alice McDermott	Relations	3
Field of Vision	Wright Morris	Relations	3
Pale Fire	Vladimir Nabokov	Relations	3
Them	Joyce Carol Oates	Relations	3
Clarissa	Samuel Richardson	Relations	3
Professor of Desire (The)	Philip Roth	Relations	3
Mating	Norman Rush	Relations	3
Tristram Shandy	Laurence Sterne	Relations	3
Fathers and Sons	Ivan Turgenev	Relations	3
Roger's Version	John Updike	Relations	3
Brideshead Revisited	Evelyn Waugh	Relations	3
Stories of John Cheever	John Cheever	Stories	1
Tales (The) (13 vols.)	Anton Chekhov	Stories	1
Hawthorne: Tales and Sketches	Nathaniel Hawthorne	Stories	1
Men Without Women (stories)	Ernest Hemingway	Stories	1
Pugilist at Rest: Stories (The)	Thom Jones	Stories	1
Short Stories of Jack London	Jack London	Stories	1
Margic Barrel (The)	Bernard Malamud	Stories	1
Complete Short Stories (3 vols.)	Somerset Maugham	Stories	1
Tales of the South Pacific	James A. Michener	Stories	1
Friend of My Youth: Stories	Alice Munro	Stories	1
Complete Stories (The)	Flannery O'Connor	Stories	1
Good Man is Hard to Find (A)	Flannery O'Connor	Stories	1
Complete Collected Stories	V. S. Pritchett	Stories	1
Close Range: Wyoming Stories	E. Annie Proulx	Stories	1
Whites	Norman Rush	Stories	1
Wild Animals I Have Known	Earnest Thompson Seton	Stories	1
Loneliness Long Distance Runner	Allan Sillitoe	Stories	1
Women in Their Beds	Gina Berriault	Stories	2
Good Scent From a Strange Mountain	Robert Olen Butler	Stories	2
Cathedral	Raymond Carver	Stories	2
Where I'm Calling From: Stories	Raymond Carver	Stories	2
World of Apples (The)	John Cheever	Stories	2
Collected Stories William Faulkner	William Faulkner	Stories	2
Collected Stories of O. Henry	O. Henry	Stories	2
Elbow Room	James Alan McPherson	Stories	2
In Other Rooms, Other Wonders	Daniyal Mueenuddin	Stories	2
Hateship, Friendship....Stories	Alice Munro	Stories	2
Love of a Good Woman (The)	Alice Munro	Stories	2
Open Secrets: Stories	Alice Munro	Stories	2
Runaway: Stories	Alice Munro	Stories	2

Table 2. Title & Author Listed by Novel Type & Grade

Title	Author	Type	Grade
Complete Tales (The)	Edgar Allen Poe	Stories	2
Collected Stories Katherine Porter	Katherine Ann Porter	Stories	2
Glimpel the Fool	Isaac Bashevis Singer	Stories	2
Séance (The)	Isaac Bashevis Singer	Stories	2
Short Friday	Isaac Bashevis Singer	Stories	2
Olive Kittenridge	Elizabeth Strout	Stories	2
Old Forest and Other Stories	Peter Taylor	Stories	2
Collected Stories of Eudora Welty	Eudora Welty	Stories	2
Complete Works (The)	Nathanael West	Stories	2
Speedboat	Renata Adler	Stories	3
Sixty Stories	Donald Barthelme	Stories	3
Him With His Foot in His Mouth	Saul Bellow	Stories	3
Decameron (The)	Giovanni Boccaccio	Stories	3
Ficciones	Jorge Luis Borges	Stories	3
American Salvage	Bonnie Jo Campbell	Stories	3
Ellis Island and Other Stories	Mark Helprin	Stories	3
Collected Stories of Amy Hempel	Amy Hempel	Stories	3
On the Island: New Selected Stories	Josephine Jacobsen	Stories	3
Family Dancing	David Leavitt	Stories	3
Shiloh and Other Stories	Bobbie Ann Mason	Stories	3
Birds of America: Stories	Lorrie Moore	Stories	3
Collected Stories of Grace Paley	Grace Paley	Stories	3
Short Stories	Luigi Pirandello	Stories	3
Presence of Grace (The)	J. F. Powers	Stories	3
Collected Stories of Jean Stafford	Jean Stafford	Stories	3
Collected Stories (The)	Peter Taylor	Stories	3
Selected Stories	H. E. Bates	Stories	1
Wonderful Wizard of Oz (The)	L. Frank Baum	Youth	1
Matilda	Roald Dahl	Youth	1
Middlesex	Jeffrey Eugenides	Youth	1
Lord of the Flies	William Golding	Youth	1
Painted Bird (The)	Jerry Kosinski	Youth	1
Separate Peace (A)	John Knowles	Youth	1
Winnie-the-Pooh	A. A. Milne	Youth	1
Goodbye, Columbus	Philip Roth	Youth	1
Leaving Brooklyn	Lynne Sharon Schwartz	Youth	1
Old School	Tobias Wolff	Youth	1
BFG (The)	Roald Dahl	Youth	2
Wind in the Willows (The)	Kenneth Grahame	Youth	2
Never Let Me Go	Kazuo Ishiguro	Youth	2
On the Road	Jack Kerouac	Youth	2
Gate at the Stairs (A)	Lorrie Moore	Youth	2
Lark and Termite	Jayne Anne Phillips	Youth	2
Catcher in the Rye (The)	J. D. Salinger	Youth	2
Adventures Huckleberry Finn	Mark Twain	Youth	2
Aunt Julia and the Script Writer	Mario Vargas Llosa	Youth	2
Charlotte's Web	E. B. White	Youth	2
Reivers (The)	William Faulkner	Youth	3
Fortress of Solitude (The)	Jonathan Lethem	Youth	3
Lion, the Witch and the Wardrobe	C. S. Lewis	Youth	3
At Swim-Two-Birds	Flann O'Brien	Youth	3
God of Small Things (The)	Arundhati Roy	Youth	3
Franny and Zoey	J. D. Salinger	Youth	3

Table 3. Bestsellers (Publisher's Weekly) 1917-2009

Title	Author	Year	Pages	Type
Mr. Britling Sees it Through	H. G. Wells	1917	449	Culture
The U. P. Trail	Zane Grey	1918	433	Frontier
The Four Horsemen of the Apocalypse	V. Blasco Ibanez	1919	471	Military
Man of the Forest (The)	Zane Grey	1920	382	Crime/Mys
Main Street	Sinclair Lewis	1921	480	Location
If Winter Comes	A. S. M. Hitchinson	1922	424	Family
Black Oxen	Gertrude Atherton	1923	352	Character
So Big	Edna Ferber	1924	272	Character
Soundings	A. Hamilton Gibbs	1925	324	Location
Private Life of Helen of Troy (The)	John Erskine	1926	252	History
Elmer Gantry	Sinclair Lewis	1927	432	Character
Bridge on San Luis Rey (The)	Thornton Wilder	1928	236	Culture
All Quiet on the Western Front	Erich Maria Remarque	1929	248	Military
Cimarron	Edna Ferber	1930	400	Frontier
Good Earth (The)	Pearl S. Buck	1931	448	Culture
Good Earth (The)	Pearl S. Buck	1932	448	Culture
Anthony Adverse	Hervey Allen & Allan McNab	1933	352	Character
Anthony Adverse	Hervey Allen & Allan McNab	1934	352	Character
Green Light	Lloyd C. Douglas	1935	364	Relations
Gone With the Wind	Margaret Mitchell	1936	1024	Culture
Gone With the Wind	Margaret Mitchell	1937	1024	Culture
Yearling (The)	Marjorie Kinnan Rawlings	1938	416	Youth
Grapes of Wrath (The)	John Steinbeck	1939	464	Family
How Green Was My Valley	Richard Llewellyn	1940	512	Youth
Keys of the Kingdom (The)	A. J. Cronin	1941	344	Occupation
Song of Bernadette (The)	Franz Werfel	1942	576	Occupation
Robe (The)	Lloyd C. Douglas	1943	520	Occupation
Strange Fruit	Lillian Smith	1944	384	Culture
Forever Amber	Kathleen Winsor	1945	976	Character
King's General (The)	Daphne du Maurier	1946	371	Relations
Miracle of the Bells (The)	Russel Janney	1947	508	Relations
Big Fisherman (The)	Lloyd C. Douglas	1948	581	Occupation
Egyptian (The)	Mika Waltari	1949	512	History
Cardinal (The)	Henry Morton Robinson	1950	565	Occupation
From Here to Eternity	James Jones	1951	864	Military
Caine Mutiny (The)*	Herman Wouk	1952	560	Military
Robe (The)	Lloyd C. Douglas	1953	520	Occupation
Not as a Stranger	Morton Thompson	1954	696	Occupation
Marjorie Morningstar	Herman Wouk	1955	584	Character
Don't Go Near the Water	William Brinkley	1956	373	Military
By Love Possessed	James Gould Cozzens	1957	576	Character
Doctor Zhivago	Boris Pasternak	1958	592	History
Exodus	Leon Uris	1959	608	History
Advise and Consent	Allen Drury	1960	616	Occupation

Table 3. Bestsellers (Publisher's Weekly) 1917-2009

Title	Author	Year	Pages	Type
Agony and the Ecstasy (The)	Irving Stone	1961	776	Character
Ship of Fools	Kathleen Porter	1962	512	Relations
Shoes of the Fisherman (The)	Morris L. West	1963	330	Occupation
Spy Who Came in from the Cold (The)	John LeCarre	1964	224	Crime/Mys
Source (The)	James A. Michener	1965	1088	History
Valley of the Dolls	Jacqueline Susann	1966	448	Culture
Arrangement (The)	Elia Kazan	1967	444	Character
Airport	Arthur Hailey	1968	224	Occupation
Portnoy's Complaint	Philip Roth	1969	304	Character
Love Story	Erich Segal	1970	224	Relations
Wheels	Arthur Hailey	1971	374	Occupation
Jonathan Livingston Seagull	Richard Bach	1972	128	Fantasy
Jonathan Livingston Seagull	Richard Bach	1973	128	Fantasy
Centennial	James A. Michener	1974	900	History
Ragtime	E. L. Doctorow	1975	288	Culture
Trinity	Leon Uris	1976	896	History
Silmarillion (The)	J. R. R. Tolkien & C. Tolkien	1977	384	Fantasy
Chesapeake	James A. Michener	1978	1024	Location
Matarese Circle (The)	Robert Ludlum	1979	544	Crime/Mys
Covenant (The)	James A. Michener	1980	288	Crime/Mys
Noble House	James Clavell	1981	1376	Culture
E. T. The Extra-Terrestrial Storybook	William Kotzwinkle	1982	60	Fantasy
Return of the Jedi Storybook	Joan D. Vinge	1983	56	Fantasy
Talisman (The)	Stephen King & Peter Straub	1984	768	Fantasy
Mammoth Hunters (The)	Jean M. Auel	1985	656	Culture
It	Stephen King	1986	1104	Horror
Tommyknockers (The)	Stephen King	1987	752	Fantasy
Cardinal of the Kremlin (The)	Tom Clancy	1988	544	Crime/Mys
Clear and Present Danger	Tom Clancy	1989	704	Crime/Mys
Plains of Passage (The)	Jean M. Auel	1990	768	Culture
Scarlett	Alexandra Ripley	1991	896	Culture
Dolores Claiborne	Stephen King	1992	384	Character
Bridges of Madison County (The)	Robert James Waller	1993	192	Relations
Chamber (The)	John Grisham	1994	676	Occupation
Rainmaker Jury (The)	John Grisham	1995	608	Occupation
Runaway Jury (The)	John Grisham	1996	560	Occupation
Partner (The)	John Grisham	1997	480	Occupation
Street Lawyer (The)	John Grisham	1998	464	Occupation
Testament (The	John Grisham	1999	480	Occupation
Brethren (The)	John Grisham	2000	464	Crime/Mys
Desecration: Antichrist Takes the Throne	Jerry Jenkins & Tim Lattay	2001	432	Fantasy
Summons (The)	John Grisham	2002	384	Occupation
Da Vinci Code (The)	Dan Brown	2003	454	Crime/Mys
Da Vinci Code (The)	Dan Brown	2004	454	Crime/Mys

Table 3. Bestsellers (Publisher's Weekly) 1917-2009

Title	Author	Year	Pages	Type
Broker (The)	John Grisham	2005	384	Crime/Mys
For One More Day	Mitch Albon	2006	197	Family
A Thousand Splendid Suns	Khaled Hosseini	2007	432	History
Appeal (The)	John Grisham	2008	496	Crime/Mys
Last Symbol (The)	Dan Brown	2009	522	Crime/Mys

* The Silver Chalice by Thomas B. Costain was listed as the bestseller for sales exclusively in 1952.

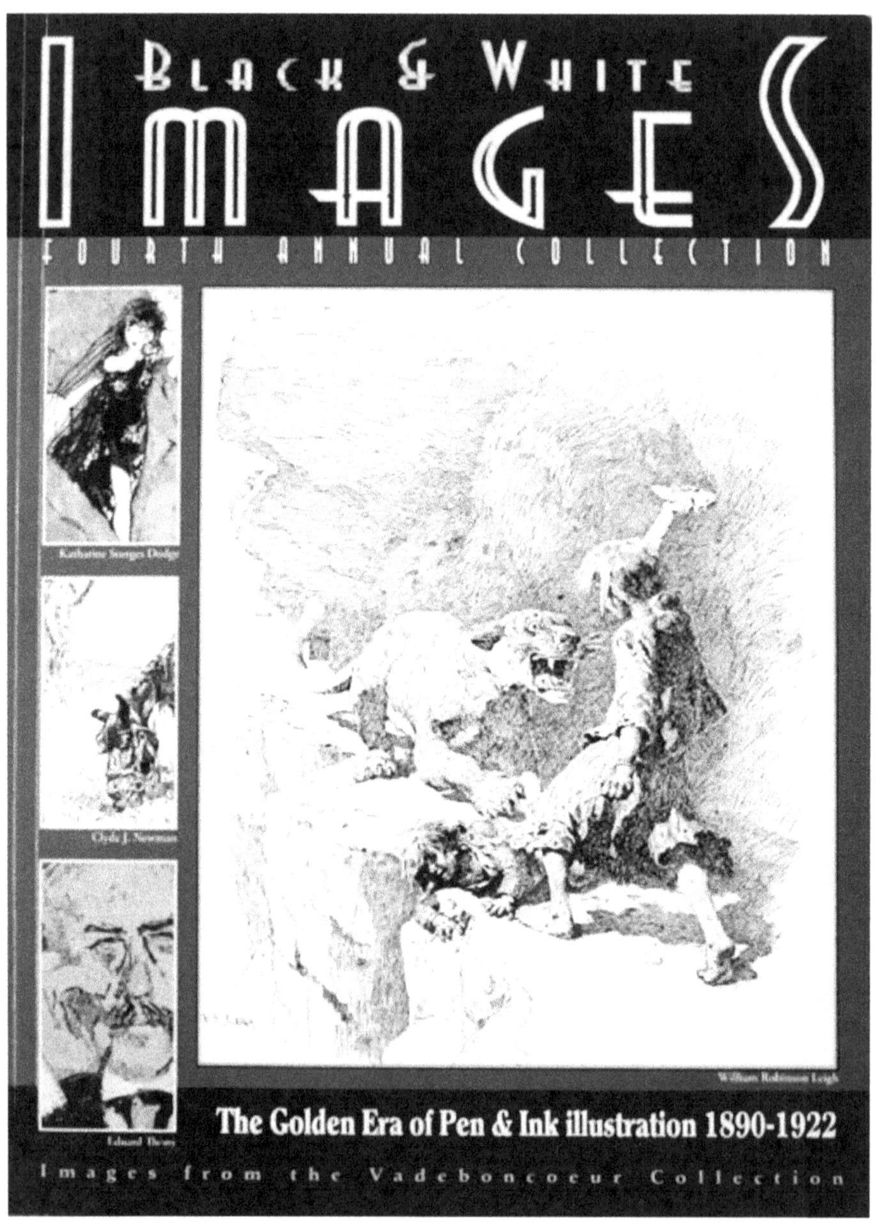

The *Vadeboncoeur Collection of Images* (in color) and *Black & White Images* are periodic picture books documenting the visual splendor of a long gone era of book and magazine illustration ended 90 years ago. All the material is new in the sense of never having been reprinted. The content is highly selective and reproduced with great fidelity.

Bibliography

The novel genre presented in 131 references and web sites. √ indicates the present author's personal favorites.

Titles are listed alphabetically under the following 19 headings:

Atlas/Landscape
Awards
Biographies, Memoirs, and Conversation
Book Clubs
Books and Collecting
Catalogs/Reference
Criticism/Reviews
eBooks
Guides and Listings
History
Illustrations, Cartoons, and Bookplates
Library Multi-Volume References
Literary Theory and Interpretation
Plot Synopsis
Quotations
The Reading Life
Subject Guide
Titles
Writing Fiction

An additional 31 titles of specialized fiction are listed in the following 11 divisions:

Adventure
Children
Crime/Mystery
Detective
Humor
Romance
Science Fiction and Fantasy
Serials
Short Story Collections
Sports
Westerns

Atlas/Landscape

— *The Atlas of Literature*, Malcolm Bradbury (Ed.), 1996.
Key places related to the making of literature, extensively illustrated with maps, drawings, and photographs.

— literarytraveler.com

— *A Writer's America: Landscape in Literature*, Alfred Kazin, 1988.

Awards

— *The Pulitzer Prize Novels: A Critical Backward Look*, W. J. Stuckey, 1966.

Biographies, Memoirs, and Conversations

An illustrative selection of 11 recent biographies.

— *Jane's Fame: How Jane Austen Conquered the World,* Claire Harman, 2009.

— *Truman Capote*, George Plimpton, 1997.

— *Raymond Carver, A Writer's Life*, Carol Sklenicka, 2009.

— *Storyteller: The Authorized Biography of Roald Dahl*, Donald Sturrock, 2010.

— *Flannery: A Life of Flannery O'Connor*, Brad Gooch, 2009.

— *Katherine Anne Porter: A Life*, Joan Givner, 1991.

— *J. D. Salinger: A Life*, Kenneth Slawenski, 2011.

— *John Steinbeck, Writer: A Biography*, Jackson J. Benson, 1990.
— *Mark Twain, The Adventures of Samuel L. Clemens*, Jerome Loving, 2010.
— *The Life of Evelyn Waugh: A Critical Biography*, Douglas Patey, 2001.
— *Thomas Wolfe: An Illustrated Biography*, Ted Mitchell, 2006.

— *American Writers series*, www.americanwriters.org. Examines selected twentieth century writers who have influenced the course of American history.

—√ *The Books in My Life*, Colin Wilson, 1998. Books that have made a difference in the author's life.

— *Conversations With American Writers*, Charles Ruas, 1985.

— *The Cambridge Companion to English Novelists*, Adrian Poole (Ed.), 2009.

— *Final Drafts: Suicides of World-Famous Authors*, Mark Seinfelt, 1999.

— *Keeping Literary Company: Working with Writers Since the Sixties*, Jerome Klinowitz, 1998.

—√ kirjasto.sci.fi/indeksi.htm. Biographies, further reading, and selected works of hundreds of writers.

— *Literary Feuds*, Anthony Arthur, 2002.

— *Literary Reflections*, James A. Michener, 1993.

— *The Literary 100: A Ranking of the Most Influential Novelists, Playwrights, and Poets of All Time*, Daniel S. Burt, 2001.

— *Namedropping: Mostly Literary Memoirs*, Richard Elman, 1999.

— *The Paris Review Interviews*, Vol. 1-4, 2009.

— *Partial Payments: Essays on Writers and Their Lives*, Joseph Epstein, 1991.

— *Some Time in the Sun: The Hollywood Years of F. Scott Fitzgerald, William Faulkner, Nathanael West, Aldous Huxley and James Agee*, Tom Dardis, 2004.

— Wikipedia.org. Easily accessible biographies of writers.

— *501 Great Writers*, Julian Patrick (General Editor), 2008.

Book Clubs

— *The Book Group Book*, Ellen Slezak (Editor) 2000.

— *The Book of the Month: Sixty Years of Books in American Life*, Al Silverman, 1986.

— *Good Books Lately: The One Stop Resource for Book Groups and Other Greedy Readers*, Ellen Moore and Kira Stevens, 2004.

Books and Collecting

— *Among the Gently Mad: Strategies and Perspectives for the Book-Hunter in the 21st Century*, Nicholar A. Basbanes, 2002.

— *Book Collecting: A Comprehensive Guide*, Allen Ahearn, 1995.

— *Casanova Was a Book Lover: And Other Naked Truths and Provocative Curiosities about the Writing, Selling and Reading of Books*, John Maxwell Hamilton, 2000.

— *On Books and Writers, Selected Essays*, Matthew J. Bruccoli, 2010.

— *A Passion for Books*, Harold Rabinowitz and Rob Kaplan (Eds.), 1999.
— *Speaking of Books: The Best Things Ever Said About Books and Book Collecting*, Rob Kaplan and Harold Rabinowitz, 2001.

Catalogs/Reference

— *Bibliography of Books, Articles, Newsletters, and Organizations of Interest to Public Library Book Discussion Groups*, Sherri McCarthy, www.penfieldlibrary.org.
— *The Cambridge Guide to Literature in English*, Dominic Head (Ed.), 3rd Edition, 2006.
— *80 Years of Bestsellers, 1895-1975*, A. P. Hackett and J. H. Burke, 1977.
— *Merriam Webster's Encyclopedia of Literature*, Kathleen Kuiper (Ed.), 1995. Note: The Cambridge Guide and Webster's Encyclopedia are similar but should be compared. New and used copies are available on the web at low price.
— *The Reader's Catalog: An Annotated Selection of More Than 40,000 of the Best Books in Print in 300 Categories*, Geoffrey O'Brien, Stephen Wasserstein, Helen Morris (Editors), 1997.
— *Thesaurus of Book Digests 1950-1980*, Irving Weiss, Ann D. Weiss, 1981. Contains 1,700 plot, theme, or thesis summaries of fiction and non-fiction books.
— Worldcatlibraries.org Over 1 billion items in more than 10,000libraries worldwide.

Criticism/Reviews

— Amazon.com Synopsis and reader reviews.
— *Bloom's Modern Critical Views* A series of selected criticism on the most widely read and influential poets, novelists, and playwrights from ancient to modern times. Current count of over 105 editions.
— *Bound to Please: An Extraordinary One Volume Literary Education*, Michael Dirda, 2005.
— Brothersjudd.com.
— *The Complete Review* www.complete-review.com. Over 1,500 fiction and non-fiction books currently reviewed.
— *Essentials of Literary Criticism*, Philip Hobsbaum, 1993.
— *Faint Praise: The Plight of Book Reviewing in America*, Gail Pool, 2007.
— *Fiction Award Winners* www.fictionawardwinners.com.
— *Internet Public Library* www.ipl.org/div/litcrit/ "The IPL Literary Criticism Collection contains critical biographical websites about authors and their works that can be browsed by author, by title, or by nationality and literary period."
— *John Hopkins Guide to Literary Theory and Criticism*, Michael Groden, Martin Kreiswirth, Imre Szeman, 2004.
— *Language of Fiction*, David Lodge, 1966.

— *Literary Criticism: An Introduction to Theory and Practice* (4th Edition), Charles E. Bressler, 2006.
— *Literary Laurels: A Reader's Guide to Award-Winning Fiction*, Sheila Cunningham, 1995.
— *Literary Theory and Criticism: An Oxford Guide*, Patricia Waugh, 2006.
— *The New York Review of Books* (semi-monthly magazine).
— *New York Times: Books* (Sunday newspaper supplement).
— *Pushcart's Complete Rotten Reviews and Rejections: A History of Insult, A Solace to Writers*, Andre Bernard and Bill Henderson (Editors), 1998.
— *The Reading List: Contemporary Fiction: A Critical Guide to the Complete Works of 125 Authors*, David Rubel (Editor), 1998.
— "Stalking the Billion-Footed Beast. A Literary Manifesto for the New Social Novel," Tom Wolfe, *Harper's*, November, 1989.
— *The Norton Anthology of Theory and Criticism*, Vincent B. Leitch (Editor), 2001.
— *The Washington Post Book World* (Sunday newspaper supplement).

eBooks
— Classicreader.com. 329 authors.
— *Project Gutenberg* Online Book Catalog gutenberg.org. Full content of over 19,000 books freely available. Excludes all copyright material which is most recent fiction.

Guides and Listings
—√ *The Book of Literary Lists*, Nicholas Parsons, 1985. A "delightful mélange" of editorial calamities, misguided rejections, printer's errors, literary hoaxes, favorites, and useful advice.
— *501 Must-Read Books*, Emma Beare (Project Editor), 2006.
— Jiffynotes.com.
— neglectedbooks.com.
—√ *Novels and Novelists: A Guide to the World of Fiction*, Martin Seymour-Smith, Editor, 1980. Close to a "single best source" on fiction covering all aspects of the craft and authors in informed and readable fashion.
— *Ninety-Nine Novels: The Best in English Since 1939*, Anthony Burgess, 1984.
—√ *Novel Guide*, Kent Halstead, 2011. 575 award winning titles and passages.
— *1001 Books You Must Read Before You Die*, Peter Boxall (Ed.), 2006.
— *The Novel 100: A Ranking of the Greatest Novels of All Time*, Daniel S. Burt, 2004.
—√ *Writer's Choice: A Library of Rediscoveries*, Linda Sternberg Katz, William A. Katz, 1983. 1,000 books considered to be unjustly neglected, overlooked, or forgotten according to a poll of over 400 writers.

History

— *American Literary History*, quarterly journal.
— *The Columbia History of the American Novel*, Emory Elliott, General Editor, 1991.
— *A History of the Novel*, Richard Freedman, 1975.
— *A New Literary History of America,* Greil Marcus and Werner Sollors (Editors), 2009.
— *Novel Reflections on the American Dream*, PBS TV documentary, 2010.
—√ *Today in Literature*, daily email newsletter. A daily literary treat.

Illustrations, Cartoons, and Bookplates

— *The Art of the Bookplate*, James P. Keenan, 2003.
—√ BPIB.com. Illustrative art with biographies of 105 contemporary artists.
— *N. C. Wyeth: The Collected Paintings, Illustrations & Murals*, Douglas Allen and Douglas Allen, Jr., 1972.
— *The New Yorker Book of Literary Cartoons*, Bob Mankoff, Ed., 2000.
—√ *The Vadeboncoeur Collection of Images and Black and White Images*, James Vadeboncoeur, subscription magazines.
— Victorianweb.org/art/illustration/illustrationov.html. Book illustrations by over 80 artists in Victorian England.

Library Multi-Volume References

— *American Writers*. Essays on American writers. (Four initial vols., 1974; 11 Supplements, 1979-2002; one Retrospective Supplement, 1998).
— *Beacham's Encyclopedia of Popular Fiction*. Signed critical analyses of works of popular literature (16 vols. through 2002).
— *Contemporary Literary Criticism*. Critical commentary and general information on more than 2,000 authors (Vols. 1-127, 1973-1999, include authors now living or who died between 1960 and 1999. Vols. 128-224, 2000-2006, include authors now living or who died since 2000).
— *Masterplots: 1,801 Plot Stories and Critical Evaluations of the World's Finest Literature* (12 vols. through 1996).
— *Short Story Criticism*. Significant criticism of the world's greatest short-story writers and supplementary biographical and bibliographical materials (92 vols. through 2006).
— *Twentieth Century Literary Criticism*. An introduction to more than 1,000 authors (40,000 titles) who died between 1900 and 1999 and interpretation of their works (179 vols. through 2006).

Literary Theory and Interpretation

— *Aspects of the Novel*, E. M. Forster, 1927.
— *The Anxiety of Influence*, Harold Bloom, 1973.
— *Creationists: Selected Essays*, 1993-2006, E. L. Doctorow, 2006.
— *How Fiction Works*, James Wood, 2008.

— *On Native Grounds: An Interpretation of Modern American Prose Literature*, Alfred Kazin, 1984.
— *Required Reading: Why Our American Classics Matter Now*, Andrew Delbanco, 1997.
— *Theory of Prose*, Viktor Shklovsky (Translated by Benjamin Sher), 1990.

Plot Synopsis
— Amazon.com.
— Acornweb.org Tightly written plot descriptions.
—√ Fictionawardwinners.com Excellent overall.
— Literature.org.
— Litsum.com.
— Mostlyfiction.com.
— Novelguide.com.
— Online-literature.com.

Quotations
— *Great Beginnings and Endings: Opening and Closing Lines of Great Novels*, compiled by Georgianne Ensign, 1995.
— literary-quotations.com.
— *The Reader's Quotation Book: A Literary Companion*, Steven Gilbar (Editor.), 1990.

The Reading Life
— *Book by Book*, Michael Dirda, 2005.
— *How to Read a Book*, Mortimer J. Adler and Charles Van Doren 1972.
— *How to Read and Why*, Harold Bloom, 2000.
— *Leave Me Alone, I'm Reading: Finding and Losing Myself in Books*, Maureen Corrigan, 2005.
— *The New Lifetime Reading Plan, Clifton Fadiman and John S. Major*, 4th edition, 1999.
— *Reading Like a Writer: A Guide for People Who Love Books and for Those Who Want to Write Them*, Francine Prose, 2006.
— *How to Read a Novel: A User's Guide*, John Sutherland, 2006.

Subject Guide
— *Read All Your Life: A Subject Guide to Fiction*, Barbara Kerr Davis, 1989.

Titles
— *Now all we need is a Title: Famous Book Titles and How they Got That Way*, Andre Bernard, 1994.

Writing Fiction
— *The Art of Fiction: Illustrated from Classic and Modern Texts*, David Lodge, 1993.
— *The Art of the Novel*, Milan Kundera, 2000.

— *From Where You Dream: The Process of Writing Fiction*, Robert Olen Butler, 2005.
— *Narrative Design, Working with Imagination, Craft, and Form*, Madison Smartt Bell, 2000.
— *On Becoming a Novelist*, John Gardner, 1999.
— *The Writing Life: Writers on How They Think and Work*, Mari Arana, Editor, 2002.

* * * * * * * * * * * * * * * *

Not included in the previous listings, but added here in recognition of their extended audience, are 11 additional fiction categories other than novels.

"I still don't think of these books (fiction genres other than novels) as, for the most part, serious reading, as Literary Reading. Let me stress that 'for the most part.' Any genre is capable of producing work of high artistic merit. James Crumley's *The Last Good Kiss* stands as a heartbreaking masterpiece of the modern 'detective' novel, just as A.S. Bhatt's Booker Prize-winning *Possession* is fundamentally, as its subtitle announces, 'a romance.' As for fantasy and science fiction, few works of contemporary American fiction can match John Crowley's *Little, Big* and Gene Wolfe's *The Book of the New Sun*, while a brilliant novel like Elizabeth Hand's recent *Mortal Love* deserves all the readers it can get."

— Michael Dirda, "As I Live and Read: One Book Lover's Plea for a Literati Nation," *The Washington Post*, 2004.

Adventure

— *The 100 Greatest Adventure Books of All Time*, Nat'l Geographic Society.

Children

— "The Angus & Robertson Kids' Top 50." Angus & Robertson.
— *Idealists, Entrepreneurs, and the Shaping of American Children's Literature*, Leonard S. Marcus, 2008.
— *A Reader's History, from Aesop to Harry Potter*, Seth Lerer, 2008.

Crime/Mystery

— *A Catalogue of Crime*, Revised and Enlarged Edition, Jacques Barzun Taylor and Wendell Hertig Taylor, 1989.
— *The Best American Mystery Stories of the Century*, Tony Hillerman (Ed.) 2000.
— "Classics of Suspense," Stanley Ellin, *Book World, The Washington Post*, June 20, 1982.

Kim, Rudyard Kipling, 1901.
A Coffin for Dimitrios, Eric Ambler, 1939.
The Spy Who Came in From the Cold, John le Carre, 1963.
The Thin Man, Dashiell Hammett, 1934.
Farewell, My Lovely, Raymond Chandler, 1940.
Gaudy Night, Dorothy Sayers, 1935.
The Daughter of Time, Josephine Tey, 1951.

Sanctuary, William Faulkner, 1931.
The Postman Always Rings Twice, James M. Cain, 1934.
A Gentle Murderer, Dorothy Salisbury Davis, 1951.
Brighton Rock, Graham Greene, 1938.
Love in Amsterdam, Nicolas Freeling, 1962.

– *Crime and Mystery: The 100 Best Books*, H. R. F. Keating, 1987.
– *The Perfect Murder: A Study in Detection*, David Lehman, 1989.

Detective

Six greatest masters or mistresses of the detective genre by P. D. James.

– Wilkie Collins (1824-1889).
– Sir Arthur Conan Doyle (1859-1930).
– Dashiell Hammett (1894-1961).
– Agatha Christie (1890-1976).
– Dorothy L. Sayers (1893-1957).
– Margery Allingham (1904-1966).

Humor

– "Comedy Tonight," 100 very amusing books, Michael Dirda, *Book World, The Washington Post*, August 16, 1998.

Romance

– "All Time Best Romance Novels Ever!" A Listmania list of 14 titles by Lindsay (graduate psychology student, CA).

Science Fiction and Fantasy

– "Best hardboiled fiction anthologies," A Listmania list of 15 titles by L. Greenberg "lgwriter49" (Astoria, N.Y.).
– "David Pringle's 100 Best Science Fiction Novels," www.strangewords.com/weirdbooks/scifi100.html.
– "Top 50 Science Fiction & Fantasy Books," 1953-2002, Science Fiction Book Club.

Serials

– *Blackwater*, Michael McDowell, Series of 6, 1983.

Short Story Collections

A representative sample of numerous short story collections.

– *American Short Story Masterpieces*, Raymond Carver and Tom Jenks (Eds.), 1989.
– *An Anthology of Famous American Stories*, Angus Burrell and Bennett Cerf (Eds.), 1936.
– *An Anthology of Famous British Stories*, Bennett Cerf and Henry C. Moriarty (Eds.), 1940.
– *Best American Short Stories of the Century*, John Updike (Ed.), 1999.
– Classicshorts.com.

Sports

– "The Ten Best Sports Books," Jonathan Yardley, *Book World, The Washington Post*, July 18, 1982.

About Three Bricks Shy of a Load, Roy Blount Jr.
Babe, Robert Creamer.
A Fan's Notes, Frederick Exley
The Glory of Their Times, Lawrence S. Ritter.
The Long Season, Jim Brosnan.
The Southpaw, Mark Harris.
The Spawning Run, William Humphrey.
The Summer Game, Roger Angell.
The Universal Baseball Association, Inc., J. Henry Waugh, Prop., Robert Coover.
You Know Me Al, Ring Lardner.

– "The Top 100 Sports Books of All time," compiled by the staff of *Sports Illustrated*, 2002.

Westerns

– *The Best of the West: An Anthology of Classic Writing from the American West*, Tony Hillerman, 1991.

– "The best westerns of all time…" A Listmania list of 25 titles by Adam "hardertheyfall" (Ohio).

– "Fast 15: All Time Best Westerns," A Listmania list by Daniel Bamberg.

* * * * * * * * * * * * * * *

FAIR USE RATIONALE AND ACKNOWLEDGEMENTS

The *Novel Guide* presents historical, biographical, and critical commentary intended to promote the general public's appreciation and selective reading of the novel genre. It is essentially a library reference, valuable in advising readers. Undoubtedly the *Guide* will increase attention given listed titles well reviewed.

Passages selected for quotation suggest the nature of the story and the author's writing style. All are brief portions (typically 200 words or less), constituting a small fraction of each novel's total content. Used for purposes of illustration and criticism, these examples are believed to fall under the fair use public domain guidelines of copyright law in the United States.

Selected works of art and photographs are an integral component of associated critical commentary and are employed here to illustrate the contributive nature these media have made to the novel genre. Many are unique historic images. All are used for educational purposes. Major works are attributed. Photos used to establish the visual identity of important authors are presented in reduced thumbnail size at low resolution. Photographs and art published prior to 1923 are in the public domain according to the copyright laws of the United States. In later instances fair use is claimed on the basis that the image is widely disseminated and in common use, or is singularly historically significant without the availability of a free equivalent. In every instance there is no possibility of commercial loss by any copyright claimant, more likely the publicity provided here will result in commercial gain to the claimant.

Acknowledgement is made to the following sources for permission to reproduce copyrighted subject matter as cited:

"Steerpike and Barquentine," page 19, Image by Mervyn Peake from *Titus Groan* (© Mervyn Peake, 1946) is reproduced by permission of PFD (www.pfd.co.uk) on behalf of the Estate of Mervyn Peake.

Caricatures by Mike Caplanis, page 75, Literary Luminaries.

New Yorker cartoons, page 76, Handelsman, J.B. © J.B. Handelsman, and page 77, Booth, George © George Booth, *The New Yorker* Collection, www.cartoonbank.com.

"Diver and Mermaid," page 63, and "Draftsman," page 78, Heinrich-Kley, Dover Publications.

"Here is Edward Bear…." by A. A. Milne, page 272, © Disney, Disney Publishing Worldwide (Used to illustrate the originality of the artist through this initial work).

Any concern regarding copyright infringement should be brought to the attention of the publisher.

Young Lady Reading by Mary Cassatt

www.ingramcontent.com/pod-product-compliance
Lightning Source LLC
Chambersburg PA
CBHW060806030726
47503CB00002B/365

* 9 7 8 1 8 8 3 2 9 8 0 9 8 *